"The narrative has the excitement of a good fantasy novel, a vivid historical setting and a lengthy, credible and satisfying plot—just the elements, in fact, that have made Lawhead a commercial success time and again."

—*Publishers Weekly*

"Engrossing with plenty of plot twists . . . Worthwhile for Lawhead regulars and historical-fantasy fans alike."

—*Kirkus Reviews*

"Here, in the story of a great gift and an even greater journey, is summoned all the magic and splendor, the brutality and the innocence of a lost era—the not-so-Dark Age when faith ruled men's hearts."

—*Smash*

"Not merely a gripping yarn—and it certainly is that—this is also a novel about faith and the tests life plants in its way. Lawhead, author of the popular Pendragon cycle of fantasies, here makes a sure move into mainstream historical fiction."

—*Booklist*

*Books by*
**Stephen R. Lawhead**

AVALON
BYZANTIUM

## THE PENDRAGON CYCLE

TALIESIN
MERLIN
ARTHUR
PENDRAGON
GRAIL

## THE CELTIC CRUSADES

THE IRON LANCE
THE BLACK ROOD
THE MYSTIC ROSE

*And Coming Soon in Hardcover*

PATRICK

# BYZANTIUM

## STEPHEN R. LAWHEAD

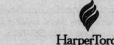

**HarperTorch**
*An Imprint of HarperCollinsPublishers*

# For Sven and Margareta

HARPERTORCH
*An Imprint of* HarperCollins*Publishers*
10 East 53rd Street
New York, New York 10022-5299

Copyright © 1996 by Stephen R. Lawhead
Cover illustration by Robert Hunt
ISBN: 0-06-105754-1

First HarperTorch paperback printing: February 2002
First HarperPaperbacks printing: August 1997
First HarperPrism hardcover printing: September 1996

HarperCollins®, HarperTorch™, and ♦™ are trademarks of HarperCollins Publishers Inc.
Avon Trademark Reg. U.S. Pat. Off. and in Other Countries, Marca Registrada, Hecho en U.S.A.

Printed in the United States of America

Visit HarperTorch on the World Wide Web at
www.harpercollins.com

20  19  18  17  16  15  14  13  12  11  10  9

# Contents

Europe and Asia Minor

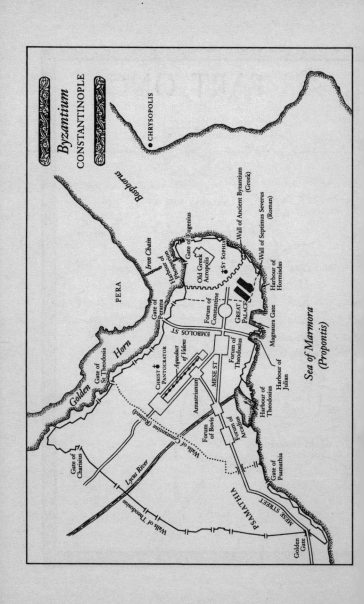

Byzantium
CONSTANTINOPLE

# PART ONE

*God be with thee on every hill,*
*Jesu be with thee in every pass,*
*Spirit be with thee on every stream,*
*Headland, ridge, and field;*
*Each sea and land, each moor and meadow,*
*Each lying down, each rising up,*
*In wave trough, on billow crest,*
*Each step of the journey thou goest.*

# 1

I saw Byzantium in a dream, and knew that I would die there. That vast city seemed to me a living thing: a great golden lion, or a crested serpent coiled upon a rock, beautiful and deadly. With trembling steps I walked alone to embrace the beast, fear turning my bones to water. I heard no sound save the beating of my own heart and the slow, hissing breath of the creature. As I drew near, the half-lidded eye opened, and the beast awoke. The fearful head rose; the mouth gaped open. A sound like the howl of wind across a winter sky tore the heavens and shook the earth, and a blast of foul breath struck me, withering the very flesh.

I stumbled on, gagging, gasping, unable to resist; for I was compelled by a force beyond my power. I watched in horror as the terrible beast roared. The head swung up and swiftly, swiftly down—like lightning, like the plunge of an eagle upon its prey. I felt the dread jaws close on me as I stood screaming.

Then I awoke; but my waking brought neither joy nor relief. For I rose not to life, but to the terrible certainty of death. I was to die, and the golden towers of Byzantium would be my tomb.

And yet, before the dream—some time before it—I had gazed upon a very different prospect. Such rich opportunity does not come to every man, and I considered myself blessed beyond measure by my good fortune. How not? It was an honour rare to one so young, and well I knew it. Not that I could easily forget, for I was reminded at every turn by my brother monks, many of whom regarded me with ill-disguised envy. Of the younger priests, I was considered the most able and learned, and therefore most likely to attain the honour we all sought.

The dream, however, poisoned my happiness; I knew my life would end in agony and fear. This the dream had shown me, and I was not fool enough to doubt it. I knew—with the confidence of fire-tested conviction—that what I dreamed would be. Sure, I am one of those wretched souls who see the future in dreams, and my dreams are never wrong.

Word of the bishop's plan had reached us just after the Christ Mass. "Eleven monks will be selected," Abbot Fraoch informed us that night at table. "Five monks from Hy, and three each from Lindisfarne and Cenannus." The selection, he said, must be made before Eastertide.

Then our good *abb* spread his arms to include all gathered in the refectory. "Brothers, it is God's pleasure to honour us in this way. Above all else, let us put aside jealousy and prideful contention, and let each one seek the Holy King's direction in the days to come."

This we did, each in his own way. In truth, I was no less ardent than the most zealous among us. Three were to be chosen, and I wanted to be one of them. So, through the dark months of winter, I strove to make myself worthy before God and my brothers. First to rise and last to sleep, I worked with unstinting diligence, giving myself to those tasks which naturally came my way, and then going out of my way to take on the chores of others.

If any were in prayer, I prayed with them. If any were at labour, I laboured with them. Whether in the fields, or the cookhouse, the oratory, or the scriptorium, I was there, earnest and eager, doing all in my power to lighten others' burdens and prove myself worthy. My zeal would not be quenched. My devotion was second to none.

When I could not think of any chore to do, I took a penance upon myself—as severe as I could devise—to chastise myself and drive out the demons of idleness and sloth, pride, envy, spite, and any others that might stand in my way. With a true and contrite heart, I did humble my willful spirit.

Then, one night . . .

I stood in the swift-running stream of the Blackwater, clutching a wooden bowl tight between shivering hands. Mist curled in slow eddies over the surface of the river, softly spectral in the pale light of a new moon. When my flesh began to grow numb, I dipped the bowl into the icy water and poured it over my shoulders and back. My inward organs shuddered with the shock of the cold water on naked skin. It was all I could do to keep my teeth from clashing, and my jaws ached with the effort. I could no longer feel my legs or feet.

Ice formed in the still places among the rocks at the river's edge and in my wet hair. My breath hung in clouds about my head. High above, the stars shone as flame-points of silvery light, solid as the iron-hard winter ground and silent as the night around me.

Again, and yet again, I poured the freezing water over my body, enforcing the virtue of the penance I had chosen. "Kyrie eleison . . ." I gasped. "Lord, have mercy!"

In this way, I held my vigil, and would have maintained it thus if I had not been distracted by the appearance of two brother monks bearing torches. I heard someone approaching and turned my stiff neck to see them clambering down the steep riverbank, holding their torches high.

"Aidan! Aidan!" one of them called. It was Tuam, the bursar, with young Dda, the cook's helper. The two slid to a halt on the bank and stood for a moment, peering out over the moving water. "We have been looking for you."

"You have found me," I replied through clenched teeth.

"You are to come out of there," Tuam said.

"When I have finished."

"Abbot has summoned everyone." The bursar stooped, picked up my cloak, and held it out to me.

"How did you know I was here?" I asked, wading towards the bank.

"Ruadh knew," Dda answered, offering his hand to help me climb the slippery bank. "He told us where to find you."

I held up frozen hands to them and each took one and pulled me from the water. I reached to pick up my mantle, but my fingers were numb and shaking so badly I could not grasp it. Tuam quickly spread my cloak over my shoulders. "I thank you, brother," I murmured, pulling the cloak around me.

"Can you walk?" Tuam asked.

"Where are we going?" I wondered, shivering violently.

"To the cave," Dda replied, a glint of mystery in his eye. I gathered the rest of my clothes, clutching them to my chest, and they started away.

I followed, but my feet were numb and my legs shook so badly that I stumbled and fell three times before Tuam and Dda came to my aid; supporting me between them, we made our way along the river path.

The monks of Cenannus na Ríg did not always meet in

the cave. Indeed, only on the most important occasions was it so—and then rarely were we all together. Though my companions would say nothing more, I discerned from their secretive manner that something extraordinary was to happen. In this, I was not wrong.

As Tuam had said, everyone had been called and all were assembled by the time we reached the *sanctorum speluncae*. We entered quickly and took our places with the others. Still shaking, I drew on my mantle and cloak, dressing as quickly as my fumbling hands allowed.

Observing our arrival, the abbot stepped forward and raised his hand in blessing. "We watch, we fast, we study," Abbot Fraoch said, his voice a rasping croak in the domed chamber of the cave. "And this night we pray." He paused, a shepherd pleased at the gathering of his flock. "Brothers, we pray God's guidance and blessing on the choice before us, for this night the *Célé Dé* will be chosen." He paused— as if searching us one last time. "May God's mind be in us, and may God's wisdom be made manifest among us. Amen!"

All those gathered replied, "Amen! So be it!"

So, it has come at last, I thought, and my heart quickened. The waiting is at an end; this night the decision will be made.

"Brothers, to prayer!" With that Abbot Fraoch sank to the floor, prostrating himself before the little stone altar.

No more was said; no more needed saying. Indeed, we had leeched all meaning from the words long ago through endless discussion and debate. Thus, having watched and fasted and studied through the dark months, we now sought the blessing of the heavenly throne. We lay down upon the bare rock floor of the cave and abandoned ourselves to prayer. The air in the cave was dense with the warmth of so many bodies, and thick with the smoke and scent of the candles. I knelt, doubled over upon myself, arms extended and head touching the stone floor, listening as the whispered invocations filled the cave with a familiar drone.

Gradually, the murmuring abated and after a time a silence deep and calm as the gravemound returned to the cave. But for the soft flaring of the candles as they fluttered, and the slow, regular breathing of the monks, not a sound could be heard. We might have been the last men on earth; we might have been the dead of another age awaiting our return to life.

I prayed as fervently as ever I have in my life. I sought wisdom and guidance, and my seeking was sincere, I swear it! I prayed:

> *King of the Mysteries, who wast and art,*
> *Before the elements, before the ages,*
> *King eternal, comely in aspect,*
> *who reigns for ever, grant me three things:*
> *Keenness to discern your will,*
> *Wisdom to understand it,*
> *Courage to follow where it leads.*

This I prayed, and meant it every word. Then I prayed that the honour I sought would be delivered into my hand. Even so, I was astonished when, after a lengthy span, I heard footsteps pause near me and felt a touch on my shoulder, and heard the abbot call my name, saying, "Rise, Aidan, and stand."

I lifted my head slowly. The candles had burned low; the night was far spent. Abbot Fraoch gazed down upon me, nodded gravely, and I stood. He passed on, moving among the prostrate bodies. I watched him as he stepped this way and that. In a little while, he stopped before Brocmal, touched him, and bade him stand. Brocmal rose and looked around; he saw me and inclined his head, as if in approval. The abbot continued on, walking with slow, almost aimless steps, over and around the praying monks until he came to Brother Libir. He knelt, touched Libir, and told him to stand up on his feet.

And there we were: we three, quietly observing one another—Brocmal and Libir in gratitude and pleasure, and myself in amazement. *I was chosen!* The thing I sought above all else had been granted me; I could scarce believe my good fortune. I stood trembling with triumph and delight.

"Rise brothers," Fraoch croaked, "look upon God's chosen ones." Then he called us by name: "Brocmal . . . Libir . . . and Aidan, come forth." He summoned us and we took our places beside him. The other monks looked on. "Brothers, these three will undertake the pilgrimage on our behalf. May the High King of Heaven be exalted!"

Sixty pairs of eyes blinked at us in mingled surprise and, for some, disappointment. I could almost hear what they were thinking. Brocmal, yes, of course; he was a master of all learning and bookwise craft. Libir, yes, a thousand times yes! Renowned for his wisdom and quiet zeal, Libir's patience and piety were already legendary throughout Éire. But Aidan mac Cainnech? It must be a mistake—the disbelief on their faces was not difficult to read. More than one monk wondered why he had been passed over for me.

But Abbot Fraoch seemed more than pleased with the choices. "Let us now thank God and all the saints for this most satisfactory conclusion to our long deliberations."

He led us in a simple prayer of thanksgiving, and then dismissed us to our duties. We left the cave, stooping low as we crawled from the narrow passage, and stepped into the dawnlight of a brisk, windswept day. Moving into the pale rose-red light, it seemed to me that we were corpses reborn. Having passed an eternity under the earth, we now awakened, rose, and quit the grave to walk the world once more. For me, it seemed a world vastly changed—new-made and potent with promise: Byzantium awaited, and I was among the chosen to undertake the journey. White Martyrdom they call it, and so it is.

# 2

e walked along the Blackwater and sang a hymn to the new day, reaching the gates of the abbey as the rising sun touched the belltower. After *prime* we assembled in the hall to break fast. I sat at the long table, much aware of my new prominence. Brother Enan, who read the Psalms for morning meal, could not contain his elation at the fact that our community was, as he put it, "to send our most revered members to help bear the great book across the seas to the Holy Emperor." Enan asked a special prayer of thanksgiving for the three chosen ones—a request the abbot granted. Then, in a mood of reckless jubilation, he read the *Magnificat*.

Listening to the cadence of those well-known words, I thought: *Yes! This is how it is! This is how it feels to be chosen, to be called of God for a great undertaking: My soul praises the Lord and my spirit rejoices in God my Saviour, for he has been mindful of the humble state of his servant. Yes!*

It was, as Abbot Fraoch maintained—and everyone else agreed—a great honour for us all. Truly, it was an honour I had sought as ardently as any of the others. Now it was mine, and I could scarcely credit my good fortune. Listening to Enan pray thanks to God for this exalted boon of a blessing, my heart soared within me. I was humbled, pleased, and proud—all three at once—and it made me giddy; I felt I must laugh out loud, or burst.

Once, during the meal, I raised my bowl to my lips and happened to glance down the long refectory table to see a fair few of the brothers watching me. The thought that they should find in me something worthy of remark roused in me a flush of guilty pride. Thus, I ate my broth and barley bread and, for the sake of my well-meaning brothers, tried not to appear too delighted, lest I appear haughty in their sight and thereby give offence.

When the meal finished, Abbot Fraoch summoned me with a gesture. I bent near to hear him. "I expect you will have much to consider, Aidan," he whispered. Having lost his voice to a Sea Wolf's blade years ago, our abbot's utterances were never more than dry whispers and raspy croaks.

"Yes, abbot," I replied.

"Therefore," he continued, "I grant you leave from your duties. Use this day to rest, to think . . . to prepare yourself." I made to protest, but he continued. "Your pursuit of this opportunity has been most vigorous. Your zeal is laudable, son. But there is more work to come, and a strenuous journey when the weather turns." He laid a hand on my shoulder. "A day for yourself now, Aidan—it may be the last you will have for a very long time."

I thanked him and took my leave, then hurried across the yard to my cell. I entered and pulled the oxhide cover over the door, whereupon I threw myself onto my pallet and lay kicking my feet and laughing. I had been chosen. *Chosen!* I was going to Byzantium! I laughed until my sides ached and tears came to my eyes and I could laugh no more.

Elation left me exhausted. As I had not slept the previous night, I closed my eyes and composed myself to rest, but my mind whirled. *Think, Aidan! Think of the places you will see, the people you will meet. Oh, it is wonderful, is it not?*

My thoughts flitted like scattering birds and, tired as I was, I could not sleep.

So, I thought to meditate. As the abbot suggested, it was an arduous journey and I must prepare myself spiritually and mentally. It seemed right to bring before my mind all the dangers and hardships that might befall us on our way. But instead of dangers, I saw vast mountain ranges swathed in cloud, and strange seas sparkling under foreign skies; I saw people thronging the streets of great cities and the courtyards of shimmering palaces. Instead of hardships, I saw eastern potentates, kings, queens, bishops, and courtiers—all arrayed in splendour to rival the glory of the sun.

Failing my meditations, I set my mind to pray instead. I began by asking forgiveness for my wayward thoughts. Very soon, however, I was thinking of meeting the emperor—how I should address him, what I might say to him, whether I should kiss his ring, or kneel . . . any of a thousand different things other than the prayer I had begun.

Since I could neither sleep nor pray, I decided to go out into the hills. The solitude and exertion, I thought, might calm my restless spirit and bring me to a more tranquil mind. I rose at once and left my cell. Quickly crossing the yard, I made my way to the gate, passed by the guest lodge and out. Continuing along the path outside the wall, I descended the shallow ditch and made my way up the opposite side, then turned onto the hill path. The once-bright day had faded under a dull sky, but the wind remained fresh and I relished the bitter bite of the cold air on my face as I walked, my breath coming in steamy puffs. The path rose steadily and soon I ascended the heights above the abbey and began making my way along the hill-top.

I walked a long time, letting my footsteps take me where they would. It was a joy to feel the fresh wind on my face while I filled my soul with the green beauty of those beloved hills. I came at last to the edge of the great wood. Not daring to enter that dark domain alone, I turned and started back the way I had come—but my mind roamed far, far ahead on unknown paths.

Thoughts of alien lands and exotic customs filled my head, and I imagined what it would be like to tread foreign soil, to taste foreign food, to hear foreign tongues speaking words I had never heard before. Even as, in my mind's eye, I clearly saw myself striding boldly through unfamiliar fields, standing before the Pope, or kneeling before the emperor, I could hardly believe that the man I saw was me.

In all, it was a pleasant enough, if frivolous, exercise, and it occupied me until I reached my favourite perch: a rocky outcrop just below the crest of the hill overlooking the monastery and the broad valley with its dark river beyond. In the windshadow of the rocks, I sat down on the grassy turf as the monastery bell tolled *sext*.

Though it was only midday, the late winter sun was already low, bathing the valley in a soft, misty light. The abbey was as I had known it from my earliest memory—unchanged and unchanging: like its oratory and scriptorium, a place of solitude and safety, where not even time, the Great Ravager, dared intrude.

Cenannus na Ríg, they call it: Kells of the Kings. In an earlier time it had served as a royal fortress—a hillfort set within protecting rings of earth and timber. But the kings long ago abandoned the stronghold in favour of Tara. Thus, while the ancient seat of Éire's monarchs boasted a sovereign presence once more, Cenannus' ditches and walls protected a monastery, and the folk of several nearby settlements as well.

I had come to the abbey as a boy. It was my father's wish that I should become a priest. Cainnech was a king and I his second son. As it was deemed auspicious for the clan to have a priest of noble blood, I was sent for foster-age, not to a noble house, but to the monastery.

I was only five summers old when I was bundled together with the length of cloth my mother had woven for me and brought to Kells. The cloth was for my cloak when I took holy vows. I wore it now, even though it was grey and the other monks wore brown, for I was a prince of my clan. Even so, any claim I might have made to the throne ended in my tenth summer when my father and brother, along with most of the clan, were killed in a battle with the Danemen at Dubh Llyn near Atha Cliath.

Upon their deaths, the kingship then passed to a man of another tribe, a cousin of my father. The day they buried my father, I buried all hope of ever taking my place as priest and counsellor to a king; nor would I become a sovereign myself as some priests had done. Not for me the world of kingcraft and courtly concerns. At first I was bit-terly disappointed, I confess. Yet, as time passed, I grew to love the life of the monastery, where every hand was busy from dawn to dusk, and all moved in precise rhythm with the cycle of labour, prayer, and study.

I devoted myself to learning, and at the end of twelve summers achieved the scriptorium, pledging myself to the vocation of a scribe—though some small part of me still yearned to embrace a larger life.

This is why, when word of the bishop's undertaking was first proclaimed among us that frosty winter's night, I determined to show myself worthy of joining such a pil-grimage. And I had succeeded, praise God! Most fortunate of men, I was going to Byzantium. Oh, the very thought delighted me; I hugged myself, rocking back and forth on the grass, and chuckling at my good fortune.

Looking down from my place on the hill, I saw the monks streaming from the chapel, returning to their work: some to the kitchens to prepare the midday meal; some to the scriptorium; some to the workshops and stores; some to the fields and woodpiles. Even though I had been granted a day of idleness, it was good to see others about their chores. I turned my eyes to the world beyond the monastery.

In the glen below the ringwall, the Blackwater ran. Across the river cattle grazed on the hillside, noses to the frosty ground, tails to the wind. And beyond, empty hills, clothed in the dusky green of winter, rose in gentle swells to the east. A smudge of smoke spreading on the wind marked the nearest settlement. Along the horizon, just below the leaden clouds, a line of palest blue appeared.

I watched as this swath of colour widened, deepening to a brilliant bird's-egg blue. In the abbey below, the kitchen bell announced dinner. I watched the brothers make their way to the refectory for their meal; but, content in my own company, I made no move to join them. Bread and broth did not excite my appetite; I feasted instead on the beauty of the day—made much the sweeter by my success.

After a while, the sun wore through the covering of cloud, and light like pale honey spread over the hilltop, warm where it touched me. I leaned back against the cold rock, closed my eyes, and turned my face to the sun, letting the thin warmth thaw my ears and cheeks. I dozed . . .

"Aidan!"

The shout, though indistinct and still far away, roused me. Opening my eyes, I saw a very large figure toiling up the hill, calling as he came. "Aidan!"

Dugal, the tallest man among us by far, approached rapidly, mounting the hillside with great bounding strides.

A warrior before coming to Cenannus, he wore the woad-stained tattoos of his clan: a leaping salmon on his right arm, and a spiral disc on his left. Upon taking vows, he had added a cross over his heart.

For strength and dexterity, he was rarely bettered: he could crush walnuts in his fist; he could toss three knives at once and keep them spinning in the air as long as he liked; I had once seen him lift a horse. By training a warrior, by inclination a monk, he was in many ways a most uncommon Christian.

I had never seen him fight, but the criss-crossed scars on his arms argued for his valour in combat. As a monk, however . . . well, let it be said that no other Latin speaker I knew could hurl a spear half so far as Dugal mac Caran. Of all the brothers, he was my best friend.

"*Mo anam!*" he exclaimed, stumping up to tower over me. "That is a fair climb on a cold day. I had forgotten it was so high." He looked around, a smile spreading slowly over his face. "Ah, but it is a fine sight to be seeing."

"Welcome, Dugal. Sit and rest yourself."

He dropped down beside me with his back to the rock, and we gazed out across the valley together. Neither of us spoke for a time, content just to soak up the small warmth the sun offered. "When you did not come to table, Ruadh sent me to find you. I knew you would be here."

"And here I am."

He nodded and, after a moment, asked, "What are you doing here?"

"Thinking," I replied. "I still cannot believe I was chosen to go with the book."

"That *is* a wonder!" Dugal said, nudging me with an elbow. "Brother, are you not pleased?"

I grinned to show him the extent of my pleasure. "In truth, I believe I have never been happier. Is that wrong, do you think?"

As if in answer to this, Dugal replied, "I brought something for you." He put his hand to his belt and withdrew a small leather pouch which he flattened and smoothed on his hand. The pouch was new, and on its side he had carefully burnished a name: Dána. The word meant "bold one"—a name Dugal had given me years ago, and one that only he used—a small jest from this prince of warriors to a docile scribe.

I thanked him for his gift, and observed, "But it must have taken you a long time to make this. How did you know I would be chosen?"

The big monk simply shrugged. "I never doubted," he said. "If anyone were to go, I knew it would be you."

"I do thank you, Dugal," I told him. "I will keep it with me always."

He nodded with satisfaction, then turned his face away. "They say the sky in Byzantium is gold," he said simply. "And the very stars are strange."

"That is true," I confirmed. "Also, I have heard that the people there have black skin."

"Everyone?" he wondered. "Or some only?"

"Some, at least," I told him confidently.

"The women, too?"

"I suppose."

Dugal pursed his lips. "I do not think I would like to see a black-skinned woman."

"Neither would I," I agreed.

We sat in silence for a time, thinking about the utter strangeness of golden skies and black-skinned men. Finally, unable to contain himself any longer, Dugal sighed: "Please God, I wish I were going with you. I would give *everything* to go."

I heard the yearning in his voice, and a sharp pang of guilt nicked my heart. Since learning of my good fortune, I had not given my friend a single thought—nor considered the feelings of any of those staying behind. Indeed, I had thought of nothing but myself and my own happiness. Smarting with shame, I cringed at this fresh evidence of my rampant selfishness.

"I wish you could go, too," I told him.

"What a fine thing that would be!" He paused, considering this daring possibility. When it proved beyond his imagining, he resigned himself with another sigh. "Ah, my soul . . ."

The cattle across the valley began lowing as they moved slowly down to the river to drink. The pale sun sloped further down, staining the undersides of the clouds the colour of butter. I noticed the wind had slackened and changed direction, bearing the scent of smoke from the cookhouse.

"*Mo Croi,*" the big monk muttered after a time, "look at the two of us. Whatever shall become of us, do you think?"

*I will go and you will stay,* I thought and, at that very moment, realized for the first time that I would be leaving every familiar thing I had ever known. I would go, and it would be months—years, perhaps—before I clasped arms with any of my friends and brothers again. The close-woven cloth of my life would be rent in ways I could not now conceive. I said none of this—how could I? Instead, I merely replied, "Who can say?"

He was silent for a while, then asked: "Will you bring me back a treasure, Aidan?"

"That I will," I promised, glad to have something to offer him in consolation. I shifted my head to look at him; he was still gazing out across the valley but his eyes were misty with tears. "Anything you like," I added.

"I hear the knives of Byzantium are the best in all the world—better even than those the Saex-men make."

"Would you like a knife?"

"Aye, that I would."

"Then I shall bring you the finest knife in all Byzantium," I vowed. "And a spear as well."

He nodded and looked out across the valley in the fast-fading light. "I should go back," Dugal said, drawing a hand quickly across his eyes. "Ruadh will be wondering what happened to me. Some of us, at least, do not have leave to sit and think all day."

"I will go back with you," I said. He stood and reached a large hand down for me. I took the offered hand and he hauled me upright with a single quick pull, and we faced one another without speaking.

Finally, Dugal turned and looked out across the valley one last time. "It is pleasant up here, though."

"I like it." I drew the air deep into my lungs and looked around again. The sun was disappearing quickly now, and the far hills gleamed a smooth frosted green with ice-blue shadows. "Sure, I will miss it."

"But think of all the new places you will see, Dána." Dugal did not look at me this time. "You will soon forget all this—this . . ." His voice faltered.

A crow flying overhead cracked the cold air with its lonely call, and I thought my heart would break.

"How I wish I was going with you," Dugal murmured.

"So do I, Dugal. So do I."

# 3

Dugal and I returned to the abbey, and to the daily round. Although the abbot had relieved me of my duties for the day, I thought best to resume them, and indeed, to increase them if I could, and in this way prepare myself for the rigours of the journey. Dugal took himself off to the brewhouse, and I continued on to the scriptorium intent on taking up my work once more.

The sun skimmed the low hilltops, casting a deep yellow light and blue shadows over the yard; I reached the door as the bell tolled *none*. Pausing at the door, I stepped aside, and a moment later my fellow scribes began trooping out into the yard. Others came from their various chores, talking loudly as they toiled up the hill to the chapel.

"Returned so soon, Aidan?" I turned to see Cellach, the Master of the Library, watching me, his head held to one side as if pondering a philosophical complexity.

"Ah, Brother Cellach, there is a task I would finish."

"Of course." Cellach started away, tucking his hands into his sleeves.

When everyone had gone, I entered the scriptorium and went to my place. The unfinished manuscript lay on

the board. I picked up my pen and stood contemplating
the line that I had last been writing. The neat black letters,
so graceful in their simplicity, seemed perfectly conceived
to carry the weight of their inspired message. Into my
mind came a scrap of verse I had written numerous times:
*Heaven and Earth shall pass away, but my Word shall never
pass away . . .*

Word of God's Word, I thought, I am the vellum and
you are the Scribe. Write what you will, Lord, that all who
see me shall behold your grace and majesty!

Laying aside my pen, I sat in the empty room, looking
and listening, remembering all that I had learned and practised in this place. I gazed at the clustered tables, each with
its bench, and both worn smooth, the hard, hard oak polished through years of constant use. In this room everything was well-ordered and precise: vellum leaves lay flat
and square, pens were placed at the top right-hand corner
of each table, and inkhorns stood upright in the dirt floor
beside each bench.

Thin light slanted in through the narrow windholes
high in the four walls. The dying wind whined as it circled
the scriptorium, searching among the chinks in the timbers
for entrance, but many hands over many years had pressed
tufts of raw wool into the cracks, frustrating all but the
most savage gales.

I closed my eyes and breathed the air. The room
smelled of peat from the small fire of turves glowing red on
the hearthstone in the centre of the room. The pungent
white smoke drifted up through the smokehole in the roof-
thatch.

It had been my chore, when I first came here, to carry
the turves, guard those embers, and keep that fire going
through the chill winter days. I would sit in the corner on
my pile of peat, and watch the faces of the scribes at their
labour, all sharp-eyed and keen as they copied out

Prophet, Psalm, and Gospel, their pens scritch-scratching on the dry vellum leaves.

I saw the scriptorium now much as I had seen it then: not a room at all, but a fortress entire and sufficient unto itself, a rock against the winds of chaos howling beyond the monastery walls. Order and harmony reigned here.

After prayers, my fellow scribes returned to their work, forsaking their talk at the door. In the scriptorium no voice was ever lifted above a whisper, and then rarely, lest the sound disturb or distract. A momentary lapse in concentration could mean the ruin of a page, and days of meticulous labour.

Taking up my pen once more, I undertook to complete the passage before me, working happily until *vespers*. We secured our work for the night and left the scriptorium, joining our brothers in the chapel. After prayers, we gathered at table to break bread for our evening meal: a watery stew of brown lentils and salt pork. Brother Fernach read from the Psalms as we ate, and Ruadh read from the Rule of Colum Cille, then dismissed us to our cells for study.

I was reading the Canticle of the Three Youths, to which I applied myself intently, and my diligence was rewarded, for it seemed as if I had only just lit the candles when the bell sounded *compline*. Laying the book carefully aside, I left the cell and joined the brothers on the way to the chapel. I looked for Dugal among them, but the night was dark and I did not see him. Nor did I see him afterwards.

Prayers were offered for the coming journey, and it put me in mind to make petition myself. So, after the service I sought out Ruadh, our *secnab*, and requested the night vigil. As second to Abbot Fraoch, it was Ruadh's responsibility to appoint the readers and vigilants each day.

Crossing the yard, I proceeded to a small hut set a little

apart from the abbot's lodge. There, I paused at the entrance to the cell and, pulling the oxhide covering aside, I tapped on the door. A moment later, Ruadh bade me enter. I pushed open the narrow door and stepped into a room aglow with candlelight. The air smelled of beeswax and honey. Ruadh was sitting in his chair with his bare toes almost touching the turf fire on the hearthstone at his feet. As I came to stand before him, he put aside the scroll he was reading and stood.

"Sit with me, Aidan," he said, indicating a three-legged stool. "I will not keep you long from your rest."

Ruadh was, as I say, secnab of our community, second only to Abbot Fraoch in the monastic hierarchy. He was also my confessor and guide—my *anamcara*, my soul friend, responsible for my spiritual health and progress.

I drew the stool to the fire's edge and held my hands to it, waiting for him to speak. The room, like most of the others, was a bare stone cell with a single small windhole in one wall, and a straw sleeping pallet on the floor. Ruadh's *bulga*, his leather book satchel, hung on its strap from a peg above the pallet, and a basin of water sat at the foot of the bed. Candles stood in iron candletrees, and on stones on the floor. The only other adornment in the room was a stone shelf which held a small wooden cross.

Many and many were the times we had sat together in this simple hut, deep in conversation over a point of theology, or unsnarling one of the numerous tangles in my wayward soul's knotted skein. I realized that this might be the last time I would sit with my soul friend. Instantly, a deep melancholy overcame me and I felt another pain of parting—oh, and there were many more partings to come.

"Well, Aidan," Ruadh said, glancing up from the fire after a moment, "you have achieved your heart's desire. How does it feel?"

"Sure, I am delighted," I replied; my sudden lack of enthusiasm declared otherwise, however.

"Truly?" Ruadh wondered. "It seems to me you express your joy in a most dour manner, Aidan."

"I am well pleased," I insisted. "It has been my only thought since I first learned of the bishop's plan, as you well know."

"And now that you have won your will, you begin to see another side to the thing," he suggested.

"I have had time to consider the matter in greater detail," I said, "and I find the abbot's decision has not made me so happy as I expected."

"Did you imagine it would bring you happiness? Is that why you wanted it so badly?"

"No, Confessor," I protested quickly. "It is just that I am beginning to understand how much I am leaving behind when I go."

"It is to be expected." He nodded sympathetically. "Indeed, I have heard it said that in order to go anywhere, one must leave the place where he is and arrive somewhere else." He pursed his lips and stroked his chin. "Although I am no authority in such matters, I am persuaded that this may be true."

My heart lightened somewhat at his gentle wit. "As always, your wisdom is unassailable, Confessor."

"Remember, Aidan," he said, leaning forward slightly, "never doubt in the darkness that which you believed in the light. Also, this: unless the pilgrim carry with him the thing he seeks, he will not find it when he arrives."

"I will remember."

He leaned back in his chair once more. "Now then, what preparations will you make?"

I had not given a thought to any specific preparations. "It occurs to me," I began slowly, "that a fast would be appropriate—a *trédinus*, I believe, would prepare me for—"

Ruadh stopped me. "A three-day fast is truly commendable," he agreed quickly. "But as we are even now observing Lent, rather than adding fast to fast, might I suggest another discipline? A spiritual fast, if you like."

"Yes?"

"Make peace with those you are leaving behind," he said. "If anyone has hurt you, or if there is anyone you hold grievance against—now is the time to set matters right."

I opened my mouth to object that I bore no one any ill, but Ruadh continued: "Hear me, my son, it is not a thing to be dismissed lightly. I would have you regard this as a matter worthy of your highest consideration."

"If you insist, Confessor," I replied, somewhat confused by his vehemence. "Still, I think a fast would be most beneficial. I could do both."

"You are not thinking, Aidan," he said. "Think! There is a time to fast, and a time to feast. The journey you will make is most arduous. Hardship and privation are the least dangers you will face."

"Certainly, Secnab, I am well aware of the dangers."

"Are you?" he asked. "I wonder."

I said nothing.

Ruadh leaned towards me across the fire. "Now is the time to gather strength for the journey, son. Eat well, drink well, sleep and take your ease while you may—store up your vigour against the day when it will be required."

"If you think it best, Confessor," I said, "then I will do it."

As if he had not heard me, Ruadh said, "Soon you will leave this place—perhaps forever, it must be said. Therefore, you must go with a free and easy heart. When you leave, leave with peace in your soul so that you may face whatever dangers come upon you with courage and fortitude undiminished, secure in the knowledge that you hold no enmity for any man, and no man holds enmity for you."

"As you will, Confessor," I replied.

"Ah! You have not heard a single word. Do not do it for me, son—*I* am not the one going to Byzantium." He regarded me with mild impatience. "Well, think about what I have said." He took up his scroll once again, signalling an end to our conversation.

"Trust that I will do as you advise," I replied, rising to my feet.

"Peace be with you, Aidan."

I stepped to the door. "God keep you this night, Secnab," I said. Suddenly overwhelmed by fatigue, I yawned and decided not to request the night vigil after all.

Turning his head to look at me, Ruadh said, "Rest while you may, Aidan, for the night is coming when no man can rest."

I walked out into the darkness and raised my eyes to a sky bright-dusted with stars. The wind had died away and the world lay hushed and still. On a night such as this, any talk of danger and hardship was surely exaggerated. I returned to my cell and lay down on my pallet to sleep.

# 4

The next day was Passion Day, and no work is done—save that strictly necessary for the maintenance of the abbey and its inhabitants. Most of us renewed our tonsure, so to be clean-shaven for the Sabbath, or Resurrection Day.

The tonsure of the Célé Dé is distinctive; the front of the head is shaved from ear to ear, save for a thin line that forms a circlet, called the corona—symbol of the crown we hope one day to receive from our Lord's hand. This must be refreshed from time to time, of course, as the hair grows back in short, prickly bristles. Renewing the tonsure is a service we perform often for one another. Thus, we are all accomplished barbers.

As the day was warm, Dugal and I took it in turn to sit on a milking stool in the yard while the other performed the rite of the razor. Our brothers were likewise occupied, and we filled the yard with pleasant, if idle, chatter. I was just drying my new-shaven head with a cloth when Cellach summoned me.

"They are calling for you," he said, and I heard the weary resignation in his voice.

"Forgive me, master, I thought we were finished."

"So did I," he sighed. "But there will be no peace until they are happy. Go to them, son. See what you can do."

Well, our part of the book was completed. Nevertheless, Libir and Brocmal, still labouring over their long-finished leaves, insisted on reviewing all the work one last time. They beseeched Master Cellach with such zeal that he gave in just to silence them, and I was obliged to help.

I arrived to find that the two scribes had carefully laid out all the leaves, placing two or three on each empty table in the scriptorium. Then, beginning at the top, they moved from table to table, inspecting the leaves, heads down, noses almost touching the vellum, sharp eyes scanning the texts and pictures for invisible flaws. I followed, hands behind back, gazing at the wonderful work and stifling little cries of delight. Truly, it is a blessed book!

Not far into their inspection, however, the two demanding scribes found a blemish. "Aidan!" Brocmal cried, turning on me so fiercely that my first thought was that the mistake, whatever it was, had been mine. "Ink is needed!"

"This can be saved," Libir intoned solemnly, his face nearly pressed to the table. "A line or two . . . See? Here . . . and here."

"Christ be thanked," Brocmal agreed with exaggerated relief, bending over the suspect leaf. "I will prepare a pen." He turned and, seeing me looking on, shouted, "What is this, Aidan? The bishop arrives at any moment. We need ink! Why are you standing there like a post?"

"You did not say what colour is required."

"Red, of course!" he snapped.

"And blue," added Libir.

"Blue and red," Brocmal commanded. "Away with you, sluggard!"

We worked through most of the day this way, for having repaired one fault, they soon found others requiring instant attention—though I saw none of the supposed errors they so cheerfully discerned. We removed ourselves from the daily round, and from the midday table as well, in order to mend the damage.

It was just after *none*, and I was standing at the mixing table, pounding red lead and ochre in a mortar, when the bell sounded. Laying aside my tools, I quickly pulled on my mantle, gathered my cloak, and hurried into the scriptorium. "The bishop has arrived!" Brocmal announced, although Libir and I were already racing to the door. Out into the yard we joined the throng making for the gate.

Ranging ourselves in ranks to the right and left of the gate, we began singing a hymn to welcome our guests. Bishop Cadoc led the party, striding forth boldly for all he was a very old man. Yet, his step was strong and his eye keen as the eagle on the *cambutta* in his hand. This sacred symbol, fashioned in yellow gold atop his bishop's staff, gleamed with a holy light in the midday sun, scattering the shadows as he passed.

There were many monks with him—thirty altogether. I watched each one as he passed through the gate, and wondered which among them were The Chosen. I wondered also who carried the book. For, though I saw more than one bulga dangling from shoulder straps, I did not see any which I thought grand enough for the Book of Colum Cille.

Abbot Fraoch met our visitors inside the gate and welcomed the bishop with a kiss. He hailed the company warmly, saying, "Greetings, brothers! In the name of our Blessed Lord and Saviour, Jesu, we welcome you to Cenannus na Ríg. May God grant you peace and joy while you are with us. Rest now and take your ease while we extend to you every comfort we possess."

To this the bishop replied, "You are kind, Brother Fraoch, but we are fellow labourers in fields of the Lord. Thus, we expect to receive nothing which you would deny yourselves." Casting his gaze around him, he spread wide his arms. "The peace of our Lord be with you, my dear children," he called in a fine strong voice.

We answered: "And with your spirit also!"

"As many as have come to you, that many more would have gladly accompanied me," the bishop continued. "I bring greetings from your brothers at Hy and Lindisfarne." He paused, smiling with pleasure. "I also bring a treasure."

Then, passing his staff of office to his secnab, Bishop Cadoc gestured for one of the monks to step forward. As the monk came near, he drew the strap of his bulga over his head and offered it to his superior. Cadoc received it, pulled the peg, lifted the flap and withdrew the book to cries of amazement and wonder all around.

Oh, it was magnificent! Even at a distance, I thought it a marvel; for the *cumtach* was not leather—not even the dyed calfskin used for very special books. The cover of Colum Cille's book was sheet silver worked into fantastic figures: spirals, keys, and triscs. At each corner of the cover was a knotwork panel, and in the centre of each panel a different gem had been mounted. These surrounded a knotwork cross, beset with rubies. In the play of sunlight the silver cumtach seemed a living thing, dancing, dazzling, moving with the rhythm of the King of Glory's creation.

Abbot Fraoch took the book into his hands, raised it to his lips and kissed it. Then he held it above his head and turned this way and that so everyone could catch a glimpse. Two years in preparation, the Book of Colum Cille was a treasure rare and fine—a gift worthy of an emperor. My heart swelled with pride at the sight.

Replacing the book in its humble bag once more, the abbot and bishop walked together arm in arm up the hill to the oratory where they held close conversation until *vespers*. Many of the monks among us, having formerly lived in either Hy or Lindisfarne, enjoyed close friendships with many of our brother visitors; some were kinsmen. They fell on one another's necks and gripped each other's arms in greeting. Everyone began talking at once. After a while Brother Paulinus, our porter, shouted for the visitors to accompany him, whereupon he conducted them to the guest lodge.

Brocmal, Libir, and I returned to the scriptorium where we worked until supper when the two scribes, failing to discover any other jot to alter, pronounced the work completed at last.

"It is finished," Libir said. "We have done our part. Lord Jesu have mercy."

"Pray God it meets with the bishop's approval." Brocmal finally allowed himself a satisfied grin as his gaze played over all the finished leaves on the tables. "Truly, it meets with *my* approval."

"You are very bards of vellum," I told them. "Though my part was small, I am proud to have been of service to you."

Both monks regarded me curiously, and I thought they might mention my contribution in their rejoicing at the completion of their labours, but they turned away, saying nothing. We then joined our brothers for the beginning of the Easter celebration—but not before securing the precious leaves.

Bishop Cadoc, as honoured guest, read the *Beati* and prayed. I listened with utmost attention, trying to determine what manner of man he might be for, though I had seen him once before, I was little more than a boy at the time and remembered almost nothing of that occasion.

Cadoc, like my old teacher Cybi, was a Briton. It was said that as a boy he had studied at Bangor-ys-Coed under the renowned Elffod, and as a young man he had travelled all throughout Gaul, teaching and preaching, before returning to Britain to lead the community at Candida Casa where he often held discourse with the most learned Eruigena. The excellent Sedulius—or Saidhuil, as he was known to us—had once written a poem in commemoration of a fine debate held between them.

Looking at the little bishop, it seemed to me appropriate that illustrious men should seek to celebrate his friendship. Small of stature and well filled with years, he nevertheless possessed the grace and dignity of a king, and exuded the health of a man still in the flush of youth. If, despite his vigour, any uncertainty still lingered, Cadoc had only to speak and doubt would vanish, for his voice was a powerful instrument, rich and full and loud, and prone to burst into song at any moment. This trait, as I have it, he shared with his kinsmen; trueborn Cymry loved nothing better than hearing their own voices soaring in song. Now, I had never heard a trumpet before, but if anyone had told me that it sounded like the Bishop of Hy singing a hymn I would have believed it.

After the meal, Brocmal, Libir and myself were presented to Cadoc. The abbot called us to his lodge where he and the bishop were sitting together with their secnabs, enjoying a cup of Easter mead. Now that the feast was begun, such luxuries were allowed.

"Welcome, brothers. Come in and sit with us." The abbot motioned us to places on the floor between their chairs. Three additional cups had been poured in anticipation of our arrival, and when the abbot had distributed these, he said, his broken voice a thin whisper, "I have been telling Bishop Cadoc about our contribution to the book. He is most desirous of seeing what you have achieved."

The bishop then asked us to describe our work. Brocmal began a lengthy account of the undertaking and how the labours had been divided among the various members of the scriptorium; Libir added observations from time to time, and Bishop Cadoc asked many questions of them both. I listened, awaiting my turn to speak, but it did not come.

It is a sign of my prideful spirit, no doubt, that I began to feel slighted—and I was not the only one. Master Cellach, under whose skillful and painstaking direction the great labour was accomplished, never received a mention, nor did any of the other scribes—and there were many. Listening to Brocmal and Libir's account, one would have thought they had produced the entire book between the two of them alone. My own hand had copied out no less than thirty-eight separate passages, filling more than twenty leaves. And I was but one of a score of scribes working in three scriptoria on three separate islands. Indeed, the men who raised the cows that produced the calves that gave their skins to make the vellum, were certainly no less important in their way than the scribes who decorated those skins with such splendid art. Then again, I reflected, there were no herdsmen going to Byzantium.

Well, it was a small thing—an oversight, perhaps. But I could not help feeling in it the sting of an insult. Pride, I suppose, will be my ruin. But Brocmal and Libir, I reckoned, were reaping their reward at the expense of all the others who would never be recognized. I determined to remedy this injustice if I could. I must bide my time, however, and await the best opportunity.

So, I sat on the floor at Abbot Fraoch's feet, sipping the sweet mead and listening to Brocmal describe the book that I knew so well—but now seemed not to know at all—

and thought about the journey, wondering what the other *peregrini* would be like. If they were anything like Brocmal and Libir, I concluded, it would be a very arduous campaign.

After a while, Brocmal finished and the bishop turned to the abbot. "You have chosen well, Fraoch," he said, smiling like a man who knows a valuable secret. "These men will serve us admirably in our endeavour."

His use of the strange word pricked my attention. Did he mean the journey . . . or, did he have another undertaking in mind? The sly expression suggested he meant something other than taking the book to the emperor.

But the abbot merely returned his smile. "Of that, Cadoc, I have not the slightest doubt." He raised the cup. "I drink to the success of our mission, brothers. May God bless you richly, and protect you always."

"Amen!" replied Cadoc, and we all raised our cups with the abbot.

The bell sounded *compline* then and we were dismissed to our prayers. "We will speak again," the bishop assured us. We bade the two good night and left the abbot's lodge, making our way to the chapel. Brocmal and Libir, in good spirits, sang as they walked up the hill. I followed behind with eyes downcast, feeling vexed with the two of them, and annoyed with myself for feeling so.

I entered the chapel and found a place along the north wall as far from Brocmal and Libir as possible. Dugal came and settled beside me, nudging me with an elbow to let me know he was there. I raised my head, but did not speak, lost as I was in my own thoughts. *Why am I always like this?* I wondered. *What is it to me if the two of them receive the honour of the bishop's praise? They earned it, after all. It was not as if they had stolen the book, or claimed more for themselves than they deserved. What is wrong with me?*

Prayers finished and I went to my cell and a disgruntled sleep. The next morning, after *maiden* prayers, we broke fast with our visitors and, since normal duties were suspended for the Eastertide celebration, everyone gathered in the yard to sing. The day had begun cool and bright, with a sky full of white clouds. As we sang, the clouds knit themselves together and closed in; a spit of rain began to fall, which eventually persuaded us back into the hall, where we settled in clumps to talk with our visiting brothers over the board.

Unlike most of Cenannus' brotherhood, I knew no one from Hy or Lindisfarne. Nevertheless, as Dugal and I moved among the tables, one of the strangers called out to me. "Aidan mac Cainnech!"

I turned to see a short, square-faced man with wiry brown hair and dark brown eyes, sitting with two other strangers. All three were watching me with evident interest.

"Go to them," urged Dugal. "They want to talk to you." He left me and went on to another table.

"I give you good greeting," I said as I approached.

"Sit you down with us," said the visitor. "We would speak with you, nothing preventing."

"I am at your service, brothers," I said taking my place at the board. "I would gladly give you my name, but it seems you have it from someone else."

"Do not think us over bold," said one of the others. "We are Cymry and curiosity is a very plague with us." The two with him laughed—clearly it was a cheerful plague. I liked them at once.

"I am Brynach," said the stranger who had called to me. "These are my brothers. No! My *anamcari*," he raised a hand to the two with him. "This long lanky reed is Gwilym." He indicated a tall spare man with thinning fair hair. "And this is Morien," he said, presenting a young man with thick black curly hair and blue eyes. "Although," he warned, "if you call him that he will never answer, for he is known to one and all as Ddewi."

"Brothers," I said, envying their easy way with one another, "I am glad to meet you. I pray your Easter with us is meat and drink to your soul." I paused, feeling the awkwardness of the question before I spoke it, but I could not help myself. "Please do not think ill of me, but I have never visited Hy or Lindisfarne, and I would know which of those two fine places is home to you."

"Neither," replied Gwilym happily. "Our home is Ty Gwyn, but lately we have spent some years at Menevia and Bangor-ys-Coed."

"Indeed," I replied. "I did not know the book was also being readied there."

"It was not," answered Brynach. "We learned of the book too late to be of material service in that part of the enterprise."

Again, my senses pricked to the suggestion of an alternate purpose for the journey—a purpose which many seemed to know. "You seem well apprised of these matters," I suggested. "Am I right in thinking that you are among those chosen for the travelling party?"

"We are, yes," Brynach affirmed.

"But you are not scribes," I blurted in surprise. "Forgive me, that did not sound as I meant it. I mean no disrespect."

"Be at ease, brother," tutted Gwilym. "Truth is a constant delight to those that love her; such beauty holds no power to offend."

"The truth is," Brynach confided, "we are not scribes. And yet, the Great King, in his infinite wisdom, has seen fit to include us in your exalted company. I hope you will accept us also." He made a little bow of his head, and put an amiable hand on the tall man's shoulder. "Gwilym, here, is an artisan for whom gold and precious stones were especially created." The monk inclined his head in easy acknowledgement of the compliment.

Brynach turned to the black-haired youth. "Ah, and this stripling you see before you is a *leighean* of rare and extraordinary gifts."

"My family have been physicians for seven generations," Ddewi explained, speaking for the first time. "And I am the seventh son of my father, who was also a seventh son." His voice and manner were quiet, hinting at unseen depths.

"Alas," said Brynach, "I myself claim no such talents or abilities enjoyed by my brothers here. My sole occupation has ever been study, and now I find I am no longer fit for anything else."

Although his modesty was genuine, I doubted that he would have been chosen if he were as humble as he professed. Before I could enquire of him further, however, he said, "Now then, Aidan, they tell me you are the finest scribe Kells can boast—"

"And not only scribe, but scholar too," put in Gwilym.

"Kells does indeed maintain many fine scribes," I allowed, "and it is true that I am one of them—albeit, the youngest and least experienced of all. My own contribution to the book is but small when compared to that of Brocmal and Libir and some others."

"But your pen has touched the blessed book," Gwilym said. "Your hands have laboured over it. I wish I could say as much."

Brynach nodded as if this were his life's highest ambition. All three glanced at one another; a sign must have passed between them, for the monk leaned near, as if to confide a secret. "May I tell you something?" he asked.

"Of course, Brother Brynach," I said.

"Those I choose to be my friends call me Bryn," he said, and motioned me nearer.

I put my head close to his, but before he could speak further, Brother Diarmot appeared. "I trust our brother has extended to you the abbey's welcome," he said stiffly. "I would not like to think he has been remiss in his duty to you, our long-awaited visitors."

Brynach pulled himself upright once more and the smile reappeared instantly. "Have no fear for our sake," he replied smoothly. "We have been made more than welcome."

"Indeed," put in Gwilym, "it is as if we had never left home."

"I am Brother Diarmot, and I am at your service. If you are hungry, it would be my pleasure to bring you something to eat."

"Thank you, brother," replied Brynach. "But no."

"Something to drink perhaps?" pressed Diarmot. He looked at me and smiled thinly. "I would have thought Aidan had offered, but I am happy to serve."

"Well," said Gwilym, "I might be tempted with some more of that excellent ale which we drank at last night's table."

"Of course," said Diarmot. "Aidan and I will bring the cups. It is the least we can do for our guests."

"Please, allow me to help you," said Gwilym rising quickly.

"No, no," replied Diarmot adamantly. "You are our guests. I could not possibly allow you to fetch your own drink. Aidan will help me."

The stubborn Diarmot loomed over me like a threat, so I rose and followed him to the kitchen to fill a jar while he found the cups. When we returned to the board, other monks had joined the three Britons, and I did not have another chance to speak to them alone. All the rest of the day I watched and waited for an opportunity, but events did not yield the desired result.

I retired to my cell that night aching with curiosity, frustrated, and resentful of Diarmot for his ill-chanced intrusion. Before sleeping, I prayed Christ's forgiveness for disliking Diarmot, and lay for a long time wondering what Brynach had been about to tell me.

# 5

Climbing the hillside in the predawn darkness, we ascend like Christ, rising from the valley of death. We huddle on the hilltop, as if shivering in the grave's cold grip, awaiting resurrection's true, unfailing light. We wait in silence, faces turned to the east, whence comes the Saving Word. Away beyond the rim of the world, daylight gathers its strength, growing and growing, until at last—the powers of darkness unable to restrain it any longer—it bursts forth in a glorious life-giving blaze. Rises up the sun victorious, Sol Invictus, renewed like Christ resurrected, as shall all men be in the Last Day. As the first golden rays ignite the heavens, we draw breath and raise our voices to the Golden Throne, "Alleluia! Hosanna! Glory to God in the Highest Heaven! Alleluia!"

Led by the Bishop of Hy with cambutta upraised, we made procession down the hill, singing the Gloria as we went. With so many guests and visitors, there was not room inside the church for everyone so, as the day was fair, the first part of the mass was conducted under the roof of Heaven. The various parts of the mass were observed: the Gradual, followed by the reading of the Gospel, and the Credo, Psalms and Offertory.

During the prayers, the visitors knelt in the yard, and then rose to form double ranks at the door for the procession of the Host and Chalice to the altar. Bishop Cadoc, aided by the abbot, continued the Service of the Sacraments at the altar. I was among those who stood outside the church, but we had no difficulty hearing. Cadoc's fine voice carried into the yard and beyond the abbey walls.

"Quanda canitus:" the bishop called as he offered the Chalice to God, "accept Jesu panem . . ."

We knelt in the glow of the Easter morning sun as our hearts warmed to the love of God. One by one, we entered the church and proceeded to the altar where we received the sacraments from the bishop's hand, returning to our places for the benediction.

It was a fine and joyful service. When it finished, we sang until the bell rang *terse*, whereupon Abbot Fraoch invited all our visitors to share our feast.

"Jesu is alive!" he rasped, raising his voice above its normal whisper. "Rejoice and be glad, my friends, for all who trust in Christ have eternal life. And as we will one day gather in Heaven's Great Hall, let us enjoy the blessings of God's rich bounty this good Easter day—a foretaste of the Feast of the Lamb."

With those words, the celebration began. To accommodate all our visitors, we hauled benches and boards from the refectory and placed them in the yard. Women from the settlements helped the cooks and kitcheners bestrew these with foods of all kinds: brown bread baked into special Eastertide loaves—round, with the shape of the cross cut in the top; cold boiled eggs—symbol of life's potency and promise; salmon and pike—fresh, salted, and smoked—on wooden trenchers; mussels and oysters; ground meal and pine kernels cooked in milk with egg and honey; roast turnips in steaming heaps; huge cauldrons of lamb stew;

pork and beef and mutton roasted with fennel and onions and garlic; goose in herbed sauce; hare stuffed with sweet chestnuts; cockerels stuffed with corn and sage; larks in elderberry; compotes of plums and raspberries and apples; and much else besides.

Aengus mac Fergus, lord of the realm, sent some of his men with Easter gifts: great haunches of venison and boar to grace our feast. They wasted not a moment setting the meat to roast on spits over fires in the yard. Divested of this duty, they quickly devoted themselves to the cellarer, and became his willing slaves, labouring mightily with the oaken vats of rich dark ale and sweet yellow mead. The vats were placed on tripods outside the entrance to the hall. Also, since it was Easter, crocks of wine were provided.

When all was ready, Secnab Ruadh called for silence and prayed God's good blessing on our festal meal. Then, taking up our wooden bowls, we broke our long Easter fast—partaking of those dishes each found most appealing. The day was given to the satisfaction of eating and drinking and harmonious conversation with friends and kinsmen. And all who gathered within the abbey walls were brother and sister, parent and child, one to the other.

After the pangs of hunger were well and truly banished, we played games. Urged on by the children of our guests, we engaged in contests of strength and skill: throwing the well-stone, lofting spears, hand wrestling, and the like. Some of the lord's men, warriors all, devised a horse race in which the riders must sit backwards in the saddle. This proved such an enjoyable spectacle that the race was run several times to accommodate everyone who wished to take part. The last race was the best, for many of the older children insisted on being allowed to ride. So that the younger ones would not feel aggrieved, some of the monks joined in, each taking a child before him so that no harm could befall the little one. This made for even more confusion and the resulting laughter made the valley resound. Oh, it was a splendid diversion!

All through the festivities, I remained at Dugal's side, painfully aware that the time for our parting was hard upon us; but, as I did not like unhappy thoughts to intrude on that glorious Eastertide celebration, I tried my best not to dwell on it. If Dugal held similar feelings, he gave no sign, enjoying himself to the full, going from ale vat to race to table and back again. Of the three mysterious visitors—Brynach, Gwilym, and Ddewi—I saw little. They seemed always to hover in the bishop's shadow, often engaged in close conversation with one or another of our elder brethren. Though the festivity flowed easily around them, the three, and Brynach especially, held themselves aloof—looking on, smiling, but seldom entering into the merriment.

So the day passed, and the sun began to drift low, flaming the western sky with red-gold. Our good *abb* summoned all the people to follow him, and we made a great procession around the cross in the yard. Once, twice, three times around, whereupon he gathered everyone in a ring around the cross and said in his grating whisper of a voice: "Behold this cross! Sure, it is naked now, but it was not always so. I would have you remember, friends, that dire and dreadful day, when the Great King's Son took the weight of the world upon his back as he hung upon Golgotha's tree!

"Woe and shame, I say! O, Heart of my heart, your people seized you; they bound you; they struck you: green reed on firm flesh, hateful fist on ruddy cheek! Wicked thorns became a crown for the sacred head; a borrowed robe mocked the shoulders of him who bore the grievous stain of mankind's sin.

"And then, no stopping the bloodlust, they took you,

piercing hands and feet with cold, cruel nails. They raised you high above the ground to die in bitter agony, your people helpless, watching.

"Hideous deed, the World Creator was spat upon as death stole the light from his eyes." Fraoch's voice cracked as the tears rolled down his cheeks. "Thunder and wind did not constrain them, rain and hail they heeded not— neither the broken voice crying out: Abba, forgive them! They know not what they do!

"Up came the sharp-bladed spear, biting deep into your wounded heart. Water and blood poured down your gleaming sides—the wine of forgiveness spilled out for all—and the Beautiful One of God breathed no more.

"Then it is down from the cross—they cannot wait to have you away! Dragged through the streets, you were, tied in a sack! Common wrappings for the corpse of the High King of Heaven, never fine linen or soft furs.

"The rock-cut tomb becomes your home, Beloved. The solitude of the turf house is your new domain, there in the bone grove. Caesar's soldiers stand guard at the doorstone lest the murderers disturb your deathsleep.

"Do they fear you even yet? They have done you to death, Lord of All, and they stand guard, looking right and left, hands trembling. Darkness falls over the earth. How not? The Light of Life has been shut up in a grave, and the greedy night is full of demon smiles.

"Friends," the abbot whispered, his voice small in contemplation of that awful night, "the enemies of light and life held great celebration then. Their revelry resounded loud in the Halls of Heaven. And the Father God gazed down in his sore grief. 'See here, Michael!' he called to his Champion. 'They have killed my beloved son. That is bad enough, but they should not rejoice so. Can this be right, that evil should exult in the death of the Only Righteous?'

"And Michael, Servant of Light, replied, 'Lord, you know it is not right. Say the word, my king, and I shall slay them all with my fiery sword.'

"Oh, but the Ever Merciful lays a finger to his lips. And it is: 'Patience, patience, all in good time. I would not be God if disaster should find me unequal to the task. Only stand you back and watch what I shall do.'

"The High King of Heaven, his great heart breaking, gazed down into that bleak grove. A single tear from his loving eye fell into that dark tomb where lay the body of his blessed son, the Prince of Peace. That tear struck the Christ full on his battered face, and sweet life came flooding back.

"The Great King turned to his Champion and said, 'Why do you tarry, friend? You see how it is. Roll aside that stone and let my son go free!' Michael, striking like lightning to the earth, put his hand to the accursed rock and, with a flick of his finger, hurled the great millstone aside.

"Up you arose! Christ Victorious! You threw aside the sack and stood. Death, that weak, contemptible thing, lay shattered at your feet. You kicked the shards aside and strode from the tomb, brave soldiers falling on their faces, slain by the sight of such undiluted glory!"

Abbot Fraoch spread his hands wide. "A thousand welcomes, O Blessed King! A thousand welcomes, Eternal Youth! Hail and welcome, Lord of Grace, who suffered all that death could do—for Adam's willful race, you suffered, yes, and gladly died. Firstborn of Life, it was ourselves you carried from the tomb, each and every one clinging to your broad back.

"So look upon the cross and rejoice, friends. Think of it, and praise Him who has the power to raise the dead to life. Amen!"

And everyone gazed at the high cross in the fiery sunset, and cried, "Amen, Lord!"

Brothers with harps, awaiting this moment, began to play. We sang: hymns, of course, but other songs as well—ancient songs, older than any of the tribes or clans that claimed them, older than the wooded hills themselves. As night enfolded us, we sang, and heard again the age-honoured stories of our race.

We went to our rest that night satisfied in body and soul, and rose the next day to continue our celebration. Through the three days of the Easter feast, I tried to prepare myself for leaving. I saw Dugal but rarely; if I had not known him better, I would have imagined he was avoiding me.

It was late the third day by the time all the visitors had gone. At *vespers*, I joined my brothers for prayer for the last time. The sun had set and it was dusky within the abbey walls, but the sky was still pale blue overhead. Two bright stars gleamed low in the east. *They say the sky in Byzantium is gold,* Dugal had said. *And the very stars are strange.*

My heart writhed within me for I longed to speak a word to him. Tomorrow I would leave, and once beyond the abbey ringwall, I would never see my good friend again. The thought upset me so I determined to take the night vigil in order to set my heart at rest.

Accordingly, I went to Ruadh to request the duty. He seemed surprised at my petition. "I would think it better for both body and soul to rest," Ruadh suggested. "Therefore, I counsel a night's sound sleep."

"I thank you for the thought," I replied. "And I am certain you advise the wisest course. But it is also my last opportunity to hold vigil before the abbey altar. Therefore, I respectfully ask your permission."

"And I give it gladly," Ruadh allowed. "It is Diarmot's duty tonight, however. You must find him and inform him of the change."

"Of course," I agreed, and made to leave the secnab's lodge. "Thank you, Confessor."

"I will miss you, Aidan," Ruadh said, following me to the door. "But I will pray for you every day at *matins*. Wherever you are, you will know that the day began with your name before the High King's throne. And each day at *vespers* I will beseech the Lord's mercy on your behalf. That way, wherever you are in God's wide world, you will know that the day ended with entreaty for your safe return."

These words moved me so that I could not speak—all the more, since I knew that he would uphold his vow through all things. He put his arms around my shoulders and hugged me to his chest. "Go with God, my son," Ruadh said. I nodded, swallowing hard, and left him.

I searched for Dugal, but did not find him—one of the brothers told me Dugal was helping with the lambing away in the next valley—and so I returned unhappily to my cell and threw myself upon my pallet. Ignoring the call to supper, I dozed awhile and awoke when the bell rang *compline*, but could not bring myself to join the brothers for prayer. I lay in my cell, listening to the sounds of the abbey settling in for the night. And when at last I judged everyone had gone to their rest, I snuffed the candle and hurried out into the darkness once more.

The moon had risen as a hard, bright ball of ice glowing in the sky. The wind which had blown all day slept now, and I could hear dogs barking in the settlement beyond the river. Moving silently across the empty yard, my shadow sharp beneath my feet, I saw no one else about.

The chapel is a plain, unadorned square of stone with thick walls and high, steeply-pitched stone roof—a place of peace and the quiet strength that comes of long devotion. The fierce moonlight had transformed the dark stone into hammered metal—bronze or, perhaps, silver. Stepping to the entrance, I lifted the latch, pushed open the heavy door, ducked my head and stepped into the spare room with its squat stone altar below a high narrow windhole; a massive wooden bookholder stood in one corner, empty now; no book is required for the night vigil. Candles sizzled silently in the tall candletrees, filling the chapel with their warm, slightly rancid scent.

Pulling the door shut behind me, I replaced the latch and started towards the altar. Only then did I notice Diarmot. "It will be my pleasure to hold vigil with you," he offered with stiff formality. My heart fell.

"Brother, there is no need," I told him. "I have taken up this duty, and will bear it gladly. Forgive me, I meant to tell you earlier, but you are free to go."

"Be that as it may," Diarmot replied with smug satisfaction. "It will be good for me to stand with you this night."

I did not relish his company, but could think of no further objection, so let him have his way. "It is not for me to deny you," I told him, and took my place at the altar opposite him.

Night vigil is a simple service of prayer. No rites attend it, save those each celebrant brings with him. Many say the Psalms, genuflecting after each one; some pray the night away, either prostrate or cross-wise; others simply wait upon the Lord in silence, meditating on the divine name, or an aspect of the Godhead.

Most often, I chose to pray, letting my mind roam where it would, placing this contemplation before the High King of Heaven as an offering. Sometimes, however, when my soul was troubled, I simply knelt and gave myself to the *Kyrie eleison*. This is what I did now. "Lord have mercy," I prayed, repeating the plea with every breath as I knelt beside the altar.

It seemed that Diarmot, however, had decided on

reciting the One Hundred-Fifty. He intoned the Psalms in a murmuring voice, bowing low as he began each one, and going down on both knees as he finished. Diarmot, like many of the brothers, was earnest and sincere—far more so than myself, I freely confess. Even so, I found it difficult to suffer him, for I had noticed that many of these monks, despite their diligence, always seemed more concerned with the appearance of a thing than its actual meaning. Sure, one heartfelt genuflection must be worth more than a hundred performed to punctuate a recitation. Most likely I am deluded in this, as in so much else.

Resigning myself to Diarmot's noisy presence, I knelt with bowed head, breathing my simple prayer, "Lord have mercy! . . . Christ, have mercy!" As I prayed, I fixed my eyes upon the gently wavering circle of light on the floor before me; light and shadow seemed to be tussling for the supremacy of the stone flagging beneath the candletree. I willed the light to triumph, but there was so much darkness round about.

Diarmot's Psalms became less a devotion than a babble as his voice droned on and on, not words at all, a sound only, a meaningless gurgle like that of a burn in full spate. The sound filled my head even as the gently wavering circle of light filled my eyes.

I entered a waking dream. It was then I saw Byzantium, and my death.

# 6

The circle of candlelight on the floor before me became a hole through which I could see a dim, formless expanse stretching in every direction to the horizon, without feature, without colour, cloud above and mist-wrack below. Alone in this empty firmament soared a great bird—an eagle—wings outstretched, keen eyes searching for a place to rest. But there was neither tree nor hill nor rock to be seen.

On and on, the eagle flew, searching and searching, but never finding; over wilderness and wasteland the bird soared. I could hear the wind's dull whine through the wide-spread feathertips as they swept the empty sky, and feel the bone-aching weariness dragging on those broad wings. Still that wonderful bird flew on, vistas of emptiness on every side, never a resting place to be found.

Then, even as those good wings began to falter, I glimpsed, far away to the east, the faint ruddy glow of the sun rising above the world-cloaking mist. Higher and higher rose the sun, growing gradually brighter, shining like red-gold in the fireglow of the craftsman's forge.

Dazzled by the radiance, I could not bear the sight and had to look away. When my sight returned, wonder of wonders! It was no longer the sun I saw, but an enormous, gleaming city, arrayed on seven hills, each summit aglow with splendour and richness beyond my most fevered imaginings. Radiant with the light of its own beauty, illumined by the fire of wealth and magnificence, this golden city sparkled like a jewelled ornament of unreckoned magnitude.

The weary eagle saw this city rising before it, and took heart, lifting its wings with strength renewed. At last, I thought, the worthy bird is saved; surely somewhere in such a city the eagle will find a place of rest. Closer and closer, the eagle flew, each wingbeat bringing it swiftly nearer, every stroke revealing a brilliance of wonders: towers, domes, basilicas, bridges, triumphal arches, churches, and palaces—all of glittering glass and gold.

Hastening eagerly towards the haven of the golden city, the proud bird, its heart quickening at the sight of such extravagant reward for long perseverance, descended, spreading wide its wings to land upon the highest tower. But as the eagle swooped lower, the city changed. Suddenly, it was a city no longer, but an immense, ravening beast possessing the hindquarters of a lion and the forequarters of a dragon, with a skin of scaly gold and claws of glass, and a vast, gaping maw of a mouth lined with swords for teeth.

The eagle twisted in the air and keened in alarm, beating its wings in retreat. But it was already too late, for the golden beast stretched out its long, snake-like neck and snatched the exhausted bird from the sky. The jaws shut and the eagle vanished.

The sharp echo of the great golden beast's snapping jaws brought me shaking from the vision. The room was dim; the scent of candle fat was strong in my nostrils. The candletree before me lay on the floor where it had fallen, the tapers either extinguished or guttering in pools of wax.

Diarmot was prostrate on the floor beside the altar, arms flung out to either side, snoring softly, asleep at his prayers.

I rose slowly, stepped to the toppled candletree, and raised it once more. The sound of its fall had roused me from my dream, but how had it become upset?

The door bumped in the wind. No doubt I had forgotten to secure the latch and a gust of wind had toppled the candletree. I moved to the door and pulled it shut with the leather thong, making certain that the wooden latch dropped into its groove. I returned to my place and renewed my posture, then began the *Kyrie* once more. But the dream remained fresh before me, assaulting my mind with its dire warning, and I could not pray. I soon gave up and simply sat thinking about what I had seen. My dreams are never wrong, but they sometimes require considerable thought to derive the proper meaning. So, I turned my mind to the purpose, but the interpretation eluded me.

When daylight's first dull shimmer gleamed in the high windhole, I rose, stretched myself, and then paused to consider whether to rouse Diarmot. Even as I stooped over him, the bell tolled *matin*, and he came awake with a start. I moved to the door and stepped outside where I was hailed by several brothers as they mounted the hill to the chapel, their cloaks whipping around their legs in a stiff northern wind. I returned their greeting with good will and drew the cold air deep into my lungs: once, twice, three times.

As I turned back into the chapel for maiden prayers, the sun lifted above the misty valley away to the east. My heart seized in my chest at the sight, for in the same instant the meaning of my dream broke upon me. The knowledge turned my blood to water: the eagle was myself, and the city was Byzantium. The beast, then, was death.

I slumped against the chapel wall, feeling the rough

stone against my back and shoulders. *Lord, have mercy! Christ, have mercy! Lord, have mercy!*

What I had seen would be. Certainty, bright and full as the sunrise even now bathing my face with light, removed even the smallest shadow of doubt. All my visions came trailing deep assurance of truth: what I had seen would happen. Time would prove it true. My death loomed before me as surely as the rising sun; I would go to Byzantium, and there I would die.

I endured prayers in a welter of dread and disbelief. I kept thinking: *Why? Why now? Why me?* But it was no good; I knew from long experience that I would get no answer. I never did.

Joining the others in the refectory after prayers, I broke fast on barley bread and boiled beef—a hearty meal to begin our journey. "Ah, Aidan, your last meal before you join the *vagabundi*, eh?" said Brother Enerch, the chief herdsman.

"Prudence, brother," advised Adamnan, sitting beside him. "When next we sit together, one of us will have supped with the emperor. Think on that."

"Think you the emperor dines with every ragged wanderer that presents himself at the Golden Gate?" wondered Brother Rhodri next to me.

Oh, they meant it for jest, but their words filled me with apprehension. Though they tried to engage me in pleasant conversation, I could not rise to their banter and quit the board after only a few bites, claiming that I must gather my belongings.

Leaving the refectory, I walked quickly across the yard to the scriptorium. The sky above had grown dismal grey; a cold, crabbed light leaked from an obscure heaven, and a fitful wind gusted over the stone walls to the west. A desolate day to match my own bleak mood, I thought.

Several of the abbey's piebald geese waddled across my

path and, as if to emphasize my distress, I lashed out at the nearest of them with my foot. The geese scattered, raising an unholy squawk as they fled. I glanced around guiltily, and repented of my hastiness as the gooseboy came running with his stick, hissing and whistling to call them back into his flock. He threw me a darkly disapproving look as he darted past.

"Look you! Keep them out from under foot, Lonny," I shouted after him.

Alone in my cell, I sank to my knees in despair. "Christ, have mercy," I moaned aloud. "Lord, if it please you, remove this curse from me. Restore my happiness, O God. Save your servant, Lord."

I poured out my anguish, pounding my fists against my knees. After a time, I heard voices in the yard outside and, rising, gazed a last time around my room. Who would have this cell after me? I wondered. Taken by the notion, I prayed for the man who would inhabit my small, bare room. Whoever it might be, I asked God to bless him richly and bring him every good thing.

Then, taking up my bulga, I put the strap over my shoulder, left my cell, and joined the travelling party in the yard.

The whole abbey had gathered to bid us farewell and see us on our way. The abbot and Master Cellach, who would go with us as far as the coast, stood talking to Ruadh and Taum. The bishop and visiting monks were assembled and ready to depart. I saw Brocmal and Libir, standing nearby, so took my place with them. Brocmal regarded me with a sour expression as I came to stand beside him, then turned to Libir and said, "One would think that any monk fortunate enough to be chosen for such a journey—against all proper expectation, mind— that monk would at least see to it that he did not keep others waiting."

This obscure rebuke was, I suppose, meant to shame me. But, as I had learned to expect no good word from those two self-satisfied scribes, the remark passed without offence. Ignoring their scorn, I searched the crowd for that one face I longed most to see. But Dugal was not there. Sick dread came over me as I realized that now, in the moment of leaving, I would go without bidding my dearest friend farewell; and once gone, I would never see him again. The finality of this realization filled me with inexpressible sadness. I could have wept, if not for all those looking on.

"Thus the journey begins!" Fraoch called, and, raising his staff high, turned and led the way to the gate. The brothers cried farewell and lifted their voices in song. They followed us to the gate, singing.

I passed through the portal and beyond the wall, and out . . . out, my feet on the path now, leaving the abbey behind. I walked on, telling myself that I would not look back. After no more than a dozen paces, however, I could not bear leaving without a last look at Cenannus na Ríg. I glanced over my shoulder, and saw the curved bank of the ringwall and, rising above it, the tall belltower; the roof of the refectory hall, chapel, and abbot's lodge showed above the wall. Monks crowded the gateway, waving their arms in farewell.

I raised my hand in reply, and saw, just passing through the gate, the ox and wagon bearing the supplies for our journey. And who should be leading that ox, but Dugal himself. The sight brought me up short.

"Oh, do move along, Aidan," Libir said irritably, prodding me from behind. "We shall never reach Constantinople with you stopping every second step."

"Perhaps he is already tired and wanting a rest," quipped Brocmal. "You stay here and rest, Aidan. I daresay we shall find the way without you."

I let them pass me by, and waited for the wagon to draw near. God bless him, Dugal had wangled himself a place in the escort party so I might walk with him. In fact, we would have another two days at least—the time it took to walk to the coast—before parting forever. This single thought gave wings to my soul.

Dugal saw me. Smiling a sly, self-satisfied smile, he welcomed me as I fell into step beside him. "You never thought I would let you leave without saying farewell, brother?"

"The thought never crossed my mind, Dugal," I lied. "Why did you not tell me?"

"I thought it was better this way," he replied, the sly smile reappearing. "Cellach was more than happy to let me come along. Someone must bring the wagon back after all."

We talked of the journey then as we proceeded down into the valley and crossed the Blackwater at the ford, following the footway east into the hills. This path was an old, old highway, marked out with standing stones along its length, and shrinestones wherever two paths crossed. The hill path overlooked the low valley, eventually coming in sight of the wide river Boann, passing the Hill of Slaine, where kingmaking has taken place since the Tuatha DeDanaan came to Éire.

There were other hills, too; and every hill along this ancient trackway was sacred, each with its stone or barrow. The gods worshiped there in times past were best forgotten. The Célé Dé left the hills and their fading gods to themselves.

Our little procession stretched out along the way, the brothers walking in groups of two or three, led by the bishop and abbot. I strolled happily beside Dugal, who walked at the head of the ox. The mysterious Britons—Brynach, Gwilym, and Ddewi—had taken places just behind the bishop and abbot. We marched without pause until midday, and paused at a stream to drink. Dugal brought the ox to water downstream of the others, and I thought to tell Dugal of my dream of death. Indeed, I had almost worked myself up to the telling, when the abbot signalled for us to continue, and we moved on.

Though dull, the day was dry; all, save me, were eager to be away. I looked out on the green hills and misted valleys, and lamented my going. Alas, it was not Éire alone I was leaving, but life as well. Thus, my joy at being with Dugal soured within me, poisoned by the terrible knowledge of my dream. I ached to share with him my burden, but could not bring myself to it. Thus I walked, heavy-hearted, alone in my misery, each step carrying me closer to my doom.

After a meal and rest, we came in sight of the Hill of Slaine standing tall and proud above the Vale of Boann, a wide, low, smooth-sloped glen. The cloud thinned, allowing the sun to show itself now and again. Sometimes the other monks sang, but my heart was not in it. Dugal must have noticed my gloomy mood, for he said, "And here is Aidan, walking all lonesome and friendless. Why are you behaving so?"

"Oh," I said, forcing a sad smile, "now that it has come upon me, I am sorry to leave this place."

He accepted this with a knowing nod, and said no more about it. We walked until dusk and made camp on the trail. As the last of daylight failed, the dark-gleaming edge of the sea could be seen away to the east. After a meal of stewed beef and barley bread, the bishop led us in prayers, whereupon we wrapped ourselves in our cloaks and slept by the fire. Strange, it seemed to me, to end a day without hearing the sound of the abbey bell in my ears.

Rising before dawn, we continued on our way along the Vale of Boann to Inbhir Pátraic, with its settlement set back a little behind sandy hills on the coast. Here, it was said, that the sainted Pátraic had returned to Éire, bringing the Good News with him. Though many doubt the truth of this—since many another place makes the identical claim—it does no harm to believe it so. The fiery saint had to come ashore somewhere after all, and the river estuary was wide and deep where the Boann met the sea—a good harbour for ships. Better, anyway, than Atha Cliath now that the Danemen were there.

We came to a standing stone which marked an ancient crossroads; here we paused to break fast and pray. After prayers, the trail descended out of the hills to the flatland of the coast. The wind had changed during the night and I could smell sea salt on the air—something I had experienced only two or three times before.

Thus, we drew near to Inbhir Pátraic: twenty-eight monks, each with his own hopes and fears. Though none, I think, as trenchant as my own.

# 7

The ship rode at anchor in the river, waiting to bear us away—the same ship that had brought the bishop and his companions from Britain. It was a low, sleek vessel with a tall, slender mast. Knowing nothing of seafaring or boats, I thought it a fine thing—if somewhat small for thirteen monks.

Upon arriving at the settlement, the head man met and greeted us in the name of his lord. "We have kept watch as you bade us," he told Bishop Cadoc. "I will send men to bring the ship now."

"My thanks and blessings on you, Ladra," answered the bishop. "We will ready our supplies and await you on the wharf."

Inbhir Pátraic was little more than a handful of mud huts perched precariously on the Boann's steep northern bank, near to the sea mouth. A small holding, the women kept swine on the water meads, and the men fished from two sturdy boats, occasionally sailing down the south coast to trade with folk along the way—sometimes venturing as far as Atha Cliath. Therefore, the place was deemed of sufficient importance that the king had paid for a handsome wooden wharf to be built and maintained. While the head

man and several of his sons rowed their small round cora-
cles out to the ship, six of us younger monks set about
unloading the wagon.

We had just begun this chore when Lord Aengus
arrived with his queen, and ten of his warriors. He dismounted at once and embraced the abbot and bishop, saying, "I am glad I reached you before you sailed, friends. My
men told me of your journey and its purpose. I have come
to bid you farewell, and beg your indulgence—for I, too,
would have you carry a gift to the emperor."

"Certainly!" cried Abbot Fraoch in a hoarse croak,
delighted that King Aengus should honour the enterprise
in this manner. "Your gift shall be a most welcome addition to our undertaking."

With that the king bade his wife approach.
Dismounting gracefully—for all Queen Eithne was a most
beautiful woman, dark-haired and fair-skinned as befitting
a Sister of Brigid—she signed to one of the warriors who
brought out a small, flat wooden casket from behind his
saddle. This, he placed in her slender hands. The queen,
back straight and head erect, carried the casket to where
the abbot and bishop stood.

"Worthy men," she said, her voice sweet and low, "I am
told the Emperor of the Romans is a man of great learning
and wisdom. Yet, even such men have need of diversion from
time to time." With that she opened the casket to reveal a
small gaming board of the kind used to play *brandub*. "The
pieces," she explained, reaching in and taking up a tiny figure,
"are gold, for the king, and silver, for the hunters."

The craftsmanship of both the casket and the gaming
board were exquisite; the individual pieces were finely
made and very costly.

"Lady," replied Fraoch, "it will be my pleasure to
deliver this gift into the emperor's hands and dedicate the
first game to your honour."

The king looked on, beaming his good pleasure. "In consideration of your service," Aengus said, "I would offer a token of my regard." He summoned three more of his men, who approached bearing three large sheepskin bundles which they placed at their lord's feet. When the first was opened, the king withdrew a cowl of fine, black wool. "There is one for each member of the travelling party," he said.

The second bundle was opened to reveal a selection of wide leather belts, while the last bundle contained new leather shoes, of the kind we made at the abbey: one piece of good thick leather cut and folded in such a way as to produce a strong, covered sandal secured by a braided leather cord. Again, there were enough to choose from so that each monk would have a new pair of shoes with which to begin the journey.

"Your generosity, Lord Aengus," Bishop Cadoc said, "is surpassed only by your thoughtfulness. We stand in your debt."

"I will hear no word of debt from you," Aengus replied, to which Queen Eithne quickly added, "Only say a prayer for us when you reach that holy city."

"It shall be done," Cadoc vowed.

The woollen hoods, belts, and shoes were passed hand to hand then, and each monk selected those items that suited him best. For myself, I was glad to have a stout belt and new shoes; the cowl would be no less welcome when the cold wind blew. I slipped the hood over my head and let it rest on my shoulders, then buckled the belt around my waist and put the shoes on my feet. The articles were finely made, and fit me well. Strangely, I felt better for wearing them. If I were going to die, at least it would be with good new shoes.

Nor was the gift giving finished yet. Abbot Fraoch called to Dugal, who brought out a number of leather water pouches and staves—a new water pouch and staff for each monk. "All our hopes go with you," the abb said. "Therefore, walk worthy of your charge in all boldness, equipped for every good work. Fear nothing, my friends. God goes before you."

We then began carrying the supplies down to the wharf. The bank was steep, as I say, and stony—and the stones slick with moss, making the footpath hazardous. Dugal lifted the bundles from the wagon and gave them into our hands, and we trundled them down to the water.

As the pile of bundles and grain bags dwindled, I worried that I would not be able to say my farewell to Dugal. "Time grows short," I told him, stepping near as he pulled the last grain bag from the wagon. "I wanted to say farewell."

"But we are not parted yet," he replied—somewhat curtly, I thought. Nor did he look at me. Instead, turning away quickly, he hefted the bag into the hands of a waiting monk, then called to the abbot that the wagon was empty.

The abbot nodded, and whispered to all around him, "Let us go down to the wharf. The ship is waiting."

Most of the brothers were already assembled on the wharf—only the bishop, abbot, and several of the elder monks stayed behind, speaking to the king and queen. I picked up a bundle and started down to the ship as the last of the provisions were being handed aboard.

As it happened, there was a particularly treacherous place where the path switched back on itself, passing between two rocks. The morning mist had made the place very slick indeed; as I had passed the spot twice before, I knew to step lightly and put my hand on the taller rock to steady myself. With a grain bag under one arm it was no easy feat, but, with care, I was once again able to avoid any mishap. Thinking, however, to call a warning to those coming behind, I paused and was just turning around when I heard a sharp, strangled cry. Someone had fallen on the path!

Fumbling for a handhold, I glanced back to see that Libir had slipped and gone down. Fortunately, Dugal was right behind him. "Brother!" Dugal shouted. "Here now! Take my hand!"

So saying, brawny Dugal reached out, took hold of Libir and hauled him upright—a tragedy narrowly averted. The elder monk, white-faced and trembling, regained his feet and pulled violently away from Dugal. "Take your hand away!" Libir cried, embarrassed, I think, by his own unsteadiness.

I turned and started down the path once more and had taken but one step when I heard a loud crack—as that of a branch struck against a stone. An instant later Libir screamed. When I looked again, he was crumpled against the bank with one leg jutting out at an unnatural angle.

"Libir! Libir!" Brocmal shouted, thrusting himself from behind Dugal.

"Stay back," the big monk warned. "Do you want to fall, too?"

The elder scribe was moaning, head back, eyes closed. Dugal edged down beside him, and carefully gathered the monk into his arms. "Easy," Dugal said. "Easy, brother. I will carry you."

Dugal straightened his back and lifted the softly moaning monk. Then, half-sitting and half-climbing, Dugal edged his way back up the bank to the top. Those of us closest to the accident quickly gathered around to see what had happened.

Brocmal pushed Dugal aside and knelt over his friend. "I told you to be careful," he said sharply. "I warned you."

"Sure, it is not his fault. The path was very slippery," Dugal observed.

Brocmal whirled on him. *"You!"* he shouted. "You did this!"

To his credit, the big monk let the remark pass. "I tried to help him," he replied simply.

"You *pushed* him!"

"He pulled away."

"Peace, brothers!" rasped the abbot, stepping in quickly. He knelt over the fallen Libir. "You have had a bad fall, brother," Fraoch soothed. "Where are you hurt?"

Libir, grey-fleshed and sweating, muttered an incoherent word. His eyelids fluttered and he lost consciousness.

"It is his leg, I think," Dugal pointed out.

Cellach, kneeling beside the abbot, lifted the monk's tunic. Many of those standing near gasped and looked away. Libir's right leg was hideously bent below the knee and gashed; a jagged stub of broken bone protruded from the wound.

"Ah," sighed the abbot heavily. "Dear God in heaven." He sat back on his heels and drew a hand over his face. "We cannot leave now," he said. "We will have to take him back to the abbey."

Lord Aengus, standing with the bishop, pressed forward and said, "Please, let him be taken to my stronghold. It is nearer, and he will receive the best of care. I will return him to the abbey as soon as he is able to travel."

"I thank you," Fraoch said doubtfully. "But it is not so simple."

"Cannot another take his place?" wondered the king.

"Yes," the abbot agreed. "Another must be chosen. But the choice is difficult. There are many factors to be weighed and considered."

"No doubt it is as you say," said Queen Eithne. "Still, it seems a great shame to tarry even a moment longer than necessary."

"Come," said Lord Aengus heartily, "you make it more difficult than it is. While I do not presume to instruct you in such matters, I would simply have you observe that the tide is flowing now. If another can be chosen at once, your journey can proceed."

Abbot Fraoch looked to the bishop, but the bishop said, "I leave the choice to you. For myself, I am happy to proceed if another can be found to take Libir's place." He indicated some of his own monks standing nearby. "There are good men with me who would serve us well. But, as Libir was one of your number, I will abide by your decision."

Fraoch hesitated, glancing around the ring of faces, determining what best to do.

"I see no harm in it," Cellach agreed. "If someone were prepared to take Libir's place, we would not have to wait. Perhaps it is the Devil's wish to thwart our purpose. I would not like to see that happen."

Though he spoke reasonably, I could tell that the master scribe saw in this turn of events an opportunity to put himself forward.

"Very well," replied the abbot slowly, regarding the unconscious Libir with an expression of sorrow and pity. "We will choose another—though it will be a bitter disappointment to this good monk."

"I do not see what else we can do," Cellach said.

"Abbot Fraoch," said Dugal softly, "would you allow me to take his place?" Before the abbot could reply, Dugal continued, "I feel responsible for Libir's injury—"

"You *caused* Libir's injury!" Brocmal cried, pressing forward again. "Abbot Fraoch, hear me: Dugal pushed Libir on the path. I saw him do it."

"Brother, please," said Cellach, "this is neither the time nor place for such accusations."

"But I saw it with the very eyes in my head!" Brocmal insisted. He threw a finger in my direction. "Ask Aidan—he saw it, too."

Suddenly, I became the centre of this dispute. I looked

from Brocmal, red face alight with anger, to Dugal, calmly, quietly, still kneeling over the stricken Libir, unruffled, apparently unconcerned by Brocmal's indictment.

"Aidan," the abbot whispered hoarsely, "I do not need to remind you that this is a serious matter. Did you see what happened?"

"Yes, abbot."

"Tell me now. What did you see?"

I answered without hesitation. "I heard a cry and turned. Libir had fallen. Dugal raised him up and tried to help him, but Libir would not—he pulled away and started down the bank on his own strength. That was when he fell."

"He fell twice?" asked Fraoch.

"Yes. Twice."

"And you saw this?"

"I heard the cry first and saw Dugal trying to help him. I saw Libir pull away; I believe he was embarrassed to have fallen. I looked to my own feet then, and I had only just turned away when he fell again."

"Not so!" shouted Brocmal. "Liar! You two are in it together. I saw you scheming, the two of you."

"Brother scribe," cautioned Fraoch gently, "you are overwrought. It seems that you are mistaken in your assessment of what happened."

Brocmal shut his mouth, but continued to glare furiously at us. The abbot turned to Dugal. "Brocmal is distraught, brother. Do not hold his anger against him. He will make amends when he is in a better mind. As for myself, I am satisfied that you tried to help Brother Libir in every way."

"I only wish he had not been injured at all."

"Sure, your quick thinking saved an old man a worse injury," Lord Aengus put in. "You have done well."

"Still, I wish it had not happened," Dugal said. He

stood up and turned to the abbot. "Good abb, though I am no scribe, I stand ready to take his place. If you will have me, so be it."

"Brother," Cellach told him, stepping near, "your offer is most noble, but you speak neither Latin nor Greek. And as you say, you are no scribe—"

Before he could finish, however, Lord Aengus said, "Forgive me, my friends. But it seems to me that you have scribes and scholars aplenty for this journey. It seems to me that a ready-handed man is wanted. Who better than a warrior to serve in this?" He placed a hand on Dugal's shoulder, as if commending him. "Forgive my intrusion, friends, but these are dangerous times. I would be to blame if I did not offer my best advice in this matter."

The bishop, nodding agreement, spoke up, "The king argues well. I think we must consider his suggestion in all seriousness."

"It may be that God has allowed this to happen," Queen Eithne suggested pointedly, "so that you would not leave your homeland without the protection of a stout warrior in your company. If *I* were choosing men for such a journey, I would travel with an easier mind if I knew that at least one of our number had served in the king's warband."

"I can think of no better warrior for such a chore," the king added, "and I have good reason to know whereof I speak."

There came a call from the wharf below. "The tide is ebbing!"

"It is choose now," Bishop Cadoc said, "or wait until another day. I leave it to you, Fraoch."

The abbot made up his mind at once. He turned to Cellach. "I am sorry, brother. I know you would gladly come with us, but you are needed at the abbey." Then, facing the warrior before him, he said, "Brave Dugal, if it is in your heart to take Libir's place, then perhaps God himself has placed this desire in you. So be it. I say you shall go. May God bless you richly, brother."

I stared on in disbelief. Dugal nodded, accepting the abbot's decision almost reluctantly. "On my life, I will do all to aid the successful completion of our journey," he vowed.

Another shout echoed up from the wharf. "The tide is ebbing! You must hurry!"

"It is settled," said the king. "Go now. We will care for your man while you take your leave." Then turning to Dugal, he said, "The world is wide, friend, and dangers crowd the day." He drew his sword and offered it to his former warrior. "Therefore, take this blade for the protection of your good brothers."

Dugal reached for the sword, but the bishop put out his hand. "Lord Aengus, keep your weapon," he said. "The Word of God is our protection; we need no other."

"As you will," the king said, replacing the sword. "Hurry now or you will not get clear of the river mouth."

Leaving poor Libir in the care of Cellach and the king's men, we made our way down to the ship. The last of the supplies had been loaded, and most of the monks had already clambered aboard. The bishop, with great dignity, eased himself over the side of the boat and took his place beside the mast. Dugal and I were the last to board.

I had never been in a ship before. "Dugal," I said urgently, "it is not big enough! Sure, it is too small."

He laughed. "Fret not. It is a stout craft." He ran his hand along the rail. "It was made to carry thirty men at need, and we are but thirteen. We will fly before the wind."

I gaped at him, still marvelling at the turn of events I had just witnessed. If the archangel Michael himself had reached down and plucked Dugal from the wharf and dropped him into the boat beside me, I would not have been more astonished.

"You are going, too, Dugal!" I cried suddenly.

"That I am, brother." His smile was broad and handsome.

"But it is wonderful, is it not?"

"Indeed," he said.

At a shout from one of the British monks, four of the brothers standing at the rail took up long oars and pushed away from the wharf.

The abbot raised his staff aloft and made the sign of the cross over us. "You go with a treasure, my brothers. May you return with tenfold riches and blessings untold!"

Then, lifting his poor, broken voice, he began to sing:

> *I set the keeping of Christ about thee,*
> *I set the guarding of God around thee,*
> *To aid thee and protect thee,*
> *From peril, from danger, from loss.*
> *Nor drowned be thou at sea,*
> *Nor slain be thou on land,*
> *Nor overthrown by any man,*
> *Nor undone by any woman.*
> *You shall hold to God—*
> *God shall hold to thee,*
> *Surrounding thy two feet,*
> *His two hands about thy head.*
> *Michael's shield is about thee,*
> *Jesu's shelter is over thee,*
> *Colum Cille's breastplate preserves you,*
> *From all harm, and the heathen's wicked wiles.*
> *The love of God be with thee,*
> *The peace of Christ be with thee,*
> *The joy of the Saints be with thee,*

*Always upholding thee,*
*On sea, and land,*
*Wheresoever you shall wend,*
*Blessing thee,*
*Keeping thee,*
*Aiding thee,*
*Each day and night of your lives for ever.*
*Alleluia, amen!*

I stood at the rail, listening to this fine song, knowing I would never see my homeland again.

The ship swung slowly out into the centre of the swift-flowing stream. The sea tide bore us quickly along, and I stood watching the green hills slide past. Those on the wharf waved us away, and sang a psalm of farewell. I could still hear that song long after a bend in the river took them from sight. I dashed the tears away with the heels of my hands, lest anyone see me.

The high banks fell away on either side and we entered a wide, low bay. "Up sail!" cried the brother at the tiller. Four monks leapt to the mast, and began tugging on ropes. A moment later the tawny-coloured sail ascended, ruffled in the breeze, shook itself, and then puffed out with a snap. Painted in white in the centre of the sail was the symbol of the wild goose: *Bán Gwydd.*

All at once, the ship seemed to gather itself and leap forward in the water; I heard waves splashing against the prow. Before I knew it, we were seaborne and on our way. I cast a long, lingering backward glance at the green hills of Éire, and bade a last farewell to my homeland. The journey was begun.

# 8

Exhilaration surged through me as the ship gathered speed before the wind, gliding out upon the smooth, glassy waves as quick and keen as any black-winged gull. The sea spread before the ship and I gaped in awe at the sight: an immense expanse of restless blue-grey water billowing to the horizon and beyond, wider and more wild than I had ever imagined. How different it appeared from the rail of a swift-sailing ship.

Gasping, the raw wind stealing the breath from my lungs, I marvelled at the speed of the boat and the power of the waves sliding by along the rail. From time to time a wave would strike the side, flinging salt spray into my eyes.

I felt the wind on my face and tasted salt on my tongue and knew what it was to be alive. I breathed deep, exulting in the racing of my heart and the cool air in my lungs. We flew!

Stupid with wonder, I stared into the sea-misted distance, and offered up the fisher's prayer: *Save me, Lord! Your sea is so big, and my boat is so small. God, have mercy!*

I stood at my place at the back of the boat, almost too frightened to move, and watched the seafaring brothers perform their labour. They worked with deft efficiency, moving naturally with the running bound of the boat, hands busy with ropes—pulling, knotting, loosing, casting—calling to one another with a familiarity born of long acquaintance.

There were six of them altogether: Connal, Máel, Clynnog, Ciáran, and Faolan—five of the *muir manachi*, that is, five sea monks, who braved deep water under the leadership of a brother named Fintán, a gaunt gristle-bone of a man who was the pilot. He stood with tiller in hand, keen eyes asquint against the sky, watching the sail and calling sharp commands which the others instantly obeyed. Obviously, they had sailed together before and had been chosen for their ship-handling mastery.

I looked around at my other companions. Bishop Cadoc had placed himself at the front of the boat, together with his advisors, the three Britons: Brynach, Gwilym, and Ddewi. At the rear of the boat, along with Fintán at the tiller, stood Brocmal, Dugal, and myself.

Thus we were thirteen souls in all; a sacred number, the number of Christ and the disciples: thirteen peregrini, chosen of God, dedicated Célé Dé each and all.

Despite the apprehension of my death, I could not help feeling proud to be included in this eminent company. And as I had not yet told anyone about my vision, I decided that I would keep this secret to myself, shouldering its bitter burden alone. This resolution pleased me oddly; I felt that in some way it would be my unsung contribution to the venture. The thought made me feel noble and worthy. I enjoyed the feeling.

As if to confirm my brave intentions, the sun suddenly cracked the clouds and poured dazzling light over the wind-stirred waves. Gazing out upon the broad, endless sweep of shimmering sea, I thought, *"Come, let the world do its worst. Aidan mac Cainnech is ready."*

I gradually settled into the plunging rhythm of the ship, and learned how to anticipate the sudden lifts and shuddering dives. The up-and-down motion was not at all difficult to master, but I found the erratic and abrupt side-to-side lurch unnerving. Whenever it happened, I seized the rail with both hands and held on, lest I tumble head-long into the sea.

Dugal, who had some small experience in ships, laughed to see my first, stuttering steps. "Stand straight, Dána," he instructed. "You hobble like an old man. Take the motion in your knees." He bent his legs slightly to show me. "It is like riding a horse."

"I have never ridden a horse," I complained.

"A Celt who has ridden neither ship nor horse? Now I have seen everything." He laughed again, and several of the sailing monks laughed with him.

"Some of us are not so worldly-wise as others," I replied.

"You will learn, my friend," Fintán called from his place at the tiller. "I daresay you will learn."

Our tutelage began at once, as the sea monks began instructing us in the ways of the rope, sail, and oar. At their bidding, we worked side by side, and I soon came to recognize seafaring as a rough yet exacting occupation, as demanding in its own way as anything encountered in the scriptorium.

When at last we finished securing the provisions and ordering the ship, I made myself a nest among the grain sacks and settled in; Dugal joined me there. "Strange the way God works, is it not?" I observed. He watched the sail swelling full in the wind. "It seems we are to be together after all."

"Indeed," he agreed, regarding the sails closely.

"Forgive me, brother, but I must know . . ." I hesitated, unwilling to speak the words.

"Did I push Libir?" he offered, guessing my thoughts.

"Brocmal thinks you did."

"I care little enough for what Brocmal thinks; let him say what he likes. What do you think?" he asked, turning his glance to me. "Did you see anything?"

"I did not see you do it," I answered. "Nor can I see how you could have pushed him."

"Then let us just say that God has favoured us highly," he said. "Truly, I do not think he meant us to be apart."

"And here I was beginning to fear I would never see you again. Who would have believed it possible?"

"We are friends," he said simply, and seemed inclined to say more, but turned his attention to the sail once more, drew a deep breath and exclaimed, "Ah, *mo croí*. The sea, Aidan. The sea! A ship is a beautiful thing, eh?"

"It is that."

We talked for a while, and then drifted into reverie, watching the slow rise and fall of the sea swell. I lay back on my grain-sack throne and closed my eyes. I did not think to doze, nor considered that I had. Nevertheless, I was startled when Clynnog, a Dál Riada Irishman, sang out: "Land ahead!"

"Already?" I wondered, rising in surprise. We had sailed little more than half a day, or so it seemed to me.

"The wind has been a fair friend to us," Fintán said, running a hand over his grizzled grey head. "Pray this weather holds."

I stepped over Dugal's sleeping form, and lurched to the side of the ship. Gripping the rail, I scanned the far horizon, but saw nothing save the great grey empty sweep of the sea—some of it glowing where sunlight touched it through a hole in the low-hanging clouds.

"I see no land," I called back to Fintán.

"There!" he said, pointing with his right hand. "Low on the horizon."

I looked where he was pointing, but still could see nothing but the rolling sea. "Where?" I shouted.

He laughed. "Keep looking."

Straining over the rail, I searched and searched, and at last began, dimly, to make out a vague shape in the misty distance—like that of a cloud bank sitting just above the firm line marking the boundary of sea and sky. I watched this murky bank for some time before observing any significant change, and at last began to see a small variation in the colour.

The ship flew towards this low-lying bank, leaping from wavetop to wavetop, ropes taut, mast-tip bending, sail straining, driving the ship's sharp prow through the deep green water. Slowly, steadily, the dark distant bank took on definition, becoming a gently undulating contour of mottled grey and green. After a time, these soft contours resolved into sharper features: stark cliff-faces of tumbled stone.

Dugal wakened and took his place beside me at the rail. "*Ynys Prydein*," he said, lifting a hand to the landscape before us.

"Have you been there before?" I asked.

"Once or twice," he said. "But it was night and I remember little of the land."

"Night?" I wondered. "Why would you go at night?"

He shrugged. "We most always went at night." Dugal paused, looking at the coastline almost wistfully. "Oh, but that was a long time ago, and I was very young."

Even as Dugal was speaking, the sky opened and light streamed down through a hole in the clouds, drenching the crag-bound coast in glorious golden rays. The sea sparkled in silver and blue, the broken rocks gleamed black as crows' wings, and the smooth-sloped hills glowed like fired emerald. This sudden beauty startled me with its intensity. I blinked my dazzled eyes and stood in awe of the sight.

And when I could take in no more, I lowered my gaze to the water and caught a gleaming flash out of the corner of my eye. I looked again and saw a swift, graceful form curving through the water; a single ripple and it was gone. I half-turned to call Dugal—and saw it again: a smooth, brown, lightly-dappled body with a face and eyes that looked right at me. "Dugal!" I cried in alarm, waving my hand at the water. "Look! Look!"

Dugal peered unconcernedly over the rail and searched the deeps. "What was it—a fish?"

"I do not know what it was," I gasped, leaning down for a better view. "But it was no fish I ever saw."

Dugal only nodded and turned away.

"There!" I shouted, as the swift-gliding creature appeared from under the ship. "There it is again! Did you see it, Dugal? Did you see it?"

He spread his hands.

"What was it?" I demanded.

"I cannot say, as I did not see it, Aidan." He spread his hands again in a gesture of serene helplessness.

From his place at the tiller, Fintán the pilot chuckled aloud, and asked: "Have you never seen a seal before, Aidan?"

"Never," I confessed. "Was it a seal?"

"Aye, it was. Dappled, you say?" He raised his eyebrows. "Then it was a young one. Keep your eyes open, brother; you will see many and many a thing in these waters."

"Seals, Dugal," I said, shaking my head in wonder.

Brocmal, standing nearby, snorted in derision and moved away. He had not altered his indignant countenance since boarding the ship, and glared at me with disapproval whenever I caught his eye.

"They commonly go in packs," Faolan informed me. "You know you are close to land when you see seals."

Within moments it seemed to me that the waters were asurge with seals—a score or more of the delightful creatures. We all gathered at the rail to watch them diving under the ship and sporting among the waves close to the prow. Sometimes they surfaced to watch us, glistening heads bobbing above the waves, their big eyes glittering like polished jet, before they turned tail-up and disappeared once more. Once or twice, they called to us with their rough, barking voices as they rolled and splashed in the water.

Fintán called a command and turned the ship. When I looked, the cliffs now loomed over us and I could hear the wash of the sea over the rocks and on the shore. We began passing south along the coast. This part of the land appeared deserted. I saw no settlements or holdings, not even so much as a single farm or the dysart cell of a recluse monk.

"There were people here once," Gwilym told me when I asked. "But they are gone now—many years ago even. The settlements have moved further inland. Look in the glens and vales, that is where you will find them now." He looked lovingly upon the land of his birth. "Only Ty Gwyn can still be seen from the sea," he added proudly. "Come what may, that Fortress of Faith will not be moved."

"Will we see it?"

"Oh, aye, tomorrow," he replied. "We will stop there for additional supplies."

As the sun began dipping towards the western sea, Fintán, who had been searching for a sheltered bay for the night, turned the ship into what first appeared as nothing more than a cleft in the cliffside. But as we sailed nearer, the gap seemed to open wider and I saw that it was really a small cove.

The water was deep and calm, allowing us to come near to the shore. Bishop Cadoc used the small coracle to reach land, but the rest of us simply slipped over the side and waded ashore. While the seafaring brothers made the ship secure, we began making camp. Dugal and I were sent in search of firewood while the others sought water and set about preparing the meal.

"We will find nothing on this barren rock," Dugal observed, glancing around at the hard slaty shingle. So, we climbed to the clifftop in order to find better pickings. Though there were no trees of any size, there were a number of dense thickets with many dead branches easily broken and gathered into sizeable bundles; these we toted to the edge of the cliff and threw down to the shore below. In a short while we had collected enough to last the night.

"Come," Dugal said, "let us spy out the land." And so we walked along the clifftop to learn what we could of the wilderness hereabouts.

Britain, so far as I could see, was no different from Éire: the same green turf and gorse over the same rock. And that was all. Still, after a day aboard ship it felt good to stretch my legs and feel solid ground beneath my feet.

We returned to the shingle and retrieved the firewood we had collected, then made our way back to camp. Fintán and his crew, instead of coming ashore, had put out fishing lines from the side of the ship, and with very little effort had soon caught enough mackerel to feed us all. While Connal and Faolan gutted the fish, Dugal and I made the fire. The fish were spitted and the spits quickly set around the perimeter of the fire to cook. Presently, silvery smoke drifted into the dusky sky, thick with the aroma of roasting fish.

I listened to the talk around me while idly turning the spit and watching the sinking sun stain the blue-green water with molten gold. The fish sizzled and the sky faded to pale yellow, and I listened to the gulls chatter on the rock cliffs above as they gathered for the night.

When at last the mackerel was cooked, I raised the spit, peeled off a strip of flesh with my fingers, blew on it a little and tucked it into my mouth. Truly, I believed I had never tasted anything so good in all my life. I also realized I had not eaten anything since breaking fast early that morning.

Was it only this morning that we left? I wondered, turning the spit before the flames. Already, it seemed the Aidan who had set off with a heart full of woe was not the same Aidan eating fish from a spit and licking his fingers.

After our meal, Bishop Cadoc led prayers. A monk on pilgrimage is excused from the daily round; the journey itself is accounted a form of prayer. Even so, we did not neglect any opportunity to refresh ourselves in this way.

We sang psalms as the stars came out, our voices ringing from the rocks all around and out over the glimmering water. With the last notes soaring into the night, we wrapped ourselves in our cloaks and slept on the shingle under the stars.

We awakened at first light to mist and low cloud. The wind had changed during the night, and now came out of the east in a low gusting breeze. The pilot and Máel stood at the water's edge, wavelets lapping at their feet, scanning the sky and talking. Cadoc joined them, exchanged a word, and then called out: "Rise, brothers!" he called. "The day is before us!"

While Clynnog and Ciáran—either side of the coracle—guided the bishop, the rest of us broke camp and waded back to the ship. Once aboard, Fintán took the tiller and signalled Connal to raise the anchor. The others plied the long oars and began turning the ship.

"Let us help them," suggested Dugal. "It will do us good to learn the seaman's craft."

He took up an oar and put it in my hands, then found one for himself. Dugal stood on one side of the ship, and I on the other. Clynnog showed me how to work the long-handled blade back and forth in the water. "More like sawing wood," he told me, "and less like stirring porridge, Aidan. Long, easy strokes. Do not turn your wrists so."

Slowly, the boat turned in the water and we began moving back out of the little cove and into the open sea once more. Once well beyond the rocks, Fintán called for the sail to be raised; the heavy fabric shook itself once, twice, caught the wind and filled. The ship slipped smoothly into deeper water, and we were away.

The pilot steered a course parallel to the land, moving south along the coast. The morning passed in a damp haze of mist and fog which clung to the cliffs and obscured the hills, leaving little to see.

We broke fast on barley bread and fish left over from the previous meal. I carried some back to Fintán at the stern, who put me to work holding the tiller while he ate. "We will make a seafarer of you yet, Aidan," he chuckled. "Just hold fast and keep an eye on the sail."

"Gwilym said we were to put in at Ty Gwyn," I said.

"Aye," answered the pilot, breaking bread. "Supplies."

"Is it far?"

He chewed thoughtfully. "No great distance."

Fintán seemed content with this answer and disinclined to improve on it, so I asked, "How far then?"

The pilot ate his bread as if contemplating the deep complexity of my question. Finally, he squinted up his eyes and said, "You will see."

Fintán's prediction proved faulty, however: I never did see the abbey called Ty Gwyn.

# 9

The wind sharpened, backing to the southeast and blowing steadily harder throughout the morning, churning the slate-grey water into stiff, jagged peaks that slammed against the prow and sides as if to drive us ashore. Consequently, our squint-eyed pilot was forced to put the ship further out, away from the coast, to avoid coming too near the land and being blown onto the rocks.

The sea swelled, lifting the ship high and holding it, before pitching it sideways into the next furrow. I found this rising-swaying-falling motion more than I could endure, and retreated to the back of the boat where I might grit my teeth and moan.

By midday, the wind had become a howling gale, piling the black waves high and spraying white foam over everything. I sat hunched in my nest among the grain sacks, clutching my stomach and desperately wishing I had not eaten the fish. Dugal, seeing my misery, fetched a stoup of water from the vat lashed to the mast. "Here, Aidan," he cried. "Drink this. You will feel better." He shouted above the wind and wave-roar, for even as far from land as we were, we could still hear the terrible thunder of the water tearing itself upon the rocks.

Placing the stoup in my hands, he watched me raise the wooden vessel to my lips, spilling most of the contents over myself due to the violent motion of the ship. The water tasted like iron on my tongue. I shivered at the taste; the shiver became a shudder and I felt my stomach churn inside me. I made it to the rail just in time to spew the ill-favoured fish back into the sea whence it came.

"Fret not, Aidan," Fintán advised. "It is for the best. You will feel better now."

This promise seemed especially remote, however, as I fell back onto the grain bags, drooling and gasping. Dugal sat with me until he was called away to help the sea monks strike the sail. This, I understood, would make the ship less easy to steer. But, as Máel explained, "It is take down the sail, or lose the mast."

"Is it that bad?" I wondered, feeling innocent and helpless.

"Nay," replied Máel, frowning, "not so bad that it cannot yet get worse."

"You mean it *can* get worse?" I wondered, apprehension stealing over me.

"Aye, it can always get worse. Sure, this is no more than a summer's breeze compared to some of the storms I have braved," he told me proudly. "I tell you the truth, Aidan, I have been shipwrecked four times."

This seemed to me a dubious boast for a seafaring man, but Máel appeared most pleased with it. The pilot called him to take the tiller just then, and I watched as Fintán grappled his way along the rail to join Brynach and the bishop at the mast. The three conferred briefly, whereupon the pilot returned to the helm. Dugal had seen this, too, and went to where Brynach and the bishop stood with their arms about one another's shoulders to keep from falling over.

They spoke together, whereupon Dugal returned to

where I sat and said, "We cannot put in at Ty Gwyn. The coast is too treacherous and sea too rough to stop there now."

"Where, then?" I moaned, not really caring any more where we went.

"We are making for Inbhir Hevren," he told me. "It is a very great estuary with many bays and coves, and not so many rocks. Brynach says we can find shelter there."

Any sight of land had disappeared in mist and cloud wrack long ago. I wondered how the pilot knew where we could be, but lacked the strength or will to ask; it was all I could do to hold to the sacking and keep my head upright.

I clung to the grain bags and prayed: *Great of Heaven, Three-One, Evermighty, who delights in saving men, hear my prayer and save us now. From torment of sea, from dolour of waves, from gales great and terrible, from squall and storm deliver us! Sain us and shield us and sanctify us; be thou, King of the Elements, seated at our helm and guiding us in peace to safety. Amen, Lord, so be it.*

Night drew on quickly and the gale, rather than abating, increased; as if drawing power from darkness, the wind mounted higher. The ropes, taut against the storm, sang mournfully as the mast creaked. Our tight little ship was tossed from trough to peak and back again, and my stomach heaved with every rise and fall. The grain sacks provided some stability and all who were not needed to keep the ship afloat gathered there to huddle together.

The last light failed and Fintán announced: "We cannot make landfall in the dark. Even if we could see the estuary, it would be too dangerous in this storm."

"What are we to do?" asked Brocmal, fear making his voice tremble.

"We will sail on," the pilot replied. "Fret not, brother. The ship is stout. We can easily ride out this storm."

So saying, he returned to his tiller, and we to our close-mumbled prayers.

Through the long darkness we prayed and comforted one another as best we could. The night wore on and on, endless, gradually passing to day once more with little alteration in the light. Day or night, the darkness remained heavy as the waves towered over us on every side.

All that dreadful day we looked for some evidence of land. But night came upon us once more, before we found even the smallest suggestion of a coastline or shore. We huddled in the bottom of the boat, clinging each to the other and all to the grain sacks. Bishop Cadoc, cold to the bone, shivering and shuddering, offered a continual litany of psalms and prayers of deliverance. The men of Éire are a seagoing tribe and we have many invocations of an oceanic nature. The good bishop knew them all and spoke them twice, and then said as many more that I had never heard before.

From time to time, one of the muir manachi would take a turn at the tiller, but our helmsman shouldered the greatest share of the burden alone—a very rock in the teeth of the storm; the Stone of Cúlnahara is not more steadfast than Fintán the pilot. My respect for that man grew with every wave that crashed over the rails.

All through the tempest-tortured night we shivered and prayed, the scream of wind and thunder of water loud in our ears. Hard pressed though we were, we kept courage keen with faith in God and hope of deliverance.

Even when the rudder pin gave way, we did not despair. Máel and Fintán hauled the broken rudder aboard and lashed it securely to the side of the boat. "We are at the mercy of the wind now," Máel informed us.

"Let Him who fixed the pole star guide us," Cadoc replied. "Lord, we are in your hand. Send us where you will."

With or without the rudder, I observed little difference in the behaviour of the boat. We were yet thrown from one wave to the next and blasted by every gale. Sea and sky continually changed places. Seawater broke over us in freezing cascades; had we taken up residence beneath a waterfall, we could not have been more severely drenched.

Three days and nights we endured this tribulation. We could neither eat nor sleep; any such comfort was impossible. When, after three days, there came no hint or evidence of the storm ending, Bishop Cadoc raised his *cambutta* and stood. Then, with those nearest him clutching him about the legs and waist to keep him from being snatched overboard by the wind and waves, the Bishop of Hy called out a *seun* to calm the storm. The charm he spoke was this:

> May the Three encircle me, May the
> Three succour me, May the Three shield me,
> Be thou ever saving me!
> Aid thee me in my dire need, Aid thee me
> in my distress, Aid thee me in every
> danger, Be thou ever aiding me!
> Nor water shall drown me, Nor flood
> shall drown me, Nor brine shall
> drown me,
> Be thou ever upholding me!
> Away with storms! Away with gales! Away with
> cruel killing waves!
> In the name of the Father of Life,
> and the Son Triumphant,
> and the Spirit Most Holy, with peace everlasting,
> Amen, Amen, Amen!

Cadoc repeated this charm three times and then sat down. We waited.

Clutching to the grain bags and to one another, the storm's savage howl loud in our ears, we waited. The ship turned around and around, rudderless, flung this way and that on the high-lifting sea swell.

Then, by some happenchance, Ciáran raised his head, looked around and sang out: "The sun!" Up he leapt. *"Sol Invictus!* The sun has conquered! *Gloria Patri!"*

Suddenly everyone was struggling up, pointing to the sky and shouting, "Glory be to God!" and praising the Ever Wise and all his saints and angels for our deliverance.

I looked where Ciáran was pointing and saw a narrow crack in the solid mass of grey. Through this crevice poured golden light in a broad, many-rayed band, piercing the night-dark sky with spears of bright morning light.

The crack opened wider allowing more sunlight to spill over the tempestuous sea. And it was almost as if the honeyed light was a balm poured onto the storm to soothe the troubled waters.

We stared at the shimmering shaft, willing it to expand and increase. But the sky closed again; the storm-clouds drew together once more, shutting out the light. Our hopes flickered out as the last ray disappeared.

Cold, exhausted from our long ordeal, we gazed forlorn and unhappy at the place where we had last seen the light. The wind gusted again and we shivered to hear it. And then, even as we hunkered down to weather the reawakened gale, the heavens split above us.

"Look!" shouted Clynnog, leaping up. "God's bow!"

I turned and saw a great arc of glowing colour shining in the air, God's promise renewed once more. Blue sky and rainbow—two of creation's most beautiful sights. We were saved. We turned our faces to the sky above, welcoming the sun's return with loud cries of joy and thanksgiving.

Fintán, the pilot, standing by the helm, called out, "Behold! The storm has flung us across the sea."

It was true. The clouds and mist had vanished, and away to the south I could make out the humped shape of land, floating on the horizon.

"Do you know the place, Fin?" asked Cadoc hopefully.

"I do indeed," the steersman replied, allowing himself a wide smile of approval.

"Then," suggested the bishop lightly, "will you yet tell us what land it is that we see there?"

"I shall," said Fintán. "Brothers, it is Armorica. Though the gales have battered us, they have performed a small service. Our crossing, though wave-tossed, has been made in half the time. We are wet and cold, truly. But God is good, he has delivered us to our destination."

"And this without a rudder?" wondered Connal.

"Yes, Con," replied Fintán, "the very hand of God was upon us, guiding us on our way. Now it is for us to do what remains." With that he began calling orders.

The muir manachi jumped quickly to their tasks. The oars were unshipped and we all set ourselves to rowing; without a rudder, use of the sail—even in a rapidly calming wind—would be useless, if not hazardous, and it was easier to steer by oar. The helmsman, meanwhile, took an extra oar and lashed it to the tiller post to serve as a rudder—enough of a rudder, at least, to help correct our rowing. The sea continued to run high and rough.

I watched the backs and shoulders of the men ahead of me—bending, swaying, hunching, to the rhythm of the song. I tried my best to imitate them, throwing the oar before me and drawing it back. I soon acquired a rough proficiency in the task, and was glad to do my part.

We rowed a goodly while, and the exertion, after three days of inactivity, roused both hunger and thirst. Gwilym and Ddewi left off rowing and began preparing a meal. It was then that they learned we had lost most of our drinking water. For, when Ddewi went to the ship's vat he found it all but empty, and that which was left tainted with salt water. The cover had come off during the storm and the good water dashed out by the rough waves.

This was not a serious problem, for we had yet a cask of water and several skins, but as these were meant to serve for our land journey it meant we would have to replenish them as soon as possible. Bishop Cadoc, Brynach, and Fintán put their heads together to determine what should be done. Since I was manning the last oar, I was near enough to overhear them.

"We must make land soon to repair the tiller," Brynach pointed out; "let it be near a stream."

"There may be a settlement," suggested Cadoc.

"Aye, there may," agreed Fintán, pursing his lips. "Do you not recognize the coast?"

"No." The pilot shook his head. "Sure, I know it is Armorica," he added quickly, "but whether we be north or south of Nantes, I cannot say."

That was the first I had heard mention of any stopping place—and yet, on such a long trip as this, we must have numerous destinations. I realized with some chagrin how little I actually knew about the journey I was embarked upon—not that it mattered very much for all that. Upon reaching Byzantium, I would die. That much I knew, and it was more than enough to occupy my thoughts.

Still, I wondered. Why Nantes? From the little I had heard of the Gaulish abbeys—and it was very little indeed—the monasteries of Gaul were unlike any known in Britain and Éire. It was often said that the continental monks were not *Fir Manachi*, that is True Monks, much less were they *Célé Dé*! Why, then, should we look to such men to aid our purpose? What interest could they have in our journey?

I thought about this as I rowed, but could make nothing of it, so contented myself with the thought that all would be revealed very soon. Bishop Cadoc and his advisors had, no doubt, good reason to hold close counsel in these matters. I determined to keep my ears open, however, to catch any stray word which might enlighten me.

When the meal was ready, we eagerly shipped oars and fell to with a will. I sat down next to Dugal and we ate our barley loaves and salt beef, and gazed upon the land to the east. The coast of Armorica, or Less Britain, as it was also known, was much closer now.

"Have you ever been to Armorica, Dugal?" I asked.

"I have not," he replied. "Although, it is said there are more Britons there now than in Britain."

"Is that so?"

"That is what they say. Samson of Dol brought them, you know. And those he did not bring, followed him anyway. They went to escape the Saexen plague." He shrugged. "Or, so they say."

"Then perhaps it is to a British abbey we are going," I mused, and told him what I learned from the conversation I had overheard.

"You may be right, brother," he agreed as Máel handed him the water jug; Dugal guzzled down a great draught and passed it to me.

"We will make a muir manach of you yet, Aidan," Máel chuckled. "If all were as earnest as you, we could rule the empire."

The water was sweet and good. I swallowed down as much as I could hold and passed the jug along to the next man. Fintán called us back to the oars shortly after that.

We rowed through the day, pausing now and then to rest and drink. The sea monks appeared oblivious to the exertion. They maintained a steady chant, marking the strike and pull of the oars with song. Those of us unused to the labour wrapped our swollen hands in strips of cloth and did what little we could at the oars. Oh, but it was hard work; our shoulders cramped and our stomachs soon ached with the effort.

The coast loomed larger with every stroke of the oars: yellow-brown hills tinged with early green, and some grey rocks, but not so many as on the south coast of Britain. Low among the hills, I could see some darker green—evidence of woodland or forest, though it was difficult to be certain at such distance. But it did not look like Éire to me. Even the water had changed colour to a pale grey-green hue. There was much seaweed floating on the surface; the wrack, torn from its watery bed by the storm, tangled in the oars and made rowing difficult—all the more so for one whose hand was better accustomed to plying nothing more unwieldy than a pen.

Keen eyes sharp on the coastline, Fintán scanned the shore for signs of a settlement. We did not think to find any habitation visible from the sea, but thought we might at least catch sight of smoke further inland. Failing that, we would work our way along the coast until we came to a river or stream outlet where we could make landfall for water and repairs.

"What will it be, Fin?" Brynach called back to the pilot. "North or south?"

Fintán thought for a moment. "North!" he decided, and pulled hard on the makeshift rudder. The ship slowly turned and we began making our way up the coast. The rowing became more strenuous now, for the sea swell remained heavy and the waves rough, and we no longer enjoyed the aid of the wind helping to push us along. We stood to our oars, fighting the waves which threatened to scuttle us with every sidewise roll.

I could feel the pull of the oars deep in my aching muscles; the palms of my hands were chafed raw and throbbed. I soon had ample cause to rue the absence of our sail, and appreciated precisely how profound was the loss of our rudder.

The sun sank toward the western sea and we had no sight of either settlement or stream. "Let us row on a little longer," Brynach suggested. "We may yet discover something to our advantage."

What he thought we might discover, I cannot say. The land beyond the shore remained dull and featureless in either direction as far as the eye could see. If any holdings *were* nearby, they were well hidden. I worked the oar and gazed longingly at the shore—mostly pebble, it appeared, with some larger rocks on the strand and standing from the water.

As the sunlight began to fade, it appeared we would be forced to abandon our plan. "Darkness is soon overtaking us," observed Brynach. "Let us make landfall and continue the search in the morning."

"Very well," agreed the pilot. "Let us just see what is beyond the promontory there," he said, indicating the high, broad headland jutting out from the shore directly before us.

Slowly, we rounded the promontory; as more of the land beyond came into view, I saw the wide sweep of a sand-rimmed bay and waves pounding themselves to froth and mist on the strand. Low sea cliffs rose behind the beach, giving way to three dark hills. A thread of white smoke drifted up from behind the furthest hill; Brynach saw it at once and sang out. We were all staring at the thin plume rising in the dusk, thinking of warm hearths and welcome . . . when Fintán called: "Ship in the bay!"

Turning my eyes to the rolling water once more, I observed a low black ship, with a high, serpent-headed prow, riding the swell and gliding smoothly into the cove. We had been so preoccupied with the smoke from the settlement, none of us had seen the other boat.

But those aboard the stranger ship had seen us.

The black ship changed its course, turning towards us

as the sail fell and a double rank of oars began stirring water. "Good," I said to Dugal standing nearby, "they can help us—tell us where we are, at least."

When Dugal made no reply, I glanced at him. His face was hard, his eyes narrowed, intent. "Dugal?" I asked.

"The only aid we will get from them," he muttered, "is help to an early grave."

I was about to ask him what he meant by such a remark when Fintán raised the alarm: "Sea Wolves!"

# 10

To oars!" cried Fintán, throwing the improvised rudder wide to turn the ship. "Row for your lives!"

I gaped in disbelief. *Sea Wolves* . . . I had heard those dreaded words all my life, and feared them. Now, confronted with the reality, I could scarce take it in.

"Row!" shouted Dugal, leaping to his place. Seizing his oar, he lashed the water with it like a man insane.

Fintán cried the cadence and we fell to the rhythm. *Bán Gwydd* turned and, little by little, gathered speed. The cadence quickened. Faster and faster, he called; faster and faster we rowed.

I kept my eyes on Dugal's broad back, not daring to raise my eyes, or turn my head right or left for fear of what I might see. Instead, I beat the water with my oar and prayed with every pull: *Lord have mercy! Christ have mercy!*

Cadoc, too, stood to his work. His fine strong voice, roused to the protection of his flock, became a keen-edged weapon. Back to the mast, he raised his staff and called on Michael the Valiant to encircle us and shelter us beneath his protecting wings. He hurled his invocation aloft with a mighty voice and all who heard him took heart.

From somewhere behind came the splash of hard-driven oars and shouts. I put my head down and rowed for dear life, all weariness forgotten.

Sweat ran into my eyes. Breath came in raking gasps and the oar grew slippery and difficult to grip. I looked to my hands and saw the oar smeared with blood.

"Row, for the love of God!" cried Fintán.

A moment later I heard a shriek and glanced over Dugal's shoulder to see the black ship dangerously close behind. A bare-chested man stood clinging to the high up-swept prow with a rope in his hand; on the end of this line was a three-tined hook. The man's arm wheeled around his head once, twice, and again—whereupon the stranger gave another loud cry and loosed his rope: it snaked into the air above the pilot's head, and sank. The hook struck the rail with a heavy clunk and bit deep.

The line snapped taut and our ship jerked in the water. This brought wild shouts of approval from those aboard the black ship. We stood to our oars, but rowing was useless. Try as we might, we could not drive the ship forward.

There came a rumbling clatter. I glanced up to see the first three ranks of rowers either side of the enemy ship had pulled in their oars and had snatched up axes and shields. All the enemy seamen were shrieking now, raising an earsplitting wail.

Dugal jerked his oar from between its stays and dashed to the tiller. "Get the hook!" he shouted. "Hurry!"

I saw now that the enemy ship was drawing closer as the Sea Wolves hauled on the rope. Fintán, Clynnog, and Faolan leaped to the grappling hook and tried to throw it off. Dugal, at the tiller, flourished the oar as if it were a weapon. The Sea Wolves howled, eagerly brandishing their axes.

Cadoc stood by the mast, calling down the aid of

angels. The rest of us struggled with our oars, desperately trying to stay out of reach of the black ship's warriors. The sea swell lifted *Bán Gwydd* high, slewing our little ship sideways, threatening to spill us all into the water. But the wave passed and the ship righted itself.

The Sea Wolves, pulling mightily on the rope all the while, were now upon us, the black ship's prow almost touching our stern. Six enemy warriors swarmed the prow, standing on the rail, ready to leap upon us.

Dugal, swinging his oar in a great arc, kept them off balance. Meanwhile, Fintán, red-faced, the veins standing from his neck and forehead, strove to dislodge the three-pronged hook.

"Aidan!" shouted Dugal. "Here!"

Taking up my oar, I joined Dugal at the stern. Bracing myself against the rail, I did my best to keep my oar in the enemies' faces. I jabbed here and there, the oar unwieldy in my bloodied hands, while the Sea Wolves, perched precariously on the rail, swiped at it with their axes, and looked for the first opportunity to jump aboard. Everyone was shouting and falling over one another in confusion.

"Row!" cried Máel, trying to make himself heard above the shouting. "Keep to your oars! Row!"

One of the Sea Wolves—a great stout giant with red braids under his war cap—swung out, holding to the slender neck of the serpent prow and slashing with an enormous club. The blow caught my oar and shivered the wood in my hands so that I almost dropped it. Máel appeared beside me, swinging an oar over his head. The Sea Wolf gave another vicious swipe with the club. Máel lowered the oar, catching the foeman on top of the shoulder. The man screamed in rage and pain, swayed, and almost fell into the sea; he was dragged back by his companions at the last instant, however. And, quicker than a blink, another Sea Wolf took his place.

The two ships were almost touching now. The sea heaved beneath *Bán Gwydd*, tipping one side-rail skyward and drowning the other in the waves. Water gushed over the rail into the boat. When the ship righted itself once more, it was half-filled with water.

"Help me!" cried Fintán.

The rope had slackened as the ship rolled over, and, for one fleeting instant, the pilot had succeeded in loosening the grappling hook—before the enemy pulled the line taut again, trapping his hand between the iron hook and the side of the ship. I dropped my oar and darted to his aid.

Seizing the hook, I put my foot against the rail and pulled with all my strength. The hook gave but little.

I heard a shriek and glanced up as a Sea Wolf leaped onto the rail. His axe split the air above my head and I fell back. Fintán screamed in pain as the iron hook tightened on his hand once more. I rolled onto my knees and grabbed the hook, jerking wildly at the one free prong as the Sea Wolf on the rail steadied himself and prepared to strike.

I saw the axe hover in the sky, and descend. In the same instant, I heard a whir in the air and an oar flew up to meet the falling blade. The axe bit deep into the oar-blade and stuck. Dugal yanked hard on the oar, jerking the foeman towards him.

As the enemy warrior toppled, Dugal lunged, throwing his elbow wide, catching the man in the chest and driving him backwards over the rail. The oar, with the axe still embedded in it, clattered to the bottom of the boat. Dugal stamped down on the oar, grabbed the axehandle and tried to pull it free as the sea swell gathered, lifting the ship and tilting it.

The axe came free, and Dugal chopped at the rope secured to the grappling hook. I saw him hacking at the rope as another Sea Wolf appeared.

"Behind you, Dugal!" I shouted. The enemy warrior threw an arm around Dugal's throat and pulled him back. But the big monk did not cease chopping at the rope: once . . . and once more . . . and crack! The rope broke. Suddenly free of the black ship, *Bán Gwydd* surged into the swell.

Sea and sky changed places. The ship rolled. I felt myself sliding and put out my hands to brace myself, but there was nothing to hold onto and I fell headlong into the swirling waves. The taste of brine in my mouth cut short my scream.

The shock of the cold water startled me. I kicked my legs and flailed my arms, swimming for the surface. My cloak and mantle clung to my limbs, dragging me down. Panic rising, I struggled. My lungs burned.

Above me, I saw a dark shape—the ship, I thought. Thrashing furiously, I swam for it, and, with one last effort, broke the surface. I only had time enough for one gulp of air, however, before another wave fell upon me.

As my head slid under, my flailing hand struck something hard. I grasped it and held on. A moment later, I managed to pull my head above the water and discovered that I was holding onto the ship's rail; the vessel was now overturned, keel up, and half under water.

The wave that overturned us had pushed the Sea Wolves well past. I could hear them jeering at us, their raucous shouts assaulting heaven with their vulgar sound.

I pulled myself a little higher up the side of the ship, and dashed the salt water from my eyes. I could see very little, for the waves towered over me on every side. But the sea swell rose, lifting the half-sunken ship, and I glimpsed the enemy vessel moving slowly away.

It appeared as if the Sea Wolves were attempting to turn their ship so to come back on us, but the waves were carrying us quickly towards the shore and, at same time, bearing them away. By the time they had turned around, I reasoned, we would be within reach of the strand. The swell rolled by and *Bán Gwydd* descended into the trough. When the next billow raised me up once more, the black ship was further away. I did not see it again.

"Aidan . . . help!"

I heard splashing behind me and turned to see Brocmal struggling in the water. Gripping the side of the boat, I leaned out, snagged the edge of his cloak, and pulled him to me. "Here, Brocmal . . . take hold."

Sputtering, shivering, he found a handhold on the ship's cladding and pulled himself up the side of the over-turned boat. I now turned my attention to finding others. "Hold on, Brocmal," I said, lowering myself back into the water.

"Where are you going, Aidan?"

"To search for others." Clutching the submerged rail, I made a circuit of the overturned ship. Reaching the prow, I swung under and started down the other side. Clynnog, Faolan, and Ciáran were clinging to the cladding.

"Aidan! Ciáran!" shouted Clynnog when he saw us. "Have you seen the rest?"

"Only Brocmal," I said. "He is just the other side of the ship. What about Dugal?"

"I saw Brynach, I think," answered Ciáran. "But no one else." He glanced around at the high-topped waves. "I do not know what happened to him."

"What should we do now?" I asked.

"We can do nothing more until we reach the shore," the seafaring monk replied. "But we are fortunate, the wind and waves will soon carry us onto the strand."

I could but marvel at his placid acceptance of our predicament. Fortunate? I do not think I would have chosen that word in this extremity.

"I will return to Brocmal," I replied, "and explain our good fortune to him."

Thus, I continued my circumnavigation of the over-turned ship and, finding no one else, came once more to Brocmal. He had pulled himself higher up the hull. I called to him to help me, but he would not give me his hand for fear of sliding back into the water. "You can climb by yourself," he told me briskly. "I dare not risk another fall."

"Clynnog, Faolan, and Ciáran are just the other side of the keel," I said, squirming up the side of the ship beside him. "Clynnog says we shall soon be ashore thanks to the wind and waves."

"What of the others?" Brocmal asked. "What of Bishop Cadoc?"

"I cannot say. Ciáran saw Brynach, but no one else."

"All drowned, I suppose," observed Brocmal. "Your Dugal included."

I did not know what to say to this, so I made no reply.

The rolling up-and-down swell of the sea grew steadily more severe as the boat drifted nearer to the shore. Now, when the ship rose up high, I could see the staggered ranks of waves breaking from the swell and pounding white and furious onto the strand and I could hear the booming roar. Soon these very waves were breaking all around and over us.

I heard a shout and looked up. The seagoing monks had climbed higher up the hull and were holding onto the keel. "Up here!" Clynnog called again. "Come up here, you two. It is safer."

I nudged Brocmal and indicated that we should join the others. He refused to move, and kept fearful eyes on the loud-clashing waves. "He says it is safer up there," I shouted. Brocmal's mouth moved in reply, but I could not hear him above the sea-roar.

"He will not move," I called to Clynnog.

"Then look out for yourself, at least," he advised.

I looked at Brocmal, shivering, clinging desperately to the hull. "I had best stay here with him," I answered.

"Then hold tight," Clynnog shouted, straining above the booming crash. "It will get rough. But when you feel the sand beneath your feet get clear of the ship as fast as you can. Understand?"

As Brocmal had made no attempt to even look at Clynnog, I started to repeat the seafarer's warning. "I heard him," the disagreeable monk muttered. "I am not dead yet."

I did not have time to make any reply, for a wave broke over the ship and from then on it was all I could do to keep my grip. The sea tossed hapless *Bán Gwydd* to and fro like so much driftwood, raising it up and slamming it down, first the prow and then the stern, spinning the boat around, washing over it in torrents. Fingers aching, shivering with cold, I clung to the cladding and prayed for deliverance.

## 11

White-frothed water surged on every side. I could hear nothing but the thunder of hard-driven waves colliding with one another as they were flung onto the beach. With each surge, I slipped lower down the side. Finally, I could maintain my grip no longer, and when a last great wave pounded over us, I was torn from my place, spun, and rolled under the water.

Dizzy, disoriented, I floundered, flinging my arms and legs about. My knee struck something firm: sand!

Gathering my legs beneath me, I stood . . . and to my surprise rose halfway out of the water. The shore was directly before me—fifty or sixty paces away. Remembering Clynnog's advice to get clear of the ship, I moved my feet and began running. I had not taken three steps, however, when I was struck from behind and thrown down. The water pummelled me and tumbled me along the bottom. As the wave withdrew, I struggled to my knees and came up spitting sand. I took two more steps before the next wave caught me; this time, however, I was able to brace myself in time and kept my feet.

*Bán Gwydd*, I saw, was now fifty or so paces away, the

three sea monks still aboard, clinging to the keel. I followed the boat, falling only once more, and dragged myself from the foaming surf to collapse on the beach. I lay there for a moment, eyes closed, heart pounding, gathering what little wit and strength remained.

"God be praised! Are you alive, Aidan?"

"Only just," I answered with a cough. I opened my eyes to see Gwilym standing over me, hair all down in his eyes, and dripping water from every pinnacle and point.

"It is Aidan!" he shouted over his shoulder to someone else. "He is not hurt." To me, he said, "Are you hurt, brother?"

"Aghh!" I answered, spitting salt water and gasping for air. Then I remembered: "Brocmal was with me! He was on the side of the ship. I do not know what has become of him."

I rolled onto my hands and knees. Gwilym helped me to my feet. "The ship is just there," he said, "he cannot have gone far." The lanky Briton began striding across the strand.

The waves had pushed the hull well up on the beach and there it had come to rest—no more than thirty paces away. Clynnog, Ciáran, and Faolan clambered over the hull and onto the beach as we approached.

"Is Brocmal with you?" I called, trying to make myself heard above the thunder of the waves.

"Alas, no," replied Ciáran. "We have not seen him."

"Who have you found?" asked Clynnog.

"Brynach and Cadoc are safe," Gwilym told us, pointing to a stand of rocks some little way down beach. "Ddewi and I are searching for the rest."

"That makes eight," said Faolan.

"Nine," added Gwilym, "counting Brocmal—if we can find him."

A cry sounded from somewhere down the beach. We turned and looked along the strand to see four figures staggering towards us; one of them, I could tell even at that distance, was Dugal. He and another monk were supporting a third between them. "It is Dugal," I said. "He has Fintán with him."

"And Con and Maél, too," said Clynnog, cupping his hands over his eyes. He and Ciáran hastened to meet them.

"That makes twelve," observed Faolan. "Only Brocmal is missing."

"He cannot be far away," I said, wading out into the water. The sun was low now; shielding my eyes against the glare, I searched the waves for any sign of Brocmal. The sea monks likewise scanned the swift-running surf. We were called away from this task by Gwilym, who shouted, "There! Ddewi has found him!"

So saying, he and Faolan began running up the strand to where Ddewi was crouched over a figure which was laying half in the water. I made to follow, but as I turned, something bumped against my leg. I looked down to see a man's head and shoulders bobbing in the wave-surge.

"Here!" I shouted in surprise. "I have found someone!" No one heard me, however, for they all continued running up the shore to help Ddewi, and I was left alone.

Grabbing hold of a bare arm, I tugged the body onto the sand as far as I could and rolled it over. I did not need the silver neck chain, nor the thick silver armband, to tell me that I had found a Sea Wolf.

A big man, with long fair hair and beard, he had a black tattoo of a boar on his upper right arm and a wide leather belt around his waist. Tucked into the belt was a long gold-handled knife. He boasted neither shirt nor mantle, but wore leggings of fine thin leather and buskins of hairy pigskin. He appeared completely lifeless; but I thought best to make certain, so I knelt and pressed my ear to the man's chest.

I was still trying to find a heartbeat when a wave

caught me from behind and sent me sprawling over the corpse. This cold embrace so disgusted me that I squirmed to my feet and started away. But I stopped and turned back. I could not leave the body where the waves might drag it back into the cold, cold sea.

"Christ have mercy," I muttered through clenched teeth. Drawing a deep breath, I seized both wrists in my hands, and dragged the body all the way past the high-water mark on the sand—a fair fifteen paces away—whereupon I sank down beside it, breathing hard.

My hasty action must have reawakened life in the corpse, for as I sat back on my heels, staring at the pale cold form beside me, the body convulsed and vomited up a bellyful of seawater. The barbarian then fell to coughing and gagging so much I thought he might drown again, so I pulled him over on his side.

More seawater gushed from his mouth and he drew a long shaky breath and moaned softly. I stood, prepared to run if he should leap to his feet and attack me. But he just lay there groaning, his eyes closed. My eye fell on the knife in his belt, and it occurred to me that it might be better if I held the weapon.

Crouching near, I stretched a cautious hand toward the hilt.

At that moment, the barbarian's eyes snapped open. The look of mingled surprise and terror in those ice-blue eyes halted me. I froze, my fingertips all but touching the handle. He noticed my fingers reaching towards his knife—and stiffened.

I withdrew my hand quickly and sat back. He blinked, his features drawing into an expression of open astonishment. I looked at him and he looked at me, neither of us moved. A kind of understanding passed between us just then, I think, for he relaxed and closed his eyes once more, pressing his face against the sand.

"What have you there, Aidan?" someone called. I glanced up as Dugal and the others arrived.

Fintán, his face pinched with pain, stood hunch-shouldered between Dugal and Connal, clutching his arm; the pilot's wrist was red and swollen, the hand limp. Maél squatted down beside me as the others gathered around, looking at the body stretched out in the sand.

"Is he dead then?" asked Clynnog.

"He was," I replied. "But he recovered."

"What should we do with him?" wondered Maél, and we fell to discussing this. We were on the point of deciding, when Gwilym returned.

"Brocmal has not drowned," he informed us. "Though he has swallowed his weight in water and sand, I expect. Brynach and Cadoc are with him."

"Then we have all survived," said Clynnog. "All thirteen—and one more besides," he added, prodding the barbarian with a toe.

The Sea Wolf awoke at the touch, and cringed when he saw the monks standing over him. Dugal, being a different sort of man than myself, stooped down and snatched the knife from the barbarian's belt in one swift motion. "Allow me to keep this for you, friend," he said.

The warrior made a grab at the retreating blade, but Dugal was quicker. "Peace. Rest easy and no harm will come to you."

From the expression of fear and bewilderment on the barbarian's face, it was obvious that he understood nothing of what we said to him. Thinking to ease his mind, I made a gentle, calming motion with my hand. He gave a jerk of his chin and lay back.

"We must move along," said Gwilym. "Bryn thinks the settlement is not far, but deems it best to find it before dark."

"The ship," said Fintán, his voice husky, "must be secured. We cannot leave it to the waves."

"Ships and settlements!" retorted Connal. "Man, will you not tell us what has become of the blessed book yet?"

Gwilym appeared unconcerned. "I expect it is safe."

"We waste light standing here," Dugal observed. "The sun is soon down."

"Never fret for *Bán Gwydd*, Fin," Clynnog said. "Come, brothers, we must hurry." He and the sea monks hastened to the overturned hull and began digging in the sand beside the rail. The hole was soon big enough for Maél to slide under, which he did. After a moment, a length of rope appeared on the sand, followed by a hammer and several wooden stakes.

We left them to the work of tying down the boat and, raising the barbarian to his feet, Dugal removed the man's belt and wrapped it around the warrior's arms, binding them to his sides. We then made our way to where the bishop and the others were waiting.

Ddewi was kneeling beside Brocmal, who sat propped against the stone, his legs splayed out before him. Brynach and the bishop stood nearby, talking quietly. They turned as we approached, and expressed surprise at the presence of an additional member to our party.

"Aidan rescued him," Dugal explained simply. "We did not like to leave him on the beach."

"Trust Aidan to save a barbarian," muttered Brocmal.

"And here I thought it was you I was saving," I told him.

Brocmal coughed and dabbed at his mouth with a soggy sleeve, then, as if this action was too much for him, sagged back against the rock once more.

"Is he well enough to walk?" asked Fintán, indicating the stricken Brocmal.

Ddewi glanced up as the pilot spoke, saw the helmsman's arm, and jumped to his feet. "He is less feeble than he appears," the physician said. "But I would have a look at that hand, Fin."

"Never fear for me, young Ddewi," the pilot said, "I can steer a ship with one paw if need be."

Ddewi, his touch at once gentle and quick, examined the swollen limb. "Can you move your fingers, Fin? Try to wiggle them." This brought a wince of pain from the helmsman, who swayed on his feet.

"None of this would have happened," Brocmal complained bitterly, "if not for Dugal. This is God's judgement on us for allowing the injustice he perpetrated to continue unpunished. Disaster will dog our steps as long as the malefactor is tolerated among us."

"Brother, hold your tongue," snapped the bishop tartly. "The issue of Libir's accident has been settled. Hear me now, Brocmal: you are not to raise the matter again, or you will find yourself subject to chastisement."

Turning to Dugal, the bishop said, "Lord Aengus was right to commend you. I do confess I feel that much safer knowing a man of your skill stands among us. May I ask you to stay beside me, brother?"

"If it would please you, Bishop Cadoc," replied the warrior.

"It would please me right well, son."

"Then say no more," Dugal replied happily. "The shadow you see beside you will be my own."

Brocmal closed his eyes and slumped back with a groan. While the physician continued his scrutiny of the pilot's wound, Brynach stepped to where I waited with the barbarian. "We will take him with us to the settlement," Brynach said. "The people there will deal with him."

"They will kill him," I said.

Brynach nodded. "Very likely," he agreed grimly.

"Then it were better for me to let him drown," I argued, feeling both angry and chagrined.

"Aye," Dugal agreed bluntly. "This one tried to split

your head with his war axe—and he would have, too, but for the seawave whelming us over."

I frowned. What Dugal said was true, but it was a bitter truth and I choked on it.

"Aidan, your concern is laudable. But we have no better choice," Bishop Cadoc said. "We cannot take prisoners. Nor would he fare better alone. We will deliver him to the lord of the settlement nearby and the decision will be his."

The sea monks joined us then, having made short work of staking down the boat. Connal espied the bishop's crosier, which had washed ashore, and gave it into Cadoc's hands. The bishop received this and, turning to Brynach, he made a stirring motion with his staff. Brynach smiled and lifted his mantle, revealing the leather bulga containing the book.

"Our treasure is safe, brothers," Bryn said. "It has pleased God to deliver us and our prize whole and hale."

Hearing this, Cadoc broke into an exaltation of thanksgiving. "Brothers," he said, lofting his eagle-topped staff, "great is God and worthy to be praised. He has delivered us from the storm, and from the hands of the wicked."

Lifting Brocmal to his feet, we set off for the settlement, singing a psalm of thanksgiving as we went. The sun had set before we gained the top of the sea bluffs, but enough light remained for us to locate the white plume of smoke once more. It seemed to emanate from between the first and second of the three hills before us. Brynach fixed the direction in his mind and strode forth boldly, leading the way. Everyone took their places behind him; as I was last in line, it fell to me to guard our barbarian.

I did not know what to do with him, so I let him walk a little ahead of me and kept my eye on him, lest he try to run away—though I reckoned that would be no bad thing, considering the reception awaiting him at the settlement.

As the ground was uneven and his arms were bound to his sides, he stumbled now and then, and I found myself having to steady him. And when it grew too dark to see the way clearly, I took his arm so that he should not fall. The first time this happened, he pulled away from me roughly and grunted his displeasure; the fifth or sixth time, however, he turned his head to look at me, the white of his eyes gleaming in the twilight. From then on, he did not resist when I laid hold of him.

Once we had left the rock-studded sea bluffs behind, the way became easier and we were able to move more quickly. The hills were well wooded, but upon approaching the first one, Brynach struck a path. Thus, we were able to walk rapidly and without fear of falling at every step. The hill was steeper and higher than it appeared in the dusk, and I was soon sweating; this, combined with the clammy dank clothes made me increasingly uncomfortable. Also, my skin itched from the salt water; my hands ached from the oars; my eyes felt dry and watery at once; my legs, shoulders, back, and sides were sore from rowing. I was hungry and thirsty, chilled to the bone and wet.

We crested the top of the first hill, whereupon Brynach paused at the top to search out the thread of smoke once more. Away to the east, a bright slice of moon rose above the low-drifting cloud. "The steading is just below," he said as we gathered around. "A goodly-sized holding, I think. You can see the edge of a field there."

He pointed down into the valley, and though I saw the smoke drifting up through the trees, I could not see the field or any hint of a settlement. We started down into the valley, still following the path—which I did not doubt would lead us directly to our destination.

Once over the crest of the hill, the wind dropped and I could hear the night sounds of the wood around us: a cuckoo called from an overhead limb, answered by another a little distance away; small, furtive rustlings in the winter detritus around the roots of the trees; the sudden flapping of unseen wings among the new-leafed branches.

It became difficult to see more than a pace or two ahead; I put out my hand to the barbarian from time to time—as much to reassure myself that he was still there, as to guide him. In each instance, the warmth and solidity of the touch surprised me; I half expected to reach out and find that he had vanished.

The wood thinned as we neared the settlement and the path widened, so that we stepped from the trees and into a clearing—the field that Brynach had glimpsed from above—to view the cluster of low, reed-thatched huts a short distance away. We halted to look and listen before moving on, but the steading remained peaceful and quiet, our arrival, as yet, unobserved.

This quiet did not last long, however, for upon reaching the middle of the field, a dog started barking, and immediately every dog in the valley had joined in, raising a din that roused the settlement dwellers and brought them running—difficult to count them in the dark, but I reckoned more than twenty men and boys in all—torches, spears, and hay forks at the ready. They did not appear overjoyed to see us.

# 12

Stand easy, brothers," Brynach said, watching the torches hasten over the field. "Say nothing until we see how they will receive us." He gestured to Dugal to come stand beside him, and the big monk took his place at the fore.

When the first rank of valley folk had drawn near, Brynach raised his empty hands and stepped slowly out to meet them. *"Pax, frater,"* he called, speaking Latin. This, added to his dress and tonsure, gave them to know that they addressed a holy man.

The head man took one look at Bryn and called to his fellows. "Hold, men. It is only some monks."

This was spoken in a tongue which, though it sounded very much like that of south Éire, used many British words and others I did not know—but the Britons amongst us understood perfectly well. "They are *Cernovii,*" Ciáran explained later. "At least, they once were."

"We are distressed clerics," Brynach said, directing his speech to the chieftain. "We are peregrini, and have been shipwrecked in the bay. Have you food and a place to rest?"

"Aye, that we have," the man said with a nod. "And you are welcome here. Is it from Dyfed you have come?"

"Yes—that is, some of us have come from Dyfed. The rest," he indicated our huddled group behind him, "are priests of Lindisfarne and Cenannus in Éire." The men of the settlement edged closer for a better look.

Brynach now gestured for the bishop to join him; as Cadoc approached, he said, "I would have you greet our superior. My friends," the well-spoken Briton called, loud enough for all to hear, "I give you Cadocius Pecatur Episcopus, Holy Bishop of Hy."

This produced an instant and gratifying response. Many of the valley dwellers gasped in amazement; several of those crowding close reached for the bishop's hand and pressed it to their lips in reverence.

"Peace, friends," the bishop said. "In the name of the most holy and blessed Jesu, I give you good greeting. Rise and stand on your feet. We are not such men as should be venerated in this way."

"You are welcome in our village," said the head man, using a word I had not heard before. "Come, we will take you there now."

Lifting high his torch, the chieftain led us across the field and into the settlement. It was larger than I first imagined: fifty or more huts, grain stores, a fine big hall, and an enclosure for cattle. There was no wall or ditch; the wood served them for protection, I suppose. And they did seem most vigilant men.

They conducted us directly to the hall where the fire burned brightly on a wide and generous hearth. We crossed the threshold and hastened to warm ourselves at the fire. Since no one gave me instruction, I brought the barbarian with me and stood beside him. He looked at me curiously, and seemed always on the point of speech—I could feel the words about to burst from him—but he kept his mouth firmly shut and said nothing.

We all stripped off our cloaks and spread them on the

hearthstones all around, and then stood as close to the flames as we might, revolving slowly front-to-back. I spread my mantle before the flames and soon my damp clothes were steaming from the heat. The fire did warm me wonderfully well.

To one side of the hearth was an enormous table made from the split log of a tree. The remains of a meal still strew the tabletop, but a command from the head man and the leavings were quickly removed. Women scurried to prepare another sitting.

"Ale!" the chieftain cried. "Ale! Tylu . . . Nominoé, Adso! Bring jars for our thirsty guests."

While boys scampered for the ale jars, our host turned to us and said, "Friends, sit and take your ease. You have had a tumultuous day, I think. Rest now. Share our meal." Placing a broad hand to his chest, he added, "My name is Dinoot, and I am leader of this *tuath*, as you would say. My people and I are happy you have found your way to us. Fear nothing, my friends. No ill can befall you here."

So saying, he led the bishop to the table and bade him sit in the prime place. The rest of us found places at the benches and, since no one told me otherwise, I brought my barbarian with me to the board.

As we moved to take our places at the far end of the table, however, Dinoot noticed the man with me was not a priest. "Bishop Cadoc," he said, putting out a hand to halt the barbarian, "forgive my curiosity, but it seems to me that a stranger has come among us."

"Ah, yes," the bishop said, remembering the warrior suddenly, and with some embarrassment. "Your eye is sharp, Master Dinoot."

"Not so sharp as some," the head man allowed, the selfsame eye narrowing slightly. "Still, I know a Sea Wolf when I see one."

"We lost our rudder to the storm," Brynach explained, "and were coming on to land—"

"Would have made a fine landfall, too," said Fintán, speaking up, "if not for a most cowardly attack." The pilot told about the Sea Wolves and shook his head with utmost regret. "Little *Bán Gwydd* is tied with ropes down on the strand."

Dinoot frowned. "The storm we knew. But I was not aware there were barbarians coursing our shores." He rubbed his whiskered chin. "Lord Marius will want to know of this."

"Your lord," asked Brynach, "he is not here?"

"His *caer* is but a half-day's walk," explained Dinoot. "There are five villages under his protection." Turning to the barbarian, who stood mute and resigned beside me, the chieftain asked, "What is to be done with that one?"

"We thought to leave the matter with you," Bishop Cadoc suggested. "We ourselves are strangers here, and are persuaded that your lord would know best what to do."

"Then I will send someone to inform him at once." So saying, the chieftain summoned one of the tribe's young men, and, after a brief word, the youth left the hall, taking two others with him. "The *machtiern* will hear of this regrettable incident by morning." His lip curled cruelly as he regarded the captive. "Trust this turd of a Dane will trouble you no more."

Rising, Dinoot clapped his hands and called for assistance. Four men hurried to him, and he said, "Throw this garbage in the midden pit and keep watch over him until Lord Marius arrives." Two of the men laid hold of the barbarian roughly and began dragging him away.

The Sea Wolf made no sound, nor offered the least resistance, but looked longingly at the table where baskets of bread and jars of ale were being laid. I saw this and my heart moved within me.

"Wait!" I shouted. The word was past my lips before I could prevent it.

The men hesitated. Every eye in the hall turned towards me, and I suddenly found myself very much the object of scrutiny. I stepped quickly to the table, snatched a loaf from the nearest platter and gave it the Sea Wolf. His childlike elation at this simple act was wonderful to behold. He smiled and clutched the bread to him. One of the men holding him reached out to take the food away.

"Please," I said, and stayed his hand.

The man looked to his chieftain. Dinoot nodded. The man shrugged and released the bread. They led the barbarian away and I took my place at table, yearning to shrink into invisibility.

Once the barbarian had been removed, the hall took life once more. The bishop and head man sat together at one end of the table. Dugal, as Cadoc requested, sat at the bishop's right hand; Brynach sat beside him—and all of them talked amiably with one another. It was good to see Dugal finding a little distinction. I had always known him to be a most able and proficient master of his own skills; unfortunately for Dugal, however, they were skills that were so rarely required at the monastery day by day. Thus, he was never offered opportunities to distinguish himself. Until now.

"That was well done," whispered Ciáran, sitting next to me. "I would not have thought of that. I commend you."

Brocmal, two places away, heard this remark, it seemed, and raised his lips in a sneer. Faolan, next to him, saw this and said, "A loaf, brother. That is all. Would you begrudge a hungry man a bit of bread?"

The imperious monk turned cold eyes on Faolan, stared hard at him, and then turned his face away without a word. He reached out and took a loaf of bread from the platter before him, broke it and bit into it.

"Let us give thanks," called Cadoc, rising from his place. He spoke a simple prayer for the food and a blessing on our hosts.

Loaves were passed and ale jars splashed drink into wooden cups and bowls. There was a warm, filling stew of salted beef and barley. The holding owned no spoons, apparently, so we lifted the bowls to our mouths and slurped down the stew, then sopped the gravy with the soft dark bread. We washed it down with great gulps of foaming ale.

Was better food ever put before me? No, there never was any to compare with that simple, nourishing fare. I ate like the starving man I was.

And while we ate, Ciáran told us what he had learned on the way to the village. "Their fathers came from Cerniu. That was long ago, however. The land here is called *An Bhriotáini* now," he told us between mouthfuls. I said the word silently to myself: Brittany.

"We are north of Nantes;" Ciáran continued, "how far north is not certain. Fin thinks the storm pushed us more east than south. Dinoot says Lord Marius will be able to tell us how far we must go to find the river."

We fell to talking about the last day's events, and the meal passed in a pleasant haze. I remember eating and laughing and singing . . . and then Ciáran was bending over me, shaking me gently by the shoulder. "Aidan— wake up, brother. Rise, we are going to our beds."

I raised my head from the board and looked about. Some of the brothers were already rolling themselves in their near-dry cloaks before the hearth; others were moving towards the door. I retrieved my cloak and fell into step behind Ciáran. We were led to a roofed byre where new straw had been laid down for us. Not caring where I slept, I stumbled to a corner, yawned and collapsed. Pulling my damp cloak over me, I laid my head in the sweet-scented hay and was asleep again as soon as my eyelids closed.

It may have been the shouting—then again, it may have been the acrid smell of smoke—that roused me from a deep, insensate sleep. I remember coughing as I awoke. The byre was filled with smoke. Eyes wide in the darkness, I stood up, not knowing where I was.

The dogs were barking. I heard the sound of running feet pounding on the earth outside. A sharp cry echoed outside in the yard, and was answered by another. I did not understand what was said.

I moved, shaking off sleep, to the doorway of the byre and looked out. Swift shapes moved in the moonlight. Smoke drifted in the night air. Looking to the hall, I saw long fingers of flame combing the roof-thatch. A figure appeared in the doorway of the hall, looked around quickly and disappeared. Again, I heard the slap of feet on the ground and turned towards the sound. I saw the glint of moonlight hard on a naked swordblade and fell back into the doorway as the figure rushed past.

A woman's scream scattered the silence like the fragments of a shattered jar.

"Wake up!" I cried. "Rise! We are attacked!"

I rushed from one sleeping form to the next, shaking my brother monks from their slumber. Outside, the dogs were in a frenzy. Shrieks sliced the still night air; the shouting increased. The first monks I roused stumbled to the doorway and out. I woke two more and then followed, darting from the byre.

A hut across the yard burst into flame. I heard screams inside, and children wailing. I raced to the hut and threw aside the hide covering; smoke billowed from the doorway. "Hurry!" I shouted, dashing inside. "I will help you! Hurry!"

A young woman, her face illumined by the quick-flickering flames, stood in the centre of the hut, clutching a small child; another brat clung to her legs, mouth wide, tears streaming down its terrified face. Sweeping the child into my arms, I dashed back outside, pulling the woman with me. Once clear of the burning hut, the mother gathered her wits and her children and, holding tight to both, made for the safety of the wood, disappearing into the shadows as she ran.

I turned once more to the yard, now seething in a turmoil of angry, shouting men—many grappling with one another, their combat hellish in the flames of burning roofs and dwellings. Someone had loosed the dogs, and the fear-crazed beasts were attacking friend and foe alike. People were streaming from the hall. I saw Dinoot dash into the open, shouting commands; Dugal emerged right behind him, brandishing a spear.

Bishop Cadoc, God save him, rushed forth, hands upraised, crying, "Peace! Peace!" Bryn and Gwilym darted behind him, desperately trying to interpose themselves between him and the attack. Heedless of his own safety, however, Cadoc darted into the thick of the fight and was set upon at once.

An axehead glinted in the confused light, cruelly swift. I heard the sickening crack of blade on bone and the bishop crumpled like a rag. I started to the place where I saw the good bishop fall, but the fight surged towards me and I could not reach him. The last I saw was Gwilym stooping over the motionless body. Then he, too, was struck down with the same axe.

"Gwilym!" I ran, shouting with all my might. I had taken but three paces, however, when all at once an enormous, broad-shouldered brute with arms as big as hams rose up screaming before me. He attacked and felled a defender with a single blow of his huge club, then straddled the body and raised the club to deliver the killing clout. My feet were already running as the heavy weapon rose over his head.

Throwing my hands before me, I hit the barbarian in the small of the back, shoving him forward as the club fell. His aim spoiled, the club struck the dirt beside his foot. Loosing a tremendous cry of strangled rage, the foeman whirled to face me. It was only then that I realized I had seen that brawny giant before, swinging from the prow of the Sea Wolves' ship.

This thought occupied me longer than wisdom would have allowed. I stood flatfooted and staring while the braided barbarian advanced, club high, ready to crush my skull and scatter my brains over the blood-soaked dirt. In the lurid light I saw the veins bulging in his neck and arms as he swung the club in a tight circle over his head, advancing with slow, murder-bent steps.

Someone shouted my name. "Aidan!" It was Dugal, running to my aid. "Run, Aidan! Flee!"

Even as Dugal raced to my defence, another foeman met him. Dugal tried to evade the attack; he lowered his shoulder and threw the butt of the spear into the man's face. The barbarian dropped to the ground and lashed out with his legs, tripping Dugal as he struggled forward. I saw my friend fall. A second barbarian leapt onto his back, hacking at Dugal's head with an axe.

"Dugal!" I screamed, and started to him. The giant with the club side-stepped quickly, blocking my path. The light caught the slick wetness on the end of the club; I saw the red glint as the club circled, preparing to fall.

A savage cry sounded behind me, but I could not take my eyes from the dread movement of the lumpen weapon. The club slashed down, falling with heart-stopping speed. At the same instant, I felt hands fasten on my left arm, jerking me sideways. The club beat the air beside my ear, and I had a glimpse of a filth-smeared face before my cowl was yanked up over my head.

The giant roared and a voice loud beside me shouted back. I made to fend off my attacker, but my arms were ensnared in my own garments. My cloak was stripped from me and wound around my head and shoulders. I stumbled forward, trying to run, and struck my head against something hard.

Blue light blazed in my eyes and I heard a strange loud buzzing in my ears as I fell.

# 13

The ground swayed beneath me. The buzzing in my ears had given way to dull, leaden ringing—like that of a poorly-cast bell. My head throbbed with a fiercely hostile ache. I could not feel my legs, nor my hands. The sky was still dark, and all was quiet. I heard the low mutter of whispered voices somewhere nearby, but they sounded like the clucking of ducks and I could make no sense of it. The air was close and warm, and breathing painful.

I made to rise. The sky burst into flaming jagged fragments of searing light. Nausea rolled over me in a wave and I slumped back again, panting with the effort.

A memory fought its way into my sluggish, half-sleeping awareness: a tiny bubble rising in a great black vat—only to burst at the moment of surfacing. What was it? What . . . what?

I heard a scream. The sound brought me to my senses as memory broke upon me with the force of an ocean wave crashing over a rock. I remembered the attack.

Eyes pressed tight against the pain, I struggled up. My shoulders and arms were swathed in heavy cloths. Shaking my arms, twisting this way and that, I fought free of the bindings—my own cloak and mantle—and threw off my cowl.

Daylight streamed into my eyes; throwing a hand before my face, I found myself gazing into the strong red glare of the rising sun. The scream sounded again and I looked up into a clear blue sky to see a white gull gliding serenely high above me. The ship's mast swayed into view.

The ship's mast! I reached for the rail above me and hauled myself shakily to my feet.

My stomach heaved again, and I vomited over the rail. When I had finished, I dragged my sleeve across my mouth and then slowly raised my eyes—this time with unutterable dread—to my new surroundings: a barbarian ship with Sea Wolves for companions. They were occupied with rowing, and paid me no attention. One brute in brown buskins, belt, and a sleeveless sheepskin mantle stood a pace or two away, his back to me. He seemed intensely interested in the distant eastern horizon where the red-risen sun was gathering its day's strength and filling the sky with light.

One of the rowers, glancing up from his oar, saw me, and called something to the brown-belted one who turned, took one look at my gaping, vomit-flecked mouth, smiled broadly, and went back to his duty. I turned my head to see what he was looking at and saw, far away, the ragged grey coastal hills of Armorica. It took me a moment to work out that we were proceeding in a northerly direction over grey-green billowy waves.

The Sea Wolf ship was long and narrow, with a high-swept prow and stern: a strong, sharp-keeled vessel. There were twenty or so rowers, with small benches for more. Behind the slender mast a platform had been established, and this was overarched with bent poles and the whole framework covered with oxhides to form a sort of enclosed stall or tent. A wisp of smoke emanated from beneath the hides, and flattened on the brisk easterly breeze.

Pain blurred my vision but there was nothing much to see anyway—a dull expanse of slate-grey water to the right of me, a dull featureless coast to the left—so I sat down again, drawing air deep into my lungs to help clear my head. I tried to think. My brain, however, refused to respond to the small demands I made upon it; all that came to me was that I was a captive.

*Captive.* The word engrossed me for an inordinate time. I savoured each lonely, helpless syllable, repeating them over and over again until the word lost all meaning. What would happen to me? What did Sea Wolves do with their captives? Slaughtered them, most likely, I concluded gloomily.

Regarding my captors, they were a filthy, noisome pack: smeared with mud and blood, and reeking of worse. When the seabreeze gusted, I could smell them and the stench made me gag.

There were twenty and two barbarians in sight; I made an accurate count. They were dressed in skins and leather, and wore broad belts of various kinds—leather mostly, but I saw several with copper and silver discs as well; most had knives or daggers tucked into their belts. Two or three wore short *siarcs*, or tunics, of close-woven cloth dyed pale yellow or brown. They seemed immoderately proud of their shaggy manes of hair: all wore their moustaches and beards long: some kept their locks in braids; some tied them back with leather thongs; others allowed their tresses to fly loose. More than half of them had some ornament worked into their hair—a bit of gold wire, a carved comb or silver trinket of some kind: a leaf, fish, bird, or hand.

A surprising number wore chains of gold around their thick necks, and everyone, from the greatest to the least, boasted other costly ornaments of various types: gold and silver rings, armbands, bracelets, brooches, and chains.

All were huge men. The smallest among them was taller than me, and the largest were bigger than Dugal.

Dugal! Oh, what had happened to him? What had become of my friends? Distracted by my own troubles, I had not spared a single thought for those I had left behind. For all I knew, the entire settlement had been slain in the attack. They might all be lying in their own blood at this very moment, the sun rising on their death-day.

*Kyrie eleison,* I prayed fervently to myself. *Lord have mercy!* Spread your loving arms around those who call upon your name in their time of need. Heal their hurt, and protect them from all harm. Please, Lord, be merciful to your people. Forgive my selfishness and pride, Lord. Save your servants . . . Have mercy, Lord, have mercy . . .

Someone shouted a gruff command. I broke off my prayer and raised my head. A fair-haired Sea Wolf with a yellow beard was standing on the platform; he shouted again, and three or four barbarians quickly pulled in their oars and hastened to where he stood. The pilot gave out a cry and two others leapt to the ropes and began raising the sail. I thought this meant that we would now be heading further out to sea, and further away from Armorica. Once under sail, the Sea Wolves shipped oars and then gathered around the tented platform. The ship held course meanwhile, running parallel to the coast. After a time, however, I saw that my first judgement was not accurate for we were, in fact, heading obliquely towards land, drawing slightly closer with every roll of the waves.

I sat huddled in my place at the prow, watching the shore. It came into my mind that I might throw myself overboard. I had no great wish to drown, but reasoned that if I chose the place carefully I might be able to swim to freedom. I could be over the side and away before anyone stopped me.

The barbarian pilot—he of the brown buskins and sheepskin jerkin—bellowed a strange word that sounded like *vik* to my unaccustomed ear. Whereupon, the sail was instantly struck and the rowers returned to their benches and oars. Though I observed the nearing coastland keenly, I could not see any hint of a settlement, nor indeed, anything at all worthy of attention. Still, as the boat drew swiftly closer, I watched and waited for a chance to make my escape.

This came much sooner than I expected, for as the ship drew close to land, the sea grew rapidly more shallow. Soon, I could see the pebbled bottom showing beneath the waves, though we were still a goodly way off. I would never have a better opportunity.

I drew a deep breath, stood quickly, and, before anyone had noticed, hurled myself over the rail. I struck the water with a splash and regretted my hasty decision at once. The sea was cold and I sank like a stone, quickly touching the bottom with my knee. Gathering my legs beneath me, I pushed away. Unfortunately, I had badly misjudged my ill-advised leap and I surfaced alongside the ship—right between the hull and the oarblades.

Seeing my mistake, I drew a deep breath and dived. Whether my plunge was not deep or quick enough, I do not know, but I felt myself caught and, though I flailed all my arms and legs with utmost effort, I could not get free. I surfaced, gasping, the end of my cloak tight in a Sea Wolf's unrelenting grip. The barbarian had simply leaned over the rail and snagged me by a trailing edge of garment.

He dragged me half-way out of the water, and then held me there—much to the delight of his barbarian friends. They all roared with mirth to see me dangling like a fish from the side of the boat. Their laughter, like their voices, was crude and rough, and it hurt my ears to hear it.

The ship drew into a small, shallow cove and turned as it came in to land. As the ship turned, I saw what the pilot already knew to be there: a river—not wide, but deep enough to admit the keel. Without pause or hesitation, the ship slid across the little bay and into the river mouth. The oarsmen pulled in their oars and used them as poles to push the boat further up the river. Oh, these were canny Sea Wolves, indeed. And strong. Only when the ship had come to rest on a broad pebbled shoal was I released—thrown back into the water like a catch deemed too pathetic to keep.

The Sea Wolf who had prevented my escape leaped into the water with me. Grasping my cloak, he stood me upright in the water, turned me to face him and shaking his head slowly, spoke to me in a warning tone of voice while shaking a dripping finger in my face. Although I could not comprehend a word he said, I understood perfectly from his manner and gesture that he was cautioning me from attempting to escape again.

I nodded, showing him that I did indeed perceive his meaning. He smiled. Then, still holding tight to my cloak, he struck me hard in the face with the back of his hand. My aching head snapped sideways and the force of the blow knocked me into the water. He grabbed my mantle and jerked me to my feet; my mouth stung and I tasted blood on my tongue.

Still smiling his broad, blithe smile, the happy barbarian drew back his hand again.

I closed my eyes in anticipation of the blow, and braced myself. Instead, I heard a sharply uttered growl. The Sea Wolf released me at once, and I opened my eyes to see another barbarian wading towards me, talking in an angry way to his companion. The first one shrugged, shook his finger at me again, released me, and walked away.

The second Sea Wolf strode to where I stood, took me roughly by the arm and led me—half-pushing, half-dragging—onto the shoal where he spun me around to face him, and struck me on the face with his open hand.

The slap caught the attention of all those nearby, but it sounded far worse than it felt; and though it brought smiles and laughter from the Sea Wolves looking on—some of these called out to the barbarian, who answered them sternly—I could not help feeling that there was no real anger or malice in the blow.

Strange to say, it was only then that I realized who stood before me: it was *my* barbarian, the one I had found washed up on the beach, the one we had taken to the settlement with us, the one to whom I had given the breadloaf. We stood facing one another now, our positions reversed utterly.

I dabbed at my split lip with the heel of my hand, and spat blood onto the strand. The barbarian took my arm again and dragged me to one of the larger rocks on the shore and shoved me down on it. He made a flattening gesture with his hand and spoke a single guttural snarl that gave me to know I was to sit still and not move, much less try to run away.

He need not have bothered; I was content for the moment to sit on the rock and dry my clothes in the sun. I *would* try to escape again, I told myself, but must wait for a better opportunity to present itself and not simply seize the first foolish chance that happened my way. This thought, added to the fact that we were still in Armorica and not out somewhere in the unknown sea, consoled me and I felt as if I were making the best of a very bad plight.

The Sea Wolves, meanwhile, set about preparing a meal. They made a small fire and brought out food from the ship, which they shared out among themselves with not so much as a glance in my direction.

One huge red-braided barbarian—I recognized him now as the brute with the club from the night raid—climbed back into the ship and seized a cask which he lifted in his arms and was about to heave onto the strand.

He was stopped by a quick shout from one of the others: a fair-haired man with long-braided yellow beard and a gold chain around his neck. This man was the one who had stood on the tented platform commanding men to his bidding.

Yellow Hair, I decided, must be the leader of this barbarian band. And although his men paid him some regard, they did not appear overly solicitous of him, nor even very attentive. Even so, he seemed to command some part of their respect, or at least a grudging obedience, for the red giant lowered the cask with a grunt, climbed from the ship and returned to his meal.

After they ate, they slept. Like pigs in the sun, they simply rolled over, closed their eyes and slept.

Any thought of slipping quietly away while they were sleeping vanished when my barbarian suddenly awoke, remembered me, and came and bound my hands and ankles with a length of braided cord. He left me in the shade of the rock, at least, where I could keep watch on my captors. This proved a dismal occupation, however, as they remained inert for the better part of the day, rising only as the shadows stretched long across the pebbled shoal.

They woke, stretched, and relieved themselves in the river. Some availed themselves of the opportunity to wash, standing in the shoals and splashing water over themselves, clothes and all. My barbarian came and untied me, pulled me to my feet and dragged me to the ship. I waded out to the waiting boat, pausing only to gulp down a few handfuls of water. For this I was lashed with the cord—half-heartedly, sure—and unintelligible abuse heaped on my poor uncomprehending head.

This proved entertaining to the Sea Wolves, who laughed to see me in such difficulty, although I did not greatly mind for, again, I sensed no genuine animosity in the exercise. I began to form the opinion that my barbarian was trying to perform a duty expected of him, but one for which he had no heart. Being a monk, I had experience of such behaviour and could recognize it quickly when I saw it.

We clambered up over the ship's rail. Once aboard, I was pushed into my place in the prow with the growled order—as I took it—to stay there. Still, he did not restrain me in any way.

I did not eat that day, nor the next. I was allowed only what water I could get for myself when we stopped. This produced no immediate concern for me; I was used to fasting and so considered this privation simply another trédinus which I happily dedicated to the Saviour God. When the others ate, I prayed: for our poor dead bishop—may God reward him greatly!—for my brothers, whether wounded or dead I knew not, for the safety of the blessed book, and for myself in cruel captivity. I prayed long and earnestly each day, though I soon learned to forego prostration or even kneeling. My captors did not like to see me in a posture of devotion, and kicked me hard if they caught me so. That was no great hardship, I reckoned, for God sees only the contrite spirit, and my reverence was true. Sure, the lack of food did not concern me, but the fact that we pressed a steady pace north filled me with unlimited apprehension. Day by day we drew further and further away from the region of Nantes, and any hope I might have sustained of ever seeing any of my brothers again dwindled accordingly. My prayers became more fervent for this, and I braced myself with endless repetitions of psalms.

One day I looked out from my perch in the prow to see that the familiar grey coast had disappeared altogether. It was not to be seen again for two days. I ceaselessly scanned the barren horizon for any sign of land, and when at last that longed-for glimpse appeared again, the land had changed entirely: low, flat, brown and featureless. Nor did the Sea Wolves sail so close to the shore as before; they ceased searching out the *viks* for rest and water and took to keeping watch both day and night.

One result of this change was that I was given a little food—the same as they ate, though far less. It was rough fare: tough and tasteless meat, unseasoned and inexpertly dried. Still, it served its humble purpose: keeping this captive alive until he should be reconciled to his eventual destiny—whether death or some worse fate, I did not know.

I stood or sat at my accustomed place, looking out at the strange, unnamed land and, whether sitting or standing, I prayed most fervently for God's Swift Sure Hand to reach down and pluck me from my onerous plight. Well, that did not happen. Instead, the sharp-keeled ship flew swiftly over the sea. North and ever north, we sailed. Only once did we see any other vessel, and this we fled.

On sighting the ship, Brown Buskins called out to Yellow Hair, who joined him at the mast. The two stood shoulder to shoulder in close scrutiny of the stranger vessel for a moment, whereupon Yellow Hair began shouting commands which sent the supine sailors scurrying to their oars. All rowed with unmatched vigour, even though the sail remained full and the wind fair. It soon became clear that we were outdistancing the stranger. After a time, the other ship gave up the chase, and the Sea Wolves cheered.

Their joy at eluding a potential rival transformed their spirits. I felt their elation, and smiled in spite of myself. So like children, I thought, in the greedy zeal of all their appetites. And, like children, only the moment concerned them. They had escaped an unwanted confrontation and their joy knew no bounds; leaping from bench to rail, they shook their spears and rattled their shields, brimming with bravado now that their supposed enemy had turned tail.

In all, it was a most instructive lesson. Nor was it wasted on me.

After that, I no longer looked to return to Armorica. The barbarians, as it seemed to me, were making for safe harbour. Turning my eyes to the north I searched those cold, black waters for any likely destination. The weather turned foul again; the wind blew hard, raising the waves. Low cloud hung over the sea, and heavy fog obscured the shore. We did not make landfall, however; the Sea Wolves apparently enjoyed the heavy weather.

When, at the end of the second day, the sun returned, the land changed again: deep bays fronting hard shingles of stone, with dark green forests rising on steep slopes behind. The hills were not high, but their upper reaches were often lost in the thick fogs of mist and cloud that festered in that inhospitable clime. I saw no settlements of any size; even single habitations were few enough. Even so, the Sea Wolves feared unchallenged passage. This I knew because, upon entering those dark seas, we took to sailing only at night, a feat the barbarians had mastered well.

The fact that they, too, might have enemies had simply never occurred to me before. But seeing how wary and trepid they became as they neared home, gave me to know that though they preyed on any they deemed weaker, they were themselves prey to others stronger than themselves and feared them with as great a fear as any they inspired. Truly, they were wolves: savagely wild, brutal, with all men's hands raised against them at each and every turn.

Thus, I kept my wits about me and learned all I could of their uncouth ways. The more I learned, the more I pitied them, for they were without redemption and not even the merest hope of salvation clung to them. God help me, I began to feel superior to them for my learning and civilization. Arrogance seized me in its gaping jaws and shook me hard; my pride swelled. I imagined that, given the chance, I might do some mighty work among them by bringing the Good News of Jesu to them. For I had heard of such things.

Indeed, had not sainted Pátraic accomplished this very feat among his former captors? This, I determined, I would do. I would become Pátraic to these Sea Wolves and earn everlasting glory.

# 14

It was a grey and green land to which we fled: cold-water bays and black rock hills bristling with tall stands of pine and birch, and small fields eked from the ever-encroaching forest and, with back-breaking care, scratched into the thin, poor soil. The settlements were small: mere huddles of timber huts scattered along the coast and at the edges of forest, or on wooded islands. Several days after entering northern waters and sailing furtively past numerous islands and bays, we came at last to our journey's end: a settlement tucked well back into a wide pebbled cove of a broad, high peninsula. Surrounded by a tall timber palisade, it appeared little more than the forest from which it had been so laboriously cleft.

There were other, smaller ships and boats, both in the bay and drawn up on the hard shingle. At the appearance of the ship, the whole settlement rushed down to the water and stood crying loud welcome. The arrival was eagerly greeted by one and all—even the hounds ran along the strand happily yapping at their masters' return. Everyone shouted, cried, and talked at once and the welcome became a joyous din.

Eager to be once more reunited with their kin, most of the Sea Wolves leapt from the rails into the water and swam to shore where they were received with great acclaim and gladness. Women embraced their husbands, children ran to their fathers; older men strode the shingle shouting and gesturing, boys brandished sharpened sticks, and young men lofted spears. Clearly, the return had been eagerly awaited.

I stood in my place at the prow, looking on. It was like any reception where families welcome husbands, fathers, and sons home from the sea. Only, these menfolk had been away on errands of pillage and plunder, scattering not fishnets but woe and death in their wake.

Yellow Hair allowed the ship to be run aground and watched while it was made fast to two stout poles set in the strand. Satisfied, he then ordered his men to bring forth the plunder. The tented platform behind the mast was quickly stripped of its hide covering and behold! five wooden caskets or chests and a veritable mound of weaponry—swords, spears, shields, and suchlike.

Red Giant stooped and gathered a chest in his great arms and, raising it over his head, gave out an enormous grunt and heaved the casket onto the shingle below. The chest splintered and burst; the sheen of yellow gold glinted in the sunlight. While two other Sea Wolves struggled with a second chest, the giant gathered a third treasure box and heaved it onto the strand beside the first. The fourth struck the others and broke open, spilling its golden treasure onto the beach.

The people gathered close about the trove and stood marvelling at the wealth arrayed there. Yet, no one—not even those who had thrown it down—made bold to touch it with so much as a fingertip. Rather, they waited until Yellow Hair had climbed down to stand over it.

This, I reckoned, was the first time the barbarians had

bridled their appetites for so long a time altogether. They all gathered close about, faces glowing with keen anticipation, eyes agleam with treasure-light, murmuring to one another behind their hands.

The chieftain spread an oxhide on the strand and then caused two of the three remaining chests to be opened and their contents poured out upon the skin. The last chest, I noticed, remained locked and was set aside; but the contents of the broken caskets were scrupulously gathered and added to the pile of gold and silver ornament and coin. And it was no mean heap. I had never seen so much wealth in one place. Sure, it was a hoard to rival that of the Tuatha De Danaan.

Then, kneeling reverently before this wealth, Yellow Hair began prodding through the mass—much, I believe, as he must have done many times over in the privacy of his shipboard hut. He found and held up a large golden cup to the delight of the onlookers who cooed like amazed pigeons at the sight. He placed the costly cup beside him and returned to the heap, whereupon, after a moment's search, he retrieved a handsome bowl which took its place beside the cup.

Next he drew out a golden chain with links as thick as a man's thumb. The barbarian leader rose, and holding the chain between his outstretched hands turned this way and that, speaking quietly the while. Then, with a wild shout, he suddenly flung the chain to Red Giant; the man's broad face split into a wide, snaggletoothed grin and he roared his pleasure, shaking all over like a bear.

Red Giant, I decided, was the chieftain's champion, and was therefore recognized before the others and awarded the choice prize. One by one, the rest were likewise rewarded by their chief—a silver brooch to one, a pair of bracelets to another; cups and bowls for some, chains and armbands for others. Everyone received something according, I suppose, to the value of his service. That they should receive such high reward for their murderous feats disgusted me. *Jesu,* I prayed, *deliver me from this den of iniquity!*

Alas, but my travail had just begun.

Great the grief! I recognized, among the hoarded gold, the fine-crafted eagle from Bishop Cadoc's staff. The proud bird had been snatched from its rightful perch and now spread its wings for the enjoyment of its captors. I beheld that holy emblem and my heart sank like a millstone. "Poor Cadoc," I murmured, "such a death was not worthy of you." At least the priceless book was not amidst the plunder; I took that as a good sign.

When the last of the golden trinkets had been dispersed, Yellow Hair fell to dividing up the coinage and silver. The larger silver objects were quickly hacked to pieces with axes—not regarding either beauty or craftsmanship— and those pieces added to the heap. I winced to see a handsome platter and several fine dishes fall to the chop, not to mention numerous brooches, pins, rings, and armbands.

Still kneeling at his work, he sorted the coins and pieces into mounds according to size and weight, and then divided them into meticulously equal stacks—one for each Sea Wolf. This done, the barbarians drew lots and chose from among the stacks according to their luck at the draw. The last pile fell to the chieftain, who scooped it up quickly, and poured the coins into his cup.

Thus were the treasures meted out. Many, I noticed, were delivered forthwith into other hands. Indeed, surprisingly few treasures remained the sole property of their recipients. For no sooner had the Sea Wolf got the goods in hand, than his wife laid claim to it; and, upon wresting the precious object from her husband's clutches, the woman knotted the family's ill-gotten wealth into a tight-tied bundle in a corner of her mantle.

Yellow Hair, having given out every last scrap of treasure, now received the adulation of his people. They acclaimed him noisily, slapping his back and shoulders; some of the women tugged affectionately on his long braided hair and beard. It was in the midst of this that my barbarian approached his leader. They exchanged a quick word and my heart seized within me as they both turned and eyed me carefully.

I saw Yellow Hair shrug in a disinterested way and then turn to the throng. He called out to them and pointed directly at me. This caused an uncertain sensation among the crowd, some of whom laughed aloud while others muttered ominously. Several moved nearer the boat for a better look, eyeing me with speculative curiosity.

One of these, a thick-browed man, raised his voice to the chieftain and was answered benignly. Yellow Hair then turned to my barbarian who nodded, his mouth firm. The thick-browed man spoke again, pointed at me, and held up two fingers. I perceived with some dismay that they were bargaining for me.

Again, the chieftain spoke, and again my barbarian nodded. The other man looked at me, then shook his head and walked away. Yellow Hair held out his hand. My barbarian reached into his belt and withdrew three gold coins which he dropped into the chieftain's palm.

Yellow Hair commanded the last treasure box to be returned to the ship, and then sat down cross-legged on the oxhide, holding his cup in one hand and his bowl in the other. At once the oxhide was taken up and lifted high, and the barbarian chieftain was carried into the fortress upon the shoulders of his people, who followed with much loud acclaim.

My barbarian summoned me from the ship, where I stood watching all that passed on the strand. I climbed over the rail and joined my new master, who put a hand to his chest and said, "Yuu-nar." Patting his chest, he repeated this word several times, nodding at me with an expression of intent expectation.

"Yu-nar," I replied, pronouncing the odd-sounding name as well as I could.

He smiled, pleased with my effort, said, "Gunnar," again, then tapped me on the chest hopefully.

"Aidan," I told him. "I am Aidan."

Gunnar appeared thoughtful. "Ed-dan," he said.

"Aidan," I corrected gently, nodding. "Aeedan."

"Aeddan," he replied.

I was on the cusp of correcting him again, when he suddenly raised his hands, took me by the throat and squeezed hard. I struggled to remove his hands, but he pressed the harder, and I began to fear he would choke me to death. My eyes bulged and I fought for breath. Gunnar forced me to my knees. Black spots crowded my vision, and I croaked, "Mercy!"

Only then did he release me. I gasped, drawing air into my lungs. Standing over me, Gunnar took a length of leather strap, such as might be used to leash a dog, and proceeded to tie it around my neck; he looped it two or three times and tied it tight. Then, with a grunt, he extended his right hand to me. I thought he meant to raise me up, so I took the offered hand. He shook off my grip and thrust his hand nearer my face.

When I made no further move, he took my head with his free hand and held it while he pressed the back of his right hand to my forehead. I understood this gesture to mean that he considered himself my master, and I his slave, indebted to him for my life, which he held in his hands.

He turned away and strode towards the fortress, stopping after a few strides to see if I was following him. When he saw that I was still on my knees, he uttered a sharp word of command—which I took to mean that I was to attend him. I rose and proceeded to the settlement behind my master.

We approached the high gates and I trembled with fear and dread. I crossed myself and invoked divine protection, saying, "Shield me with a mighty shielding, Lord. Let Michael, Chief of Hosts, go before me into this dread place. My soul between thy hands, Great King, thy wings surrounding me in this sea of unrighteousness. So be it!"

Thus sustained, I made the sign of the cross over my heart and entered the fortress, passing through the enormous gates and into that heathen domain.

I had never seen a barbarian habitation before, but I had heard men tell of the settlement at Dubh Llyn; apart from the absence of the river, this might have been that very place. The dwellings were large, squat mud-and-timber lodges with steep-peaked thatched roofs; there were seven of these lodges, each one made to serve fifteen or twenty people.

One great structure stood apart from the others, holding centre place within the timber walls. Two slender birch poles stood before this dwelling, their tops adorned with wreaths and boughs of fresh-cut branches tied with white and yellow rags. Even without the birch poles I would have known the place as Yellow Hair's hall.

Passing among the dwellings and across the wide yard, Gunnar and I followed the throng between the birch poles and into the great hall. The room was a dim and very forest-like, with the boles of trees standing the length of the hall, their branches obscured in the smoky darkness of the roof. These rooftrees were painted: red, white, and yellow, but one—that nearest the western corner where the king had his chamber, though it was little more than a stall such as often given to horses—was painted blue.

Sooty torches fluttered in their iron sconces, casting a

dim filthy light over all within. The length of the room was lined with sleeping nooks or stalls, some of which were fronted by screens or skin hangings for privacy. Round wooden shields hung from the upper beams above clusters of spears. Two long boards on trestles faced the hearth, with low benches running the length of the boards on either side. The floor was strewn with reeds and straw; dogs sprawled lazily underfoot, or sniffed around the legs of the newcomers.

All lords are alike in the ostentation of their dwellings, and the barbarians are especially given to excessive display. Yellow Hair's chair was a big, oaken throne with rings and bosses of iron; his hearth was wide and deep, stone-lined, with huge iron firedogs to support the vast logs he kept burning day and night. An enormous bronze cauldron hung by a double-linked chain from a tripod; the contents of this kettle bubbled and spluttered.

Lord Yellow Hair strode directly to the gurgling pot and, taking up a long flesh-fork, thrust the implement into the stew. He brought up a steaming hunk of meat which he brought to his mouth and from which he worried off a chunk. Chewing heartily, he swallowed the gobbet down, then turned to those looking on and called in a loud voice: "*Öl!*" he cried. "*Öl! Fort!*"

Several young boys scampered away, returning a few moments later with foaming bowls of brown ale—the preferred drink of all Danemen. Yellow Hair drank deep, emptying the bowl into his mouth and quaffing the heavy liquid in great gulps. When he finished, he wiped his yellow moustache on his sleeve, passed the bowl to his champion, and swaggered to his throne, turned to the watching crowd and, with exceeding ceremony, sat down.

This, I believe, was an awaited sign, for no sooner had his lordly rump touched the polished oak, than the entire hall lurched into frantic motion. Instantly, men were jostling one another for places at the board while women darted here and there, and everyone in full cry. The noise! Chaos reigned. My head swam.

Gunnar took his place with the other Sea Wolves who had settled themselves at the board. I was made to stand behind him—not a bad place to be, for there I could observe the bustle of the hall without getting trampled in it—while all around me the people of the settlement prepared a feast.

Ale jars and bowls began appearing, brought to the board by the serving boys running through the hall. The Sea Wolves guzzled down the frothy brew, elbowing one another impatiently, slapping the board with their hands and crying for more. Cups and jars and bowls circled the hall, passed hand to hand.

Several men entered carrying a large vat which they set on an iron stand beside their lord's throne. They proceeded to plunge empty bowls into the vat, and withdrew the vessels full and foaming, and flung them into the maelstrom. Watching the men drink with such zeal, I became aware of my own clawing thirst, but no one gave me anything to drink—nor did I think it likely that they would.

As the Sea Wolves settled to their drinking, the women and girls hastened forth with baskets of black bread. The sight of all those fine round loaves brought the water to my mouth and a sharp ache to my poor empty stomach. I watched as basket after basket was placed upon the board and men took up loaves—two and three at a time!—broke them and stuffed them into their mouths.

Meanwhile, several men busied themselves at the fire. Two iron standards were established on either side of the hearth, and when this was accomplished and the flames brightly hot, the men vanished, only to reappear bearing the whole carcass of a cow on a long iron spit. Three spitted pigs and two sheep followed, and all were placed on the standards to turn slowly over the flames. Soon the crack and sizzle of burning fat was added to the chatter of the flames, and the great hall filled with the savoury aroma of roasting meat.

I thought I would swoon.

To divert myself from my dilemma I looked elsewhere around the hall and saw, sitting on a stool in a darkened corner, a bent old man; what is more, this man was staring at me most intently. When he saw that I marked his gaze, he rose and shuffled forth—more bear than man, so he seemed, for he was dressed in the shreds of filthy rags and his head weaved back and forth as he walked.

His features were begrimed with soot and dirt, and the few straggles of hair left to him were a tangled mat of straw and dung. Round-shouldered and lame, he shambled out of his corner to stand before me, regarding me with eyes so wide and lustrous I assumed he must be mad.

This wretched being stood looking at me for some time, then leaned forward and put his face up next to mine, reached up a grimy hand and rubbed the top of my head—whereupon he laughed out loud, expelling a breath so foul that I gagged and beat the air with my hand. He laughed the more, and I rocked backwards on my heels almost to falling over.

The old man gave my shaven forehead a last pat, opened his mouth in a toothless grin and said, "What is your name, Irish?"

Startled, I gaped at him. "I am—" I paused, trying to remember my name. "Aidan!" I said. "My name is Aidan."

The odd creature smirked and squirmed. He indicated Gunnar sitting at the board a pace away. "Caught you, boy, did he?"

"He did that," I answered.

The stranger laughed and shook himself all over as if this revelation were a singular pleasure to him. "Verity,

verity," he said and, still laughing, began to sing: "The Sea Wolves go *a-viking* and fetch back Irish meat and bone. Gold and silver are more to their liking, but these wolves would devour stone!"

I stared at him in amazement, wondering how this vile being came to speak Latin. Sure, it was a lazy and much-eroded Latin, but the cleric's tongue nonetheless.

"Who are you, man?" I asked.

"Scop, I am," he replied, "and Scop ever more."

"Scop?" I wondered—an unusual name for a most unusual man.

"It means soothsayer, boy. *Skald*, the Northmen say; you would say *bard*." He laid a dirty finger beside his nose in a knowing way. "I am Truth Speaker to Rägnar Yellow Hair." At this he indicated the man on the throne with a reverential wave of his hand.

"His name is Yellow Hair? Truly?" I wondered aloud.

"It is that. Mind him, now. He is lord of the Geats and Oscingas." He raised both fists and clashed them together. "Two tribes, mark you. Many knives owe him blood. He is a most worthy gold-giver." Scop closed one eye and peered at me closely. "Be you slave or hostage, Irish?"

"Slave, I believe." I told him about the brief bargaining on the beach.

The old man nodded and placed a sooty finger on my leather collar. "Slave you are, indeed. But that is for the best. Slaves are often treated better than hostages. You might have done worse, Irish—might have done worse. There are places where the shaven men still bring a fair price."

Just then Rägnar saw the old man and called for him. Scop shambled away, laughing and smirking as he went. I stared after him, wondering what manner of man it was that I had just met. I had little time to think about this, however, for Gunnar summoned me.

"Aeddan!" he shouted, craning his neck.

I stepped nearer and he thrust his empty cup into my hands. "Öl!" he ordered, pointing at the vat.

Taking the cup, I made my way to the vat where the boys were busily filling the drinking vessels. I watched how they plunged the bowls and jars into the vat and did likewise. I returned to my place and delivered the jar into my master's hands. He nodded with a self-satisfied smile, well pleased to have his bargain producing such good return so quickly.

I took my place behind him once more to observe the revelry. The sight of so much food and drink, devoured with such vigour, made me weak with hunger. I gawked at the baskets of mounded bread, and the glistening meat slowly turning on the hearth; I gazed wistfully at the foam-rimmed cups and bowls continually raised and lowered the length of the board; I heard the rising cacophony of shouts and coarse laughter and hands slapped upon the board. The roister swirled throughout the hall and I stood forlorn, and contemplated a long dry day and hungry night stretching out before me.

When the meat was roasted, the carcasses were divided and the joints carried to the board where the barbarians fell upon them like the wolves they were. I watched them warm to their feast—hunch-shouldered at their meal, hands grasping, fingers tearing, heads down, teeth sunk in succulent flesh, rich hot juices running from hands and flowing down chins—eating and eating, stuffing themselves to repletion and beyond until, sated, they flopped forward onto the board to sleep. Sure, no wolf pack ever snored more loudly or slept more soundly.

And when they woke, they fell to eating and drinking again. Their first hunger appeased, they settled into a less frantic consumption. Now they desired amusement to heighten their pleasure, and they began calling upon their skald to provide them songs.

Up rose Rägnar Yellow Hair from his throne and cried aloud, "Scop! *Siung* Scop!"

At this the revellers began pounding the board with hands, cups, and jars. "Scop! Scop!" they called. "*Siung! Siung!*"

Out from his noisome corner the Truth Singer shuffled, head wagging slowly side to side as he limped towards the throne, where he stooped to embrace his lord's legs. Rägnar cuffed him and pushed him away, but there was no violence in the blow. Drawing himself upright, old Scop straightened, shaking back his rags—a dirty bird preparing to take flight.

The hall fell silent, anticipation grew keen; the revellers licked greasy fingers and leaned from their benches expectantly as the ragged man, his throat quivering with the effort, opened his mouth and began to sing.

# 15

I t is ever the Lord's good pleasure to hide his more precious gifts in the most unlikely places—earthen vessels hold the rarest treasure after all. Though I have enjoyed many and many a song raised by some of the best voices in the world, I never heard anything to match the sound that issued from old Scop's throat. It was not beautiful, never that; but it was true. And in its truth was a beauty surpassing that of all the golden ornaments Lord Yellow Hair had bestowed.

It is said that time vanishes in the song of one blessed of the Word Giver—so the ancient Celts believed. Well, I believe it now, too. For so long as Scop sang, holding each within the hall in thrall to him, binding them like slaves with his subtle, artful chain, time itself stood bound, its relentless flight arrested, unable to move.

I could not understand the words, which were sung in the thick unlovely speech of the Danefolk; but the broad sense of his utterance I perceived as well as my own mind, for the expressions of both his voice and countenance were miracles of transformation. He sang deeds of valour, and the very blood stirred within me and I yearned to feel strong steel against my hip and thigh. When the song became joyful, he beamed forth with a radiance unknown to any save those who behold Sweet Jesu himself in beatific visions. When the song grew plaintive, sorrow crushed him down with such a weight I feared he would perish; tears streamed freely down the upturned faces of his listeners, and, may Christ have mercy, I wept, too.

The song finished, and when I dried my eyes Scop had disappeared. I came to myself, blinking, staring around as one roused from a waking sleep. The hall slowly resumed its raucous life; the feasters returned to their gluttony, shaking themselves free of their bard's enchanted coils.

Ale and meat and bread were brought and placed before the revellers in perpetual supply. Now other dishes and delicacies began appearing also: apples baked in honey, stewed fish with onions, fat boiled sausages, pork with lentils, dried plums swimming in ale. Now and then someone would rise from the table and totter to one of the sleeping nooks, or stagger from the board to vomit or relieve themselves, and another would take the empty place.

Every so often, the merrymaking was leavened with a quarrel as men's tempers, whetted and abetted by drink, overtook them. All of these fights came to blows, and two ended with both combatants prone and unconscious— much to the demented delight of the onlookers, who cheered lustily whenever anyone drew blood.

Thus the feast trundled noisily on: a drunken brawl in a muggy hall reeking of smoke, blood, piss and vomit. Whether night or day, I could not tell: tired, hungry, thirsty, it was all the same to me. I longed to crawl into one of the many sleeping nooks along the walls, but each time I made to slip away, Gunnar would rouse himself and order me to fetch him more ale.

Treading my way to the vat, stepping carefully among the bones and shards of broken vessels that now lay strewn over the floor, I noticed that the serving boys often snatched a furtive drink from the vessel they were filling before returning it to the board. This, it seemed, was how they obtained their food and drink: pilfering it while no one was looking.

Provoked by this thought, I stepped to the vat, leaned over and plunged the cup into the cool brown liquid. I smelled the heady sweetness of the ale and my thirst overcame me. Before I could think to stop myself, the cup was at my lips and the ale sliding down my throat. Ah, bliss! I had only tasted such fine beer once or twice in my life, and drank this down greedily.

Lord help me, for I could not help myself, I drained the whole cup down, then hastily refilled it, whereupon I turned and stepped quickly away—only to find my way blocked by a hulking Dane.

He glared at me and said something, which I could not understand. I bowed my head and made to step around him, but he caught my arm and twisted it, shouting his demand the louder. I could not make out what he wanted, but he eyed the cup in my hand, so I offered it to him.

"Nay!" he thundered, and with a violent swipe of his arm sent the jar flying from my hands. The metal cup sailed through the air, spewing ale in a shower all around and striking the board a few paces away. Those nearby stopped and stared.

The angry barbarian shouted something at me again and, when I made no answer, seized me in his arms and lifted me off my feet. He crossed to the vat with a single swift step and shoved me hard against the oaken tub—forcing my head down towards the frothy liquid.

Fortunately, the vat was no longer full. The top of my head touched the foam, but I was able to keep my face out of the drink. All those looking on laughed to see this odd contest.

The Sea Wolf roared with anger and, seizing my legs, lifted me, intent on thrusting me bodily into the vat. I grabbed the iron rim and held on with all my might. The wood and metal was sticky slick, however, and I could not maintain my grip. Lower and lower I slipped while all those looking on laughed all the harder at my predicament.

Unable to hold on any longer, I took a deep breath as my head plunged beneath the frothy liquid. Bubbles prickled my nostrils and ears; I shook my head furiously, and managed to catch another breath before my head was forced under again—further this time, and though I thrashed around, flailing my arms and kicking my legs, I could not get free. I stopped struggling to save what little air I had left in my lungs, and prayed for deliverance.

*Father God, defend me,* I thought. *It would be a sorry shame to let your servant drown in beer!*

Even as I loosed this prayer, I was yanked backwards, overturning the tub and spilling all the ale. I rolled onto my back, gasping for breath, squirming on the ground and shielding my head with my hands and arms against the heavy blows falling on me.

I glimpsed a red face swaying over me and heard an outraged cry. The Sea Wolf seemed to grow another head, for another face appeared on his shoulder, and it was Gunnar's. All at once the teetering barbarian toppled, sprawling over me with my master on his back.

The two rolled like snakes entwined, thrashing and sliding in the beer. I squirmed free of the fight and drew myself up a little apart. The hall's inhabitants, roused from their various stupors, quickly formed a ring around the combatants and goaded them on with taunts and cheers.

"Hrothgar!" shouted some. "Gunnar!" cried others.

Rägnar leaped up on the seat of his throne, clattering a spear against a shield, drawing the crowd's notice long enough to make himself heard. He shouted a command and the rabble surged forward, gathering up the fighting men and sweeping them out of the hall and into the yard where, cheering and shouting, they quickly reformed the ring.

Though the Dane called Hrothgar was larger, Gunnar was quicker and fearless: he stood head-to-head against the big barbarian taking each terrible blow and giving the same—again, again, again, the fists struck, face and neck and shoulder and stomach. Blood flowed from noses and mouths, and still they traded blows, any one of which would have stunned a horse.

Hrothgar, unable to find any advantage over his opponent, broke off abruptly. He stepped back, lowered his head and charged like a bull, bellowing as he came. Gunnar remained motionless, his feet firmly planted. Hrothgar closed on him and appeared to whelm him over, but the barbarian's arms closed on empty air. For, quick as a flick, Gunnar dropped to his knees, seizing Hrothgar around the neck in the same swift motion. The startled barbarian gave out a strangled cry and followed his head to the ground.

Hrothgar made to rise, but my master was on his back. Gunnar joined both hands together, raised them over his head and brought them sharply down on the back of his adversary's neck between the shoulderblades. Hrothgar gave out a grunt like that of a killed ox, and put his face to the ground; he tried once to rise, but his legs collapsed and he hugged the earth in a wide embrace.

Gunnar stood, wiping blood from his eyes and mouth, while the crowd clamoured out his name. He cast his gaze around the ring and raised his arm in triumph. All at once the throng rushed forward, seized Gunnar, raised him up, and carried him into the hall to celebrate his victory.

I watched them go, but made no move to follow. For

the sun was shining on a fine bright day and I had no wish
to return to that dark, stinking hall.

"They were fighting about you, Irish."

I turned. "Scop!" The sight of him surprised and
alarmed me. He stood red-eyed and haggard; sweat ran
from him in rivulets down his neck. "Why would they
fight about me?" I asked. "What did I do?"

"You drank from *Jarl* Rägnar's ale vat, and then offered
the cup to Hrothgar." He shook his head in mock disapproval. "Most impolite that was."

He turned and began shuffling away. I called him
back. "Stay. Please, Scop. I have been looking for you. I
thought you would sing again."

The shabby skald slowly turned his head and gave me
a sly wink and smile. "I throw my pearls to these swine
only with greatest reluctance," he replied. "I sing when it
suits me."

"Does this not displease Rägnar, your lord and master?"

Scop frowned and thrust out his chin. "*Jarl* Rägnar is
my lord, but he is no master to me. I sing when I choose."

"But are you not a slave?"

"I was once. No longer. It took twenty years, but I am
a free man now."

"Forgive me, brother, but if you are free, why do you
stay? Why not go back to your people?"

The ignoble bard shrugged and shook back his rags.
"This is my home. These are my people."

"That I can scarce believe," I told him.

"Believe it, boy; it is the truth," he spat, flaring suddenly. "God abandoned me here and left me to die. But I
did not die. I lived, and while I live, I am my own man and
I serve no one but myself alone."

"Then tell me, if nothing prevents you, how do you
know Latin?"

Scop turned and began hobbling away. I fell into step a pace behind him. "Please," I insisted, "I would know how it is that you speak the cleric's tongue."

I thought he would not answer, for he limped on without heed. But after a dozen or so paces, he stopped abruptly and turned. "How think you I came by it?" he demanded. "Think you I found it at the bottom of my mead bowl? Or perhaps you imagined I went a-viking with the Sea Wolves and plundered it from some poor defenceless priest?"

"I thought no ill, brother," I soothed. "But it seems a very mystery to me, that is all."

"A mystery?" he wondered, rubbing his blackened neck with a dirty hand. "Dost speak to me of mysteries, Irish?" He glared at me. "Ah, mayhap you think your own speech mysterious."

"Nothing could be less so," I answered. "I am a priest. I was taught in the abbey."

"Well, I likewise learned my tongue that way."

"Indeed?" I could not keep the surprise out of my voice.

"Why amazed?" he countered defiantly. "Is that so unchancy? Do you find it beyond your narrow ability to believe?"

"I find it," I confessed, "most unlikely."

"Then tell me," he challenged, "which is the more unlikely: that you should find yourself a slave of the Danes, or that I should be sent out a priest among them?"

So saying, he gathered himself in his rags and stumped off, tatters flapping like the bedraggled feathers of a great, ungainly bird.

I did not see him again for, after more eating and drinking, and sport—the throwing of hammers and axes and, heaven forbid it! even pigs, which they caught and hefted into the air to the loud acclamation of their fellows—

Gunnar took his leave of his lord, bade farewell to all his kinsmen, gathered his weapons and plunder in a leather bag, and departed the settlement, taking me with him—tied to him by a long rope around my waist.

We walked through close-grown forest all the day, moving exceedingly slow, for Gunnar's head hurt him and he stopped often to lie down. During one such rest, I made a meal from the fragments of bread and meat he had in his bag. My master could stomach no food, but raised no objection when I ate. Thus, I broke my long fast on hard bread and rancid meat—poor fare, but welcome nonetheless. After my meal, I untied myself and searched among the forest plants and found some *ffa'r gos*, which I crushed and mixed with clear-running water from a nearby stream. Upon straining out the pulp I gave it to Gunnar to drink— which he did, but not before I drank some first. He slept again and upon waking seemed in much better spirit.

At night we camped on the trail; Gunnar made a fire and we slept on either side of it, moving on again when the birds woke us at dawn. Once the bread and meat were gone, we had nothing to eat; still, we stopped often to drink from the sweet streams that abounded in that land. I looked for berries, and found some, but they were unripe.

We walked by day, Gunnar striding ahead, the bag on his shoulder, and myself trailing after. Though the bag was weighty, Gunnar would not allow me to touch it, preferring to tote it himself. We must have made an unusual sight, I reflected: master labouring under his load while the slave sauntered along empty-handed behind. But he would have it no other way.

As my master did not deign to speak to me—not that I would have understood him if he had—I had ample time to think. Mostly, I thought about my brother monks, and wondered if any had survived, and if so, what had become of them. Would they return to the abbey? Would they continue on to Constantinople? Since the blessed book had not turned up with the plunder, I reckoned some of the brothers may have escaped, and that our treasure had not been discovered.

I felt secure in this belief, reasoning that if the book had been found, it would certainly have been taken; and if it had been taken, I would have seen it shared out among the barbarians as payment for their hateful deeds. I had not seen it, so I considered it had not been stolen. This gave me hope that perhaps the pilgrimage would proceed—without me, it is true, but it would continue.

I made this my prayer, as I walked along, that however many of our company yet survived, be they many or few, would yet journey on and reach Byzantium with the emperor's gift. This produced in me a peculiar feeling: a curious mingling of remorse and relief: remorse for the lives so suddenly required in the Red Martyrdom of this pilgrimage, and relief that I would not now have to join them.

For, despite my current enslavement—which would seem to thwart the fulfillment of my dream—I still did not doubt that I would die in Byzantium. Even so, I will not tempt heaven by denying that relief may have outweighed remorse in my heart. I was ever a contrary creature, I do freely confess it.

As dusk fell on the fourth day, I noticed that the forest thinned somewhat and, as the first stars began glowing in the sky, we stepped out from the wood and into a wide meadow clearing. In the centre of the clearing stood a huge timber house with a barn and cattle enclosure hard by. Two neatly-ploughed fields lay west and south of the house, green shoots showing golden in the lowering light.

Gunnar took one look at the house and loosed a wild whoop that resounded across the meadow. Dogs began barking, and within the space of three heartbeats I could see two black canine shapes racing towards us; a moment later, these were joined by three human figures—two of which were women, judging by their dress.

The dogs reached us first and Gunnar greeted them as happily as if they had been children long lost to him and given up for dead. He hugged them to him and kissed their muzzles time and again, calling their names and stroking their glossy coats. They were big dogs, with large heads and powerful jaws. I was heartily glad that I was with Gunnar just then, for I did not doubt these same creatures would joyfully rip the throat from any intruder.

My master met his kinfolk with as much zeal as he had shown in greeting the dogs. The women—though one, I now saw was little more than a girl—were clearly glad to see him, embracing him many times, pressing kisses on his face and neck, clutching at his hands and arms. The elder of the two, I soon learned, was Karin, his wife; the younger was called Ylva, and was a kinswoman of his wife, and helped them as a serving maid.

The third figure was a lad, tall and slender, and younger than he first appeared. At the boy's approach, Gunnar left off kissing his wife and gathered the youngster into a fierce embrace. I feared the boy would be crushed, but he survived, laughing and hugging his father. After another round of kissing and embracing, the boy turned to gawk at me.

His father saw his wide-eyed stare and, clapping a heavy hand to my shoulder, said, "Aeddan."

The boy dutifully repeated the name, whereupon his father placed his hand on the boy and said, "Ulf."

He presented the women next, calling each by name, which I repeated until he was satisfied that I could utter them properly. Karin, his wife, was a sturdy woman with a broad, kindly face; her hair was light brown and her eyes green as the sea. Her movements were deft and, I quickly learned, perfectly matched to her purposeful manner. She was a most practical woman, accomplished in all the craft of her kind. And sure, no tyrant ever ruled with more aplomb; her authority in her house was absolute.

Ylva, her young kinswoman, was a sylph of a girl, bright as sunbeams, slender and fair as a woodland flower. Her hair was pale yellow and her brow was straight; her arms and breasts were shapely, her hands long-fingered. She was as much a joy to the eye as to the mind, for as I came to know her better, I found her quiet, thoughtful, and easy in her manner.

Ulf was a boy through and through, a happy lad, fond of fishing and hunting and berry picking, and full of youthful high spirits. He adored his father, and if not for the fishpond would rarely have left Gunnar's side.

These, then, were presented to me one by one, and all welcomed me, not as a conquered enemy, but as a guest or kinsman. I felt, in spite of the harsh treatment I had received on the journey, that having now arrived at Gunnar's holding, I had been admitted into the warm embrace of this family. Perhaps life in the cold northern forests is harsh enough as it is without adding to its bitterness unnecessarily.

With a clap of his hands and a shout, Gunnar sent the hounds racing back across the meadow to the house. He laughed to see how they ran to his command. Ulf, unable to contain himself any longer, gave a whoop and dashed after the dogs, as Gunnar, throwing his arm around Karin's shoulders, gathered his wife to him and proceeded to the house, his stride long and swift. He threw back his head and began singing loudly, to the amusement of the ladies, who laughed and joined him in song.

Gunnar's leather bag, forgotten for the moment, lay on the ground at my feet. Like a good slave, I slung it onto my back and followed my master home.

# 16

I stayed that night in the barn with Gunnar's ox and cows. He did not bother to chain or restrain me in any way, and I soon learned why. As the moon rose in the tall pines, the wolves began to howl. Sure, I had heard wolves before, but never so many or so close. From the sound of their mournful wailing, I reckoned they must be swarming on the very edges of the forest. The barn was secure enough—a very fortress, for Gunnar had no wish to lose his valuable animals; but the howling kept me awake long into the night, and I fell asleep with the sound in my ears.

In the morning, the maid Ylva came to rouse me and bring me to the kitchen. The Danefolk build their dwellings in such a way as to make the kitchen part of the house itself, and no small part, either. Indeed, Gunnar's house was a fair likeness of Rägnar's hall, save that he had made a sleeping loft among the rooftrees above the table. This loft was reached by a ladder and overlooked the hearth below. Adjacent to the hearth was a nook where the ale and water tubs were kept, and a low door leading to a small storeroom. At the end of the hall, there was a place where animals could be kept in bad weather; this was strewn with straw and had a manger for feeding them.

I broke fast with the family, and began what was to become our custom: Gunnar and his son sitting on the bench at the hearth-end of the board, and myself at the stable-end perched on a three-legged stool with a wooden bowl balanced on my knee, while Karin and Ylva fluttered from hearth to board, cooing over the preparations. The Danefolk, I learned, liked their meals unbearably hot, and began almost every meal with a thick barley gruel which they slurped down from big wooden bowls, sometimes with wooden spoons, but most often without.

When the gruel had been eaten and the bowls collected, then bread, meat, and pale white cheese was served. If fruit was in season, that was offered, too; Gunnar especially loved the bitter blue currants, and a puckery little red berry they called *lingön*, which Karin prepared in a boiled compote Gunnar poured on his bread. This sauce was so tart I could never get it down without honey.

There was sometimes fish—fresh when they could get it, though usually salted or preserved in a solution of brine and vinegar, or lye. The lyefish, or *lütfisk*, stank to heaven with a stench to bring tears to the eye. They ate this abomination boiled in milk, and professed to like it; but the stink alone made the gorge rise in my throat and I could in no way abide it.

If there was no fish, then sausages were served— boiled or roasted, it made no difference. Occasionally, there was a kind of meat which was prepared by soaking whole pork haunches in brine for several months and then hanging them in the rooftrees over the hearth so that the smoke would preserve them. This treatment made the meat turn bright red, like raw beef, but the taste was magnificent—sweet and succulent and salty all at once. I always enjoyed the *rökt skinka*, and ate as much of it as often as I could.

The Danefolk liked their meat; they liked their bread, too—heavy and dark, served warm from hearth or oven. I soon grew to enjoy this strange custom. Karin's ale was the same as her bread: dark, rich, and filling, and with a sweet taste that reminded me of nuts. Once Karin put spruce berries in the brew, to produce a most unusual beer. I could not drink it, but Gunnar thought it a wonderful diversion from his normal drink. Sadly, they disdained wine—which, after all, was difficult for them to procure—but I made up for that lack by acquiring a taste for Karin's dark brown ale.

I ate, as I say, with the family. To his honour, Gunnar never stinted in his care of me where food was concerned, nor was I given inferior fare: I ate the same food as my master, and in similar portions. And it shames me even now to say that I indulged myself sinfully, utterly without regard to the Rule of Moderation. How often I asked for more!

I still see Karin's broad, kindly face glowing with pleasure—and the heat of the hearth—as she laid the food on the board, her hands red from work, but her braids neat and her clothing spotless as her kitchen. She was a meticulous, hard-working woman, and enjoyed nothing more than to have the fruit of her labour admired and made much over. Sure, this was no hardship at all for any fortunate enough to find a seat at her table; her offerings, while simple, were never less than superb.

There were two, however, not so fortunate in this respect—though in others perhaps they were far more so than I. These were Odd, the labourer, and Helmuth, the swineherd. Both were Saex-men, and both slaves. Odd was a large fellow, patient, tireless, and very nearly mute. Helmuth, a man of mature years, was a well-mannered and even-tempered soul, who, despite all appearances, happily possessed a smattering of learning, as I soon discovered.

Owing to the pig stink that permeated his clothing
and person, poor Helmuth was never allowed inside the
house. When it rained or snowed he slept in the barn, but
when the days were fine and warm, Helmuth slept outside
with heaven's vast starfields his only roof. Even had he not
preferred it, he would have done so anyway to guard his
precious swine from the wolves. Odd, when he was not
working, stayed always with Helmuth.

That I should take meals with the family while my
brother slaves ate alone outside or together in the barn,
caused me some little anguish on their account. But as no
one else seemed to think it any hardship, and Odd and
Helmuth were apparently content, I very soon came to
accept the arrangement.

After breaking fast that first day Gunnar, accompanied
by young Ulf and the two hounds, went out to examine the
state of his domain. In all it was a handsome holding,
everything well made and neatly ordered; he was justly
proud of what he had accomplished in the harsh north-
land. For his part, little Ulf was proud of his father; I
observed that he never left his father's side the whole day
long.

We walked the fields together, Gunnar and Ulf chattering away, myself lagging behind as, now and again, my
master stopped to inspect some part or portion of his holding: a ploughed field, a new calf, an iron binding for a
door, the level of grain in the granary, the fishpond, a
length of newly-woven hurdle fencing—anything that
came to hand. A blind man could have perceived how
much this rough brawny Dane loved his land, concerning
himself with every detail of its husbandry.

All that first day we traversed the boundaries of
Gunnar's realm—a lonely island fortress, as it seemed to
me, set in an evergreen sea, cut off from the wider world.
As the days passed, I felt more and more distant to the

world I had known. Our little abbey, by contrast, was a busy port on a well-travelled route where trade was conducted not in silver, but in words.

Gunnar had saved me from certain death, that I will not deny. But the cost of my salvation was high indeed. I felt lost and very, very alone. Accordingly, I began to pray the daily round, and to say psalms when I had the chance. One night, at table, I prayed aloud over the meal while my master and his family looked on in amazement. So taken aback were they by this peculiar behaviour, it did not occur to them to prevent me. In time, they came to expect it and waited for me to say the prayer before eating. The ritual, I suppose, appealed to them. I have no idea what they made of it.

That first evening, however, when I raised my head from the prayer, I found Gunnar staring at me. Karin stood at his shoulder, also gazing at me, and prodding her husband insistently. He spoke a few words to her and she desisted.

The next morning, my master took me to Helmuth and, using a complicated series of gestures, indicated that I should pray again as I had the night before.

This I did.

The effect this produced upon the swineherd was extraordinary. He threw down his stick, sank to his knees and cried out, clasping his hands, his lips quivering in thanksgiving as huge wet tears filled his eyes and rolled down his cheeks. Then up he leaped, clutching me by the arms and crying, "Alleluia! Alleluia!"

Gunnar watched this with a bemused expression on his face. Helmuth subsided after a moment, and fell to murmuring to himself. Gunnar spoke a few words to him, whereupon the swineherd seized his master's hand, kissed it, and blubbered enthusiastically. The baffled Dane nodded curtly to his slave, then turned on his heel and left us there together with the pigs.

"Master Gunnar says I am to be . . ." Helmuth paused, searching his dusty memory for the proper word. "Heya! I am to be pupil—nay, not pupil . . . *scólere*, nay . . . teacher! Alleluia!" He beamed ecstatically, and I had the uncomfortable feeling that I was seeing zealous Brother Diarmot in another guise.

"I am to be the teacher of you," Helmuth continued. "You are to be pupil to me." He studied me for my reaction.

"Forgive me, friend, I mean no offence," I replied, "but how is it that every skald and swineherd knows and speaks good Latin?" I then went on to tell him about Scop.

"Scop!" he cried. "Scop it was who taught me. An excellent man, Scop. I was sent to him as a boy to sit at his feet and learn the *mirabili mundi*! I was one of his best pupils!"

"He was still a priest then."

"Priest he was, yes," Helmuth confirmed, "and his name was Ceawlin, a most holy and righteous man—a Saecsen, like me. He taught me the love of Jesu and the veneration of the saints, and much else. I thought to be a priest myself," he halted, shaking his head sadly, "but that was not to be." He looked at me. "Though it is long since I have heard the Mass, I still believe. And I often speak to the All Father—I ask him to send me someone to talk to. He has sent you, I think."

We talked as best we could: despite what I had said, Helmuth's Latin was not good, and it was polluted with many strange words in several languages. Even so, in the days to follow, we began to understand one another better and I pieced together the story of how he came to serve Gunnar. With many hesitations and much misunderstanding on both sides, Helmuth eventually explained about the war that left old Åke the Reticent and his bellicose son, Svein, dead, and Rapp the Hammerer on the throne. "Rapp was no believer in anything save the war hammer in his hand," Helmuth observed bitterly. "Rapp made slaves of all the undead. No, ah—he made slaves of those who yet lived—"

"The survivors."

"Heya, the *survivors*! Some he sold; some he kept. He reckoned Saecsens useful, so he kept Ceawlin and me; he thought we might make good hostages if the Saecsenfolk attacked him. We served in his hall until he died."

"What happened then?"

"He had twice boychilds—"

"Two sons. He had two sons."

"Heya. Thorkel, the elder, and Rägnar, the younger. After Rapp died—choking on a marrow bone in his drinking hall—Thorkel took the throne. He was not a bad jarl, but he was no Christian man, either."

"What happened to him?"

"He went a-viking," Helmuth said wistfully, "and never returned. They waited two years and then made Rägnar *kung*."

"King?"

"Heya. Yellow Hair has been kung ever since." The swineherd shrugged. "The people like him because he is more generous than his father and brother ever were. Whatever he has, he gives away with all regret—no regret, I mean."

"Including his slaves."

Helmuth sighed. "Including his slaves, heya. He gave me to Gunnar's father, Grönig, who made me his swineherd—though I can read *and* write, mind—and here I have been ever since. I make no complaint; I am well treated."

"Have you never tried to escape?"

Helmuth spread his hands and opened his eyes wide. "Where would I go? There are wolves in the forest, and wild men everywhere else." He smiled a little ruefully. "My place is here; I have my pigs to look after." He looked around, counted them quickly to assure himself that all were still in sight.

"What of Odd?" I asked.

"Gunnar bought him to work the farm," Helmuth said, and explained how a blow on the head when he was captured had deprived Odd of all but the simplest speech. "Slow-witted he may be, but Odd is a hard worker, and very strong." He paused, then said, "I would know, Aeddan—"

"Aidan," I corrected.

"I would know how is it that you come to be here. Has Gunnar won you, or did he buy you in Jutland at the slave market?"

"He captured me," I answered, and told him about the night raid on the village—careful to omit any mention of the pilgrimage or the treasure. "Then, when we reached the settlement, he gave Yellow Hair three gold pieces for me."

"Gunnar is a good master, heya," Helmuth told me. "He seldom beats me, even when he is drunk. And Karin is a woman worthy of praise in any tongue; she is master of the kitchen, and all that passes beneath her—" he hesitated, "eyesight?"

"Gaze," I suggested gently. "All that passes beneath her gaze."

"Heya. They are good people," he said, adding thoughtfully, "Gunnar says that he shall carve out both our tongues if I do not teach you to speak like a Dane before the next full moon."

With such an attractive incentive before us, we began my formal instruction that very morning. Helmuth, faltering and tongue-tied, grew more certain as more memories of his childhood occupation under Ceawlin's tutelage came back to him. After a shaky beginning, we soon worked out a system of learning whereby I would point to a thing saying the Latin word—thereby helping Helmuth recall his learning—to which he would reply with the appropriate word in the northern speech. I would then repeat this word aloud many times to impress it on my memory.

After many days of such discipline, I obtained a rough sense of the tongue—if sense it was—and could name a good many of the common things around me. Helmuth gradually introduced words that implied an action: to chop, to dig, to plant, to make a fire, and so on. I found in him a willing teacher and easy companion, good-natured, patient, eager to help. What is more, I no longer thought he smelled of pig dung.

Odd, finished with his day's work, would sit and gaze at us in bewildered amazement. What he thought about it, I never knew, for in all the time I knew him, I only ever heard him grunt.

During these days, Gunnar made few demands on me. I chopped wood for the woodstore, fed the chickens, carried water from the well, helped Odd feed the cows and mend the hurdles when the cattle kicked them down; I helped Helmuth with the pigs, removed ash from the hearthplaces, changed the straw in the barn, spread manure on the fields, dug stumps; I helped Ylva pluck geese and pull weeds . . . In short, I performed whatever tasks needed doing, but my toil was no more arduous or burdensome than any I had known at the abbey. Indeed, my master often preferred the more demanding tasks for Odd and himself. And in any event, no one worked harder than Karin. Thus, I formed the conclusion that Gunnar had no real need of another slave. Whatever reasons he had for buying me from Rägnar, labour was not one of them.

I continued to take my meals in the house, and began to feel as much a part of the family as Ylva or Ulf. Sure, I was treated no worse than either of them. And when I learned to put word to word, forming crude, and often amusing, sentences, my master praised me highly and professed satisfaction with my progress—so much so that the day of testing came soon after my first halting conversation with him.

Hoping to put my mind at ease, I determined to ask what happened the night of the raid. "Do you know what became of my brothers?" I asked, fumbling over the words.

"It was very dark that night," Gunnar observed mildly.

"Were they killed?"

"Maybe," he allowed, "some men were killed. I do not know how many." He then explained that, owing to the confusion which ensued upon the sudden arrival of the lord and his men, he could not be sure of anything. "The jarl appeared and we ran away, taking only what we could carry. We left much treasure," he concluded sadly. "But I do not know about your friends."

The next morning Gunnar roused me in the barn and told me that he and Helmuth were taking some of the pigs to Skansun. "There is a market," he told me. "It is one day's walk. We will stay the night and return home. Do you understand?"

"Heya," I replied. "Am I to go with you?" I asked, hoping for a chance to see something of the wider world once more.

"Nay." He shook his head solemnly. "You are to stay with Karin and Ylva. Ulf will go with me, and Helmuth, too. Odd will remain with you. Heya?"

"I understand."

"Garm I will take with us; Surt I leave here to guard the cattle."

A short while later, we were standing in the yard bidding the travellers farewell. Gunnar spoke a word to his wife, charging her, I think, with the care of the farm, then called the black hound, Garm, to him and strode from the yard without looking back. Ulf fell into step behind him, and Helmuth, with the pigs, met them at the end of the yard. We watched them out of sight, and then turned to our chores.

The day was good and bright, the air warm and full of insects, for summer was speeding on. Odd and I spent the morning working in the turnip field and, after a midday meal, Ylva and I filled a small cauldron with the previous day's milk which had been left to stand, built a small fire in the yard, and began making cheese. Once the milk was gently simmering, we left the tending of the pot to Karin, and I returned to the field.

The first intimation I had that the situation was other than I believed it to be was when, at sunset, I happened to look up from weeding the turnips to see both Gunnar and Ulf striding across the meadow with Helmuth and his pigs straggling along some distance behind. Thinking something terrible must have befallen them, I dropped the hoe and ran to meet them.

"What has happened?" I gasped, breathless from my run. "Is something wrong?"

"Nothing is wrong," Gunnar replied with a slow, sly smile. "I have returned."

"But—" I waved a hand towards Helmuth, "what about the market . . . the pigs? Did you change your head—ah, mind?"

"I did not go to the market," my master informed me. Ulf laughed aloud, as if they had perpetrated a handsome jest.

I glanced from one to the other of them. "I do not understand."

"It was the watching-trial," Gunnar explained simply. "It was in my mind to see what you would do when I was not here to guard you."

"You watched me?"

"I watched you."

"You watched to see if I would run away, yes?"

"Yes, and—"

"You did not trust me." The realization that I had been tested—albeit in a gentle and good-natured way—made me feel stupid and disappointed. Of course, I reckoned, a master has every right to test the loyalty of his slaves. Still, I felt ill-used.

Gunnar regarded me with a deeply puzzled expression. "Do not take on so, Aeddan. You have done well," he said. "I am satisfied."

"But I was never out of your sight," I complained.

Gunnar took a deep breath and drew himself up. "I do not understand you," Gunnar said, shaking his head from side to side. "I," he thumped himself on the chest, "I am well pleased."

"I am not well pleased," I told him flatly. "*I* am angry."

"That is your concern," he replied. "For my part, I am pleased." His expression became haughty. "You think yourself a learned man, heya? Well, if you knew the proper way of things in Skania, you would be pleased too."

With that he strolled away, smug with contentment. Later, as I lay in my straw bed, I repented of my shameful behaviour. Sure, Gunnar was a good master; he fed me well, and since coming to the farm had not raised a hand against me. I had no just cause for my bitterness. I resolved to ask his forgiveness the next day. Alas, I never got the chance.

# 17

I heard a noise in the yard and awoke. It was dark yet, but the sun rose as I stepped from the barn. Gunnar was bidding farewell to Karin, who pressed small loaves of bread into little Ulf's hands. Helmuth was already on the trail, stick in hand, waiting with the pigs as they rooted for mushrooms in the undergrowth. Farewells made, Gunnar turned and called Garm, the larger of the two black hounds, to him, and strode from the yard, his son and dog hurrying after him.

"Where has Gunnar gone?" I asked, coming to stand beside Karin.

"Gunnar and Helmuth have gone to the market," she replied. "They would have done this yesterday if not for the watching-trial."

"I understand," I told her, feeling slightly cheated of the chance to make amends.

"Yes," she affirmed, nodding her head. "They will return tomorrow. You bring wood."

So, I began my chores, first bringing wood to the kitchen and then fetching water. Odd appeared with hoe in hand, and shuffled his way to the field, where I soon joined him. We worked together in amiable silence until

Karin called us to our first meal of the day. We sat in the yard in the warm sun with our wooden bowls full of steaming porridge which we ate with the aid of hard brown bread.

After breaking fast, Odd returned to the field, and I repaired the handle of his hoe, which had worn loose; I sharpened the blade and Karin's kitchen knife as well. Then I helped Ylva skin three hares she had caught in a snare during the night; we quartered the small carcasses and stretched the pelts on little frames to dry. Then I led the cows down to the pond for water, and spent the rest of the morning watching them.

After the midday meal, I returned to the field where I worked weeding the turnips until the sun began to sink behind the trees. Upon reaching the end of the last row, I straightened and looked back. Though I was a slave, I did my work with as much care as if I had been at the abbey. This I did to please Gunnar, and, more importantly, to please God. For Holy Scripture teaches that a slave is to serve his master well and in this way win him to the Heavenly Kingdom. This I set myself to do.

I was admiring my handiwork when Odd grunted at me from across the field. I turned and looked where he was pointing: two dark figures approached, moving boldly from the cover of the forest and towards the house.

Holding tight to the hoe, I ran to the house as fast as I could. "Karin! Karin!" I shouted. "Someone is coming! Hurry, Karin! Someone is coming!"

She heard me and came running from the house. "What is this great noise you are making?" she demanded, scanning me quickly from head to toe.

"Someone is coming," I repeated. "There!" I pointed behind me to the meadow. "Two men."

Karin squinted her eyes and looked towards the forest.

Her frown deepened. "I do not know them," she said, mostly to herself, and then loosed a stream of speech I could not understand. I looked at her and, having no words for this situation, shrugged.

Karin became urgent. "Ah!" she cried. "Ylva! The pond . . . fetch her. Hurry!" she said, already dashing for the house. "Bring Surt! Hurry!"

Across the yard and behind the barn, I ran, my feet pounding the bare earth path leading down to the fishpond in the little dell north of the house. It was not far, and I found young Ylva, her mantle raised to her hips, wading in the water. Her back was to me, and she turned as I came sliding down the muddy bank to the water.

"Aeddan, heya!" she called, cheerfully. "Come swimming."

The sight of her pale white thighs, so round and firm, so delicately tapered to her comely knees, brought me up short. For a moment I forgot why I had come there. I stared at her fair flesh, and fought to regain my tongue once more. "I—it is . . ." I forced myself to take my eyes from her legs. "Someone is coming. We must go. Hurry!"

I turned and started back up the slope. I reached the top and looked back; she still stood in the water and had made no move to follow. "Come, Ylva!" I shouted, glancing around the banks of the pond. "Surt!" I called. "Heya, Surt!"

Understanding me at last, the young woman splashed lightly from the water, lowering her mantle as she came. I had a last glimpse of those lovely legs as she climbed the bank. "Surt!" she called to the dog. "Heya, Surt! Here, Surt!"

There came a crash in the underbrush as the great black hound bounded onto the path behind us and stood looking expectantly, his mouth open, tongue lolling. Ylva ran to him and laid a slender hand on his chain collar. "Home, Surt!"

We three raced back to the house to find Karin, fists on hips, as the strangers entered the yard. Odd appeared around the corner of the house, hoe in hand. Surt took one look at the two men, gave a low, warning rumble deep in his throat, broke from Ylva's grasp and ran to Karin's side where he stood growling. I heard Karin say, "Who are you?"

They ignored her and came ahead a few more steps. Surt snarled, hackles raised like knives. "Stand you there," Karin called again, and added something that I did not catch.

The men stopped, and looked around the holding. One of them was fair, the other dark; both were bearded and both tall, well-muscled fighting men. The dark one had a long braid over his shoulder, and the fair one wore his hair close-cropped. They carried spears and had swords on their hips with long knives tucked into their sword-belts. Neither, I noticed, owned a cloak, but one had a leather tunic, and the other a sleeveless siarc. Their tall leather boots were well worn.

"Greetings, good woman," replied the fair-haired stranger at last, turning his eyes lazily toward us as he spoke. "It is a warm day, heya?"

"There is water in the well," Karin said. The chill in her voice more than matched the barbarian's cool arrogance.

The cold-eyed stranger's gaze flicked onto Ylva, and lingered there. "Where is your husband?" he demanded.

"My husband is about his business."

The men exchanged glances. "Where does your husband's business take him?" asked the dark man, speaking for the first time. His voice, unlike his appearance, was pleasant and inviting. "Far?"

"Not far," Karin said. "He is near."

The stranger said something which I did not understand.

He smiled reassuringly, taking a slow step closer as he spoke. Odd shifted uneasily, and Surt growled.

Karin's reply was short and defensive, as it seemed to me; I did not know what she said. I moved to stand beside Odd, wishing that Gunnar's watching-trial had been this day rather than yesterday. Karin spoke again—a challenge, I thought.

The fair man made his reply, and I heard the words: "King Harald Bull-Roar," and "a message," and "free men of Skania." Thus, it seemed to me communication of some importance, and I rued my scant knowledge of Danespeak, limited as it was to farm chores.

Karin asked them about this message, I think; her tone was sharply suspicious.

The dark stranger replied. "Gunnar's ears . . ." I heard him say, then: "We will speak to him now."

"We owe fealty to no lord but Rägnar Yellow Hair," Karin told them flatly.

"Rägnar Yellow Hair," sneered the fair barbarian, "owes fealty to Harald Bull-Roar."

"No doubt," continued his dark companion smoothly, "Yellow Hair himself would tell you the same if he were here. Unfortunately . . ." He spread his empty hand in a gesture of helplessness; I observed, however, that his right hand came to rest on the hilt of his sword.

"If you refuse to—" I did not know the words, "—Gunnar now," said the other, "it will go ill with you."

"My husband is not here now," Karin declared. "Tell me the message, or wait for his return."

The dark man seemed to consider this. His eyes turned once more to Ylva, standing silent beside me. "We will wait," he decided.

Karin nodded curtly, said something about the well and barn, then turned and walked stiff-backed to the house, summoning Ylva to her as she went. The king's men watched her go; though they said nothing, their silence fairly bristled. Nor did I like the way they looked at Ylva, for I saw menace in their long-lingering stares.

Odd and I returned to our chores. The cows were in the meadow and, with Surt's help, I made quick work of herding them to the cattle enclosure. I finished the milking and poured out a drink for the dog, then took the milk to the house.

I was just entering the yard when I heard voices; they seemed to be arguing. Quickening my pace, I rounded the corner of the house to see Ylva standing before the barn between the two barbarians. The fair-haired one had her by the arm, and she was trying to pull away from him, but he gripped her too tightly. The men were talking to each other, and to Ylva, in a joking way, all smiles and coaxing tones. Ylva, however, seemed to be pleading with them—to release her, I think—and her expression was one of fear.

I placed the milk jar by the door and entered the yard. "Ylva," I called, as if I had been looking for her. "Karin is waiting." I said this as I walked to where they stood. "Go to the house."

Ylva turned at her name, and implored me with her eyes. "I must go," she told the men.

"No," said the fair-haired stranger. "Stay and talk with us."

"Twenty silver pieces," said the dark man, ignoring me. "I will give twenty."

"Twenty!" mocked his companion. "That is more than you—"

I could not understand any of what he said next, but his friend replied, "You know nothing, Eanmund." To Ylva he said, "For a good wife, I will give twenty-five silver pieces. Are you a good wife?"

"Please," said Ylva, her voice a small frightened thing, "I must go." She said more, which I took to be pleading for release.

"Heya!" I called, stepping forward with much more boldness than I felt. Pointing at Ylva, I said, "She is wanted in the house."

The fair-haired man released Ylva, and turned on me. Placing both hands flat against my chest, he shoved me backward. "Get away, slave," he shouted.

Ylva, momentarily free, made to dash away. She had taken but three steps, however, when the dark man caught hold of her once more. He pulled her roughly towards the barn, talking to her in a rough manner. I struggled to my feet and was about to run for Karin, when I heard a strange, strangled cry.

I turned to see Odd, holding tight to his hoe, advancing with short, swift steps to where we stood. His face was flushed with rage. "No, Odd!" I shouted at him. "Stay back."

To the barbarians, I said, "Let her go. Please! Odd does not . . ." my poor language deserted me, "he does not think—" that was not the word I wanted. *Understand!* "Please, he does not understand."

"Odd!" shouted Ylva. "Stay back." She said more, but to no avail, for he came on, gripping his hoe like a weapon. He made his curious, mewing roar again, and I realized that he was trying to say her name.

Fearing the clash to come, I turned and raced to the house, calling for Karin. Whether she heard my call, or had been roused by the shouts in the yard, Karin appeared in the doorway just as I reached the house. "Hurry!" I said, pointing to the barn where the strangers, still holding tight to Ylva, were confronting Odd.

"Nay! Nay!" she cried, already running for the barn.

A thought sprang into my head: *Surt!*

I hastened to the cattle enclosure, calling the hound as I ran. Surt heard me and met me on the path. Laying hold to his collar, I said, "Follow, Surt!"

And then it was swiftly back to the yard to find Ylva and Karin shouting at Odd, who appeared to be hugging the fair-haired stranger, while the other king's man hammered on his back with the pommel of his sword. Closer, I saw Odd lift the man off his feet in a crushing embrace.

The fair one's eyes were squeezed shut against the pain as he kicked his legs to free himself. At last, his friend landed a blow at the base of Odd's neck. The big slave gave a grunt and dropped his catch. The fair man fell to the ground where he lay gasping, and Odd staggered backward and went down. The dark man stooped to his friend, and Karin took Ylva by the arm and pulled her away.

Surt, seeing his people mistreated, growled and surged forward. As the fight appeared to be over, I kept a tight grip on his collar; it was all I could do to hold him back. We had almost reached the place where Karin and Ylva were standing, when the fair-haired barbarian struggled to his feet. He stood, clutching his ribs, and cursing. Blood dripped from the corner of his mouth.

Then, snatching the sword from his companion's hand, he turned to Odd, who was sitting on the ground, holding his head and moaning. Without so much as a word, the fair man thrust the swordpoint into Odd's chest.

Poor Odd looked up in surprise. His hand grasped the naked swordblade and tried to pull it out. But the fair stranger forced the blade deeper, his face a leer of brutal glee.

Ylva screamed. Karin shouted and thrust the girl behind her.

I saw the wicked blade withdraw, red and streaming, and I saw the barbarian's arm rise to strike again. Odd fell back and tried to squirm away. Before I knew what I was doing, my fingers had loosed their grip on the dog's collar.

"Go, Surt!" I cried.

There came a sound like a rippling whir. The fair-haired man glanced up to see death hurtling towards him in the shape of a black hound. The dark man made a clumsy grab as the blurred shape flew past him.

The king's man turned, sword glinting in his upraised arm.

Surt, fangs bared, was still three paces away when he leapt. The weight of the hound upon his chest threw the stranger to the ground. A truncated scream echoed in the yard as the hound's jaws closed on the man's throat.

The dark man lunged forward, but Surt was already shaking the life from his fair-haired victim. Karin shouted for Surt to stop, but the beast had the taste of blood in his mouth and would not release his kill.

Snatching up the fallen sword, the dark man gave a quick chop at the base of the dog's head. The great hound collapsed and rolled to the side, fangs still sunk in his victim's wound.

The barbarian writhed on the ground, a peculiar gurgling sound coming from his torn throat. All at once, he gave a great spluttering cough, spewing blood in a crimson mist. His limbs snapped rigid. He arched his back off the ground and then subsided with a wheezing sigh as the air rushed from his lungs.

Karin and I ran to where Odd lay; he appeared serene and thoughtful as if contemplating the cloudless sky. But the eyes that gazed up were looking into another realm. Blood no longer flowed from his wounds, and breath no longer stirred his lungs.

Dull silence claimed the yard. My head throbbed with the sound of my own blood rushing in my ears. I turned from the vision of death to see Ylva, hands pressed to her mouth, trembling in every limb, sobbing. My first impulse was to rush to her and offer comfort. But I had no sooner turned and taken a single step towards her, when I was halted by a snarl of rage: "Slave!"

The dark stranger rose from where he knelt beside

the body of his friend. Sword in hand, he advanced slowly, spitting words which I could not understand. His meaning was clear enough, however; he meant to kill me. No doubt he would have slain me, too, and as easily as he had killed the hound, if not for Karin's swift intervention.

"Stop!" she shouted, putting out her hand to the stranger. "This is Gunnar Warhammer's land, and you have killed his slave and dog—" she said something else I did not catch, but she pointed to Ylva, and I guessed she meant that the threat to Ylva would be reported, along with the slaying of Odd and Surt.

Foaming with rage, the dark barbarian advanced. The blade in his hand rose to my throat. I saw the hatred in his eyes, but felt strangely calm, as if it all had happened a long time ago and to some other Aidan.

The swordpoint swung nearer.

The blow caught me on the side of the head—not the sword, but the fist gripping the handle. I fell at once, blinded by the pain, and lay waiting for the final stroke that would part soul from body. I was dimly aware of Ylva's wailing; she was shouting and crying for the bloodshed to stop.

I heard Karin shout again, and I looked up to see that she had seized the stranger's sword arm and held him from completing his thrust. "Enough!" she cried. "Would you kill *two* of Gunnar's slaves?"

The king's man hesitated; the swordpoint wavered as he weighed his choices. Karin, her brow dark and threatening, spoke a warning in a low voice, and the sword arm slowly relaxed. Glowering murderously, the king's man sheathed the blade and, with a dark-muttered oath, turned away. Head throbbing, I climbed to my feet and brushed myself off.

Karin stepped to Ylva and spoke sharply to her. The

young woman's wail subsided to a ragged whimper. "Come," said Karin, gathering Ylva under her arm. To the king's man and myself she said, "Bury them."

The two women walked slowly and with great dignity back to the house, leaving me and my enemy to deal with the corpses. Together we dragged the bodies down to the duck pond and, using Gunnar's wooden shovel and part of an iron ploughshare, dug two graves in the soft earth of the bank. As it happened, I did all the digging, for as soon as we reached the pond, the king's man sat down and would do no more, so I performed the task alone.

When I finished, the stranger stripped his friend's body of all valuables—including swordbelt, boots and jerkin. He then sat down again and watched as I rolled them into the graves. The dark man gave me to know in muttered threats and gestures that if he had his way, I would soon be joining them there.

I did not like to see Odd go to his rest without the least regard paid to his passing. True, he was no Christian man, but it seemed to me that he was still a child of the Eternal Father, and deserved to be treated as such. Indeed, if I had been a better monk, I might have told him about the Everliving Son, and he might have believed. So, I made a prayer for him. As I pushed the dirt over his body, I said these words:

"Great of Heaven, you pour your gifts upon all who walk your world below, pagan and Christian souls alike. Odd, here, was a slave, and worked hard for his master. He loved Ylva, I think, and died trying to protect her. Jesu said that there is no greater love than that shown by a man who lays down his life for a friend. Sure, I know Christians who would not do as much. Therefore, account this to Odd's credit, Lord. And if there is any room in your banquet hall for a man whose life was lived by such light as he had, then please let Odd join the heavenly feast—not for his sake, mind, but for the sake of your own dear Son. Amen, so be it."

The king's man glared at me as I prayed, and when I finished, he seized me by my slave collar and spat in my face, and then spat into the grave. Jerking hard on the collar then, he forced my to my knees, whereupon he kicked me in the stomach, once, and then again—releasing his hold on my collar with the second kick, so that I fell backwards into the grave and landed on top of poor Odd's corpse. The king's man then began throwing dirt over me, as if he would bury me alive.

In a little while he tired, however, and sat down again. I climbed warily from the grave, and continued with the burials, pausing to make a prayer for the stranger, too. "Lord God," I said, "I give you a man who lived by the sword. His deeds you know; his soul stands before you now. In judgement, Lord, remember mercy. Amen."

The dark man stared at me as if in amazement. I do not know what he found to astonish him so, but he did not spit at me this time. I finished pushing the dirt over the bodies and pressed the earth down, marking the graves with a round stone fetched from the pond. I also buried the dog in a shallow grave beside the two men, but said no prayer for the beast. When I finished, I looked around, but the king's man was gone. Nor did I see him when I went back to the house.

That night, I lay for a long time unable to sleep, a curious, unsettling feeling fluttering in my breast. It was not fear of the king's man, or worry that he would try to harm us in our sleep, no. It was the thought that I had caused the death of a fellow human being—pagan barbarian though he was. One moment he existed and now he did not, and I had brought this about.

Even so, I held no remorse for the deed. What I had done, I did to save Odd. Shameful to say, my only regret was that I had stayed my hand. My heart and mind, my whole being was consumed with the certainty that had I loosed Surt sooner, Odd would still be alive.

Sure, I knew I should feel deep grief and guilt for a sin of such iniquitous magnitude. Christ save me, I could not find it in me to repent. Thus, I lay on my bed of straw, trying to work up a sincere feeling of remorse for the hateful act. Oh, but defiance had me in its wicked grip; I knew beyond all doubt that had I to do it again, I would not hesitate. At last, abandoning sleep altogether, I made my way down to the fishpond where I stripped and stood to my waist in the water reciting the Psalms—the chastisement I had previously favoured.

Alas, the water was not cold enough to produce true penance. Rather, I found the cool, still water refreshing on my skin, and the deep stillness of the night a balm to my soul. In the end, I could but admit defeat; I hauled myself from the water and fell asleep on the bank as the pale slivered moon set in the trees.

# 18

Gunnar returned at dusk the next day. The king's man had waited through the long summer day, maintaining a sullen, brooding vigil in the woods. I saw him once or twice while I was fishing. Later, I was cleaning the fish when Gunnar called, announcing his arrival. The master of the holding came striding into the yard, singing out for his wife and cup. I rose from my work and went to meet him, my stomach churning with dreadful anticipation.

They were standing in the yard by the house. Little Ulf fidgeted under his mother's embrace; he had a new knife tucked into his belt. And Helmuth, I noticed, was wearing new leather boots, and carrying a bundle of cloth.

"Where is this stranger?" Gunnar demanded as I joined them. The happy greeting had faded into sour suspicion.

"I have not seen him since the killing," Karin said.

Gunnar, his face squeezing into a scowl, turned to me.

"He helped me to—ah," I tried to think of the word.

"Bury them." Karin completed the thought for me. "He helped Aeddan to bury the bodies."

"There were two of them?" growled Gunnar, his anger rising.

"Yes, two. One killed Odd, and then Surt killed him," I explained as best I could. "The other killed Surt."

"Surt killed one?

"Heya," I said.

"They said they are King Harald's men. They came for you, husband," Karin told him, and continued, but I lost the thread. ". . . they said only Gunnar must hear this message."

The two began speaking to one another so rapidly that I could not follow what they said, but I think they were discussing how the killings had taken place; I know Ylva's name came into it, and also my own, for Gunnar turned to me and demanded something which I did not understand. I shook my head helplessly.

Helmuth, standing near, said, "Gunnar wants to know if it is true that you loosed the dog."

To Helmuth I said, "Tell him that I only thought to protect Odd, but I did not act swiftly enough to prevent the attack."

My master said something else and placed his question again. Helmuth relayed his words to me. "He asks if you loosed the dog. Tell him the truth."

"Yes, I did that," I replied, and, Jesu forgive me, I confess I felt no guilt.

"Good," Gunnar said gruffly.

Just then Helmuth raised his pigstaff and pointed across the yard. "Master Gunnar," he said, "here he comes."

Gunnar took one look at the approaching stranger, and turned to Karin and Ylva. "Go into the house and stay there."

Karin took Ulf's hand in her own and pulled him away with her. As they disappeared into the house, Gunnar started forward to meet the stranger. "You two will come with me," he said, gesturing for Helmuth and me to follow.

"Is that the man?" Gunnar asked as I fell into step with him.

I nodded. "Yes."

When only a few dozen paces separated us, Gunnar halted and waited for the stranger to approach him. He looked little worse for his night in the woods, though none better either; his hands were dirty, and his eyes red from lack of sleep. When he came near enough, Gunnar called out to him. I understood some of what was said, and Helmuth explained the rest later.

"You say you are King Harald's man," Gunnar said curtly. "I ask myself, what would your king do to men who raped his kinswoman and killed his slave and hound?"

At this, the warrior blanched. "No one raped your kinswoman," he muttered. "We only wanted to talk to her."

"What of Odd? As he did not understand your speech, no doubt you thought he would understand your sword. I think he understood you well."

"Eanmund killed him," the dark man replied. Raising an accusing finger at me, he said, "*He* killed Eanmund. He loosed the hound. As to the girl, we did not know she was your kinswoman; we thought she was a slave."

"Because of you," Gunnar said, "my good slave is dead, and my hound also. What have you to say to this?"

"If you think yourself aggrieved, take your complaint to the king. For myself, I say only this: My name is Hrethel and I am accustomed to holding council in the halls of jarls and kings, yet you keep me standing here like a slave or foreigner."

"Do you expect the welcome bowl even now? After bringing death and strife to my house, you think I should pour out my best ale for you?" Gunnar laughed harshly. "Be thankful I do not pour out your blood instead."

"I am a man of rank," the stranger said. "I merely meant for you to bear that in mind.

"Then cease your worrying on that point," Gunnar sneered haughtily. "I know well what manner of man I have before me."

Hrethel frowned, but abandoned any further attempt to gain the better of Gunnar. "The message I bring is this: King Harald Bull-Roar has proclaimed a *theng* to commence the first full moon after next. As a free man and land-holder of Skania, the king charges you to attend."

Gunnar's eyes narrowed. "But I am Jarl Rägnar's man."

"Rägnar Yellow Hair has pledged fealty to Harald. Therefore, you are summoned along with your king. If you fail to attend, your lands will be seized in forfeit to King Harald."

"I see." Gunnar stroked his chin thoughtfully. "Is there nothing more? This message might easily have been given to my wife or my slave. I am thinking that if you had done so, my slave and my good hound would still live."

"I am charged by my king to deliver the message to the jarls and free men of Skania, not," Hrethel sneered, "their wives and slaves. This I have done, and now I will leave you."

"Go your way," Gunnar told him. "I will not prevent you. I will go to the theng—of that you may be certain. For I intend to bring your crime before the king."

Hrethel nodded, his frown indignant. "That is your right."

He turned on his heel and walked from the yard, across the meadow and into the forest. Gunnar watched him out of sight and then turned to me. "We will go to the council, you and me," my master said, pressing his finger into my chest. "You saw what happened. This you will tell the king."

If the message Gunnar received troubled him, he gave no sign—neither that night, nor in the days to follow. Life on the small holding continued as before, but without Odd there was that much more for everyone else to do. I took on most of his chores, but considered it no hardship, for it meant I could speak more often with Helmuth. I applied myself to the work of the holding, and no less diligently to my speech, practising the rough tongue with Helmuth as often as I could, and also on my own. I began speaking with more precision as my confidence increased; I reckoned that if I were to give an accounting before the king, I would benefit from increased fluency, and this thought inspired my efforts. Helmuth helped me with the speech I would make; he questioned me as if he were king of all the Danes, and I answered him over and over again until I could offer a clear account of all that happened the day Odd was killed.

When I was not practising, I prayed as it seemed right to me, and my mind turned again and again to my brothers on the pilgrimage. I often found myself wondering where they were, what they were doing, and what had happened to them since I last saw them. I prayed for them in the daily round, praying the protection of Michael Militant and his angels to shield them on their way.

Summer drew on and the days passed; the time for the theng approached. One day a free man from a neighbouring holding came to speak to Gunnar. His name was Tolar and he was on his way to market; he stopped for a meal, but did not stay the night. I do not know what they talked about, but Gunnar was very thoughtful when he left.

From that day Gunnar began to grow short-tempered and particular. He found fault in everything; no one could please him. Once or twice, he even shouted at Ulf. In fact, one evening just before we were to leave he became so unpleasant that I left the house to sit outside on a stump in the yard so that I might eat my meal in peace without his complaining. I was enjoying the warm evening and the long northern twilight, saying vespers aloud to myself when I became aware that someone had crept up beside me.

I opened my eyes and raised my head to see Ylva

standing over me with her hands clasped, as mine had been, in an attitude of prayer.

"You are singing again to your god, heya?" she observed.

"Yes."

"Perhaps this god of yours would help our Gunnar."

I did not know what to say to this, so I merely agreed. "Perhaps."

"Something preys on Gunnar's mind," she declared quietly. She knelt down in the grass beside the stump. "He is worried about the theng. He fears it will go ill with him there."

I turned to look at her face in the soft dusky light. It was a beautiful face in its way, fine-featured and good-natured, with deep brown eyes and a small, straight nose. Her long braids were still neat after a whole day's labour. She smoothed her mantle with her hands. Her clothing carried the scent of the kitchen.

"Tell me about this—this theng," I suggested.

"It is the *theng*," she answered. "It is a . . ." she hesitated, thinking how best to describe it, "a place where jarls and free men go to talk."

"A council." I drew a circle in the air.

"Heya," she nodded brightly, "it is a talking-ring."

"Has Gunnar any purpose—ah, no, that is not right." I thought for a moment. "Reason! Has he any reason to fear this council?"

She shook her head, peering at her hands in her lap. "None that I know. Always before, he welcomes the theng. Every day everyone drinks the king's öl and gets drunk. It is enjoyable for them, I think."

"Ylva," I said on sudden inspiration, "would you do something for me?"

She looked at me suspiciously. "What is this you wish me to do?"

"Would you . . ." I did not know the word, "ah, would you cut me?" I patted my bristly forehead. "Here?"

She laughed. "You want me to *shave* you!"

"Heya. I want you to shave me. If I am to stand before the king, I must look like a . . . ah—"

"Shaven one," she said, supplying the barbarian term for priest.

"Yes, I want to look like a shaven one. Will you do this?"

Ylva assented and fetched Gunnar's razor and a bowl of water. She settled herself on the stump and I on the ground before her, and, at my direction, she renewed my tonsure with swift strokes of her deft fingers. Karin, concerned over Ylva's absence, came out to look for us and, when she saw what we were about, hurried back to the house and called Ulf and Gunnar to see as well. They thought the sight immensely humorous and laughed loud and long at me.

Well, if the sight of a monk's tonsure gave them pleasure, so be it. Laughter, I reckoned, was the least trial a priest of the Holy Church might endure. Anyway, there was no spite in it.


Tolar arrived the day before we were to leave for the king's council. He and Gunnar were good friends, I soon discovered. They often accompanied one another to market, or, on such occasions as this, to the theng. The next morning, Karin, Ulf, and Ylva came out into the yard to see us away.

Karin wished her husband well, and gave him a bundle of food which he put in the bag at his belt. Ylva also wished Gunnar well on his journey. Then, turning to me, she said, "I made these for you to eat on the way."

She pressed a leather pouch into my hands, and, leaning

close, kissed me quickly on the cheek. "May your God go with you, Aeddan. Journey well and return safely."

Then, overcome by her own boldness, she ducked her head and hurried back into the house. Thunderstruck, I watched her disappear through the door. My cheek seemed to burn where her lips had touched. I could feel the colour rising to my face.

Gunnar had already turned away, but Tolar stood looking on, smiling at my embarrassment. "Made these for you," he said, chuckling to himself; he tapped the bag in my hand as he moved past.

Ulf and Garm accompanied us as far as the edge of the forest, whereupon Gunnar sent them back with a last farewell. We then turned to the trail and began walking in earnest; Garm, nose to the ground, ran ahead, searching out the trail and circling through the brush on either side. We rested and watered at midday, and while the others napped I took the opportunity to examine the pouch Ylva had given me; inside were five hard, flat brown disks. They smelled of walnut and honey. I broke off a piece of one, tasted it, and found it sweet and good. I ate half a disk then, and made a habit of eating half each day.

Thus, we progressed: walking steadily, taking only two or three rests each day, stopping early and rising at dawn to move on. It was not until the evening of the third day that I learned of Gunnar's misgivings. We had stopped by a brook to make camp, and he was sitting with his feet in the water. I removed my shoes and sat down a little apart from him. "Ah, it is good after a long day's walk," I told him. "We have forests in Éire, but not like this."

"It is a very big forest, I think," he replied, looking around as if seeing it for the first time. "But not as big as some."

He dropped his gaze, and his expression clouded once more. After a moment, he drew a deep breath. "They are saying that Harald is increasing the tribute again. Rägnar owes Harald a very large tribute, and we must all help to pay. Each year it grows more difficult." He spoke more to himself than to me, as if he were merely thinking aloud. "Harald is a very greedy man. However much we give him, it is never enough. He always wants more."

"That is the way with kings," I observed.

"You have greedy kings in Irlandia also, heya?" Gunnar shook his head. "But none as greedy as Harald Bull-Roar, I think. It is because of him that we go a-viking. When the harvest is not good and the winter is hard, we must find silver elsewhere."

He was silent for a time, looking at his feet in the water—as if they were the cause of his trouble. "Such raiding is hard for a man with a wife and son," he sighed, and I felt the weight of his burden. "It is all right for the younger men; they have nothing. Raiding teaches them many things useful to a man. And if they get some silver they can get a wife and a holding of their own."

"I see."

"But it is not so easy now as it was when my grandfather was a young man," Gunnar confided. "Then, we only raided in times of war. Or to find wives. Now we must raid to satisfy the silver-lust of greedy jarls. That is not so good."

"Heya, not so good," I sympathized.

"I do not like leaving Karin and Ulf. I have a good holding—the land is good. But there are not so many people nearby, and if anything should happen while I am away . . ." He let the thought go. "It is not so bad for the younger men; they have no wives. But who will be hearthmate to Karin if I do not return? Who will teach Ulf to hunt?"

"Perhaps King Harald will not increase the tribute this year," I suggested hopefully.

"Nay," he murmured, turning woeful eyes on me, "I have never yet heard of a jarl such as that."

# 19

After walking four days—in a more or less easterly direction—we came to a big river bounded by wide water meadows on either side. In the centre of the meadow on the far side of the river stood an immense stone, marking the council ring, the theng place. On the broad flat lea, and down below on the gentle slopes of the riverbanks, were ranged a number of camps, most with rush-covered huts, though some boasted ox-hide tents.

We crossed the meadow and made our way along the riverbank to the fording place. "Ah, look, Tolar," said Gunnar, pointing to one of the tents. "There is Rägnar's tent."

Tolar nodded.

"Perhaps they can tell us why we have been summoned like this."

We waded across the river, and Gunnar and Tolar were hailed by men from various camps, whom they greeted genially as we passed by. Some looked askance—watching me with unfriendly eyes—but no one stopped or challenged me. Perhaps it was because I had been given the task of holding tight to Garm's collar, lest he bound away to fight with one of the other dogs guarding the various camps. However it was, I was relieved that no one demanded an explanation of me, and I was content simply to observe.

I had supposed, living among barbarians, that I had grown indifferent to their habits and appearance. I was wrong. The sights that met my eyes as we made our way through the various encampments almost made me gape with amazement. I saw men—and women too, for there were many women in attendance—covered in the skins of wild animals, looking more feral than any of the beasts whose pelts they wore; and there were others who wore nothing at all, and whose bodies were stained with strange designs in blue and ochre. All were big, for the Danefolk are an exceedingly large race, and many, although full-grown, were fair-haired as maidens; but, whether fair or dark, most all of them wore their locks braided in long thick ropes of hair, decorated with feathers, leaves, shells, and wooden ornaments.

I could but shake my head in wonder.

Some barbarians, lately arrived, greeted their kinsmen with cries and much commotion; others worked at building shelters and sleeping places. Everyone talked loudly, with much shouting and bellowing. Oh, they are a noisy breed; I could scarce think.

The mingled scents of food cooking over various fires brought the water to my mouth, even as the smoke stung my eyes. We passed by several small camps and cooking fires, and I looked with longing at the roasting meat and bubbling cauldrons.

The tent of Rägnar Yellow Hair was a white-spotted oxhide, around which ten or more men sprawled, lazing the day away, waiting for the council to begin. At our approach one of them raised a hand and sang out, alerting anyone who cared that Gunnar and Tolar had arrived.

"Hey, Gunnar."

"Hey, Bjarni. Are you winning the battle?"

"We are holding our own, I think," the man said with a yawn. "The king is not here. He is drinking öl with King Heoroth and the jarls."

"Where can we make camp?"

"There is a good place behind the tent—so I was told."

"Very well, we will take it," Gunnar said, and Tolar nodded his agreement. "But please do not trouble yourself. We would not disturb your much-needed rest."

"Come drink with us later," Bjarni said, closing his eyes. I think he was asleep again before we had walked six paces.

We three spent the rest of the day making camp: I gathered stones from the river to make a fire-ring; Gunnar chopped wood from the huge mounded store of sawn logs King Harald had provided; Tolar gathered reeds from the riverbank. We were about our preparations when Rägnar returned to his tent. Gunnar and Tolar went to greet their lord, leaving me to arrange the bundles of reeds on the ground so we would not have to sleep on the bare earth.

Thinking we would soon require a cooking fire, I began stripping dry bark to use as kindling. I was about this task when a rough voice captured my attention. Raising my head, I looked around. An enormous man stood over me, glaring down from his height. My heart sank.

"Greetings, Hrothgar," I said, hoping to placate the man who had tried to drown me in the king's ale vat. I lay aside the wood and sat back on my heels.

"Slaves are not permitted here," he said, and made other remarks which I could not follow. His speech was slurred with drink, and difficult to understand.

I did not know what to say, so I simply smiled inoffensively and nodded.

Reaching down, he grabbed my collar and hauled me upright. He held his face close to mine. "Slaves are not permitted here." His breath was foul and he stank of sweat and sour beer.

"Gunnar brought me."

His eyes narrowed. "You are a slave, and you are a liar."

"Please, Hrothgar—I want no trouble."

"Nay," he said, a vicious grin spreading across his bloated face, "it will be no trouble." He pushed me away hard, and I fell sprawling to the ground. "Now I will show you what happens to slaves who use their tongues for telling lies. Stand up on your feet."

I rose slowly, a sick feeling spreading through my inward parts. Glancing around quickly, I hoped to see Gunnar returning, but I did not know where he had gone and I did not see him anywhere.

I thought to call out, and opened my mouth to do so, but Hrothgar's fist was flying towards my face before I could draw breath to shout. I ducked under the blow and stepped lightly aside. He turned and swung again, and I ducked again.

"Stop, Hrothgar. Please, stop," I pleaded, moving another step to the side.

"Stand still!" he bellowed.

His booming voice drew the attention of some of the nearer barbarians. They began shouting to one another that there was a fight to be seen, and we were quickly surrounded by a ring of interested onlookers. Some of them called for Hrothgar to catch me, while others urged me to elude him. I took the advice of the latter, and moved slowly sideways, step by step. Each time the great hulking Dane swung at me, I moved aside, sometimes ducking under the blow, sometimes bending backwards out of his reach. And each time he missed, Hrothgar cursed and grew more angry.

Soon he was sweating and puffing, his face red and ripe to bursting.

"Let us cease now," I said. "We have no quarrel, you and I. Let us end this and walk away."

"Stand still and fight!" he roared, mad with rage and drink.

He swung again, and I ducked. But I had gone to that well once too often, and this time he anticipated my movement. As his right hand swung over my head, he threw his left fist low to catch me. Alas, I saw it too late.

The blow caught me on the jaw. But, drunk as he was, there was no real force in the swing. I fell back, more from surprise and losing my balance, than from the force of the swing. Hrothgar thought he had felled me, however. I let him believe this.

"You have beaten me, Hrothgar. I cannot fight any more."

"Stand up!" he raged. "I will knock you down again."

"My legs will not hold me. You have defeated me."

"Stand on your feet!" He stooped and snatched up a piece of wood—one of those I had been stripping. This he threw at me. The throw was clumsy and I rolled easily aside.

I made a chore of climbing to my feet, shaking my clothes all around. With a mighty growl, the barbarian swung at me. I leapt away, side-stepping once again. Hrothgar, unbalanced by the force of his swing, toppled forward onto his knees. This brought a great peal of laughter from those looking on, and a roar of rage from Hrothgar.

"Please," I said, "let us stop now, Hrothgar. I cannot fight any more."

He pushed himself up and lunged at me, throwing wide his arms. I jumped lightly back and he hugged the earth. Again the throng laughed, and I realized that they were calling for me to defeat him. I gazed around the ring of faces and saw Gunnar and Tolar standing in the forefront jeering with the rest.

"Gunnar, what shall I do?" I called, barely making myself heard above the crowd.

"Hit him!" Gunnar called back. "Hit him hard!"

With a grunt and a curse, Hrothgar heaved himself onto his feet once more and stumbled forward. The crowd cheered more wildly, shrieking with approval and delight. In the same instant I saw a glinting flash out of the corner of my eye.

I turned just in time to see the knife blade slicing up through the air. I jerked my head away and felt the blade-tip nip my chin. I fell backwards, landing on my rump. Hrothgar, unable to keep his balance, fell forward and landed atop me, trapping my legs beneath his bulk. One swift slash and he would cut my throat, or gut me like a fish.

Desperate to shift him, I kicked and heaved, but could not move my legs. Hrothgar, still gripping the knife, made a clumsy swing. I threw myself back and heard the thin whisper of the blade in the air—and I heard a crack as my head struck something hard: the piece of wood Hrothgar had thrown at me. My hand closed on it at once. If I had any thought at all, it was only to use the wood to fend off the knife.

Hrothgar, laying crossways on my legs, lunged blindly. His arm went wide, and his head flopped down with the effort. The rounded mound that was the back of his head presented itself to me and I struck it. The wood bounced off the barbarian's skull with a hollow sound which so surprised me that I swung again—harder.

Hrothgar gave out a grunt and lay on his face in the dirt.

A moment later, Gunnar and Tolar were rolling the

brute aside. Men came forward to slap me on the back, and declare what a quick-witted fighter I was.

"I did not mean to hit him so hard," I said to Gunnar. "Is he injured, do you think?"

"Hrothgar hurt?" Gunnar chuckled, much amused. "Nay, nay. His head will ache as much from the öl as from the puny knock you gave him."

I observed the prostrate body doubtfully. "I fear I have only made matters worse. Hrothgar will be very angry with me now."

Gunnar waved aside my worry. "Nay, by the time he wakes up, he will have forgotten all about it. Still, I think you were lucky," Gunnar observed affably.

Tolar the Taciturn nodded in sage agreement.

"I should teach you to fight. That way you would not be forced to rely on luck—she often proves a flighty bed-mate."

"Heya," confirmed Tolar in a tone that conveyed years of bitter experience.

Rägnar Yellow Hair approached boldly, his counte-nance severe. Scop, his Truth Sayer, fluttered at his side like an overgrown buzzard. Rägnar glanced from Gunnar to me; I expected the worst. He held out a silver coin which Gunnar accepted and tucked into his pouch. With a dark glance at me, he turned and walked away. Scop flapped after him.

There came a sound so strange and loud that it halted any further talk; everywhere men stopped and stared at one another.

"That will be Harald Bull-Roar," Gunnar said, looking away towards the river.

"There!" shouted Bjarni, standing before the tent. "Jarl Harald arrives!"

I looked where the man was pointing and saw, moving among the trees and shrubs along the river, a red-and-white expanse. To a man, the whole camp began walking to the river, where, after a few moments, the huge thundering bellow sounded again and a ship sailed into view.

The vessel was sharp-keeled and long, its prow rising high to end in the fierce, fire-eyed, serpent-toothed head of a dragon; the stern rose likewise to become a forked tail. Both stern and prow had been painted red and yellow; the ship's sides were black, and the sails alternating red-and-white in broad handsome stripes. Fresh-limed shields hung on the rail, and ranks of oars bristled from the sides. Ah, yes, it was a sight to stir the heart and make the blood run swift in the veins.

Those gathered on the banks hailed the fine vessel with lusty shouts; some, overcome with zeal, leaped into the water and swam to the ship to clamber up the sides and join the warriors at the rail. The bellowing sounded again, shaking the very ground beneath our feet, and I saw that this extraordinary noise was produced by two enormous battle horns manned by two barbarians each, who took it in turn to blow into the instruments, lest one of them grow faint.

Rägnar, surrounded by his men, rose to watch the arrival. "A fine-looking ship," he observed. "Had I a longship half so good, it would be Harald paying me tribute, and not the other way."

Lifting a hand to the vessel, which was now coming to rest against the bank, Gunnar said, "Ship? I see no ship, Jarl Rägnar. Nay! It is our silver tribute I see before us—with dragon head and banded sails now, but it is our silver just the same."

"Indeed," Rägnar agreed bitterly. "And now that I see the trove of wealth we have given him, I am sick at heart."

Tolar nodded and, on sudden inspiration, he spat.

They continued complaining like this, each one having his say, but all the time their eyes kept stealing over the long, sweeping lines of the ship and its high, handsome sails. And step by step they moved down to where wooden stakes were now being hammered into the earth for the ropes which would secure the vessel. I found myself walking beside Scop.

"So! The monk becomes a warrior," he sneered. "Mayhap warriors will now wield pens."

"The beer unhorsed Hrothgar," I said. "I merely provided a soft place for him to fall."

Scop made a nasty grunt and reached up a filthy hand to pat my clean-shaven tonsure. "Shaven One," he cooed malevolently.

Ignoring his foul mood, I said, "I did not think to see you again."

"Ha!" he scoffed. "Dost think it a happy surprise?"

"I do," I replied, annoyed at his disagreeable manner. "And I thank God for it, too."

The Truth Sayer looked sideways at me. Seizing me suddenly by the arm, he spun me to face him. "Look around you, Irish. Is this your precious abbey? Are these your brother priests?"

Before I could make an answer, he put his filthy hand upon my neck and drew me close. "God abandoned me, my friend," he whispered with strangled rage. "And now, Aidan the Innocent, he has abandoned you!"

With that, he stumped away quickly, taking himself back to camp alone. I watched him go, frustrated and angered by his impudence and presumption. Shaking off the disgust of his provocation, I continued on to the riverbank and rejoined the others gathered there.

King Harald had arrived with all his house *karlar* and three of his five wives. Some of the other women who had come with their men noticed and made much of this fact. Several warriors dropped over the side of the ship and into the water; they waded onto dry land, while others readied a number of long planks made from split pine trees. The planks were placed between the rail and bank, and made secure by the men on the bank.

Only then did Harald Bull-Roar deign to show himself. And when he did it was to the astonished delight of the throng.

# 20

King Harald Bull-Roar, Jarl of the Danefolk of
Skania, arose from the ship like Odin himself,
arrayed in blue the colour of a northern midnight;
he stood in the bright sunshine, glinting of gold and silver,
his long red beard brushed and its ends braided. Gold
sparkled on his chest, at his throat and on each wrist;
seven silver bands were on his arms, and seven silver
brooches secured his cloak.

He stepped to the rail, and I saw that he was bare-
footed. Gold and silver bracelets gleamed at his ankles. He
was a big man: deep-chested, with thick-muscled arms,
and long, strong legs. Standing tall upon the rail, a king in
the prime of life, he gazed with quick, intelligent eyes
upon the assembled host.

A king is a king anywhere, I thought. Harald had the
same regal bearing of any lord I had ever seen. Sure, he
and Lord Aengus were brothers under the skin; each laying eye to other would have recognized royalty. Of this I
had no doubt.

Raising his hands in salutation, he opened his mouth
to speak and I saw that youthful battles had left him with a
livid scar from chin to throat. He spoke in a voice both

deep and loud, turning this way and that, and spreading wide his arms as if to embrace all those thronged below him on the bank.

The substance of his speech seemed to be about setting aside differences during the council. I think he called on everyone to sit down together in peace as free men in order to best decide what to do—or something like that. It is the sort of speech all lords make when they want their way, and there was much sceptical grunting and clearing of throats.

Then, without the least hesitation, Harald lifted one bare foot and stepped from the ship's rail into the air. Some of the women gasped, but they need not have worried. For as the king stepped out from the rail, a hand appeared and caught his foot. Another hand joined the first, and the king took another step. Two more hands—those of the warriors who had set out the planks—caught the king's right foot and bore him up.

In this way, Jarl Harald was conveyed onto the river-bank, carried by his house karlar as he stood upright—a most impressive feat. For the rest of the day, it was all anyone talked about: "Did you see how they carried him?" "Heya! The king's feet never touched the earth!"

Harald Bull-Roar was carried to the place where his tent would be erected; a red oxhide was spread upon the ground and the king sat down to receive the homage of his people. Everyone came before him, some to lay themselves at his feet, others to bestow gifts of honour and welcome. The jarl accepted his honours with good grace, and I found myself liking the man for his easy deference, despite any misgivings Gunnar or Rägnar might have had—and I did not doubt their fears were genuine, and with ample reason. But Harald was a winsome man: all smiles and bright confidence, always bringing his people close with a gesture or an intimate word.

I watched as he sat upon the red oxhide, calling his noblemen by name, disarming them with flattery and praise. Even before the theng began, the king was plunged deep into his campaign. Men approached him, wooden in speech and movement, full of doubt and mistrust, only to rise again a moment later, beaming, conviction and faith rekindled by a word and a touch.

Oh, Jarl Harald was a very master of kingcraft: subtle, shrewd, persuasive and reassuring, slaying his opponents' objections before they knew to contradict or oppose him.

Sure, I had seen such power once or twice before. For all his gold and silver, this barbarian lord reminded me of Bishop Tudwal of Tara, renowned for his composure, his confidence, his easy mastery of men.

Nor did Gunnar and Tolar, for all their apprehensions, remain aloof from the king's considerable charm. I waited as they performed their duties of respect; they returned glad-hearted and confident once more. When I asked what the king had told them to bring about such a change, Gunnar demanded, "Have I ever said a word against the king? You must learn to be more trusting, Aeddan."

This advice brought a concurring nod from Tolar.

Of all the jarls and free men I observed, only Rägnar remained aloof from the king's winning ways. Perhaps he knew too much of kingcraft to be easily swayed by the methods he himself employed from time to time. Perhaps he found it hard, being a lord, to allow himself the indulgence of complete conviction. Many tribesmen depended upon him and his judgement; whatever others might think or do, his own thoughts and actions were circumscribed by his obligations. Thus, Rägnar Yellow Hair could not give complete allegiance to any man, and still remain king in more than name only.

Proud men are all alike. No doubt he resented having Harald over him. Paying tribute was bad enough; he did not like to be seen bowing low as well. I imagine it might have been the same with some of the other lords, but I could not observe them all. Even so, it seemed that when the ceremony of greeting had been concluded, the battle was over and the king had claimed the field. He had, it seemed to me, sowed seeds of hopeful anticipation among the people and then withdrew to let those seeds sprout and take root.

Sure, the mood of the camp that night was buoyant with expectation; all across the meadow, men gazed at one another over the fire and speculated on the council: What would tomorrow bring? What would the king propose?

Though I had no part in the proceedings—nothing they decided could possibly affect me one way or another—I could still feel the intense anticipation of the assembly. It was late into the night before anyone could sleep.

Early the next morning, a single large drum summoned the jarls and free men to the theng-stone. We were breaking fast when the drumming began. Gunnar and Tolar stood at once. "It is beginning," Gunnar said, throwing aside the bone he was gnawing. "Hurry! We will sit in the forerank."

Unfortunately, everyone else had the same notion; hence the call became less a summons than the start of a race, as from all the scattered camps the men hastened to the meeting place. The few women stood to look on with longing, though some boldly followed their men to the nearest allowable perimeter of the council ring—a boundary marked out by a circle of small boulders.

Emboldened by the womenfolk's example, I took a place at the outer ring, while Gunnar and Tolar elbowed their way towards the centre of the circle. The best places were already taken, so I stood in the press, straining for a view of the proceedings. At first, nothing appeared to transpire, but then I noticed an old man hobbling around the theng-stone, shaking a gourd filled with pebbles. Muttering and mumbling, he staggered in a strange, stiff-legged gait around and around the upright stone.

"Skirnir," someone nearby said, and I guessed that was his name. He was, I decided, one of those curious creatures known as a *skald*—probably, he was advisor and counsellor to King Harald.

Dressed in a short, ragged siarc and breeches of scraped deerskin, old Skirnir continued his muttering incantations for a time, and then lay aside the gourd and, picking up a wooden bowl, spattered a liquid—perhaps oil of some kind—onto the standing stone using a small bundle of frayed birch twigs which he grasped in his right hand. Each time he dipped the twigs into the bowl he called the god's name; and each time he shook the oil onto the rock, he sneezed.

When he had circled the great stone a number of times, he placed the bowl upon the ground and then, placing his hands in the oil, proceeded to speckle the surface of the rock with handprints—sometimes patting the stone with his palms, and sometimes hugging it in a wide-armed embrace. While he was thus employed, King Harald emerged from his place among the onlookers; he had something tucked under his arm, but I could not see what it might be.

After the skald finished anointing the stone, he turned to the king and gestured for the object he carried, which turned out to be a chicken. Before I could think why Jarl Harald should be holding a chicken, the king lifted the bird, raising it high for all to see, then gave it to Skirnir who likewise raised the bird—once, twice, three times, lifting it on high—then offered it to the king, who took its head and beak into his mouth for a moment. A strange sight, that: the king standing before the people with the head of a live chicken in his mouth.

Then the skald gave a loud shout and started to shake all over. His hands and shoulders quivered, his legs shook and his body trembled. All at once he seized the chicken and held it high; he began to spin, trembling all the while. Around and around he spun, whereupon he gave his arm a sharp jerk. There came a crack and the chicken's head snapped off in his hand. The poor bird began running and hopping and fluttering; old Skirnir, keen-eyed, followed its headless flounderings on hands and knees, observing the pitiful bird's death throes. Blood spattered onto the skald and onto the stone.

Everyone held their breath, leaning forward in keen anticipation, as the chicken's flopping gradually diminished. At last, the sorry bird lay still, its feathers quivering gently while it died. Then up leaped Skirnir, and with a loud voice proclaimed the omen favourable—although he did so in such an uncouth speech that I could not make out all he said. The people seemed pleased, prodding one another and nodding solemnly.

Let it here be known that I place no confidence in oracles or omens; neither do I believe in the old gods. Their powers, if any, derive from the will of those who persist in such faulty thinking. I do not say the old gods are demons only—though many wiser heads assure me that this is so— but they are hollow vessels, incapable of bearing the weight of men's belief. In elder days, people clung to such gods as they could find. All was darkness then, and men fumbled in ignorance for anything to hold against the savage night.

But, see, the light has come; day has dawned at long last! That is good news. And it is no longer acceptable to worship those things embraced in darkness. That is my belief. If I did not condemn the barbarians for their misguided faith, perhaps I may be forgiven what some of my more zealous brothers would certainly consider my sinful lack of piety and devotion. No doubt, if they had been in my place they would have scorched the very earth itself with the fire of their transforming righteousness.

But I am a weak and sinful monk, I freely confess it. Even so, I have resolved to tell the truth. Judge me how you will.

After the omen had been judged auspicious, Skirnir proclaimed the theng commenced. Gathering his gourd, bowl, and chicken carcass, the skald withdrew and Harald came before the assembly, declaring himself pleased that so many had answered his summons.

"My kinsmen and brothers," he called in his deep bull voice, throwing his arms wide as if to embrace the assembly. "It does cheer me greatly to see you standing before me, for we are indeed a mighty people. I ask you now: Who is able to stand against the Daneman when he is roused in wrath? Our skill is both dire and formidable. The might of our arms is feared by all the world. Who is able to stand against it?"

Harald thrust his arm in the air as if brandishing a sword, and cried, "Who is able to stand against the Daneman when the wrath of Odin fills his veins with fire?"

Murmured voices rejoined with assurances that no one could stand against the wrath of the Danefolk. The king then commenced a long speech in which he described how all the world trembles when the longship keel slices the deep waters, and how all the world cowers in fear when the Sea Wolf hunts the sea trails. These sentiments were conveyed with much thrusting of imaginary swords and rattling of imaginary spears on invisible shields.

The murmurs now chorused agreement; several cheered, encouraging the king aloud. Most remained silent, but everyone was intent, eyes and ears keen, eager for their great Jarl to declare what had moved him to summon the theng. Seeing that he had them on his side, Harald moved to the heart of his concern.

Now, I have heard of warriors who can leap from one horse to another in full gallop and never miss a stride. This feat Harald now performed. "Brothers," he said, "I know that the yearly tribute weighs heavily on your shoulders. I know that such a burden is difficult to bear."

The king said this with convincing sympathy, as if it were some other lord that had imposed this onerous weight upon his people. He then declared, with an expression of utter conviction, that he would be a vile king indeed if he stood by and did nothing to ease the weight of law from his people's shoulders.

This produced a minor commotion as the people tried to work out what Harald could possibly mean. "Therefore," the king said, "I have devised a means by which the tribute . . ." The king's listeners leaned forward expectantly. "—by which the tribute may be *forgiven*."

Sure, this caused such a stir among the listeners, the king was forced to repeat his astonishing decree, not once only, but three times. "You have heard me, heya," he assured them, shaking his fists in the air. "Your tribute will be forgiven."

Harald allowed a moment for this news to make its way to the rearward ranks and to be passed to those standing beyond the stone circle. He stood erect, fists on hips, his smile broad, red hair gleaming in the sun; he fairly beamed confidence, assurance streaming like heat from a flame.

The king went on to describe how he had set his mind on a venture which would bring wealth and riches to every free man in Daneland. He threw his arms wide and begged them to hear him out. The shouting all but overwhelmed his booming bull voice. Harald begged them to listen; he pleaded for their indulgence, and told them that he had determined to go to Miklagård, where there was silver and gold beyond measure, and where even the lowest slave was far wealthier than the richest king of Skania.

The people were amazed at the king's audacity: Did you hear? *Miklagård!* they said. The king is going to Miklagård. Think of that!

"Now I ask you, brothers," Harald continued, his bull voice thundering above the excitement his announcement had created, "is it right for the slaves of the south to enjoy more wealth than the kings of the north? Is it right that we, Odin's favoured children, should break our backs in toil—ploughing, reaping, chopping wood, drawing water—while brown slaves sit idle in the shade of fruiting trees?"

He let the question hang in the air to do its work.

"No!" cried a voice. It sounded very like Hrothgar to me. "It is not right!" shouted another. And everyone seemed to agree that this state of affairs could not be allowed to continue.

Harald waved his hands for order. He continued, speaking reasonably, and somewhat reluctantly, as if merely acquiescing to the prevailing view—a view which he had no great wish to further himself. He spoke of how he had vowed in his heart to ease the burdens of his people. He said he would go to Miklagård, if that is what they wanted, and he would bring back the wealth of the southern slaves. He would bring back this wealth and use it to better the lives of the Danefolk. He would bring back such wealth that they would not have to pay tribute due him. He would bring back wealth to make even the greediest among them satisfied. He would do all this and more, *if* that is what they wanted.

He thrust his hand towards the river where his huge new ship lay at anchor. That ship, that very ship, he declared, was the swiftest of any ever built in Skania. He would go with this selfsame ship and he would lead the war host to the city of gold. And he, Harald Bull-Roar, would fill that great fast ship with such treasures as would make all other kings sick with jealousy when they saw what wealth his jarls and freemen would enjoy.

The people could not take such amazing good fortune quietly. They hugged themselves and one another, and cried out and leapt with joy at the prospect of so much wealth within such easy reach. They acclaimed their king and his wisdom and foresight. Here was a king, truly, who knew what was best for his people.

"For this reason," Harald said when the outcry had spent itself once more, "I will forgive the yearly tribute, which is due me as your lord!"

Again, the king was overwhelmed by a seatide of acclamation, and was forced to wait until it had abated before wading on.

"I will forgive the yearly tribute," he repeated, speaking slowly. "Not for one year only will I forgive the tribute. Not for two years! Not for three years—or even four!" he cried. "But for five years will I forgive the tribute to any man who will arm himself and follow me to Miklagård."

Oh, he was a shrewd lord. I do not think that anyone even noticed the subtle trap he had laid for them in his words. All they heard was that the king was forgiving the tribute for five years. They did not yet perceive that in order to receive the benefit of the forgiven tribute, they all had to follow him to Miklagård and help him fill his treasure chests with raid and plunder.

Harald called them kinsmen, he called them brothers. He bade them to fly to the south where wealth beyond measure awaited them. He made it sound as if they had but to take shovels and scoop it off the ground. He flung wide his arms once more. "Who is with me?" the king cried, and they all shouted their approval, surging forward, fighting among themselves to be the first to pledge support for the inspired plan.

Having won his way, Harald quickly declared the council ended, lest, I believe, any dissenting voices should be raised to spoil his impressive victory. Yet, who would have dissented? Even Rägnar left the council ring with his scowl of protest softened into a thoughtful, if not benevolent, smile.

The king then declared that the day should be given to feasting and drinking. To this end, he caused three great ale vats to be placed in the centre of the camp with orders that every vat should be continually replenished from his shipboard store throughout the remaining days and nights of the gathering. He then offered three oxen and six pigs to be roasted for the feeding of his people.

The celebration following Harald's bold decision complimented the king's exuberance full well. That night the daring Jarl's name and far-thinking, even visionary, abilities were lauded in cup by one and all. Around each fire-ring, men, their faces glistening with grease from the rib bones in their hands, licked their lips and proclaimed Harald Bull-Roar the finest king who ever trod the earth on two legs. They hailed him a true and noble lord; a kindly ruler whose only thought was ever for the benefit and uplifting of his people; a man among men, wise beyond his years and beyond his time; a brave and courageous, yet essentially sympathetic, sovereign who could dream and dare great things on behalf of his people.

They had, of course, the king's skald, Skirnir to help them remember these flattering sentiments. The skald roved the meadow, hopping from camp to camp to sing songs in praise of his patron, finding willing, if somewhat bleary-eyed, listeners for his spirited performances.

When the day was done and the last reveller collapsed

onto his fire side pallet, it was agreed that this year's theng was the best since Olaf Broken-Nose killed an ox with his bare hands.

And that night, as the deep summer stillness lay heavy upon the sleeping celebrants, I dreamed again.

# 21

A tawny owl swept low over the meadow on silent wings, eyes wide in surprise at finding so many humans strewn over its hunting ground. With a muted shriek of irritation, the bird flew off along the river.

The wind rose, gusting gently, rippling the meadow grass and making a strange, fluttering hiss. I heard the sound and stood up from my mat of rushes and looked around. Gone were the tents and fire-rings; gone were the people sleeping on the ground; gone was the theng-stone and gathering place. Even as I watched, the meadow changed and became a sea: the slow-waving meadowgrass became billowing waves and the pale flowers flecks of foam scattered over a rising swell.

I wondered how it was that I should stand upon the waters, but the ground I stood upon had become the curving deck of a ship. The ship itself could not be seen in the gloom, but I heard the wind-snap of the sails, and the slash of its sharp prow through the waves.

The sky above was dim; there was neither sun, nor moon, and the few stars were strangely configured. The ship carried us swiftly over dark, unknown waters, the rest of the seafarers and I—for though I could not see them, I could hear the others working nearby, talking low in muttered whispers to one another. I stood at the rail, gazing out into the misty distance toward an unseen horizon.

I do not know how long we sailed; a year, a day, an age of years . . . I cannot say. The wind did not fail, nor the ship alter its course. But the waters gradually changed from the cold grey of northern storms to a deep brilliant blue. I searched the far flat horizon for any sign of land—a rock, an island, the clouded hump of a hill or mountain—and I searched in vain. All was sea and sky and queer stars in alien skies. Still the ship ran boldly before the wind, swift-gliding as a winged gull.

Gradually, the sky began to change; it softened and grew pale, then blushed with pearly light the colour of rose petals. The hue deepened and became seamed with gold which swirled and brightened, fusing into the arc of a great, shining disk of blazing light, still half-hidden below the sea line. It was then I knew I faced the east, and we flew towards the rising sun.

On and on we sailed. The sun rose higher, its rays piercing the eastern sky with swordblades of shimmering light—so bright I had to close my eyes and turn my face away. When I looked again, it was not the sun I saw, but a vast golden dome: the enormous rising sphere of a palatial roof, supported on pillars of white marble the size and girth of the tallest trees. I marvelled that a palace so huge should float on the fickle sea. But as we drew swiftly nearer, I saw that this eastern extravagance rested on a spit of land; the contours of the palace's walls and many-chambered halls hugged the steep hump-backed hill. This hill rose from the sea to divide three vast waterways, and three great peoples.

A sound arose from the sea and land. At first I thought it must be the soughing of the water upon the rocky shore, for the soft thunder rose and fell with the regularity of waves. Closer, the sea thunder resolved into human voices singing in a curious, breathless chant.

And then I was standing inside an enormous chamber wrought of many-coloured stones whose roof was vast as the great curved bowl of heaven—so large that the sun and stars burned in its high firmament. Light poured down in curtained shafts and I moved from the shadow of a mighty pillar towards the light, treading across stone polished smooth by centuries of slow, reverential steps.

As I walked forward, I heard someone call my name. I looked up into the dazzling light and saw the face of a man. He gazed on me with large, sad eyes, and an expression of infinite love and sorrow. "Aidan," he said gently, and my heart moved within me for I knew it was Christ himself who spoke.

"Aidan," he said again, and oh! my heart melted to hear the sadness of his voice. "Aidan, why do you run from me?"

"Lord," I said, "I have served you all my life."

"Away from me, false servant!" he said and his voice echoed like the crack of doom.

I squeezed my eyes shut and when I opened them again, it was night once more and I was lying on the ground beside a fire burned to embers.


The celebration following King Harald's announcement proceeded through the next day with no sign of abating. Since Hrothgar's failed attempt at killing me, no one had so much as raised an eyebrow at my comings and goings. Even my beefy tormentor, whom I had seen several times after the fight, appeared to take no further interest in me. Perhaps, as Gunnar had suggested, he possessed no memory of the scuffle.

Gunnar, like everyone else, was intensely occupied

with the feasting and drinking, and required little of his slave, leaving me free to wander where I would. Thus, I used my liberty to withdraw to a quiet place and pray. It was not easy to find such a place, but a shaded birch bower on the riverbank served as a chapel in the green. Cool, peaceful, the earth soft with thick-grown grass . . . I spent most of the day there away from the loud revel of the camp.

I sang the psalms and performed the *lúirch léire*, the cross-vigil and, feeling penitent and contrite for my lapse in daily worship, recited the Canticle of the Three Youths, whose ordeal in the furnace of fire always produced in me a renewed enthusiasm for devotion.

Thus, I passed the day happily, and, as a reward for my diligence, indulged in one of Ylva's sweetmeats; the taste in my mouth gave me pleasant thoughts of her, which I enjoyed as much as the honeyed morsel. Returning from my wildwood cell, I happened to pass by the place where the king's ship lay anchored; a movement aboard the vessel caught my attention, and I saw two women emerge from the tented covering behind the mast. A third figure stepped from the tent—King Harald himself. He spoke a word to the women, and then disembarked by means of the planks; there were no house karlar to bear him aloft this time.

He saw me lingering near the ship and stopped. As he appeared about to speak, I also halted. The king stood for a moment staring at me, his forehead low, his gaze menacing. He turned away abruptly, as if the sight of me offended him, and stalked back to his camp, apparently deep in thought, swinging his right arm like a weapon.

Returning to camp myself, I found Gunnar, Tolar, Rägnar, and several others sitting around an empty tub with cups in their hands, trying to decide who should go and fetch more öl.

"I think Jarn and Leif should go," Gunnar was saying. "Tolar and I went last time."

Tolar, staring at his empty cup, nodded forlornly.

"You speak the very truth, Gunnar. But you are forgetting that Jarn and I went twice before," replied the one called Leif. "I think you are forgetting this."

Rägnar raised his cup and drained it. "Well then," he said, "it seems that I must go." He made to rise.

"Nay, jarl," said Leif, putting out his hand to stay his lord, "we cannot allow that. It is for us to go."

"Then I hope it is soon that you are going," Rägnar replied. "For I fear I will grow too old to raise my cup."

Leif sighed heavily, as if shouldering an immense and onerous burden, "Come, Jarn," he said, making no move to rise. "Our luck is not with us. It seems we have drawn the black stone once again."

I stepped into the camp and all eyes turned hopefully to me. "Aeddan will fetch the öl!" cried Gunnar. Pointing to the empty tub, he said, "More. Bring more."

I nodded, stooped to the wooden tub, and picked it up. "But he cannot carry it alone," Gunnar pointed out. His eyes swept the ring quickly. "Tolar must go with him."

Tolar raised his head, glanced at Gunnar, shrugged, then put down his cup and stood.

"Come, Tolar," I said. "Let us hope there is still a drop or two left."

"We must hurry," said Tolar. Grasping the ale tub, he took it from me and hefted it to his shoulder. "This way," he said, striding rapidly away.

Sure, he had never spoken so much at once, nor moved so swiftly. I fell into step beside him and we hastened to the place outside the stone circle where the king's cooking fires had been established. There were more pigs on the spits, and an ox sizzled slowly over the fire. A stack of casks had been brought up from the ship; several of these had been breached and were being emptied into the larger vats. We joined the others waiting there and watched the golden-brown liquid sloshing into the vats, in a beautiful creamy froth, drawing the slightly sweetish, yeasty scent into our nostrils.

"Ah!" I said to Tolar, "I wish I had a lake of ale."

He smiled and regarded me knowingly.

"Had I a lake of öl," I said, raising my hand in the age-old bardic gesture, "I should hold a great ale-feast for the King of Kings and Lord of Lords; I should like the Host of Heaven to be drinking with me for all eternity!"

Tolar smiled, so I continued, reciting the Brewer's Prayer: "I should like to have the fruits of Faith flowing in my house for all to taste; I should like the Saints of Christ in my own hall; I should like the tubs of Long-suffering to be at their service always. I should like cups of Charity to quench their thirst; I should like jars of Mercy for each member of that angelic company. I should like Love to be never-ending in their midst; I should like the Blesséd Jesu to be in the Hero's seat.

"Ah, *mo croí*, I should like to hold an everlasting ale-feast for the High King of Heaven, and Jesu to be drinking with me always."

I do not know what Tolar made of this outburst— probably I had rendered it poorly in the tongue I still spoke so inelegantly, but he endured it with a vague smile. When the vats were replenished, we elbowed our way to the edge and plunged our tub into the foamy depths. Together, holding tight to the rope handles with both hands, we carried the tub back to our camp, careful not to spill even the smallest drop along the way.

The others praised our diligence and skill as they crowded round with cups in hand. "The Shaven One," Tolar said, meaning me, "has charmed this öl with a rune to his god."

"Is this so?" wondered Rägnar.

"I said a prayer my people know," I explained simply.

"You respect this god of yours," said Leif, cocking his head to one side.

"He does that," Gunnar assured him, taking some pride in this fact. "Aeddan has not ceased making prayers to his god since he came to us. He even makes prayers over our supper."

"Indeed?" asked Rägnar wonderingly. "Scop never does this. He was of the Shaven Men, I am told. Is this something your god demands of you?"

"It is not a demand of the god," I replied. "It is—" I paused, desperately trying to think how to describe devotion. "It is a thing we do out of gratitude for his care of us."

"Your god gives you food and drink?" hooted the one called Jarn. "Now I have heard everything!"

Talk turned to whether it was worth a man's time to hold to any gods, and which ones were best to worship. Leif insisted that it made no difference whether a man worshipped all of them or none. The debate occupied them for a goodly while, the ale vat supplying the necessary moisture when throats grew hoarse from argument.

Finally, Rägnar turned to me. "Shaven One, what say you? Is it that men should obey the old gods or give them up?"

"The gods you are speaking of," I replied carelessly, "are like the chaff thrown to the pigs; they are the dried grass knotted and burned for kindling. They are worth less than the breath it takes to speak out their names."

They all stared at me. But the öl was making me feel expansive and wise, so I blustered on. "The sun has set on their day, and it will not rise again."

"Hoo! Hoo!" cried Jarn derisively. "Hear him! We have a *thul* among us now. Hoo!"

"Quiet, Jarn," growled Rägnar Yellow Hair. "I would hear his answer, for this question has vexed me sorely many years." When silence had been enforced, he turned to me. "Speak more. I am listening."

"The god I serve is the Most High God," I told them. Jarn snorted at my presumption, but I ignored him and blundered on, mangling the few words at my disposal, but pushing on regardless. "This God is the Creator of all that is, and ruler of all Heaven and Earth, and of the unseen realms, both above and below. He is not worshipped by way of stone images or wooden idols, but in the heart and spirit of those who humble themselves before him. It is ever his desire to befriend and welcome the people who call upon his name."

Leif spoke up. "How do you know this? Has anyone ever seen this god of yours? Has anyone ever spoken to him, eaten with him, drunk with him?" He took a long pull on his cup. The others reinforced themselves likewise.

"Ah!" I answered. "Many years ago, this very thing came to pass. God himself came down from his Great Hall. He took flesh and was born as an infant, grew to manhood and astonished everyone with his wisdom and the wonders he performed. Many people believed and followed him."

"Wonders?" sneered Jarn. "What are these wonders?"

"He brought dead people back to life, restored sight to men born blind, gave the deaf to hear. He touched the sick with his hands and they were healed. Once, at a wedding feast, he even turned water into öl—"

"*That* is a god worthy of worship!" cried Leif enthusiastically.

"Heya, but the jarls and truth-singers of that land could not abide his presence," I continued. "Despite the good things he did and taught, the skalds of the kings feared him. So, one dark night, up they leapt and seized him and dragged him before the Roman Magister; they accused him falsely and demanded that he be put to death."

"Ho!" shouted Gunnar, growing excited by the tale. "But his followers raised the battle cry and descended upon the Romans and slew them. They cut off their heads and hands, and made a feast for the crows."

"Alas," I informed him sadly, "his followers were not warriors."

"Nay? What were they then, jarls?"

"Neither were they lords. They were fisherfolk," I told him.

"Fisherfolk!" hooted Jarn, who acted as if he had never heard anything so funny.

"Yes, fisherfolk and shepherds and the like," I replied. "Thus, when the Romans seized him, all his followers scattered to the hills lest they should be caught and tortured and put to death also."

"Ha!" laughed Rägnar scornfully. "I would not have run away. I would have driven them down with my spear and axe. I would have stood before them with my shield and fought them like a man."

"What happened to this God-man?" wondered Gunnar.

"The skalds and Romans killed him."

"What are you saying!" cried Leif, aghast with incredulity. "Is it that this god of yours was killed by the Romans? If he was truly creator of the world, he could take any form he wished. Why did he not change himself into a fire and burn them up? Could he not seize them and crush them with his mighty strength? Could he not send the death wind among them and slay his enemies in their beds?"

"You are forgetting," I said, "that he had become a man and could do only what a man might do."

"He let them kill him?" hooted Leif. "Even my hound would never allow such a thing."

"Maybe your hound is a better god than the one Aeddan worships," Jarn suggested maliciously. "Perhaps we should all worship Leif's hound instead."

"Is this so?" demanded Rägnar, frowning with concern. "He let the Romans kill him? How could this happen?"

"The Roman warriors chained him and took him out; they stripped him, tied him to a post, and beat him with the iron-tipped lash," I said. "They beat him so hard the flesh came off his bones and his blood covered the ground. Even so, he did not cry out."

"That is manful, at least," put in Gunnar, much impressed. "I am certain Leif's hound could not do that."

"Then, when he was already half dead, they laid a timber door post on his shoulders and made him carry it naked through the city, all the way to Skull Hill."

"The Romans are cowardly dogs," spat Rägnar. "Everyone knows this."

"The Romans took him and laid him on the ground . . ." Putting aside my cup, I lay down and stretched myself in the cross position. "While a warrior knelt on his arms and legs, another took up a hammer and spike, and nailed each arm and leg to the timber beam. Then they hoisted him up and stuck the beam in the ground, leaving him to hang there until he died."

My listeners gaped.

"While he hung high above the ground, the sky grew dark. The wind blew fierce. The thunder roared through the sky-vault."

"Did he turn into a storm and strike them all dead with thunderbolts?" wondered Gunnar wistfully.

"Nay," I said.

"What did he do?" asked Jarn suspiciously.

"He died." I closed my eyes and let my limbs go limp.

"It is just as well," sniffed Jarn. "If your god is so weak and useless as that."

"Odin once sacrificed himself in such a way," Rägnar pointed out. "He hung on the World Tree for nine days and nights, allowing his flesh to be consumed by ravens and owls."

"What good is a dead god?" asked Leif. "I have never understood that."

"Ah, now you have hit upon the most important point," I told them. "For after he was well and truly dead, the skalds caused him to be taken down; they put him in a cave and sealed the entrance of the cave with a huge stone—a stone so big not even ten strong men could shift it. This they did because they feared him even in death. And they made the Roman warriors to stand guard over the tomb lest anything should happen."

"Did anything happen?" Rägnar asked doubtfully.

"He came back to life." I leaped up from the ground, much to the astonishment of my listeners. "Three days after he died, he rose again, and broke out of the cave—but not before he had descended into the underworld and freed all the slaves of *Hel.*" I used their word, for it very nearly signified the same thing: a place of tortured souls.

This impressed them greatly. "Heya," nodded Rägnar in approval. "And did he wreak vengeance on the skalds and Romans who killed him?"

"Not even then did he demand the blood price. In this he showed his true lordship: for he is a god of righteousness, not revenge—life and not death. And from before the ages of the world he had established loving kindness as the rooftree of his hall. He is alive now, and for ever more. So whoever calls upon his name will be saved out of death and the torment of Hel."

"If he is alive," demanded Jarn scornfully, "where is he now? Have you seen him?"

"Many have seen him," I replied, "for he does often reveal himself to those who diligently seek him. But his kingdom is in heaven where he is building a great hall wherein all his people can gather for the marriage feast when he returns to earth to take his bride."

"When is he returning?" asked Rägnar.

"Soon," I said. "And when he returns the dead will come back to life and he will judge everyone. Those who have practised wickedness and treachery against him, he will exile to Hel where they will mourn for ever that they did not heed him well when they had the chance."

"What of those who held to him?" asked Leif.

"To those who have shown him fealty," I explained, "he will grant everlasting life. And they will join him in the heavenly hall where there will be feasting and celebrating for ever."

My listeners liked this idea. "This hall must be very big to hold so many people," observed Gunnar.

"Valhalla is large," offered Rägnar helpfully.

"It is bigger than Valhalla," I said confidently.

"If it is so big, how can he build it by himself?" wondered Leif.

"He is a god, Leif," answered Gunnar. "Gods, as we know, can do these things."

"Also," I added, "he has seven times seven hosts of angels to help him."

"Who are these angels?" asked Rägnar.

"They are the champions of heaven," I told him. "And they are led by a chieftain called Michael who carries a sword of fire."

"I have heard of this one," put in Gunnar. "My swineherd Helmuth speaks of him often."

"He cannot be much of a god if fisherfolk and swineherds can call upon him," scoffed Jarn.

"Anyone may call upon him," I said. "Kings and jarls, free men and women, children and slaves."

"I would not hold to any god my slave worshipped," Jarn insisted.

"Has this god a name?" asked Leif.

"His name is Jesu," I said. "Also called the Christ, a word which means jarl in the tongue of the Greekmen."

"You speak well for this god of yours," Rägnar said; Gunnar and Tolar nodded. "I am persuaded that this is a matter worthy of further consideration."

They all agreed that it was just that: a matter worthy of further consideration. And such deep cogitation required the aid of öl, to which they applied themselves forthwith. Such strenuous thought, it was then suggested, should not be undertaken without the strength provided by a full stomach; it would be folly to even contemplate such a task without proper sustenance. Thus, the talk quickly turned to who should go and fetch the meat which was soon to be coming off the spits.

In the end, Gunnar, Leif and I went to claim our portion of the meat. We ate and drank amiably, and I fell asleep thinking that, whatever else happened to me in the days to come, my time among the barbarians had not been entirely wasted.

# 22

The next morning, King Harald held court in the ring of stones. Anyone with a grievance, or anyone seeking redress, could come before him for a judgement. This custom is roughly similar to the way it is done with the Irish kings and their people. Perhaps it is the same everywhere; I cannot say. But I understood the process well enough just by watching how the people behaved: they came before the king, sometimes singly, sometimes in pairs, with their supporters behind them for encouragement. They then declared the nature of their grievance and beseeched the king, who sat upon a wooden plank resting on two stones, for his decision.

King Harald seemed to enjoy the proceedings, leaning forward eagerly, hands on knees, listening to the complaints, and making up his mind, often very quickly after only a few questions. I watched the faces of those who went before him, and most often the people appeared to come away satisfied with the justice they had received.

Several times, however, there were scowls and dark mutterings as the aggrieved stumped off to lick their wounds. That is also the way of it in Éire, for it is not possible, even in all fairness, to please everyone, and there is no pleasing some people ever.

As we stood waiting for our turn, I wondered whether Gunnar would be pleased with his judgement, for it was the king himself he held to fault. What would Harald Bull-Roar do?

When called at last, Gunnar strode forth boldly, pulling me along and making me stand beside him. The king looked at me, and his glance put me in mind of our previous meeting; something of the same curious thoughtfulness appeared in his expression.

Lifting a hand to Gunnar, he recognized my master as a free man of Rägnar's tribe and asked him what it was that concerned him. Gunnar answered forthrightly, saying that it was a matter of grievous concern, involving nothing less than the murder of a trusted and long-serving slave.

The king agreed that this was indeed a serious affair. "It would seem," said the king, "a matter for grave consideration." He paused long enough for those gathered around to enjoy his wit, and then said, "You call it murder, why?"

Gunnar replied that he called it murder indeed when a man's slaves were attacked by armed men—indeed, king's men!—attacked and killed without cause. "Odd did not have a weapon," he concluded. "Not even a rock."

"Now that you bring it before me," Harald replied, "I seem to recall that I sent two karlar into that region and only one returned. Perhaps you can tell me how this happened."

Gunnar, anticipating the question, had his answer ready. "During the attack, my good hound killed the man who murdered my slave. For this my hound was killed also. Thus, you can see that I have lost a hound and a slave for no reason. It is not a loss I can easily bear."

The king was not swift to agree with Gunnar, but

allowed that hounds did not kill king's men unless provoked. "Who provoked the hound?"

"The karlar," Gunnar answered.

"And who loosed the hound?" asked Harald, suggesting that he knew more about this incident than he had revealed.

"This man, my slave," said Gunnar, indicating me. "He loosed the hound."

Harald Bull-Roar's eyes became hard and his features grew rigid. "Is this so?" he demanded.

I think he expected me to deny it, or to try to explain it away somehow. It took him aback when I simply replied, "It is true."

"Did you know the hound would kill my man?"

"No, lord," I answered.

"Did you think it might happen?"

"Yes."

"You thought the hound might kill a king's man," Harald's voice grew angry and loud, "and yet you loosed the dog anyway?"

"I thought it would be no bad thing if the hound stopped the karlar from killing Odd."

At this, Harald grew puzzled. I think he had made up his mind how this would be settled, but my admission had put a slightly different face on the thing and he now wondered what to do. Looking away from me, he said to Gunnar: "You have lost a slave, and I have lost a warrior. I will pay you for your slave—"

"And hound," added Gunnar respectfully.

"I will pay you for the loss of your slave and hound," Harald said, "and you will pay me for the loss of my warrior. I will tell you now, my warrior was worth twenty gold pieces. Your slave, I think, was not worth half so much."

"No lord." The colour had drained from Gunnar's face;

he was no longer so eager for justice as he had been only moments before.

"How much then?" demanded the king.

"Eight pieces of silver," Gunnar suggested.

"Five, perhaps?" wondered the king.

"Six," allowed Gunnar. "And six for the hound."

"If we grant that twelve pieces of silver are worth two of gold, you still owe me eighteen gold pieces for the death of my warrior," said the king. "Pay me now and the matter is settled."

"Lord," said Gunnar ruefully, "I have never held so great a sum in all my wealth, nor has my father, nor his father before him. Not even Rägnar Yellow Hair has so much gold." On sudden inspiration, he added, "All we have, we give to you in tribute."

King Harald dismissed this with an impatient wave of his hand. "I care nothing for that. We have made a bargain. You must find the way to pay your part, heya?"

"Though I sell all I have, I could never raise so much wealth," Gunnar said.

Harald seemed to soften then; he lifted a hand to his chin and appeared to consider what could be done to help Gunnar out of his predicament. He granted that it was not good to leave affairs like this unsettled, and conceded that the attack had been fomented by his karlar in the first place.

"Taking this into account," he concluded, "I will not demand the full blood price. The gift of your slave will suffice."

Gunnar, not quite believing his good fortune, made no further protest but agreed at once, lest the king change his mind. Harald summoned one of his men, who stepped to the king's rough throne. The king put out his hand and the warrior gave him a leather bag from which the king withdrew a handful of silver coins. "I would not have you think ill of your king," he said and, selecting a few coins from his hand, motioned for Gunnar and me to approach.

"For the loss of your slave," Harald said, pouring six silver coins into Gunnar's outstretched hands. Then, as if thinking better of his offer, he took three more coins and added these to the others. "For your hound," the king said, and gave Gunnar six more silver pieces. "Heya?"

Gunnar glanced at me and shrugged. "Heya," he replied, greatly relieved. With a flick of the king's hand, my master retreated gratefully, tucking his silver into his belt. The warrior stepped up and took me by the arm; I was brought to the king's throne. Harald Bull-Roar reached out, seized hold of my slave collar and pulled me down to my knees.

"You are my slave now," he said. "Do you understand this?"

I indicated my submission with a bow of my head, whereupon I was hauled to my feet and shoved roughly back behind the king and made to stand with the king's other servants. Even as I was struggling to adjust to this startling turn of fortune, I was thinking that the king had planned his justice very carefully. I think that from the moment he had seen me on the riverbank, he had begun scheming and this was the result.

I found my place among the king's following of serving men and slaves. Once out of sight, the king seemed to lose interest in me and, since no one gave me anything to do, I stayed out of the way and observed the ordering of his court. I learned little for my effort, however, for there was no order to anything.

At the conclusion of the theng the next morning, everyone bade farewell to friends and kinsmen, most of whom would not be seen again until the next summons brought them all back to the council ring. The forest trails round about echoed with the sounds of homewarding

Danefolk calling to one another, and whooping with loud exuberance at the heady prospect of sailing into fame and fortune with Harald Bull-Roar.

For, before dismissing them to their various journeys, the king had stood at the fierce dragon prow of his handsome ship and restated the terms of his offer: anyone who followed him to Miklagård would be exempt from paying tribute for five years and would also gain a share in the treasure to be won. Sure, most of the free men and nobles had pledged to join the king straightaway.

Most, I say, but not all. Rägnar Yellow Hair did not pledge his support and, following their lord's reluctance, neither had Gunnar or Tolar, nor several of Rägnar's house karlar, though these, it must be said, were less than pleased with their jarl's opposition to the plan.

When the last of the people had gone, the king boarded his ship and we started down the river. I found a place at the rail and watched the theng-place disappear behind us. Sorrow overwhelmed me at the thought that I would never see Ylva or Karin again, nor Helmuth, nor little Ulf, nor even Gunnar. They had been good to me, and I never had the chance to bid them fare well. I did what I could, however, and prayed for them, and asked the Lord Christ to send an angel to be with them. As I did not know what kind of master Jarl Harald might be, I prayed for myself, too, that I would prove worthy of my calling.

After three days, travelling both day and night, we arrived at the river mouth and, after another day's travel north and east along the coast, came to the king's holding at a tiny bay called *Bjorvika*: little more than an armed camp with a low turf wall raised around a double handful of mud-and-thatch houses, and a stout timber dock for his ships, of which there were three. The dragon longship was the largest, but the other two had twenty benches each.

The king's holding, I soon learned, was but one of

three. In addition to his port, Harald maintained a summer settlement, with fields and cattle, and a winter holding where he drank and hunted during the cold months. As he planned to sail from Skania with the next full moon, the king had brought only those people he would need to the port settlement; the rest remained elsewhere.

In the days to follow, I roamed the holding at will, and even explored the furthest extent of the small cove without raising objection. Occasionally, I was given some small chore to do—carrying wood, fetching water, or feeding the pigs. One morning, two of the king's men came and replaced my leather collar with one of iron, whereupon they took it into their heads to beat me. They hit me and kicked me so hard I lost consciousness and could hardly walk for three days. Otherwise, I was left to myself. This, despite the fact that everyone was busy dawn to dusk readying supplies and provisions for the king's great raiding journey.

For myself, I determined that I would use my time to improve my mastery of the Danefolk speech as much as I could, and I rehearsed that uncouth tongue until my lips grew limp and my head ached. Even so, time hung heavy on me, and I thought often of Gunnar and his family, and wished I was back with them.

The season turned, passing swiftly from summer to a chill, damp autumn. The wind changed and blew more insistently from the north and east; the sun sank ever lower in the sky. I marked the changes and occupied myself as best I could, being careful to stay out of the warriors' way lest any of them take the opportunity to beat me again. Then, two days before the king was to leave, he suddenly remembered me, and I was summoned by one of the karlar to his hall.

Harald's hall was much like Rägnar's—slightly larger, perhaps, but essentially the same. Nor was there much difference in the affairs conducted there. The hearth was large and accommodating, the benches long, the board wide and perpetually filled with men eating and drinking any time of the day or night. Unlike Rägnar, however, Harald Bull-Roar had an oaken throne established at the south side of the hearth; the back of this huge chair was shaped like a great shield, with boss and studs of polished bronze, and a rim of silver secured with golden nails. The king's bare feet rested on a low stool covered with the white winter pelts of young seals.

The warrior pushed me before the throne and left without a word. The king, who was talking to one of the advisors forever clustered about the throne, saw me out of the corner of his eye and sent his confidant away. Placing his hands on his knees, Harald stared at me in no friendly way, slowly squinting his eyes as if what he saw standing before him was not altogether to his liking.

"They tell me," he said after a moment, "that you speak to yourself. Why is this?"

I answered straightaway. "It is to learn the ways of the Danefolk speech."

He pursed his lips, accepting this answer without comment. Then, as if making an observation: "You are of the Shaven Ones."

As no answer seemed required of me, I remained silent.

"Do you understand what I am saying to you now?" the king demanded.

"Yes, jarl," I replied. "I understand."

"Then make an answer."

"It is true, lord, I am of the Shaven Ones."

"And do you know the making of *runor*?"

"Lord, forgive me, I do not know this word. What is runor?"

The king puffed his cheeks in exasperation. "*Runor* . . .

runor! Like this—" Harald clicked his fingers impatiently. One of his men produced a rolled-up skin, which the king unrolled and thrust at me.

I looked at it and saw that it was a crudely drawn map with a list of settlements down one side; next to each settlement was a terse description of the people who lived in the region and the trade to be had there. It was written in Latin, and I told the king that if these were what he called runor, then, yes, I could indeed read them without difficulty.

If I thought this would please Jarl Harald, I was mistaken. He snapped his fingers again and another scroll appeared. "And this?" he demanded, throwing the roll at me.

Unwrapping the roll, I gazed at the antiquated document. "This I can read also," I told him.

"Tell me what is written there," he said, making of the request a challenge.

Glancing at the parchment again, I saw that it was a tally of some sort—such as might be made of goods in a storehouse; it was written in Greek. I shared this observation with the king, whereupon he said, "Nay, nay. Speak it out."

I began to do so, but had only uttered half a dozen words, when he stopped me. "Nay! Tell it in Danespeak."

"Forgive me, jarl," I said, and began again. "Barley, six bags . . . salt bacon, three sides . . . oil of olives, seven small casks . . ."

"Enough," said Harald distractedly. He looked at me hard, as if trying to decide whether to press me further, or banish me from his sight forever. After a moment, he appeared to resolve something within himself, for he lifted his hand and summoned two of his karlar, who approached carrying a wooden trove box; the box was bound in iron bands and had an odd peaked top like the roof of a house.

The treasure box was opened and a square object wrapped in cloth lifted out, and placed in the king's hands. Harald took the cloth-wrapped bundle into his lap and began unwrapping the long binding strips. I caught a glint of silver as one by one the strips of cloth fell away. Then the king was holding the thing and beckoning me forward.

I do not know what I expected to see. But the sight that met my eyes made my heart leap into my throat. I gasped at the sight of it, and stared in heart-sick astonishment at the object in his hands. For there, almost within my very grasp, lay the cumtach of Colum Cille.

Not the whole book, no—that would have held no interest to a marauding Sea Wolf—but the great book's gem-crusted silver cover was more than pleasing to their greedy eyes.

*Kyrie eleison*, I breathed. *Lord have mercy! Christ have mercy!*

King Harald opened the cover and I saw that a few leaves yet remained—three or perhaps four, not many; likely, they had come away in the haste of pillage. To my holy horror, the king took one of these pages and cut it from the others with his knife. It was all I could do to keep from crying out. The Book of Colum Cille was desecrated.

"Speak it," said the king, offering the sacred page to me.

But I could not speak. With trembling fingers I lifted the fragment to my eyes—one of the initial pages of the Gospel known as Matthew's Book—and looked once more upon the richly glowing colours and the impossibly intricate braiding of the knotwork cross, the spirals and keys and triscs—all the while thinking: Great Father, forgive them, they know not what they do.

"Speak it!" commanded the king again, more sternly this time.

Mastering my distress, I forced myself to calmness

under the king's gaze. It would not do, I thought, to allow
him to see that I held any knowledge of the book. Even
then, my very heart breaking, I reckoned my best hope of
remaining close to the treasure was to betray no attach-
ment.

Turning the page in my hands, I scanned the lines—
the page was one of those written in our own abbey. I
opened my mouth and read out the passage—I do not
know what I read. The words swam before my eyes, and it
was all I could to do keep my hand steady. One line, and
then another—my voice ringing hollow in my ears: "Now
when Jesu was born in Bethlehem in Judea during the
reign of Herod the King, behold, Magi from the East came
to Jerusalem—"

"Enough!" roared Harald, as if the sound hurt his ears.
He stared at me for a moment, silence coiling at his feet
like a length of rope. The hall grew hushed; everyone
waited to see what he would do.

I stood uncertainly under his gaze, trying to determine
if I had betrayed my knowledge of the book. Though he
regarded me closely, I think it was not myself the king
heeded. Rather, it seemed that some other matter now
preyed on his mind. My reading was perhaps part of his
preoccupation, but not the larger portion.

At last, he lifted a hand abstractedly and gestured me
away. Willing strength to my legs, I turned to leave the
hall, but had not walked more than three paces when he
called me back.

"Shaven One!" he shouted suddenly, as if in
afterthought. "You will come with me to Miklagård."

# 23

The wind was high and the day fair as we rounded the dark brooding headland of the Geats and sailed onto a grey, windscoured sea. I did not know where we were, less yet where we were bound. I had no idea at all where Miklagård might be, nor did I care. I might have been sailing into hell with the devil himself on my back— and it would have made not the whisker of a difference to me.

I stood on the deck of King Harald's ship as a man determined. Having pondered long over it, I had decided that I could not stand aside and allow the sacred cumtach to be defiled by the barbarians. Come what may, I would risk all to preserve the treasure for which my brothers had given their lives.

Alas and woe! Preserving the holy object meant abetting the wickedness of King Harald. Christ have mercy!

Still, man can only do what is given him; this had been given me and this I could do. Harald, I decided, would receive my help so long as it meant I could keep the sacred cumtach within reach. And if by helping him I furthered his hateful schemes, so be it. I would pay for my sins as all men must, but though I forfeit my soul's eternal peace and endure the flames of torment everlasting, I would save the silver cover of Colum Cille's book.

Sadly, the priceless book itself was gone—evil the waste of that fair creation!—but the cumtach remained. What is more, it remained close at hand: Harald had brought the silver book cover with him; he kept it in the peaked box in his shipboard dwelling along with two other caskets full of gold and silver he thought the journey would require.

I cared nothing for the caskets and their treasures, but I meant to watch over that peaked box with the very eyes of an avenging eagle.

Oh, my determination had grown fierce in the harsh certainty of my predicament. All else—my life before, and, yes, ever after—was as nothing beside the hard grit of my new-found fortitude. If the decrees of happenchance required firmness, I would be a rock, a very fortress of resolve.

On the day the four longships sailed from Bjorvika, I hardened my heart to my new vocation: advisor to a marauding Sea Wolf whose gold-lust would consume the lives of many. Harald Bull-Roar meant to seize all he could set hand to, and his grasp was great indeed.

Whether King Harald's plan was madness itself, or pure cunning, could not, with any lasting satisfaction, be decided. Opinion swung all too readily both ways, and often vacillated from one extreme to the other depending on the day and the direction of the wind. When the wind howled cold and raw from the north, everyone grumbled that it was insane to leave the warmth and safety of the hearth so late in the season. When the sun shone fair and the breeze blew brisk from the west or south, they all agreed that no one would expect a raid so late in the season and that this fact alone would win them much plunder from the unsuspecting inhabitants of Miklagård.

Rain or sun, it was all the same to me. I maintained my place in the king's company, anticipating his next command, but keeping my distance. I did my duty, performing my service as a slave, but extending myself no further. If Harald's evil ambition was to be restrained, it would have to be by God's hand, not mine. I was that vessel made for destruction—that jar of promise, perfect from the master potter's hand, but marred in the kiln, and now deserving only to be crushed beneath his heel and cast away.

But God is good. He took pity on me and sent me friends to comfort me. Gunnar and Tolar, anxious to be forgiven five years' tribute, had decided to go to Miklagård after all; as their own lord, Rägnar Yellow Hair, refused to support the king's raiding scheme with either men or ships, they were given places aboard Harald's. This cheered me immensely, for I had missed them more than I knew. And since I was no longer Gunnar's slave, they treated me as one of their own.

We were but two days at sea and I was sitting near the stern with my back to the rail, soaking up a brief ray of sunshine near the end of a rain-riven day, when I heard a voice say, "You are looking sad, Aeddan."

"Am I?" I opened my eyes to see Gunnar, Tolar and another man standing before me. The stranger was tall and fair-haired, his ruddy face well-creased and his pale eyes cast into a permanent squint from gazing at the horizon in every kind of weather.

"You look as if you have lost your only friend," Gunnar said, pursuing his observation.

"I suppose it is because I am missing my nice dry bed in your barn. It is difficult to sleep on the bare board of a bouncing ship."

Gunnar turned to the stranger. "You see? I told you he was Irish."

"He is Irish all right," the man observed placidly. "My

cousin Sven once had an Irish woman. He got her in Birka for six bits of silver and a copper armband. She was a good wife, but had a very bad temper and would not allow him any other women. Always she said that she would gut him like a fish if he even thought of bringing another woman home. This vexed him sorely, I believe. She died after only five years—I think it was a wolf got her, or a wildcat. That was unfortunate for him. Sven could not easily afford another wife like that."

"Unfortunate indeed," I agreed. "You are the king's helmsman. I have seen you with him. I am Aidan."

"And you are the king's new slave," said the stranger. "I have seen you also. Greetings to you, Aeddan. I am Thorkel."

"We have sailed together before—Thorkel, Tolar, and me," Gunnar said. "This is the third time for us, and everyone knows the third time brings very good luck."

Tolar nodded sagely.

"They are saying you are a Christian," the pilot informed me. "They are saying it is bad luck for the king to trust a Christian; they fear it will prove poor raiding once we get to Miklagård." Thorkel paused, distancing himself from the rumour-mongers. "Well, people say many things; most of it is foolishness, of course."

"Aeddan is a priest," Gunnar declared blithely, raising a hand to my overgrown tonsure. "He speaks very well for his god. You should hear him sometime."

"So?" wondered Thorkel. "A Christian priest? I have never seen one before."

"It is true," I affirmed, and resolved to find a razor somewhere and restore my tonsure.

The seaman passed a speculative eye over me, and made up his mind at once. "Well, even so, I cannot think trusting a Christian is any worse than trusting one's luck to the moon and stars, and men do that readily enough. I think you are harmless though."

From this moment, Thorkel and I became friends. As I had no particular duties, I often spent the better part of every day in his company—sometimes sitting on his bench at the tiller, other times standing with him at the rail as he scanned the sea with his keen blue eyes. The tall helmsman undertook to tell me whatever he could about our progress, not that there was always much to tell. Aside from a few vague landmarks—hills, rocks, rivers, farms, and suchlike—there was little to be seen or mentioned.

We plied the wave-worried seas. Autumn storms were gathering and the days were growing cool and short in the northern realms. Thorkel steered a steady course along unfamiliar shores, and the king resolutely resisted any forays into unprotected settlements—not that many opportunities presented themselves; signs of human habitation were few along the darkly forested coast, for we were pursuing the little-known, and less trusted, northern route to our destination. More difficult than the southern route, the northerly course had the singular advantage of shortening the journey; by how much the journey might be reduced was anyone's guess. Some wagered that we would be drinking öl in Harald's hall for the *Jul*, or mid-winter feast. The pessimists among us tended to think it would be high summer once more before we tasted any of the king's beer.

Thus, coursing from headland to islet to promontory, we made our way along the misty coastline, pushing ever eastward. Truly, the Eastern Sea is a friendless expanse of cold black brine traversed only by solitary whales and other monsters of the foam-flecked deeps. I saw no other ships save the three following in our wake.

Twelve days after setting sail, we came to the place Thorkel had begun searching for three days previously: the mouth of the River Dvina. Pausing only long enough for the ships behind to catch us up, we then turned into the deep channel of the river and began the southern course of our voyage.

A peculiar voyage it was, too; for we left sea travel behind and sailed the inland waterways: south down the Dvina and Dnieper, passing through the lands of Gårdarike and Curled and other trackless places, the barbarian realms of the Polotjans and Poljans, Dregovites, Severians, Patzinaks, and Kazars. Twice we were attacked—once in daylight while under sail. Our adversaries rose up out of the reed-beds, yelling shrilly and throwing stones and sticks; when we did not stop, they gave chase along the river, bouncing over the rocky banks on shaggy little ponies—a sight which made the Sea Wolves laugh, and occasioned great mirth for many days after.

The second attack came during the night four days into the great portage over the hills between the Dvina and the deep, long Dnieper. The fight was savage and brutal and lasted until midday. At King Harald's command, Thorkel and I and five others retreated to the longship to guard the sails and stores. I took no part in the fighting, but watched it all from the rail, praying Michael Militant's shielding for Gunnar and Tolar, whom I could see from time to time, toiling amidst the smoke and blood and shouting.

What a peculiar creature is a man, wayward as the wind and just as fickle. Many of these same Sea Wolves had attacked my own dear brothers, killed how many I do not know, ruined our pilgrimage, and stolen our chief treasure—and in similar circumstances. Yet, and yet!—here was I, hands clenched in fervent prayer, pouring out my heart for them, praying with all my might that they should overcome the marauders. It was, I suppose, God's way of showing how far I had fallen. Sure, no additional proof was needed.

Harald lost seventeen men altogether: eleven dead, and

the rest carried off for slaves. The foemen lost far more—scores, I think—but we did not stop to count them, nor did we take slaves. As soon as the battle broke the Sea Wolves hastened to the ships and, taking up the ropes, we moved on until we came to a more sheltered place in an oak grove. There we stayed the day, resting and tending the wounded. At dawn the next morning we continued the portage as if nothing had happened, the previous day's clash all but forgotten.

Few settlements were of any size to warrant attention. One of the few, however, was a timber fortress called Kiev—a trading settlement in the possession of a tribe of Danefolk called *Rhus*, I think. Here we were to exchange some of King Harald's silver for fresh meat and other supplies.

"This Kiev is perhaps a day or two past the shallows," Thorkel informed us a few days after the attack. We had spent the day poling the ships through muddy shoals—a tedious and oppressively tiresome labour. Thorkel, Gunnar, Tolar, and I were sitting at a small campfire on the riverbank beside the ship; we had begun taking our evening meal together, breaking bread with one another and dipping it into the same pot.

Why Harald tolerated this odd communion between his slave and his men, I cannot say. But then, neither had I worked out why he wanted me in the first place. The whole business was inscrutable to me. Still, I took comfort in the familiar companionship of Gunnar and the others; I am not ashamed to say they were my friends.

Although he had never been so far south, Thorkel seemed to know the region well; Gunnar remarked on this, whereupon the pilot smiled and leaned forward confidentially. "I have a skin, you see," he confided, tapping the side of his nose meaningfully. What he meant by this, I soon discovered, was that he had an oiled sheepskin on which was drawn a crude map.

"Here is Kiev," he said, unrolling the skin which he kept inside his shirt. The rivers were black scratches and the settlements brown spots. He placed his finger on one of the spots, and then, moving further down, stabbed at another brown spot. "And here is Miklagård. You see? We are almost there."

"But we have a very long way to go yet," I pointed out.

"Nay," he replied, shaking his head and frowning at my ignorance. "All this," he indicated a blank expanse above Miklagård, "here and here—all this is calm water. We can easily cross that in three or four days if the wind favours us."

He passed the skin to me and I held it to the fire and bent my head low over it. Much worried and wrinkled, the skin was dirty and faded, but there were yet legible a few letters and fragments of Latin words. "How did you come by this map?"

"My father was Thorolf, helmsman to Jarl Knut of the Straying Eye; he bought it from a helmsman in Jomsborg," Thorkel declared proudly. "This fellow got it from a merchant in Frencland—or was it Wenland?—I do not remember which. It is very valuable."

Thorkel's map soon proved its worth. Two days later we arrived at the trading settlement known as Kiev.

# 24

Set on the broad bank of the Dnieper, Kiev had grown from a small Danish trading outpost into a large market town carved out of a forest of birch, beech, and oak, surmounted by a hill on which was erected a large timber fortress where, it was said, the masters of Kiev stowed all the silver they took in trade. Furs of mink, marten, beaver, and black fox, silk cloth from the east, swords and knives, glassware and beads, leather, amber, ivory in walrus tusks and horn of elk and reindeer—all this and more passed up and down the river, and the trading lords of Kiev took their toll in silver *denarii* and gold *solidi*.

There were seven ships moored along the riverbank when we arrived, and two more joined us soon after; these had come up from the south where their crews had spent the summer trading with the Slavs and Bulghars. They were Danemen—some of them were from Sjálland, and others were from Jutland—keen traders all. Indeed, it was Danes from Skania who had settled Kiev to begin with, and most still spoke the Danish tongue, albeit with a strange embellishment.

King Harald ordered his four ships to be roped

together and ten men to stay behind to guard each one, as
he did not trust the other Danes to leave his boats in peace.
Not until he was satisfied with these precautions did he
allow anyone to go ashore, and then not until everyone
had sworn a solemn blood oath not to breathe a word of
our destination, lest any of the other Sea Wolves took it
into their heads to raid the City of Gold and ruin our
chance of taking the citizens by surprise.

Then the king gathered his karlar around him and
made his way into the market. The first thing he did was
buy a goat, a sheep, and four chickens, which he took
directly to a place in the centre of the market surrounded
by a half-circle of tall poles. The ground underfoot was
damp, and the place stank of blood and rot; the skulls of
various animals lay scattered about the open ring of posts.

Harald advanced to the centre of the ring. There,
before an upright post carved with the likeness of a man,
the king threw himself down upon his face. "Jarl Odin," he
cried aloud to make certain everyone heard him, "I have
come from afar with four longships and many good men.
We have come seeking good trade and much plunder. And
now I have brought you this fine offering!"

So saying, he raised himself up, drew his knife and
promptly slit the throats of the animals which his karlar
held for him. Beginning with the goat and the sheep, he
slaughtered the poor beasts and collected some of the
blood in a wooden bowl as it gushed onto the ground; this
blood he smeared on the post and flung onto the surrounding poles. The chickens he beheaded and threw into
the air so that the blood could spatter all around, on the
post and also the poles, which were Lord Odin's wives and
children. When the animals were dead, the king divided up
the carcasses, leaving choice pieces for the god and sending the rest back to the ship for his supper.

This commotion was, I think, performed more for the

purpose of impressing the Kievan merchants than any
desire on Harald's part to honour Odin, Thor, and Freya.
But despite the bawling and thrashing of the animals and
the king's loud proclamations, the bloody sacrifice failed to
elicit even fleeting interest from Kiev's populace. No doubt
the tired spectacle bored them.

The rite observed, King Harald strode confidently into
the marketplace and arranged for water, grain, and salt
pork to be supplied to his ships. The men, meanwhile,
took it in hand to discover the other, less overt—but by no
means less prominent—trade of Kiev. There were large
dwellings at one end of the market square below the
fortress before which were long benches, and on these
benches were assembled a number of young women who,
like everything else in Kiev, were for sale. One could purchase them outright for a price, and many men found suitable wives this way. For a lesser price, however, one might
purchase a small measure of wifely companionship.

It was this companionship which appealed most to the
Sea Wolves. Harald had forbidden anyone to bring a
woman aboard his ships, and anyway most of the men had
wives at home. The king had less prurient concerns on his
mind, however.

He was not seeking trade or companionship, but information. Thorkel had heard it said—and so his map seemed
to indicate—that south of Kiev lay enormous whirlpools
and cataracts which could smash even the strongest ships.
Harald wished to know how these dangers might best be
avoided; he hoped, if possible, to find a guide, or at least to
learn what other traders knew of the river further south.

To this end, Harald wandered the marketplace, pre-
tending to admire the wares and engaging the various
traders in conversation. At the king's behest, Thorkel and I
accompanied him on his sojourn among the merchants in
the event our skills were required. Most of the merchants,

as I say, spoke Danish, or could at least make themselves understood in that tongue. Even so, we learned little for our efforts, as the merchants were interested only in dealing and trade and kept steering any inquiries towards the value and quality of their particular wares. On all other subjects they were reticent to the point of rudeness.

"I am thirsty," Harald declared at last. We had walked the length and breadth of the market, enduring shrugs, silence, and insults for our trouble. "Some öl, I think, will help us decide what to do."

Crossing the market square, we directed ourselves to one of the larger houses, distinguished by the small mountain of ale casks stacked haphazardly outside. Several women were sitting on the bench, watching the activity of the market and enjoying the thin sun. At our approach, they began preening for us, to show their virtues to better advantage, I suppose. They were odd-looking women: black, black hair as fine as spider wisp, and deep dark eyes lightly aslant in full-cheeked faces round as moons, firm-fleshed short limbs with skin the colour of almonds.

The king paused to observe them, but found little to his liking and walked on into the house, which had been constructed on the order of a drinking hall, but with an upper gallery where, from sleeping places like stalls, people could look down on the proceedings below. Long benches lined the walls, with boards and trestles set up around a large square central hearth. A few men sat at the tables eating and drinking; more sat on the benches with jars in their hands. The huge room was loud and murky and dim, for there was neither windhole in the wall, nor smokehole in the roof, and everyone seemed bent on shouting at one another. One step into the room and I felt the gorge rise in my throat from the stink of vomit, dung, and urine. Filthy straw covered the floor, and skinny dogs slunk along the walls and cringed in the far corners.

Harald Bull-Roar had no difficulty in making his presence known. He strode boldly into the room and cried, "Heya! Bring me ōl!" The whole house shook with the force of this demand, and three disheveled men scrambled to serve him—each with a jar of ale and several large cups. They sloshed the rich dark beer into cups and thrust them into our hands. I got one, but Thorkel and Harald got two each, which they guzzled down greedily—to the ardent encouragement of the jar-bearers, who vied with one another to keep our cups supplied.

I drank my first bowl at once, and then sipped the second slowly and looked around. There were men from many different tribes and races, most of them new to me: big, burly, fair-haired men dressed in pelts; short swarthy men with quick slender hands and hooded eyes above noses like hawk beaks; long-limbed, slender pale-skinned men in long, loose-fitting clothes and soft boots of dyed leather; and others whose appearance made me think of arid desert places. The only tribes I recognized were either men from our own ships, or other Danes. There were no Britons or Irish at all.

As the king and Thorkel drank, they let their feet take them where they would. The king's boldness and conspicuous good will drew other northmen to him, and he soon had assembled an amiable group of sailors and river traders. From these he began coaxing the information he sought. "You must be brave men indeed," the king observed, "if you have been in the south. For it is said that only the bravest boatmen dare face the rapids south of Kiev."

"Oh, they are not so bad," boasted one great shaggy Dane who smelled of beargrease. "I have twice been as far as the Black Sea this summer."

"Ah, Snorri!" chortled his companion. "Twice, to be sure, but once was on the back of a horse!"

"The other time was with a ship." The big man bristled. "And difficult it is to say which is the more dangerous."

"They say," continued Harald, directing more ale into the cups, "there are ten cataracts, each larger than the last, and each big enough to swallow ships whole."

"It is true," said Snorri solemnly.

"Nay," said the small man with him, "there are not so many as that—four perhaps."

"Seven at least," amended Snorri.

"Maybe five," put in someone else. "But only three are large enough to swamp a ship."

"What do you know of this, Gutrik?" big Snorri challenged. "You stayed all summer in Novgorod with toothache."

"I went there seven summers ago," Gutrik said. "There were but four cataracts then and I do not think the river has changed so much."

"If only your memory was as reliable as the river," taunted another man lightly. "I myself have seen six."

"Of course, six," sneered an increasingly belligerent Snorri, "if you count the little ones as well. I myself took no notice of them at all."

Thorkel, though still holding cups in both hands, drank from neither, but listened to each man intently, trying to patch a whole truth from the various scraps each man contributed. "I am beginning to think that none of them have been down the river at all," he whispered to Harald at last.

"Then that is what we must discover," replied the king. Turning to the men, who now numbered seven or so, he said, "You all speak like men of considerable experience. But, aside from Snorri, who has been down the river this very summer?"

Each one looked to the other and, when they found no

answer, gazed into their cups. Then the man called Gutrik spoke up. "Njord has been downriver," he declared. "He has just returned with the ships this very day."

"Heya," they all agreed, "Njord is the very man for you."

"Find Njord," Gutrik assured us, "and you will learn all there is to know about the Dnieper. No man knows it better."

"A piece of silver for the first man to bring this Njord to me," said the king, withdrawing a small silver coin from his belt. "And another if that be soon."

Three of the men disappeared at once, and we settled back to wait. Thorkel and the king continued to talk to the rest, but I grew curious and looked around. It soon became apparent that the house had much more to offer than food and drink. From time to time, one of the women from the bench outside would enter, towing a seafarer behind her. Sometimes they would go up to the gallery to one of the sleeping stalls and lie down together; more often they would simply find a seat on one of the benches along the wall and copulate in full sight of anyone who cared to look.

This happened so casually, and occasioned so little notice from anyone that it might have been pigs or dogs in heat, rather than human beings. I saw a man enter the house and go directly to his friend who was engaged in such intercourse. The two exchanged greetings and spoke for a few moments, then the first man sat down on the bench beside the amorous couple while his friend continued the sexual act to its consummation, whereupon the two men then changed places and the second man took up where the first man had left off.

The iniquity of it was breathtaking. I could only shake my head in despair. But they were barbarians, after all. It did me good to remember this from time to time.

As it happened, Njord was similarly occupied in another house nearby. When he had finished his drink and his woman, he came along with Gutrik, who claimed his silver by presenting the pilot to King Harald saying, "The best helmsman from the White Sea to the Black stands before you. I give you Njord the Deep-Minded."

The man who stood before the king could not have been less impressive. A wizened stick demands greater consideration. Njord was a hump-shouldered, long-boned, jug-eared Dane with skin creased and tanned to leather from the wind and sea salt; like Thorkel, he was squint-eyed, and his long moustache all but covered his mouth. His hands were rough from the ropes and tiller, and his stance splay-footed from maintaining his balance on the slanted boards of a heaving hull. The hair on his head had been blasted to a mere grizzled wisp of sun-faded grey. He looked like a gristle-bone the dogs had gnawed clean and discarded.

"Greetings, friend," bawled the king. "We have been hearing of your skill and knowledge from your friends. They speak most highly of your shipwise abilities."

"If they do me honour, my thanks to them," replied the pilot with a small bow of his round, grizzled head. "If they do me insult, my curse on them. I am Njord, Jarl Harald, and my best greetings to you."

"Friend," said the king expansively, "it would cheer me to have you drink with me. Cup bearers, be about your work! More öl! Our bowls are empty and our throats are dry!" Turning to Njord, he said, "All this talk has made me hungry, too. Let us sit down and eat together, and you can tell me of your journeys."

"A man must be careful when sitting down with kings," observed Njord narrowly, "for it is a costly business paid out in life and limb."

I understood then why he was called Deep-Minded, for it soon became apparent that he believed himself a philosopher with a gift for expressing his insights in witty aphorisms.

The men around him stared, but the king threw back his head and laughed. "Too true, I fear," Harald conceded happily. "But let us hazard health and fortune, heya? Who can say but it may prove worth the risk."

Thorkel and I found a place for the king and his strange new friend. Gutrik, Snorri and the rest joined us, shoving aside others in order to remain near enough to reach the meat and ale that soon began appearing on the board. So we settled down for a meal that stretched all the way to dusk, and ended with the king and Njord exchanging solemn, if drunken, vows: the pilot to guide us past the treacherous cataracts, and the king to reward him handsomely out of the proceeds of his business venture. The precise nature of this venture, I noticed, Harald failed to articulate.

The small matter of Njord's obligation to lead his own jarl's ships on their homeward voyage was quickly overcome when Harald offered to repay the pilot's share of the summer's spoils as compensation for the loss of his services. The ship's master was summoned and quickly agreed; the bargain was struck on the spot.

Having obtained all he came for and more, the king was now eager to depart. Up he rose from the table, and hastened for the door, trailing a considerable body of serving men, each demanding payment and shouting at the top of his lungs to make himself heard above the others. The king's progress was halted at the door; he turned and reached into his belt and brought out a handful of silver. This he delivered to the foremost server, saying, "Share this out among yourselves as you deem best."

The serving men gaped in astonishment at the paltry reward and shouted all the more loudly. "This is our reward?" they shrieked incredulously. "A whole day's food and drink, for *this*?"

But the king merely raised his hand in admonishment as he stepped through the door. "Nay, I will hear no word of thanks. For the pleasure was mine alone. Farewell, my friends."

Njord nodded his head in admiration of Harald's aplomb. "There breathes a king indeed," he muttered.

Even though it meant exchanging one stench for another, it was good to be quit of the drinking hall, I thought, as we passed the wooden post of Odin with its rancid gifts. A whole day weltering in the sun had made the putrefying sacrifices most pungent. Yet, on the whole, the stink of rotting meat was preferable to the noisome stew of smoke, sweat, faeces, sour beer and vomit dished up in the drinking hall.

There was no one aboard ship but the guards—not the same ten who had been left behind to watch the vessels, for these had been replaced earlier in the day by kinsmen who had sated themselves on both cup and copulation, and who were now fast asleep on deck. The sleeping men were roused and commanded to retrieve their fellow shipmates.

Separating the Sea Wolves from the delights of Kiev proved far more difficult than anyone could have foreseen. The pleasure houses were large and contained many rooms—some of which were completely enclosed, for those seeking more private expression of the carnal arts—and each house and room had to be searched and the seafarer led or, more often, carried back to the waiting ships.

The moon had risen and gained its peak by the time all Harald's raiders were assembled once more and the ships pushed away from the bank. Fortunately, rowing was not required; the southward flow of the river carried us along. Thus, no one was forced to grapple an oar and disaster was held at bay.

The next day, however, we were not so fortunate.

Below Kiev the Dnieper passed through ragged hills that squeezed the river into a swift-running stream carving its way through high stone banks barely wide enough to admit the ships. Sure, an oar held either side would have been scraped to splinters. It was all Thorkel could do to keep the keels centred in the deepest part of the channel. All day long he wore a brow-furrowed haunted look, as if he expected calamity to overtake us at any moment. Njord, on the other hand, spent the day with his head under his cloak, sleeping off the revel of the night before.

When he finally emerged, the worst of the passage was behind us and the water had grown placid once more. "Ah, you see now," he declared, looking around, "this is splendid. I think you are a true helmsman, friend Thorkel. Your skill is equal to mine in every respect save one." He declined to say what the singular lack might be, but went on to pronounce upon the seaworthiness of the ship instead. "Oh, but it is a fine ship, heya? I think so. Stout-masted, but easy on the tiller—a fine longship all in all."

"We have always thought as much," replied Thorkel a little stiffly. "But I am glad to hear you say it."

"In three days the contest begins, however," Njord continued. "The first cataracts are not so bad—little more than rapids. We shall go through four of them very easily, for the water is not so swift this time of year. When the spring rains flood the valleys, it is an entirely different matter. We have good reason to thank our stars it is not spring."

"What of the remaining cataracts?" wondered Thorkel.

"Every man acquires debts," answered Njord cryptically, "but only a fool borrows trouble." He walked away, running his hands over the smooth rail.

"I did not care to borrow it so much as to merely catch a far-off glimpse," muttered the pilot.

The Lord Christ himself said that each day's cares are sufficient to the day and that tomorrow's worries are best left for the morrow. This I told Thorkel, who only blew his nose at the notion and would not speak to me the rest of the day.

# 25

The first three cataracts were mastered with poles. As Njord had predicted, the water was low in the pinched crevices through which the river pushed its way to the Black Sea. Using the ends of the oars, we poled the boats slowly around the rocks—now bracing, now guiding, now pushing—until we reached calm water again. By the time we had cleared the third cataract, King Harald was wishing he had not brought so many ships with him; after the fourth, he was contemplating the wisdom of leaving two boats behind and retrieving them later.

Greed awakened just in time to persuade him that he would need all his ships to carry the plundered wealth of Miklagård away, and that, if anything, he was foolish not to have brought more and even larger vessels.

The fifth and sixth cataracts taxed the strength and endurance of every crewman, save the king and ten warriors who stood on the bank to guard the supplies against ambush. A devious local tribe known as the Patzinaks liked, according to Njord, nothing more than to lie in wait where the boats were most vulnerable.

Toting burden after burden, I aided the laborious process as each vessel was beached and unloaded: every grain sack and water butt, each cooking pot, every spear and sword, all the ropes and sails and rowing benches. When every vessel was but an empty hull, the men stripped off their clothes and waded naked out into the swirling, waist-deep water where they shouldered the ropes—some at the bow and others amidships—and with brute force hauled the unwieldy vessels along. Some of the crewmen employed oars to fend the hulls off the nearer rocks, and the whole party proceeded slowly, keeping as close to the bank as possible to avoid being swept out into swifter water and thrown against the sheer rocks. Once the ships were safely past the danger, all the supplies and weapons were trundled downriver and loaded into the craft once more.

This labour occupied the whole of two days for each cataract. And if the first six were not bad enough, the seventh cataract was by far the worst. Not only were there rocks and whirlpools, but also two falls to be traversed. Njord, who had until now been less help than the king thought sufficient, was not forthcoming with a ready solution.

"What are we to do?" demanded the king, growing impatient in the face of the impossible task before us.

"A man may journey by many roads," observed Njord sagely, "but only one way leads to his destination."

"Yes, yes," growled Harald. "That is why I have brought you with me. Show us the way to go."

Njord nodded, his narrow eyes became slits, and his teeth gnawed his lower lip as if he were working out a complicated calculation. "It is difficult," the grizzled pilot conceded at last. "Your ships are too big."

"What is this!" roared the king, making the earth tremble with the force of his cry. "Have I taken you this far only to be told my ships are too big?"

"It is not *my* fault your ships are too big," Njord answered petulantly.

If ever a man stood on sinking sand, Njord was that man; yet, he seemed oblivious to the danger he faced at that moment. "If you had asked me," the pilot sniffed, "I would have told you."

"Is there anything which you will yet tell me?" wondered the king, his voice menacing and low. I could almost hear the knife sliding from its sheath.

Njord pursed his lips and stared at the water with an expression of deep inscrutability. "If the mountain is too tall to climb," he pronounced suddenly, "then you must go around." Turning to the king, he said, "Since you ask my advice, I tell you the ships must be carried."

The king gaped at him in disbelief.

"Impossible!" cried Thorkel, unable to contain himself any longer. He thrust himself forward to appeal to the king. "Strike his worthless head from his shoulders and be done with him. I will do the deed gladly."

Njord's frown deepened. "If this is how you would repay the best advice you will hear the whole length of this river, then give me my part of the reward now and I will be gone from your sight."

"No," said the king firmly, "you will stay. The ships are here, little thanks to you. Now it is for you to earn your silver and get them safely across the cataract, for that is what you agreed to do. Fail in this and you will have the reward you deserve."

Emboldened by these words, the slight pilot stirred himself from his indolence and began ordering the preparation of the boats. "Stand you aside," he said, "and watch well what I shall do."

As before, the ships were emptied. Then Njord began to display the acumen for which he was acclaimed, but of which we had heretofore seen so little demonstration. He ordered the oars to be removed and the masts struck. He commanded tall fir trees to be cut from the forest and trimmed of all branches; other trees were cut to use as levers. Then the empty hulls were pulled from the river and dragged with ropes over the bank on the round logs.

It must be said that, once begun, Njord warmed to his task and acquitted himself well. He seemed always to know just the right place where a lever would be needed, and could foresee difficulties before they arose and took steps to overcome them, or at least mitigate their severity. By day's end we had one ship beyond the rapids and another half way along.

That night we camped on the bank and commenced again the next morning in a chill rain which began at daybreak. The rain made the task more difficult, for the paths grew muddy and the men's feet slipped, and the wet poles were difficult to grip. However, the remaining vessels were smaller than the king's longship, and could be moved more quickly and with somewhat less effort. Night found us with the last two ships more than half way along the dry course. At dawn the Patzinaks attacked.

King Harald was the first to perceive the danger, and it was his bull roar which roused the work-weary Danemen from their sleep. If not for this, I have no doubt we would have been slaughtered where we lay. Up we rose as one man, spears in hand—for raiding Sea Wolves always sleep with a weapon ready, especially when on land.

The Patzinaks were small and dark and shrewd, striking with quick, furious thrusts of their wide-bladed spears and axes before darting away again. All the dodging and feinting made them hard to hit. This frustrated the Sea Wolves, who much preferred a foe to stand his ground and trade blow for blow. The Patzinaks had encountered Danemen before, however, and had learned best how to deal with a more powerful opponent.

Harald saw how they meant to wear down his men, or perhaps through frustration to draw them into a fatal blunder, so he signalled his men to retreat to the ships and make their stand on the riverbank. There, with backs to the solid oak hulls, they stood to face the feisty Patzinaks.

When the foemen saw that the Sea Wolves would no longer be drawn into the open, they soon lost interest in pursuing the fight further. But, far from discouraged, they simply changed their stratagem; retreating a short way off, they held council and elected an envoy to proceed under the sign of the willow branch.

As the envoy approached, the king motioned me to him. "We will speak to them, you and I," he said. "Though I think we will hear little to our liking."

When the Patzinak party had come within fifty paces, they halted and waited for us. The king, ten of his house karlar, and myself went out to meet them. The king, frowning mightily, scanned the ranks of foemen, sharp disdain furrowing his brow and making his lip curl.

Up spoke the envoy's leader, uttering an unintelligible stream of gibberish. When this produced no effect, he tried another tongue, which was, if anything, even more incomprehensible than the first. Seeing that neither of us understood him, he abandoned this speech and tried yet a third: "I give you good greeting, men," he said in sorry Latin.

This I understood well enough and replied in kind, telling Harald what he said.

"We see that you are not afraid to fight," the envoy continued smoothly. "Therefore, it has pleased our lord to allow you to pass through our lands unmolested."

I repeated his words to King Harald, whose response was ready. "Your lord has a most peculiar way of expressing his pleasure," the king grumbled. "Yet, I have been worse hindered. Fortunate for your lord and for all who follow him that I have lost no men, for we would certainly be having a very different manner of discussion at this moment."

"That is indeed true, Your Greatness. For this, you can thank my lord, who ever extends his hands in brotherhood to those who desire his friendship." The envoy, a slight dark man who was missing most of his right ear, paused, smiled affably, and added, "Of course, such friendship is best established with due and proper consideration." He rubbed the palm of his right hand with the fingertips of the left.

"It seems to me," replied Harald, once I had conveyed the envoy's words to him, "that your lord extends his hands for a more tangible reward than brotherhood alone."

The envoy smiled and shrugged. "The demands of friendship are many, and not without obligations of their own. A man of your undoubted eminence must certainly find this to be so."

King Harald shook his head when he heard this. "They are cheerful thieves," he told me. "Ask them how much silver it will take to establish this bond of friendship between us."

I asked, and the envoy answered: "It is not for me to say, Gracious King. Rather look at your men and ships and weigh their worth in your sight. As you are a man of obvious rank, I am certain you will behave accordingly."

Harald considered this and summoned one of his karlar who hastened back to the longship, returning on the run with a small leather bag. Reaching into the bag, the king drew out a silver armband.

"This is for friendship," he said, placing the silver in the Patzinak envoy's outstretched hand. "And this," Harald continued, reaching in again, "is for the friendship of my men." He placed a smooth-polished yellow gem in the envoy's hand. "And this," he said, reaching into the bag a third time, "is for the future good will between our peoples should we happen to pass this way again." He placed a green gem beside the yellow one, then closed the bag and passed it back to his man.

"I would have thought," said the envoy, peering disappointedly at the objects in his hand, "that a man of your estimable worth would have placed a much higher value on the friendship between our peoples."

"I desire only the merest acquaintance," was Harald's retort. "I do not wish to marry your lord or any of his people, agreeable though they may be."

The Patzinak envoy did not like this. He sighed and pulled on his chin, gazing at the loot in his hands and shaking his head sadly from side to side as if he were contemplating a tragic mistake. "I am loath to believe," he said at last, dropping the treasure into the bag at his side, "that your new friends hold so little value in your eyes. I fear it is most distressing. No doubt when my lord hears of the small esteem in which you hold him, he will require additional blandishments."

"How foolish of me," replied Harald upon my relation of these words, "I have forgotten to mention that in addition to the silver and gems which you have so swiftly hidden from sight, I am also giving you and your wealth-lusting lord the gift of your lives." The Sea Wolf king paused to await the effect his words would have; and when the envoy raised protest against this line of reasoning, Harald said, "What? Do you place so little value on your own heads?"

With that, he drew his axe and prepared to signal his men to renew the fight. The Patzinak envoy gaped at him and said, "Now that I understand you better, I am amply persuaded of your earnest desire for our friendship. Therefore, I will endeavour to present your generous offer to our lord. Still, I would remind you that you must pass this way again when you return home. And I would beg you to consider well what manner of welcome you wish to receive upon your return."

"Let us find what we find," growled Harald, growing tired of the game.

"Then go your way," the Patzinak envoy said. "I will tell my lord to prepare the welcome you deserve."

"That is my fondest wish," replied Harald, drawing his thumb along the edge of his axe.

"So be it." With that, the envoy signalled to his men and they withdrew at once.

"That was well done, jarl," said one of Harald's men. "Will they attack again do you think?"

"I think not," replied Harald. "We have purchased safe conduct this time. But we are forewarned: next time it will be more costly."

Returning to the ships, we prepared to continue on our way. By day's end all four ships were once again in the water and drifting peacefully downriver. As the moon was bright enough to steer by, we did not rest, but continued on through the night. Daybreak found us far away from the Patzinak lands, and well beyond the last of the obstacles standing between King Harald Bull-Roar and the City of Gold.

# PART TWO

*May the Everlasting Christ*
*Go before you all your days,*
*And take you in his loving clasp,*
*Whether braving storm-torn Western seas,*
*Or treading death-dark streets in*
*The Golden Cities of the East.*

# 26

The Black Sea, so far as I could tell, was no darker than any other I had seen, and when the sun shone the surface of the water gleamed like polished jade. But the sun was a rare visitor, for the days were often grey and the dawn mist which lay thick on the water now remained well past midday. Still, the air was warmer than I would have imagined; and if it grew chill at night, when the sun shone it grew almost pleasant.

By what I could see from the longship's rail, I reckoned we had come to a land of tight-clustered hills. The hills, rising dull brown beyond the cragged shore were not high, but they were dense with small, shrubby trees and thorny bushes. Sometimes I glimpsed bony sheep picking their way among the prickly branches, searching for food, but I did not see any people.

Harald, considering his fleet more than a match for any foe, proceeded boldly, sailing by day and coving at night. One evening the wood gatherers returned to camp with some of the peculiar sheep: tall, rangy, thin-haunched, long-necked, with mottled fleeces of brown and grey—more goat than sheep, to look at them. We slaughtered the beasts and put them to roast on spits over the campfires. The meat was strong and tough, and the burning tallow made our eyes water. None of the men could stomach the fare. Even Hrothgar gave up after a while, saying his belt would be more tender, and would no doubt taste better. After that miserable meal, no one troubled the sheep any more.

The experience put me in mind of Christ's parable. It could be no easy task to separate those sheep from goats; it would take a shepherd who knew his flock and could call them by name. Sure, it would take a good shepherd.

Several times, early in the morning, we saw fishing boats; small craft, carrying only two or three men who plied the water with long oars, they presented no interest to the Sea Wolves, who sailed by without molesting them. When, after sailing three days, we came in sight of our first settlement, Harald gave orders that no one should turn aside to plunder. With the prospect of unlimited wealth now almost within reach, he did not care to waste his efforts on such small pickings.

"They can have nothing worth taking," he said, frowning with disdain. "Besides, we can always sack them on the way home."

Over the next days, the settlements grew more numerous. Feeling that we must be getting near to Miklagård, the king exercised greater caution in his approach. Accordingly, we sheltered in coves during the day, emerging at dusk to sail the misty waters until dawn. I took my place beside Thorkel at the tiller, watching the sky. Though the sea lay deep-misted and obscure beneath a mantle white and dense as wool, the sky shone bright with stars beyond measure.

All night long we watched the dazzling sky, ablaze with unfamiliar stars. Contemplating this wonder, Dugal's words came back to me: the very stars in the sky are strange.

*Oh, Dugal, if you could only see them,* I thought. I would give anything for you to stand on this deck beside me with your eyes straining heavenward and the starlight on your handsome face.

"We are near," Thorkel said, pointing out over the rail to the west.

I looked and saw the lights of a fair-sized settlement, the glow of hearthfire, candle, and rushlight from a hundred or more dwellings—some huddled low, near the shore, and others scattered higher in the hills.

I did not see why this should mean that we were any nearer our destination. "Do you know this place?" I wondered.

No, Thorkel said; he had never seen it before. So, I asked him how it was that he thought a settlement on the sea betokened nearness to Miklagård.

"For a Sea Wolf, you have much to learn," Thorkel replied. "People do not build a settlement on the water unless they are secure behind the defences of a wall."

Squinting my eyes, I searched the shoreline, stark in the silver of bright starlight. "You are mistaken, Thorkel. I see no wall."

The tall pilot smiled. "Miklagård," he said, "is their wall."

He spoke the truth, for the next night we passed between two close headlands and entered a narrow steep-sided strait. As daylight broke in a milky haze in the east, the great city itself stood revealed. We all gathered at the rail to gaze upon this awesome sight. I looked out across the dawn-misted sea to a settlement of vast extent, flung upon the humped backs of seven hills: great domes of palaces pushing head and shoulders over tight-clustered white dwellings—like the rounded crests of mountains soaring above the clouds—all gleaming in the dawnlight like stars sown upon the earthly firmament.

A strange feeling of recognition came over me as I stared out across the water. Dull dread began pulsing through me with the quickening beat of my heart.

Turning to Thorkel, I said, "This is never Miklagård."

"How not?" he replied. "There are not two such cities in all the world."

"But I know this place," I insisted, the recognition strong in me now.

"That could be," the pilot allowed sagely, "for it goes by many names." He lifted a hand to the city-spread hills. "This is the renowned City of Gold, Constan's City—"

"Constantinople," I said, growing numb from crown to sole.

"Heya," Thorkel agreed amiably.

"Byzantium." The word was a whisper of disbelief on my fear-numbed lips.

"That is a word I do not know," the helmsman said. "For the Danes it is always Miklagård."

I passed a trembling hand over my face. I was a doomed man, sure; and a stupid man also. Thinking I had escaped the dire consequence of my dream, I had instead sailed straight to it.

But there was no time for ruing my fate. Harald, seeing the nearness of his prize, ordered the warriors to ready the attack. His bull voice bawled a dizzy stream of commands which were repeated on the other ships. Within moments, barbarians were dashing about the decks of all four ships pulling on armour and dressing themselves for battle. The clatter of the commotion was horrendous.

I saw Gunnar darting amidst the confusion and called to him. "Aeddan!" he cried. "Today we fill our troves with treasure, heya!"

*Yes, and today I die,* I thought. Death awaits me in Byzantium. To Gunnar, I said, "But the king cannot expect to attack the city now. Would it not be better to wait until dark?"

"Nay," he answered, jerking tight the lacings of his mail shirt. "We would get lost in a city so big after dark. How would we find the treasure houses? Better to attack now while the city still sleeps."

"But the guards will see us." My voice sounded shrill and frantic in my ears.

"And the sight of us will frighten them so they will throw wide the gates of the city."

"At the sight of you, Gunnar Warhammer," said a nearby barbarian, "they will certainly bring out the treasure by the wagon load."

The warriors fell to arguing about who would carry away the most plunder in the day's looting, who was the bravest and who the most timid, who would achieve renown and who earn disgrace, and which weighed more, an iron battlehelm or a sceptre of gold. This banter was accompanied by loud shouts and outrageous boasting. They were, I noticed, growing more and more excited all the while; and it came to me that they were rousing themselves to battle heat. By the time we reached the shore, they would be slavering Sea Wolves.

I retreated to my place by the mast and hunkered down. I did not know what else to do. Of course, I would not fight, nor take part in the looting. If I had any thought at all it was to stay aboard the ship and keep out of sight. Perhaps if I did not set foot on Byzantine soil, I would not die.

Even that bare hope was taken from me, however, when King Harald, magnificent in his battledress, emerged from his tented platform and saw me crouching at the mast. "You!" he shouted. "Aeddan! Come here."

I rose and went to him. Oh, the king was splendid: his hair was bound beneath a leather cap; iron bands encircled his arms, and his shirt was fine-ringed mail; on his hip he wore both a sword and a long knife; from his belt hung an iron war axe; he carried a short, thrusting spear in one hand, and a warhelm in the other.

"I want you beside me," he said gruffly. "For when I seize the ruler of Miklagård, I will need you to translate his surrender for me."

My heart sank in the sick feeling spreading through me. Not only would I set foot in Byzantium, I would be in the first rank. What is more, alone of all the attackers, I would have no weapons and no shield with which to defend myself.

*This is how I will be killed,* I thought. I will be cut down in the forefront of the attack. When the spears and arrows of the defenders began whistling around our heads, I would be among the first to fall.

Harald glanced at the sky. "It is a fine day for a fight," he announced, placing the warhelm upon his head. "Come men," he cried, stepping to the mast. "To oars! To oars! Let the weak tremble in their beds and curse their day of birth! Let the strong make ready their graves! Let all men fear the Sea Wolves' cry!"

The gold-lust was on them now; they leapt to the oars and began rowing toward the shore. I crouched beside the mast, leaning against the solid oak for strength, praying the Kyrie over and over under my breath. "Lord, have mercy! Christ, have mercy! Lord, have mercy! Christ, have mercy! . . ."

All around me, men, gleaming hard in their war array, bent themselves over the oars, driving the ships to the rhythm of our swift-beating hearts. With every dip and pull of the oars, the hills of Byzantium drew nearer.

Harald Bull-Roar stood on his platform, feet wide, swinging his war axe over his head and calling cadence to the rowers. Deep voice booming like a drum, he bellowed, banking his warriors' courage high, inflaming their blood-lust with crude exhortations:

"Cold strake cuts wave!" he cried. "Axe-Wielder swiftly glides! Curved hull pushes wave! Sword-Striker hastens to the weapon storm!

"Doomed skulls roll! Severed limbs twitch! Hungry death delights in the battle banquet!

"Come, wolf! Come, raven! The meat-feast awaits! Drink deep of the red cup in the Worm King's hall!"

Raving like a madman, the king roared, whipping himself and his men into a battle frenzy.

"Gold-Giver, Ale-Pourer, Rich Provider, I am Jarl Harald Bull-Roar! Attend me Corpse-Makers, Hewers of Men, for I will deliver wealth into your hands. I will cause rivers of gold to flow over the Champion's feet, and showers of silver to fall from the skies!

"Steel-Clashers! Sword-Breakers! Widow-Makers! Hasten now to glory. Follow your Wealth-Thrower to the Hero's Hearth where cool gold quenches battle heat. Fly! Fly! Fly!"

Faster and faster we flew, the knife-edge dragon prow slicing through the calm water. Did ever a man hasten so to his death?

Constantinople, unsuspecting in the milky dawn, drew ever closer—as if it were the city flying towards us rather than the other way. I seemed to see death sweeping nearer with every oar-stroke, and yet I could not take my eyes from that place. The closer we came, the larger it grew: a colossus, a seven-humped wonder on its vast splayed thumb of a peninsula thrust into the sea. Soon I could see the dark seams of streets like tangled cords winding among the masses of square white dwellings. A filthy pall hung over the heights—smoke from hearthfires beyond counting, drifting, coiling, gathering in a thick brown pall of billows.

We drove swiftly on, making directly for the nearest landfall. Even from the sea, however, we could see the city's high protecting wall rising straight from the water. Harald was not dismayed; he directed the ships onward for a closer look. But what he saw dashed cold water on his overheated scheme. For, rising up like a sheer red cliff-face from the water's edge, stretching out of sight to either hand, encircling the entire city stood a thick curtain of brick and stone ten men high. On the water below, small tenders ferried tradestuff to and fro along the waterfront.

One look at the size and extent of Byzantium's wall, and the Sea Wolves faltered. I could feel the shock of discovery course through the ship like the tremor of an unexpected wave. Harald bawled for the longships to halt, and suddenly rowers were dragging their oars in a desperate attempt to slow our forward flight. The last vessel did not receive Harald's command until too late, causing it to collide with the one just ahead. A dozen oars on both boats were snapped and broken, and rowers cursed and writhed in pain, clutching injured limbs. The resulting confusion brought howls of outrage.

Ignoring the fuss, Harald, standing high on his platform, scanned the wall. Some of the small tenders, seeing our sudden approach, hastened to draw near, jostling among themselves to be the first to reach us—thinking, I suppose, that we had trade goods to unload. Each would be the first to provide this service.

As the tenders drew closer, the men aboard hailed us in Greek. It had been long since I had heard this language spoken aloud, and it sounded strange in my ears. Still, I was able to pick out a few words and phrases from the thick gabble of voices.

Suddenly, angrily, Harald called out to me. "What are they saying?" he demanded.

"They are offering to unload our ships," I replied, moving to the rail. "They say they will do this for fifty *nomismi*."

"Unload our ships!" the king cried. "What is this nomismi?"

"I do not know—money, I think."

"Tell them who we are!" the king commanded. "Tell them we have come to sack the city. Tell them we are after wealth and plunder."

Leaning over the rail, I called to the nearest boat in which two men with white woollen caps stood beseeching us loudly. I told the men that these ships belonged to Lord Harald, who was a fierce warrior, and that we had come from Daneland in search of wealth. The boatmen laughed at this, and called to some of their friends in other craft, who also laughed. I heard the word *barbari* relayed from boat to boat. They then told me how matters stood in the emperor's harbour.

"What do they say?" asked Harald gruffly, his patience wearing thin.

"They say *everyone* comes to Byzantium seeking wealth," I answered. "They say there are no more berths in the harbour, and you dare go no further unless you are prepared to meet the guards of the harbour master."

"To *hel* with their harbour master," growled Harald. Whirling away, he ordered the rowers to proceed up the channel along the northern shore.

We continued on our way, more slowly this time, and accompanied by a score of small craft, each with boatmen shouting and hailing us in shrill voices. Numerous vessels, large and small, thronged the way and it was all Thorkel could do to steer us through the obstruction without colliding with one or another of them. Hence, we proceeded with much shouting and cursing and waving of arms, using the oars as much for shoving other craft out of the way as for rowing. The commotion accompanying our tedious progress was deafening, the upset complete.

The ships had not travelled very far, however, when we came upon an enormous iron chain. Fixed to gargantuan rings set in the wall, the chain—each link as big as an ox!—stretched across the entire channel from one bank to the other, closing the waterway to all larger craft. Small boats could pass easily under this chain, but the longships of the Sea Wolves were halted within sight of many fine houses and several palaces.

Perplexed, frustrated, Harald Bull-Roar, King of the Danes, gaped at the chain in disbelief. Not knowing anything else to do, he ordered some of the warriors to destroy it. Leaning from the rails, the barbarians began chopping at the nearest links with their axes. The attack made no impression on the ponderous barrier, and the men soon gave up altogether. Even prodding it with oars, they could not so much as make the great chain swing.

King Harald commanded his pilot to turn the ships and follow the shoreline south, thinking to find some weakness in the city's defences the other way. The rowers renewed their labour, although with somewhat less zeal than before, for the inner waters were far more crowded with ships and boats. Pushing through them all was a torturous tactic, but the Sea Wolves persevered, and eventually rounded the peninsula to find a busy port with not one but three or more harbours, and the largest of these was, like the rest of the city, protected by high walls.

Harald ordered Thorkel to make for the first of the harbours, and we soon came within sight of the quay, but could go no further for the number of ships and small craft jamming the harbour entrance. The king was still puzzling what to do next when a large, square-hulled boat approached. This boat contained ten or more men dressed in fine red cloaks, and carrying spears and small round shields; they wore ornate helmets of burnished bronze on their heads, and short red breeches which ended just above the tops of their tall leather shoes.

The foremost man of the group was a short man who made himself appear taller by way of a high horsetail crest on his helmet; he stood at the prow of their boat holding a rod with a bronze ball on the end. This fellow began hailing us and gesticulating with the rod; those with him called out in loud angry voices.

Some of the Sea Wolves laughed at the presumption of these men; thinking they had come to fight us, the Danes began taunting them, shouting, "Is this the mighty warhost of Miklagård?" and "Who are these maidens we see before us? Have they come with kisses to greet us?"

Squinting with suspicion, Jarl Harald glared at the men in the boat. "Find out what they are saying," he demanded, shoving me roughly towards the rail.

I hailed the leader of the men in Greek, and he made a reasonable reply. I thanked him for speaking simply and slowly, for my tongue was not accustomed to such speech, and told him I would convey his words to the king.

"I am the *quaestor* of Hormisdas Harbour," the man said importantly, and told me simply and directly what to tell the king.

"Well?" rumbled Harald impatiently. Sweat was running down his face and neck, for the sun had climbed past mid-morning and now shone as a hot, dirty disk in a grey-white sky.

"The man says you must pay the harbour tax," I said, and explained that the men in the boat were part of the harbour guard charged with collecting money and keeping order.

"But did you tell them who I am?" growled Harald.

"I told them. They say it makes no difference, you must pay the harbour tax like everyone else."

"To hel with their harbour tax!" roared Harald, giving

vent to his frustration at last. "We will lay siege to the city and starve them into submission!"

This sentiment brought grunts and growls of approval from barbarians looking on. They, like their lord, were frustrated and anxious. The size of the city dismayed them, and they sought release for their consternation in familiar, if foolish, action.

"A siege is a fine thing, of course," observed Thorkel mildly. "But it is such a large city, Jarl Harald, and we have only a hundred and sixty men with us. Even if we had ten times as many, I fear we would be hard-pressed to surround it."

Harald, glaring hard, made to dismiss his pilot, but one of the king's house karlar spoke up. "Perhaps it would go better with us," he suggested gently, "if we were to pay this tax and seek entry into the treasure houses some other way."

"I am a king!" bellowed Harald. "I receive tribute from jarls and free men. I pay tribute to no one."

Nodding sympathetically, Thorkel stepped near his lord. "Nay, jarl," he suggested, "do not say it is tribute. Think of it as casting a little grain to fatten the goose for the feast."

Harald looked at the enormous walls, and cast an eye over the wide sweep of the busy bay. There then came the sound of something heavy knocking against the hull of the ship. I peered over the rail to see the harbour guard striking the side of our ship with his ball-tipped rod.

"We cannot stay here all day," he said. "Pay the tax or I will summon the guard ship."

I replied that we were discussing how best to make this payment, and asked for a few moments in which to make our decision. To the king I said, "They are demanding an answer, Jarl Harald. What will you do?"

He stood paralysed by indecision, gazing up at the city walls which seemed to loom over us like a high range of mountains barring our destination. After a few moments, the guard resumed his assault on the hull of the longship.

He shouted words to the effect that we were rousing the wrath of the emperor, and stood in danger of increasing the tax by our refusal to pay. This, I told to the king.

"Agh!" cried the king in frustration. "A man cannot think with all this din. How much?" he shouted. "How much to send them away?"

Leaning over the rail once more, I asked how much was required. "Four hundred and fifty nomismi," answered the guard. "One hundred for each of the small ships, and one hundred and fifty for the large."

Harald agreed reluctantly, and gave me a silver coin which he pulled from his belt. "Ask him its worth," the king ordered, and summoned one of his karlar to bring a purse from his trove box.

I stepped to the rail and held up the coin. "We are ready to pay the tax now," I said. "Please, tell me how much this silver coin is worth."

The quaestor rolled his eyes elaborately and replied, "I will come aboard your ship." So saying, he and two of his men, assisted by others in the boat, climbed to the rail and were soon standing before the barbarian king.

"The coin," demanded the tax collector, thrusting out his hand, "give it to me."

Placing the coin in his outstretched hand, I said, "The man you see before you is Harald, King of the Danes of Skania. He has come to pay his respects to the emperor.

The harbour guard made a sound through his nose as if this information meant nothing to him. "He may pay what he likes to the emperor," replied the man, examining the silver in his hand, "but first he must pay the quaestor." Holding up the coin, he said, "This silver denarius is worth ten nomismi."

I counted out the twenty coins Harald had given me, and then turned to the king. "We have paid two hundred," I told him, "we must pay two hundred and fifty more."

Harald, frowning mightily, emptied the remaining coins into his hand, counted them, and ordered another purse to be brought; from this he extracted seven more coins and gave them to me also. The Sea Wolves looked on, amazed and aghast that their king should be giving silver to this upstart of a fellow.

When I had counted twenty-five additional denarii into the tax man's hand, he said, "Two more."

"Two more?" I wondered. "Have I miscounted them?"

"No, you have counted correctly." Reaching into my hand he took up a coin. "This," he said, "is for keeping me waiting." Then, taking another coin: "And this is for causing a disturbance in the harbour."

"I most heartily apologize," I answered. "We were unaware of the customs of this place."

"Now you know," replied the quaestor, tucking the coins into his purse. Then, reaching into a pouch at his belt, he withdrew a thin copper disk. "Nail this to the prow," he instructed. "It shows that you have paid the tax."

With a flick of his hand, he turned and, aided by his two men, began lowering himself over the rail. Glancing at the disk, on which was embossed the image of a ship under sail, I asked, "Please, I would know when we must pay again."

"You are free to come and go in the harbour until year's end," the tax man replied without looking back. "Should you return to Constantinople after that, you must pay again."

Upon offering this information to the king, Harald scowled fiercely and declared that by year's end he intended to be back in his own hall enjoying the wealth he had taken in the plunder of Miklagård. This plundering, he vowed, would commence without further delay.

Seizing me by the arm, the king put his sweaty face near mine. "And *you*, Shaven One," he growled, his voice thick with threat, "will lead us to the nearest treasure house."

# 27

In order to plunder a treasure house, it would be necessary to go into the city and find one. Various ways of accomplishing this strategy were discussed and in the end it was decided that, to avoid arousing the suspicions of the populace, only three or four warriors should go ashore and search out the best places to attack. Further, it was decided that since I alone spoke the language of the place, albeit poorly, I should lead the landing party.

Strangely, the thought of setting foot in Byzantium did not alarm me overmuch. The shock at finding myself arrived at the place of my death had quickly faded, and a sense of resignation to the inevitable settled in its place. I felt as if I were being pulled along by events too complex to understand, and too powerful to resist. I was a leaf tossed in the gale, a feather cast onto the storm-maddened sea. There was nothing I could do but ride out the tempest.

I prayed to the Heavenly Father to do with me what he would. I also prayed that I might somehow be spared aiding King Harald in his odious scheme of theft and slaughter. Having struggled through all things to remain a good monk worthy of the Célé Dé, I did not wish to begin a life of crime now—so close to the Judgement Seat, as it were. Far better, I decided firmly, to die opposing Harald than to approach the Throne of Heaven reeking of sin, with the blood of innocents on my hands.

It came to me that *this* was how I would die—with the king's sword at my throat, as punishment for refusing to accompany him ashore. The thought produced not fear, but despair, for it seemed a cruelly meaningless end to life. God be praised, my despair was short-lived. Jarl Harald considered scouting duty beneath him, preferring instead to remain on the ship awaiting our return. "Three of my karlar will serve me in this," he said, and turned his attention to choosing who should go.

He summoned the man who had suggested paying the harbour tax—his name was Hnefi, and the king trusted him for the sagacity of his advice; Harald also called forth a warrior called Orm the Red, who, in addition to being adept with sword and spear, was light of foot and stealthy. The king was on the point of selecting the third member of the party when I suggested that it might serve our purpose to have at least one warrior I knew and trusted, who could speak to the others should the need arise.

Harald, his patience growing brittle once more, asked if I knew such a man. I told him I did, and named Gunnar. "Very well," the jarl agreed impulsively, "let Gunnar Warhammer go with you."

Thus, we four found ourselves clambering over the side of the longship and into one of the many small boats still jostling one another for our service. Dropping into the boat, I told the boatman that we desired to be put ashore at the nearest city gate.

"A wise choice, my friend," the boatman said agreeably. "Rest yourself and worry for nothing. You will soon be there. My name is Didimus Pisidia, and I am at your service. You have chosen well, for this is the best boat in all

Byzantium. I will pray to God your wisdom is rewarded a hundredfold."

"I thank you, friend Didimus," I replied, and confided that as we knew nothing of Constantinople, we would be grateful for any guidance he might be able to offer.

"Ah, you are the most fortunate of men," the boatman replied, "for you are in the presence of one to whom the city is a Garden of Delight. You may place your full confidence in me. I will certainly give you the best guidance you could desire, never fear."

Hnefi and Orm dropped into the boat just then. Orm, supposing it his duty to show me my place, pushed me roughly aside. Unsteady in the small boat, I fell against the side. "Say nothing!" he warned. "I am watching you."

Gunnar, coming behind them, interceded for me, saying, "Let him be, Orm. He is the king's slave, not yours."

"Tell this man to take us to the nearest gate," Hnefi ordered, settling himself in the bottom of the boat.

"I have already done so," I replied. "This is what I was doing when Orm struck me."

Hnefi nodded curtly. "I am the leader now," he said. "You will do what I tell you." He gestured to the watching Didimus and said, "Now tell this worthless fellow to get about his work or we will gut him like a fish."

To Didimus I said, "We are ready to proceed now, if you please."

"It is my pleasure," answered the boatman, pushing away from the longship with his hands. "Sit down, my friends, and worry for nothing. This is the best boat in all Byzantium." He took up the long oar at the stern and, standing with his foot on a bench, waggled the oar back and forth. The boat turned and drew away from the longship.

Those watching from the rail called out for us not to carry off all the treasure, but to save some plunder for them. Orm answered by blowing his nose at them, and Hnefi told them their time would be better spent looking to their weapons than worrying about us.

Gunnar settled himself beside me against the curved side of the boat. "Why did you choose me?" he asked.

"I thought it might be helpful to have someone I could trust beside me." As he made no reply, I asked, "Why? Would you rather have stayed behind, Gunnar?"

"Nay," he answered with a shrug, "that is no concern of mine." He looked out at the city for a moment, and then glanced at me sideways. "I thought you might have a different reason."

"Quiet!" snarled Orm. He kicked me with the toe of his boot.

"Orm," said Hnefi, "I am the leader here. If you cannot remember that, I will leave you in the boat while we go and find the treasure."

Orm grumbled and took out his knife and began polishing the blade on his *breecs*. To me, Hnefi said, "Keep your mouth shut. When I want you to speak, I will tell you."

I turned my attention to the city, bobbing nearer with every dip and stroke of Didimus's oar. From the water, very little of Constantinople could be seen—only where the hills raised their heads did I mark any of the city behind the walls. These walls, however, were most impressive. Brick and stone in alternating courses had been used to create an enclosure both high and stout, and bearing a distinctive red-and-white banding, making it like no other wall I had ever seen. Along the top of the wall, people were moving—city guards perhaps, though I was too far away to be certain. Here and there, I could see the tops of trees—a few pines, and the bare branches of others which had lost their leaves.

The sea came up to the very foundations of the wall,

allowing only a very narrow causeway which served a varied collection of stone and timber quays, large and small, new and old; around each of these, ships clustered like feeding piglets crowding one another at the sow.

And such ships! I saw vessels with two and three masts, and some with more than one deck. There were so many different coloured sails, I quickly lost count—and the cargoes of the ships were even more varied. I saw bags and chests, casks and jars and baskets beyond number. Sure, if a boat could carry it over the sea, it would be found in Constantine's city.

Didimus steered a snaky course through the clotted harbour; we passed along the unending quayside, dodging the larger boats and searching for a place to make our landing. As we drew nearer the quays, I became aware of the stink. The water grew foul with garbage and excrement, and refuse of all sorts, for the slops were continually tossed overboard into the bay. This fulsome effluent made for a ready stench as potent as any I had encountered.

Our boatman seemed not to mind, however; he worked the oar with his arms, smiling and singing the while, pointing out any of several landmarks when it occurred to him to do so. Orm and Hnefi watched him with low suspicion and ill-founded contempt, and kept their mouths firmly shut as if they feared revealing the king's loathsome plan.

When at last we bumped against a tier of stone steps fronting the quayside before an enormous gate, I was glad to put the stink of the bay behind me. I turned to thank the boatman, but remembered Hnefi's warning and dutifully held my tongue. Orm stepped from the boat, and Gunnar followed, both seemingly oblivious to Didimus, who was calling to us and holding out his hand for payment.

Hnefi, ignoring the boatman, said, "Come, Shaven

One, you will go before us. I do not want you wandering from sight."

"Forgive me, jarl," I replied, "but we must pay him."

The barbarian regarded the boatman impassively, and said, "Nay." Hnefi turned his back and stepped from the boat without further word, leaving me no choice but to scurry after him.

"Please! Please, my friends," bleated Didimus. "I have given you faithful service. You must pay me now! My friends! Please! Listen to me, you must pay now! Ten nomismi! Only ten!"

I paused on the steps long enough to say, "I am sorry, Didimus. I would pay you, but I have nothing."

Seeing that he would not be paid, Didimus began crying curses at us, and calling for the harbour guards to come and beat us. I ran up the steps with his shouts of "Thieves! Thieves!" burning in my ears.

The three Danemen were waiting for me at the top of the steps. "That was wrong," I complained to Hnefi. "We should have paid him."

Hnefi merely turned away.

"He might have helped us," I insisted. "Now he is calling for the guards to come and beat us. We should give him something."

I felt the sting of Orm's blow against my teeth before I knew he had lifted a hand. "Do what you are told, slave," he told me, shoving me hard. I fell on the stone steps and would have tumbled into the water, but Gunnar grabbed me by the arm and kept me from rolling over the edge.

I climbed to my feet and followed them up the stairs. We walked towards the wall, the Danes moving cautiously, their hands on the pommels of their swords. Pausing at the entrance to the city, Hnefi turned to me and said, "You go first. We will follow."

The gate was a huge double timber door banded with

iron. People were passing through it by the score, many laden with burdens of various kinds—some pushing small two-wheeled carts, and others pulling wagons, but most bearing bundles on their backs. Above the gate hung a red triangle of cloth with a symbol on it sewn in white; I did not recognize the symbol and could not think what it meant.

We joined the throng moving through the gate, and reached the entrance only to be hailed by a man in a green cloak, wearing a round black cap of wool, and carrying a short rod of brass. "Disca!" he cried without enthusiasm. He held out his hand impatiently.

"Forgive me, lord," I said, "I do not know what you want of us."

He turned a weary eye on me, then glanced at the barbarians. If their appearance alarmed him, he hid his fear right well. Noticing my slave collar, he said, "Which of these men is your master?"

"He is," I pointed to Hnefi.

"Tell your master that barbari are required to obtain leave of entry from the Prefect of Law."

"I will tell him," I replied. "Perhaps you could be so kind as to tell me where we may find the Prefect of Law."

Stifling a yawn, he raised the brass rod and pointed to a booth set up in the shadow of the gateway. "Over there."

I thanked the man and explained to the Sea Wolves what he had said. We walked to the booth to find a small, bald-headed man sitting in a cushioned chair beside a table on which sat scales and a pile of small copper discs. I stood before him for a moment without arousing his attention, which seemed to be wholly occupied with a brown spot on his green breecs which he scratched with a long fingernail.

"If you please," I said, "we were told to obtain leave to enter."

"Ten nomismi," he said without looking up.

Turning to Hnefi, I translated what the Prefect of Law had said. Hnefi gave a disapproving grunt and started walking away. Orm and Gunnar hesitated, shrugged, and followed. This brought an immediate response.

The Prefect glanced up, saw the barbarians entering the city and shouted, "Stop!" in a very loud voice. He leaped to his feet and ran after Hnefi. "You must pay!" the bald man shouted. "Ten nomismi!" He shook one of the small copper discs in the Sea Wolf's face.

Hnefi seized the man's hand and relieved him of the disc. He tucked the copper into his belt and continued on his way. The man stared incredulously and then began shouting. "Guards! Guards!"

Ignoring the outcry, the Sea Wolves walked on, and I followed. We had not moved ten paces when we were stopped by eight red-cloaked guardsmen who simply appeared in our path. Each wore a bronze helmet and carried a short, thick spear. Their leader carried a bronze rod, not unlike that of the harbour master save that, instead of a ball on top, the soldier's rod had a lion's head.

"Halt," said the foremost guard—a young man, little more than a shaveling youth, he nevertheless bore himself with an air of placid authority.

"They did not pay!" the old man screeched. "They did not pay for the disca!"

The guardsman looked at the barbarians, and then at me. Choosing me as the more likely to make an answer, he said, "Is this true?"

"I must beg your pardon," I said. "We have only just arrived in your city and know nothing of the customs here. It may be that, through ignorance, we have—"

"Pay him," he said, waving aside my explanation.

"Ten nomismi," said the Prefect, tapping his open palm.

Turning to Hnefi, I said, "They say we must pay for

the copper disc—it is our leave to enter the city. Without it they will take us prisoner and throw us into the hostage pit." I did not know if this last was strictly true, but I thought it might communicate the situation in a way he would best understand.

"If we pay," asked Hnefi, "we will go free?"

"Yes."

Frowning, he reached into the pouch at his belt and brought out a silver denarius which he handed to me. I gave it to the Prefect, who puffed out his cheeks in exasperation. "Have you nothing else?" he demanded.

"Please," I said, "I do not understand. Is it not enough?"

Before the Prefect could reply, the young guardsman answered, "It is too much." Indicating the coin, he said, "The silver denarius is worth one hundred nomismi." To the Prefect, he said, "See you give them the proper amount in return."

Glaring at the guard, the bald man grumbled, took hold of my sleeve and said, "Come this way."

He pulled me with him back to the booth, where he made a great show of placing the single coin in his scales and adjusting the weight. When at last he was satisfied with the heft of our silver, he reached under the booth and brought out a leather bag full of coins—bronze, copper, silver, and gold—and began counting bronze and copper pieces into my hands. The bronze pieces were marked with Greek letters: some with E, some with K, others with M and I. These letters, I supposed, ascribed certain values to the coins; but he counted them so rapidly, I could get no idea what they were.

The Sea Wolves, always keen-eyed for business matters, watched this operation with interest. When the Prefect finished, Hnefi made me give the money to him. "First ten, and now a hundred," he observed, "it seems our silver coins increase their value wonderfully well. Jarl Harald will be hearing of this."

I thought about all the silver we had given the harbour guard, but thought it best not to say anything. Orm needed no reminder, however. "And so will the harbour master, I think."

The Prefect of Law then counted out two more discs, which he gave to Orm and Gunnar. When I held out my hand for one, he shook his head. "It is only for the barbari," he explained, and said that the disc gave them leave to enter the city as often as they liked until the year's end. "But," he warned tartly, "they must use only the Magnaura. All other gates are forbidden to them."

"I understand," I told him. "But tell me, please, which is this Magnaura gate?"

The bald man regarded me with an expression of disgust. "That!" he snapped, flapping his hand at the doorway behind us. "That is the gate you must use. Be off with you!"

He dismissed us then with a curt gesture and settled himself in his chair once more. We continued on our way, moving swiftly past the watching guards. Having purchased the freedom of Byzantium, the barbarians were desirous of discovering just how far this liberty might extend.

## 28

W ithin moments of leaving the gate, we were lost—a fact which did not come to our attention until very much later, however, for we walked the close and winding streets, wandering where curiosity took us, searching for the chief treasure house of the city. What had seemed a simple, straightforward matter aboard the ship was quickly shown to be monumentally complicated when standing in the middle of a road ebbing and flowing with people like a restless tide. Our first attempts to gather our wits provoked angry shouts to get out of the way.

"Move on! Move on!" cried a guardsman who happened by. "You cannot stop here. Move on!"

"He says we must move along," I told the Danes.

"Where should we go?" wondered Gunnar.

"Let us follow that man," suggested Orm, pointing to a fat man trailing a long purple cloak. "He will certainly lead us to a treasure house."

"I am the leader," Hnefi reminded him. "I say we shall go the other way."

Thus we proceeded, progressing deeper into the city until we came to a wide street lined with dwellings which for size and the expense of their construction were not to be equalled. They were very palaces.

"You see!" Hnefi crowed proudly. "I know how to find good treasure. Follow me!"

The greedy Sea Wolves strode boldly, declaring loudly which palace should be raided first and which they thought contained the most wealth—no easy decision, as it happened, for *every* house we saw seemed to possess a grandeur far exceeding any we had ever encountered, and at each and every dwelling the Sea Wolves stood in the street, gazing at the imposing edifice and swearing solemn oaths that here before them stood what was certainly the chief treasure house of the city. And they were happy in this thought until we came to the next.

One street was lined with mansions two and three floors tall, and where the walls of the lowest floor were blank-faced brick, save for the door, the walls of the upper floors boasted windholes covered with glass. I had never seen glass windholes before, but there they were. And on every house in the street! Many of the mansions, if that is what they were, had ornately carved doors, and painted lintels; one or two of these structures boasted carved statuary affixed to plinths beside the windholes. Many were topped with tiled roofs on the slant, but more grand dwellings had flat roofs from which green foliage could be seen. I had heard that wealthy Romans did this, but I had never encountered such wealth before. If that was not enough, nearly every house possessed another feature unknown to me: an extension of the upper floor which overhung the street. These protuberances—remarkably substantial, many of them—were faced with wooden screens which, I suppose, could be opened to allow the cool evening air into the upper rooms.

That a city the size of Constantinople should contain such mansions and palaces was to be expected. But there were scores . . . hundreds! I walked in a daze of disbelief. I could not comprehend such wealth, nor could I imagine whence it came.

The Danes were beside themselves with delight. They argued continually over which palace must contain the most treasure, and which they should plunder first. Orm was for rushing boldly into any or all of them and simply stealing whatever valuables came to hand. Hnefi was of the opinion that King Harald would want to make the decision which house to plunder.

"But Jarl Harald is not here," Orm complained, his reckoning, as ever, unassailable.

"Then we will wait until he arrives." Hnefi was adamant that we should arouse no undue suspicion among the inhabitants of the city. He reasoned that if we began breaking into every house we saw, it would alert the people and they would certainly be on their guard when we returned for the raid. "It is for us to look and discover where the best treasure is to be found," he declared. "We can come and get it tomorrow."

Orm accepted this with some reluctance, saying, "I still think we should take something back to show the king."

Gunnar agreed with Hnefi, and allowed that it would go ill with us if we aroused the wrath of the people. Alone of the Danes, he appeared cowed by the immensity of the city, growing quieter by degrees—as if he would gladly slink away into the shadows.

So we continued, wandering this way and that, looking at the houses and observing the people. In this part of the city we did not see many inhabitants about, and those we did meet seemed to race about their errands with unseemly haste. Perhaps the look of the barbarians frightened them; I cannot say.

Nevertheless, I saw enough of the citizenry to form the

opinion that the Constantinopolitans were in every way an average race: neither very tall nor unduly short; neither exceptionally dark-skinned nor light; in countenance, neither ugly nor remarkably fair. They appeared sturdy of physique, with short strong limbs and compact bodies—more suggestive of vigour than brute power, hardy rather than graceful.

In preference, it appeared the women wore their hair long with the strands wound into coiled tresses; the men were given to full beards which they wore oiled and elaborately curled. Their clothing, for the most part, consisted of a simple cloak worn over a long siarc, or mantle, with voluminous breecs for men, and a gown for women. The cloth of these garments was plain, light-coloured rather than dark, and adorned with brooches and other such jewellery. And everyone, men and women, seemed inordinately fond of hats.

I have never seen a race so given to hats as the people of Byzantium. Everyone who could afford even the most rudimentary covering wore something on his head, be it a scrap of heavy woollen cloth folded into a peak, or strands of straw woven as a sunshade and tied into place with rags. Many of these hats seemed to possess official sanction and were worn as badges of office. Others seemed to be following the dictates of some convention, the sense of which I could not penetrate.

We ambled along in stupefied reverie, gawking at everything, until, "Listen!" hissed Gunnar.

The Sea Wolves stopped as one, and held their breath, listening. "What is it?" wondered Orm, after a moment.

"It sounds like an animal," observed Hnefi. "A large one."

"Nay," said Gunnar. "It is people."

"There must be very many of them," agreed Orm.

"A battle!" cried Hnefi. "This way! Hurry!"

Off they ran towards the sound, clutching their weapons in the hope of winning plunder for themselves. I hurried after them so that I would not be left behind. Ahead of us the street widened and I could see movement and colour in the light beyond.

And then I found myself standing in a market square—the largest, busiest, noisiest market I had ever seen, thronging with hordes of people and all of them bawling at the top of their voices. Merchants stood beneath rich-woven canopies crying the virtues of their wares to one and all, wheedling with their customers in any of six languages while prospective buyers sauntered slowly by, eyeing each item and bargaining with undiluted fervour. Strange battle this, but a form of combat nonetheless. The various sounds of commerce melded together to produce the monstrous din we had heard.

Drawn into the maelstrom, the Danemen stumbled forth, still holding tight to their weapons. I had taken but a half-dozen paces when my eyes watered and I began sneezing. Directly before me was a stall boasting spices the like of which I had never known: deep red and dusty yellow, black, orange, pale green, and white. These mysterious spices were heaped into pyramids of casual abundance: brown mounds of powder that smelled like peppered honey—cinnamon, I learned later; black deeply pungent spikes, which were cloves; three or four kinds of pepper, yellow turmeric, earth-coloured hills of cumin and coriander, bright red chilies ground to fine crimson powder, golden peaks of ground almonds, and little round, stone-coloured beans called chickpeas. The mingled scents created a perfume so intensely pungent I could not see, and had to hurry on.

Beside the spice merchant was the first of many stalls selling green produce. I stopped and stared down the long line of stalls at vegetables of every kind under heaven:

leeks, onions, garlics, lentils, little red objects called capsicums, cucumbers, green finger-like things called okra, cabbages, any of a dozen varieties of beans and squash and melons. Nor was this all. Indeed, it was not even the least part of all I saw. It was as if the whole world had sent its goods to this marketplace: everything from gold and silver to salt and pepper, live animals and Egyptian leather, Macedonian pottery and Syrian wine, magic potions and Holy Icons blessed by the Bishop of Antioch. If one could think of it, there was someone selling it in the market.

One merchant sold only *olives*—fifteen or twenty different varieties! This astonished me more than anything I had seen before. Sure, I could not tell one olive from another in the dark; I had never even seen an olive before. But looking at bowl after bowl of olives—green, black, purple, and more—it occurred to me that any civilization which could concern itself in such detail with such a small and insignificant fruit must possess powers beyond imagining.

Twenty kinds of olives! Think of it!

No king of Éire, however powerful or wealthy, had ever seen, let alone tasted, one solitary olive. Merely undertaking the transportation would have squandered nearly all of Éire's energies and resources. Yet, here in Byzantium, even beggars could eat olives grown in the furthest outposts of the empire. How, I asked myself, was it possible to measure such an achievement? To this, I had no answer.

Unfamiliar with such casual displays of wealth, the market was, for me, less a place of commerce than a revelation of magnificence unrivalled by anything I had known. After but a few moments, I could comprehend no more; and though I continued walking through the marketplace, looking at everything on offer, my mind simply refused to credit it.

As we passed a stall selling brass bowls and cups and other small objects, the merchant suddenly called out in Danespeak: "Heya! Heya! Come here, my friends."

The Sea Wolves stopped and stared at the man. "This man is a Dane!" said Orm.

"Then he is like no Dane I ever met," observed Gunnar.

"He is, I tell you," insisted Orm, who turned and began speaking rapidly to the man, who simply smiled and spread his hands with a shrug.

"Gunnar is right," decided Hnefi, "the man is no Dane."

Disgusted by what they considered a shabby ruse, the Sea Wolves stalked away. But the brass-seller was not the last to hail the barbarians in their own tongue, for as we made our way along the close-set stalls, other merchants called out to us in Danespeak. At first wary, then charmed, the simple feat, repeated so frequently, soon amazed the Sea Wolves almost as much as the wealth on display. They continually stopped to engage the various sellers in conversation—which did not run far beyond the first few words of greeting on the seller's part before lapsing into Greek or, sometimes, Latin, or some other tongue.

Hunger overtook us as we wandered the lavish stalls. Orm complained loudly that the sight of so much food was making him light-headed. Gunnar said that bold plunderers such as we needed sustenance to keep our wits keen and strength ready. Hnefi suggested that the food would not be good for us; unaccustomed to it as we were, it might make us sick. Orm and Gunnar protested so vehemently at this that Hnefi finally relented. Having a bellyache, he said, was far preferable to listening to the others piss and moan about how hungry they were.

Hnefi decided that we should eat nothing more unusual than salt fish; the others agreed, so we went in search of one of the fish-sellers we had seen earlier. While we were looking, however, we happened upon a man standing at a brazier of glowing coals over which he roasted long strips of meat wrapped on long wooden skewers. The meat sputtered in the heat, sending up an aroma that brought water to the mouth.

Orm took one sniff and stopped in his tracks. He and Gunnar stood side by side, transfixed by the sight and smell of the sizzling meat. The man, his face glowing in the heat of the coals, saw that he had acquired interest in his wares, and called out, "Heya! Heya!"

"How much?" asked Hnefi, pointing at the skewers.

The man shook his head.

"How much?" demanded Hnefi, speaking more loudly.

The man simply smiled wide and shrugged his shoulders. "Forgive me, my friend. I do not understand," he said in Greek.

"He is asking how much for one of the spits you have roasting there," I told the man.

"Ah!" he laughed, "a learned slave we have before us. Welcome to Great Constantine's city, my friend."

"How do you know we are newly arrived?" I asked.

The man laughed again and said that everyone else in the world knew very well that the skewers cost two nomismi. "How many would you like, my friend?"

"Four," I replied, and told Hnefi to give him eight of the small brass coins.

When the money was counted over, the man allowed us to choose our skewers. The Danes wolfed down the meat in gulps and demanded more, which the man happily supplied for eight more coins. Taking our meat-sticks, we continued on through the maze of market stalls, chewing the meat from the sticks and looking at all around us. The Danes moved like men in a dream.

As we passed along a row of stalls selling incense and

perfume, our progress was arrested by the sight of a most regally beautiful woman being borne through the market in a chair on poles. Four slaves carried the chair and a fifth held a round sunshade made of stiffened cloth attached to a slender cane. The woman—a queen, certainly—wore a robe of shimmering blue silk; her hair was elaborately curled and heaped high on her elegant head, and her painted face was impassive as she regarded all beneath her.

The Sea Wolves decided to follow her and see where she went, hoping to mark the place so that they could return and plunder it later. So, we followed the chair-bearers from the market as they started down one of the many streets radiating from the square.

The way was narrow and dark, the dwellings so close-built that little light from sun or sky made its way down to the street. Men hurried to and fro, or stood in huddled clumps talking to one another; some glanced at us as we passed, but most ignored us. Apparently, the sight of wild barbarians wandering the streets was nothing new to them, although we saw no other Sea Wolves that day.

The buildings here were of more humble construction, their roofs steeply pitched, their façades far less ornate than those we had seen previously. There was little glass to be seen and no statues. The path itself was unpaved save for a narrow strip of flat stone down the centre. We made our way along, and eventually came to a place where two roads crossed. Carts and bearers filled the street at this junction and it was all so confused we quickly lost sight of the queen and her chair. We stood in the centre of the crossroads and tried to decide which direction to take. Thinking to return to the wealthier district we had seen before, Hnefi chose the right-hand way, though it was darker and even more narrow than the one before.

We had walked but a dozen paces when a low, broad door in the wall suddenly banged open and out on a gust of hot air rushed a wooden cart pushed by two men, stripped to the waist and sweating. The cart was full of fresh-baked bread, and the smell from the open doorway halted us in our steps.

"*Bröd!*" cried Orm, running after the men. He caught the cart, stopped it, and grabbed a loaf from among those stacked in the cart. The men yelled at him, snatched it back, and hurried on again, shouting at him as they went.

Seeing how Orm had fared, Hnefi turned to me. "Get us some of this bread," he said, and sent me after the cart.

I caught up with the men and fell into step beside them. "If you please," I said, "we would like to buy some of your bread."

"No! Not for sale!" one of the bakers shouted irritably.

"We have money," I said.

"It is impossible," the other baker said. "This is *theme* bread."

"Forgive me, I do not understand."

"Theme bread!" repeated the first baker. "Theme bread—bread for the soldiers. We are not permitted to sell on the streets. You will get us into trouble. Go away."

"I am sorry," I replied. "But we are hungry. Perhaps you can tell us where we can buy bread like this."

"Fie!" muttered the first baker, pushing away.

But the other man paused long enough to say, "Try over there." He pointed to an open doorway a little further along the street.

I shouted my thanks to the men and returned to where the Danes were waiting. "They say we can buy bread there." I showed him the house the baker had indicated. We made our way to the place, whereupon Hnefi withdrew a handful of coins from his pouch, selected a small one marked with a K and gave it to me. "Buy it for us," he ordered.

Regarding the tiny coin doubtfully, I promised to do

my best and entered the dark doorway. The interior of the building was warm and lit only by the fire from an enormous oven. A large fat man in a leather apron together with a skinny boy were stoking the flames with chunks of chopped wood. On the floor beside them was a small mountain of loaves still hot from the oven.

I greeted them and explained that I wished to buy some bread. The man wiped his hands on his leather apron and held out his hand for the coin. "All of it?" he asked.

"Yes," I said.

He shrugged, stooped to the stack of still-warm loaves, selected three and held them out to me. I took them with thanks, whereupon he selected three more and gave those to me as well. I thanked him again, and received three more loaves. These bread loaves were not large, but nine of them were enough to fill my arms. I thanked him for his generosity and he placed two more loaves atop the others and bade me farewell.

Staggering back into the street, I rejoined the amazed Sea Wolves. "All this," wondered Hnefi, "for only one coin?"

"Yes," I told him. "I could not carry any more."

"We can live like kings in this place," remarked Orm. With that, the Danes helped themselves to the bread, each taking three loaves, leaving me with two, which was more than plenty. We strolled on happily, tearing off pieces of bread and eating as we walked along.

The thin warmth of the day began to fade as the sun sank lower and the night clouds crowded in. The streets became shadowed and the sky took on a pale purple cast. Hnefi grew concerned that we should make our way back to the ship to tell what we had learned of the city. It was only when we turned and tried to retrace our steps that we discovered our predicament; we had wandered so far and by such a circuitous path that the process soon proved utterly futile.

"You will ask the way to the harbour," Hnefi commanded. We had paused at a paved open space near a cluster of stalls selling woven cloth and dyed wool. Two streets
led away from this small square: one uphill in what seemed
to be a westerly direction, and the other downhill to the
north. Neither way seemed likely to lead to the harbour,
which we imagined to lie somewhere to the south, though
this was in no way certain, as Gunnar thought it must certainly be to the east, and Orm was convinced that it was
due west.

"Ask that man," Hnefi ordered, pointing to an old man
hurrying by with a bundle of sticks on his back.

I went to the man and hailed him. "Pardon me,
father," I said, "I was hoping you could tell me the way to
the harbour."

The old man glanced at me and, without stopping,
said, "Follow your nose."

"A strange thing to say," remarked Hnefi when I told
him. "You must ask again."

I tried another passerby, who told me that we should
take the uphill path. Though we hastened on our way, the
sky was growing dark by the time we reached the top of
the hill to find another square surrounded by several large
buildings and a view of the city to the east and south.
"Heya!" shouted Orm, pointing to the east, "Gunnar was
right. There is the harbour."

Gunnar made no reply, and when I turned to him, I
saw that his attention was wholly occupied with a large
white structure behind us. "Look," he said, indicating the
roof.

I saw where he was pointing and my heart leapt within
me. A gold cross stood at the apex of the roof, gleaming in
the last light of the setting sun, and this had caught
Gunnar's eye.

I was instantly seized by an overwhelming desire to

run to the place and throw myself on my knees before the altar. I stood staring at the cross and thought: *I have arrived at last. I have crossed many oceans to be here, but here I am.* I thought I should tell someone about the pilgrimage. The brother priests in Constantinople should know of this; I should tell them.

Without thinking, I started away towards the church. Alas, I had walked but three steps when Hnefi grabbed me roughly by the arm. "Stay here!" he snarled.

Orm misunderstood the significance of Gunnar's interest. "It is not gold," he said.

"Most likely brass," added Hnefi. "It is not worth taking."

Ignoring them, Gunnar said, "It is his sign—just as you said, Aeddan."

"Yes, it marks a church," I told Gunnar. "A place where the Lord Christ is worshipped."

We were thus involved when the big double door swung open. There came the peal of a bell from inside the church, and a procession of priests emerged carrying candles and cloth banners on poles. Dressed in long dark robes, they moved out into the street, singing a psalm in a slow, undulating chant. Their tonsure was the Latin kind, unlike mine; their clothing, however, was similar to that worn by the western monks, but more richly ornamented. Several of the priests wore long silk scarves around their necks—the *orarion*—embroidered with crosses in gold thread; the sleeves of their robes were long and also ornately patterned.

Leading the procession was a bishop carrying an eagle-headed crozier and wearing a mitre. He was followed by a pair of monks wearing white chasubles: one of them carried a large wooden cross, and the other the image of the Christ painted on a flat wooden panel. The painting showed Jesu nailed to the cross, eyes lifted heavenward, pleading mercy for those who had crucified him.

The sound of priestly voices lifted in song filled me with a rare delight. It seemed half a lifetime since I had heard the psalms sung out—though the singing was in Greek. Still, I felt a thrill ripple through me at the familiar words: "Praise God in the heights, all ye men! Praise the Lord of Hosts, all creatures on the earth below!"

Gunnar put his head near mine. "It is *him*!" he whispered. "It is the Hanged God you told us about. It is the same one, heya?"

I told him that it was the same god, and that the cross had become Christ's sign.

"Even in Miklagård?" wondered Gunnar. "How can this be?"

"He is everywhere," I replied. "And is everywhere the same."

"Then it is true," he concluded, much impressed. "All you said of him is true."

Orm, overhearing this, decided to give us the benefit of his vast knowledge of religious matters. "You are mistaken, Gunnar," he declared flatly. "Do not let this Shaven One lead you astray. That was certainly some other god, for how can the same one be in two places at once?"

"There could not be two such gods," Gunnar maintained. "Aeddan said he was hanged on a cross by the Romans. There he is, and there is the cross."

"The Romans kill *everyone* on the cross," Orm replied, enjoying his superior intelligence. "They cannot all become gods."

Hnefi had grown impatient with the talk. "The Shaven Ones are going down the hill," he said, indicating the priestly procession. "We will follow them—perhaps they will lead us to the harbour."

The priests moved slowly, and we followed at a short distance, keeping them in sight by the light of their candles. As I walked along, I began thinking how I might speak to these priests. We were, after all, brothers in Christ, and having come all this way it seemed important that I should declare myself in some way to the leaders of the church. And then it struck me that perhaps, by some priestly means, they had word of my brothers. At this prospect, my heart beat a little faster.

We followed the procession down the long hill, past more houses, their upper windholes glowing from within with warm yellow light; we passed another market square, empty now save for a few homeless dogs fighting over scraps. At one place we passed alongside a truly large aqueduct, around the walls of which were clustered a number of crude shelters that appeared to be made of discarded wood and refuse, thrown together anyhow. Before some of these people sat hunched over small fires, cooking bits of food on twigs. They watched us silently as we passed.

The stars were bright in the sky by the time the priests arrived at their destination: another church, somewhat larger than the last, with a rounded roof and rows of glass windholes high up in the walls. Candlelight flickered on the glass, beckoning me inside. A pang of longing arrowed through me, and I yearned to go inside and observe the eventide Mass. Just to be among others of my kind would have been bliss. But the Sea Wolves had got the scent of the harbour in their nostrils now, and would not stop long enough to allow me to go inside the church.

"Perhaps I should ask someone the way to the ships," I suggested to Hnefi, though I could smell the dank fishy scent of the water. "I could go into the church and speak to one of the priests. Maybe one of them could lead us, and then we would not get lost."

"Nay," replied Hnefi, starting off down another dark street. "I can find the harbour now. This way."

"But it is growing dark. We may yet lose our way."

He gave a grunt by way of reply. "Move along, slave," Orm said, stepping behind me and shoving me forward.

"Let him be," Gunnar said on my behalf. To me he added, "Come, Aeddan, do not anger them. As it is, I think Jarl Harald will not be pleased when he learns how we have fared this day."

Hnefi's unerring nose led us to the harbour. The city gate was closed, but a four-man guard stood watch at the small door and upon presentation of our copper disci, they allowed us through. The bay was dark and calm; the water glimmered with the lights of cooking fires and lanterns from the ships laying at anchor. The small boats had vanished, however. We walked up and down the quay looking for a boat to take us out to the ship, but there were none to be seen anywhere.

"We will have to swim," declared Hnefi.

"But we do not know which ship is ours," Orm pointed out. "We cannot swim to every ship in the bay."

They fell to discussing how best to proceed, when Gunnar said, "Listen! Someone is calling."

There came a voice from the water. Stepping to the edge of the quay, we looked down to see a single small boat with a man sitting at the stern holding a small lantern on a pole. I recognized the upturned face.

Upon seeing us, he called out again, and I answered, "Greetings, Didimus. Do you remember us?"

"I remember everyone, my friend. Especially those who do not pay."

"That was unfortunate," I replied. "I am truly sorry. But perhaps we are in a better disposition now. Will you take us back to our ship?"

Hnefi pushed in beside me. "What is he saying?"

"He says he will be most happy to take us back if we pay him."

"How much?" asked Hnefi suspiciously.

"Twenty nomismi," Didimus answered when I asked him.

"Two coins," I reported to Hnefi. "But we must pay before he will take us."

"It is better than swimming," Orm pointed out hopefully.

"Heya," agreed Hnefi. "Tell him we will pay. One coin now and one when we have come to the ship."

"Come to the steps then," said Didimus when I relayed the Dane's offer to him.

We walked to the steps where Didimus met us with the boat. Hnefi pulled five or six of the bronze coins from his pouch. Selecting two, he gave these to me and directed me to pay the boatman.

"Hnefi says I am to give you one now," I told Didimus, placing the coin in his outstretched hand. "I am to give you the other when we have arrived."

Holding the coin to the light, he saw the K mark and said, "But it is too much."

"I am certain he wants you to have it," I lied. "He thanks you for waiting."

"May God be good to you, my friend," said the boatman, tucking the coin away.

We climbed into the boat and settled ourselves as before. The Sea Wolves remained silent, but Didimus, pleased with his reward, felt like talking. "I knew I would see you again," he said. "Your first day in the City of Gold—did you fare well?"

"It is a very great city," I answered.

"Perhaps more brass than gold, though."

"Perhaps," I agreed. "Have you been waiting all day for us to return?"

"Not all day," the boatman replied, smiling at his own ingenuity. "But I knew you would return to your ship sooner or later, never fear. So, I watched the gate until it closed."

Working the long oar with swift, efficient strokes, the boatman quickly brought us to the longship. Hnefi hailed those aboard; some of the men leaned over the side to haul us up. As the others climbed into the longship, I gave Didimus the second part of his payment. "May God reward your patience and perseverance," I told him.

Holding the coin to the light of the lantern, his face arranged itself into a wide grin of pleasure. "My friend," replied Didimus happily, "he has done so already, never fear."

Raising my hands, I was pulled up the side of the ship and dragged over the rail. "Until tomorrow, my barbarian friends," called Didimus as I turned to face an extremely angry king.

# 29

Jarl Harald Bull-Roar, King of the Danes of Skania, could not understand why he had been made to stand waiting aboard his ship all day while we roamed the city spending his coins. How difficult could it be, he thundered, to locate the treasure? To the hiss and flicker of torches, he stood with his arms crossed over his chest, frowning mightily, demanding an answer to this mystery. Gunnar and I remained silent before his simmering wrath, while Hnefi and Orm strove to explain.

"It is very difficult, Jarl Harald," Hnefi said. "This Miklagård is far larger than we knew. It is not easy to find a treasure house."

"But finding a drinking hall is not so difficult, heya?"

"We found no drinking hall, jarl," replied Orm. "We could find only wine."

"So! You have been drinking wine," growled the king dangerously.

"Nay, jarl," put in Hnefi quickly. "We were looking for the chief treasure house, as you commanded us to do. We saw very many things, including many fine dwellings. I am certain they contain much plunder."

Harald liked the sound of this, so Orm embellished it.

"It is true, Jarl Harald. There are hundreds of these houses—thousands, perhaps. The treasure they hold is more than we could carry away though we had ten ships."

"You saw this treasure?" inquired the king. "You saw so much gold and silver?"

"Nay, Jarl Harald," replied Orm, "we did not see the gold or silver. But these dwellings are surely the halls of kings."

"The halls of kings!" scoffed Harald. "In their hundreds and thousands, you say. But I ask you: how is it that Miklagård contains so many kings?"

"Perhaps they are not *all* kings," allowed Hnefi judiciously, "but they are wealthy men. For who else can build such palaces?"

The king scowled at his scouts, and tugged at the ends of his moustache as he tried to determine what to do. Finally, turning to Gunnar and me, he said, "Well? What have you to say to this?"

"It is as Hnefi and Orm have told you, Jarl Harald," replied Gunnar. "There were too many palaces to count, and some of them must contain treasure worth plundering."

"Some of them, heya," grunted the king in gruff agreement. "That is likely the way of things. What else?"

"We drank no öl, nor even wine," Gunnar said, "although we did eat a little bread and some meat grilled on sticks. Also, we saw a market to make Jomsburg and Kiev seem like pig wallows."

"That I should like to see," muttered Harald.

"Truly, this Miklagård is the greatest city ever known," put in Orm enthusiastically. "It is like no other on this earth."

The king gave the warrior a dark look, preferring Gunnar's more plausible account. Turning once more to Gunnar, he said, "Even I, who did not go into the city, can see that it is a large settlement. Are there many soldiers guarding the gates?"

"Jarl, there are more people of every kind than I have ever seen in one place before, and there are guards at every gate: eight at least, and I do not doubt there are many more elsewhere."

"If this is so, how did you gain entrance?"

"We were made to pay to enter the city." So saying, Gunnar brought out the copper disk he had been given. The king took it and examined it closely.

"It cost ten nomismi," Gunnar explained.

"And that is another thing you should know," Hnefi said suddenly. "It happens that the silver coins we carry are worth a *hundred* nomismi, not ten."

The king swung from Hnefi to Gunnar for confirmation. "It is true, jarl," replied Gunnar. "They told us this at the gate. Ask the Shaven One; he spoke to them about this very thing."

Harald's face clenched like a fist as the enormity of the theft practised against him became apparent. "Is it true?" he asked, his voice husky with pent-up rage.

"Yes, lord," I told him, and explained what the soldier at the gate and the Prefect of Law had told me.

"I will nail the thief's head to the mast," growled the king. "I, Harald Bull-Roar, make this vow."

All thoughts of plunder were quickly forgotten as the discussion swung to how the king might best carry out his revenge on the dishonest harbour master. There quickly emerged a crude, but effective plan which the Sea Wolves were only too able to carry out. In celebration of their loathsome scheme, the king shared out öl, and everyone drank his fill. I did not drink with them, however, but hunkered down beneath the dragonhead prow and watched the barbarians stoke their courage with liberal lashings of ale.

A little after sunrise, the harbour of Hormisdas began to stir and one of the Sea Wolves climbed the mast, establishing himself at the topmost part to search for ships which might be making entrance to the harbour. But there were no ships on the horizon, so he climbed down again and we waited. After a while, Harald ordered him aloft once more and the search was repeated, with no greater success than before.

After the third search, the king said, "We will not wait any longer." He then gave the order for the anchor to be brought up and, using the oars, the Danes steered Harald's longship towards one of the nearer craft the king had marked out. They moved the vessel in a most stealthy manner, giving the impression it might be drifting of its own accord. They did this so that they would not arouse suspicion, for what they had in mind was wicked and cruel.

When we had come close enough to the neighbouring ship, they threw out iron hooks to secure the vessel, whereupon six Sea Wolves leapt onto the deck of the captured ship and, using firebrands lit for the occasion, immediately set its sail ablaze.

Fortunately, there were few people aboard the other ship, the merchant, pilot, and most of the crew having gone into the city with tradegoods the day before. The flames and smoke woke the remaining crewmen, however. Up they rose to see their sail alight and their vessel overrun by barbarians. Severely outnumbered, the strangers were in no mood to resist, and put up no fight whatsoever. They simply sat down on the deck and gave themselves up to their fate.

This pleased Harald, for he was not interested in losing any men. The burning sail gave off black smoke, which pleased the king even more. "Heya!" he cried. "See here! They are coming! Loose the ropes!"

As the king expected, the harbour guard, alerted by the fire, raced to the disturbance in haste, arriving in time to see the Sea Wolves return to their own ship and push off from the other. Observing that the harbour guard was coming to aid them, the crew of the burning vessel leapt up and began calling for the guard boat to arrest the barbarians' escape.

Harald made a show of trying to turn his ship, as if to flee, but was easily overtaken by the boat of the harbour guard. They came alongside, shouting at the Sea Wolves and shaking their spears.

"Shaven One!" cried Harald. "What are they saying?"

"They are saying to halt at once, or face the emperor's war fleet."

The Sea Wolf king smiled at this and said, "Then I suppose we must stop." He called to Thorkel to ship oars, and then thundered to his men in a roaring voice: "Prepare to be boarded!" To me, he said, "Tell our thieving friend that we are stopping now."

Taking my place at the rail, I called down to the harbour master, standing at the prow of the boat. "We are halting now," I told him. "The king will allow his ship to be boarded."

"Then stand well back," the quaestor answered angrily. With a forward motion of his hand, he signalled his men to scale the side of the longship. There were eight guards altogether, each armed with a spear and a short, broad-bladed sword.

When they had all come on deck, the harbour master swaggered to where Harald stood and demanded to know why he had attacked the other boat, to which—once I had translated the question—King Harald replied placidly, "I found the sight of them annoying."

"Do you not know that it is an offence to molest a ship in the emperor's harbour?" demanded the quaestor.

I conveyed the man's words, and Harald replied: "And is it an offence in the emperor's harbour to steal a man's silver?"

"Of course it is," replied the guard. "Do you claim that they tried to steal your silver?"

"Nay," confessed Harald, "they are not the thieves—it is *you* who have stolen my silver." The words were scarcely out of his mouth when the entire company of barbarians rose up with a terrible shout and threw themselves upon the guardsmen. The struggle was brief, and the Sea Wolves were able to disarm their outmanned opponents with little effort and no bloodshed.

Then, seizing the quaestor, Harald hurled the thief onto the deck, and placed his foot on the man's neck. The guardsmen squirmed to see their master treated so, but they were disarmed and held in the iron grip of Danes inflamed with righteous anger, and there was nothing they could do.

The quaestor shouted and thrashed around, demanding to be released. Jarl Harald, his bare foot well placed to crush the official's neck, ignored the commotion and called for his sword. The blade appeared and was placed into his outstretched hand.

"What is this?" the quaestor croaked from the ship's deck. "What . . . ?" Appealing to me, the captive shrieked pitifully, "Tell him, agh! . . . must release us at once . . . wrath of the emperor! Tell him!"

The king indicated that I should relay the prisoner's words; I convinced Harald to free the man's throat sufficiently to allow the wretch to speak, then repeated the quaestor's threat. Harald laughed. "Good! I have not killed a thief in a long time. I will enjoy telling his master why I have done this." With that, he raised the sword.

"Wait!" cried the writhing captive.

"Tell him to hold still," Harald instructed, "or it will not be a clean chop."

"What? What?" gasped the quaestor.

"He says you'd better lie still or the blow will not be clean."

"Tell him it was a mistake," shouted the quaestor. "Tell him I will give it all back."

"It is too late," I told him. "King Harald has determined to take revenge on you for the way you cheated him yesterday. He no longer cares about the money."

"Then what does he want?"

"He wants to nail your head to the mast of this ship," I answered. "And I believe he will do that very thing."

Harald removed his foot from the quaestor's neck, and placed the edge of the sharpened sword against the soft flesh; the tender skin parted and a few large drops of blood trailed down the doomed man's neck and splashed onto the deck.

"Does he know who I am?" the captive shrieked.

"He believes you to be the man who made him a fool before his men and stole his silver," I replied.

"You are making a mistake!" wailed the captive.

Harald put his foot on the man's back and raised the sword above his head, preparing to strike.

"No! No!" shrieked the quaestor. "Wait! Listen to me! I am an important man, a wealthy man. You can ransom me!"

"What does he say now?" wondered Harald, squinting his eye as he judged where the blade would fall.

"He is saying he is a man of some importance and that you might consider holding him for ransom."

Harald cocked an eyebrow at this. "Who would pay?"

I relayed the king's question to the captive, who said, "The emperor! I am the emperor's man, and he would pay for my release." Tears fell from the wretch's bloated, red face and the smell of fear wafted from him like a rank perfume.

King Harald listened intently while I translated the tax collector's words, and considered the new possibility presented to him. "How much?"

"The king wants to know how much he might expect in ransom," I told the quaestor, who was now sweating so much that the rivulets formed a puddle beneath his head.

"Twice as much as I took from him," the captive said.

King Harald shook his head firmly as I gave him the harbour master's words. "Tell this ignorant fellow that I have slaves worth more than that. Besides, I will get all the silver I can carry when I plunder the city. Nay," he said dismissing the opportunity, "I will have his head on my mast, and this will be a warning to all who think to plunder Harald Bull-Roar's silver."

This I told the Quaestor of Hormisdas Harbour, who sputtered with rage and frustration. "It is impossible! Do you understand what I am saying? No barbarian has ever plundered this city. You will all be killed before you set foot inside the gate. Release us at once, and I will plead clemency before the emperor."

"Plead mercy for your men instead," I told him. "For unless this Daneman hears a better reason than you have given, you and all your men will be dead before the emperor's fleet can stir an oar." The quaestor's men shifted uneasily and muttered imprecations to their superior. Still I could see that my speech fell somewhat short of persuasion, so I added, "Trust me; I speak the truth. I am a slave, and I shall die in this city anyway. My life is in God's hands; I am content. But you—you have it in your power to save yourself and the lives of your men."

The harbour master squeezed shut his eyes. "The emperor will pay, I tell you! He will grant you whatever you ask. Spare me!"

I told Harald what the desperate man had said, and added, "Think of it, jarl, the emperor himself paying tribute to Harald, King of the Danes—that would be a wonder, would it not?"

A smile appeared on the king's face and he agreed that, yes, it would be a wonderful thing to have the emperor bowing to him with the ransom in his hands. He made up his mind at once. "I will do it."

Taking his foot from the man's neck, he yanked the quaestor to his feet and stripped him of his belt and boots, and took the ring off his finger; he then gathered his horse-tail helmet and bronze-knobbed rod of office. All these items were tied up together in the quaestor's red cloak, whereupon the king gave orders that if he did not return before the sun had set, the captives were to have their throats slit, their heads nailed to the mast, and their corpses thrown into the harbour. He then chose twelve men to accompany him ashore—Hnefi, Orm, and Gunnar, who had been ashore the previous day, and myself as interpreter, were foremost in the landing party. As the king made ready his departure, I turned to the quaestor. "Is it true that you answer to the emperor?"

"That is true," he muttered sullenly.

"Then pray the emperor considers your life worth saving."

# 30

Harald exulted in his triumph. The very thought of obligating the emperor delighted him; it appealed equally to Harald's sense of fairness and to his vanity, for he imagined catching one of the emperor's minions in theft granted him a hold over the great ruler, who would be honour-bound to redress the injustice.

That Harald and his Sea Wolves had come to Constantinople with the sole purpose of robbing the emperor and as many of his subjects as possible was a detail which failed to impose itself on the barbarian mind. Even so, the Danes possessed a powerful, if peculiar, sense of honour; I had seen it amply demonstrated before. In truth, I had no idea what would flow from this action, but considered that if it prevented bloodshed, it would be no bad thing.

The Sea King commanded his three other vessels to come alongside and shield the dragonship in case anyone should try to interfere; he brought men from the other ships to help keep watch over the hostages, and charged his Sea Wolves to arm themselves for battle and await his return with utmost vigilance.

"I go to collect the honour-debt," Harald proclaimed

as he prepared to depart. "Thus will I be the first king of the Danefolk to receive tribute from the emperor of Miklagård." Truly, the man was drunk with arrogance.

The king, having arrayed himself in his finest clothing, took his place in the quaestor's boat and commanded his men to row. The Sea Wolves made short work of driving the small boat through the crowded harbour, and we soon made landing at the steps below the Magnaura Gate and proceeded through that great portal. Our mission was almost thwarted before we had set foot in the city, for upon seeing the barbarians the prefect of law leapt from his table and demanded to see our disci. Harald, on his way to collect a ransom, was not in a humour to pay anything for the privilege of entering the city, and refused.

When the king continued on his way, the prefect called the guards, shouting, "Stop them! Stop them!" until the gatemen appeared, weapons ready, and blocked our way with their spears. Harald was of a mind to fight them, but seeing the young guardsman who had helped us the previous day, I begged the king to stay his hand while I explained the matter to this official.

"So, it is you again," the guard said. "I thought you might have learned your manners yesterday."

"It is more serious this time," I said, and told him as quickly as I could that the quaestor and his men had been taken hostage.

"You can prove this?" he inquired. I motioned to Gunnar to bring the bundle; under the king's watchful eye he untied it and allowed the guardsman to look inside. Upon seeing the harbour master's belongings, he said, "So, you have taken him. Do you wish to tell me why you have done this?"

"That is a matter for the emperor alone," I replied. Having experienced something of the ways of the city, I reckoned that our best hope of gaining the emperor's ear lay in saying as little as possible to anyone else, for men are curious by nature and like to see a mystery resolved.

"Aeddan!" thundered Harald, who was, I observed, quickly losing patience with the trivial restrictions the city contrived to throw in his path. I bowed before the king and begged the chance to negotiate safe passage to the emperor's palace, asking only for the luxury of a few moments to do so. The king grunted gruff approval to this plan, so, bowing once more to my barbarian master, I turned to the guard.

"The king is growing impatient. It is in his mind to collect a ransom in exchange for the quaestor and his men; to this end, he means to see the emperor at once."

"You will never succeed," the guardsman informed me. "The palace guards will not allow you into the palace precinct. Should you attempt to force your way in, they will kill you."

"Please, help us," I said.

"Me!" he protested. "It is none of my concern."

"If you do not help us, the quaestor and eight of his men will die before the sun has set. Harald Bull-Roar has decreed that the captives' heads will adorn his mast if he does not return with the ransom; he has four ships of fighting men waiting to carry out this vile deed. Although your soldiers may try to prevent it, much blood will be shed on both sides and the harbour master will die anyway."

"So that is the way of it," he said, regarding the barbarians carefully. He weighed the situation in his mind for a moment. "Quaestor Antonius is a prick who thinks himself a patriarch," he said at last. "I am willing to assume you have good reason for taking him captive. Still, you should know that he possesses a measure of influence with those in authority, and if you have gambled poorly you will find yourselves in chains—or far worse—for your trouble."

Before I could protest that we had ample provocation for our rash act, he lifted his hand. "Say nothing. It is, as you say, a matter for the emperor alone. But I will advise you, as a friend, that if you hope to win the emperor's favour in the matter, you must bring him a pledge of surety."

"I do not understand," I confessed. "What is this *surety*?"

"It is a token," he said, "a sign of good faith given to indicate the high rank of your lord, and convey the importance of your petition."

"Why should we need such a token?" I asked. "The quaestor's ring, rod, and helmet would seem proof enough of the importance. And Harald is as you see him—a very king of his kind. His rank cannot be doubted."

"What you say is true, of course," agreed the guardsman. "But Quaestor Antonius is well known and respected at court. You are neither. Should you come before the emperor—which, I warn you, is most unlikely—and demand ransom for his majesty's harbour master, you would most readily advance your cause if you showed yourselves to be men of wealth and power in the custom of this city. This is best accomplished by the display of surety."

"But we hold the harbour master and his men hostage," I pointed out.

"Yes, and the less said about that the better," the guard advised, "if you hope to see the emperor."

I began to understand. "Then the greater the value of the object given in surety, the greater faith is demonstrated in our word."

"Precisely," agreed the guard.

"And if the emperor will not redeem his man?" I wondered.

"Then God help you," the guardsman concluded, "and God help the harbour master."

I stood daunted by the challenge of extracting a ransom from the emperor. And, as if to press his point further, the guard added, "Do not try the emperor's patience, my friend. Prison is the least torment awaiting a false accuser." He paused, regarding me doubtfully. "It is a risk, yes. Nevertheless, this is how affairs of this nature are conducted in Constantinople. I thought you should know."

I looked the guard in the eye. "Why are you telling me this? Why are you helping us against your own countryman?"

The guardsman lowered his voice, but held my gaze steadily. "Let us say that, unlike many in this city, I care about such things as honesty and justice."

"Friend," I asked, "what is your name?"

"My name is Justin," said the guardsman. "I am Chief of the Magnaura Gate *scholarii*. If you wish to pursue the matter further, I will lead you to the emperor's court, although, as I say, it is doubtful you will be admitted."

"Then we shall leave it in God's hands," I told him.

"Amen."

I went to Harald, who fumed at being made to stand waiting while lesser men flapped their tongues. "Well?" he demanded. "Speak! What did he say?"

"That man is the chief of the guards, and has said he will lead us to the emperor's court. But we are forewarned: it will go ill with us if you do not also bring a token to attest your rank and signify the importance of your business—something to prove you are trustworthy.

"Proof! I will present the thief's head for my proof!" declared the king.

"Nay, Jarl Harald," I said, "that will not do." And I explained as best I could the strategy given me by Justin, including what would likely happen if the emperor was displeased by our ransom demand. On sudden inspiration, I offered the observation that perhaps if the emperor was not inclined to redeem his servant, he still might be persuaded to make reparation for the theft and return the silver.

The king's brow wrinkled in thought as, surrounded by the bewildering formalities of the city, he seemed more willing to consider the possibility of simple restitution. "It seems to me," I suggested, "that we have nothing to fear, as we are certain of the truth of our claim."

The king hesitated. What had begun as a simple collection of an honour-debt was rapidly growing into a legal contest he no longer understood.

"Jarl Harald," Gunnar said, speaking up, "would you rather some other king was first of all Danes to win tribute from the emperor's hand? You would do well to consider this, I think." He paused, allowing the king to feel his prize slipping away, then added, "Do as Aeddan advises, and the tale will be told in every hall in Daneland. You will gain greater renown than Eric Hairy-Breecs. I think that is a thing worth all the silver in Miklagård."

"I will do it!" cried Harald, making up his mind at once. Turning to Hnefi, he said, "Take four men with you and bring the treasure box from the ship."

Had I been thinking more clearly, I would have known what this meant. Alas, I was so preoccupied with steering our ship of concerns successfully through the rocky sea before us, the significance of Harald's words passed me by.

I told Justin that the king was sending men back to the ship to bring the required surety, and he said, "Come along, then. I will leave some men to escort the barbarians when they return. The palace is not far; we will await them there."

The Chief of the Magnaura Gate then appointed several of his guardsmen to escort Harald's men to the longship and thence on to the palace of the emperor. He then motioned the rest of us to follow him, and thus our odd company was allowed to pass into the city without so much as a single nomismi changing hands. Justin and I marched together at the front of the parade, leading a procession of proud, awestruck barbarians and their escort of soldiers at the rear. As Justin had said, the emperor's palace was no great distance from where we had entered, although it lay in the opposite direction from the way we had gone the previous day, so I recognized nothing from before.

King Harald, looking regal if slightly bewildered, strode like a conqueror through the streets of Constantinople, much impressed by everything he saw. His head swung this way and that, but he kept his mouth firmly shut—unlike the rest of the Sea Wolves, who exclaimed aloud at each new marvel to meet their eyes. The fine big houses occasioned much speculation about the wealth inside, and the first glimpse of the amphitheatre brought exclamations of wonder and delight—much to the amusement of the citizenry of Constantinople, many of whom stopped to watch our curious company pass by.

Had anyone known what the barbarians were saying, they would not have been so amused, I think. The Sea Wolves were astounded by the sight of so much wealth, and eagerly discussed how best to get it for themselves: whether it was advisable to slay the owners outright, or simply seize the valuables and kill only those who resisted; whether to burn individual houses, or put the whole city to the torch . . . I was heartily glad the onlookers taking such delight in the display understood nothing of what the Sea Wolves said.

When we came in sight of the palace walls, the talk turned to strategies for sacking such an imposing place. The difficulty, from a barbarian point of view, was that the palace presented itself not as a single house or dwelling, but a cluster of buildings scattered within a walled compound—a city within a city. The prevailing opinion was that it should be plundered like any other settlement: fires should be set and the inhabitants slaughtered as they fled the flames. The barbarians could then loot the place at their leisure, providing the soldiers did not interfere. The Sea Wolves had no idea how many soldiers the emperor commanded, but judging from the look of the gate guards they reckoned their own superior strength and stature more than a match for any number of shorter, more lightly-equipped defenders. The somewhat benign appearance of our small escort of red-cloaked guards did nothing to arrest the barbarians' swift-racing avarice.

Curiously, as we neared the palace, the houses became more crude and haphazard in their construction. The grand and spacious villas of the wealthy were steadily replaced by habitations of meaner design, each more rude than the last until, in the very shadow of the palace walls, the dwellings were little more than hovels: bits of wood stuck up against the wall and covered over with branches and rags. The entire length of the wall in either direction supported these pathetic structures, about which swarmed a horde of filthy beggars.

Before we knew what was happening, we were surrounded by a seething mass of dirty, ragged people, all crying for alms. Some of these wretches waved withered limbs or stumps in our faces, others exposed gangrenous wounds running with pus. The barbarians, though uncouth themselves, were appalled by the poverty of this stinking throng and lashed out angrily whenever any of the beggars pressed too close. The guardsmen, well accustomed to the stench and noise, took the lead and pushed the overbearing crowd back with their shields and the butts of their spears. We eventually reached the gate where we were met by a company of blue-cloaked guards who, upon taking one look at the barbarians, drew their weapons and challenged us at spearpoint.

"Halt!" shouted the chief guard. "Halt or be killed."

The Danes, seeing spears lowered, thrust themselves forward to wage battle—at which point our escort of guards joined ranks with their countrymen. Justin raised his voice above the rattle of shields and shouted, "Scholarae Titus! Let us through! These men are with me—I am escorting them to an audience with the emperor."

The guard called Titus signalled his men to stay the attack, and said, "Explain this procession."

"We are on a . . . diplomatic mission—a matter of the highest importance."

Eyeing the barbarians, Titus said, "I cannot allow it."

"Listen to me," Justin said, stepping close. "There are lives at risk. The Quaestor of Hormisdas Harbour has commissioned us," he lied. "We must get through at once." He then signalled to me to bring the bundle, which I took from Gunnar and brought to him. Unknotting the cloak, Justin held it open for his comrade to inspect. "I am hoping to resolve the incident without bloodshed."

Titus shifted through the items in the bundle. "They have weapons," he replied firmly. "I cannot allow barbarians beyond the gate with weapons. It is my head, and I consider *that* the highest importance."

Turning to me, Justin asked, "Your king must agree to leave his weapons behind."

Motioning for Harald to join us, I quickly explained to him the conditions of entry. He frowned and shook his head dangerously, saying, "Nay. I will not go into that place unarmed. We will burn it down instead. Tell them that."

Turning to Justin, I said, "Lord Harald asks what assurances you offer that he will not be attacked should he and his men surrender weapons."

Justin, observing the thrust of Harald's chin, turned

back to the other guard. They held close conversation for a moment, and then Justin motioned me to join them. "My friend Titus begs to inform your king that within the palace precinct, influence and negotiation have replaced brute force. We are not barbarians here. If the king would hold converse with the emperor, he must put aside his arms and proceed peaceably."

This I told to Harald, who considered the situation for a moment and wondered, "Is it a trap?"

"I do not think so, Jarl Harald," I answered. "In any event, you still have the quaestor for a hostage—his life and those of his men remain in your hands whether you hold a sword or not. Truly, I believe you must obey these guards if you wish to see the emperor—and collect your honour-debt."

"I will do it," replied the king, making up his mind at once.

"Very well," said Titus, when I had conveyed the king's words to him. "Tell him to get on with it."

Harald commanded the Danes to give their axes, swords, and hammers to the soldiers for safe-keeping, which they did with no little grumbling and suspicion. I noticed, however, that the small knives which all Sea Wolves carry close to their bodies—under their belts, or in their boots—did not appear among the items given over for safe-keeping. Justin then instructed Titus regarding the expected arrival of the surety. That settled, Scholarae Titus signalled the gatemen, who stepped aside and opened the big door, allowing us to pass quickly through, leaving the rabble and noise behind.

Once inside the walls, we found ourselves in what seemed an enormous garden at one end of a long, tree-lined pathway. High walls divided this palace precinct into several smaller partitions so that wherever one looked the eye met the blank expanse of some wall or other. Rising above the walls, here and there, were the branches of trees and the rounded tops of domes, many with crosses at their peaks.

The ground rose gently, as the emperor's palace was situated astride the crown of a hill overlooking the Sea of Marmora, shimmering dull blue to the south. Led by Justin, our motley assembly—consisting now of eight barbarians, nine guards, Justin, Titus, and myself— trooped up the path towards another wall in which was set a gate large enough for horsemen to ride four abreast; what is more, an entire house had been constructed above this enormous portal where guards and watchmen lived.

Passing through this portal we entered another garden with several more tree-lined marble walkways. There were clusters of buildings scattered haphazardly around this inner compound: kitchens, stores, dwellings of various kinds, and several large chapels. The buildings were mostly of stone—fine coloured marble from the quarries of lands throughout the empire—and most had wide windholes covered with clear glass, and not only this, but also coloured tiles of blue and green affixed to their upper portions, so that the slanting sunlight made the heights of these habitations gleam like gems.

There were six handsome black horses grazing in the grassy places, untethered and unwatched. When I remarked on this, Justin merely replied that the emperor, a former stableboy, liked his horses.

*Sure, Heaven itself has touched this place with its glory*, I thought. The magnificence of these grounds was the envy of the world, and I could scarce believe I was walking in them.

Within this inner precinct were no fewer than four palaces and three additional chapels. As we walked along, Justin told me which they were. "That is the Octagon," he said, pointing to one of the structures, "the emperor's private quarters. And over there," he pointed to another imposing palace, "is the Pantheon—where the empress and the court ladies stay. And there is the Daphne Palace, and the one beside it is Saint Stephen's church."

"What is that one?" I asked, pointing to a large stone building with a high triple-domed roof of red clay tiles which rose above the tops of the trees.

"The Triconchus Palace," replied the guard. "It is the new state throne-room; Theophilus built it. But the emperor prefers the old throne-room in the hall of the Chrysotriclinium." He indicated yet another enormous building of yellow stone. "We are going to the old throne-room."

"And what is beyond that high wall over there?" I wondered, pointing behind the throne hall.

Justin smiled, "That, my friend, is the Hippodrome. If you survive this day, you may see some races there. The emperor is fond of horses, as I say, and so of racing."

Jarl Harald, growing wary of the talk between us, growled at me and demanded that I either translate, or keep silent. I told him that Justin was telling me about the emperor's liking for horse racing. He snorted at this, saying, "Horses are costly and they eat too much."

The array of fine buildings and gardens was staggering. The inner precinct alone was many times larger than the whole of the abbey at Kells and, confronted with so many walls and buildings, I quickly lost any sense of direction. On and on we walked, passing through gates and doorways—one after another, beyond counting—and I began to be aware of a detail that had earlier escaped my notice; the Great Palace, beneath the lustre, was decaying.

Despite the richness, the precinct wore an air of weariness—as if, beneath the patina of opulence, the buildings were old and tired and sad; the bright fire of their first splendour was faded now to only a glow. The path beneath our feet was white marble, but the expensive stone was discoloured and cracked; tufts of grass grew up through the cracks. The bronze crosses atop the chapels were dull green, not gold, and the colourful façades were missing many of their tiles. Several trees along the pathway were dead.

Here and there, as if to counter the decrepit appearance, masons were busy at work atop wooden scaffolding, restoring damaged sections of some buildings, and renewing the façades and roofs of others. Indeed, when I listened, the principal sound to meet my ear was that of hammer on chisel.

The marble walk ended at a large square building of pale yellow stone which supported a huge dome flanked by two smaller domes. Two trees grew on either side of an arched doorway, casting pale blue shadows in the thin autumn light across a paved foreyard. There was a stone water trough shaped like a bowl directly before the door, and here we halted.

"Tell your king that he may choose two men to come with us," Titus said, and indicated that the rest were to wait at the entrance with the soldiers. "When the others arrive with the surety, one of my men will alert us."

I conveyed these instructions to the king and he chose Hnefi and Gunnar to accompany him, giving instructions to the rest to attack and burn down the palace if the war cry sounded. This they vowed to do and then stretched themselves out on the grass to wait.

Justin, looking on, said, "Are you certain you wish to proceed? You have much to lose by continuing."

I glanced at King Harald, who had quickly mastered his amazement. It would not be long before he was again calculating the extent of his grievance in blood. "We have much to gain, also," I said. "We will follow wherever the path leads."

"It leads through here," he replied, indicating the massive central doorway deep beneath high stone arches. "Beyond this door beats the heart of the empire."

# 31

Stepping into the doorway, Titus rapped on the door with his bronze rod. In a moment, a smaller door opened within the larger and a gateman peered out. "Scholarae Titus, Chief Guard of the Bucoleon Gate," he said. "I am bringing emissaries to the emperor."

The gateman regarded the barbarians, then shrugged and opened the door; Titus motioned for us to follow and we were admitted into a stone-paved yard bounded by high walls on all four sides. Thick vines grew on the walls, the leaves of which had coloured and were beginning to fall. The breeze swirled in the square, sending dry leaves rattling across the stone-flagged yard. The sound made the place seem desolate and empty.

The gateman secured the door behind us and then led us to yet another in one of the walls. This door was also wood, but tightly bound in thick iron bands as wide as a man's hand and studded with large bronze nails. Blue-cloaked guards with long-bladed lances stood on either side of the door, regarding us with bored curiosity. The gateman took hold of an iron ring and pushed one of the great panels open; stepping aside, he indicated that we should proceed.

Having done what he promised, Titus left us to our fate. "I will return to the gate and send the surety when it arrives," he told Justin and departed.

The room we entered was immense. Light came in through four round windholes above, illuminating four large paintings: one of Saint Peter, one of Saint Paul, and the other two of royal persons—judging by their purple robes—one male, the other female: an emperor and empress, I supposed, though I could not say who they might have been. The walls were pale red in colour, and the floors white marble.

Save for low benches which lined the north and south wall, the room was bare of furniture—but not empty, for a goodly number of men in various kinds of dress stood about, some of them talking quietly to one another, others simply looking on. They watched us enter, their glances sharp and unwelcoming. Some had the wan, desperate appearance of men who had spent long years in captivity; others seemed sly and calculating, appraising our potential value. The sight of three barbarians and a travel-worn monk with a guardsman in tow did not excite them, however, and they quickly turned back to their own affairs.

The room, for all its size, was close, the air heavy and stale, and slightly sour. If ambition has a scent, I thought, then I am smelling it now.

In the centre of this anteroom stood a pair of great bronze doors, twice a man's height and covered with images of riders on horseback following the hunt. A huge bronze ring hung in the centre of each door, beneath which stood a man carrying a double-headed axe on a pole. Red horsetails were affixed to the hafts of the axes, and these guards carried small round shields on their shoulders and wore sleeveless red tunics with wide black belts. Their hair was shaved from their heads, save for a single knot which hung down over their temples. The face they presented to the world was fierce indeed, and all who held discourse within that room came under their merciless scrutiny.

Catching my glance, Justin said, "They are the *Farghanese*—part of the emperor's bodyguard."

He had just finished speaking when we were approached by a man holding a wax tablet and stylus. He glanced disdainfully at me, and at the barbarians, before turning to the chief guard. "Who are these men and what are they doing here?"

"This man is a king of his kind, and he comes seeking audience with the emperor."

"The emperor grants no one audience today," replied the pompous man.

"With all respect, Prefect, there has been trouble at the harbour."

"This trouble," sniffed the prefect, "requires the emperor's attention? I should have thought it more a matter for the emperor's guard."

"They have made hostages of the Quaestor of Hormisdas Harbour and of his men," replied Justin. "Any intervention by the guard will result in the deaths of all concerned. As I am only a scholarae, I have no authority to endanger the quaestor's life. But if you wish to take it upon yourself to settle the matter, Prefect, I bow to your superiority."

The official, who had been about to write something on his tablet, raised his eyes and glanced at Justin; his head whipped around and he regarded the barbarians. Weighing the odds, he made up his mind at once. "Guards!" he cried.

The two Farghanese leapt forward at the prefect's shout. Harald roared an order, and the Sea Wolves drew knives and prepared to meet the attack. The courtiers in the near vicinity threw up their hands and scattered with a great commotion.

"Stop!" Justin shouted. Seizing me by the shoulder, he cried, "Make them stop! Tell them it is a mistake!" To the prefect, he shouted, "Do you want to get us all killed? Call them off!"

Throwing myself before Harald, I said, "Wait! Wait! It is a mistake! Put up your blade, Jarl Harald."

"I told you they were in earnest!" Justin hissed in exasperation. "For God's sake, man, let the emperor deal with them."

The prefect seemed to reconsider his hasty action. He spoke a word and the Farghanese relaxed; they raised their axes once more and the danger passed.

Shaking his robes in agitation, the prefect glared around him like a master who has discovered his servants quarrelling. "I am citing you, scholarae. You know the proper conveyances," he informed Justin tartly. "I need not remind you that official protocols exist for precisely these occasions. I suggest you remove yourself from here at once and take the barbarians with you."

"Yes, prefect. And what of the quaestor?"

Lowering his eyes to the tablet, the man pressed his stylus into the soft wax. "As I have already told you, the emperor is seeing no one. He is preparing an embassy to Trebizond, and is spending the next few days in the company of his advisors. All affairs of court are suspended. Therefore, I suggest you take your concerns to the *magister officiorum*."

"I believe the magister is in Thrace," Justin pointed out. "I understand he is not expected to return to the city until the Christ Mass."

"That cannot be helped," the prefect answered, working the stylus against the wax with deft strokes. "In any event, it is the best course I can recommend." Glancing at me, and then at the Danes he added, "That will allow them time to bathe and clothe themselves properly."

I conveyed the prefect's words to Harald, who merely grunted, "I will not wait." With that, he stepped forward and produced a gold coin from his belt.

Taking hold of the tablet, he pressed the gold coin into the soft wax. The prefect looked at the money and at Harald, then brushed his long fingers across the coin. As the official's fingers closed on the gold, the king seized him by the wrist and squeezed hard. The prefect gave a startled cry and dropped his stylus. Harald calmly pointed to the entrance.

"I think he means to see the emperor now," remarked Justin.

The Farghanese bodyguard moved to the prefect's defense once more, but the prefect waved his free hand to ward them off. "In Christ's name, just open the doors!"

The two guards stepped aside and pulled on the bronze rings; the doors swung open and Harald released the official's hand. The prefect led us into a small screened room, the *vestibulum*, where we were instantly met by a man in a long white robe carrying a slender silver rod—the *magister sacrum*, he was called. Tall and grey and gaunt, his face pitted and scared, he gazed upon us severely. Addressing the prefect, he said, "What is the meaning of this unseemly intrusion?"

"There has been some trouble at Hormisdas Harbour," the prefect answered. "These men are responsible. The emperor's attention is required."

The magister made a face as if he smelled something foul. "You will not speak until spoken to," he intoned, addressing himself to the uncouth visitors, "and then you will make your replies as succinct as possible. When addressing the emperor, you may call him by his official title, *basileus*, or sovereign lord, either is acceptable. It is customary to keep your eyes averted when not speaking to him. Understood?"

Harald looked to me for explanation, and I relayed the magister's rules to the king who, much to my amazement, burst into a broad grin as he learned the Byzantine protocols. With a heartfelt, "Heya!" he slapped the unsuspecting magister on the back with his enormous paw.

The courtier maintained his rigorous dignity, however, and without another word led us into the emperor's hall. We stepped from the vestibule into a room without equal in the world: high and wide, the space beneath the ceiling dome was vast and filled with the light of ten thousand candles. The walls, floors, and pillars were deep-hued marble, polished so smooth that their surfaces reflected like mirror pools. The glint of gold met the glance on every side: gold was woven into the fabrics of clothing, in the mosaics covering the walls; all the fitments and furniture of the room were gold—candletrees, chests, chairs, tables, bowls and ewers and urns—the very throne itself. The whole room was bathed in the honeyed gleam of that most precious metal.

What shall I say of the wonder of this hall and its renowned occupant? In the centre of the vast room sat a golden throne raised upon a tiered dais, and tented over with a cloth of gold. Three steps—carved from porphyry, I was told, and polished to the smoothness of glass—led up to the dais, and at the topmost step was the emperor's footstool. The royal seat itself—more couch than throne, double-backed and large enough for two big men to sit comfortably—was established directly beneath the great central dome. In the apse of the dome was the largest image I have ever seen, a mosaic of the Risen Christ, ablaze with glory, and beneath his feet the words "King of Kings" in Greek.

In clustered ranks about the throne stood a veritable

crowd of people—courtiers of various kinds, I decided; nearly all were robed in green, or white, or black, save those closest to the throne who were Farghanese and, like the warriors standing guard at the door carried pole-axes and shields.

At our first steps the sound of a rushing wind commenced, and a moment later the most exquisite music filled the air. It was like the music of pipes and flute and every rushing wind that I had ever heard. And thunder, too, yes, and everything that sang under heaven. I had never heard anything to equal it, nor ever have again. It was, I think, the sound of heavenly majesty rendered audible to the earthly ear, and it seemed to come from a great golden casket a little behind and to one side of the throne.

I might have discovered more about the source of this glorious music, but I had eyes only for the throne and the man sitting in it. For, occupying one side of the wide throne and regarding us openly, was Emperor Basil, robed in deepest purple that glistened and shimmered in the light.

The splendour of the room and the opulence of all around me combined to make me suddenly conscious of my own appearance. Glancing down, I noticed to my embarrassment that my once-fine cloak was stained and torn; my mantle was filthy and ragged at the edges. Raising a hand to my head, I felt that my hair had grown and my tonsure needed renewing, and my beard was matted and unkempt; an iron collar hung about my throat. In short, I looked more like one of the beggars that swarmed the walls of the Great Palace, than an emissary of the Irish church. But I was not an emissary. In truth, I was what I appeared: a slave.

So this is how I came to the emperor: not dressed in the white robe and cloak of the peregrini, but in travel-worn rags and a slave collar; not surrounded by my brother monks, but in the company of rough barbarians; not led by the blessed Bishop Cadoc, but beside a pagan Danish king; not bearing a priceless gift, but bargaining for a hostage.

Ah, vanity! God, who has no use for pride, had seen to it that I remained humble before his Vice-Regent on Earth.

Raising my eyes once more, I found myself looking into the face of the most powerful man in all the world, and it was the face of a clever monkey. Before I could properly take in the sight, the magister sacrum raised his rod and cracked it down hard on the floor.

At the same instant, the golden throne began to rise in the air. So help me Michael Valiant, I tell the truth! The throne, which looked like a Roman camp chair, save larger and made of gold, simply lifted itself into the air to hover before us—as if raised by the superb melody issuing from that golden *organ*, as they called it.

Before I could grasp the contrivance of this wonder, the white-robed magister struck the floor with his rod again and made a flattening motion with the palm of his hand. Justin sank to his knees and stretched himself facedown, flat on the floor. I followed the guard's example, but the barbarians beside me remained standing, oblivious to the insult they provoked. The music swelled, and then stopped. I held my breath—I do not know why.

The next voice I heard was that of the emperor himself. "Who disturbs the serenity of these proceedings with such unseemly clatter?" he inquired; his voice was even and deep, and came from a place high above us.

To my alarm, Justin whispered, "Here is your chance, Aidan. Tell him who you are."

Climbing quickly to my feet, I squared my shoulders, swallowed hard and replied, "Lord and emperor, you see before you Jarl Harald Bull-Roar, King of the Danes of Skania, together with his slave and two of his many warriors."

A faint twitter of laughter greeted my salutation, but it quickly died when the emperor muttered, "Silence!"

"*Basileus*, they seem to have gained their way by guile," said the magister sacrum, anxious to absolve himself without seeming irresponsible.

"So it does appear." Scanning the barbarians, the emperor said, "The king may approach. We will speak to him face to face."

The official gave a crack of his rod and motioned for the king to answer the summons. I moved to Harald's side. "He would speak to you," I told him, and together we stepped forward.

The floating throne descended slowly to its base, and before us sat Emperor Basil, a small, bald-headed man; olive-skinned like his Macedonian countrymen, he possessed the short limbs and compact frame of a horse soldier. His eyes were dark and quick, and his hands—resting on the arms of the throne, fingers drooping from the weight of his patriarchal rings—were small and neat.

"In the name of Christ, Sovereign of Heaven, we greet you, Lord of the Danes," he said, offering a bejewelled hand to Harald, who bore himself with regal dignity.

Justin touched my shoulder, indicating that I should convey the emperor's words to the king, which I did, and added, "He means for you to kiss his hand. It is a sign of friendship."

"Nay!" replied Harald. "I will not." He then told me to ask the emperor whether he would ransom the life of his thieving servant now, or see his headless corpse thrown into the harbour.

"What does he say?" asked the emperor of me. "You may speak for him."

"Sovereign lord and emperor," I replied quickly, "Harald Bull-Roar, Jarl of the Danmark and Skania says that he regrets he cannot observe friendship with you until he has presented the purpose of his mission."

"So be it," replied Basil, taking up the matter at once. He spoke cordially, but his manner gave me to know that there were to be no further pleasantries wasted on the rude barbarians. "What is the nature of his concern?"

"He demands to know your business here," I said to Harald.

"Then tell him," ordered the king angrily. "Tell him we offer him a chance to redeem the life of his thieving harbour master."

"Emperor and lord," I began, "the king says that he would like it known that he has made hostages of Quaestor Antonius and his men, and now awaits your offer of ransom for their lives." This I said and told how, upon arrival in Constantinople, we had immediately been cheated by the quaestor. "My lord Harald captured the harbour master and would have taken the man's head, along with those of his men," I explained, "but the quaestor told us that the emperor would certainly pay a great reward for the sparing of his life. Thus, my lord Harald, Jarl of the Danes of Skania, seeks the emperor's ransom."

Basil made no reply; to be sure, his face betrayed nothing of his mind, so I gestured to Gunnar to bring forth the bundle once again. I placed it on the floor, unknotted it, and spread the red cloak. There, for all to see, was the quaestor's helmet, rod of office, and official ring. The emperor leaned forward slightly, squinted at the display, and then leaned back with a puff of agitation.

"Where is Quaestor Antonius?"

"He waits aboard Lord Harald's longship, basileus, with his men as well."

Turning his head slightly, Basil called for the prefect to join the proceedings. The magister hastened to summon the prefect, who approached the throne. Speaking to me, the emperor said, "Tell the king that I am sending this man to bring the quaestor. He must release him to the prefect, so that we may resolve this matter." He then directed Justin to accompany the prefect.

Upon relaying the emperor's words, Harald protested. "Nay!" he bellowed. "The emperor must pay the ransom if he desires the release of his man. This is everywhere understood," he added.

So, I explained to the basileus that Harald's men would not release their captive until they received word from their jarl that the ransom had been paid. Sure, I spoke more bravely than I felt, and stepped back to see what would happen next.

Far from showing his displeasure, however, the basileus merely nodded and instructed the prefect to bring him a bowl from one of the tables. This the official did, fetching a handsome golden bowl which he placed before the throne. "Give it to the king," Basil said, whereupon the prefect delivered the bowl into the barbarian lord's hands.

Well pleased with the weight and craft of the bowl, Harald granted his assent. Calling Hnefi to him, he charged him to attend the prefect and bring back the quaestor. "Tell the karlar the ransom has been paid," Harald said, then whispered, "but do not release the thief's men—this bowl does not buy *their* lives." The three left at once, whereupon the magister returned us to the anteroom to wait with the others detained at the emperor's pleasure.

While we were waiting, Titus appeared with the four barbarians Harald had sent to bring the surety. The newcomers were full of admiration for all the wealth they had seen along the way and wanted to know how much the emperor was giving for the quaestor's life. "It is difficult to say," Harald allowed ruefully, his golden treasure hidden beneath his cloak. "In this place, nothing is simple, I think."

The magister returned for us eventually. We entered the throne-room to find Justin and the quaestor standing before the emperor. "Quaestor Antonius," intoned the emperor gravely as we resumed our places, "we have been hearing about some of your recent activities. Have you anything to say in this regard?"

"Sovereign lord," replied Antonius at once, his voice, like his expression, pure defiance, "a serious mistake has been made by these men. Possessing no knowledge of the currency of Constantinople, they have erroneously calculated the worth of their coinage and so believe themselves to have been cheated."

"A reasonable explanation," replied the emperor mildly. He pursed his lips as if in thought, laced the fingers of his hands together and brought them to his chin. After a moment, he spoke again, directing his question to Harald, "The harbour tax is paid in silver. Have you other coins like those you delivered to Quaestor Antonius?"

"I do," replied Harald, speaking through me. Withdrawing the pouch kept under his belt, he opened it and shook a few silver denarii into his hand.

These he passed to the emperor, who examined them briefly and selected one, observing, "They were not minted in Constantinople, but we believe such coins to be in plentiful supply here and elsewhere." Showing the coin to Harald, he said, "What is its value?"

"One hundred of your nomismi," replied the Danish king, when I had explained the question.

"Who told you this?" wondered the emperor mildly.

"That man." I conveyed the king's words, and Harald pointed to Justin. "Indeed, if not for the scholarae's aid, I have no doubt there would have been bloodshed and loss of life." This last I added on my own, thinking it important that Justin's part should receive its due.

The emperor merely nodded and continued with his

examination. Holding up a silver coin, Basil asked, "What say you, Quaestor Antonius? Tell me the value of this coin."

"One hundred nomismi, basileus," the quaestor answered stiffly.

"So," Basil smiled. "We have established the question of value." Addressing the harbour master, he said, "King Harald of Skania has made claim against you, Antonius. He says you have reckoned but ten nomismi to the denarius. Is this so?"

"Exalted basileus," replied the quaestor, "it is *not* so. Such an error could not be made. The barbarian is certainly mistaken."

Basil pursed his lips. "Then the fault is the king's alone."

"Lord and emperor," replied the quaestor, adopting a more reasonable tone, "I do not say it is the fault of anyone. Indeed, I believe no one is to blame. I say only that the ways of Byzantium may be confusing to one so newly arrived. I have already explained this to him, but he chooses to believe otherwise."

"There," the emperor said, spreading his hands as if satisfied that he had penetrated to the heart of the mystery at last. "A simple miscalculation. As no harm has been done, we are happy to allow the matter to end here and send you about your business with our own good wishes." He paused, observing the effect of his words. "We excuse your ignorance, as we forgive the disturbance of our peace. Return the bowl, and we will speak of this matter no more. What say you?"

Harald's face clouded as I relayed what the harbour master had said and explained the emperor's words to him. "With respect, Jarl Harald," I said, "he is giving you a chance to withdraw your complaint without incurring the wrath of the empire. It appears the judgement has gone against you."

"Tell him about the token," Harald commanded.

"Lord and sovereign," I said, apprehension creeping over me, "the king has brought a token of surety which he would like to put before you in consideration of his complaint."

This revived the emperor's interest.

"There are barbarians waiting in the anteroom, basileus," the prefect volunteered. "Shall I cause them to be admitted?"

"By all means, prefect," said the emperor. "It seems we are to be overrun by barbari until this matter is resolved."

Some of the courtiers laughed politely and the prefect hastened to summon the remaining Danes. A few moments later, the bronze doors opened and four Sea Wolves stepped from the vestibule, two of them carrying the peaked treasure box between them. I saw the chest and my heart beat faster. The Danes came to where Harald stood and placed the treasure at his feet.

"Well?" asked the emperor impatiently.

"Basileus," I said; it was all I could do to prise my eyes from the peaked box, "King Harald has placed before you the assurance of his honour in this matter."

"Has he indeed?" With the merest movement of his wrist, Basil summoned the magister, who opened the lid of the treasure box to reveal, Jesu help me!—the silver cumtach. Sure, Harald would bring *that* as his pledge of faith and honesty. The book was gone, but the sacred cover had found its way to the emperor nonetheless. Oh, but it was not the way I would have chosen to deliver it.

The official knelt down, withdrew the priceless cover from its resting place and, still on bended knee, placed it at the feet of the emperor. Basil leaned forward, allowing the imperial eye to rest upon the exquisite silver tracery and jewels of the cover. Then Harald stepped forward and laid the emperor's golden bowl alongside the silver cumtach.

"We see by this that you place a very high value on your word, King of the Danes."

The quaestor stared at the treasure incredulously, and I imagined that he was on the point of recanting his version of the events. But the moment passed, and the harbour master kept his mouth firmly shut.

"Magister," the emperor called, beckoning the official to him. He whispered something into the official's ear, whereupon the man nodded once and departed, walking backwards from the room. "Now we may learn the truth," Basil declared and, in afterthought, added, "as God wills."

# 32

Emperor Basil commanded that music should be played, and the wondrous organ we had heard on entering began once more. We waited, listening to the heavenly sounds of that most extraordinary instrument. The Danes grew restless; unaccustomed to spending so much time without shouting, drinking, or fighting, they shifted from one foot to the other with growing agitation. "How long are we to be made to stand here like this?" demanded Harald loudly.

"Peace, Jarl Harald," I soothed. "I believe the emperor is working out a plan."

He subsided with a growl and contented himself with scrutinizing the gold on display. Hnefi and Gunnar talked openly of how their fingers itched to be close to such riches, and yet unable to steal any for themselves. I might have been embarrassed by this, but as no one else knew what they said, it made no difference.

The emperor, for his part, deigned not to notice his barbaric guests' coarse behaviour. He sat back in his throne, folded his hands over his stomach and closed his eyes. When I thought he must be asleep, he roused himself and said, "Slave, come here."

There were no slaves near, that I could see. So it took me by surprise when he raised his hand and beckoned me. "Forgive me, basileus," I said, edging a hesitant step forward.

The emperor motioned me nearer, and held out his hand for me to kiss. I did so, and remained standing before him with my eyes downcast—as I had seen the magister do.

"We perceive that you are a learned man," Basil said. "How came you to be a slave to these barbarians?"

"Lord emperor, I was on a pilgrimage with my brother monks when our ship was attacked by Sea Wolves." I explained briefly about surviving the shipwreck and finding the Gaulish village. I concluded, saying, "The settlement was attacked that same night and I was taken captive." Indicating the cumtach resting in the box at the foot of the throne, I said, "The silver book cover offered to you as surety once belonged to us."

"Indeed?" wondered the emperor. "And your brother priests? What became of them?"

"Sovereign lord," I said, "I wish I knew. As it happens, I hoped the emperor might tell me."

Basil regarded me with a look of studied amazement. "We might tell you?" He laughed. "Although the emperor's knowledge of the events in the empire is exhaustive, it is by no means infinite. Why would a man of your learning imagine that we could provide you with an explanation of so obscure an event?"

"Forgive my presumption, basileus," I said, "but the pilgrimage of which I speak was to Constantinople; it was, in fact, to seek audience with yourself, sovereign lord, and present you with a gift both rare and precious."

"Truly?" The emperor professed himself to be fascinated and commanded me to explain further. "You have gained the imperial ear, bold priest—at least until the magister returns. Tell us more of this wonderful tale."

In all my days of captivity, I had never dared think, even in whimsy, that I might stand before the emperor and regale him with the story of my misfortune. But I was keen to learn the fate of my brothers, so up I spoke, casting aside all trepidation. I told the basileus about the abbey at Kells, and the making of the book; I told him about the choosing of the thirteen to make the pilgrimage, the preparations for the trip, and the storm that drove us across the sea and into the Sea Wolves' path. "I assumed the pilgrimage would continue without me," I said. "But unless the emperor tells me he has seen them, I must conclude that my friends turned back, or were killed in the raid as I feared."

Emperor Basil sat for a moment, thinking, and then said, "What is your name, priest?"

"Sovereign lord," I answered, "I am Aidan mac Cainnech."

"Aidan," he said, "it grieves us to tell you that your brother priests have not arrived in Constantinople. They have not come before us here. Devoutly do we wish it were otherwise, for judging by the cover alone, it would have been a gift worthy of veneration, and a tribute to your monastery's devotion. We are truly sorry."

The magister sacrum returned just then, and the emperor summoned him. I made to step away, but the emperor said, "Stay, priest." So, I remained beside the throne.

"Basileus," the magister said, "the *komes* have returned."

"They may enter," allowed Basil, and the magister withdrew. The emperor's smile grew sly as he said, "Now let us see what breed of vermin we have caught."

The magister reappeared, leading three young men, all dressed alike: they wore long, close-fitting tunics of yellow and blue with wide sleeves, and yellow breecs with the leggings tucked into the tops of high boots; short, gold-handled swords hung from their belts. The foremost of the three—slender as a sword, with dark hair and fine, sharp features—advanced swiftly to the throne and prostrated himself. "Rise, Nikos," said the emperor, recognizing the courtier. "Rise and declare before this exalted assembly that which you have discovered."

"Basileus," answered the man named Nikos, when he had regained his feet, "it would seem that our quaestor has been a very industrious man, and richly blessed of God in all his dealings."

"Enlighten us further." The emperor turned his gaze from the courtier to the worried visage of the harbour master.

Komes Nikos, a dark-haired young man with keen black eyes in a smooth, handsome face, held out his hands and two of the courtiers who had entered with him advanced bearing a large earthen jar. Nikos took the jar, raised it, and held it aloft. "With God and these men as my witnesses, this jar was found in the home of Quaestor Antonius, lord and emperor," he announced, his voice trembling slightly with the effort, for the jar appeared heavy. "With your permission, basileus."

Basil nodded, and Nikos let the jar fall. The pottery vessel struck the polished marble floor and smashed into splinters, releasing a cascade of gold and silver; hundreds of gold solidi and silver denarii splashed onto the floor.

Nikos, stooped, filled his hands with the coins, and let them spill from his fingers. "It would seem our estimable quaestor is either a most frugal man, or a most dishonest one. I am intrigued, emperor." He regarded the ashen-faced quaestor. "I would know how he acquired such wealth."

"Quaestor Antonius," called the emperor, "come forward and explain how you came by these riches. For we are persuaded that a man with a salary of two solidi a year could never hoard so much. Perhaps you sold property?" suggested Basil reasonably. "Perhaps you wagered on a race? Perhaps the Greens have given you the festival money for safe-keeping?"

Antonius stared sullenly at the money on the floor. "You had no right," he muttered to the courtier.

"By decree of the emperor, I was given the right," replied Nikos succinctly. His manner was that of a man enjoying himself with immense satisfaction, and immense restraint.

"We are waiting, Quaestor Antonius," said the emperor, raising his voice. "How did you come by this money? We require an answer."

Antonius, looking shaken and afraid, nevertheless raised his head. "Sovereign lord, the money which was found in my house is the inheritance of my family. It came into my possession with the death of my father, eight years ago."

"You certainly come from a very wealthy family, Quaestor Antonius," observed Nikos, his tone insinuating and accusing. "By the look of that pile, your father must have owned half of Pera."

"My father was a shrewd man of business," allowed Antonius. "It is well known. Ask anyone who had dealings with him."

"Shrewd indeed," said Nikos, stooping again to the heap of coins. He withdrew a handful. "It seems he must have saved much for the future—and well *into* the future. See here!" He held up a gold coin. "This solidus was struck only last year. And this one the year before. In fact," he sifted through the coins in his hand, examining them closely, "as I look at them, I cannot see any older than three years. Yet, you say they came to you eight years ago."

"I have been changing them—old for new," Antonius

replied smugly. "I prefer new coins; they have a more uniform weight."

The slippery quaestor appeared to be wriggling away. His explanation, though hardly believable, was at least plausible; and, more importantly, there seemed to be no way of disproving it. Sure, he had anticipated this day a thousand times and had devised his story well.

I looked at the coins on the floor, and saw the silver cumtach of Colum Cille in the thieving quaestor's hands. The silver! "Sovereign lord," I said, surprising even myself with my suddenness, "if I may speak."

The emperor nodded slowly, his eyes on the quaestor.

"There are silver coins among the gold. Perhaps they might be examined as well." So saying, I bent down and stretched my hand towards the heap of coins.

Komes Nikos stopped me; taking hold of my wrist, he said, "Allow me to assist you, friend." Though he spoke politely, his grip on my wrist was uncompromising, and there was no friendship in his eyes.

I withdrew, allowing the courtier to sort through the pile, picking out the silver denarii. In a moment, he had retrieved a handful, and then turned to me. "There are not so many silver as gold," he said, "but a fair few. What is your interest in them?"

"Only this," I said, and walked to where King Harald stood silent and slightly bewildered; I held out my hand to him. "Your silver, Jarl Harald," I said, in Danespeak. "Give me some coins."

"What is happening here?" he asked, withdrawing the pouch from his belt at the same time. "What are they saying?"

"Patience, lord, it is soon over, and I will tell you everything."

The king grudgingly placed the coin bag in my hand and I returned to my place by the throne. Nikos had already seen what I had in mind, and said, "Reach into the purse, and take out a coin. I will take up one also. Now, show them to the emperor."

We both extended our hands with a coin on the palm. Emperor Basil examined each denarius in turn. "They are the same."

Nikos took several more coins from among those he had retrieved and inspected each one. "They are all the same, basileus."

"I would know, Quaestor Antonius," the emperor said, "how the coins of this Danish king have come to be in your possession. Do you maintain that they were also part of your shrewd father's bequest?"

"Lord and emperor," the harbour master replied, "those denarii are the most common coin in the empire, as everyone knows. Rather ask how this barbarian king came into possession of coins minted in Constantinople."

"These were not minted in Constantinople, Quaestor Antonius," said the komes. "They were struck in Rome, and all commemorate Theophilus." Stooping again to the heap, he sifted through the coins, withdrawing the silver until he had them all. These he counted. "Basileus," he announced, rising, "I would have you know that there are forty-five Roman denarii."

The emperor glared at his tax collector. "It appears that you have, to the very coin, the precise number of denarii this king has charged you with stealing. What is more, each is a Roman coin of the exact stamp as that from the barbarian's own purse. If you can explain, then do so."

The harbour master, brazen to the last, shrugged. "It is merely an unlucky chance, basileus," he said. "Nothing more."

"Oh, it is too much for chance, we think," declared Basil pointedly. The emperor gazed with cruel satisfaction at the unhappy quaestor and said, "Allow us to suggest another, altogether more logical possibility: that you stole this silver from these men and put it in the jar with the intention of changing it for solidi—along with all the rest of the denarii you have been stealing in the course of your duties. Further, Quaestor Antonius, it is our belief that, judging from the considerable extent of the evidence we see before us, you have been abusing your position as Master of Hormisdas Harbour for a considerable length of time." Emperor Basil sat upright in his wide throne. "That will stop."

"Sovereign lord," said Antonius quickly, "the gold is mine, I swear it on the holy name. I am telling the truth; it is my bequest. With all respect, you cannot believe these barbari."

"Respect?" asked Basil. "We wonder that you use such a word. You have shown little respect to us, or to your position. Still," the emperor said briskly, "though the silver is no longer in question, it is not proven that you stole the gold."

So saying, Basil beckoned the magister to him. The court official brought a wax tablet of the kind the prefect carried, and gave it to the emperor. Taking up the stylus, Basil began to write.

"Basileus," ventured the quaestor hesitantly, "it was but a small transgression. It is not a matter for prison certainly."

"We agree, Quaestor Antonius, it is not a matter for prison. That would be a cruel waste of a man of your impressive talents, and a loss to the empire. It is clear to us, however, that your present position is, shall we say, constricting to you."

Glancing up from his writing, the emperor allowed himself a thin smile. "The imperial mines are always in need of men such as yourself—men with an appetite for wealth, and an eye for the glint of silver. We are certain you will find the company of like-minded men most invigorating."

The former harbour master's mouth dropped open; he closed it and swallowed hard. "No . . . no . . . please Holy Jesu, no," he murmured.

Basil, having dispensed justice to his satisfaction, dismissed the matter. "Transportation has been arranged. You will be the guest of the emperor until your ship sails." He made a signal with his hands and five of the Farghanese stepped forward at once. Basil passed the wax tablet to the magister, and flicked his hand towards the bronze doors, saying, "Take him from here."

"My money!" said the quaestor, struggling forward as the guards took hold of him. "That is my money."

"Your gold will remain with us," Basil replied. "Wealth of this magnitude would only prove a hazard where you are going. In this, we are showing you far more charity than you ever showed us."

The bronze doors opened and the prisoner was hauled into the anteroom. He made one last attempt to remonstrate with the emperor, but the leading Farghanese silenced him with a sharp blow to the mouth and he resigned himself to his fate and allowed himself to be led away.

Emperor Basil gestured that the gold and broken pottery should be cleared away. Komes Nikos turned to King Harald and presented him with the recovered silver coins. "Your denarii, lord," he said, dismissing the king with a word.

Harald accepted the silver and then, in an act I have pondered often since, he stepped to the foot of the throne and, directing me to translate his words, said: "Most Noble Emperor, I tell you the truth: I came here to plunder your treasure stores and take to myself as much as I could carry back to Skania."

The emperor received this confession with good grace. "You are not the first to entertain such notions, Lord Harald."

When I had relayed Basil's words, the Sea Wolf king continued, "Now I find myself before you, and I look around me," he glanced around with wide-eyed admiration, "and I see such wealth as men in my country cannot imagine." Gesturing to the pile of gold coins on the floor, Harald said, "What is more, I see that men in your service are rewarded far more richly than can be told."

The emperor nodded with satisfaction. "You have had but a glimpse of the wealth and power of the Holy Roman Empire, and you realize the futility of clashing with that power. In this, you show wisdom, Lord Harald."

"It is true," agreed Harald readily, when I had translated the emperor's words. "And I ask myself, if a mere servant can amass such wealth, what may a king do? I have with me four ships and one hundred and sixty men. We have come seeking plunder, but will stay to gain wealth and renown in friendship with you, Great Jarl. Therefore, I place myself, my men, and my ships at your service, Most Noble Emperor."

Even as I conveyed these words, I wondered at Harald's audacity. Was he so confident, so arrogant, as to believe all his men would follow him in this grand gesture? So naïve as to believe the emperor would accept his offer, and even reward him for it?

In this, I was the innocent. For, wonder of wonders, the Holy Emperor of Rome, Sovereign Lord of All Christendom, regarded Harald Bull-Roar, barbarian lord and plunderer, narrowly, as a man calculating the value of a horse, and made up his mind at once. "We accept your offer, Lord Harald. You will have seen that men of valour are welcome in my service, and they are indeed paid well. That you are seafaring men argues well in your favour: we have need of swift messengers just now, for the southern waters have become dangerous due to Arab raids.

"Therefore, let us put your fealty to the test. We are readying an envoy to Trebizond which will require an escort. Accept this service, and we will make you part of the imperial fleet. As it happens, the conventions of war at sea allow the victor to keep any spoils he should acquire when engaging an enemy. Naturally, we would extend this privilege to you, and even pray that you prosper."

Harald, when he had heard the cast of the emperor's thought, heartily approved of the plan. "We will meet your test, Lord Emperor," he said. "Your enemies will become our enemies. Our victories will be victories for you. I, Jarl Harald Bull-Roar, pledge this with my life and the lives of my men."

Perhaps Jarl Harald, himself a man of authority, recognizing a power far greater than his own had adopted the most prudent course; perceiving the might of the empire arrayed against him if he pursued the raiding scheme, his shrewd barbarian mind had contrived the best possible solution. Or perhaps God, toiling away unseen and unknown in the fertile soil of Harald's immortal soul, had sown the seed which now bore its unexpected fruit. However it was, the result both astonished and amazed me.

"We accept your pledge, Lord Harald," replied the emperor graciously. "And we will pray the Heavenly Father richly rewards your loyalty. Return to your ships and prepare yourselves." Gesturing to the magister, who produced his wax tablet, the emperor took up the stylus and began to write. "We will send the *protospatharius* to you tomorrow to arrange for provisioning. The envoy sails in three days' time." Passing the tablet back to the magister sacrum, Basil held out his hand for the king to kiss.

This time, Jarl Harald Bull-Roar bent his neck, and sealed his allegiance with a kiss. The emperor stood up from his throne and retrieved the golden bowl that lay at his feet and presented it to the wily Dane; then, descending from the dais, he stooped, and with his own hand swept a fistful of gold coins from the heap on the floor and poured them with a magnificent clatter into Harald's bowl as a wealthy merchant dispensing alms to a favourite beggar. The barbarian king smiled so broadly, and with such manifest delight, that the emperor repeated the gesture. I could not help noticing, however, that the silver cumtach received no further mention, and lay forgotten at the foot of the throne.

Basil then dismissed his new ally, saying, "Serve us well, King of Skania, and the glory and treasure you seek will be yours, as God wills."

Harald thanked the emperor and took his leave, saying he would return to his ships and await the emperor's pleasure. Then, following the magister's lead, we were removed from the imperial presence—eyes averted, we walked slowly backwards from the throne. Upon reaching the doorway, I paused for a last lingering glimpse of the marvellous hall, when the magister put his hand on my shoulder.

"The basileus would speak with you alone," he said, indicating the throne. I looked up to see Emperor Basil beckoning me to him. "Tell your king that you will be returned to him when the emperor has finished with you."

Harald, happy with his gold, grunted his gruff approval, and I retraced my steps to the throne wondering what God's Vice-Regent on Earth could want with me.

# 33

"We live in uncertain times, Brother Aidan," the emperor said, his tone at once familiar and imperious, "as you have seen evidenced this day: trusted officials use their powers to rob and steal for their own gain, and barbarian raiders argue for justice and pledge loyalty."

The emperor had ordered everyone from the throne-room save his imperial bodyguard. These men stood ranged around the throne, expressionless, eyes neither watching nor looking away. There was no one else to hear what the emperor said to me.

Raising a hand to the Farghanese bodyguard surrounding his throne, he said, "Look you now and tell us who stands closest to the emperor?"

He seemed to expect an answer, so I said, "Are they barbarians, sovereign lord?"

"Your master is a barbarian, and we have seen many such before. We labour under no illusion, Brother Aidan, we know we faced an enemy who came to steal and kill; he told the truth about that, yes, but we knew anyway. And yet, when given the chance—we know well who placed that chance within his grasp, Subtle Priest—when given the chance, this rough barbarian showed himself more trustworthy than the man born and bred to his office.

"Trust is the heart of the matter here. Who does the emperor trust? His friends? Friends sick with envy and the venom of spite, who would sooner slit his throat than bend the knee? Does he trust his officials? All the scores upon scores of nameless, grasping functionaries who would sooner poison his drink than kiss his ring? Perhaps he trusts his sons? Men who are either too young to shoulder the burden of state, or who are themselves ambitious and over-eager for the crown?"

He appraised the effect of his words, and nodded with grim satisfaction. "You begin to see how it is. For every work the empire requires, the emperor must weigh out the loyalty of the man he asks to perform the task. For most duties, scant loyalty is required, and one man may serve as well as the next. For some tasks, however, great loyalty is necessary—and then the choice becomes much more exacting."

As he spoke, I began to feel a strange sensation in my stomach—like fear, or dread, but neither—as if I had made a momentous wager and was now about to discover whether I had won or lost.

"Komes Nikos, as you have seen, is a loyal and trust-worthy servant," Emperor Basil continued. "He stands close to the throne. Scholarae Justin is poised for swift advancement; his diligence and honesty will find particular reward. We have need of such men always, and that is why we seize on them whenever and wherever we find them.

"Brother Aidan," he looked at me with his clever dark eyes, "we see such a man standing before us now, and we are loath to let him escape our sight."

"Then you must also see, sovereign lord," I told him, raising my hand to the iron ring on my neck, "I am but a slave."

The emperor's response was sharply contemptuous. "You disappoint us, priest. Little do you comprehend the power of an emperor if you imagine *that* to be an impediment. Allow us to reassure you, brother monk, the ability to reward the friends of the empire is well within our grasp."

"Forgive me, sovereign lord," I said. "I am ill-taught in courtly ways. I have spoken out of place."

The emperor leaned back against the cushions of his throne. "Never fear, we will not command you against your will. It is your loyalty we are most anxious to procure, not your obedience." The emperor smoothed the purple silk of his robe with his hands.

"Your pilgrimage has not been in vain, brother priest. You are well placed to be of service to us. It may be that the chore we have in mind is the very task to which God himself has called you. Hear us, Brother Aidan; your work has only begun."

"Sovereign lord," I replied, my thoughts roiling in confusion, "command me how you will, I am your servant."

Basil smiled a lipless smile of thin satisfaction. "Good. We are pleased, brother monk." Beckoning me closer, he said, "Listen carefully, this is what we would have you do."

I attended with utmost care while the emperor explained that the whole of the imperial attention was concentrated upon the embassy to Trebizond. It was, he said, a matter of utmost delicacy. "Naturally, the empire has enemies of many kinds—enemies whose aims are not always easy to discern. Therefore, we must avail ourselves of every protection for the good of the empire." He looked at me with disarming candour and said, "Secrecy has its uses, brother priest. If you know how to keep a secret, we would welcome your presence in Trebizond. More, we would reward it."

I replied that discretion was a virtue, and one which

had served me well in the abbey. The emperor then shared his secret concern and asked me to be his eyes and ears in Trebizond, to observe all that took place and report to him upon my return to Byzantium. When he finished, he asked if I understood. Upon receiving my assurance, he stood abruptly. The Farghanese all moved back one pace. Making a gesture of dismissal, the emperor said, "Come to us when your journey is completed."

"As you will, basileus." I bowed my head and stepped backwards as I had seen the others do.

The emperor summoned the magister to usher me from the palace. "The gateman," Basil said, "is he still with us?"

"He awaits your pleasure in the anteroom, basileus," replied the white-robed courtier.

"Tell him that he is to return this man to his ship," the emperor commanded, adding as he thought of it, "but there is no hurry, we believe, so tell the guard that he is to show our servant whatever he wishes to see and experience of our city." Glancing at me, he said, "And by all means, he is to feed the man. Give him a solidus for this purpose, magister."

"As you will, sovereign lord," replied the courtier.

Once again, I was dismissed and led from the hall. Basil allowed me to reach the door before calling, "God grant you a safe voyage, brother priest, and a swift return. Until then, let us both anticipate the pleasure of discussing what you will do with your freedom."

Upon emerging from my audience, I found Justin waiting alone in the anteroom; all the others had gone. The magister beckoned him to us and placed a gold coin in his hand, charging him with the emperor's orders. The magister then turned and disappeared into the vestibule, and we were left to make our way out of the palace.

"So!" exclaimed Justin as we stepped outside at last. "This is one day I will not soon forget."

I agreed heartily that I had never experienced anything like it before.

"You are a remarkable fellow, my friend." He regarded me with genuine admiration. "The quaestor sent to the mines, and the barbarian hired as a mercenary—my scholarii will never believe me." He stopped and looked at the coin the magister had given him. "A whole solidus," he said, drawing a deep breath, "and there is still daylight! Now then, what pleasures will you command this evening? By the emperor's command, I am at your service."

"It has been a very long time since I set foot inside a chapel. If it is not too difficult, I would like to go to church and pray."

"The only difficulty will be to choose which church to favour with our presence—there are hundreds in Constantinople. We could go to Saint Stephen's," he indicated the nearest cross rising beyond the wall, "where the emperor and his family pray on certain days. Or, I could take you to the Hagia Sophia—every visitor to the city wants to go there."

"Please, if it is not too much trouble, I would like to go where you pray."

"Where I pray?" wondered Justin. "It is only a small church near my home. There is nothing at all remarkable about it. You have all of Constantinople to choose from, my friend." Though he protested, I could see that he was pleased with my choice. "Let me take you to Saint Sophia's."

"I would rather see your church. Will you take me there?"

"If that is what you want, of course." Together we left the Great Palace, and made our way down from the walled precinct, slipping through one of the small gates close to the Hippodrome. We followed a narrow, twisted, high-walled pathway behind that enormous edifice and emerged onto a wide, tree-lined street. "This is the Mese," Justin told me. "It is the longest street in the world, and it begins there at the Milion." He pointed to a tall, free-standing column set in a square a short distance away.

"Where does it end?"

"At the Forum in Rome," he said grandly. "This way; my church is not far."

Turning west, we walked along the wide street which was, he told me, the city's chief ceremonial route. "All the emperors and armies march along the Mese and go out through the Golden Gate when they leave on campaigns. And, whether in triumph or defeat, they return the same way."

The Mese swarmed with people in the cool evening—as if, having finished work for the day, the entire population of the city was now making its way home—most of them carrying the items for a simple supper: a loaf of bread, a few eggs, an onion or two, and oily packets of spiced olives. The more fortunate, however, might pause and enjoy a meal at one of the innumerable eating and drinking places lining the Mese—*tabernas*, Justin called them. These could be recognized by the bright-coloured standards with names painted on them—names like House of Bacchus, The Green Charioteer, or Leaping Lark. Statues of Greek and Roman gods stood outside most of these tabernas, along with smouldering braziers on tripods.

If the sight of glowing charcoal on a chilly night was not enough to draw hungry people in, the owners of the eating places stood beside their braziers, cooking meat on spits and imploring passersby to stop and avail themselves of the hospitality offered. "Come in, come in," they would call. "My friend, it is warm inside. The wine is good here.

Tonight we have roast pork and figs. You will love this food. Come in now; there is room just for you."

The aroma from the braziers and that of the unseen kitchens combined to form waves of scent, lush and dense, which ebbed and flowed about us as we made our way down the longest street in all the world. After passing a number of these tabernas, my mouth began to water and my stomach to growl.

Justin, however, seemed impervious to both the aroma of the food and the pleas of the taberna men. Ignoring all but the path before us, he pushed on. We passed a magnificent church—the Church of the Sacred Martyrs, Justin informed me—and all at once, the bells began. First just one, probably from Saint Sophia's, which was followed quickly by another from a church further off, and then another, and still others, near and far, until the whole of Constantinople rang with the sound. Even to one long accustomed to the tolling of the daily round, I could but marvel at this multitude of chimes: bells of every tone from high, clear-voiced celestials, to deep-toned earthshakers. From every corner of the city came the blessed sound—a boon of peace at the close of day.

We turned onto a narrow street and joined a throng making its way to the church at the end of the packed-earth path. The doors of the church were open and candle-light spilled out onto the street and onto the heads of those crowding through the doorway. "This is the Church of Saint Euthymi and Saint Nicholas, where I worship. There are many more beautiful churches, but few more crowded."

We waded into the press at the door and squeezed in to find places next to one of the pillars. Candles blazed in every corner, and lamps hung from elaborate iron grids suspended above the heads of the crowd. Indeed, there were so many people packed together so tightly, that I could hear but little of what the priests said. Even so, I know there were numerous prayers and I recognized the reading as coming from the Gospel of Saint Luke.

In this, it was very like one of the services performed at the abbey, but the similarity ended when the worshippers began to sing. Their song was unlike any I have ever heard. I do not know how this music was achieved, but it seemed to fill the entire church with a buoyant, uplifting sound of many parts which somehow blended and united to form a single voice of admirable strength. I was considerably moved and impressed, and felt a longing in my heart for the monks of Cenannus na Ríg. DeDanaan's children rejoice in the best voices of any in the world, and I would have given much indeed to hear them attempt this new way of singing.

Aside from the music, the worship was, as I say, much the same as I had known before—except for the fact that, instead of kneeling or prostrating themselves for prayer, the people stood upright; and instead of clasping their hands, they lifted them up. Also, the priests used far more incense than we would have allowed at the abbey. Indeed, they seemed intent on filling the church with clouds of fragrant smoke.

In the end, this became too much for me. It may be that the import of the day, together with the lights and sounds and smoke and the press of the crowd, combined to overwhelm me. One moment I was standing beside Justin, listening to the priest speak out the benediction, and the next moment I was slumped against the pillar and Justin crouched beside me with a worried expression on his face.

"I felt a little light-headed," I told him as soon as we were outside once more. It was dark now, and a chill wind blew off the sea. "But I feel better now. The air has revived me."

"I do not wonder you fainted," he replied. "You have walked over half the city today, and on an empty stomach." He frowned reprovingly. "It is time to eat."

Reaching the Mese, we continued west a short way, arriving at a crossroads. Justin turned onto the right hand street, which was steep and dark and quiet, and led me a few dozen paces to a small house with a low door and a high step. As we approached, I heard laughter from within. On the doorframe hung a wooden placard painted with the image of a roast fowl and an amphora of wine.

He thumped on the door with the flat of his hand. "I am from Cyprus," Justin told me, pausing in his assault on the door. "The man who owns this house is from Cyprus, too. All the best food comes from there. It is true. Ask anyone."

At that instant the door opened to reveal a man with a black beard and gold ring in his ear. "Justin!" he cried at once. "So! You have not forgotten us! You wish a meal, yes? You shall have one." Justin then showed the bearded man the coin given him by the prefect. The man grinned widely. "What am I saying? A meal? You shall have a feast! A feast I shall give you." Turning to me, the man said, "Welcome to my house. I do not know you, my friend, but already I can see that you are twice blessed."

"How so?" I wondered, as charmed by his effusive greeting as by the exquisite aromas washing over us from the warm rooms inside.

"It is simple. You have chosen to visit the finest taberna in all Constantinople, and this in the company of the most excellent soldier in all the empire. Oh, the night is cold. Come in, my friends!" he cried, almost pulling us over the threshold.

Closing the door quickly behind us, he said to me, "I am Theodorou Zakis, and I am honoured to have you in my house. The worries of the day cannot reach you here. Please, follow me."

He led us up a narrow way of stairs to a large room with a handsome bronze brazier glowing in the centre, like a hearth, around which were scattered a number of low couches. Several of these were occupied by men reclining in groups of two or three over large platters filled with various dishes. There were also a few small tables set into alcoves formed by wooden screens. One table was placed in that part of the room which overhung the street below and it was to this table Theo brought us.

"You see, Justin, I have saved this for you. I know you prefer it." Turning to me, he added, as if in secret: "Soldiers always prefer tables. I do not know why." He pulled out the table then, and positioned the two low, three-legged stools. "Sit! Sit you down. I will bring the wine."

"And bread, Theo. Lots of bread," Justin said. "We have had nothing to eat all day."

Our arrival occasioned but little interest in our fellow diners. They carried on with their meal as if we did not exist. I thought this most unusual until Justin explained that it was customary and no one thought it rude. "Have you no tabernas in Ierne?" he inquired.

"No. It is a new thing to me—but then, everything in this city is new to me."

"When I first came to Constantinople four years ago, I had no friends so I came here often, even though I could not afford it so easily. I was only a legionary then."

"Do you have family?"

"A mother and sister only," he replied. "They live in Cyprus still. I have not seen them for seven years. But I know they are well. We write to one another often. It is one of the blessings of life in the emperor's army—a soldier can send letters anywhere in the world and be certain they will arrive."

Theo returned with a double-handled jar shaped like a

small amphora, but with a flat bottom. "For you, my friends, I have saved the best. From Chios!" he announced, producing two wooden cups which he placed on the table beside the jar. "Drink this, and forget you ever tasted wine before."

"If we drink all this," laughed Justin, "we will forget everything."

"Would that be so terrible?" Laughing, Theo retreated—only to return a moment later with four loaves of bread in a woven basket. The bread was still warm.

"Tell me, Aidan," Justin said, pouring wine into the two wooden cups, "what did you think of the emperor?"

"He is a very great man," I answered, taking up one of the loaves and handing it to Justin.

"Indeed, indeed," he agreed good-naturedly, breaking the loaf in half. "That goes without saying. He has done much to benefit the city and the empire."

In the manner of Constantinopolitans, Justin said a prayer over the meal. It was not unlike one which might have been heard over a meal at the monastery. The prayer finished, I took up another loaf and broke it in half, releasing a yeasty gush that brought the water to my mouth. We ate and drank for a time, savouring the bread, warming to the wine.

After a while, Justin observed, "This may be a Roman city, but it has a Byzantine heart, and a Byzantine heart is, above all, suspicious."

"Why suspicious?"

"Need you ask?" Justin said, his smile becoming secretive and sly. "Nothing is simple, my friend. Every bargain masks betrayal, and every kindness is cunning in disguise. Every virtue is calculated to the smallest grain, and bartered to its best advantage. Beware! Nothing is as it seems in Byzantium."

This seemed to me unlikely, and I told him so. But Justin grew insistent.

"Look around you, priest. Where great wealth and power reside, there suspicion runs rampant. Even Rome in its greatest glory could not surpass the wealth and power Constantinople possesses now. Suspicion is a necessity in this city: it is the knife in your sleeve and the shield at your back."

"But we are Christians," I pointed out. "We have dispensed with such worldly conceits."

"You are right, of course," Justin conceded, emptying his cup for the second or third time. "No doubt I have lived too long in this city. Still, even Christians hear the rumours." Leaning forward over the table he lowered his voice. "It is said that our former emperor, Basileus Michael, died from a fall. But does a man lose both hands at the wrist by slipping in the bath? Even the emperor's friends say Basil the Macedonian's ascension owes less to divine appointment, than to the skillful application of the blade." Justin silently drew a line across his throat with his forefinger.

The King of Kings, Elect of Christ, God's Vice-Regent on Earth entangled in murder? How could anyone say such a thing aloud, let alone think it? Was this how the citizens of Constantinople spent their days—in vicious speculations and wicked calumny? Ah, but he had already drunk a fair amount of strong wine, so I forgave him his slander and paid no heed to what he said.

The taberna owner returned and placed before us two clay bowls of milky broth and two wooden spoons. He left again without a word, drifting to another party of three reclining on couches. In a moment all four were laughing out loud. I raised my bowl to my lips to drink, but Justin stirred his soup with a spoon and I was reminded how I had slipped into the ways of the barbarians.

"Any sorrow at Michael's passing was buried along with his blood-sodden corpse, I should think," Justin said lightly, raising his spoon to his lips and blowing on the hot broth. "He was a profligate and a drunkard, bringing the city to ruin with his extravagance and dissipation. It was well known he seduced and bedded Basil's wife—and not once only, but many times, and that Basil knew. Indeed, some claim that one of our emperor's sons is not his own, and that only because the cuckold's wife had produced a royal bastard was the hapless Basil allowed to take the purple and become co-ruler."

Glancing around quickly to see if anyone had heard him, I saw to my relief that the other diners appeared oblivious to our talk. "How can you say such things?" I demanded, my voice a hoarse, offended whisper.

Justin shrugged and swallowed down the broth. "I do not say Basileus Michael was an evil man, only that he was a weak one."

"Weak!" I gasped.

My companion raised the corner of his mouth in a grim smile. "We have had Popes and Patriarchs that would make poor dim-witted Michael seem a saint by comparison. It is said that Phocus kept two Abyssinian boys as lovers, and tortured heretics for the amusement of his dinner guests. Theophilus, they say, killed two brothers and a son to get the throne. Basil has his son Leo locked in prison this very moment."

Lifting the bowl to his mouth, Justin spooned down the broth. I gaped in disbelief. "You are not eating, Aidan," he observed over the top of the bowl. "Do you not like the soup?"

"It is not for lack of an appetite that I refrain," I retorted sharply. "I am aghast at the callous way in which you defame the Holy Emperor. I am appalled at the facile way in which you repeat vilest slander. Even if the smallest crumb of what you say is true, it should move us to pray pardon and forgiveness for our fallen sovereign, rather than to repeat malicious gossip."

Justin lowered the bowl. "I have upset you. My words were ill-chosen. Forgive me, brother, it is the way we speak here. On my life, I meant no offence. I am sorry."

His contrition softened my anger, and I relented. "Perhaps I have over-stated my objection. I am a stranger here, after all. If I speak when I should listen it is for you to forgive me."

"No, you are right to remind me of my misplaced charity," replied Justin, setting aside the bowl. Retrieving the cups, he handed one to me. "Now, for the sake of this fine meal, let us put all such unpleasantness behind us and drink a health." Handing my cup to me, he said, "Let us drink to our new friendship." He raised his cup, and I raised mine. "To the friendship of Christian men!" he said.

"To Christian friendship," I said, tipping the cup to my lips.

We ate in silence for a time, sipping our wine, and dipping bread in the golden broth. I began to feel genuinely revived. Justin was just refilling our cups yet again when the owner's wife came to the table with a wooden platter bearing a roast chicken—for each of us! The platter covered the whole of the table, forcing Justin to put the cups and jar on the floor. She lay the platter before us and stood, admiring her handiwork before urging us to eat and enjoy.

"Now," said Justin lightly, "let us pay our respects to these neglected birds. It would be a sin to let this food go cold." Pulling his knife from his belt, Justin began cutting into the chicken before him, indicating that I should do the same. When I hesitated, he said, "Have you no knife?" Before I could reply, he said, "Of course not. Here, take mine." He offered his to me. "Forgive me, Aidan, I keep forgetting you are a slave."

The birds were stuffed with almonds and sweetmeat spiced with cumin and honey, and surrounded with small, leaf-wrapped parcels containing minted lambsmeat, lentils, and barley. Every mouthful, every morsel, was a revelation of wonder. Each bite was a delicacy which I, shameful to say, gobbled greedily, immersing myself in the exotic flavours. Remember, I had never tasted lemons before, and I discerned their splendid tang and aroma in most of the dishes, even the soup. I had never eaten vine leaves, nor aniseed, nor olives, nor half of the spices used in that meal.

It is my belief that I have never tasted food so sumptuous and fine, and to eat in the company of another Christian was a blessing to me. I recalled the meals at the abbey table, and rebuked myself for all the times I had felt less than charitable towards any of my brothers, especially Diarmot.

The memory put me in mind of Éire, and I felt a pang of regret for my brother monks in Kells. I missed my friends and the steady, slow-revolving wheel of the daily round. I missed hearing the psalms and prayers, and the gospel reading at the eventide meal. I missed Abbot Fraoch, and Ruadh, and Cellach; I missed the scriptorium, and the feel of a pen in my hand. And, God bless him, I missed Dugal.

Ah, mo croi, I thought, what has become of you?

"I have not eaten so well, nor in such good company since I left Kells," I told Justin when we had taken the edge from our hunger.

"I have been wondering about this," he said, "How did a priest of Ierne come to be a slave to wild barbarians?"

Thus, while picking out choice morsels from the platter before us, I told him of my sojourn among the Sea Wolves of Skania. I told him about the abbey, and my work there, and about being chosen for the pilgrimage, and the book we had made for the emperor, the cover of which he had seen this very day. "That was crafted by the brothers of Hy," I said. "The barbarians destroyed the book."

"Do you belong to a sect?"

"I am of the Célé Dé. The words mean Servants of God," I told him, and explained that ours was a small community of monks who lived simply, prayed continually, worked to support ourselves and maintain the abbey, and served the people of the region in various ways.

Justin attended carefully to all I said, asking questions now and then, but mostly contenting himself to listen. The wine loosened my tongue, and I talked—far more than I would have thought possible—through all that remained of the meal and on and on. When it came time to leave, Justin paid the taberna man, who bade us good night and farewell, sending us on our way with small sweet cakes to eat as we made our way home.

"But you still have not said how you came to be Harald's slave," Justin said as we started down the Mese once again. "This is a story I wish to hear."

So, as we walked the near-empty street I told him about the work of the three monasteries, making the book and its silver cover, and the unhappy pilgrimage to Constantinople. I ended saying, "I have been fortunate. At least I have arrived. I have no idea what has happened to the others. I fear the worst."

"As to that," replied Justin, "I have friends among the scholarii on the gates. I will speak to them. There is little that passes in or out of the city that the gate guards do not know. One of my cohorts may have heard something about your brothers." Turning, he lifted a hand to the Magnaura Gate standing before us. "We have come to the end of our way. Come, let us find a boat for you."

Justin spoke briefly to the guard on the gate, and the man let us through the night door. There were still a few small craft waiting at the bottom of the steps, and Justin bargained with the boatman and paid him. "He will take you to the ship. Good night, Aidan," he said, helping me into the boat.

"Thank you, Justin," I replied. "Thank you for all you have done for me this day. I will pray God rewards your kindness a thousand times over."

"Please, say no more," he answered. "I have my reward: the emperor favours me with his gold, I have bread and wine with a brother . . . it is a good day for me." Raising his hand in farewell, he said, "Remember, I will seek word of your friends. I should learn something in a day or two. Come see me when you can."

"How will I find you again?" I called as the boat pushed away from the quay.

"I am always at the gate," he said. "Farewell, my friend. God keep you."

"And you. Farewell, Justin."

# 34

The next morning, King Harald prepared to receive the protospatharius aboard the longship. I marvelled at the eagerness with which this red-bearded plunderer donned the garb of civilization. I watched him stride about the deck, ordering the ship for inspection by the Overseer of the Fleet, and I thought: yesterday he was but a raiding rogue, and today he is a loyal defender of the empire.

At midday the anticipated official arrived in a small boat with four men in blue cloaks; they all wore brown belts and low-crowned, wide-brimmed black hats, and a black cloth pouch hung at his side on a leather strap over his shoulder. As an official of the imperial court, he carried a rod of ebony which had a bronze knob on either end.

The overseer and his men came aboard bearing greetings from the basileus and a parchment document recognizing the jarl and his men as mercenaries in service to the emperor. "I am Jovian, Protospatharius of the Imperial Fleet," he told us, and presented the sealed parchment to Harald, who received it with genuine gratitude, and sat bathed in bliss as I read it out to him. The two then sat down to a meal of black bread and fish and öl; they ate and talked most amiably and then applied themselves to the business at hand: negotiation of the amounts and methods of remuneration for Harald's service.

The emperor, it transpired, had placed the value of Harald's service at a thousand nomismi each *month*. There ensued some confusion over this, however, and it was explained that a month was to be understood as the duration of time between one full moon and the next.

"That is a hundred silver denarii every month," I told him. "I think that is very good, Jarl Harald."

Hnefi and Orm, sitting close by, heard the number and could not believe their good fortune. "Jarl Harald," they said, "it is more than we got raiding all last summer!"

But the marauding Dane was not accustomed to accepting the first offer. "It is enough for me and the use of my ship perhaps," he allowed cannily. "But I have four ships and a hundred and sixty men. What am I to give them?" While I translated his words, the king fixed the courtier with an uncompromising stare.

"I did not know you had so many men," replied Jovian. "Perhaps some allowance might be made for them." After a brief conference with his underlings, he said, "Shall we say two thousand nomismi? One thousand for you and your ships, and another thousand for your men. What say you to that?"

"That is less than ten denarii for each man," Harald complained.

"But it is more than most of them have ever held in their hands at once," pointed out Hnefi.

"Nay," declared Harald with a slow, obstinate shake of his head. "Ten for each man." I conveyed the king's answer.

"Eight, perhaps," suggested the overseer cautiously. "And I will allow your men a share of the theme bread."

Harald listened to the offer, considered it, and extended his hand in the barbarian manner. The protospatharius regarded the king's hand with a bemused expression.

"It means he has agreed," I informed the official. "If you agree, clasp his hand thus—" I made a shaking motion with my hands to show him how it was done.

Jovian grasped the Sea King by the hand and sealed the bargain. That settled, they then turned to a discussion of the rights, privileges, and duties of the Danes as new-made subjects of the realm. Lastly, they decided how, when, and where provisions for the voyage were to be collected, and the means by which the Sea Wolves were to join the other ships of the imperial fleet making their way to Trebizond. Needless to say, I spent the day translating between them; it was tedious, but I learned much to my advantage about the emperor's fleet, and the nature of the voyage under contemplation.

I understood that it was to be more than a simple trading party, although trade was indeed part of it, for Trebizond, owing to its location at the furthest extent of the eastern frontier, had long supplied Byzantium with its silks, spices, jewels, and other essential luxuries which, I quickly learned, the Arabs controlled. Each year, a great fleet of merchant ships made its way to Trebizond for the trade festival which was held in the spring. Delegations from all over the world attended the festival.

Recently, however, the Byzantine delegation had been running afoul of Arab pirates who preyed on ships passing to and from the market, which created the necessity of sending an escort of warships to protect the merchants—a costly exercise, and one which the imperial navy would rather avoid, all the more since the ships were increasingly needed elsewhere. For this reason, the emperor was risking the winter seas in order to send an envoy to arrange for a council with an entity called the Caliph of Samarra. If the council proved successful and the raiding could be brought under control, much expense and bloodshed might be avoided at next year's festival.

It was late in the day when the protospatharius finished his business and departed. I begged leave to return to the city, thinking I might worship again in one of Constantinople's churches, or even receive word from Justin as to the fate of my brother monks, but Jarl Harald would not allow it. He demanded I tell him what had passed between the emperor and myself the day before.

I had hoped he would not ask, but in the event I had already decided that I would tell him the truth—at least, as much of the truth as I could without betraying the confidence of the emperor.

"You returned to the ship late in the night," the king pointed out. "I am wondering what use the emperor made of my slave."

"Jarl Harald," I answered, "it is true that I was long absent from your side. The emperor wished to speak with me about the voyage to Trebizond."

"I see," the king replied, in a way that suggested he did not see at all why the emperor should bother himself about me.

"I believe he was grateful to you for bringing the harbour master to justice," I suggested, side-stepping the issue slightly.

"Ah, yes," replied Harald, as if remembering the incident was a strain on his mind, "the harbour master. Nothing else?"

"The emperor believes that he cannot trust many of his court officials," I offered. "That is why he makes such liberal use of mercenaries—men who prosper with his success, but have nothing to gain at his demise. He is well disposed to reward those who earn his pleasure."

"This Basil is shrewd, I think. He uses well the tools of his craft," Harald mused. "Did he ask about me?"

"About you, Jarl Harald? No, he did not ask me anything about you, or your affairs. But I can tell you that he appeared well satisfied with the bargain between you and him. In any event, he said no more about it—only that he found such alliances useful because he could place little trust in others."

"Heya," observed Harald absently. Obviously, I was not saying what he expected to hear. He was silent for a moment, and then said, "You will stay on the ship until we sail. This I have decided."

He dismissed me then, and I went to the prow of the ship and hunkered down in the sharp V-shaped nook formed by the high-swept keel and sides. There, below the fierce painted dragonhead, I turned my face to the planks, closed my eyes, and tried to impose some small order upon the chaos of my thoughts. Sure, this had been a most confusing run of days for me, and I was feeling the strain of trying to swim against the tide of swift-moving events.

To begin: I had arrived at the city of my death. Strangely, this no longer frightened me. I suppose I had lived long enough with the knowledge for any fear and dread to have abated. And now that I was here, I felt nothing—save an ambiguous curiosity. My lucid dreams never foretold falsely, however; experience had long ago taught me that what I saw never failed to come about. Still, I had arrived in Constantinople, I had walked abroad in the city, and yet I lived. I did not know what to make of that.

Nor did I know what to make of Justin's suggestion that word of my brother monks might be forthcoming. For if they had reached Constantinople, the emperor certainly would have known. Even without the gift of the book, they would have sought audience with him. Reason suggested the pilgrimage had not succeeded, but hope argued otherwise.

And then there was the emperor's secret. What was I to make of that?

"We have now a chance for peace with the Muhammedans of the Abbasid," the emperor had told me once we were alone together. Although peace is always a laudable aim, and worthy to be pursued at all times, who or what these *Muhammedans* might be, I did not know. But this was why the emperor wished me to attend the embassy to Trebizond: "We require an impartial witness, canny priest," the emperor said. "We require someone who will watch and remember all that passes there—someone who will not be suspected, someone unknown."

The basileus had then gone on to imply that if I agreed to report the proceedings of the meeting between his emissaries and those of this caliph, I would be freed from my captivity to Harald. Sure, I was sore tempted. What man would choose to remain even a moment in slavery if granted the opportunity to end it at a word?

Oh, but I was also cautious. Try as I might, I could in no way discern the emperor's motive in this. Perhaps he only meant to help me—to reward me with my freedom, let us say, for bringing the thieving quaestor to justice. Although, if that were in his mind, he could have done it then and there.

I pondered the emperor's words, turning them over in my mind. And I paid special heed to all that passed between Harald and the fleet overseer, hoping for a hint, however small, of what or who the emperor feared that he should take such illicit precautions. I learned much, but nothing to betoken any apprehension; nor anything that would answer the most vexing question: why had the emperor chosen me?

Perhaps, as he had intimated, the emperor could not spare any of his trusted men for this errand, and since, as Harald's slave, I was bound to go with the ships anyway, he merely decided that I might perform a useful service. Still, I asked myself: was it really so difficult to find loyal men?

Likely, it was an act of impulse and nothing more. This I told myself, but could not help thinking that something more sinister lay behind it. No doubt, I was over-influenced by Justin's vile gossip—I confess it did disturb me greatly. Sure, it had been most careless of him to speak so. Had I been a better priest, I should have imposed a penance on him so that he would refrain from repeating gossip, were he to be so tempted in the future.

These thoughts circled in my restless mind, never alighting, never settling. In the end, however, it came to this: the Holy Emperor himself had commanded my service. As a priest of the church, I was forsworn to obey.

*Suspicion*, Justin said, *is the knife in your sleeve and the shield at your back.* I forced the thought from me. But the guardsman's words kept coming back to me: *Where great wealth and power reside, there suspicion runs rampant.*

Such were my thoughts, swarming in my brain like wasps. In the end, I gave up trying to order them, and simply poured out my heart to God. I prayed for a goodly time, but received no solace, so stopped after a while and sat quietly, listening to the talk of the men around me. After a time, I rose and busied myself with other things.

The next day the fleet overseer sent a man with a map showing our destination and the route by which we would go. Both king and pilot studied the map and, with me as interpreter, questioned the man closely and at length. The map was much more detailed and accurate than any Thorkel had ever seen, and revealed much of the southern seas, heretofore unknown to the Danes. When they had learned all they could, Harald dismissed the man and no sooner had his feet left the planks than the king ordered me to make a copy of the map for him. Despite using the most primitive tools—a seabird's feather for a pen!—I persevered, and even found the labour enjoyable. I could not resist the urge to embellish the new map with a few triscs and a band of knotwork down one side. The quill, though crude, served well enough, and I found myself enjoying the practice of my former craft so much that I drew, over the empty Southern Sea, a wild goose, symbol of the Holy Spirit—a blessing to all who should behold the map in years to come. My work occupied me the rest of the day, and took my mind off wanting to go ashore.

The following morning, the ships were moved to the Harbour of Theodosius, which served the emperor's fleet, being nearer the imperial storehouses and granaries. All through the dreary, rain-dashed morning, I watched as the wagons trundled onto the quay and sacks and baskets of provisions were bundled into the waiting ships. I watched, looking for any opportunity to leave the ship; despite Harald's orders I still hoped for a brief word with Justin. After a while the rain stopped and a dull, hazy sun appeared. Sea gulls wheeled in the air, diving for garbage in the harbour. As midday approached, I began to fear that Harald would keep his decision, and I would not have another chance to go into the city.

Happily, as the last of the sacks were being stowed, Gunnar came to me. "Heya, Aeddan," he said by way of greeting. "Jarl Harald says Hnefi and I must go and collect our share of bread." He passed me a small square of parchment on which was written a number; the parchment bore an imperial seal. "The king says you are to go with us in the event we are questioned by those in authority over the loaves."

This was the chance for which I had been hoping. Tucking the parchment into my belt, I said, "When the jarl commands, we must obey. Come, let us hurry."

"Heya," agreed Gunnar, regarding me dubiously.

Summoning two from the score of small boats working the harbour, we departed with a party of ten to fetch bread for all four ships. One of the small privileges of serving in the imperial forces was this allowance of bread which could be obtained from any of several imperial bakeries in the city. Even though all four of Harald's ships were full-laden with provisions, the king was intent on receiving everything due him. Bread had been granted in his bargain with the Overseer of the Fleet and if the emperor decreed free bread for his servants, then Harald wanted each and every loaf.

Despite the fact that we were now in the emperor's employ, we were still barbarians, and so continued to use the Magnaura Gate. This meant returning to Hormisdas Harbour, but the boatmen did not mind for it meant a greater fee for them. We arrived and I wasted no time making for the gate. Leaving Gunnar and Hnefi with the gate prefect to purchase entry disci for the others, I ran over to where the guardsmen stood at their post. Justin was not among them, nor was he anywhere to be seen.

"Where is Scholarae Justin?" I asked, speaking to the nearest soldier.

Glaring, the man appraised me with contempt. "Move off," he growled.

"Please," I said, "it is important. I was meant to see him here. I must know where he has gone."

"It is none of your concern," the guard said, and was on the point of moving me along by force, when one of the others interceded.

"Tell him what he wants to know, Lucca," the other said. "It will do no harm."

"You tell him," replied the first. He blew his nose at me and turned away.

"If you know where he is," I said, appealing to the second soldier, "I would be grateful of your help."

"Scholarae Justin has been reassigned," said the soldier. Regarding me more closely, he asked, "Are you the priest called Aidan?"

"I am."

The soldier nodded. "He said to tell you he could be found at the Great Palace."

"But where?" My heart sank at the prospect of trying to locate him in that warren of walls, halls, residences, and offices—assuming I could even gain entrance. "Which part of the palace?"

The guard shrugged. "He did not say. Probably he is at one of the gates."

I thanked the soldier and left, wondering how I would ever be able to return to the Great Palace, and even if that could be accomplished, how to go about finding Justin.

# 35

Gunnar and Tolar were waiting for me when I returned to the prefect's booth. "Well," Gunnar said, looking down the crowded street, "we must now find a bread-making place."

Glancing around, I noticed the people passing to and fro through the gate; many were bearing burdens, and some of these were led by others who walked ahead, clearing the way. On a sudden inspiration, I said, "Far easier to say than do. We all know what happened last time we went a-viking in this city."

"Jarl Harald was not so pleased with us as I thought he would be," Gunnar conceded. Tolar nodded grimly.

"No, he was not," I agreed. "The best way to avoid incurring the king's wrath would be to find someone to guide us."

"You have good ideas, Aeddan," Gunnar said. "But I do not think Hnefi will allow us to do this."

Thinking quickly, I said, "How much silver do you have?"

Gunnar regarded me warily. "No more than ten pieces," he replied.

"Good," I said. "That should be enough. Perhaps we

will not need them." Regarding the others waiting a few paces away, I said, "Now let us ask Hnefi."

A short consultation ensued in which Gunnar and Hnefi argued over the notion of hiring a guide. "This Miklagård is a large and confusing settlement, as you know," Gunnar pointed out. "If the jarl were here, he would certainly use a guide, I think."

"Jarl Harald would never use a guide," Hnefi insisted. "And I will not use one either. We are Sea Wolves; we will find the way ourselves."

The Danes looking on nodded their agreement; opinion, I could see, strongly favoured Hnefi's position.

"You are wrong, Hnefi. In this place it is far better to have someone to show us the way," I insisted.

"We did not fare so well last time on our own," added Gunnar. "The jarl was very angry with us. This is worth remembering, I think."

"*You* use a guide," sneered Hnefi, as if this were insult enough. "I would never consider such an undignified thing."

"Very well. We will use a guide," I declared, "and we will deliver the bread to the ships before you."

"You speak above yourself," he growled. "I do not listen to the gibber of slaves."

Seizing the moment, I made my challenge. "Then let us make a wager and see who is right."

"It was your fault that the jarl became angry," Hnefi replied carelessly. "I am not listening to you."

"You only say that because you do not wish to part with your silver," I observed, half-fearing he would strike me. "You know I am right, but it pains you to admit it in front of your friends." I indicated the Danes who stood looking on with mounting interest.

As expected, Hnefi took the bait. "I do not make wagers with slaves." He drew himself up haughtily. "Besides, you do not have any silver."

"That is true," I conceded. "However, Gunnar's purse is full."

"Not so full that it cannot hold more," replied Gunnar grandly. "Come, Hnefi, let us make a wager if you are not afraid. Three pieces of sil—"

"*Ten* pieces of silver," I put in quickly. "Ten denarii to the first one to reach the ship with half the allowance of bread."

Gunnar hesitated, peering doubtfully at me.

"Ha! You are not so certain now, Gunnar Big-Boast?" the haughty Hnefi gloated. "Ten silver pieces is too much for you, heya?"

"I was merely thinking how best to spend my winnings," replied Gunnar smoothly. "It is difficult to know what to do with so much silver all at once. A man should plan these things. I am thinking that I may have to buy a bigger purse."

Tolar chuckled.

"Go your way," Hnefi sneered. "We will see who returns to the ship first." Hnefi turned to the onlooking barbarians. "You men are free to choose. Who will go with Gunnar, and who will go with me?"

This invitation occasioned a brief discussion of the merits of both sides. A few were intrigued and might have sided with Gunnar, but the safer bet was deemed to lay with Hnefi. The barbarians, it seems, trusted their battlechief more than they trusted a slave and an unknown guide.

"Perhaps you should give me your silver now," mocked Hnefi, "it appears you are alone with your slave-friend."

"Tolar stands with me," Gunnar replied.

"But the rest go with me."

"How will you carry so much bread—just the three of you?" called one of the barbarians.

"That is no worry," Hnefi laughed. "They will never find any!" He gestured to the shore party to follow him, and they all moved off in good spirits, discussing how to help Hnefi spend his winnings.

"He is right," observed Gunnar gloomily. "Even if we find the baking place first, we will never be able to carry so much bread by ourselves. I have made a very foolish wager."

"Be of good cheer, Gunnar," I said lightly. "Worry not, neither be afraid. God stands ready to aid those who call upon him in time of need."

"Then do so now, Aeddan," Gunnar urged. "We are but three against ten."

Standing in the street I offered up a prayer that God would lead us speedily to the nearest bakery and allow us to prevail. The prayer pleased Gunnar enormously. He told me that a god who helped men win wagers was a god worth knowing.

"Now then," I said, "it only remains for us to find a guide."

I ran back to the quay, where a search of the harbour quickly produced the desired result. "There! There he is," I cried. "Hurry, help me call him."

Gunnar, Tolar, and I stood on the quayside waving our arms and shouting like madmen, and in a short while, the little boatman stood before us. "Greetings, Didimus," I said, "we have need of a guide. Can you find someone for us?"

"My friend," he replied happily, "you say to Didimus 'find a guide', and I say to you: look no further. Before you stands the finest guide in all Byzantium. The city holds no secrets for Didimus. You may place your entire trust in me, my barbarian friends. I will soon take you anywhere you want to go."

He scurried down the steps to his boat, secured it to an

iron ring in the quay wall and returned at once, eager to lead us on. "Now then, where do you wish to go? Perhaps you wish to see Hagia Sophia, eh? The Church of Holy Wisdom, yes? I will take you there. The Hippodrome? I can take you there. Follow me, my friends, I will soon show you everything of interest in this city."

If I had not stopped him, he would have been away at once. "A moment please, Didimus," I said. "We have urgent business to conduct, and for this we require your aid."

"I am your servant. Consider your affairs successfully completed." He smiled, looking from me to Gunnar and back again. "Where do you wish me to take you?"

"To the nearest imperial bakery."

"A bakery!" The little boatman made a sour face. "The whole city is before you! I will take you to Hagia Sophia! You will enjoy this greatly."

"By all means, let us go to the Church of Saint Sophia," I replied, "but first it is of utmost importance to visit the bakery to fetch the bread allowance for the ships."

Didimus shrugged. "If that is what you wish, it is soon accomplished. Follow me."

He strode out smartly, calling out for people to clear the way before us. Gunnar appeared worried. "Never fear," I told him as we started off. "We will prevail. You see? God has already answered our prayer."

Following our chattering guide, who seemed determined that we should appreciate as many of the sights as possible along the way, we threaded our way along narrow, close-crowded streets. As it happened, the closest imperial bakery was very near the granaries, which were no great distance from the harbour. We arrived after a short walk. "Here, my friends, is the bakery," said Didimus, pointing to the white-painted building before us.

Save for the column of smoke drifting from the clay

pipe in the roof, it might have been a stable. He stepped to the blue door and banged on it with the flat of his hand, and a voice called out from within. "He says to wait," the boatman informed us.

We stood in the street, watching the people hurry by around us. The dress and appearance of the wealthier Byzantines amused and amazed me anew: their lavish and extraordinary attention to each item of clothing and every curl of hair was extraordinary. I saw three men walk by, deep in ardent conversation, the foremost of them pounding his fist into his palm. Each of the men wore long cloaks over bright-coloured, richly embroidered tunics, the shoulders of which were stuffed with cloth to make them appear larger—absurdly so, it seemed to me. Their hair was long and heavily oiled, and arranged in well-ordered coils—beards, too. As they passed, they saw Gunnar and Tolar, and put their noses in the air, turned their faces away, and hurried on as if they smelled a repulsive odour. I felt slightly offended, but Gunnar laughed at their pomposity.

After a time, the blue door opened. "Here!" called a fat man in a close-fitting brown garment; his hair and clothing were powdered almost white with flour. He took one look at us and shouted, "Be gone! Away with you!" Before we could move or speak, he pulled in his head again, slamming the door behind him.

"A most unfriendly man," observed Didimus. He made to knock on the door again, but Gunnar stepped forward, indicating that he should step aside. Motioning for Tolar to stand at the door, he knocked sharply.

We waited and Gunnar knocked again, using the handle of his knife this time, and almost rattling the door off its hinges. A moment later the man, angry now, thrust his head out. "You! Stop that! I told you to be gone!" He made a dismissive gesture with his hand.

Quick as a flick, Gunnar seized the baker by his fat

wrist, yanked him through the doorway and out into the
street. The baker sputtered in outrage and spun around,
but Tolar had swiftly stepped behind him into the doorway
and was now blocking his retreat.

"My friend," I said. "We have business with you."

"Liar!" snarled the man. "I bake for the emperor alone.
Neither pagani nor barbari taste my bread. Now, get you
gone before I call the scholae!"

"These men also serve the emperor," I told him flatly.
"He has sent them to you to collect our bread allowance."

"Again, I call you liar," the baker sneered; his face had
turned very red and he seemed about to burst. "I have
never seen you before. Do you think it is so easy to steal
bread from me? I am not like those others who give the
politikoï to anyone who asks and then charge the state
exorbitant fees. My bread is honest bread and I am an honest man!"

"Then you have nothing to fear from us," I said, trying
to soothe him. "The men you see before you serve in the
barbari bodyguard. They have come to fetch the politikoï,
as you say, for the ships escorting the trade delegation to
Trebizond."

The fat baker stared at me. "I am Constantius," he
said, calming somewhat. "If you are from the emperor,
where is the sakka?" He thrust out his hand, palm upward.

"What is that?" I asked.

"Thieves!" the baker cried. "I thought so! I knew it! Be
gone, thieves."

"Please," I said, "what is this sakka?"

"Ha! You do not know politikoï; you do not know
sakka! If you were indeed Farghanese," he sneered, "you
would know what it is. I would not have to tell you."

Gunnar followed this exchange with a perplexed
frown on his face, watching every move carefully, his hand
ready on his knife.

"We *are* emperor's men," I insisted, "but we have never done this before. The ways of Byzantium are new to us."

"The sakka is given you by the logothete to tell me how much bread to allow," said the baker. "You do not have one, so you get no bread. Now, get out of my way. I have wasted enough time with you."

Understanding came to me at once; I reached into my belt and produced the small square of parchment Gunnar had given me. "This is the sakka you require, is it not?"

Constantius snatched the parchment from me, glanced at it, and shoved it back at me. "It is impossible. I do not have so much bread. Come back tomorrow."

"We need it today," I said. "Is there some other bakery to which we can go?"

"There are other bakers," Constantius replied stiffly. "But it will do you no good. No one has so much bread ready to carry off at once."

"Can you bake it?"

"Of course I can bake it!" he cried. "But I cannot do it all at once. If you want so many loaves you must wait."

"We do not mind waiting," I said.

"Wait then," he snarled. "But you cannot wait here. I will not have barbari lurking outside my bakery. It is not seemly."

"Of course," I agreed. "Tell us when to return and we will come back when you are ready."

"The four of you?" he wondered. "You cannot carry so much."

My heart sank. "Why? How much bread is it?"

Glancing at the parchment once more, he said, "Three hundred and forty loaves."

"We will bring more barbari to help us," I replied. "We will fetch them now."

"You say you have ships," said Constantius. "Where are they?"

"In Theodosius Harbour," the boatman replied.

"It is not far," the baker observed. "I will bring them to you when I have finished."

"There is no need," I told him. "We would be most happy to carry—"

"No, I insist. Leave it to me," he said. "This way I know you do not sell them on the way back to your ships."

"Very well, I only thought to save you trouble. We would be most grateful for your service. There are Danish ships—longships, four of them."

"They are easy to find." He ducked his head, then turned abruptly. Tolar made to block the door.

"Let him through," I said. "This man has work to do on our behalf." Tolar moved aside, allowing the baker to pass.

Constantius disappeared into his bakery once more, calling, "I am an honest man, and I bake an honest loaf. You will see me at the harbour—but do not look for me before sunset!" With that, he slammed the door again.

"What has happened here?" wondered Gunnar.

I explained to him all that had taken place. He listened, shaking his head. "I should not have wagered so much money," he said gloomily. "Sunset is a long time. Hnefi and the others are certain to return to the ships before us."

"You are forgetting that we have the sakka." I then explained the purpose of the small, but all-important square of parchment he had given me, and which I had just passed on to the baker. "No one will give them bread without it."

"Heya!" said Gunnar, his frown turning to a grin and spreading wide. "I should have wagered more."

"Gunnar Big-Boast," chuckled Tolar.

"Unless Hnefi swiftly learns to speak Greek," I added, "they will not soon realize their error. By the time they think to find us, we will have the bread aboard the ships."

"Very shrewd, my friend," observed Didimus. "You are a very Hercules of the intellect. I salute you." He thrust his hand in the air in a rough rendition of the imperial salute. "Now then, as we dare not linger here, I will take you wherever you wish to go."

"Please, could you take us to the Great Palace? There is someone I must see."

"I will take you, never fear," replied Didimus, "and then I will take you to the Hagia Sophia, and you will light a candle for me that the All-Wise God will give me shrewdness like yours. Follow me."

# 36

The guards at the Great Palace turned us away. None of them had ever heard of Justin, but they knew he was not of the gate contingent, for there had been no new appointments for more than a year. One of them suggested, however, that he might be part of the inner-palace scholae. "You could look for him there," the guard told me.

"If you will kindly tell me where to go, I will do as you advise," I replied, and was promptly told that it was impossible unless I had official business beyond the gate.

"But my business is with the Scholarae himself," I explained.

"No one is allowed into the inner-palace precinct without a formal summons," the gateman insisted. I thanked him for his help and resigned myself to leaving the city without seeing Justin again.

"Now we will go to The Church of Divine Wisdom," said Didimus, leading us back through the swarms of beggars who made their homes along the palace walls. "We will light a candle for your friend. We will perhaps light many candles."

Gunnar seemed well disposed to seeing the sights of

the city one last time before sailing, and Tolar had seen nothing of Constantinople at all, so was happy to follow wherever we went. "I do not care where we go," Gunnar said, 'so long as I am there to collect my winnings from Hnefi."

"It is no distance at all," Didimus said. "I will return you to your ship in plenty of time, never fear. You are talking to the best guide in all Byzantium. Come with me, my friends, and I will show you the Hippodrome and the Forum of Augustus on the way."

The Hippodrome was impressive. The forum was a hollow square surrounded by two hundred columns, mostly taken from Greek temples, Didimus told us, because no one remembered how to make them like that anymore. I did not believe this, but the columns were definitely much older than the forum, so perhaps there was a small grain of truth in what he said. As imposing as these structures were, however, they shrank to insignificance beside the awesome achievement of the Hagia Sophia.

Heaven bless me, the Church of Holy Wisdom is a holy revelation made visible—a testament of faith in stone and mortar, a prayer in glass and tile and precious metals. The wonder of the world, it puts antiquity's much-vaunted architectural spectacles to shame. Sure, God himself inspired this church, and guided each and every labourer—those who put hand to trowel and beam, no less than he who conceived and drew the plans.

Just outside the forum, we four fell into step with the crowd entering the church, and passed directly into the first of two separate halls. Like many others, we paused before a chandler's stall for Didimus to purchase candles and incense, then walked quickly into the second, larger hall which was lined with huge slabs of red and green marble. The vaulted ceiling overhead was decorated with myriad stars and crosses picked out in gold. Above the towering bronze doors before us was a mosaic of the Virgin and Child; the divine infant held a small cross in his hand as if to bless all those who passed beneath his beneficent gaze.

Pushed along by the throng, we were swept under the mosaic, through the gate called Beautiful, and into the *nave* of the church. If from the outside Hagia Sophia's imposing red bulk appears heavy—a veritable mountain of brick and stone whose ponderous slopes rise above the surrounding trees, an enormous domed and mounded eminence girded about with massive masonry walls and giant supporting buttresses—on the inside, it is all light and air.

To step through the great bronze doors is to enter one of Heaven's own halls. Golden light streams from a thousand windholes, striking glints and gleams from every surface, falling from a dome as wide and open as the very sky. Miracle of miracles, there are no roof-trees of any kind at all under Sophia's dome—nothing obscures the glance or obstructs the eye as it soars up and up and up toward the exalted heights. The majestic dome hangs high above the marbled floor as if suspended from heaven by angelic hands.

The floor, as expansive as a plain, is all fine, polished marble; the double-tiered galleries high above the floor are marble also, deep-coloured and striking to the eye. There are screens and panels of marble, painstakingly carved with every manner of design: intricate geometrics, crosses, suns, moons, stars, birds, flowers, plants, animals, fish—everything, in fact, that exists in heaven and earth. The galleries are lined with enormous porphyry columns, the capitals of which have been carved into the shapes of plants; so cunningly have the sculptors practised their craft, it is as if the columns support masses of vines, luxuriant with leaves.

The galleries and corridors seemed endless; the high-pillared arches rose in tiers one above another. Above these were tall arched windholes, hundred upon hundred, admitting heaven's light. Though there must have been a thousand thousand people within the body of the church, such was its size that it could comfortably accommodate two or three times more again.

Almost every ceiling and pediment was covered with mosaics of the most elaborate design. The monks of the scriptorium are divinely adept at the intricacies of highly complex and sophisticated patterns; but even our good master at Kells could have learned much to his advantage from a close study of Sophia's panels and ceilings. Sure, the majesty of the church stole the breath from our mouths. Incapable of speech, Gunnar, Tolar, and I could but gape and stare, staggering from one marvel to the next, minds numb with wonder. And still we stared, drinking in each incredible sight as if it would be the last thing we would ever see.

Gunnar grew increasingly subdued, but not from boredom or lack of appreciation. Far from it! He gazed with amazement upon all he saw, and from time to time pointed out details of workmanship that I had missed. But his comments grew increasingly few and far between, and though he still appeared eager to capture every sight before him, his enjoyment took on the quality of rapture. Once, turning to see if he was still with me, I saw him standing before one of the gigantic carved screens, staring as if in a trance. He had his hand raised to the figure of a cross which had been carved into the panel as part of the design; and he was tracing the shape with his finger, repeating the motion again and again.

Gunnar seemed especially fascinated with the cross. Passing beneath the centre of the dome, I felt a touch at my shoulder and looked round to see the stout barbarian staring straight up at a golden mosaic of the largest cross I have ever seen. "His sign," Gunnar whispered, in a voice made small with awe. "It is everywhere."

"Yes," I answered, and explained that the cross was revered even as far away as Éire, the furthest limit of the empire. "Although the cross of the Byzantines is slightly different from the cross of the Celts, and that of the Romans is different again, yet they all honour the self-same sacrifice made by the Lord Christ for all men."

"So much gold," remarked Gunnar. Tolar nodded sagely.

Didimus led us to the left side of the nave where a free-standing panel had been erected to hold a number of large images painted on flat wooden boards. These icons bore the images of Christ, and various apostles and saints, which the people of Byzantium especially venerated. Before the panel, which Didimus called the *iconostasis*, rose a series of boards in stepped ranks which held the candles placed there by the worshippers. Taking his candles, Didimus lit one from those already burning, and placed it in one of the few empty holes in the plank. He stood for a moment rocking slightly back and forth, before taking a bit of the incense and sprinkling it over the flame. The incense struck the flame with a puff of fragrant smoke.

"There," he said, turning to us, "I have sent a prayer through Elijah that Holy Jesu will give me your shrewdness, and I have sent one through Barnabas that God will give me your barbarian friend's strength."

I conveyed these words to Gunnar, who appeared much impressed with this procedure. He held out his hand to Didimus for one of the candles. While Tolar and I watched in amazement, Gunnar lit the candle and performed the little rocking motion in imitation of the boatman. I wondered what had moved him to pray—and what he said—but thought it uncouth to ask.

Both Gunnar and Tolar were dazed by the grandeur of the church—especially the extravagant use of gold and silver throughout, which continually amazed them. It is no exaggeration to say that the gleam and glitter of these rare metals everywhere meet the eye, especially as one approaches the sanctuary—to which Didimus led us next. Rising from the floor is a circular platform, the *ambo*, reached by two flights of wide, low stairs to the right and left. The ambo is surrounded by a series of pillars with gilded capitals which support a shelf bearing a multitude of lamps and crosses—some silver, some gold, and many adorned with pearls and gems.

"We can go no further," Didimus explained once we had pushed our way to the edge of the platform. "No one but churchmen and high officials are allowed beyond the ambo."

"In Éire," I said, "anyone can come to the altar. It is God's table and all are welcome."

The little boatman looked at me curiously, as if he had never heard of anything so peculiar. "The choir stands there," he continued. "On high days there is always a choir." Pointing beyond the ambo he indicated a sort of raised walkway. "That is the *solea*," he told me, "it is used by the priests and emperor when approaching the altar. The chancel screen is solid silver—so they say."

The chancel was enclosed on three sides by an open lattice-work screen of gleaming white, radiant in the light of all the lamps and candles. The chancel screen had a series of columns which supported a low parapet on which stood a number of priests and court officials, all dressed in the colours of their kind: priests in white robes, courtiers in red and black. The columns and parapet were faced in silver, and the light of candles and lamps hanging down allowed the eye to feast on the rich metalwork: images of the Christ, and the Virgin, prophets, saints, angels, seraphim, and imperial monograms.

The chancel with its screen and parapet formed an

inner sanctuary for the altar standing just beyond. The worshippers were not allowed beyond the ambo and solea, but the parapet was fairly low, and the altar was raised, making it easy for the gathered congregation to view the ceremony taking place at the altar.

The altar was of rose-pink marble, surrounded by a sort of tent of gold. "That is the *ciborium*," Didimus said when I asked him. "The stone comes from Damascus," he said, paused, and added, "or Athens."

The fabric of the tent-like shelter was wefted with threads of gold, and sewn with jewels—ruby, emerald, topaz, and sapphire—arranged in patterns. The light of all the lamps and candles, and the sunlight streaming down from the windholes above, struck the ciborium and suffused the altar with a heavenly glow. The entire sanctuary seemed to radiate pure, golden light, bathing and engulfing not only the altar, but those attending it, too.

For, sitting in a golden throne to one side of the altar, was the basileus. He was holding a lighted candle in his hands, looking bored and perturbed. Flanking him on either side were two young men in long purple robes; beside them stood two more men in priestly white. Gunnar pointed out the emperor to Tolar, who seemed somewhat disappointed in the look of the jarl's new master. But he kept his observations to himself.

A priest wearing a long stole embroidered with crosses stood at the altar holding a censer which he swung back and forth on a chain. This task completed, he backed away, bowing before the altar. Then another priest—an older man with a small, flat hat upon his white head—approached the altar, bowed three times, raised his hands, and began speaking very quickly and very low. Still speaking, he began performing some service there. Everyone seemed most intent on the actions of this priest, but I could not make out what he was doing.

After a time, this priest also retreated and there came the peal of a bell. "We should go now," Didimus said abruptly, "otherwise we will be caught in the crowd and we will not reach the ship in time."

Taking one last lingering glance at the magnificent altar, I could see that the service was ended and those around the altar had commenced their procession along the solea. People around us were already streaming back through the nave. We hurried as best we could, but there were so many people that we were soon halted by the crush at the doors.

"There is another way," said Didimus. "Hurry!"

He led us across the nave to one of the great galleries, where we turned and began running down the long corridor, arriving at a long, switchback ramp. We joined the people making their way down this ramp and eventually tumbled out into a narrow street behind the church. A high wall lined with trees rose directly before us, and a double row of soldiers had formed a rank across the street which stretched away to the right and left; holding their bronze-topped rods lengthwise across their chests, they blocked the right-hand side of the street, to prevent the crowd from following the emperor and his courtiers who were walking in procession back to the Great Palace.

Most of the people strained for a look at the emperor; many called out to him, seeking impromptu audience. But it was not the emperor who caught my eye as the crowd surged forward. I took one look at the rank of soldiers and turned to Gunnar and Tolar. "Stay here, both of you. Wait for me." To Didimus, I said, "I have found my friend. Wait here."

Pushing through the crush, I elbowed my way to the forefront of the throng, enduring many knocks and curses along the way. Tight-pressed as I was, I managed to get one arm up and began waving and shouting: "Justin! Here I am!"

Turning, he caught sight of me and beckoned me to him, pushing people out of the way with the butt of his spear. "I have been looking for you," I said upon reaching him.

Taking my arm he pulled me aside. "We cannot talk now. Come to me tomorrow—the east gate. I will watch for you."

"But I am leaving at dawn tomorrow," I told him. "I was afraid I would not see you again."

He nodded and glanced around, as if he feared someone might be watching him. "Pretend you are resisting me," he whispered.

"What?" I did not understand. "Why should I—"

"Act like you are trying to get by me," he urged, raising his rod, and holding it with both hands across his body. "Stand aside, you!" he shouted, pushing me backwards with the rod. "Stand aside."

I fell back a step or two, and Justin pursued me, pushing me back further. When he had shoved me five or six paces back, he said, "Aidan, listen to me: I have word of your friends."

My heart clenched in my chest. "What? Tell me. What have you heard?"

"Keep quiet. We should not be seen together." He glanced around quickly and said, "They were here—"

"Here! In Constantinople!"

"Shh!" he hissed. "Be quiet and listen. They were here—they were seen."

"When?"

"Just after First Fruits, I think. They—"

"How many?"

"Eight or ten, perhaps—I cannot say for certain. They were led by a bishop, and were taken to the monastery of

Christ Pantocrator upon arrival. They stayed with the monks there."

"But what happened to them?"

"They left again."

"Without seeing the emperor? I do not believe it."

Justin shrugged. "They were seen to depart."

"Who saw them? How do you know this?" I could feel myself growing frantic.

"Quiet!" he said, pushing me back with the rod. "I have certain friends."

One of the scholarii took an interest in the exchange between Justin and me, and started towards us. "Trouble there?" he called.

"It is nothing!" Justin replied over his shoulder. "This fellow is drunk. I am dealing with him." Pushing me again, he said, "Hear me, Aidan: the komes knows about this."

"The komes . . . Nikos?"

"The one who helped trap the quaestor, yes," Justin answered. "My friend said Nikos met with them twice—the last time was on the day they left. That is all I could discover." He looked around quickly. "I must go. I will try to learn more if I can."

The chief guard called again. The other soldiers were already moving off. "Trust no one, Aidan," said Justin, stepping quickly away from me. "Beware Nikos—he has very powerful friends. He is dangerous. Stay far away from him."

I made to thank him and bid him farewell, but he was already running along the narrow street to join the other soldiers. I turned and made my way back to where Didimus and the Danes were waiting. I pushed through the crowd, thinking: *They are alive! My friends are alive! At least most of them are alive, and they reached Constantinople after all.*

"That was the warrior from the gate," Gunnar said as I joined them. "The one you were looking for?"

"Yes, that was the one."

"And he told you what you wanted to know?"

"Yes," I said tersely. I did not care to discuss it further—certainly not with Sea Wolves who were the cause of the ruined pilgrimage, and all the other troubles in my life. Instead, I turned and strode along the street. "Come," I said, "we must hurry if we want to be at the quay when the bread arrives."

"Heya!" agreed Gunnar. "The sooner we collect the winnings, the happier I will be."

"Didimus," I called, "lead us back to the ships. Quickly, now! We do not wish to miss Constantius."

"Most fortunate of men are you," cried the little boatman cheerfully, "for you are in the company of one who anticipates your every whim. I have already thought of this, and I have devised a special route to take you. No boat this time, yet, never fear, we will reach the harbour before the sun sets."

True to his word, Didimus brought us to the harbour just as the sun sank below the western hills. "You see!" he said. "There is your ship, here are you, and the sun is only setting. And now I must go home to my supper. I bid you fare well, my friends. I will be leaving you now. If I have been of service to you, I am happy. I need nothing more." Smiling in anticipation of his reward, he added, "Naturally, if people wish to show their appreciation . . ."

"You have done us good service, Didimus," I told him. "For that we are grateful."

Turning to Gunnar, I explained that we must pay the boatman for his help, reminding him that without Didimus, we would not have been able to win the wager.

"Say no more," replied Gunnar expansively, "I am feeling generous." Opening his leather bag, he produced a handful of nomismi and began counting them out.

Didimus's face fell when he saw the coins. Nudging Gunnar, I said, "Truly, he has been a very great help."

From among the coins Gunnar selected a silver denarius, and held it out to Didimus. The boatman's smile instantly returned. "May God Himself bless you richly, my friends!" he gasped, snatching the coin and tucking it quickly out of sight. Seizing my hand, he raised it to his lips and kissed it. Then he kissed Gunnar's hand as well, and departed, saying, "Next time you need a guide, call on Didimus, and you will have the best guide in all Byzantium, never fear!"

"Farewell," I called. Didimus quickly disappeared among the workers and boatmen making their way to the city, and we hurried to the place where the longship was still moored to the quayside.

We had just reached the ship and were about to go aboard when we heard Hnefi call out, "Ho! It is no use hiding. We have seen you."

"Heya," replied Gunnar affably. "And I see you have found your way back to the ship. That is a triumph for you, Hnefi. You must be very pleased."

"If I am pleased," said Hnefi, strolling up as if he owned the harbour, "it is because I see you standing there empty-handed. You should have stayed with us." Some of the other Sea Wolves arrived, staggering slightly, and looking dazzled by the day's experience.

"I see that you have found a drinking hall," Gunnar observed. "No doubt the öl has helped ease the sting of your defeat."

"Wine!" cried Hnefi. "We have been drinking wine—and that in celebration of our victory! I will take my silver now."

Some of the Danes aboard ship gathered at the rail to observe this exchange. They called to their shipmates below and were told of the wager between Gunnar and Hnefi over the bread.

"I wonder at you, Hnefi," Gunnar replied, shaking his head sadly. "It must be that you have forgotten the most important part of the wager. I am looking, but I do not see the bread."

"Are you blind, man?" replied Hnefi. "Open your eyes."

So saying, he turned and called a signal to the remaining five Sea Wolves of his party just then straggling up. I saw that they were bearing large cloth bags on their backs. At their leader's signal, they came to where we were standing, and slung their bags to the quay. "Behold!" cried Hnefi, opening the nearest bag. Thrusting his hand inside, he produced a small brown loaf. "I give you bread."

Gunnar stepped to the sack and peered inside; it was indeed full of small brown loaves. "It is bread," confirmed Gunnar. "But I am wondering how you obtained it."

The Sea Wolves on the quay and those aboard ship began clamouring for the wager to be settled. As I suspected, numerous additional wagers had been struck, and now the winners wanted their take.

"I do not understand," Gunnar said, shaking his head. "How did they do it?"

We were not to wonder long, however, for at that moment, there came a shout from the quay. I turned to see Constantius the baker, pushing a cart loaded high with fresh bread in big, round fragrant loaves. Behind him a young man pushed a second cart filled equally high. "Here!" he shouted. "Here you are! I have found you."

He forced the cart through the midst of the barbarians, hollering at them to make way. "Just as I promised," he declared in a loud voice, "I have brought the politikoï. 'Do not worry,' I said, 'I am a man of my word.' And now you see, eh? I was telling the truth. I am an honest man. Here is your bread."

I thanked him, and said, "These Danes do not understand

your speech. If you will allow me, I will tell them what you are saying."

"By all means, you must do that. Let understanding increase."

To Hnefi and the others, I said, "As you see, Constantius here has brought the bread allowance—and not half only, but the whole of it."

"Heya," he agreed confidently, "it is a shame for you that he arrived too late."

"How so?" challenged Gunnar. "You see the bread before you."

"We brought bread also, and we arrived with it before you," Hnefi replied. "Therefore I have won the wager."

"That is by no means certain," said Gunnar. "I do not know what it is that you have brought in those bags of yours, but it is not the bread we were sent to fetch."

"You know it is bread!" charged Hnefi. "You have seen it with your own eyes."

King Harald arrived at the rail and demanded to know why so many men were standing idle when there were provisions waiting to be brought aboard ship. Hnefi quickly explained about the wager, adding, "As it happens, I have won. But this worthless Dane refuses to admit his defeat and pay me my winnings."

"Is this so?" asked the king.

"I do refuse, Jarl Harald," answered a defiant Gunnar, "for it is not my custom to pay when I win a wager. I pay only when I lose. Hnefi insists on having it the other way, I think."

This response delighted the onlooking Sea Wolves, many of whom laughed, and began cheering for him.

"What is all this commotion?" wondered a bemused Constantius, finding himself surrounded by barbarians in full cry.

While I explained the dispute, the king made his way to

the quay to settle the argument himself. "Clearly, you cannot both have won this wager," opined Harald judiciously. "One of you has won, and the other has lost. That is the way of things." Seeing that he had achieved general agreement on this fundamental point, he pressed on. "Now then, it appears that Hnefi has returned first with the bread."

"Hnefi has indeed returned first," allowed Gunnar. "But he has not brought the bread he was sent to fetch."

"And yet I see before me sacks of bread," Harald pointed out equably.

"No, Jarl Harald, this is not so. While there may be loaves in those sacks, it is not the bread given by the emperor. I only have returned with the proper loaves, as this baker will certainly attest. Therefore, I have won and it is for Hnefi to pay me."

"Proper loaves?" howled Hnefi, colour rising to his already florid face. "Bread is bread. I returned first: I win."

"Anyone may stuff stale loaves into a bag and hope to claim the prize," maintained Gunnar with cool disdain. "It means nothing."

Harald hesitated. He looked thoughtfully at the cart full of loaves, and at the sacks lying on the quay. The matter, apparently so straight-forward only a moment before, had taken an unexpected twist, and he was no longer certain what should be done.

Mistaking the king's hesitation for unwillingness to accept the bread, Constantius, standing next to me, whispered a suggestion. Listening to him, an idea came to me how the dilemma might be solved.

"If I may speak, Jarl Harald," I said, putting myself forward. "I believe there may be a simple way to discover who has won the wager."

"Speak then," he said without enthusiasm.

"Taste the bread," I advised. "As we will all be eating this bread for many days, it seems right to me to have only the best brought aboard. There is only one way to prove which is best—taste it and see."

Gunnar acclaimed the suggestion. "That is excellent counsel." Retrieving a loaf from the pyramid on the cart, he offered it to the king. "If you please, Jarl Harald; we will abide by your decision."

While Harald pulled off a portion of the bread, I explained the trial to Constantius. "That is not what I meant," the baker said. "But it makes no difference to me. I bake an honest loaf, as anyone can see."

Pulling a loaf from Hnefi's bag, the king broke it and, with some little difficulty, pulled off a piece. He chewed it for a moment and swallowed—again with difficulty, for the bread was tough, owing to its staleness.

"Well?" demanded Hnefi impatiently. "Which is it to be?"

"As I am king," said Harald, holding up the brown loaf from Hnefi's bag, "this bread is good enough for men at sea. Indeed, I have tasted far worse many times."

"Heya!" agreed Hnefi, swelling up his chest. "It is what I am telling you—"

"But," continued Harald, cutting him short, "this bread is far superior in every way." He broke another piece of the white bread, put it in his mouth, and chewed thoughtfully. "Yes, this is food for kings and noblemen. So, I ask myself, which would I rather be eating?"

Turning to Hnefi, he said, "The loaves you have brought are fit only for fish." With that, he tossed the remains of the brown loaf into the water. To Gunnar, he said, "Bring your loaves onto the ship. This is the bread we shall have on the voyage."

The new-made loaves were quickly taken from the carts, passed to those at the rail, and stowed away. Others gathered around to watch Gunnar and Hnefi settle their wager. "Cheer up," said Gunnar, "you did well.

I am surprised you found any bread at all. Fate was against you."

"Fate!" muttered Hnefi, producing his leather bag. He began counting silver denarii into Gunnar's outstretched palm. "Next time, I will keep the Shaven One with me," he said grudgingly, "and then we will see how well *you* fare." This was the first time Hnefi had shown me any respect or consideration, and it pleased me greatly.

"It is not Aeddan who helped me," replied Gunnar, dropping the coins one-by-one into his bag. "It was this god of his. I lit a candle to this Lord Jesu and prayed him to help me win. Now, you see for yourself what has happened."

"You were lucky, that is all," said Hnefi. He and those with him stumped off to console themselves as best they could.

"Even if I do not get another piece of silver," Gunnar remarked, "this has been a most rewarding voyage. My Karin and Ulf can live for three or four years on what I have now."

"With so much silver in your bag," observed Tolar, "we will be calling you Gunnar Silversack from now on."

Once the carts were unloaded, Constantius was eager to be away as it was growing dark. I bade him farewell and thanked him for his help. Gunnar, feeling all the more generous since he had won the wager, gave the baker ten nomismi.

"Tell your friend to keep his money," Constantius said. "I am well paid by the emperor for my labours."

When I told this to Gunnar, he shook his head and pressed the money into the man's hand. "For the cart, and for the boy," Gunnar said, and I conveyed his words to the baker. "A drink or two, after your labours. Or, light a candle to your Jesu and remember me."

"My friend," replied Constantius gallantly, "tell him I will surely do both." He bade us farewell and retreated quickly, he and the boy, pulling the empty carts behind them.

Overcome by his good fortune, Gunnar pressed a silver denarius into my hand also. "If not for you, Aeddan," he said, "I never would have won the wager."

"If not for me," I corrected him, tucking the total of my earthly wealth into the hem of my cloak, "you would never have made the wager."

"Heya," he laughed. "That is true also."

I climbed aboard the ship and watched the sun set in a dull glow of red and gold as violet shadows slowly stole the seven hills from sight. Only then did it occur to me that I had stood in the greatest church in all the world, and I had not breathed a single prayer, or offered up even the most fleeting thought of worship. That never would have happened at the abbey. What was wrong with me? The thought kept me awake most of the night.

At dawn the next morning, as the oars were unshipped and the longships rowed silently from the harbour, I stood at the rail and, living still, looked my last upon the city of my demise.

# 37

So we came to Trebizond. I will say nothing of the voyage, save that it was wholly uneventful and unremarkable. Even the weather remained indifferent: dull days, neither fair nor foul, warm nor cold, completely wet nor entirely dry. We sailed in party with seven other ships—five large merchant vessels and two smaller craft belonging to the imperial fleet. Rumour had it that one of the imperial ships contained the envoy, and the other a vast amount of treasure. Harald's four long-ships provided an effective escort; I cannot think many pirates would be bold enough to challenge a pack of Sea Wolves.

Soon after leaving Constantinople, a deep melancholy settled in my heart and filled me with gloom. With nothing of consequence to do aboard ship, I spent many days brooding over all that had happened to me since leaving the abbey.

At first, I considered that my dolorous feelings derived from some failure on my part—though, try as I might, I could not determine what this failing might be. Then it came to me that it was God who had failed, not me. I had done all in my power to remain a faithful servant; I had borne all my misfortunes with as much courage and grace as I possessed, and had even tried to advance the knowledge of his lordship in the world. Others might have dared and achieved more in this regard, I do freely confess it, but I had done what I could—even to the extent of laying aside any care for my life for his greater glory.

This, I believe, was what cast the shadow over my soul. I had been willing to die, had faced the day of death without fear or regret—but I did not die. Strange to say, this brought neither relief nor joy but seemed instead a cruel deception for if my life was not required, why did God allow me to dream so? And if he had decided to spare my life, why had he forced me to endure the slow torment of imminent death without granting me the comfort I would have gained from knowing my life was no longer at hazard?

None of this made sense to me. No matter how I thought about it, God always came out seeming churlish and small, and wholly unworthy of my devotion. I had been willing to give—indeed, had *given* to the utmost of my ability—heart and mind and soul to him. I had dedicated the whole of my life to God, and he had not so much as acknowledged the gift. Far from it! He had ignored it completely.

This thought made me feel more alone than ever I had been in my life up to now. I was a lost man—the more since I had formerly consoled myself thinking that I was about some holy purpose, and that God cared for me. Truth, they say, is a cold and bitter draught; few drink it undiluted. Sure, I drained the cup this time.

I had once imagined myself a vessel made for destruction. I knew now that the destruction I feared was complete. I was undone. Even the bleak hope of a martyr's death was denied me. I had been willing to die, and to suffer the Red Martyrdom would have been a noble and godly thing. But no more. All holiness, all consolation of faith, all grace was refused me. In desperation I ran my hands through my hair, which had grown long now; my tonsure was gone. I looked down at my clothes—little more than rags. My transformation was finished: I looked like Scop!

In the bitterness of this hateful realization, I heard again the old Truth-Sayer's words—hateful words, mocking words, but true: *"God has abandoned me, my friend, and now, Aidan the Innocent, he has abandoned you!"*

This, finally, was the cause of my despair: God had abandoned me among strangers and barbarians. When I ceased to be of use to him, he had cast me aside. Despite the glorious promises of the holy text—how he would never leave nor forsake his people, how those who worshipped him would be saved, how he cared for his children and answered their prayers, how he raised up those who honoured him and cast down the evil-doers . . . and all the rest—he had forsaken me.

The grand promises of Holy Scripture were empty words, mere sounds in the wind. Worse, they were lies. Evil-doers prospered; the prayers of the righteous went unanswered; the God-fearing man was humiliated before the world; no one was saved even the smallest torment: good people were made to suffer injustice, disease, violence, and death. No heavenly power ever intervened, nor so much as mitigated the distress; the people of God cried to heaven for deliverance, but heaven might as well have been a tomb.

Oh, I saw it all clearly now. I saw, stretching out before me as wide and empty as the sea, the same stark desolation Scop had seen. `Bitterness and confusion looped serpent coils around me; joy and hope turned to ashes in my heart. Had I lavished my devotion on a lord unworthy of veneration? If that was true, I did not see how I could live. Nor indeed, why I should want to continue drawing breath in a world ruled by such a God.

If only I had met my death in Constantinople, I would have been spared the agony of the torment I now felt. I might have died an ignorant man, but I would at least have died a happy one.

The Danes could not understand my distress. When duty permitted, Gunnar, and sometimes Tolar and Thorkel, came to sit with me at the prow. We talked and they tried to cheer me, but the black rot had taken hold of my soul and nothing any of them said could ease the pain. The rest of the barbarians took no interest in my plight whatsoever. Harald and his karlar were delighted with their new and highly-paid prominence as defenders of the empire. Accordingly, the Sea Wolves remained continually wary, for they had it in mind to seize any ships that tried to attack, hoping to augment their pay with plunder. But, aside from a swift-disappearing flash of sailcloth on the seaward horizon, we saw no marauders. All eleven ships arrived safely in port sixteen days after leaving Constantinople.

As the rock-cragged hills above Trebizond came into view, I turned with great reluctance and resignation to the task set before me, and determined that if the emperor required a spy, a spy I would become. Since I was no priest any more, I might at least try to earn the freedom promised me. All things considered, this seemed the most sensible course, though I little knew how or where I should begin, nor less yet how to insinuate myself into the proceedings.

Feeling as I did—alone and forsaken in a godless world—I decided simply to let fate fall as it would. Sure, it was all one to me. Accordingly, the moment the planks touched the long stone quay, the emperor's envoy sent word to King Harald that his presence was required. He was to bring with him twenty of his fiercest and most loyal warriors; the emperor's emissaries desired a bodyguard—to enhance their prestige, no doubt. The rest of the Danes would remain at the harbour to provide protection for the merchant ships. Apparently, the more brazen Arab pirates operated from the very quay, looting full-laden ships before they even left the harbour.

The Danes quickly established the watch, ranging themselves along the quayside in guard groups of three or more. Meanwhile, in response to our command, we assembled on the quay beside the envoy's vessel—twenty warriors, Jarl Harald, and myself—to receive our instructions from the imperial envoy, a tall, thin-shanked old man with huge ears and a face like a goat's, complete with a small, wispy white chin beard. The envoy's name was Nicephorus, and he served as *eparch*—which, as I was informed with elaborate disdain, happened to be a particular variety of very senior court official, eighteenth in rank to the emperor.

As we stood on the quay, waiting to conduct the eparch and the members of his company to the place of meeting, I was startled and dismayed to see the Komes Nikos emerge from the eparch's ship. He walked directly to where Harald stood, glanced at me and gave a slight-but-perceptible nod of recognition before addressing himself to the king.

"The eparch sends his greetings," Nikos said coldly. "It is expected that you will place yourselves under his command while we remain in this city. The eparch's desires will most often be delivered through me. Is that agreeable to you?" Although he asked the question, his manner implied that it would be this way whether Harald thought it agreeable or not.

I relayed these words to my master, who nodded and grunted his rough approval. "Heya," he said.

"Then you will follow me," Nikos said imperiously. "We will escort Eparch Nicephorus to his residence."

We left the quay, walking slowly so that the merchants and dignitaries behind us were not left too far behind. In this way we entered the city, moving in stately procession along a narrow central street.

From the sea, the city had seemed little more than an overgrown fishing village, which is how it had begun. And though it apparently boasted some of the most varied and important markets in the empire, it still possessed something of its old nature in the small, tidy, and quiet streets lined with simple, lime-white houses of the square Greek kind we had been seeing ever since entering the Black Sea.

To my inexperienced eye, the city appeared compact, confined as it was to the low hills between the rough crags rising behind, and the sea spreading before. There was a handsome colonnaded forum, a wide house-lined central street, a basilica, two public baths, a small colosseum, a theatre, numerous wells, a taberna, and three fine churches—one formerly a temple to Aphrodite. The whole was surrounded by a low wall and deep ditch of Roman construction.

As I came to know the place, I discovered a feature which charmed me more than anything else I saw, and these were pools which threw water into the air for the sheer delight of the sight and sound alone. These fountains, I was to discover, the city possessed in profusion—sometimes with carved marble statuary, sometimes merely with unshapen stones for the water to play over, but almost always in the midst of a small, carefully-tended green or garden, where people might sit on stone benches beside these pools, talking to one another, or simply enjoying a moment's peace in their daily activities.

On the day of our arrival, Eparch Nicephorus was received in the forum by the magister and spatharius, who stood at the head of a small group of lesser officials, extending their hands in friendship and greeting.

"On behalf of Exarch Honorius and citizens of Trebizond, I welcome you," said the magister, a short, stock-legged man with a round face and a black beard. "His eminence the governor sends his greetings, and wishes you a fruitful stay in our city. He regrets that he is unavoidably detained in Sebastea, but assures me that he will endeavour to join you before your business here is completed. In the meantime, we have prepared a house for the envoy's use. You will be taken there in due course, but first we thought you might like some refreshment after your long journey.

"I am Sergius, and I am at your service during your sojourn here." The magister spoke politely enough; indeed, wonderfully so, in precise and polished Greek. But the man lacked genuine warmth, I thought; there was no light of friendliness in his eye, nor enthusiasm in his voice. He was a tired musician, performing his old song with little liking for those he was meant to entertain.

The spatharius, on the other hand, more than made up for his superior's lack of zeal with an overabundance of good will. A young man, but with many grey hairs in his dark hair and beard and a fleshy paunch beneath his cloak, he all but quivered in his desire to please. His name, he told us, was Marcian; and he proceeded to fawn over the eparch in an oily, obsequious way that put me in mind of a pup overanxious for its master's favour.

The two of them—weary minstrel and his pandering dog, as it were—led us along a wide street lined with the tall, flat façades of fine houses whose windholes were all shuttered against the day. The magister stopped before a large, square house set a little apart from the others. At first, I thought this was where we would stay, and welcomed the prospect as it was easily the finest house I had ever had the pleasure to enter.

Nikos ordered a dozen of the Sea Wolves to mount

guard outside the house, though there was no one in the street at all. Then Sergius conducted us up the steps, through the wide door and into a large vestibule; the walls were painted pale green, and the floor was a single huge mosaic depicting a Greek god—Zeus, I think, judging from the trident—surrounded by a dance of the seasons. Passing through the entrance room, we came into a large empty marble hall, through this, and out into a small, stone-paved square open to the sky. Though it was not a warm day, the sun off the white surfaces produced an agreeable warmth. In the centre of the square was a fountain, which produced a gentle, soothing sound. The principals arranged themselves in chairs while slaves in green tunics hovered around them bearing trays of food and drink.

As leader of the eparch's bodyguard, King Harald was required to attend this reception of welcome, although he had no real part in it, nor did anyone deign to address him. He was allowed a chair—which I stood behind—but the only ones who betrayed any interest in him were the slaves who brought him cups of wine. I do not think Harald noticed the slight, preoccupied as he was with the drink and sweetmeats.

Komes Nikos spoke at length of matters in Constantinople, supplying his hosts with the intimate gossip they desired, and in a most amusing, if deprecating, way. He provoked laughter several times with a witty description of some person known to his listeners, or an event of general interest.

"What is it they laugh about?" Harald asked me after one such outburst. I told him that Nikos had just made a clever observation regarding one of the palace officials. The king regarded Nikos through narrowed eyes for a moment. "A fox, that one," he remarked, and turned back to his wine.

The eparch, I noticed, said little. When he did speak,

his comments were restricted to the purpose of his visit—a quality which made him seem dry and tedious next to Nikos's smooth, and occasionally artful, ebullience—and he seemed to endure the reception, rather than to enjoy it. When at last he came to the end of his fortitude, Nicephorus stood abruptly and said, "You must excuse me, I am fatigued."

The spatharius leapt to his feet and almost upset himself in his scramble to assist the eparch. The magister rose more languidly, and with an air of resignation. "Of course," he said, "how foolish of us to prattle on like this. I hope we have not exhausted you. I will take you to your residence now. It is not far. I will summon a chair at once."

"Not for me, if you please. I have spent too many days confined to the bare boards of a ship," the eparch replied. "I shall walk."

"As you will," replied the magister, somehow implying that this was yet one more demand he was obliged to accommodate, however wearisome.

The house provided for the eparch was the governor's own, and it was magnificent. More palace than house, it was supplied with exquisite furnishings, all tastefully displayed, and all placed at the eparch and his party's disposal. The entrance vestibule was of white marble, as was the hall, which featured a mosaic of Bacchus, Cupid, and Aphrodite in a wooded vale. Built in the style of a Roman villa—a central courtyard surrounded by long wings—the house contained enough rooms for all of us.

"We hope you will find this to your liking, eparch," the magister declared, his tone and expression combining to imply the opposite of his words. "We have endeavoured to anticipate your needs. Naturally, if there is anything you require . . ." He let the words drift away, as if finishing the thought were too much bother.

Nikos took it in hand to order the household, informing

me so that I could explain the arrangements to Harald. "The bodyguard will stay in the north wing. However, no fewer than ten guards will be required to remain on watch day or night. Is that understood?"

I conveyed the instructions to Harald, who indicated that he understood. "Very well," continued the komes, "the eparch and I will stay in the south wing, and you," he directed his words to me, "will also stay in the south wing. In fact, you are not to return to the ships. Should the eparch require someone to order the guard, he will want you close at hand."

Jarl Harald was not pleased with this development, but grudgingly agreed when it was pointed out to him that he had no other choice in the matter. I considered this protection unnecessary. The city appeared peaceable enough; nowhere had I seen anything to argue for such fastidious precaution. But, as soon as the baggage began arriving from the ship, I learned the reason for Nikos's concern, for the emperor had sent his emissary with a whole shipload of baskets, crates, and boxes. These were carried into the house and placed in a room which had been prepared to house it—that is to say, emptied of all other furniture— and a double guard placed at the room's only door at all times.

I reckoned by this that the crates and boxes contained valuables, and I was not the only one. Harald, too, realized which way the wind blew in Trebizond. Harald and his Sea Wolf guards became diligent in the extreme—though I think it must have chafed them raw to have to guard the very loot they had previously hoped to steal. Even so, from the moment Eparch Nicephorus set foot in the villa that day, he did not stir so much as a pace without a full complement of armed barbarians. More dutiful bodyguards there never were.

My own position was ambiguous. Komes Nikos had

said the eparch required me to remain close at hand; beyond this, I was given nothing to do. True, I served as Harald's interpreter, but no other duties were forthcoming. It seemed to me that Nikos simply wanted me close so that he could keep an eye on me, though why he should concern himself in this way, I could not say.

Aside from the tedium, the situation suited me. I had not forgotten Justin's warning to stay far away from Nikos; on the other hand, he was possibly the only person who knew what had transpired with my brother monks during their sojourn in Constantinople and, what is more, why they left without completing the pilgrimage—that is to say, without seeing the emperor. It seemed a mystery to me, and I reckoned my best chance of solving it lay in remaining close to Nikos. Toward this end, I began searching for ways to worm myself into the proceedings.

As it happened, this was not as difficult as I first imagined. As Harald's interpreter, I was very often present when orders were given and instructions conveyed. Consequently, I chanced to see the eparch from time to time, and I never let pass an opportunity to ingratiate myself to him—not in any overt way, mind, but subtly and with some wit, so that Nikos might not find any reason to suspect me.

A word here or there, a greeting perhaps—these were my tools. Thinking that the eparch might be a devout man, I contrived to sing a verse or two of a psalm in his presence, once when it might seem as if I did not know he was nearby. Another time I contrived to be praying in the courtyard, in Latin, when he passed by. Although he said nothing, he stopped and listened for a while before continuing on his way.

Gradually, I came to his notice. I knew my work was succeeding when once I entered a room he also occupied, and his eyes shifted in my direction. A tiny gesture, indeed, but I never failed to reward his notice with a smile, or a reverent bow of my head, such as I might give any esteemed superior. It does me no credit, I fear, to say that I achieved my aim without seeming to have done anything at all. Indeed, I succeeded far better than I could have hoped.

One day, walking down the corridor to my own room, I passed the open doorway leading to the courtyard. The eparch was there and called me to him, saying, "Brother, come here."

I went to him, dutifully, as if this were my habitual function. "I call you brother," he said, "because you are, or were, a priest. Well? Am I wrong?"

"By no means, eparch," I replied respectfully.

He allowed himself a satisfied smile. "I thought so. I am rarely wrong about men. I have heard you praying, you know, and singing; you have a fine voice. I enjoy hearing you."

"You flatter me, eparch."

"What are you called?" he asked.

"My name is Aidan," I told him simply.

"Where were you born, if I may be so bold?"

I noted his fatherly tone, and told him I was born in Éire and was, for the most part, raised by monks at the monastery at Kells. "Do you know Éire?" I asked.

"Alas, no," he said. "It has not been my privilege to have travelled so far as that."

We talked awhile of these and other things, and he dismissed me to my duties. But from that day, Nicephorus began including me in various ways—slowly at first, to see how I took to the work, but with greater frequency when he saw that I enjoyed the proceedings. Very soon, I found myself acting as Nicephorus's personal servant. Indeed, the eparch took pity on my shabby appearance and bought me some new clothes: a grey cloak, breecs, and a long mantle of pale green and a siarc to go with it—plain, but all finely made and handsome for that. "The eparch would not have you mistaken for a beggar," said the servant who brought me the clothes.

Harald, already unhappy with our enforced separation, did not like this, and told me so. "It is not right. I will speak to the jarl eparch, and tell him he must get his own slave, or pay me for the use of mine."

"You must do that, of course, Jarl Harald," I agreed. "However, there might be some value in sitting so close to the eparch's chair."

He regarded me with a suspicious glare. "What do you mean?"

"The eparch is a man of authority; he has great power and influence with the emperor. A well-placed slave might learn much to his master's advantage while serving such a man," I argued.

The suggestion appealed to Harald, as it placed him at the heart of events once more. He had, by his own admission, begun finding guard duty slightly tedious, and had recently been thinking how he might make more of his position. Insofar as serving the eparch allowed me to report to the jarl items of interest he might not otherwise have learned, Harald was more than happy that my service should continue.

Nikos, however, took a rather different view. The inflection of his voice, the guarded glance of his eye, the trifling slight—indeed, in every one of a hundred tiny ways, the komes gave me to know that he thought the situation improper and unacceptable. But, since the eparch could do as he pleased, I remained privy to many of the ensuing deliberations.

In this way, I came to know the eparch very well, and to respect his deep knowledge and even deeper sagacity. Sure, I have met many intelligent men, but never one so widely read on so many diverse subjects; his learning admitted no impediment. I also found him to be an astute judge of men, as he had said—a fact which no one else seemed to appreciate.

More and more often, I found myself standing behind the eparch's chair when he met with this official delegation, or that group of merchants. Harald, as I say, tolerated my attendance at these preliminary councils, so long as I conveyed to him afterwards something to his benefit. He questioned me closely whenever we were alone, more often than not asking exceptionally perceptive questions about the various matters discussed—always paying special attention to travel routes and borders, the strength of various local tribes, and so forth.

But, I race ahead of myself. The caliph's envoy did not arrive in the city until twenty days later, and we did not meet him for seven days after that. All of which gave me a long, unobstructed view of friend Nikos; and what I saw confirmed what Justin had said of the seemingly loyal, devoted courtier: here was a ruthless and dangerous man.

# 38

The Amir J'Amal Sadiq arrived twenty days after our own landing, as I say; he approached the city on horseback, leading a retinue of noblemen, slaves, and other servants numbering well into the hundreds, along with herds of sheep, cattle, and horses. Receiving word of his approach, Nikos dispatched the imperial bodyguard to the city gate to escort the Arabs into the city.

The amir advanced at the head of his company directly to the shadow of the gate, then stopped. His was the first Arabian face I had ever seen, and it seemed to me the visage of a bird of prey: sharp featured, lordly, proud. His skin was dark brown; his eyes, hair, and beard were deepest black. He wore white: from the top of his head, wrapped in a long winding cloth called a *turban*, to the soles of his feet, encased in fine white leather boots. The brightness of his snow-white clothing against the darkness of his skin and hair made for a striking appearance.

The envoy did not enter the city that first day; instead, he sent a messenger to beg of the magister permission to occupy the flat land at the river's edge below the city's eastern rampart, for the Arabs would not stay within the city, but insisted on erecting their tents outside the walls. Tents, yes, but not crude skin structures stretched with rope over poles; they were as far from that as mud huts from a palace. The tents of the amir were made of cloth woven of a multitude of colours, and most had multiple rooms within.

They raised these tents on the banks of the river which passed beside the city, and there they remained for three days without stirring from the camp. And then, early in the morning on the fourth day, a messenger from the camp appeared at the door of the eparch's palace bearing a small blue-enamelled box.

As it chanced, Nikos was in the city and the eparch was breaking fast in the courtyard; the first people the messenger encountered were the ten barbarians Nikos insisted stand guard every moment of the day and night. Not knowing anything else to do, they called me to speak to the man. Since Constantinople, the Sea Wolves had come to value me as a mediator between them and the Greek-speakers, who they thought spoke gibberish. As they could not make themselves known to anyone else, the bodyguard at the door came to me. "A man has come, Aeddan," said the Dane named Sig.

I went outside to meet an Arab on a pale, sand-coloured horse. Seeing that I was but a slave, he dispensed with the formal salutation, and said simply, "May the peace of Allah be upon you. I bring greetings in the name of my master the amir." The messenger spoke in precise, unhesitating Greek and asked if the time were convenient to speak to the eparch.

"If you would come with me," I replied, "I will take you to him."

Sliding from the saddle, he followed me, walking a pace behind and to the right. I brought him to the courtyard where he greeted the eparch more formally, apologized for disturbing his meal, and placed the blue box in the eparch's hands, saying, "A gift from Lord Sadiq, who will be pleased to receive the eparch tomorrow at the *hour* he finds most felicitous."

"Please tell your master that I would be delighted to attend him. I will come at midday."

"As you will." Raising his hands shoulder high, palm outwards, the messenger bowed once, and departed without another word.

The eparch was in the habit of eating his first meal of the day alone at a small table in the courtyard; sometimes a brazier was placed beside the table to take the chill from the morning air. Though the sunlight was thin and the days were not warm, with or without the brazier's fire he preferred the open air of the courtyard to any other room. When the messenger departed, I turned to leave him in peace. Putting out a hand to me, he said, "Stay, Aidan. We will see what the amir has sent me."

I took my accustomed place beside his chair and asked, "What is this 'hour' of which he spoke?"

Eparch Nicephorus turned in his seat and addressed me as a teacher might an esteemed pupil. "Ah!" he said, extending his forefinger to the sky above. "The Arabs conceive of the day as divided into twelve courses—a wheel of twelve spokes, you see—each corresponding to one of the zodiacal phases. It is their belief that the sun passes through these twelve phases as it moves through the day. They hold each division to contain the aspect most favourable for various activities, and do nothing without first consulting the heavens in order to determine the best course for any action they contemplate."

The Arabs then were extending the same courtesy to the eparch which they themselves expected. The eparch understood this, and he appreciated the nobility behind it. Laying aside his plate, he took up the enamelled box and opened it; inside was a single diamond the size of a wren's egg lying in a nest of red silk. Removing the gem, he held it before him, turning it in the morning sun. It glittered hard fire in the yet dim light of the courtyard.

Nikos appeared at that moment, saw us talking, and stiffened. His smile was once more in place by the time he reached the table. "I see the greeting has come at last," he said, indicating the blue box with its costly gem.

"The amir will receive us tomorrow," the eparch said. "We will go to him at midday, I think. They consider that propitious."

"With all respect, eparch," replied Nikos stiffly, "would it not be better to summon them to attend us here—and at a time of our choosing? We should not be seen to obey their summons."

"It is a fine point you raise," allowed the eparch, "but inappropriate to the particular circumstance."

"On the contrary," said Nikos, "it is most pertinent. With respect, eparch, I would not like our leniency to be misconstrued as vacillation or weakness. We should command them to attend us—not the other way around."

"It is never weakness to show good will toward those one hopes to persuade," replied Nicephorus gently. "The amir will recognize the generosity of our acceptance, and consider it accordingly." The eparch raised an admonitory finger. "These Arabs are a proud race; they do not willingly allow themselves to remain in debt or obligation to anyone. You would do well to remember this."

"Of course, eparch." Nikos inclined his head in a stiff bow and withdrew. I did not see him again until the next day when we assembled the party that was to greet Amir Sadiq—and then I saw why: Nikos had arranged, at considerable pains, for a number of horse-drawn chariots to take us to the Arab camp.

Eparch Nicephorus emerged from the house, took one

look at the long line of chariots awaiting us in the street, and said, "Send them away, Nikos. Send them away! We will walk to the amir's camp."

Blinking in disbelief, the komes said, "Walk? With all respect, eparch, we cannot be seen to *walk*."

"Why not?" asked the eparch lightly. "People walk here and there about the earth, their business to perform. This I have seen myself, and, try as I might, find no shame in it."

"But the magister and the officials—they will deem it improper and undignified to walk."

"I was not aware that we were trying to impress the magister and his minions with our exalted position."

"Eparch, please, I would not have expected you to adopt this tone. Believe me, I care as little as you for the opinion of the magister. But it is the amir's opinion we must consider now."

"Then let me reassure you," said Nicephorus, "it is my sole consideration."

"No less than mine, eparch—"

"Is it?" The eparch's voice became firm, and his eye keen. "I do wonder, Nikos." Dismissing the matter, he said, "But never mind. The amir is waiting; let us depart. Bring the gifts."

Nicephorus started off down the street alone. Nikos watched him for a moment, and I saw the rage welling up within him; he all but shook with fury. Then, as quickly as it had flared, he forced the anger down again. Turning quickly, he signalled Harald to send the bodyguard ahead.

The magister, waiting a little distance apart with a group of city officials, came forward then. "I see the eparch has changed his mind," he said, watching the lanky old man striding down the street.

"Unfortunately, yes," agreed Nikos with seeming

reluctance. "I fear we must accustom ourselves to his unpredictable humours."

That was all he said, but the doubt sown with those few words would quickly grow to a sizeable crop.

By the time our party reached Trebizond's eastern gate, Nikos had arranged us in well-ordered ranks, reclaiming some semblance of the pomp he had hoped to inspire. Passing through the gate, we crossed the ditch bridge and proceeded in procession towards the camp. Seeing that we approached on foot, Amir Sadiq mounted a welcome party and met us on the way.

I will never forget the sight of him, sitting on his fine grey horse, dressed all in white, dazzling in the pale winter sunlight. He reined in his mount, slipped from the saddle in a single, fluid motion, and advanced open-handed to greet the eparch. The caliph's envoy was not a big man, but he exuded an air of such dignity and dominion that he seemed to tower over all around him. He was lithe, rather than muscled, and moved with the grace and subtlety of a cat.

Though they had never met before, the amir strode directly to Nicephorus and bowed. He said something in Arabic which sounded like, *Al il'allah*, and then, without the least hesitation said, "Greetings in the name of the Great al'Mutamid, by All Wise Allah, Khalifa of the Abbasids. I am J'Amal Sadiq, Amir of the Abbasid Sarazens, and I welcome you to my camp."

The eparch inclined his head in acknowledgement of the salutation. "Greetings, Amir Sadiq. In the name of the most noble Basil, by the grace of God, Elect of Heaven, Co-Regent of Christ on Earth, Emperor of the Romans, I welcome you," replied the eparch. "I am your servant, Nicephorus."

"You must now forgive me, Eparch Nicephorus," said the amir, "I have exhausted my small store of Greek words. From now on I will employ the aid of my advisor." Raising his hands, he clapped them twice, and said, "Faysal!"

A young man, only slightly older than myself, appeared beside his master as if out of nowhere. I recognized him at once as the messenger who had brought the invitation the previous day. Bowing low, Faysal proceeded to relate the words of his master to the Greek-speakers present. Facing one another, eparch and amir traded additional greetings and salutations for a time, including those of the lesser officials of both sides in their turn. They then exchanged gifts: gold armbands for the amir, and a gold bowl for the eparch.

"It is our custom," said J'Amal Sadiq through his interpreter, "to take refreshment at this time of day. I would deem it the greatest of honours if you would consent to join me in my tent."

"The honour, Amir Sadiq, would be ours entirely," replied the eparch. "But we could not consider setting foot inside your tent without extracting from you a promise to dine with us another day."

"Most certainly," answered the amir. "I will await the day with enormous anticipation."

The delegation then proceeded to the tent, which stood centermost in the midst of the camp. As Harald was to remain outside the tent with his barbarian guardsmen, I took my place beside him to wait, thinking that would be as close as I would get to the proceedings. But, as the eparch stepped to the entrance of the tent, he half-turned, looked around him—noting the magister and spatharius, Nikos, and the others making up his party—then saw me standing with Harald. "You there! Priest!" he called, more gruffly than was usual when no one else was near. "Come here. You will attend me."

"We do not need him," said Nikos quickly. "Let the slave remain outside with the barbarians where he belongs."

Turning on Nikos suddenly, almost fiercely, the eparch charged, "Do *you* speak Arabic?"

"You know I do not," answered Nikos, frowning at the question. "But—"

"Then you need bother yourself no further with my decision," replied the eparch archly. Turning once more to me, he said, "Follow me."

I saw the komes's eyes narrow as I stepped past him. Once inside the tent, I confessed: "Eparch, I do not speak Arabic." I whispered so as not to be overheard.

"Do you not?" he wondered absently, and spoke in such a way that I could not tell if he knew this fact before I told him, or not. "Never mind, it makes no difference."

Altogether, the delegation made a party numbering close to thirty, with another fifteen or so Arabs in attendance. The tent held us all, and with room to spare. We sat on the floor, but that is not to say we sat on the ground. No; for the ground, which had been but grass and dirt, was now transformed into a patchwork of brilliant colour, owing to the Arab habit of flooring their tents with thick-woven lengths of cloth of the most striking design and colour—*every* colour known to the weaver's art, in fact. The effect of these coverings, or rugs, was to bewitch the eye, even as their design delighted the intellect. Along with the rugs, which formed a handsome floor, there were cushions for leaning or sitting upon—all of which made for as comfortable and satisfactory a shelter as I have encountered anywhere.

When we had all assembled inside the tent, the amir ordered the refreshment to be served. This he accomplished without uttering a word; a simple clap of his hands, and immediately, a dozen servants appeared bearing silver platters, each dish larger than the last, and each containing foods the like of which I had never seen. The biggest platter held a whole roast lamb and required the strength of two slaves to carry it.

The platters were placed within reach of the guests on low wooden tripods, whereupon the servants retreated, only to be replaced by others bearing silver jars and trays of silver cups. A hot drink was poured out and the cups distributed to one and all, myself included. Taking his cup, the amir raised it, spoke a brief burst of Arabic, and then drank; the rest of us followed his example, placing our lips to the rim to sip the steaming liquid, which tasted of flowers and honey. It was hot and sweet, but refreshing for that.

The amir then showed us how to dip from the platters, holding our sleeves with the left hand and using the fingers of the right hand to select the choice morsels. Some of the delegation from Trebizond grumbled at this manner of eating, begrudging the lack of knives; they picked among the platters like fastidious birds, none too courteous in their comments, nor over concerned, it seemed to me, with offending their host. But Nicephorus behaved regally, licking his fingers and smacking his lips in appreciation of the delicacies before him. For delicacies they were, of that I have no doubt.

For his part, Amir Sadiq professed himself delighted that the eparch should enjoy himself so. Several times, he chose out a particular tid-bit and gave it to the eparch. This, I quickly learned, was a gesture of friendship; to be fed by the hand of the noble ruler was considered an especial honour among them.

They ate, and when the appetites of the officials and their men were met, I—along with the other servants—was given to eat of several of the dishes, and found them strange to my taste, but not overly disagreeable. One or two contained a potent spice which produced heat in my mouth and warmed me so that the sweat stood out on my forehead. I thought I might swoon, but the feeling passed.

While eating, the eparch and the amir talked. Alas, I

was not close enough to hear what they said, but they seemed to find the measure of one another quickly, and were not displeased with what they found. The eating and talk continued in a leisurely way until there came the sound of someone wailing outside the tent. The voice droned on in an undulating chant, and we all fell silent to hear it, save the amir, who rose, bowed to the eparch, spoke a word and departed. His men followed him, leaving only the servants and translator behind.

"Please," said the young man, "my lord Sadiq begs to be excused as it is his hour to pray. But you are his honoured guests and you are welcome to remain as long as you wish. Eat and drink your fill."

The eparch rose and said, "You will convey our thanks to your lord, and tell him that we have enjoyed ourselves in his company. It is with deepest regret that we must leave."

We left the camp and returned to the city, and to the governor's house where the eparch began preparations for receiving the Arabs.

This, then, began my first acquaintance with the Muhammedans, who, I promptly learned, were not pagans, as I had first supposed, but a people who worshipped the same God as Christians and Jews, and, like them, revered the Holy Word. They knew somewhat of Jesu, but, like the Jews, did not hold him to be the Christ. Nevertheless, they were extremely devout, and very exacting in their ways and lived according to a set of laws laid down in a book, the Qur'an, written by one called Muhammed, a mighty prophet indeed. The chief tenet of their belief was, as I came to understand it, complete and utter submission to the will of God, a state which they called *islam*.

That night, as I lay in my bed, in the palatial house in Trebizond, I dreamed again.

# 39

In the between-place where waking and sleeping meet, I found myself standing in darkness. The features of the room could not be seen, but it was cool and damp, and I could hear shouts and cries of men echoing, as if at a distance, along stone corridors. The room where I stood was foul with the stink of urine and excrement, and acrid smoke.

I did not know how I came to be there, nor what sort of place it was. Nor could I recall how long I had been in this room—if room it was. But I heard the cries of men all around, and it seemed to me that I was waiting, and perhaps had been waiting a long time for someone to arrive, though why . . . I could not say.

I became aware of some other presence in the room. I raised my eyes and saw a man standing before me. This man was of the brown-skinned race, and stood glaring at me, his arms folded across his chest, as if offended by the sight of me.

"If you please," I ventured, "why am I here? What have I done?" As I spoke these words, it came to me that I was a captive in prison.

"Silence," replied the man. His voice was command

itself. Unfolding his arms, I saw that he clutched a book-roll in his hand. He thrust this at me and said, "Read it out."

Taking the scroll, I unrolled it and began to read—though the words felt strange in my mouth, and sounded odd in my ears. I read, spilling these alien words into the darkness of the room, until the brown-skinned man shouted, "Enough!"

He then snatched the book-roll from my hands, saying, "Do you understand what you have read?"

"No, lord," I replied.

"And do you not realize where you are?" he asked.

"Of that I am far from certain," I told him. "But it seems a kind of prison. Am I a captive, then?"

The brown-skinned lord laughed at me. "A prison?" he chuckled. "Does this truly appear a prison to you?"

With that, he clapped his hands and I was no longer standing in a damp, stinking room in the dark. Indeed, I was sitting on a gold-brocaded cushion in a room larger than a hall. Ranged before me were trays of food, and I wore robes of finest silk.

"Eat," directed the man. Again, it was a command, and no kindly invitation. "Take your ease."

I reached towards the nearest tray to take up some food, for I was suddenly overcome with a powerful hunger. As I stretched my hand towards the tray, I caught sight of my wrist extending from the sleeve of my robe. The flesh of my wrist was red and scarred. I pulled back my hand and looked at it, then examined the other wrist—it was scarred as well, but I had no memory of how those scars could have come there.

I heard the sound of a horse neighing. I turned from my bewildered inspection to see another brown-skinned man sitting upon a white horse. The man was dressed in robes and turban of sky blue, and held a spear in his hand.

Upon seeing me, he raised the lance, levelled it, put spurs to his mount and urged it forward.

The horse leapt to the spur and charged. Before I could move, horse and rider were hurtling down upon me. I saw the horse's nostrils flaring wide. I heard the hollow beat of fast-flying hooves upon the polished marble floor, and the stinging rip of the honed spear-head slicing through the air.

I turned and tried to run, but something held me fast, and I saw that my arms were restrained by two big men with skin the colour of ebony. Gripping me tightly, they threw me to my knees. The rider appeared before me then; his horse had disappeared and he carried not a lance, but a sword which he proceeded to heat in a brazier. He thrust the blade into the flaming coals and drew it back and forth along its length. The metal grew dull and then began to blush, and then to glow. Withdrawing the blade from the fire, he advanced to where I struggled on the floor.

He spoke a word I could not understand and one of the black men snatched a handful of my hair and yanked my head up, while the other squeezed my jaws and forced my mouth open.

It was dark now. All I could see was the glowing steel as the fiery blade swung nearer.

I could feel the heat on my face. I could hear the wispy sigh of the hot metal in the cool air.

They pulled my tongue from my mouth.

The sword rose up sharply, and hovered before falling. In that instant, I saw the face of the warrior illuminated in the dim fireglow. It was the face of the Amir, J'Amal Sadiq.

He regarded me dispassionately before commencing his stroke—no anger, no hatred, merely a grim serenity as the blade fell, severing my tongue. I screamed, and went on screaming. My mouth filled with blood.

I awoke to the echo of a shout still reverberating down

the empty corridor outside my room, and the taste of blood in my mouth.

The next days were given over to the preparations for the feast with which the eparch would welcome the amir and his noblemen. There were many long and serious consultations about what the Muhammedans could or could not eat. It seemed that the Arabs would not abide pork in any form, nor shellfish—which the fish market of Trebizond excelled in supplying—nor certain kinds of vegetables. Nor did they drink wine, or ale.

These constraints occasioned endless discussion among those whose duty it was to prepare the meal. I came to know this because the eparch bade me observe in the kitchens and bring word of the arrangements as they progressed. The master of the kitchen was a sour man called Flautus, who begrudged every demand the eparch placed upon him. He went out of his way to construe offence, and grumbled prodigiously at every opportunity. In this way, he instilled in his helpers and all who laboured in the kitchens a loathing of the Arabs well before they arrived.

Why he should complain so, I was not to discover. However, Nikos recognized the quality of the man and wasted no time inflaming Flautus' animosity to the full. I learned the way of it when, having been sent to the kitchens on a minor errand, I saw Nikos talking to the kitchen master. The latter was chopping a bit of meat with a cleaver, dropping the implement with increasingly violent strokes. Upon seeing me, Nikos broke off his talk and approached me.

"Brother Aidan," he said, his tone lightly menacing, "it is good to see you taking an interest in the eparch's affairs. He does not overly burden you, I trust?"

"No, komes," I answered, "I am content."

"King Harald does not begrudge someone else the use of his servant, I suppose?"

"Jarl Harald is pleased to have me help where I can. I feel certain he would complain if it were otherwise."

"Good." He looked at me a moment, as if trying to read my thoughts. "You know, Aidan," he continued, speaking as if he were confiding an intimacy, "I have not forgotten your aid in helping bring the treacherous quaestor to justice. I have not forgotten that day."

"Nor have I."

"And I still cannot help wondering what moved you to do such a thing. It was no affair of yours certainly."

"But it was, Komes Nikos," I replied. "It was my lord Harald's affair and I serve my lord."

"And in serving your lord you gained the favour of *my* lord, and freedom for yourself, too. Yes?"

"But I am not free," I pointed out. "I am still a slave."

"Yet you entertain hopes of freedom, I presume."

"I do, komes," I said, and added: "It is a hope most slaves cherish."

"You are to be commended for keeping this hope alive, friend Aidan." Without raising his voice, or altering his speech in any way, his bearing had become threatening. "If I may be so bold as to suggest, I can be of help to you, priest. I enjoy a certain influence where the emperor is concerned."

"I will bear it in mind."

"I am certain that you will."

He left the kitchen then, and Flautus watched him go. When I looked at the cook, he averted his eyes and pretended not to listen. He began chopping the meat again, slamming the cleaver hard against the bone and gristle as if it were an enemy. I concluded my business there quickly, and hoped to avoid future discussions with Nikos.

When the preparations were complete, the invitation was sent to Amir Sadiq to come the next day after his evening prayers. The messenger returned with word of the amir's acceptance saying, "He is bringing fifty of his men with him, and two wives."

"Two wives?" wondered the eparch. "I know nothing of his wives. Did he say anything more about them?"

"Only that they are to accompany him," replied the messenger.

The next day, a little after sunset, the amir and his retinue arrived. Jarl Harald and forty of his best barbarians lined the street before the house, saluting the amir as he passed. I wondered who had taught them to do that, and guessed it must have been Nikos's idea. Upon reaching the doorway, King Harald himself opened the door for the amir to pass through.

Lord Sadiq entered the banqueting hall, followed by his own bodyguard of fifteen tall Sarazens carrying small round shields of silver, and long silver spears. In the centre of the ranks, surrounded by Sarazens, walked the two women—if women they were, for they were covered head to foot in long, flowing robes of pale yellow silk, veiled and wrapped so only their large dark eyes showed.

I was intrigued. Never had I seen women so captivating and so cosseted. Slender and graceful as willow wands, their robes glittering with golden threads, they moved with silent elegance, setting the air a-quiver with the gentle sound of tiny bells. I caught a fragrance as they passed— sweetly exotic, dry, but rich and full like that of a desert flower. The scent seemed to beckon, and my heart moved within me.

Aloof, yet near, they were very goddesses; close enough to touch, yet unreachable, they were vulnerable as lambs, surrounded by warrior guards bristling with lethal intent. It took all the strength at my command to turn my gaze from them lest I offend the amir. Even so, I stole glances whenever I might. Though I could not see their faces, I imagined such beauty and loveliness to accompany those fair forms as belong to angels, and my imaginings were far short of the mark, I know.

The Arabs were received with good grace by the eparch, who offered his hands as a sign of respect. The amir took the eparch's hands in his own and the two exchanged greetings. Nicephorus presented Sadiq with the gift of a gold neck chain, and three gold rings for each of the amir's wives. Each of the noblemen in the amir's retinue received a silver cup.

The amir bestowed gifts also. He summoned his servants who brought forth wooden chests. These were opened to reveal fine silk robes, alabaster jars of precious oils, and beautiful enamelled boxes; inside each box was a ruby. As these and other gifts were distributed, Sadiq presented Nicephorus with a purple silk robe of the kind much prized throughout Byzantium; it was edged in gold, and there were small golden crosses woven into the fabric. He also gave the eparch a sword of the kind his own bodyguard carried: silver, with a slender, curved blade.

I marvelled at the lavishness of the amir's gifts, even as I wondered at the reason behind it. The eparch's presents were fine and good, but the amir's were exquisite. Yet, if the eparch felt uncomfortable with the uneven exchange, he gave no sign.

After the formal acceptance of the gifts, the party sat down to the meal: the Byzantines to low couches, the Arabs to cushions on the floor. They watched one another warily across the narrow aisles along which the servants bore trays and platters of food. To describe the fare is to demean it, for words alone cannot suffice, but impart only the barest hint of the sumptuous feast served that night. As there was no one to say me otherwise, I joined in with a will. The meal was a rapture, every mouthful a delight from the small green, brine-soaked olives, to the honey-roasted quails. And the wine! As fragrant as balsam and light as a cloud, it filled the mouth with the freshness of fruit and the softness of a summer's night. The Arabs drank—not wine, but a sweet drink made from honey, spices, and water which Nikos had ordered to be prepared especially for them.

The grand worthies of Trebizond affected to seem unimpressed. They reclined on their couches and nibbled stoically from their knives as if it were a grim duty to dine on such handsome fare. I tell you the truth, it was a sin the way they behaved before the bounty of that table. But I more than made up for their transgressions; I know I did my best, relishing every morsel as only a grateful man can do.

Nicephorus and the amir sat together on cushions, the eparch having abandoned his customary couch in deference to his guest. Established on a low dais, the two overlooked the feast, surrounded by those of highest rank and privilege. Nikos was second to the eparch, followed by the magister and the spatharius, who both wore the expressions of men being forced to attend a grave-digging. Midway through the feast, Nikos rose and went out, returning a short while later followed by four men bearing a huge golden ewer on a carved wooden pallet. People exclaimed aloud at the appearance of this impossibly costly object; the hall rang with the acclaim.

Nikos led the servants through the centre of the hall and came to the foot of the dais. "Emperor Basil sends his regards to the amir," he said, speaking in a voice loud enough to be heard throughout the hall. "He has asked me to deliver to you this ewer on his behalf, to be given to the caliph as a token of the high esteem with which he values his future friend."

This pronouncement sent a flurry of quick-murmured whispers through the hall. Some men actually gaped in amazement at the generosity—not to say profligacy—of the gift; the cost was staggering.

At Nikos's command, the servants poured the specially prepared drink from the great ewer into silver pitchers with which other servants began filling the cups of the celebrants. When the last of the elixir had been poured, Nikos raised his cup and said, "I drink to the health and long life of the emperor and the caliph, and to friendship and peace between our peoples!"

Everyone lifted high their cups and drank. And it was in that moment, when all were occupied, that there came a shout from the entry vestibule and into the hall rushed eight or ten men. Dressed in long black Sarazen robes, the lower portions of their faces covered; they dashed along the centre aisle, screaming and shouting, swords and spears flashing in the candlelight. Without the slightest hair of hesitation they seized the golden ewer and, before every eye, bore it off. Men struggled to their feet and attempted to bar the way, but the thieves had already made good their escape. Before anyone could act, the robbers and their prize had disappeared.

The eparch was stunned. The magister and spatharius stared in frozen amazement. The amir's colour deepened with shame and rage that men of his own race should perpetrate this brazen crime in the very house in which he was a guest. He stood at once and ordered his bodyguard to give chase, kill the thieves, and bring back the golden ewer. The Sarazens rose as one and took up their weapons.

But Nikos prevented them. He held up his hands and called out. "Please! Please! Be seated. I beg you please be seated. They are gone; no one has been hurt. There is no cause for alarm. The true crime would be if we allowed these robbers to interrupt our enjoyment of this feast.

Therefore, I beg you: take no thought for what has happened here tonight. It is nothing—a trifle only. Do not be dismayed."

He turned to the servants who still stood with the silver pitchers in their hands. He summoned the nearest to him and spoke a word in his ear. The servant signalled the others and they all went out.

"My friends," said Nikos, "return to your pleasure. Let it be as if nothing has happened." He flung out his arm and pointed to the hall entrance where the servants had once more appeared, bearing an even larger ewer than the one that had been stolen. "You see!" he cried. "No ill has befallen this night. The largesse of the emperor is all sufficient. Enjoy! Enjoy!"

If the sight of the first ewer amazed and delighted the banqueters, the sight of the second silenced them with astonishment. Even so, I could read their thoughts as if they were written on their faces: How was it possible that two such objects should exist? And could they both be given to the caliph? The magnitude of expense! Only a god can afford to bestow such gifts!

More sweet drink was poured from the second ewer and carried through the hall to refill the cups. Nikos renewed his pledges of good will, and slowly the banquet resumed, but with much more interest than before.

The next day, the whole city bubbled with the excitement of the bold robbery, and how the quick-thinking komes had saved the honour of the amir with his extraordinary gesture. An act of true nobility, they called it; largesse on an unprecedented scale. The magister and spatharius were busy morning to night spreading word of the robbery, and a reward was quickly offered for the capture of the thieves and the return of the ewer.

Only the eparch appeared ill-pleased with the komes's behaviour in the affair. I found him just after midday in the room he used for holding council. "Eparch," I said, moving to where he sat, fists balled on the arms of his chair, "you asked me to tell you when Nikos returned. He is here now."

"Tell him I wish to see him at once."

I turned and started away, but Komes Nikos came sweeping in the door at that moment, full of zeal and assurances. "We will find the ewer, never fear," he said. "I have men searching throughout the city. I have every confidence that it will soon be returned."

"What of the dignity of our guests?" demanded the eparch. "Will that also be returned?"

"You are aggrieved, eparch," observed Nikos. "I assure you, I am doing all to resolve this unfortunate incident."

"I *am* aggrieved," replied the eparch tartly. "I am angry. The offence to our guests was unpardonable. The amir was gracious enough to accept my assurances that the matter would be most seriously pursued."

"So it is," the komes said. "You have my every pledge. The perpetrators shall be apprehended and brought to justice. If you will heed a word of counsel, I think you put too much trust in the Danes. They are the ones who should be held responsible for this. If not for their negligence, this crime would not have been committed."

"How so?" demanded Nicephorus. "They remained at their posts throughout—exactly as you placed them. Even the slaves say no one entered or left the house once the Danes had taken their positions. I think we must look elsewhere for the perpetrators."

Nikos started to object, but the eparch dismissed him with an exasperated flick of his hand. "You may go, Komes Nikos," he said. "Go and give your assurances to the magister and his monkey. I am certain they will be more easily persuaded. Go! Leave me. I wish to think."

The komes affected offence at this brusque treatment.

"If I have displeased you in some way, eparch, I am sorry. I would only remind you that it is, after all, a most delicate and unusual situation. We must proceed with all caution and circumspection."

"Yes, yes. I am certain of it," he replied, his irritation increasing. "Go then, cautiously and circumspectly, by all means. But go."

Nikos stalked from the room. The eparch watched him go, and then said, "You heard him, Aidan?"

"Yes, eparch."

"He said the ewer would soon be returned. I wonder where they will find it—in the kitchen, or in the stable?"

"Eparch?"

"He is dirty with this. I know it." Turning to me, he said, "Thank you, Aidan. You may go. I am tired. I will lie down now."

He rose wearily from his chair and walked to the door, paused, and said, "Can I trust you, Aidan?"

"I hope you can," I told him.

"Then I will tell you something," he said, motioning me to him. As I stepped near, he placed a fatherly hand on my shoulder—the gesture reminded me of Abbot Fraoch. Putting his mouth to my ear, he whispered, "Beware the komes, Aidan. He has marked you for an enemy."

This did in no way surprise me. Still, I said, "I believe you, eparch. But why should he think me an enemy?"

He offered a thin, mirthless smile. "Because you have penetrated his duplicity. Discovery is what he fears most of all; it is the one thing treachery cannot abide."

# 40

T he golden ewer came to light a day or two later—
found, they said, in a ditch outside the city walls. It
was undamaged, for the most part, save for a dent
in one side, and a bent handle which looked as if someone
had tried to pull it off. King Harald growled when I told
him of the treasure's recovery. "It was dropped where they
knew to find it," he snarled.

The jarl had taken a sour view of the event from the
beginning. He held that the theft impugned his honour and
that of his men, and insisted the raid had been created
solely to disgrace him. "There were no thieves," he argued.
"Once the amir arrived, no one entered or left the hall. No
one came near."

"Perhaps the thieves were already inside the house," I
suggested. "Perhaps they were hiding."

"Heya," he agreed. "The thieves were inside the house.
That is so. On Thor's beard, the jar was never stolen."

"But I saw it. I was there. They rushed in and took it."

"Nay," he replied, his voice a low rumble. "Did you
ever hear of a thief parting with such a treasure once he
had it in his hands? I never did."

"Maybe they feared pursuit," I suggested. "They hid it

in the ditch and hoped to come back for it later—when no one was looking."

The barbarian king shook his head firmly. "The time when no one was looking was when they threw it away," the jarl replied, and I was forced to admit that in matters of stolen treasure, his knowledge and experience were far superior to mine.

Gunnar and Tolar had their own views. "Who profited from the theft?" Gunnar asked pointedly. "Find that man, and you have caught the thief."

In the event, those responsible for the supposed raid were never found; and, since the ewer was recovered, the search was halted and speculation ceased. Interest turned instead to the peace talks between the eparch and the amir which commenced a few days later. They alternated meeting places, sometimes within the city, and sometimes in the Arab camp. Sometimes the magister and certain prominent citizens took part, sometimes various merchants from Constantinople, and sometimes only the eparch and amir alone but for their interpreters and advisors. I also attended a few of these discussions, but found them exceedingly dull.

Winter deepened around us all the while; the days, though chill and often damp, were never cold. Nor did it snow, except for the high tops of the mountains far to the north and east. Sometimes, a southern wind would stir the leafless branches and the day would be almost warm. Even so, with the approach of the Christ Mass, Trebizond began to shake off some of its seasonal lethargy. I noticed a steady stream of newcomers arriving in the city. When I remarked on this to one of the merchants—who, by virtue of having traded gemstone and marble in Trebizond for twenty years, was sometimes included in the eparch's delegation—I was told this was but a trickle that would eventually become a flood.

"Just wait and see," he said. "By Saint Euthemius's Day there will not be an empty room in the whole city. Every doorway will become a bed. You watch. It is true."

We at the abbey, like every holy community, honoured certain saints with feasts on particular days: Saint Colum Cille's day was special to the monks at Kells. And though there were many eastern saints unknown in the west, it still seemed odd that any day should be more highly regarded than the Christ's Day Mass. "I had no idea the saint's day was so well observed here," I told him.

"Some come for Euthemius's feast, I suppose," he allowed with a shrug of indifference. "But most come for the *fair*."

I had heard this word before, of course, but his use of it was strange. Upon inquiring, I was told that a fair was a gathering, not unlike a market, where people might buy and sell, and also enjoy special entertainments and diversions over many days. "The Trebizond fair is well known," the merchant assured me. "People come from the far ends of the empire and beyond just to attend—Christian and pagan alike, everyone comes."

He spoke the truth with no exaggeration. For the Christ Mass came and went, strictly observed, yes, but stiffly and with very little warmth. I did attend a Mass, out of curiosity rather than desire, and I could not find it in my heart to pray. The worship seemed perfunctory to me; even the singing lacked interest. All in all, I thought it a dismal observance—though, perhaps my own feelings of desolation coloured my perception; I was still bitterly disappointed with God, and in no fit mood to regard the birth of his son, to whom I was no longer speaking.

Deep in my innermost soul, I must have entertained the notion that a miracle of reconciliation would take place for me during that most holy and joyous observance: that my Lord Christ might look down in pity and mercy upon me, take hold of me, embrace me as his son, and raise me up once more to my proper place in the Great Kingdom. But no. God, ever aloof, remained hidden in his obscure Heaven, silent and uncaring as ever. Or, if he did favour mankind with the light of his presence, it was upon some other corner of the earth that he shone. The glad tidings of great joy were, I suppose, bestowed upon others.

The only glimmer of anything that even faintly resembled happiness or good will came from the barbarians. The Sea Wolves made a noble and determined attempt at a celebration: *jultide*, they called it—a seven-day orgy of eating and drinking and fighting. They contrived to brew their öl, and procured six sheep and four bullocks for roasting, though they would rather have had an ox or two and some swine. As there was nothing to prevent me, I joined them for part of their festivities at the quay where they had taken over a sizeable portion of the wharf, having erected large tent-like shelters made from their ship's sails.

"I am missing Karin's rökt skinka," Gunnar confided three or four days into their celebration. "And her lütfisk and *tunnbrod*—I miss those also. My Karin makes the best lütfisk. Is this not so, Tolar?"

Tolar nodded sagely, and stared into his cup. "The *glögg* is good."

"True," agreed Gunnar solemnly, then confided: "I have never had glögg before, Aeddan. In Skania, only very wealthy men may drink it as it is made with wine, you know. But maybe we are all very wealthy now, heya?"

"Heya," Tolar replied, then thought perhaps he had said too much, for he rose abruptly and went to find a jar to refill the cups.

Thorkel and two other Danes staggered by just then and settled at the table with us. "Aeddan, old Sea Wolf!" cried Thorkel. "I have not seen you for fifty years!"

"You saw me yesterday, Thorkel," I told him.

"Ah, yes, so I did." He smiled happily. "This is the best *jul* ever, but for the snow." He paused, his smile fading in a sudden upsurge of melancholy. "It is a pity about the snow." He shook his head sadly. "I miss that."

"Not the cold, however," amended Gunnar.

Tolar, just returning, overheard this remark and shook his head solemnly. He did not miss the cold, either.

"Nay, not the cold," agreed Thorkel wistfully. "You can keep the cold." He looked at me blearily, guzzled his drink, and asked, "What do the folk of Irlandia do for the jultide?"

Though I had no wish to discuss it with drunken barbarians, that is exactly what I did. "We have no jul, but celebrate the Christ Mass instead," I told them, and went on to explain something about it.

"And is this god the same as the one hanging on the gallows?" wondered the pilot. "The one Gunnar is always jabbering about?"

"It is called a *cross*," Gunnar corrected him. "And it is the same god. Is that not so, Aeddan?"

"That is so," I agreed. "He is Jesu, called the Christ."

"How do you know so much about this?" inquired one of the Danes with Thorkel.

"Aeddan here was a priest of this god, and he was my slave before Jarl Harald got him. He knows all there is to know of such matters."

"Beware, Gunnar," warned the other Dane, "you may become a priest yourself if you are not careful."

"Ha!" cried Gunnar in derision. "But I will tell you one thing: this Christ of Aeddan's helped me win the bread wager against Hnefi and the others. Ten pieces of silver, if you will remember."

The others were much impressed with Gunnar's revelation, and demanded to know whether this Jesu would help them win wagers, too.

"No, he will not," I told them, bitterness welling up in me like venom. "He does not help anyone! He does what he pleases and heeds nothing of men or their prayers. He is a selfish, spiteful god, demanding everything and giving nothing. He is fickle and inconstant. Sooner pray to your rune stones—at least a stone will listen."

Stunned by my sudden and heated outburst, my companions stared at me for a moment. Then Gunnar, a slow, sly, suspicious smile spreading across his broad face, said, "You are only saying that because you want to keep this god to yourself. You do not want us to know about him. That way he is yours alone."

They all agreed that this accounted for my sudden contrariness regarding this Christ, and determined among themselves that whatever I said, the opposite must be true.

"You cannot make fools of us so easily," Thorkel declared. "We can clearly see there is more here than you are telling." Lifting a hand to the city behind us, he pointed to one of the crosses atop the largest of the churches. "Men do not raise worship halls to gods who do nothing for them. I think you are trying to lead us astray. But we are too smart for you."

The discussion was curtailed just then when a wrestling match began. Two big Danes stripped off their clothes, laved olive oil over themselves and began to grapple with one another on the quay. A crowd quickly gathered around them, and wagers were made. The fight, however, settled into a rather lacklustre and disappointing tussle. The spectators were on the point of abandoning interest in the contest when one of the wrestlers, stepping too near the edge of the quay, fell into the harbour. His opponent, seeing his chance, dived into the water after him, seized him, thrust him under the surface and held him there until the unfortunate wretch collapsed from lack of air. He would have drowned if the other had not let him up when he fainted.

This produced a most remarkable consequence, for no sooner had the first wrestler been hauled from the water than another Sea Wolf threw off his clothes and jumped into the harbour. He, too, was bested and was soon dragged unconscious from the cold sea. The next to enter the fray fared better. He bested the first opponent and the next three in turn, but fell to the fourth, who then took on all comers.

This water wrestling proved enormously popular with everyone. Even King Harald tried his luck, and lasted through three opponents before succumbing. With each new contest, wagers were laid and money changed hands. The sport continued for two days before they had had enough, and everyone agreed that it was one of the best jultide games they had played.

Thus, we wintered in Trebizond. Gradually, the days began to lengthen and the weather to turn. When at last the sea roads opened once more, the ships began arriving from other parts of the empire. The eparch and amir looked to the conclusion of their talks, and the merchants to returning home. Meanwhile, streaming into the city by all and every means, came a veritable torrent of people, from as many tribes and nations as could be counted.

The city became an enormous marketplace, with the streets as stables; people offered sleeping places in their houses and were paid handsomely for their hospitality. Harlots also arrived in numbers to ply their particular trade among the populace of fair-goers. Consequently, the sight of men and women copulating in doorways and behind market stalls became wearily commonplace as the pursuit of this occupation succeeded.

The forum was transformed into a welter of people, many of whom congregated in clumps around certain of their favourites, be it teacher, seer, or soothsayer. There were Magi from the East whose knowledge of the stars and their movements was vast as the heavens themselves. They held forth with their observations and argued among themselves for supremacy. They also provided those seeking their counsel with close-studied readings of the star-courses and other celestial signs, by which many set great store. Apparently, one solitary consultation was enough to produce a reliable reading of an individual's future.

This fascinated me, I freely confess, for my own dreams have shown me that there are ways of knowing and seeing which are beyond the common abilities of most people. Also, I was curious to know what another might make of my circumstance. Condemned to a death I did not die, slave to a barbarian king, and a spy for the emperor, could my life be ordained by heaven and written in the stars?

When curiosity overcame better judgement, I plucked up my courage and entered into one of these consultations with a wizened old Arab named Amet, whose face was so wrinkled and dark it looked like a dried fig. He was, he said, a Magus of the Umayids who had learned his craft after long and arduous tutelage in Baghdat and Athens.

"All praise to Allah, and to his Glorious Prophet also," he said in lilting Greek. "I have faithfully served two amirs and a khalifa. Sit with me, my friend. I tell you the truth: I alone have devised a means by which the future is revealed in utmost clarity. You may rely upon my *observation*—you see! I do not use the word prediction as so many do; for to describe what has been written for anyone to see is not prediction, is not foretelling; it is reading merely—you may rely on my scrutiny with complete confidence. Now you must tell me everything you wish to know."

We sat down together on cushions in the tent-like stall he had erected beside a column on the forum's eastern

side. I told him I had reason to inquire after my future—
not from any desire for personal gain, or even happiness,
but from a sense of duty.

"Why duty?" he asked, tilting his head to one side.
"You say duty, which implies obedience? Why do you use
this word?"

His question caught me up. "I do not know." After a
moment's thought, I said, "I suppose it is because I have
always sought to be an obedient servant."

"A servant must have a master; who is your master?"

"I am a slave to a king of the Danemen."

The old Arab dismissed my reply with an impatient
gesture. "He is not your master, I believe. He is your
excuse merely."

"Excuse?" I thought his use of the word inept, but was
intrigued nonetheless. "I do not understand."

Amet smiled mysteriously. "You see? I already know a
great deal about you and we have only begun speaking to
one another. Now perhaps you will tell me the day of your
birth."

I told him, and he asked, "The time of day, what was
it? Be as precise as possible; it may be important."

"But I do not know the precise moment," I replied.

He clucked his tongue and shook his head at my ignorance of a detail of such momentous significance. "Give me
your hand," he said, and I complied. After a cursory glance
at the palm, he turned it over and then released it.
"Morning," he said. "Near dawn, I believe, for the sun had
not yet risen."

"The time-between-times!" I said, as memory came
singing back to me over the years. "My mother always said
that I was born in the time-between-times—when night
had finished, but day had not yet begun."

"Yes," replied Amet, "that would be the hour. The day
we have established already." He raised a bony finger

towards the roof of his tent. "Now we will look to the heavens."

Though he did not move from his cushion, he nevertheless bestirred himself to great activity. Producing a beaded cloth pouch which he wore on a rope around his neck, the old magus withdrew a disk-like object of shining brass, passed his hand over it reverently, and then, pushing here and lifting there, erected two additional appendages which he deftly adjusted. Raising the object with the aid of a small brass loop, he put his eye to a hole in one of the arms, performed some small, inexplicable manoeuvres, and turned his face to the sky outside the tent.

"It is called an *astrolabos*," he told me, lowering the disk, folding the arms and replacing it in the pouch. "To him who knows its secrets, this device reveals wonders. What is your name?"

"I am Aidan," I told him. "Has your device revealed any wonders about me?"

Placing a fingertip to his lips, he turned to a squat earthen jar employed to hold a number of scrolls. Selecting one of these, he unrolled it and held it before him for a moment. He glanced at me, frowned, threw the scroll aside and selected another. "Aedan," he said, pronouncing my name like a Greek.

The second scroll apparently met with his approval, for he smiled and said, "You did not tell me you were a seer, Aedan."

"But I am not a seer!" I protested. Even so, the shock of recognition coursed through me.

"The stars never lie," he scolded. "Perhaps you are a seer, but have not yet discovered this gift." Retrieving the first scroll, he studied it once more, only to discard it again in favour of a third which he withdrew from the baked earth jar. "Strange," he said, "to find a lord who is also a slave. Wisdom leads me to doubt this, but experience has taught me that truth does often run contrary to wisdom."

"I was a prince of my tribe," I told him, "but I put aside nobility long ago to become a servant of God. I was a priest for many years."

"Ah, I see! A servant of the Most High, Allah be praised! Servant and slave, yes. This is important." He lay aside the scroll and folded his hands in his lap. "Now I must meditate on this matter. Farewell, my friend."

"I am to leave?"

"Leave me now, yes. But return tomorrow and we will talk again, God willing."

"Very well," I agreed, rising to my feet. "Good day to you, Amet."

"God go with you, Aedan, my friend." He touched his forehead with his fingertips and, closing his eyes, arranged himself in an attitude of meditation, legs crossed, hands resting on his knees.

I left him like that, a small island of calm in the midst of the swirling eddies of the busy market. On my way back to the eparch's residence, however, I debated within myself whether to go back to him, for I had begun to doubt whether any good could come of knowing whatever Amet might tell me. By the time I reached the eparch's door, I had decided that my own premonitions of the future were confusing enough; it would be better for me not to know any more than I knew already.

This I told myself a hundred times over, and resolved to stay away. But the heart is desperately wicked, and men often fail to do what is best for them. Alas! My once solid resolve had dwindled to such a weak, enfeebled thing, that the next day I crept from the eparch's house and hurried with hasty steps to the magus's stall.

# 41

The Bishop of Trebizond did not approve of the fair; indeed, he abhorred it entirely, by reason of the fact that it led God's most vulnerable children into doubt and error. He particularly disliked the potion sellers who preyed on the childless, the crippled, and the easily confused. "Worse than poison!" was his judgement on the concoctions they dispensed. "Dogs' piss and vinegar would do a body more good," he concluded, "and that you can get for nothing! They sell their vile concoctions at exorbitant rates to those least able to afford them, and then give their poor victims pernicious lies to swallow along with their foul elixirs. Soothsayers! Diviners! Magicians! I condemn them all."

Despite the bishop's censure, the people flocked to the fair, and most seemed to enjoy it—especially the farmers and village folk, many of whom brought their animals to the city for sale and trade. I respectfully submitted to the bishop that they could hardly be held to blame who had no priests to teach them or offer a better example.

"I have no qualm or sympathy for the *pagani*," Bishop Arius asserted with some vigour. He had come to the eparch's residence to pay his respects to the imperial envoy and, seeing that I was a monk—for so he perceived me—inquired after me while waiting for Nicephorus to receive him. We fell into discussion of the crowded conditions in the city, and one subject led onto another, as they will. "Unbelievers are none of my concern; they can do what they please. But Christians should not be seen supporting such confabulations. The wickedness proceeding from these fairs cannot be exaggerated."

"Indeed," I allowed, "yet there are Christians among the astrologers and seers. I was always taught that such practices were an abomination."

"Then you were well taught," replied the bishop tartly. "All such devilry is an abomination in the sight of God. Those are no true Christians you saw holding forth with the seers and soothsayers."

"Are they not?"

"Be not deceived, son. They are *Paulicians*." He said the word as if it were the name of a particularly hideous disease.

I had never heard of this sect, and told Arius so.

"Would that no one had ever heard of them," he said pointedly. "Forewarned is forearmed, so know this: they are members of a heretical sect which promulgates the instruction of a misguided apostate—a man who styled himself a teacher, yet whose teaching was far, far removed from that of his blessed namesake."

He spoke with such vehemence, I wondered what they could believe that would arouse such wrath. "These Paulicians," I inquired, "is it that they believe a false doctrine? Or that they lead others astray with their teaching? Either way, why not simply excommunicate them and ban the belief?"

"That was done," the bishop affirmed, "and accomplished with admirable vigour. But as sometimes happens, driving them out of the church has only made the sect stronger. It is no longer simply a matter of belief; their very existence is an offence against Heaven and all true Christians. What is more, they have amassed such power in certain quarters so as to choke out the very truth. Their doctrine—if the word can be used—is a perverted accretion of errors, lies, and half-truths." Arius appeared to have swallowed something sour. "These Paulicians propound that God created only the heavens and the celestial lights, while the Evil One created earth and all upon it. Every other tenet of their belief flows from this."

I observed that many people held such views—if not overtly, then at least in their tacit response to the world. "Many who call themselves Christians," I suggested, "behave in such a way as to reveal a true belief in no way dissimilar to that which these Paulicians teach."

The bishop rolled his eyes. "How well I know it, my friend. I have been twenty-eight years in the church, mind. No, no, it is not their assertion of an evil creator that is most offensive—if only they had stopped there! How much misery would have been prevented, only God can say. But they compound their sins, and go on adding lie to lie.

"For example, they say that the Lord Christ was merely an angel sent from Heaven to wage war against the Evil One," Bishop Arius replied, his mouth squirming with distaste. "They insist that the Virgin Mary is but an ordinary woman, unworthy of devotion, or veneration, or indeed any special consideration. They hold not to Holy Scripture at all, and preach that all men are free to follow their own dictates since the laws laid down by God were for the Hebrews of old, and no longer concern right-thinking human beings. Accordingly, they do not believe in marriage, or any other sacrament, nor the primacy of the church, nor even baptism."

"Shocking, to be sure," I conceded, warming to the debate. How long had it been since I had discussed such matters of doctrine in a learned manner? "Still, they sound harmless enough." Heresies abounded in the East, as everyone knew; and many were much worse than the benighted Paulicians.

"That is where you are wrong," the churchman corrected. "They are not content to preach and teach, but persist in fomenting riots and uprisings in the provinces."

"Over baptism?" I wondered aloud.

"Over taxes," corrected the bishop. "Four thousand peasants and farmers were killed the last time. For this cause, and all the rest, they were purged from Constantinople. It is our misfortune that they fled east and now reside almost wholly in these much-disputed territories—at least, that is what is said. I have reason to believe, however, that very many yet reside in Constantinople, secretly, gnawing away like rats at the substance of the Holy Church. Rumour has it that some have even wormed their way to the very foot of the throne."

"What do they want in Trebizond?" I wondered.

"They come here for the fair, like everyone else," replied Arius. "They come from Tarsus, from Marash and Raqqa in the south, where it is said they have made alliance with the Muhammedans. In exchange for allegiance, the caliph allows them to practise their abominable religion. They are ever seeking converts among the discontented."

I was on the point of asking him for a description of these Muhammedans when Nicephorus appeared and I was dismissed, whereupon I left the house and hastened to my consultation with Amet.

As I walked along the much-constricted street to the forum, I could not help reflecting on the fact that despite whatever Bishop Arius might say, the fair was well-attended by the humble churchgoers of Trebizond. Tiny golden crosses were purchased right alongside glass amulets to be worn as protection against the evil eye—for if angels stood ready to aid the God-fearing, then demons were just as eager to harm them; and if Christians could command angels, then the wicked could certainly command devils.

In this and other ways, it seemed to me that most of the bishop's flock were far closer to these Paulicians he despised, than to his orthodoxy. Still, it was merely a matter of passing interest; I told myself that I was finished with such tedious matters of the faith. The rise or fall of an obscure sect was nothing to me.

These thoughts occupied me as I made my way among the magicians' stalls set up in the forum: crystal-gazers and potion-makers, men who foretold the future in the livers of freshly killed animals, the amulet-sellers, purveyors of incense and readers of knucklebones and gopher sticks.

In the encampment of the astrologers, I found Magus Amet in much the same posture as I had left him the day before. He opened his eyes at my arrival, welcomed me, and bade me to sit, patting the cushion beside him. Then, turning to a copper pot which was steaming over a small fire, he lifted the vessel and poured a thin brown liquid into two tiny glass cups sitting on a brass tray. Holding the tray, he offered me a cup, saying, "Refresh yourself, my friend."

Accepting the cup, I lifted it to my lips. It was very hot, so I hesitated. "Drink! Drink! It will not harm you," Amet said. Taking up his cup, he sipped the hot liquid noisily into his mouth. "Ah! Most refreshing, you will find."

The stuff smelled vaguely herbal, so I sipped at it and found the taste not unpleasant—a little like rose petals combined with tree bark, and something slightly fruity. "It is very nice, Amet," I said. Even as I swallowed down the elixir, my heart began beating faster for word of what he had to tell me.

"You are wondering," he said, "if I have discovered anything of interest to you."

"That I am," I granted, "though I must confess that all my teaching prior to this moment has warned me against trifling with the forces of darkness."

"Forces of darkness?" Amet raised his eyebrows high. "Hoo! Listen to you! If that is what you believe, then be gone from me. Shoo! Go away."

"Truly," I told him, shaking my head, "I no longer know what I believe."

"Then allow me to assure you, my sceptical friend, that I have not spent my life in the pursuit of trifles. The same God—the very same—who set the stars in motion guides my sight along Future's course. This is my belief."

We sipped our drink in silence for a time, and then Amet put aside his cup and slapped his knees with the palms of his hands. "I have discovered many things about you, my friend," he said. "Whether they are of interest to you is another matter, and one which you alone must decide. Shall I tell you?"

"Yes, tell me. I am not afraid."

The old man's eyes narrowed as he looked at me. "Fear comes into your mind very quickly. When I said you were a seer, you protested to me that you were not. Yet I know that you are, and I think you have seen something of what the future holds for you, or fear would have no place in your thoughts."

"It may be as you say," I allowed vaguely, trying not to give away any more to him than that. If his abilities were genuine, and I truly hoped they were, I wanted to learn from an untainted source.

"Since that is the way of it," Amet continued, "what can I tell you that you do not already know?"

This seemed to me a ruse—a trick to coax the ignorant or gullible into revealing more about themselves, details which the seer could then claim as proof of his veracity and craft. "Pretend I know nothing of which you speak, for indeed—with all respect, Amet—you have told me nothing."

The old man's wrinkles rearranged themselves into an expression of deepest pity. "Very well," he said, choosing a scroll from among those in his basket. He unrolled the parchment and studied it for a moment, then began to read aloud. "All praise to Allah, Wise and Magnificent, Ruler of Realms, Progenitor of Peoples and Nations! Blessings to all who honour His name." So saying, he bowed his head three times, then raised his eyes to me and said, "You, my friend, are destined for greatness." Holding up a finger, he warned, "But this will not be won without great sacrifice. This is God's decree: virtue is purchased in the marketplace of torment; he who would be great among men must first be brought low. Amen, so be it."

The old seer's pronouncement was unexpected and disappointing; it was, in fact, considerably less than I had hoped. My heart sank low to hear what I considered an extremely meek and ordinary announcement—nothing more than a dubious and ambiguous declaration united to a tired aphorism. Was this the wisdom dispensed by the Ruler of the Universe?

"I thank you, Amet," I said, trying to conceal my disappointment. I replaced my cup on the brass tray and prepared to take my leave. "I will heed your words."

"You are disappointed," the magus said. "I can see it in your eyes. You think me a fool."

"No," I said quickly. "I think—that is, I hoped you would tell me something I did not know."

"And I have already said that I can tell you nothing

you do not already know, yes?" He frowned fiercely. "Speak plainly, priest. Why did you come to me?"

"I thought you might tell me about my death."

He peered at my face as if at one of his scrolls. "At last we come to it," he said.

"Have you seen this?"

"It is tempting fate to speak of death. Since you insist, however, speak of it we will."

Closing his eyes, he placed the palms of his hands over his face and began to rock gently back and forth. This continued for a little time, and then he whispered, "Amen".

Opening his eyes, he regarded me with a strange expression. "You have recently escaped death, and you will again. Your enemies are never who they seem, but be warned: your true enemy is very near; his hand is concealed and ready to strike."

Although this was scarcely less vague than what he had said before, I felt a thrill of recognition as he spoke.

"A captive you are, yet you will change one captivity for another before your true nature is revealed. This is not to be wondered at, neither feared. For your salvation is assured, though your safety is ever in doubt." Raising his hands either side of his face, palm outward, Amet bowed three times, saying, "This I have seen. May Allah, Ever Merciful, be praised!"

We made our farewells, then, and I offered the old magus the silver coin Gunnar had given me. "It is all I have," I told him, "but you are welcome to it."

Amet refused, however, saying that if he could not accept money from another seer, still less could he take it from a slave. "Spend it on yourself, Aedan," the seer called after me as I left. "The small joy it brings will be the last you will know for a very long time."

As I had nothing else in mind, I determined to do as he suggested, and the notion stimulated me. I had rarely had any money, and had never spent any on myself. I stood looking around, wondering how best to dispose of my coin. Sure, anything could be bought in the market— from wart potions to Persian parchment and red parrots.

What should I do with the money? The question posed something of a dilemma. The experience of spending was so peculiar to me that with the whole of the market before me, I was stymied—by the multiplicity of choice as much as by the singularity of the experience.

I wandered through the market and the nearby streets rapt in thought over this unexpected problem. I examined soft leather shoes, and silk rugs; I considered buying a knife, and then thought I might like a small purse of fine leather—but, having bought it, I would have nothing to put in it.

*Enjoy*, Amet had suggested. What would I enjoy?

Just as I posed this question my eye fell upon a young woman standing beside a pillar beneath a covered colonnade. She was swathed in finest silk of red and yellow, and on her feet were white sandals with straps of braided gold. Her hair was dark, and fell about her shoulders in a mass of tight curls. I must have stared too openly, for she noticed my glance, smiled, and beckoned me with a gesture I had seen many times since coming to Trebizond.

In truth, it was only upon seeing her crook her finger in that certain way that I knew the trade she practised. Though it brings me no honour to say it, even as I took my first step towards her, I made up my mind to avail myself of her services. As I had never done this before—indeed, I had never lain with a woman—I did not know how the bargain was struck. Instantly, I was overwhelmed by the most delicious uncertainty. My heart began to beat fast, and my palms grew damp. When I opened my mouth to speak, I found the words strange on my tongue.

Recognizing inexperience when she saw it, the young

woman smiled. Shifting her garment slightly, she revealed to me one smooth, shapely white shoulder. My eye travelled down to the swell of her breast to see the rosy tip of her nipple before she adjusted her garment once more. "Would you like to come with me?" she asked. Her voice was not as lilting or as sweet as I had imagined it would be, but it was agreeable nonetheless.

Not trusting my voice, I simply nodded. She smiled again, and stepped behind the pillar. I followed, almost trembling with excitement, and noticed that there were other women waiting further back in the shadows. They took not the slightest notice of us.

"Do you have money?" She put out her hand to stroke my arm.

I nodded again. "Yes."

She smiled again, and put her hand to the side of my face. The touch tingled on my flesh. Thinking that this is where the act began, I raised my hand to her cheek. She pulled her clothing aside to expose her breast. "Let me see the money first."

I reached into my belt and withdrew the silver coin. The young woman stiffened. "More," she said. "Show me more."

Perplexed, I said, "This is all I have."

Shrugging her clothing back into place, she pushed me from her. "Ten denarii!" she sneered. "I do not even bend over for less than fifty."

Stunned by the sudden change in her demeanour, I repeated, "It is all I have."

She regarded me with the harsh, unyielding eyes of a judge, and must have decided I was telling her the truth. "Come with me," she said, stepping further into the shadowed row of columns. I followed, growing more excited with every step. We passed three or four other prostitutes—none as fair as the one who led me, however—and continued on until we came to a place well out of sight of the street. I thought she was going to have pity on me, but in this I was disappointed.

The young woman halted and turned towards me. "There," she said, pointing into a dark-shadowed recess, "Delilah will have you."

Peering into the shadows, I saw a human form huddled against the stone. "Delilah," called the young prostitute, "I have brought you a fine young man." She turned and started away, laughing. "Farewell, ten denarii!"

The figure in the shadows rose and lurched forward. A face emerged from the darkness. Little more than a mass of ratty hair and wrinkles, the ageing prostitute looked at me with sly approval. "Ten denarii," she said, and opened her mouth to show me that she had no teeth. Delilah then gave me a toothless smile and said, "Like a baby," she cooed. "Only ten denarii."

She hobbled closer. I became aware of a rank, sickly smell. Disgust, more than the stench, drove me back. The ageing whore followed, clutching at my clothes. "Do whatever you want," she screeched. "Only ten denarii."

Sickened at the thought of coupling with such a creature, I edged backwards, desperate now to get away. She shambled after me, grasping at my clothes. Turning from her, I fled, running back along the columns and the waiting women. They laughed, and called scorn upon me as I ran past, looking neither right nor left.

My face burning with shame, I stumbled into the street once more. I could hear the mocking laughter of the prostitutes ringing in my ears long after they were out of sight, though this was no doubt all my imagining. Hoping for nothing more than to lose myself in the market crowd, I walked aimlessly for a time, until my composure returned.

Sure, I felt humiliated, and deeply disgusted with myself for even thinking to behave in such a shameful manner. Abhorrence claimed me, and I abandoned myself to a wallow of loathing, berating myself for my ignorance and stupidity, as well as for the folly of my disgraceful actions.

Curiously, however, this feeling did not last. It was not long before I began to think that, as the thing stood, nothing had happened and no one had been hurt. As for myself, I had suffered nothing worse than embarrassment. Thinking this, some small part of my self-respect revived. What is more, I still had my silver coin.

Thus, much chagrined, I resumed my inspection of the market stalls. Alas, it was hopeless. Try as I might, I could not think of anything I would enjoy doing with the money. At last, I chanced upon the thought of procuring a meal at a taberna—like the one Justin had bought for me. But to enjoy it, I would need a friend to share the feast, and I had none. I thought of buying wine and taking it to the quay to drink with Gunnar and Thorkel and Tolar. *If Gunnar were here*, I thought, *he would know what to do.*

For a moment, I considered going to find Gunnar, but the more I thought about it, the more offensive the idea became. Had I become so devoid of creative volition that I required a master's aid and approval for even so small a thing as spending a coin? Had I embraced slavery so completely that I could no longer decide for myself?

Chastised by these thoughts, I determined to purchase a meal, as that had been the last thing I had truly enjoyed for its own sake alone. The forum was not the best place for this, so I went in search of the taberna I had seen when first entering Trebizond. I found the central street and began walking along it in the direction of the harbour. The narrow way was crowded as midday approached, and the street merchants were at their busiest. It was all I could do to find the place, and when I at last pushed my way to the door, I found it closed and locked. No one answered my knock, but when I persisted, a boy put his head out of a windhole above the street and told me to come back in the evening and the master would be happy to serve me.

Discouraged, I moved off down the street where I found a man selling bread, and another selling roast birds, chops of pork, and such like. I bought two fine loaves and a roast fowl, and continued on until I came to a woman selling wine. I bought a jar of sweet red Anatolian wine and, with the last of the money purchased some olives. As I was then very close to the harbour, I continued on towards the seafront, where I thought I might find a place to sit down and eat in peace.

Indeed, I reached the harbour and settled down on a large coil of rope and a heap of fishing nets at the water's edge. Carefully placing the wine jar on the quay so that I would not spill it, I untied the roast fowl and began to eat. It seemed odd to me, sitting there alone, but as I ate and watched the ships come and go in the harbour, I began to take pleasure in my simple meal. The food was good, the day was fine; I could look across the harbour to where the Danish longships were docked, and almost make out individuals among the figures moving around on the wharf.

Very soon, the sun and wine, and a stomach full of bread and roast chicken, united to make me sleepy. My eyelids grew so heavy I could not keep them open, so I lay back in my nest of rope and netting to sleep.

It was late when I awoke; the sun was well down, flaming the western sea and tinting the sky deep yellow. I rose with an aching head and made my way back through shadowed streets to the governor's house, and slipped in quietly, hoping no one had cause to remark upon my absence. Aside from a fleeting twinge of guilt over my small transgression, I reflected that I had enjoyed myself after all.

But then I wondered what Amet had seen that inspired him to exhort me to a day of pleasure. Was it really the last day of peace and happiness I would know?

# 42

Negotiations between the eparch and the amir concluded when all parties agreed to honour the safety of travellers, especially merchants and the like who habitually traversed disputed borders. The routes themselves might remain under contention, but all recognized that it was best for everyone if trade continued unhindered. What is more, both emperor and caliph vowed—through their emissaries—to take whatever steps necessary to halt the pirating and raiding on both sides.

Furthermore, they agreed that these simple measures, if strictly upheld, could lay a solid foundation for increased cooperation, perhaps even reconciliation in the future. Towards this end, they proposed to meet again the following year to plan a council at which the emperor and the caliph could meet face to face and exchange tokens and treaties of peace.

Spring, early in this part of the world, was soon upon us and that meant the beginning of the trading year. Hence, Nicephorus was eager to return to the emperor with word of the envoy's success, for the sooner word of the peace accord could reach Constantinople, the sooner the merchants could resume trading with full confidence—

and the sooner imperial coffers would begin enjoying fresh infusions of tax money, foreign and domestic.

"If you will pardon me, eparch," said Nikos the day after Amir Sadiq had departed. There had been a great farewell feast to celebrate the successful conclusion of the council, and the amir had been sent off with gifts of assurance and good will—the treasure the Sea Wolves had guarded, in fact. The eparch was preparing to sail the next day.

"Yes, yes, what is it, komes?" replied Nicephorus impatiently. He was sitting at the small table in the courtyard, looking at various documents having to do with the business just concluded.

"I see you are busy. Therefore, I will speak plainly."

"By all means."

"I think it a mistake to return to Constantinople at once." Nikos was so intent on making his point that he failed to notice me standing just inside the door. I had brought the eparch his cloak; the day had turned cloudy, and he asked me to fetch it for him.

"And why is that?" wondered the eparch, laying aside the parchment he was reading.

"We have had pledges and assurances before, but it has not stopped the predation."

"Are you suggesting the amir has lied to us, or deceived us in some way?"

"Not in the least," answered the komes quickly. "I am as certain as you are that Amir Sadiq is a just and honourable man."

"Then what *are* you suggesting?" The eparch glared at Nikos. "Come now! Be quick about it. You proposed to speak plainly—do so!"

"I am simply suggesting," Nikos said with elaborate patience, "that the news of our achievement may not receive the welcome it rightly deserves."

"And why should you imagine that?" snapped the

eparch, already dismissing the komes from his mind, if not from the room. He turned back to the parchment he had been perusing.

"For the simple reason that no one will believe it."

The eparch glanced up from his work, regarded Nikos, then said, "Ridiculous."

"Is it?" countered the komes quickly. "Who will be the first to test the soundness of the treaty? If I were a merchant, I do not think I would be overeager to risk life and livelihood on the naked assurance of . . ." He hesitated.

"Say it, komes," demanded the eparch. "On the naked assurance of a silly old man. *That* is what you were going to say, is it not?"

"To risk life and livelihood on the assurances of an unknown Arab emissary," corrected Nikos smoothly. "It seems to me that without additional surety, shall we say, the agreement we take back with us will be seen as yet another empty promise offered by the duplicitous Muhammedans—a promise ordained to be broken as soon as the first trade vessels leave the Bosphorus."

This arrested the eparch's attention. He raised his head slowly and turned to the komes. "Yes, I am listening. What do you propose?"

"A simple demonstration," answered Nikos.

"A demonstration," the eparch intoned flatly. "What sort of *demonstration* do you have in mind, komes?"

"A journey, nothing more."

The eparch's mouth turned down at the corners. "I am disappointed, komes. I expected something much more creative and intelligent from you." Flicking his hand dismissively, Nicephorus said, "It is out of the question. You are too late with your anxious worries. We are leaving as soon as the ships are provisioned and ready. The merchants are anxious to return to Constantinople, and so am I. The emperor is waiting."

"It need be nothing very elaborate, or very far," continued Nikos as if he had not heard the eparch's decision. "What better way to announce the success of the treaty than to declare before the emperor and the assembled merchant princes that you personally have inaugurated the new peace with a journey over one of our more troubled trade routes, and found it to be completely satisfactory?"

The eparch regarded Nikos closely; I had seen the same look on the face of a man trying to determine the age of the horse he was buying. "You have a destination in mind, I presume?"

"The short journey to Theodosiopolis should suffice. It would take only a few days, and amply serve the purpose."

The eparch considered this, tapping his fingertips together. Finally, he said, "It is a meritable idea, Komes Nikos. I think you should do it—"

"Good," replied Nikos swiftly. "I will make the arrangements at once."

"On your own," continued the eparch, more forcefully. "That would allow me to stay here and prepare for next year's council. The governor is expected in a few days, and I could greet him and relate the details of our agreement. It would be time well spent. You go."

"But I am not the eparch," Nikos pointed out. "I could not—"

"It makes no difference. The journey is largely symbolic anyway. It will carry the same significance whether I go along or not."

Komes Nikos seemed about to make an objection; I could almost see the protest forming on his lips. But he checked himself and said, "Very well. If that is your decision."

"That is my decision," replied Nicephorus precisely.

"I shall leave in the morning. Good day to you, eparch." He turned suddenly and, for the first time, saw me standing just inside the doorway. His face stiffened; he crossed the room in quick, long strides. "Beware, meddling priest," he whispered under his breath as he passed. "Beware."

"Ah, Aidan, you are here," called the eparch, beckoning me to enter. "The day has grown cold. I am chilled to the bone."

Unfolding the cloak, I placed it around his shoulders. "I could light the brazier," I offered.

"Too much bother," he said. "I will not stay out here much longer. The light is failing." He looked at the doorway, as if expecting to see Nikos standing there. "Did you hear what he said?"

"Yes, eparch."

"What do you think?"

"I know nothing of these matters," I answered.

"But you know Nikos," the eparch pointed out. "You know him and, what is more, you distrust him—as do I." Nicephorus paused, ordering his thoughts. "I distrust him because I do not know where his true loyalties lie. He is ambitious, I believe. Many young men are ambitious, and I have seen more than my share; but in our friend Nikos, ambition serves an end I cannot see." Turning stiffly to me, he asked, "Was he lying, do you think?"

"You would know better than I, eparch," I answered. *Suspicion,* Justin had said, *is the knife in your sleeve and the shield at your back.*

"I think we must assume that he was. But if so, I cannot see any possible gain in it—for him or anyone else. Can you?"

"No, eparch." Even as I answered I felt the creeping damp of the prison cell I had seen in my dream. I shivered and looked around me; the courtyard had grown dim as daylight waned. "It is getting dark. Shall I not light the brazier for you?"

"No, no, that will not be necessary," said the eparch, rising. "I am going to my room." He folded the parchment and tucked it under his arm as he started for the door. "Walk with me, Aidan."

I fell into step beside him and we entered the corridor. "I do not know how you came to be slave to the Danes," he said, "but I want you to know that I intend speaking to the emperor on our return."

"Eparch?"

"About your freedom, son," he said in a fatherly tone. "It would be a sad waste of your talents to spend the rest of your life translating Greek for barbarians. We must do something about that, I think."

"Thank you, eparch," I replied, for I could think of nothing else to say.

"We had best keep this between ourselves for now," he cautioned. "It would be less awkward when the time comes."

"Of course."

"Tell Flautus that I will take my meal in my room," the eparch instructed. "I have had enough of celebration feasts for awhile." We had reached his door; he opened it and dismissed me. "Oh, Aidan," he said calling me back, "would you ask Jarl Harald to place a guard at my door tonight? I think I would sleep a little better for it."

"Yes, eparch; at once."

He thanked me and I took my leave, going straight-away to find Harald and arrange for the guard. Taking the eparch's concern to heart, I also remained out of sight that night, behaving as a dutiful slave and staying close to Harald. But nothing happened, and the house remained quiet. I went to sleep thinking: Nikos departs tomorrow and we will not have to worry about him any more.

The next day, Nikos prepared to leave, leading a group of thirty barbarian guards and a dozen opportunistic traders desirous of an escorted journey to Theodosiopolis. He spoke briefly to the eparch and left the villa, whereupon Nicephorus went in to break fast in his customary fashion. I served him at table whenever I could so that I might remain privy to his affairs.

Thus, the eparch was just sitting down when Nikos returned. "A matter of urgency has arisen," he said, striding quickly into the courtyard. "It requires your attention."

The eparch's expression of anger gave way to bewilderment when the magister and another man appeared in the doorway behind Nikos. The eparch rose to his feet and bade the men to enter.

"Forgive my intrusion, eparch," the magister said quickly. "I am glad to have arrived before it was too late."

"Too late?" wondered Nicephorus.

"Ah," said the magister, glancing at Nikos, "too late to prevent the komes from leaving."

The eparch frowned. "Why should that cause you concern, I wonder?"

"I will explain," offered the magister.

"It would be a kindness," allowed the eparch.

"Consul Psellon," he indicated the man beside him, "has just come from the governor with a message for you."

"I see. May I have it, please?" Nicephorus held out his hand.

Magister Sergius nudged the man, who put his hand into a fold of his cloak, and withdrew a thick square of parchment tied with a black silk band and sealed with a red spot of wax. "It is the exarch's seal, you see," volunteered Sergius.

"Thank you for that observation, magister," intoned the eparch. "No doubt I would have failed to appreciate that detail. I am, as always, indebted to you."

Sergius coloured and made to further his explanation,

but Nikos cut him off, saying, "Thank you, magister. I think we are fully capable of assessing the importance of this document without your assistance."

"Of course." The magister subsided gratefully.

Eyeing the magister and consul in turn, the eparch took up the bundle, untied it, broke the seal, unfolded the heavy parchment and began to read, his lips moving over the words as he scanned the document. "This is most interesting," he observed upon finishing. "Most interesting, indeed."

Without waiting to be asked, Nikos snatched up the parchment and began to read. "It *is* from the governor," he observed, still reading.

"So it would appear," mused Nicephorus, staring at the magister and consul with an expression of rank scepticism.

"He is asking us to join him in Sebastea," Nikos continued. "He says there is word of—" he broke off abruptly, glancing at the eparch. "It is a matter of extreme urgency," he finished lamely.

"Apparently," conceded the eparch, still staring at the two before him. "When did this message arrive?" he asked.

"Just this morning," declared the magister. "I came directly to you the moment Psellon arrived."

"I see." The eparch's eyes narrowed. "So you knew the contents of this message, did you?"

"By no means, eparch!" The magister all but shrieked at the implication. "But I knew it to be important—Psellon told me that much."

Consul Psellon nodded vigorously. "It has come directly from the governor's own hand," he confirmed.

"Oh, most certainly it has," agreed the eparch sourly. "Yet, knowing nothing of the message—save its importance—you travelled night and day to bring it to me."

"Of course, eparch," Psellon replied.

"How many travelled with you?"

Psellon hesitated; his eyes shifted to the magister, who stared straight ahead.

"Come!" said the eparch sharply. "The question is perfectly simple. How many travelled with you?"

"Four others," answered Psellon uncertainly.

"I see. You may go, both of you." Nicephorus dismissed Sergius and Psellon with a disdainful gesture, and watched them until they left the room. "What have you to say of this?" inquired the eparch of Nikos when they had gone.

"I think it fortunate that I was detained," the komes replied. "Since I am ready, very little additional provision need be made. We can leave the city by midday. I will make the arrangements."

"I take your answer to mean that you believe this communication to be genuine?"

"Certainly," said Nikos, "I think it safe to say Exarch Honorius seeks only the good of the empire."

"Of that I have no doubt," agreed the eparch, "no doubt whatever—*if* Honorius wrote it."

"I see no cause to question the veracity of the document," said the komes mildly. "It is in the governor's hand, and carries his seal after all."

"Yes, it does. I see that it does." The eparch, his expression one of doubt and bafflement, sat down slowly in his chair.

"Now, then, if you will excuse me, I will make the necessary arrangements. I assume we will want the Danes to accompany us?"

"Yes, yes," replied Nicephorus, his gaze vacant; his mind was clearly on other matters. "Make the arrangements by all means."

In three strides Nikos was gone, and with not so much

as a glance in my direction, though he must have known I
was there the whole time. The eparch sat in his chair staring at the half-folded parchment as if it were an object he
had never seen before. As no one else was near, I went to
him.

"Eparch? Can I help you in any way?"

"Honorius sends word of betrayal," he announced
absently. "He says we must come to him."

As the eparch was deeply distracted, I plucked up my
courage and asked, "May I see the message?"

"If you wish," he said. He made no move to hand it to
me, but he watched me while I read.

The message was terse and stilted, indicating that the
caliph planned to use the completion of the peace council
to renew hostilities between the Arabs and Byzantium. As
details of this treachery were too sensitive to impart by
messenger, the governor requested the eparch to join him
in Sebastea at once, and suggested travelling with a bodyguard.

"You are a man with some experience of the written
word," Nicephorus said when I finished. "Can you tell me
anything of the man who wrote this?"

The script was Greek, and written in a bold, confident
hand; each letter was neatly formed and orderly, if slightly
small. "I would say the man was a scribe," I ventured, "a
monk, perhaps. He writes distinctly—his words are well-
chosen. Is it truly the governor's hand?"

"Yes, it is," answered Nicephorus. "And that is what
worries me most."

"Then I do not understand, eparch."

"I know Honorius, you see. We served together in
Gaul, and again, briefly, in Ephesus long ago." he confided.
"I do not think Nikos or anyone else in Trebizond knows
this, and I have told no one since coming here. But I will
cut out my own tongue before I confess he wrote that letter.

"Look at it!" he said, with mounting agitation. "The greeting is wrong. We are old friends, Honorius and I. He knew I was coming—knew I would be staying in his house. Yet, he sends the message, not to me, but by way of the magister. What is more, he addresses me not as a man he has known for forty years, but by title only, as if I were a mere functionary of the emperor he had never met."

I began to see what concerned the eparch now, and agreed that it did seem strange. The wording of the letter was stiffly formal—precise, yet distant. "Do you suspect forgery?"

He shook his head. "No; he wrote it. But I cannot believe he wrote it to *me*."

"Perhaps he did not wish to betray your friendship—should the letter go astray."

"Perhaps." The eparch's tone suggested he thought otherwise. "That letter betrays precious little, it seems to me."

"You suspect another reason for sending a message such as this," I concluded. "What could it be?"

"That is what I am asking myself," he said, shaking his head slowly. He rose from his chair, his food untouched. "I fear we must make ready to leave, Aidan," he said, crossing the courtyard. "Please, inform Harald."

"What about the letter?" I asked, indicating the parchment still lying on the table.

Misunderstanding my question, the eparch replied, "No doubt all will become clear once we arrive in Sebastea."

He left the courtyard and returned to his room. As no one else was around, I picked up the letter and examined it again. It appeared neither more nor less odd than before; I thought, *it may be genuine after all*. Folding it carefully, I retied the black band, and tucked the document inside my mantle with every intention of returning it to the eparch. Then I hastened to find Harald and alert him to our unexpected change in plans.

# 43

The gates of Trebizond were open wide and the road stretched out before us. It was a little past midday, the sun bright in a late winter's sky; the air was cool, but the sun warm on our faces and backs. The road to Sebastea was a well-travelled path—deep-rutted owing to the rains, and the recent invasion of visitors attending the fair.

Nikos travelled on horseback, and the eparch rode in an enclosed wagon, pulled by a two-horse team; three additional wagons and teams brought the provisions. The Sea Wolves, over a hundred in all, marched in two long columns either side of the wagons, spears and axes in their hands, shields on their backs.

Although Nikos kept insisting that we did not need so many, the eparch had decided to take the largest bodyguard at his command. Leaving behind only enough men to guard the ships, Harald, glad for the change of routine, had formed a veritable army to escort us to Sebastea. And there were others with us, too: a fair few of the traders and merchants attending the pagan fair—regarding the free use of an armed bodyguard as an opportunity too valuable to miss—decided to make their return journey a few days early, swelling our ranks considerably. Thus, we formed a body of perhaps two hundred or more altogether.

The first two days the weather remained good: fair and bright, the sky cloudless. The third day dawned grey, with a thin, miserable rain lashed by a rough north wind. The Sea Wolves seemed not to mind the cold and wet, singing now and then, and talking to one another in loud, raucous voices. The wagons themselves rumbled along with much groaning and shouting from the drivers, sometimes in the road, more often out of it, for the ruts often became too difficult for the horses.

I kept my place behind Jarl Harald, who walked beside the eparch's wagon. Tolar and Thorkel had been left behind with the ships, but Gunnar had been chosen to go with us, and he walked with me sometimes, and we talked. The chatter, though trivial, occupied the tedium, but did little to keep my mind from the cold. I had become used to the mild winter weather and the icy damp seeped into my bones and made me shiver despite my cloak and mantle.

We marched from daybreak to midday, and then stopped to rest and eat at a place where a river crossed the road. The stream—little more than a muddy rivulet this time of year—became a torrent in late spring, it was said, and eventually joined the Tigris far to the south. Across the river, the road divided. Theodosiopolis lay two days' journey to the east, and Sebastea four or five days south and west.

After we had eaten and rested, we forded the stream and continued on. The small sheep-herding villages grew fewer and further apart as the land gradually became more rugged; the hills became steeper, the valleys deeper. Small trees and sparse grass gave way to rocks and prickly shrubs of various kinds. The wind began to screech and moan as it scoured the bare rocky hills, making a cold, lonely sound.

The travelling company, so spirited the first few days, sank into silence and melancholy.

The next day was worse. The rain settled into a dull, spitting patter and continued through the day. I wrapped my sodden cloak around me and thought about the warm security of the scriptorium aglow in the ruddy blaze of a peat fire. Ah, mo croi!

Day's end found us in a cramped little gully between two steep hills. Having just made one arduous climb, and not yet ready to face another, we stopped to make camp, grateful at least for the respite from the wind. The ground was rocky and uneven and, except for a few diminutive, bedraggled-looking pines, devoid of vegetation. A stony cliff rose sheer from one side of the road; on the other, a narrow, deep-sided ravine contained a stream which was beginning to flow swiftly now due to the recent rain.

There was nothing to use for firewood, and what little fuel we had was needed to cook our evening meal, thus we spent a cold night huddled close to the rock face where the rain could not get at us so easily. Just before dawn, I was awakened by water dripping on my neck, leaking down from a rock directly above, so I got up and stumbled to the eparch's wagon and crawled beneath it.

This, I believe, is what saved me.

I had only closed my eyes again, when I heard a sound like the cracking of tree roots in the earth. I listened for a moment, and it came again—but from a direction I could not discern. Then I heard a rumbling sound like thunder, but closer and sharper. I opened my eyes. The sound instantly became a loud clattering crash and heavy objects began striking down, shaking the very ground.

In the dim half-light of an overcast dawn, I saw the sheer cliff-face in motion: rocks and stones, falling, sliding, collapsing, tumbling down upon us. I rolled further under the wagon, drew up my legs and cowered behind a stout wheel just as a huge stone struck the back of the wagon and shoved it sideways.

Men caught in the slide awoke screaming in terror and alarm as the rocks fell upon them. Many, however, were crushed in their sleep, never knowing what killed them.

The fall subsided almost as soon as it had begun. The last stones thudded to the ground and then all was still, and deathly quiet.

The silence gave way to the moans of the injured. I crept from the shelter of the wagon to see that the base of the cliff had been obliterated by the rockslide. I stood slowly and peered through the murk of the dust-thick air; all around me lay misshapen heaps of shattered stone.

I moved cautiously forward, trying to see if there were men I might help. I took two steps and heard far above me the pattering clatter of loose pebbles raining down. Fearing the rockslide had begun again, I glanced up and glimpsed instead a figure moving quickly back from the edge of the clifftop. In the same instant, I felt, rather than heard, a swift surge of movement and I jumped aside as a horse clattered by. There was someone in the saddle and it was Nikos. He blew past me like an evil wind, and disappeared into the dust and murk behind.

There was no time to wonder about this, for I heard a loud shout, which was answered at once by the roar of a multitude, or so it seemed. I turned to see swarms of men running down the steep hill before us.

The camp slowly stuttered to life. The eparch appeared. I ran to him. He stared at me in the dusky light. "Where is Nikos?" he demanded angrily.

"I saw him riding away," I answered, pointing out the direction behind me. "We are being attacked!"

Out of nowhere, King Harald appeared, long-axe in hand, leaped onto the nearest wagon and began bellowing his battle-call. Within moments there were Sea Wolves everywhere—though far fewer than there had been before—running, shouting, calling their swordbrothers to rise and fight.

Weapons glinting dully, the warriors raced to join battle as the first foemen reached the camp. The ring of steel on steel and the shouts of fighting men filled the valley and echoed through the ravine. I had no weapons—and would not have known what to do if I had—but determined to stay with Eparch Nicephorus and protect him if I could. This proved no easy chore, since he insisted on rushing directly into the thick of the fight to lend his aid.

"Here! This way!" I shouted, pulling him back from the toiling bodies before us. Indicating a supply wagon nearby, I said, "We can see best from there." Hastening to the wagon, I paused to help the eparch into the box, and then climbed up myself. We stood together and watched the fearful clash.

The enemy were not large men—at least, not when set against the Sea Wolves—but they were many and dressed in dark cloaks and turbans, making them difficult to see in the pre-dawn light. Even so, in those first desperate moments of battle, it seemed as if the superior strength and battle-skill of the Danes would win out. For the Sea Wolves stood to their grim work, shoulder to shoulder, each man protecting his neighbour's unshielded side, forcing the oncoming enemy back and back, one step at a time.

"You see, eparch!" I cried. "They are driving them away!"

The eparch, keen-eyed in the murk, said nothing, but gripped the sides of the wagon and stared at the dread battledance before us.

I looked in vain for Gunnar; I could not see him anywhere, and feared he must have been among those killed in the rockslide.

The Danes howled their full-throated battle cries, and I

understood why they were called wolves. The sound was uncanny, striking fear into the heart, and weakening even the most stalwart will. Jarl Harald was fearless, standing in the front rank, his axe swinging with practised and deadly accuracy. Men fell before him—some shrieking in agony, some toppling silently, but all with startling rapidity. The axe-blade bit deep, its appetite insatiable.

As the first flush of battle passed, it became increasingly apparent that the Danes were even more sorely outnumbered than my first estimate. It may be that more and more enemy were arriving—reserves held back from the initial attack were perhaps being committed now—for it did appear that the numbers of dark-cloaked foe were swelling.

Slowly, painfully, the flow of battle turned against us. The eparch and I stood in the wagon and watched with growing horror as the Sea Wolves were inundated and engulfed by the ever-growing tide.

"Pray for them, priest!" Nicephorus cried, seizing me by the arm. "Pray for us all!"

Alas, I could not. God had forsaken me, and I knew my prayers would fall like infertile seed on the hard ground of God's stony heart. For all the good my prayers would do, I would have a better chance of saving us all by taking up a spear, and I knew well what a sorry warrior I would be.

I was spared further meditation on my worthlessness, however, by the sudden appearance of a grim-faced warrior waving a bloody war hammer. "What are you doing?" shouted the warrior. "Get out of there!"

I was jerked off my feet and pulled bodily from the bed of the wagon, then hurled to the ground where I lay squirming in an effort to get away. The eparch likewise was hauled kicking from the wagon and dropped, scarcely less gently, beside me.

"Aeddan!" shouted Gunnar, "you will be killed standing up like that." Before I could say anything, he shoved the eparch and me beneath the wagonbed. "Get under there," he instructed sternly, "and stay until I come back for you."

He was gone again before I could speak a word to him. The eparch asked, "What did he say?"

"He said we are to keep out of sight until he returns."

"But I can see nothing from here," complained the eparch. He endured the ignominy of our position for but a moment or two longer, and when there came a great shout from the battleline, Nicephorus bolted from beneath the wagon, shouting, "I will not be seen hiding like a coward!"

I ran after him, seized him, and pulled him back to the wagon. We did not go under it again, but we did stand beside it to watch the battle. What we saw, however, filled our mouths with bile. Everywhere, the Danes were being driven down. The ranks of the enemy had swelled the more, and were in danger of overwhelming all resistance.

Even as we watched, there came another great shout and the dark foe surged as one, throwing back the defenders ten paces at once. Another shout, another surge, and the forerank buckled and gave way. The resistance was breached and our defences in imminent danger of being overwhelmed.

Harald was a canny battlechief; he would not allow himself to be surrounded so easily. Realizing the peril, he raised his bull roar and began calling the retreat. The Viking warriors fell back and soon were passing along the road. Gunnar ran to us. "The battle is lost," he said, breathing hard. "We must flee while we can. This way. Go!"

So saying, he spun me around and began pushing me ahead of him. "This way!" I shouted to the eparch. "He will protect us!"

Back along the road we fled, past the broken mounds of rock which now marked the graves of Danes, merchants and their families, running for our lives. The traders who survived, having seen how the fight was turning, were already fleeing up the hill; I could see them before us, bent beneath the burdens they sought to save.

The first of the traders reached the crest of the hill and fled over the top. Seeing their escape, we all ran the harder to make good our own.

Alas and woe! It was not to be.

No sooner had the escaping merchants vanished from sight than they reappeared once more, flying down the hill and screaming for everyone to turn back. Not comprehending the significance of their screams, we proceeded on a few more paces. Two heartbeats later there arose before us an enemy host as great or greater than the one that came behind. They seemed to spring up out of the hilltop to sweep swiftly down upon us.

"Stay down!" cried Gunnar, pushing me to the ground even as he ran to engage the attackers. Reaching up, I pulled the eparch down beside me, and we hunkered there, half-crouched by the roadside, as merchants and traders streamed back wailing in terror as they ran. Some still carried their wares on their backs.

Caught between two enemy forces—one behind and an even greater one before, the Danes had no choice but to fight on to the last man, or surrender.

It is not in the Sea Wolves to surrender.

Harald rallied his men—now numbering fewer than eighty, I reckoned—and renewed the fight. Bellowing like a mad bull, he called on Odin to witness his valour, then he and his remaining karlar rushed to meet the new threat with such ferocity that the enemy was momentarily staggered. The onrushing ranks halted and were in some places thrown into confusion as howling Sea Wolves, gripped by the blood-lust of battle, drove headlong into them. The sound of the clash was deafening—men screaming, cursing, crying as they fought and died.

Oh, it was a dreadful slaughter. The Danes fought with astonishing courage, time and time again performing startling acts of savage and wonderful daring. I saw Hnefi—arrogant, prideful warrior that he was—fight without a weapon when the broken stub of his sword was struck from his hand. Rather than retreat to find another blade, he darted forth, grabbed his foe, lifted him high, and threw the man into a knot of advancing enemy. Four men went down and Hnefi leapt upon them and slew them all with their own spears.

Another Dane, surrounded by six or more foemen, his spear broken and knowing he faced his death, took hold of the edge of his shield and, with a loud cry of defiance, began spinning around and around, the shield forming a wide arc. Two ambushers who tried to dart in under the shield to stab him with their spears had their skulls cracked by the iron rim; another lost his own weapon and darted aside just in time. The three that were left retreated to a safe distance and then threw their spears at once. The Viking was struck twice, but turned one of the spears on his attackers and killed one and wounded another before he succumbed.

Gunnar I glimpsed in the killing heat of the fray, leaping and whirling like an enraged animal, his hammer a blur of steel and blood about his head. I heard the awful sound of bones snapping and breaking beneath the fury of his blows. He charged and charged again. Two of the dark enemy fell to a single smashing stroke; he felled a third before the second struck the ground.

The dark adversary swarmed all around us, straining to the fight, their shrill voices keening as they waved their slender swords. The eparch and I hugged the earth as the onrushing enemy flowed over and around us. More and more pressed in from every side, and the valiant Sea Wolves strove to hold them off. Never did men fight and die with such abandon. If the battle could have been won with fearlessness alone, the Danes would have stood unchallenged on the blood-soaked ground in the end. But there were simply too many attackers, and too few defenders. One by one, the brave Danes were dragged down and killed.

The last thing I saw was Harald Bull-Roar staggering under the weight of two assailants on his back. With a mighty shrug he threw them off, but two more leapt upon him, and then two more, and he crashed down. The dark-cloaked adversary overwhelmed us and the battle was over.

For a moment all was quiet, and then the enemy raised their victory chant. They stood on the battleground, weapons lofted high, cheering themselves and jeering at their victims. One look at the hillside, however, told me there was nothing worth cheering about. The dark ones had paid a fearful price for their dubious victory.

The enemy dead lay in heaps upon earth stained with their blood. The wounded, and there were scores, lay moaning where they had fallen, or stumbled dazed and shaken over the corpse-strewn hill with bewildered expressions on their ashen faces; still others sat and wept into their wounds.

The chanting stopped and the victors turned their attention to searching the bodies. Instinct told me to remain perfectly still. I thought that if I appeared as merely one more corpse among so many, I might be overlooked. Cautiously, carefully, I put my mouth next to the eparch's ear to tell him my plan.

"Do not move," I whispered. "They may think us dead and leave us alone."

He did not hear me, so I whispered a little louder and

gave him a surreptitious nudge with my arm. "Did you hear me, eparch?" I asked, looking at his face. His eyes were open, and he was still watching the hilltop where the battle had been fiercest. "Nicephorus?"

It was then that I saw the spear protruding from between his shoulders and knew that he was dead. I stared at the wicked spear in disbelief. *How is it possible,* I wondered, *for a man to die so quietly? Why him and not me?*

In the turmoil of battle, his life had been violently taken and I, lying right beside him, had not even noticed. I felt shame and disgust and outrage all at once. I wanted to leap up and start running—to run and not stop running until I had put the hateful battle and the blood-soaked earth far behind me.

Unaccountably, I began to tremble. My limbs shook, my body jolted, and I could not stop the shaking. Seized by paroxysms I shuddered and convulsed uncontrollably. It was all I could do to press my face into the dirt and hope the enemy would pass me by.

Someone must have seen me shaking, for the next thing I knew, my arms were gripped and I was jerked upright and dragged up the hill between two attackers. We came to a place where a number of enemy were standing in tight ranks around a group huddled on the ground. The ranks parted and I was thrown in among those kneeling there. I saw King Harald, head down, bleeding from his nose and mouth, and realized that these few, myself included, were the last left alive.

Still trembling, I quickly scanned the group and counted twenty-one; of those I knew, only Harald and Hnefi numbered among the survivors. Twenty-one left from more than a hundred warriors, and who knew how many merchants—all dead. Alas, the killing was still not finished.

One of the dark-cloaked victors, his sword notched

and dripping red, strode to the nearest Dane, grabbed a handful of the man's hair, jerked back his head and cut the victim's throat—much to the amusement of the ambushers looking on. The Sea Wolf slumped to the ground, closed his eyes and died without a whimper. The warrior next to the dying Sea Wolf, unwilling to lay down his life for the delight of the enemy, struggled to his feet and threw himself upon the man who had killed his friend. Somehow, he succeeded in getting his hands on the foeman's throat. The Sea Wolves urged him on enthusiastically. It took three hard sword chops on the back of his neck to kill him.

After the third Sea Wolf had his throat slit, the others stopped cheering and resigned themselves to their fate.

*This is how I shall die,* I thought. *This, finally, is how I shall die—murdered with barbarians by an unknown enemy.*

"Christ have mercy!" I muttered. The words were out of my mouth before I knew what I was saying—a reflex trained by long habit only. I no longer believed, nor even expected that the Lord Christ would even hear my prayer, much less answer it.

The man kneeling next to me heard my outburst, however, and said, "You pray to your god, Aeddan. That is good. I think only your Christ can help us now."

I looked at the man, stared at him; the voice I recognized, but the battered face I no longer knew. "Gunnar?" One eye was horribly bruised and blood trickled down his face and neck from a gash in his scalp; his lips were split and bleeding, one ear was all but torn away, and there was a hideous blue-black knot on his forehead. "Gunnar . . ." I hardly knew what to say. "You are alive!"

"For a little yet," he whispered, wiping blood from his eyes. "But if your Christ saves us this time, then I, too, will worship him."

Just then, a fourth prisoner was yanked to his feet so that the dark-cloaked foe could impale him with a spear.

Two enemy warriors held the Sea Wolf while a third put a spear through his belly.

"No one can save us now," I said bitterly.

"Then farewell, Aeddan," Gunnar said.

The unfortunate Dane was still twitching on the ground when the leader of the dark ones arrived, seated on a brown horse. I suppose he had directed the battle from a safe distance, and now that it was over, felt sufficient courage to come and inspect the spoils, such as they were.

He rode directly to where the prisoners were being slaughtered and slid from the saddle. Taking hold of the man who had murdered the last prisoner, he struck the warrior twice in the face, and shoved him away hard. Then he turned and began shouting at the others; I watched the mirth disappear from their faces. They put up their weapons and the killing stopped at once.

"He works fast, this Christ of yours," whispered Gunnar knowingly. "What is that one saying?"

"I do not know."

"They are Arabs?"

"Maybe," I answered. "But they do not speak like the amir and his people."

The leader of the dark ones shouted some more commands, and then climbed back onto his horse and rode away. The few remaining prisoners were then bound hand-to-hand, one to another, with rope made of leather strips. We were prodded to our feet at spearpoint and made to stagger back down the hill over the still-warm corpses of the fallen.

The dead lay in very heaps on the ground: whole families cut down as they ran, Danes in tight battle groups, toppled over one another. It was as if a forest had been laid waste, the trees levelled and left where they dropped. Women and children and merchant men lay in silent scores upon the bloody ground, ridden down and slaughtered, their bodies hacked, split, broken and discarded. The stink of blood brought bile to my mouth; I retched and gagged, and closed my eyes to shut out the sight.

*My God,* I wailed within myself, *why?*

I lurched blind over the uneven ground, stumbled, and fell over a battered corpse—a mother with her infant clutched tight in her arms, both pierced with the same spear. *Christ have mercy!* I cried. But there was no mercy for them, or for anyone else that day. God had abandoned them, like he abandoned everyone in the end.

I passed the body of the eparch, still lying with the spear in his back, an expresssion of contemplation on his face. I heard the strangled call of a crow and looked to the corpse-strewn hillside where the carrion birds were already commencing their cruel feast. I hung my head and wept. Thus, I began my long torturous walk to the caliph's mines.

# PART THREE

The shade of death lies on thy face, beloved,
But the Lord of Grace stands before thee,
And peace is in his mind.
Sleep, O sleep in the calm of all calm,
Sleep, O sleep in the love of all loves,
Sleep, beloved, in the Lord of life.

# 44

A thousand curses on his rotting corpse!" muttered
Harald, bringing the pick down sharply on the
stone. "May Odin strike his treacherous head from
his worthless shoulders."

"And feed it to the hounds of hel," Hnefi added, and
spat into the dust for emphasis. He raised his pick and
swung it down as if he were smiting an enemy.

Harald swung the pick high and smashed it down once
more. "As I am a king," he intoned ominously, "I will yet
kill the traitor who has brought us to this slavery. Odin
hear me: I, Harald Bull-Roar, make this vow."

He was talking about Nikos, of course; and the vow,
though heartfelt and infinitely sincere, was not new. We
had all of us heard the same promise, with slight varia-
tions, ten score times since coming to Amida where we had
been sold in the Sarazen slave market. Danes were considered too wild and barbaric to be used in any way other
than for the most brutish labour. Thus Harald, together
with the sad remnant of his once-fearsome Sea Wolf host,
had been purchased by the caliph's chief overseer and
promptly put to work in the silver mines.

To be a slave was a humiliation intolerable to

Harald, who would have preferred death a thousand times over—save for the fact that it would have placed him beyond revenge, and wreaking his vengeance on the one who had brought him to such ignominy had become the sole aim and purpose of his life. The Roaring Bull of Skania was now intent on keeping himself and his few men alive with the hope of returning to Trebizond, reclaiming his ships, and sailing to Constantinople to rend Nikos body from soul in the most brutally painful way possible.

It was Jarl Harald's belief that Nikos had betrayed us to the enemy—a conviction which the captive Danes supported with the undying zeal of true believers. Sure, I was no dissenter. I thought Nikos guilty, too, but could not work out why he should have done such a thing. Hundreds of people on both sides had died to further Nikos's dark design. But what was the gain? I kept asking myself. What hidden purpose did it accomplish?

Following the ill-fated battle, our captors had pursued a relentless pace through a wasteland of arid hills and rock-filled ravines. Settlements were rare, the land desolate and unfriendly. We rested little, and ate less; our captors gave us only enough sleep and food to keep us on our feet. Since so little of our time was taken up with resting or eating, we had ample leisure to speculate on our plight and the chances of making good an escape, and did so as we walked along. All our contemplation counted for nothing in the end, however; we neither escaped, nor learned the nature of the fate awaiting us.

Twelve or thirteen days after the ambush, we arrived footsore and hungry in Amida, with its low buildings of white-washed mud, and were marched to the open square of wind-blown dust they called a market. It was only when—along with another group of thirty Greek captives—we were herded into the ragged, thorn-infested hills north of Amida, that the nature of our fate penetrated our hunger-dazed minds: we were consigned to the caliph's silver mines.

These mines were no great distance from Amida, which, to my best reckoning, lay far to the south and east of Trebizond, well beyond the borders of the empire, and deep in Sarazen lands. Some of the Greeks with us knew of the caliph's mines; I heard several of them talking, and what they said did not make for glad rejoicing.

"It is death they have given us," said one slave, a slight young man with curly dark hair. "They work you until you drop."

"We could escape," suggested the captive beside him, an older man. "It has been known."

"No one ever escapes from the caliph's mines," replied a third, shaking his head slowly. "This is because anyone who tries is beheaded at once, and the guard who is responsible is disembowelled with his own sword. Believe me, they make certain no one escapes."

I relayed what the Greeks were saying to Harald, who merely grunted and said, "That may be. Either way, I do not intend to remain a slave very long."

The mines occupied the whole of a tight, many-folded valley at the foot of a range of high barren hills. A single road passed into the valley, overlooked by guard posts on either side along its length, with three or four Arab guards at each position. At the valley entrance a great stone wall had been erected with a huge timber gate through which all who would come or go must pass.

Once beyond the gate, we entered a veritable city of small white-washed dwellings built from packed mud where the guards and mine overseers lived, many with their families, judging from the clots of women and children we saw here and there in the cramped, winding streets. Harald saw this and laughed. "They are slaves like us!" he hooted, and called all his men to heed and remember this.

Yet, slaves we were, and we were housed in long low huts outside the entrances to the various pits, of which there were many—perhaps several score—scattered in among the folds of the valley floor, and up among the slopes and crevices of the hills themselves. The huts were nothing more than a roof and a rear wall with a few partitions; they remained open at the front, like pig sties; there were no doors to keep out the wind, and the men slept with their legs and feet outside. But as we were somewhat further south, the weather was milder, and it seldom rained.

The first day was taken with fitting shackles. All the slaves wore iron leg chains held in place with iron bands around the ankles. Some of the Sea Wolves were so big that the normal bands were too small, and larger ones had to be made. As an extra precaution, because of the size and ferocity of the Danes, the overseer decided to bind each Sea Wolf to another with a short length of chain so that they could not move so quickly or adroitly. This safeguard failed to impress Harald, who deftly manipulated the pairings so as to match those who fought best together with one another.

"You never know," he explained. "It might prove useful."

Because I was not a warrior, I was paired with Gunnar, who volunteered to look after me.

Shackled and chained, the next morning at dawn we were given our tools—short-handled picks for chipping and prying, and small hammers for breaking rock—and led into the shaft that we were to work, along with a dozen Greek slaves, mostly fishermen from an island called Ixos, whose boat had been driven off course by a storm. There were four guards—two for every group of fifteen or so slaves—and each shaft or pit had an overseer, which meant that we laboured under five keen-eyed Arabs. All the guards were armed: some with wooden staves, and others with short, curved swords, but all carried horse whips, which they applied with dexterity born of long practice.

The shaft was a tunnel driven directly into the hill which opened into a large cavernous room, from which several dozen smaller tunnels radiated in all directions. The work was arduous, but simple. Each slave pair was to take a finger shaft and, using our picks and hammers, pry the precious metal from the unyielding stone. So that we might see what we were doing, we were given small lamps. These were crudely fashioned of baked earth and held a horse-hair wick and measure of olive oil. The lamps were lit from a torch kept burning in the centre of the cavern, beside a tub of oil used to fill the lamps.

After twenty days, my hands toughened and my blisters no longer bled; after forty days, I no longer smashed my fingers against the rocks with the unwieldy pick. Sometimes, we were able to work near other Danes and we could talk to them. Mostly, however, we were kept apart, save for meals—which were little more than flat bread and a thin, watery cabbage soup—and at night when we were taken back to the huts to sleep.

We worked every day, with no rests—except during the more important Arab holy days, and then it was not for us, but for the guards, that we were allowed a day of peace. These days were infrequent, and always welcomed with profound, if pathetic, gratitude. And so the days passed.

The only solace—if solace it could be called—derived from the fact that the Sea Wolves actually enjoyed finding the silver. They would have gladly dug up all of Byzantium to get such wealth if they had but known where to dig. Thus, they approached the work with a sly enthusiasm that was exceeded only by the ingenuity with which they hid the silver they found.

Of course, they did not hide all of it; Jarl Harald made certain that they provided a fair account of their work to our Sarazen slave masters. It would not do, he said, to make the overseers suspicious. "Better to keep them happy," Harald counselled, "then they will leave us alone."

Thus, the chief overseer received a goodly portion of the silver the Danes mined, and seemed content with his new slaves—content, and oblivious to how much wealth they actually unearthed. I do not exaggerate when I say that the Sea Wolves obtained half again as much as they gave up. And all that they kept for themselves, they hid against the day when they would escape. In concealing their wealth, they showed a genius that rivalled their proficiency in finding it. Truly, the Danes are supreme masters at hiding treasure.

The same guards remained always with us, though the ones that watched us during the day were relieved from duty at night. Thus we came to know very well their habits and dispositions. It was during the changing of the guard, when the night watch arrived and were settling themselves, that Harald took the opportunity to pass along his thoughts for the day.

Usually, this communication took the form of whispers relayed one person to the next down the line, although sometimes—when the guards were very lax—Harald gathered us together to exhort us and praise our efforts personally. It was important to do well, he insisted, for that way we would win our freedom the sooner. Never forget, he insisted, that the king was working on a plan of escape.

We could speak this way to one another, because no one else understood Danespeak. Most of the guards knew some Greek, and a few could speak it fluently. As time went on, I began to learn a word or two of the Arab speech, but no one knew what the Sea Wolves said to one another, which Harald considered a good thing since it meant none of the Greek slaves or Arab guards could betray us. This, he maintained, would make our escape all the easier when the time came.

When we weren't plotting escape, we concocted ingenious tortures for Nikos. That traitor died a thousand times over, each death more hideously painful and protracted than the last. Thoughts of revenge kept many a man going through the endless days of mind-numbing, body-wracking labour.

Gradually, the season passed and the desert land blushed briefly—tiny spots of crimson and gold flowers flecked the bleak hillsides—and then the sun entered its summer house and the heat began to oppress us mercilessly. I could match neither the Sea Wolves' ardour nor their greed, and so the work went ill with me. As summer progressed the mine-shafts grew hot and stifling; the dust choked me, the darkness weakened my vision. I continually knocked elbows and knees, arms and legs against the rocks, and the oil lamps burned my hair. I found the dull gleam of silver meagre compensation for the loss of my freedom and slow starvation.

Gunnar bore the hardship more easily than I, maintaining an even temper, encouraging me when my spirits faltered. To take my mind from my misery, he made me talk to him about the Christ, which I did, at first grudgingly, though as time went on I found maintaining such virulent rancour tedious. Sure, I still felt a cold, hard place in my soul, and my resentment towards God was more, not less. But arguing over theology gave us something to occupy our minds, which is the better part of survival, I believe.

In our quiet periods, when the guards were close by, he would think about all I told him. Then, at meals, or when we reached the vein we were working—far from the guards' eyes and ears—he would ask me questions that had occurred to him. In this way we proceeded, and he began to learn some skill in close-reasoned argument. His was a practical mind, not quick or nimble, but solid and untroubled by much in the way of extraneous philosophy. Thus, most of what I told him came to him fresh, and the few superstitions that he held were easily swept away. In short, he revealed a genuine facility for the subject at hand.

Even though I no longer believed . . . no, I did still believe, but as one rejected by God—cast out from the hearth of faith, as it were—I found to my surprise that I could speak the words of faith, and explain them, without having them touch me. Strange perhaps, to be so angry at God and yet eagerly participate in reasoned discourse about him and the wonder of his ways, but that is the way of it. Curious, too, that Gunnar's interest in the faith should increase as my own waned.

As summer drew on, the vein of ore our group had been working dwindled. Eight of us were taken to another pit nearby and put to work with the fifty or more slaves who laboured there. This pit was larger than the one we had left, with more shafts and tunnels and corridors. There were Bulgars among the slaves, as well as Greeks, and several black Ethiopians, along with some others. Gunnar and I had never seen a black man before, but after getting used to them, we agreed that they were a handsome race in all. Perhaps slavery makes a man look at such things differently, but, save for the swart hue of their skin, they seemed more like us than not.

We seldom saw them, however, because the pit overseer was a harsh and cruel master who made them rise before dawn to begin work; thus, they were already toiling away by the time we arrived. Likewise, they were made to work past dark, so that we quit the mine before they did.

A few days after starting at the new pit, Gunnar found

a particularly productive vein which lay at the end of a long tunnel that had not been worked recently. We crawled in on hands and knees, clutching our oil lamps and pushing our tools ahead of us.

When we came to the end of the shaft, Gunnar stood up. "Look here, Aeddan," he said, raising his lamp. "There is no roof."

Standing beside him, I looked up to see that indeed the shaft had opened out into a wide crevice whose top, if there was one, was somewhere far above us, lost in the darkness our feeble lights could not penetrate. "There is much silver here, I think," he observed. "We will get a—"

"Listen!" I hissed.

"What is the—"

"Shh! Be quiet!"

We listened for a moment, holding our lamps high in the silence.

"There is noth—" Gunnar began.

"There it is again!" I insisted. "Listen!"

The faint echo of the sound I had heard was already fading, and the sound did not come again. "Did you hear it?" I said.

"It was water dripping," Gunnar confirmed.

"Not water," I replied. "*Singing*—someone was singing. It sounded like Irish."

"You are hearing things," he answered, placing his lamp in a notch someone had carved. "It was water dripping. Come, let us find some silver or we will not get anything to eat today."

We worked through the day, and though I listened intently all the while, I never heard the sound again; nor did I hear it the next day when we returned to the shaft. Three days later, however, the pit overseer made us go to another shaft, near where some others were working. The veins here were so interwoven that there were many connecting rooms and corridors, and sound travelled easily, if confusingly, from one to another. We had just found a good place and had begun working, when I heard the singing again. Gunnar allowed that he had indeed heard something, but that it did not sound like singing at all. "More like crying or weeping," he said.

I became so agitated, that I upset the lamps and spilled out most of the oil. "Now we have to fill them again," I sighed, for it meant a long crawl back to the primary shaft.

"Then we must hurry," Gunnar reminded me, "or we will be scratching our way in the dark."

We left our tools and made our way back to the main gallery and the oil tub. Two other slaves were standing at the vat when we got there, so we waited our turn. As it happened, the pit overseer appeared just then, and began shouting angrily at us. I suppose the sight of four slaves standing idle offended him; perhaps he thought we were trying to avoid work, for he ran at us, uncoiling his whip.

The lash caught me around the throat before I could dodge away; I was yanked to the ground. The guard, under whose less suspicious eye we had been filling our lamps, ran forward and began striking the others with his wooden stave. His first blow struck Gunnar, who fell down beside me clutching his head. The other two slaves, in a clumsy attempt at protecting themselves, pushed the guard aside. Seeing they had overcome him so easily, they kicked him a few times for good measure.

This action made the overseer livid; he began cursing and shouting like a madman, and striking wildly with his whip. The other two slaves, seeing the furor they had caused, ran away, quickly melting into the shadows while Gunnar and I rolled on the ground, writhing under the lash. I heard people shouting, and saw that a number of nearby slaves had come to investigate. I pushed myself up on hands and knees, and, with Gunnar beside me, tried to scramble out of the way of the whip and its crazed wielder.

Unfortunately, this action was seen as trying to avoid further punishment. The overseer, in a spitting rage, renewed his frenzied attack. I felt the lash rip across my shoulders—once, twice, and again. Pain lit my vision with crimson fireballs. I rolled on the ground, tangling with Gunnar, to whom I was chained at the ankle. We could not move fast enough to avoid the whip.

Each stinging lash tore at my flesh. My eyes filled with tears and I could not see. I began shouting for the whipping to stop. I shouted in Greek, I know, and in Danespeak. I cried out in every tongue I knew and begged for mercy.

And miracle of miracles, my cries were answered!

For all at once I heard a shout that sounded like, "Célé Dé!" The whipping instantly ceased: abruptly and in midstroke, the whip went taut and the slave master's arm froze. There came an odd cracking sound and, in my somewhat confused vision, the furious Arab seemed to rise from the floor to hang in the air.

He hovered above me for a moment, his bewildered face growing round and red; he gasped for breath, but could not breathe. Suddenly, the slave master flew sideways through the air and I did not see him any more. The instant he disappeared, another face swung into view above me—a face which for all the world looked like someone I knew.

Still squirming in pain, I gaped, gulping air to keep from passing out. A name came to my lips. I spoke it out.

"Dugal?"

# 45

ugal!" I rolled to my knees, straining up at him. "Dugal, it is myself—Aidan! It is Aidan here." I lurched towards him. "Do you not know me, man?"

Dugal stared at me as if at a monster risen from the bowels of the earth. "Aidan!" he cried, leaning closer. "Sure, I knew it was you! I heard you cry out and I knew it must be Aidan. But . . . but, you—" Words failed him.

"The same and no other," I replied, and made to stand, but my legs would not hold me and I fell again. Tears came to my eyes and I wept like a child to see my dearest friend once more.

Dugal gave a shout of triumph so tremendous that the whole mine reverberated with the sound. In one swoop, he raised me up and enfolded me in a fierce hug. The touch of his hands on my raw shoulders made me cry out in pain, whereupon he dropped me to my feet again.

"Dána!" he cried. "Christ have mercy, brother, what are you doing here?"

"Dugal, I can hardly believe it is you," I said, dashing tears away. "I was certain you were killed . . . the battle—I saw you fall."

"That I did, but the blow was never fatal." He beamed at me with such joy, it warmed my heart to see it.

Gunnar, still lying on the ground, climbed to his feet to stand beside me—as we were still chained together, he had nowhere else to go—and he gazed at Dugal with an expression of slightly amazed admiration.

"This is Dugal," I told him, "my brother monk from Éire."

"I remember him," replied Gunnar.

"God bless you, Aidan," murmured Dugal, gripping my hands tight in his own. "And here was I thinking you were lost forever. Oh, but it is a fine thing to see you again."

"And you, Dugal." I hugged him to me, feeling the solid flesh and bone beneath my clasp, as if to make certain that it was no mere phantom. "Ah, mo croi, I have so much to tell you, I cannot think for wanting to say it all at once."

We fell silent, just looking at one another. Dugal's hair and beard, like my own, had grown long and shaggy. I had never seen him without his tonsure, and long hair made him look more like a Sea Wolf than a monk. His clothes, like mine, were little more than filthy rags, and he was powdered with rock dust head to heel, but had he been covered in mud with a beard to his knees, I still would have known him as my own reflection.

There came a shout from some of the slaves looking on across the way. Gunnar prodded me in the side and said, "I think our trouble is not finished yet."

Into the pit rushed five or six additional guards; the Arab with the wooden stave led the way, pointing to us, and to the pit overseer still lying crumpled on the floor where Dugal had hurled him. Before we could move, the guards seized us by the arms and dragged us out of the pit and into the bright sun outside. It had been many days since I had had the full light of a noonday sun in my eyes, and it was a fair few moments before I could see.

I stumbled over rocks and fell, pulling Gunnar down with me; we rolled and writhed, regaining our feet only to fall again as the guards dragged us down the hillside. Battered and bruised, cut in a hundred places, we were finally brought to a huge chunk of stone which surmounted a heap of jagged rock shards discarded from the mines. At various places, iron spikes had been driven into the stone to which chains and shackles had been affixed to iron rings. The three of us were chained to the rock and left to bake and swelter in the heat.

As the sun was directly overhead, there was not so much as a shadow wherein we might find refuge. So, we sat with our eyes squinted tight against the blinding light, sweating, our pallid, sun-starved skins slowly turning fiery red.

"I am sorry," Dugal apologized after awhile. "I have brought this misery upon us. If I had not seized the guard, we would not be here now."

"That may be so," I answered. "But if you had not pulled the madman off me I might have been killed. At the very least, we would never have found one another."

"True," he allowed. "That is very true."

"What will they do with us, do you think?" I wondered.

"God knows," replied Dugal. "For myself, I do not care what happens. It is the Red Martyrdom for me, one way or another." He paused, dismissing the thought from his mind. "Ah, well, we are in God's hands, Aidan. He will see us right whatever ill befalls us."

At his words, anger welled up inside me. But as I did not care to contradict him, I said, "Tell me, Dugal, how did you come to be here? Tell me everything; I want to hear it all."

"I wish there was more to tell. In truth, we had an easy time of it—for the most part, that is." He opened one eye to a narrow squint and regarded me. "But you, Aidan, *you* must have tales worth hearing. Tell me how you have fared."

"I will, and gladly, but after you, brother. Now then, after the Sea Wolves attacked the village and I was carried off—what happened?"

Casting his mind back, he began to tell me about all that had taken place since I had last seen him. He described the night raid and its aftermath, saying, "We lost two only: Brocmal and Faolan were killed; Faolan died outright, and Brocmal followed a day or so later. We buried them at Nantes and continued on, taking three brothers from the abbey to complete our number. Forgive us, Aidan, we reckoned they had taken you for a slave."

"Truly, that is what they did."

"I wanted to go and search for you, but Bishop Cadoc said you were in God's hands now and that we would never find you again."

"Cadoc! Is he still alive? Where is he?"

"He is alive, yes, and he is here," Dugal told me. "We are all here—leastwise, those of us left."

Although I dreaded the answer, I had to know. "How many—how many are here?"

"Four only," came the reply. "Cadoc, Brynach, Ddewi, and myself."

"And the rest?"

"Dead . . . all of them dead."

My heart sank within me as the faces of my brother monks passed once more before my inward eyes. I saw them again as I had seen them in life, each smiling and laughing, calling to one another greetings of fellowship and good will. I saw them and regretted the loss of their lives. They were gone: Maél, Fintán, Clynnog, Brocmal, Connal, Faolan, Ciárán, Gwilym—all of them gone.

"A friend in Constantinople told me that ten of you had been there."

"Aye, we were," confirmed Dugal gloomily. "Would that we had stayed there; the monks were good to us, and we were learning many things from them—and teaching them as well."

"What happened?"

"I do not know the whole of it," he answered. "Bishop Cadoc made application to see the emperor—to present him with the book, and to put forth an appeal regarding some other concerns which the Britons had prepared. I cannot say what these concerns might be, but Brynach knows."

"Did you see the emperor?"

"No," he shook his head slowly, "we never did. Cadoc and Brynach were told by palace officials that our request would take time to be recognized. We were welcome to stay with the monks at Christ Pantocrater, so we settled in to wait. After a time, a man of the court came to see Cadoc. He asked to see the gifts we had brought, and was most helpful. The bishop showed him the book and lamented the loss of the silver cumtach. This man said that our appeal would be more favourably looked upon if the gift were restored. He said he would try to help us replace it."

"And did he?" I wondered, scenting the unmistakeable whiff of treachery.

"Indeed," Dugal affirmed readily and without rancour. "He arranged for us to go to Trebizond where, it was said, the finest silversmiths in the empire would help us make a new cover for the blessed book."

"Who was to help you in Trebizond?" I asked, growing excited. "His name—what was his name?"

"I do not think I ever heard it," Dugal replied with a shrug. "He was something called a magis . . ." He paused, struggling for the word.

"Magister?" I suggested. "Magister Sergius?"

"The very man!" cried Dugal. The memory of unhappy events intruded and he concluded solemnly, "We came in sight of Trebizond, but never reached the city. Sarazen pirates attacked our ship just off the coast. Those of us who were not killed outright, were brought here." He looked at me and a smattering of his former spirit returned. "I never thought to see you here, Dána. Truly, it is a wonder."

"And the other man, the one who arranged for your journey—his name, was it Nikos?"

"Aye," confirmed Dugal, in a tone of amazement. "How is it that you know this?"

"It is less a wonder than you think, Dugal," I replied bitterly. "The same men were helping us, as well. I see now that they were helping themselves from the beginning."

"Are you saying they betrayed us?" Dugal's incredulity was genuine. The possibility had never occurred to him. "You are certainly wrong, Aidan. I cannot think why anyone would wish to betray a handful of poor monks."

"Nor can I, Dugal." I agreed, and told about how we had been attacked by men lying in wait for us on the road. "It was Nikos who led us there, and only Nikos escaped. Indeed, he fled before the slaughter began."

The big monk shook his head in bewildered resignation. "If I had known the book would be the death of so many, I would have thrown it in the sea with my own two hands. And to think I have protected it through all things . . ."

It took a moment for Dugal's meaning to come clear. "But does it yet survive?"

"That it does," confirmed Dugal, glancing darkly towards Gunnar. "Despite its shameful treatment, and no thanks to some."

"Are you certain? You know this to be true?"

"Yes, the book endures. Cadoc keeps it; he has it hidden away."

"You cannot mean that it is here!"

"Indeed, I mean that very thing."

"Here?" I persisted. "In this hell hole?"

"Where else should it be?" he asked. "Never fear, the book is safe and will remain so. No one knows we have it."

Just then, Gunnar groaned and woke up. He struggled upright. "Heya!" he shouted, fighting against the chains.

"Peace," I soothed. "Be still. They are gone for the while. Rest yourself."

He looked around, blinking his eyes, taking in our predicament. He saw Dugal, frowned, and slumped back against the rock, but said nothing.

Dugal's eyes narrowed. "How is it that you can speak to this—" he hesitated, "this murdering barbarian?"

"Hear me, Dugal," I declared seriously. "Gunnar is my friend. He has saved my life not once or twice only, but many times—often to his own hurt. He is a barbarian, true, but he is also a believer and that must be accounted to his favour. I trust him as I trust you."

Dugal frowned and looked away. "No doubt you have a different view of things," he conceded. He was silent for a moment; I saw his lips moving, and after a moment he said, "I still would know how you came to be here, brother."

"It is a long and tedious story, Dugal," I said, despair yawning before me like a chasm black and deep. "Are you certain you want to hear it?"

"And does the sun still rise in the sky?" he said. "Come, brother, we are together now, but who knows how this day will end?"

"Very well," I agreed with a sigh, and began to tell him about my sojourn among the Danes, how I came to be first Gunnar's and then King Harald's slave, and the Sea Wolf king's grand scheme to raid Constantinople. I told him about meeting the emperor, and about how Jarl Harald had given the silver cumtach to Basil as a token of surety in a legal dispute, and the Viking longships had become part of the imperial fleet.

I spoke a long time, pausing now and then to relate what I was saying to Gunnar, who grunted his rough agreement. Oh, it was a fine thing to speak my mother tongue once again. I talked more in that short time than I had in many a day. I told Dugal briefly about my few days in the city and Harald's bargain with the emperor, and more, and at last concluded, saying, "We were sent to Trebizond to serve as bodyguard to the Eparch Nicephorus, who negotiated peace with the Sarazens."

Likely, we would have gone on talking endlessly, but the sun's heat became oppressive and our tongues cleaved to the roofs of our mouths for lack of water. Gunnar, his head hurting him terribly from the blow he had endured, cautioned us to preserve what little strength remained us, so we closed our eyes and lay back against the rock and waited.

The day ended in a white blaze which gradually turned deep yellow as the sun fell behind the ragged hill line. The shadows crept out and covered us, and night slowly folded us into its dark heart. We remained chained to the rock through the night. I slept fitfully, sometimes waking to stare up at the immense star-dazzled skybowl. It seemed to me that all the eyes of heaven gazed down upon us, pitiless, cold, and silent. No cheerful light bathed or soothed us; a hard, merciless glare, stark in judgement, mocked our pains instead.

I recalled the times I had prayed beneath these selfsame lights, imagining them angels eager to bear my prayers to the throne of heaven. But no more. The pain in my shoulders and on my livid flesh was nothing compared to the torment of my soul. Had it done any good, I would have poured out my agony to the Lord of Souls. *Ha! Sooner*

*plead to the stars, Aidan, and beg mercy of the wind; either
way, the answer will be the same.*

Misery, I have learned, is not content. It is restless and
multiplies without ceasing. If I, for the merest space of a
heartbeat, imagined that my tribulation was soon to cease,
the truth soon struck me hard in the teeth: my torment
was only beginning.

They came for us at dawn.

# 46

Six guards and the pit overseer that Dugal had man-
handled arrived as the sun rose on another blistering
day. The overseer, one side of his face bruised and
discoloured, glared down upon us with a malicious sneer;
he spoke out a lengthy discourse which we could not
understand, then motioned to the guards with him. They
leapt forward, unshackled us, and bound us each sepa-
rately; our hands were crossed and tied together at the
wrist. Then, passing their staves through our arms with a
guard on either end, they half-carried, half-dragged us
away.

We were brought to a large dwelling at the edge of the
guards' settlement. In the bare yard outside the white-
washed dwelling stood a thick wooden post with an iron
ring fixed to its top. Leaving Gunnar and Dugal in a heap
to one side, they threw me against the post and, taking a
long leather rope, tied my hands to one end and put the
other end through the ring. The whipping post was half
again as tall as a man, so that when the rope was pulled
taut, I was stretched full height, with my weight resting
only on the tips of my toes.

As this was happening, I noticed that the chief overseer

of the mines came out from the dwelling to stand looking on, his arms crossed over his chest. Under his gaze, I was stripped naked, and the guards then began to bludgeon me with their wooden staves—slowly at first, alternating their strokes, taking it in turn to hit me, first one and then another, striking wherever they would. Oh, but they were thorough. Very soon there was not a single place on my body that had not been pummelled—save for my head; I suppose they did not care to knock me senseless, so they avoided hitting my head lest I pass from consciousness, and thus beyond their torture. Neither did they break the skin, for loss of blood would have had the same effect, and it was clear they wished to prolong the agony as much as possible.

With the aching sting of the first blows, I felt the helpless frustration of the victim; futility, potent as pain, overwhelmed me, as I experienced the most wretched helplessness. My soul recoiled in horror at my own weakness. Tears came to my eyes, and I was ashamed of myself for weeping. I bit my lips to keep from crying out, wishing with all my soul that the ordeal would stop.

As the beating continued, however, it soon became apparent that my torturers had merely been warming to their task; the blows became sharper, and more keenly judged. Again and again, I was struck in the places where I was certain to feel the most pain: forearms, shins, knees, elbows, ribs. At the same time, the rope was pulled even tighter and I was lifted off the ground entirely, so that I could not brace myself even by so much as a single toe.

With each blow, my body jerked and swung uncontrollably—only to be struck again while still swinging. The guards laughed at this. I heard their voices, ringing in the yard and any sorrow I had felt for myself vanished utterly, consumed in a sudden surge of white-hot rage.

Never had I known such anger. Had it been a flame,

the entire mining settlement would have been scorched to ashes, every house and all the inhabitants: men, women, and children. I ground my teeth on my lips until the blood ran down my chin and onto my chest, and still I did not cry out. Far away, as if from a great remove across a vast distance, I could hear Dugal praying out loud for me, beseeching God on my behalf. The exercise was but a meaningless act born of desperation, and I scorned his useless prayers.

When at last they took me down, all my wounds had spread and fused into a single massive bruise which pulsed agony through me with every gasping, rattling breath. Blinded by pain, I could not see properly; I was conscious, though—some small part of my mind remained aware. I knew that my limbs were intact and that none of my bones were broken. I knew that Dugal was now undergoing the same torture I had just received.

I knew also that I was a changed man, for the insane rage had consumed me from within, and my heart was now as cold and hard as a spent cinder.

When they had finished with Dugal, and then with Gunnar, they bound our hands behind our backs and tied them to our ankles. We were made to kneel in the sun like this during the hottest part of the day. My awareness drifted; sometimes I knew where I was and what had happened, and other times I thought I was alone in a coracle on the sea. I could even feel the waves undulating beneath me, now lifting my little boat high, now dropping down once more.

It seemed to me as I lay in the bottom of the boat, a solitary cloud drifted in front of the sun; the shadow passed over me and I opened my eyes to see that the cloud had an unusual shape and solidity. Roused by this curiosity, I looked again, and saw that the cloud had the face of a man, and that its white billows were the folds of a turban;

two dark eyes in that face regarded me with deep apprehension and concern. This baffled me, for I could think of no reason why my torturers might distress themselves over my plight.

I heard a voice like the buzzing of an insect, and realized that the man whose face hovered above me was speaking. He seemed to address me, but I could not understand what he was saying. Then he raised his head and spoke to someone else. Yes, he addressed someone else; his face contorted in anger as he looked away from me. Someone shouted, and the man shouted back in reply as he disappeared from view. I had not the strength to raise my head and see where he went. But even as he vanished, it came to me that it was a face I knew—I had seen this man before— he had a name, and it was a name I knew, but could not say. Who was he?

This question gnawed at me through the day; I kept remembering the face and thinking about it until the sun began to sink low in the dust-hazed sky, and the guards returned to give us another beating. As before, we were hoisted up onto the post, and set upon with wooden staves. The only difference was that this time they struck flesh already bruised and wounded, and which had had ample time to swell. Thus, the second battering was even more painful than the first.

The hard place within me refused to yield, however; I did not cry out. Neither did I endure the full brunt of the punishment, for after the torture began in earnest, the pain became too great and I passed into blessed oblivion. The next thing I knew, water was being poured over me, to revive me. I awoke to throbbing agony, every muscle and bone aflame with pain. When the first wave of pain had passed, I found that the sky was dark, and that we were receiving the attentions of a small man in a large black turban. The fellow gave us each a drink of water, holding our heads for us so that we would not drown when the water gushed down our throats. After easing our thirst, he examined our limbs. Where the skin had burst from swelling, he rubbed a soothing salve into the wound.

This was done under the silent scrutiny of the chief overseer, who stood before his house watching all that was done for us. Satisfied that no bones were broken, the little man turned to his superior, bowed once very low and departed, muttering to himself.

The guards bound us hand and foot once more and left us to our anguish for the night. The pain of my bruised body kept me awake all night, and I lay on my side in the dust—too sore to move, but too aching to lie still—thinking that death would be a mercy, and one we would certainly be denied.

I thought, too, that the punishment we were enduring was far in excess of any crime we might have committed. We had laid hand to a guard, I do not deny it, but that we should be subjected to such savage punishment, was an absurdity I could not understand. It made no sense to me, but then, I reflected, very little of what happened in this world made any sense at all. To believe it did . . . *that* was absurd.


At dawn the next morning, we were roused by the blowing of a horn—a trumpet, I think. From somewhere on the hillside came the dull bell-like tolling of someone beating a length of iron. In a little while the whole of the mining settlement was astir. People came from their houses to assemble on one side of the dusty square outside the chief overseer's dwelling. I heard someone moan beside me, and turned my head to see Gunnar awaken and take in the gathering throng.

"It seems we are to have witnesses to our torture today," I remarked.

"It is not our torture that brings them," replied Gunnar. "They have come to see us die."

He was right, of course. In a little while the other slaves began arriving, taking their places opposite the settlement dwellers on the other side of the square, where they stood in ranks behind the guards who had brought them. I looked for Cadoc and the other monks, and for Harald and the Sea Wolves, but I could see none of them in among the crowds.

When everyone had taken their places, the chief overseer appeared, accompanied by the pig-eyed underling who had directed the previous day's torture. This fellow walked about with upraised hands until everyone became silent; then he deferred to the chief overseer, who stepped forth to speak out a short address. At its conclusion, the master of the mine clapped his hands. Out from the throng of onlookers stepped three men. Two of them carried a wooden block, and the third a curved sword twice the size of an ordinary weapon. This great sword's blade was burnished so that it gleamed in the morning light.

"At least we will not have to suffer another day of beatings," Gunnar observed. "I do not think I could tolerate that."

He made it sound as if he had come to the end of his good temper. In truth, he had come to the end of his life. We were not to be given a quick, painless death, however. No sooner had the block been set up nearby, than two horses were led out into the square. I could not understand what it meant, but Gunnar knew.

"I have heard of this," he said, and explained that the victim was tied to the two horses, which were then driven in opposite directions, thereby stretching the condemned man's body between them. When the bones of the back separated sufficiently, the sword was used to hack the poor wretch in half. "The unlucky one sometimes does not die all at once," he added.

Dugal had not stirred, and I made to wake him, but thought better of it and let him sleep on. *Let him enjoy the little peace he has left,* I thought; *at least he will enter glory well rested.*

As it happened, his rest ended almost at once. For as soon as the horses were brought to stand either side of the block, four guards came to where we lay and laid hands to Dugal, jerking him awake violently. He gasped in pain at his rough handling, and his head fell limply forward.

I decided then what to do. Drawing together what little strength I possessed, I pushed myself up onto my knees. Black waves of pain broke over me as I raised my head. Placing one foot flat on the ground, I gritted my teeth and stood, tottering and wavering like an infant. The agony of that simple act brought tears to my eyes; I heard a roaring boom in my head, and somehow lurched forward a pace.

"Take me!" I said, my voice a raw rasp.

The guards turned to stare at me; one of them said something I did not understand, and the others returned to their task and dragged Dugal away.

"Leave him alone!" I shouted, almost collapsing with the effort. "Take me instead."

Another shout met my own. From across the yard the chief overseer called to the guards and pointed at me with his staff. The four guards dropped Dugal at once and started for me instead. I turned to Gunnar. "Farewell, Gunnar Warhammer," I whispered with the last of my strength. "I am glad I knew you."

"Say not farewell, Aeddan," he said, struggling to his knees. "Wait for me in the otherworld. We will go to your God together."

I nodded, looking my last upon my battered friends.

Then the guards seized my arms and hauled me to the block. We passed the place where Dugal lay. I saw that he had lost consciousness again. "Farewell, brother," I said, though I knew he was past hearing. "You were ever a true friend to me, Dugal."

We reached the block whereupon I was thrown to the ground, and they began lashing my hands together. They had almost finished the chore when a commotion arose from across the yard where the slaves were assembled. I heard shouting, and to my surprise I recognized both the voice and the words.

"Stop!" cried the voice. "Let me take his place."

Out of the corner of my eye, I saw the figure of an old man hobbling forth as quickly as his wracked body would allow. After a moment, I realized that it was Bishop Cadoc. Gone were the robes and cloak, and gone the eagle-topped cambutta, but his voice was strong and powerful as ever. One of the guards ran to thwart him, but the chief overseer gestured to the man to allow him to come forth.

"Take me instead," Cadoc said quickly, puffing with the effort of crossing the yard. I saw then that he was ill, for his eyes were hazy and his breath a laboured wheeze. He stepped nearer, gesturing to the chief overseer to help explain his words. "I will take his place. I will take all their places. Take me, and let them go," he said, offering himself.

"Please, Bishop Cadoc, it is better this way," I pleaded. "I am content and ready to die. God has forsaken me, and I have nothing left. Let it end now."

The mine overseer looked from one to the other of us, and decided, I suppose, that he would get more work out of me than out of Cadoc, for he uttered a gruff command and the guards took hold of the bishop. Taking the rope from me, they tied the old man instead.

"Cadoc!" I began, "It is not right that you—"

"Listen to me, Aidan," he said, gently. "There is not much time." I made to protest to the chief overseer, but Cadoc stopped me, saying, "I am dying, Aidan. I am nearly gone."

"Bishop Cadoc . . ." I cried in agony.

"Peace, brother," he soothed. "I have reached the end of my life and I am ready to join my king. But you, Aidan, must live. There is much to do and your life is just beginning."

His hands tied now, they pulled him roughly to the ground and bound his feet. Cadoc seemed oblivious to the mistreatment. "You were well chosen, brother. Never doubt that. God will not forsake those who call upon his name. Cling to him, Aidan. He is your rock and your strength."

They lifted him to the block and lay him over it, face down, his thin shoulders and legs falling to either side. A rope was passed through the tight leather bonds joining his hands, and another between his ankles; these were then tied to the horses' harnesses.

"Always remember," he said, turning his face to me for the last time, "your life was bought with a price. Remember that when doubt overtakes you. Farewell, Aidan."

He then turned his head and closed his eyes. I heard the familiar drone of the Lord's Prayer.

The chief overseer spoke out a command, and the pit guard, whip in hand, stepped to the block, pushing me aside. I could not stand and fell to the ground where I rolled in torment on my bruised back. Another guard, a tall, well-muscled dark-skinned Sarazen, took his place on the other side of the block. He reached out his hand and received the curved axe.

At a nod from the chief overseer, the pit guard gave out a cry to the horses. His whip uncurled in the same instant and the crack echoed in the yard. The slaves all shouted at once. The horses started forth. Poor Cadoc's body snapped taut like a scrap of rag. The whip cracked again as the pit guard lashed the horses to their work.

There came a hideous popping sound from Cadoc's body as the very bones and sinews gave way. Hearing this, the tall guard swung his axe up over his head and down again in one swift motion. The blow was ill-placed, however, for the blade bit deep into the good bishop's side just above the hip, opening a terrible gash. Out spewed blood and entrails.

Cadoc cried out. The whip cracked again, and the horses stretched him further. "Kyrie!" he screamed, his great voice crying not in pain but victory. "Kyrie eleison!"

Unable to look away, I stared in horror as the curved blade slashed again, this time catching Cadoc in the small of the back. The bones severed with a snap and the horses stumbled forward. I saw a gush of bright, bright red, brilliant in the sunlight, as the bishop's body split in half.

Cadoc gave a last cry as the fore-half of his severed trunk, suddenly free, slewed forward. "Kyrie!" he gasped as the breath of life fled his lungs.

The Arab onlookers raised a shout—a word that sounded like "Bismillah"—calling over and over again. The slaves, ranged opposite the cheering crowd, fell into a sullen silence as the two halves of the good bishop's corpse were loosed from the horses and dragged off to one side, leaving a dark trail in the dust. My mouth filled with bitter bile and my stomach heaved, but there was nothing in my gut to throw up. I gagged instead.

Reeling, I felt my hands caught up and quickly lashed together with a strong leather thong. Numb horror stole over me; I raised my eyes to meet the triumphant, mocking sneer of the pit guard, and the truth broke over me: Cadoc's sacrifice was meaningless and I was next to die.

The chief overseer had no intention of showing mercy; he killed an old man who had outlived his usefulness as a slave and, just as surely, he would now kill us. The bishop's gesture, so grand and selfless, an expression of ultimate compassion, was shown to be the act of a blundering old fool. *That* was the truth, brutal as the Sarazen sun beating down upon the white dust square, blighting all beneath its unrelenting gaze.

My mind squirmed with dread. I was to die like Cadoc, hacked in half like a meatbone, my inward parts spilled out onto the dusty ground. "Bastard!" I spat at the chief overseer, rage flaring through me with the intensity of the white-hot sun above. "Satan take you all!"

The smug Arab only laughed, and gestured his men to tie my feet. They pushed me to the ground, and took hold of my legs. I tried to kick at them, but my legs were bruised and stiff from the torture I had endured, it was all I could do to bend them, and the next thing I knew, I was slung up into the air and placed upon the blood-stained block.

I heard Gunnar shout something, meaning to instill bravery, I think, but I could not hear what it was. All I could hear was the sound of my own heart wildly pounding in my ears. I felt the ropes being passed between my wrists and ankles, and made secure. All I could think was that this was not my fate; my death was otherwise ordained. That I should leave life so miserably was a monumental injustice.

The ropes snapped tight.

My arms and legs stretched taut. In a moment the horses would be driven forth and the wicked blade would slice into my side.

Images cascaded through my mind in a mad, meaningless rush. I glimpsed the green hills of Éire, and the faces of my brother monks going up to the chapel. I saw Dugal striding across the pasture, carrying a lamb, and laughing. I saw Eparch Nicephorus peeling an orange with his long fingers. I saw Gunnar's son Ulf, running with his fishing pole down the path to the pond, and Ylva feeding geese on meal held in her apron. I glimpsed Harald Bull-Roar standing beneath the handsome prow of his dragon ship, and the purple hills of Byzantium misty in the distance. Lastly, I saw my own hand working over a leaf of close-copied vellum at my desk in the scriptorium, pen quivering in the candlelight.

The crack of the pit guard's whip brought me to myself once more, and to the sudden, searing ache in my shoulders and back. I felt the sinews in my sides stretch. The ropes groaned as the horses pulled the harder.

I heard the whip crack again, and liquid fire spurted into my veins. Instantly, every muscle and bone was aflame. I cried out, and my voice sounded strange in my ears—like the hoarse blat of a ram's horn when it is blown. The sound came again and I thought, *How strange to make such an undignified noise at the moment of death.*

Another voice wormed its way into my consciousness—Gunnar or Harald, I could not tell which—was shouting for all he was worth. The words were odd, though, and I could not make out what he was saying. A thick black cloud descended over me then, and I took a deep breath, and another, greedily, knowing it would be my last.

I felt the axe-blade strike my back. Oddly, it did not hurt. Indeed, it seemed a relief, for the terrible straining tension went out of the ropes.

*Ah!* I thought, *this is how it ends. The pain simply stops and then you die. Perhaps I am dead even now. If so, why do I still hear the shouting?*

# 47

I felt my body lifted up and lowered to the ground. The mist cleared from my eyes and I saw that I was now sitting on the blood-soaked ground with my back against the block; a stranger stood over me, brown-skinned, dressed in a long blue robe and cloak, and white turban.

My mind was beclouded; I could make nothing of what was happening around me. I heard someone speaking rapidly and looked around to see a man sitting on a fine white horse, spear in hand, his face hard and angry. With him were four mounted warriors in blue turbans, holding spears and long blue-painted shields.

It came to me that this was the same man I had seen the previous day. Apparently, he had returned and was not well pleased with what he saw; he sat on his horse, berating the chief overseer in a loud voice. They were arguing in Arabic so that I did not know what they said, but the chief overseer was shouting and shaking his fists at the stranger on the horse.

The white-turbaned stranger, grim-faced, eyes narrowed, turned in the saddle and gestured to the warrior standing over me. At once the warrior began untying my wrists and ankles. He was quickly joined by another warrior and together they raised me between them. I could not stand, so they were forced to bear me up.

Livid with rage, the chief overseer started towards the two warriors supporting me. He took a quick step, and I saw the glint of a blade in his hand. Another few steps and he would reach us. There was nothing I could do to prevent the attack. Indeed, I had not the strength or wit to so much as cry out to warn my protectors.

Then a curious thing happened: as the chief overseer drew back his arm to strike, a sharp-angled metal point appeared in the centre of his chest. He shuddered forward a step or two, and then stopped to look down as a bright red bloom of blood spread from the protruding point. The knife fell from his hand, and he clawed at the thing in his chest, raking his fingers against it.

The chief overseer staggered forward one more step and then crashed to his knees. Staring at me, he gave a choked cry and pitched forward face-down in the dust. The long shaft of a spear stood upright in the centre of his back. The slaves began shouting as one, ecstatic that their tormentor had been struck down.

The white-turbaned man moved his mount to where the fallen overseer lay and retrieved his spear without so much as rising from his saddle. Spear in hand, he called in a warning voice to the guards and slave drivers who stood looking on, and then motioned for the two warriors holding me to follow. They carried me to a horse and hoisted me onto it. I could not sit upright, but slumped on the animal's neck and clung on with the last of my strength. Soon we were racing headlong down through the narrow streets of the mining settlement towards the gate—one warrior leading my horse, and another riding alongside, keeping me in the saddle. The flight was almost as painful as any of my beatings and I cried out with every jolting step.

I do not know how far we fled—once beyond the gate, I swooned and cannot remember anything more until I awoke in a dusky twilight. The stranger in the white turban was kneeling beside me, pressing a wet cloth to my forehead. When he saw that I had wakened, he held a cup to my lips and gave me water to drink.

"Allah, Most Merciful, be praised," he said, "you awake in the land of the living."

I gazed at the man's face as he spoke, and I remembered where I had seen him before—with the amir, in Trebizond. "I know you," I told him, my voice a rasping whisper in my ears.

"I know you, too. I am Faysal," he replied. "I have been looking for you."

"Why?" I asked.

"That is for Lord Sadiq to tell," he replied.

"My friends—" I said, remembering Gunnar and Dugal suddenly. I tried to sit up; pain burst behind my eyes and I fell back, panting with the effort. My shoulder felt as if it were being prodded with white-hot irons.

"I know nothing of your friends," Faysal replied bluntly. "But tell me, is Eparch Nicephorus dead?"

Unable to speak, I nodded.

"We are taking you to the amir. He is in Ja'fariya, which is several days' ride from here."

I roused myself to protest. "Please," I gasped, "I cannot leave my friends."

Faysal seemed not to hear. He rose, saying, "Rest now and regain your strength."

Though I slept the remainder of the day, by nightfall my condition had worsened. I could no longer lift my head, much less stand, and it hurt to breathe. My whole body pulsed with pain, especially my shoulder and deep in my chest. Waking by firelight, I found Faysal sitting beside me, his dark eyes shadowed with worry.

"Drink this," he said, offering me a cup. "I have brought you some food also."

I raised my hand and reached for the cup and pain seared me from elbow to neck. Tears came to my eyes. I lay back groaning and gasping for breath.

"Please," Faysal said, and proceeded to loosen my clothing. Though he worked most gently, even the smallest movement caused me to cry out. He took one quick look and sat back on his heels. "It is not good," he told me. "The bones of your arm have been separated from their place. I can help you if you will allow me—though I warn you, there will be much pain."

As I could not imagine anything more painful than that which I had already endured, I gave my silent assent. Faysal left me then, and I heard low, urgent voices for a moment before drifting into unconsciousness again. Returning some while later, he roused me and said, "It is best done quickly."

Kneeling before me, he motioned to two of the men with him to attend me. They lifted me to a sitting posture, and one put his arms around my waist and the other held me about the chest. "Put this between your teeth," Faysal instructed, placing a tight-folded cloth in my mouth. When he was satisfied with these precautions, Faysal took my arm between his hands and slowly raised it until it was level with my shoulder; I winced and bit into the cloth, but did not scream.

Slowly, slowly, Faysal rotated my arm. Pain burst in bright fireballs; I felt him tighten his grip on my arm, and I closed my eyes.

Without the least warning, he pulled my arm straight out. In the same moment, the man holding my chest pulled me back. I heard a grating pop as my arm gave way. I thought I would swoon with the pain. Instantly, Faysal released his grip and the pain ceased. "There," he said, taking the cloth from between my teeth, "the bone is returned to its proper place."

They then crossed my arm over my chest and bound it there with a long strip of cloth torn from one of their cloaks. This finished, I fell back sweating and shaking with exhaustion. Faysal covered me with a cloak and I slept until dawn when they brought me water and a little bread dipped in honey. I was able to swallow a bit of it, and felt somewhat revived.

I could not stand. Every limb had been bludgeoned and every joint cruelly twisted. The bruises on my flesh were dark, angry blue-black in colour, and there was not a solitary patch of skin that was not discoloured; due to the swelling, the skin had burst in several places. Faysal did not like the look of my wounds and told me so. "I fear for you, my friend," he said. "I think we dare not stay here any longer."

Since I was in no way fit to sit a horse, they constructed a carrier of sorts made of a wide piece of stout cloth slung between two horses and tied somehow to the saddles. Into this sling I was placed, like a baby bundled into a cradle, and we set off.

Clearly, Faysal was anxious to reach Ja'fariya, for we did not stop all that day, and only once the next day. I lay in my sling, drifting in and out of consciousness. The riders were such masterful horsemen, that I rarely suffered the slightest bump or jolt, but swung gently to the rhythmic swaying of the horses.

The incessant, drumming ache in my joints and muscles—every part of my body had either been bludgeoned or stretched—increased through the second day. My right shoulder still throbbed, and the pain in my chest was gradually replaced by a burning sensation which made breathing difficult. My periods of awareness grew shorter and my sleep deeper; I could rouse myself, but only with extreme effort, and as time passed that effort no longer seemed worthwhile. During my brief periods of lucidity, I reckoned we were travelling rapidly, but could not tell in which direction. We rested only briefly during the hottest part of the day, and pushed on well into the night.

Once, I awoke, opening my eyes to see the full moon hanging like a glowing face above me, perfectly round and ablaze with pale gold light in a sky of deepest blue. Stars in their hundreds of thousands gleamed like so much silver dust scattered by a wildly generous hand. I did not know if I was still in my sling, or lying on the ground, and felt a distinct urgency to learn which it might be, but soon passed into unconsciousness without discovering the answer to this mystery.

Another day passed—or, then again, it may have been the same day, or one of a long succession of days, for all I could tell—and we arrived at the amir's palace. I cannot say which way we had travelled, nor how long the journey lasted—two days, four, or maybe less or more—such was beyond my ken.

All I can say with certainty is that I awoke suddenly to find that I was being carried along a panelled corridor to the accompaniment of hushed voices. They brought me to a small, bare cell of a room where I was placed on a covered pallet. Sunlight slashed into the room through a narrow slit of a windhole; dust motes swirled lazily in the sharp shaft of light. Those who had carried me to the room departed and I was left alone for a moment.

My head felt as if it were made of lead-covered stone; I tried, but could not raise it, and the effort brought waves of black dizziness besides. I closed my eyes—only for a moment, or so I thought—and when I opened them again, my clothes had been taken away and I was now covered by a thin white cloth. My arm was still bound to my chest with a winding cloth, and what little I could see of the rest of my body was grossly swollen and discoloured; the blue-black bruises were turning a hideous purple colour. A clear fluid oozed from the places where my skin had burst from the swelling. My mouth was dry and my eyes burned—indeed, I felt as if I were being slowly roasted from the inside.

I heard a movement beside me, and Faysal appeared; he squatted at my bedside, peering doubtfully into my face. "You are awake, my friend?"

I opened my mouth, and made to answer, but no sound came out. Faysal, seeing my difficulty, raised my head and brought a shallow bowl to my lips. The bowl contained honey water which I drank, and it seemed to free my tongue. "Where am I?" I asked; the voice I heard was not my own; at least, I no longer recognized it as mine.

"Lord Sadiq's palace," he answered. "Do you have much pain?"

It took me a moment to think about this. Yes, I decided, there was pain—a continual, insistent pulsing ache in every limb and muscle—but I had become used to it. "No more than before," I answered in the same husky, wheezing, unfamiliar voice.

"The amir wishes you to know that he has sent a messenger to bring a physician from Baghdat. He will arrive tomorrow, if it pleases Allah. Meanwhile, we will do all that may be done to preserve your life. You must help us in this by eating and drinking what is given you. Do you understand what I am saying?"

I nodded.

Faysal sat for a moment, an expression of keen appraisal on his face; had I been a horse, I do not think he would have given much for me. "It is important to the amir that you live," he said, as if I might require persuasion. Finally, he rose to go, but as he stepped to the doorway, he said, "Kazimain is skilled in healing. Lord Sadiq has ordained that she shall attend you until the physician comes. Do whatever she says."

He left me then, but I heard him speaking to someone in the corridor outside. After a moment, the voices stopped and a young woman entered the room. She carried a small brass platter with flat bread and fruit, and small brass bowls. Kneeling, she placed the platter beside me, and began tearing the bread between her long fingers.

When she finished, she took a bit of bread, dipped it into one of the bowls, and held it to my mouth. I opened my mouth and she fed me; the bread was soft and the sauce sweet. I chewed and swallowed, whereupon the process was repeated until I had finished. She then gave me another drink, and prepared to feed me some more bread. All at once I was overwhelmed by exhaustion; sleep, like a rolling billow of the ocean, pulled me down into its dark depths. "No more," I murmured, fighting to keep my eyes open.

The young woman replaced the bread, picked up the brass tray, and stood. "Thank you, Kazimain," I whispered in my own tongue.

My use of her name surprised her, I think, for she paused to look at me curiously before turning and vanishing from my sight. That expression of surprised curiosity occupied my shattered thoughts for a goodly while—indeed, for far longer than anyone might have imagined. It was the last thing I saw, or remembered seeing, for a very long time. During the night, late and alone, I lapsed into a fevered sleep from which they could not wake me.

# 48

Alone and in darkness I wandered, a spirit lost and unaware, clouds of unknowing bearing me wherever they would. I descended to the realm of the dead, the dominion of lost souls who, in an earlier age, ended their lives in the underworld as shades in a lightless, hopeless eternity. In this state, I endured: beyond caring, beyond feeling, beyond all desire . . . save this and this alone: to wreak vengeance on the one who had betrayed me.

I no longer feared death, but I refused to die while the man who had brought about my suffering still lived and drew breath. Whatever life was left to me, I would devote to avenging myself and all those who had likewise suffered and died at his hands. This I vowed with all my heart. If I was to die and endure the torment of an everlasting existence beyond God's grace, so be it! But before I lay down in my grave, I would savour the cold solace of revenge.

That thought flickered in my consciousness like the flame of a solitary candle. Whenever I felt myself drifting away, the flame drew me back, holding me with its feeble, guttering light. It seemed I spent a lifetime like this, hovering between life and death. I heard voices speaking in obscure tongues; sometimes I dreamed strange dreams of exotic places beneath suns of burning white. Oft-times I had visions wherein I was laboured over by beings in white robes who administered draughts of healing elixirs.

Then one day I came to myself; awareness returned and I heard someone close beside me singing—a low, lovely voice, though the words were unknown to me. I opened my eyes to see Kazimain sitting beside me, dressed in palest bird's-egg blue, a bag of crimson silk in her hand. The honey-yellow sunlight of a late afternoon was pouring in through a high-arched open windhole behind her. Outside, I could see rooftops—a few red-tiled and pitched, and some with bright white bulging domes like great eggs; most were flat, however, with canopies of various colours strung over ropes; many had plants, or even small trees. I saw several tall, finger-thin towers with pointed tops soaring above, striving like spears above the rest.

From the bag in her hand, Kazimain withdrew a few kernels of barley and, half-turning, placed these on the white stone windhole ledge. Even as she withdrew her hand, a small grey-green bird appeared, cocked a bold bead of an eye at her, and began pecking at the kernels.

"A friend of yours?" I asked. Though my voice was but the faintest gasp of a whisper, she spun round as if I had screamed aloud. She gave me a wide-eyed, horrified look and fled the room. I heard her pattering footsteps grow fainter as she ran away.

I turned my attention to the room. It was the same bare cell I had known before: only the low pallet of carpets for my bed, beside which had been added two large cushions on the floor and a wooden stand bearing the weight of a large brass platter containing fruit, and a pitcher and jars. The walls were rose-coloured, and the floor white marble. Save for the windhole, there was nothing else to be seen.

My injured shoulder was still wrapped, but my other

arm was free, so with small, slow, aching movements I grasped and drew aside the thin cloth which covered me to get a better look at my battered limbs. The bruises were still there, of course, in their hundreds; they were deep-coloured, but they had lost the awful purple hue and were now the ghastly yellow-green tinge of old wounds. The swelling had gone, however, and the throbbing ache as well; what is more, some of the smaller cuts were almost healed over. By this I surmised that a fair amount of time had passed—days, at least; possibly many days.

Though I possessed no recollection of how long I had been unconscious, my mind was clear. Aside from the bruises, my body felt reasonably sound. Determined to prove this for myself, I took a deep breath and pushed myself up into a sitting position. The attempt was a disaster: instantly, black flecks swarmed in my eyes, and pain seared through my head. A sound like churning water filled my ears, and I collapsed on the bed.

A moment later, the sound of voices and rushing feet beyond the doorway alerted me to the arrival of visitors, so I quickly pulled the light coverlet over myself just as a white-turbaned man with skin the colour of polished mahogany and a nose like a hawk's beak appeared in the doorway; he was dressed in white and wore a circular medallion on a thick gold chain around his neck.

Kazimain hovered behind him, her dark eyes shining with excitement. Seeing that I was awake, the man raised his hands heavenward, threw back his head, and loosed a long, heartfelt paean. Then, composing himself once more, he proceeded to my bedside and bent over me. He placed a cool hand on my forehead, and gazed searchingly into my eyes. He reached down and took me by the hand and pressed his fingers to the underside of my wrist.

After a moment, he turned and spoke to Kazimain, who ducked her head and withdrew from the room. Then, taking hold of the cloth, the man pulled the covering aside and knelt down, pressing his fingers here and there, and glancing now and again when I winced at the pain his probing caused. Next, he took my head between his palms, moved it this way and that, touched my chin and opened my mouth to peer inside.

These obscure ministrations finished, he sat back on his heels and proclaimed, "Allah, All Wise and Merciful, be praised! You have come back to us. How are you feeling?"

This he said in a soft, lilting Greek and, though I understood him quite well, it was a moment before I could make an answer. "Who are you?" I did not mean to be so blunt, but I did not think my voice strong enough for more than the simplest utterances.

"I am Farouk al-Shami Kashan Ahmad ibn Abu," he replied and lowered his head in an elegant bow. "I am court physician to Amir Sadiq and his family. To you, I am simply Farouk." He raised his hands and professed himself well pleased with my recovery. "By Allah's will, you are summoned once more to life. Greetings and welcome, my friend; the peace of Allah be with you."

"How long?" I asked, swallowing hard.

"It has been my pleasure to serve as your physician these last seven days."

*Seven days!* I thought. *A long time to lie at death's threshold.*

I was still pondering the meaning of this revelation when another man, larger and darker than Farouk, entered the room carrying a brass bowl of steaming water and a roll of linen cloth, which he placed on the floor beside the physician. "A bath for you," he said, shaking out the linen cloth into a large square. "Have no fear, Malik will assist."

On the whole, it was more in the nature of a trial than a simple bath. Malik, who throughout the entire ordeal uttered never a word, levered me up into a sitting position, and proceeded to rub me with the wet cloth. I am certain he worked as gently as he could, but even the slightest touch hurt, and when he raised my arm, tears came to my eyes. I bit the insides of my cheeks to keep from crying out, and even so did not succeed. Farouk watched the procedure with cool interest, speaking now and then an instruction to Malik, who obliged without reply. I slowly perceived that, along with his bathing, Malik was systematically moving and massaging all my joints and limbs and would not stop until every part of me had been examined in this fashion.

I gritted my teeth and endured, until Farouk commanded Malik to desist, and the abuse ceased. I lay back painful and aching, but refreshed nonetheless. The water with which I had been bathed was infused with lemon—a bitter yellow fruit highly regarded in the east, but unknown in the west—which imparted an astringent quality to the water which both refreshed and soothed me.

"We will leave you in peace for the moment," Farouk told me. "Meanwhile, I will inform Amir Sadiq of your splendid return."

"I must see him," I said, my voice urgent, if slightly ragged. "Please, Farouk, it is important."

"I have no doubt that it is," the physician replied.

"When can I see him?"

"Soon," he said. "In a day or two, perhaps, when you are feeling better. I can tell you that the amir is most eager to speak to you as well."

Despite the amir's professed enthusiasm, it was a good many more days before I saw him. Farouk visited every day, however, sometimes with Malik, other times with Kazimain. She was often hovering nearby, and it was Kazimain who brought my food each day; occasionally, she stayed and waited while I ate. I found her quiet company entirely agreeable.

Some days were better for me than others, but on the whole I felt my strength returning. I also felt the hard place inside me, gnarled and tight, clenched like a fist full of walnuts, deep down inside where nothing could reach it ever again. Two things I kept there: my will to vengeance, and the determination to free my friends.

My recovery proceeded apace, especially after Farouk succeeded in getting me on my feet: *that* was another ordeal, far more miserable than the bath, and far more painful—so much so that I fainted the first time and Malik had to carry me back to bed. Nevertheless, under Farouk's keen and compassionate eye, I grew strong once more. My appetite returned and I began to eat with vigour. Kazimain continued to come to my room each day—it was like the sunrise to see her each morning—and Faysal looked in on me from time to time.

Gradually, with much slow and painful exercise, the stiffness in my limbs and the ache in my joints diminished. I was able to shuffle around the bare confines of my room without collapsing or fainting. My shoulder still pained me, but I could tell that it was healing. The winding cloth was changed every few days, allowing Farouk the opportunity to examine my shoulder and arm. He assured me that no bones had been broken, and that without Faysal's crude-but-effective treatment I would not be so well off. "You were very fortunate," he insisted. "It could have been much worse."

One day, after I had expressed mild discontent at remaining in my room all the time, Farouk told me he thought it was time I saw more of the palace. The next evening, Kazimain brought a bundle of green and blue cloth tied with a wide band of red silk. This she placed on the bed beside me, departing again at once. Using my good hand, I worried loose the red silk band and unfolded the cloth. There were two garments, both thin and lightweight; the first was a long, loose blue robe, and the second a billowy green cloak like those Farouk and Faysal wore.

As no one was about, I shrugged off my mantle and, with some difficulty, pulled on the robe. I was still trying to adjust the voluminous garment when Farouk arrived. He crossed the room to me in quick steps, picked up the band of red silk and put it around my waist, tied it expertly, and suddenly the robe felt right on me. He stepped back, raised his hands and proclaimed: "As the light hidden beneath a bowl shines out when the covering is taken away, I see a new man revealed."

"I feel like a very old man," I remarked. "I can hardly move."

"The heat of the day has passed," he declared. "I have come to take you for a walk." Putting a hand to my elbow, he led me to the door and out into a low corridor that seemed to stretch on and on into the distance; doorways opened off the corridor to the right, and large, pointed windholes to the left. The walls and floors were coloured marble, and the lintels polished wood. I saw that my room was the last one at the furthest end of the corridor.

"This is the amir's principal residence," Farouk informed me. "Lord Sadiq has a summer palace in the mountains, and a house in Baghdat. I am told they are both fine houses. Perhaps you will see them one day."

His comment awakened my latent curiosity. "Why am I here, Farouk?"

"You have been brought here to recover your health," he said simply.

"So you have said. Is there no other reason?"

"You remain here at the pleasure of Amir Sadiq," the physician said, adjusting his answer slightly. "I am not privy to my lord's purposes."

"I see. Am I a slave?"

"We are all of us slaves, my friend," said Farouk lightly. "We merely serve different masters. That is all."

We walked on—my own gait a laboured, hobbling shuffle. My legs felt as if I were dragging blocks of marble from my ankles. Eventually, we reached the end of the corridor and I saw a wide stairway leading down to rooms below, and another stairway leading up. A gentle breeze, fragrant with the scent of roses, was drifting down into the corridor from above. "What is up there?" I asked.

"It is the roof garden of the amir's wives," answered Farouk.

"I would like to see it. May we go there?"

"Most certainly," he said. "It is allowed."

Taking the steps one at a time, very slowly, we ascended to a softly warm summer evening. The sun had just set and the sky was tinted an exquisite golden hue with fiery purples and dusky pinks over hills of slate blue. The sky itself was immense, and stars were already glinting overhead. There were other large dwellings nearby, but the amir's was the largest, and overlooked them all.

The palace roof was a flat expanse onto which hundreds upon hundreds of plants had been arranged in clay pots of all shapes and sizes, and placed around a raised central pavilion made of slender wooden slats woven in open latticework, and overdraped with red-and-blue striped cloth. There were small palm trees, and fronded shrubs large and small, and flowers, many of which had closed their petals for the night. It was the roses, however, that caught my attention, for the air was heavy with their fragrance, and everywhere I looked, I saw whole thickets of tiny, sweet-scented white roses, which seemed to breathe their luxurious perfume upon the evening air in silent sighs.

While we were yet standing at the top of the stairs, there came a strange, chanting wail from across the city. It seemed to emanate from one of the slender towers I had seen from my bed. This sound waxed and waned eerily, and was quickly fortified by other chants and wails.

Upon listening for a moment, it occurred to me that I had heard this very sound before, though I could not remember where or when. "What is that?" I asked, turning to Farouk.

"Ah!" he said, reading the expression on my face. "It is the *muezzin*," he explained, "calling the faithful man to his prayers. Come." He turned and led me towards the pavilion where he sat me down upon a cushion. When I was thus settled, he said, "If you will please excuse me, I will return momentarily."

Farouk took himself a few paces away, turned his face to the east, bowed low three times, then knelt, placing hands flat before him and touching his nose to the ground. I watched him perform this curious ritual, rising now and then to bob his head up and down once or twice, before lowering his face again.

Though I did not doubt my physician's sincerity, his actions put me in mind of the gyrations some of the monks at the abbey would perform, with their genuflecting and kneeling and prostrating themselves, up and down, down and up, repeating the same words over and over again in a high reedy voice until they formed a meaningless gabble.

Farouk continued for a short while, then he rose, bowed to the east, and returned to where I was sitting. "The night is growing cool," he announced, "and I do not think it wise for you to become chilled. I shall return you to your room now."

He helped me to rise from the cushion, and we began shuffling back to the stairs, and had just reached them when the chanting began again. This time, however, the cry did not come from the finger-thin towers, but from the streets below, and it was not one person only, but many voices. I looked to Farouk for an explanation. He simply smiled, and lifted a hand to the raised edge of the roof.

I turned and we made our way to look down into the street where a huge crowd, a veritable multitude, thronged the narrow streets, and they were all chanting and crying out in attitudes of imprecation, as if beseeching the amir for recognition or a favour. I watched them, but could form no opinion of their actions. "What do they want Farouk?"

"They want your health, my friend," he answered.

He chuckled at the expression of incredulity that appeared on my face. "Who are they?" I wondered. "What can they know of my health?"

"It has become known in the city that the amir's new slave is ill," Farouk said, spreading his hands wide. "The people have come to pray for your recovery."

"Why tonight?"

"This night is no different from any other since you came," he told me.

"They come *every* night to pray?" I wondered. "For me?"

The physician nodded and cupped a hand to his ear. After a moment he said, "They ask God to raise up the amir's servant. They entreat Allah, All Wise and Compassionate, to restore your health, and bring you once more to happiness and prosperity. They ask the Holy Angels to stand over you and protect you so that the Evil One may no longer ravage your body and spirit. They ask God's peace and blessing on you this night."

The chanting prayers continued for a time, weaving a curious, ululating music in an unknown tongue. A sharp crescent moon had risen low and now gathered radiance in the night-dark sky. I felt the soft warmth fading in the air, and smelled the evening's sweet perfume. The strangeness of the place swirled around me like currents in a pool of hidden depths; I shivered to think of plunging myself in those exotic waters. Oh, but I was already immersed to the neck.

Their prayers finished, the people began creeping away. In a few moments, the streets were empty once more and silent. I gazed down into the now-quiet darkness with a feeling of curious astonishment. That all those people, unknown to me as I to them, should intercede for me—a mere slave in the amir's house—was more than I could credit.

Sure, I could not help thinking that it would not have happened in Constantinople, or anywhere else in the Christian world that I knew. Indeed, I had stood before the emperor, Christ's own Vice-Regent on Earth, the very Head of the Church Universal, and had received not so much as a cup of cold water, or a kindly word—and I a fellow Christian! But here, a stranger in a foreign land, I had received a continual outpouring of prayer from the moment I had arrived. All this time, they had prayed for me, a stranger unseen and unknown.

Such care and compassion, such blind faith, both astounded and shamed me. That night I lay long awake thinking about what I had seen, and fell asleep wondering what it could mean.

# 49

We walked to the rooftop garden again the next day, and lingered there a little longer before shuffling slowly back to my room. Exhaustion dogged my last few steps and Farouk helped me undress, whereupon I collapsed onto my bed with a groan, feeling as if I had worked the entire day heaving heavy boulders over a wall. I slumped back onto the cushions and Farouk drew the covering over me. I was asleep before he left the room.

He returned the next morning as I awoke. A tray of fruit, bread, and a steaming hot drink lay on a wooden tripod beside the bed. When he saw that I was awake, he sat down and took my hand in the peculiar wrist grip he had used before. He looked at me thoughtfully for a long moment, then replaced my hand, and said, "You are making a good recovery, my friend. As it happens, Amir Sadiq would like to see you today. Shall I tell him you are feeling well enough to sit with him?"

"Yes, of course, Farouk. I would be happy to speak with him whenever he wishes."

The physician smiled. "Then I will suggest that you speak together this morning while you are feeling strong. You can rest again, and then we will walk a little. Yes?"

"Certainly," I replied. "Whatever you think best. I owe my life to you, I think. If not for you, I would have died."

The white-robed physician held up his hands in protest, and shook his head. "No, no, no. It is Allah, All Wise and Merciful, who alone heals. I merely made you comfortable so that this healing might take place." He regarded me with his gentle, dark eyes for a moment. "For myself, I am only glad you are feeling better."

"Thank you, Farouk," I said.

He rose to his feet and said, "I will leave you now and return when I have spoken to the amir. It would be best if you would eat everything I have brought for you. We must begin rebuilding your strength."

Upon receiving my promise, he left me to myself. After a time, Kazimain appeared as I was finishing a bunch of blue-black grapes—the only fruit on the tray which I recognized. She smiled when she saw me, and came to the bedside, knelt, and selected a spherical fruit with a red skin; it looked a little like an apple, but had a tufted knot at one end, and the skin was very tough. She showed me how to break it open, speaking a word as she did so, but I could not make out what it was. Farouk returned just then, bearing a bundle of clothes, and said, "She is telling you that the name of this fruit is *narra*. The Greeks call it by another name, but the word escapes me."

Kazimain pushed her thumbs into the leathery red skin, gave a twist of her wrists, and the fruit split in two, revealing an interior of hundreds of tightly packed seeds, glistening like rubies. She broke off a small section, loosened a few of the little jewels into her palm, and offered them to me.

I took a gemlike seed and put it in my mouth. The tiny juice-filled pip burst on my tongue with a tart sweetness.

"You must take the whole handful at once," advised Farouk with a laugh. "It will take you all day otherwise."

By the handful, the narra was too astringent for my taste, so I went back to the grapes and ate them with a little of the bread. When I finished, Kazimain departed to allow Farouk to dress me in the clothes he had brought: a robe and cloak of green-and-blue striped silk, finer than those I had worn before, and a red silk belt. "You must be suitably arrayed for your audience," he explained, and showed me how to arrange the robe and tie the belt properly.

"Ah, you look a man of elegance and purpose," he declared, acclaiming the result. "Now, the amir is waiting. I will lead you to him. And if you will allow me, I will instruct you in how to conduct yourself in his company."

"I would be grateful," I replied, even though I already had a fair notion of what he expected, which I had learned through observations of the few meetings I had attended when the eparch met with the Arabs in Trebizond.

"It is easily told," said Farouk, leading me from the room. "I will explain as we go."

We started down the long corridor, passing the stairs leading to the roof garden. Instead of going up, this time we turned and descended to the lower level, and into a great hall. "This is the receiving room," explained Farouk, "but, as this is not a formal audience, the amir will see you in his private apartments. It is customary in these circumstances for you to bow upon greeting him. Simply do as you see me do," he told me. "You may invoke Allah's blessing upon him, or you may simply remind the amir that you are his servant awaiting his pleasure."

We made our way across the long reception room, and Farouk explained several other things he thought I might like to know about the ordering of the household. A high, narrow door stood at the end of the room, and Farouk indicated that we were to go through; he pushed open the door and we entered a vestibule with but a single low door at the end of it; the door was rosewood and its surface studded with gold-topped nails arranged in flowing design. Before this door stood a guard with a curved axe on the end of a long pole. Farouk spoke a few words and the guard turned, pulled on a leather strap and the door swung open; the warrior stepped aside, touching his hand to his heart as Farouk passed.

Bending our heads, we passed under the low lintel. "Remember," whispered Farouk, "your life is in his hands now."

With that, we entered a chamber more akin to one of the amir's tents than a palace: tall slender pillars, like tent poles, held up a high roof, peaked in the centre; both ceiling and walls were covered with red cloth that billowed gently in the breeze from four vast windholes which made up a large curved alcove wherein Amir Sadiq and three women sat on cushions, a huge brass tray of food before them. The windholes were covered by enormous pierced wooden screens which allowed both air and light into the room. Through the intricately carved screens, I could see the shimmer of water in a small pond, and I could hear the splash of a waterfall.

At our appearance, the women rose and departed without a word. Farouk bowed from the waist and greeted the amir; I imitated the gesture, but stiffly.

"Enter! Enter!" cried Sadiq. "In the name of Allah and his Holy Prophet, I welcome you, my friends. May peace and serenity attend you while you are my guests. Sit and break fast with me. I insist."

I made to protest that I had eaten already, but Farouk gave me a warning glance and replied for both of us. "To share bread with you, my Lord Sadiq, would be a pleasure most profound."

The amir did not rise, but spread his arms wide in welcome. "Please sit beside me, Aidan," he said, indicating the cushion at his right hand. "Farouk," he said, nodding to his left, "please allow me to come between you and your estimable charge."

"Very soon he will be no longer in my care," replied the physician genially. "In no time at all I shall be on my way home to Baghdat."

"There is no hurry, my friend," said Sadiq. "You are welcome to stay as long as you like."

"Thank you, my lord," answered Farouk, inclining his head slightly. "My affairs are not so pressing that I must rush away all at once. With your permission I will stay until my services are no longer required."

Turning to me, Sadiq said, "It is good to see you standing on your own two feet. You are feeling better, I think."

"I am most grateful to you," I said. "Without your intervention I would have died. My life is yours, Lord Sadiq."

"Allah makes some men of iron, others of grass," the amir replied lightly. "You, I think, are the first material. Now, if you will excuse me, I have exhausted my small supply of Greek. Farouk will convey your words to me, if you agree."

I conceded readily, and remembered that Sadiq had deprecated his Greek-speaking abilities upon meeting the eparch. I watched as he began heaping food into small brass bowls, and thought that perhaps the subtle amir spoke Greek much more fluently and skilfully than he let on. Certainly, he understood more than he allowed. I wondered why he should pretend otherwise.

He placed his hand on my arm, and spoke to me a long burst of their tongue-twisting speech. Farouk, dipping a square of flat bread into a bowl containing a creamy white mixture, listened for a moment, and then said, "The amir says that he is sincerely glad you have survived your ordeal. He knows that you will be concerned about your position in his household, but wishes you to remain at ease in this regard. Later, when you are feeling stronger, there will be time to give this important matter the consideration it deserves. Until then, however, you are considered merely a guest under his roof."

"I thank you," I replied, speaking through Farouk. "Your thoughtfulness is laudable. Again, I am in your debt, Lord Sadiq."

The amir seemed happy with this reply—or with the one which Farouk relayed to him; I suppose it amounted to the same thing. Sadiq regarded me with a directness and an intensity of interest, eating olives and spitting the pits discreetly into his curled fist, nodding to himself from time to time. I ate from the bowl before me, too much aware of his scrutiny to taste much of what I was eating.

"When last we met it was in the company of the eparch," he said, speaking through Farouk. "I have been told that he is dead. If this is true, I am sorry."

"It is true," I answered, my voice going flat; I felt the heat of hatred stirring within. "We were ambushed on the road. Eparch Nicephorus died in the attack, and two hundred or more were slaughtered with him."

"It is a shameful thing which has befallen you," replied the amir gravely; Farouk gave me his words: "As I believe you to be a trustworthy man, I ask you to trust me when I tell you that I had nothing to do with the contemptible ambush. Nor, to the best of my knowledge, did any other Sarazen tribe. This I believe, for I have made it my affair to discover the truth of this incident from the moment I learned of it. Nevertheless, the truth is ever elusive, and I have yet to obtain it in full."

He watched me while Farouk spoke, measuring my response. When I made no reply, he said, "What can you tell us about the ambush?"

"We were travelling to Sebastea and were attacked by

Sarazens," I told him bluntly. "We were more than two hundred—including merchants and the eparch's bodyguard. The enemy came upon us as we slept. Only a handful survived."

Sadiq nodded gravely, and Farouk conveyed his next question to me, "Why do you think they were Sarazens?"

"They were dressed in Arab clothing," I replied, casting my mind back to that hateful day. "Though it is true they spoke a tongue I had not heard before, I saw no reason to believe they were not what they appeared."

"Now, if I may ask, why were you going to Sebastea?"

"The eparch had received a letter from Governor Honorius claiming that the caliph practised treachery upon us and would not honour the peace which Amir Sadiq and the eparch had agreed."

Sadiq made a lengthy reply, which Farouk translated: "This letter was certainly a lie. For reasons you cannot know, the khalifa is most desirous of honouring the peace agreement. Even now he looks with great anticipation to the day when he and the emperor meet face to face to exchange bonds of good faith." He stared at me intently, almost willing me to believe him. "But that need not concern us at this moment."

"Eparch Nicephorus did not believe the letter;" I told him as the memory came back to me, "he thought it a ruse."

"Yet, he proceeded to Sebastea regardless. Why do you think he did that if he believed the letter a deception?"

"I cannot say," I replied. "It may be that he felt he could not risk taking a chance. Or, it may be that he thought that going to Sebastea was the best way to prove the letter false and, perhaps, catch the real traitor. Whatever the reason, I know he suspected treachery—not from the caliph, perhaps, but certainly from some other. He knew the governor as a friend; and he could tell from the letter that, though it was in Honorius's hand, the information it contained was false."

After Farouk had relayed my words, the amir mused upon them for a little time, then asked, "Did Eparch Nicephorus tell you who he suspected of fomenting this treachery?"

"No, lord; he never did," I answered. "But I have reason to believe that it was Komes Nikos. You might remember him as the eparch's aide."

Sadiq's eyes narrowed at the name. "I remember him. This would be a most serious breach of trust for such a man," he cautioned through Farouk, "*and* a most serious accusation for one to make against another."

"I do not make it lightly, or without just cause," I answered. "Two hundred or more people were slaughtered in the ambush, and the few who survived are slaves now; Nikos alone escaped—indeed, he fled the camp on horseback before the attack commenced. And, if that alone were not cause enough, the eparch's expedition was not the first organized by Nikos to end in catastrophe."

The amir wondered at this, so I explained briefly about the pilgrimage, and how my brother monks had come to grief acting on Nikos's counsel and following his guidance. When I had finished, Sadiq conceded, "This puts the matter in a most revealing light. But please tell me," he continued, "do your brother priests yet live?"

"Three only are left alive," I answered. "They are slaves in the same silver mine to which we were sold."

"That is also highly suggestive," the amir remarked through his interpreter. "I discern the shape of a single hand in this disastrous series of events. And I believe you have correctly identified the owner of that hand." His smile was quick and sly. "We, too, have our spies, my friend," he explained. "And what you have told me confirms much of what I have discovered since learning of the ambush and the eparch's death."

He then stood up and clapped his hands twice, quickly and loud. Instantly, a young man appeared, bowed, and approached. The amir spoke to him very rapidly for a moment, whereupon the young man bowed again and departed, his face impassive. "The amir is sending a messenger to the khalifa," Farouk told me.

Amir Sadiq sat down once more, and took up a brass pitcher which sat on a tripod over a candle flame; he poured three tiny cups of steaming liquid, and passed one each to Farouk and me. Raising his cup, he threw back his head and drank it down in a single swallow. I did likewise, and found it a sweet, yet refreshing brew. He then selected a small seeded bread loaf, which he broke in three parts, giving a portion to each of us. We ate for a time, listening to the play of the water outside. When the amir addressed me once more, Farouk translated his words thus:

"I am mindful that you have suffered much on account of affairs that were not of your making," he said. "Still, peace is every man's concern, just as war is every man's curse. You have acquitted yourself with admirable courage through the ill that has befallen you. For this, I commend you highly.

"When word of the ambush reached me, I began searching for any survivors, hoping to find at least one who could tell me what had taken place. You must forgive me for not finding you sooner; the khalifa's slaves are many, and it was not known to which master the survivors, if any, might have been sold. You can be sure that I was as pitiless in my search as the blazing noonday sun. Not even the shadows remained where I had passed!

"The treachery, about which the governor's letter warned, truly exists I fear. But it is not on the part of the khalifa. This I can demonstrate most convincingly, but for now please accept my assurance that it is so. From what you have told me, added to what I have already learned, it seems likely, if not completely undisputed, that the Komes Nikos is acting in alliance with an Armenian faction within Arab borders. As to the attack, I am persuaded that no Sarazens were involved. Those who attacked you were Armenians."

I suppose my dull-witted incomprehension was obvious; Sadiq, studying my reaction, nodded slowly, and then said something very fast to Farouk, who said, "The amir asks you to accept this supposition—for the present at least."

"As you will, Lord Sadiq," I said, "but why should these Armenians wish to do this? I cannot see the benefit of such betrayal."

"The answer remains unclear," conceded the amir. "Even so, I have no doubt that we shall soon discover their purposes: deeds worked in darkness cannot remain hidden in the light. In the meantime, know that I am taking steps to alert both the khalifa and the emperor to this treachery. It is to be hoped that my warning does not come too late.

"And now, my friend," he concluded amiably, "your estimable physician has cautioned me against overtiring you. We will speak again very soon."

Farouk made to rise, but I remained seated. "If you please, Lord Sadiq," I said firmly, "I was not the only one to survive the ambush. There are others, good friends, still enslaved at the mines."

"Their fate, like the fate of all men, remains in Allah's hands," replied the amir when Farouk had conveyed my concern. "But from what Faysal has told me, I think I can tell you that there will be no more killing or torture at the mine. The overseer was a coward and a fool; no doubt he deserved the fate which befell him. The new overseer will not soon forget the example of his predecessor."

"When can they be released?" I asked, apologizing for the bluntness of my question. Farouk frowned, but passed my question along regardless.

"As to their release," Sadiq said, "I would ask you to appreciate that it is a most complicated matter. It may take some time, but I will see what may be done. Be patient, my friend. All is as Allah wills it to be."

Thus, my audience with Sadiq was ended. I wanted to question the amir further, but Farouk warned me off with a glance; rising quickly, he claimed the blessings of the day on behalf of Lord Sadiq, and we departed. Once in the great hall outside, the physician led me from the amir's apartments. When we had passed well beyond the doors, he said, "Let us walk outside a little. The sun is not yet hot, and it will do you good to have fresh air in your lungs."

"Thank you, Farouk," I replied, irritably, "but I would rather return to my room if you do not mind. I am tired." In truth, I wished to think about all I had learned.

"Please," the physician insisted. "It may be that I can tell you something to your benefit." He nodded slowly as I relented, then taking my arm, led me away, saying, "Come, I will show you the jewel of the palace—a delight to the ear as well as the eye!"

# 50

We crossed the spacious hall and passed through a high-curved doorway and out into another world. Green and deep-shaded, shadows abounding, the garden of the amir was a cool haven amidst the oppression of heat and dust of the land beyond the high walls. Monkeys and parrots flitted here and there among the upper branches of the leafy canopy above. Water glinted and sang among the shadows, trickling through brook-like channels, gathering in darkling pools hidden beneath saw-toothed palms and splay-leafed flowered creepers. The liquid song of rippled run-and-trickle played lightly on the ear, murmuring reminders of peace and calm. The paths were many and interlacing, marked out with flat stones to pursue an idly wandering course around a large pond where imperious swans held sway, gliding serenely over the breeze-ruffled water.

Farouk led us along one path and then another, taking turns at random, until we were well beyond the palace precinct and any listening ears. Turning aside into a shady bower, he settled himself on a stone bench and offered me the place beside him. "Let us talk a little," he suggested, "before continuing our stroll."

The small exertion of the morning had all but exhausted me, and I was grateful for the rest. "This is magnificent," I remarked as I settled myself on the low bench.

"The amir is a man of many talents," Farouk said, "architecture is not the least of them. This palace was built to the plans he drew with his own hand—the garden as well. Plants and trees from every corner of the Persian empire find their home here. It is a living work of art."

He looked around him, appreciating qualities of the garden which were, no doubt, veiled to my untutored eye. After a moment, his mouth framed a word, hesitated, and let it go. We sat for a while in silence before he said, "The path of life is rarely straight, I find. It twists and turns always unexpectedly."

This did not seem to require any comment from me, so I made none. The balm of the garden seeped slowly into me as I sat in the dappled shade. After a time Farouk continued. "We live in difficult times, my friend."

"Truly," I replied.

"As the amir rightly suggests, you have borne much for a cause of which you know next to nothing. You desire an explanation, and no doubt deserve one." He did not allow me an opportunity to comment on his observation, but proceeded straightaway. "However, you must understand that Lord Sadiq cannot, at the present time, offer you the accounting you desire. I am certain that he will attend to this matter once he is free to do so. Until then, perhaps you will allow me to be of some small service in this regard?"

His words were carefully chosen, if somewhat circuitous, but pricked my curiosity nonetheless. "By all means," I replied magnanimously. "Please, continue."

"As it happens, our Great Khalifa al'Mutamid, like the amir, is a many-talented fellow. His achievements are legend, believe me. Still, he is human, after all. Thus, I think you must agree that it is difficult for a man of several occupations to excel in them all equally."

"Such a man is very rare," I allowed, as Farouk seemed to want assurance that I followed his meaning—though why he persisted in speaking as if he were giving a formal oration, puzzled me.

"Unfortunately, al'Mutamid is perhaps not so rare as his people believe him to be."

"I see. Some people, I suppose, might have difficulty accepting these human limitations," I ventured, adopting Farouk's tone. "Such men might confuse the mere mention of weakness with treason, for example."

"Or worse!" he quickly put in. "Like an arrow, your intellect has penetrated straight to the heart of the matter, and just as swiftly."

"Such things are not unknown in the land where I was born," I told him. "Where kings rule, lesser men must always take heed for themselves. The truly benevolent lord is a wonder of the world."

"Precisely!" Farouk rushed on, "al'Mutamid is a gifted poet, and his calligraphy far surpasses any seen in a hundred years! Two hundred! And his disputation on theological subjects is rightly renowned far and wide." He paused, willing me to understand.

"Naturally," I allowed, "with so many interests it must be difficult to treat more mundane matters with equal consideration. By necessity, some pursuits will prosper while others languish."

"Sadly, that is the way of things completely," agreed Farouk. "Still, God is good. Our khalifa is blessed with a brother who has made it his duty to shoulder the affairs of state to which, by necessity, the busy khalifa cannot address himself."

"It seems a splendid arrangement," I observed, "and

one which allows both men to fully devote themselves to the pursuits for which they are best suited."

"By Allah!" cried Farouk. "You have grasped the truth entirely."

"Even so, I do not see why this should cause Amir Sadiq undue concern. It seems to me he could direct to either man those matters which concern him, sparing the other needless worry."

"Alas," replied Farouk sadly, "it is not so simple as that. You see, although he is the khalifa's brother, Abu Ahmad is not entitled to wield the authority he, from time to time, must necessarily assume.

"I see how that would make Abu's position somewhat delicate."

"Amir Sadiq is the last in a long and illustrious line of Sarazen princes and is pledged at birth to serve only the khalifa, and him alone. His loyalty must remain forever beyond the taint of suspicion."

"Of course."

"If even the most insignificant breath of a word hinting that the amir entertained a divided loyalty were to reach the khalifa, Sadiq's death would follow as the night does the day."

"That swiftly?" I mused.

"That swiftly," agreed Farouk, "yet not so rapidly that he would not have leisure to witness the bloody executions of his wives and children, and all his household before his own eyes were put out and he himself was impaled and his head carved off with a dull blade."

"Loyalty is a virtue ever in short supply," I agreed.

"As you are a foreigner," Farouk remarked, "you cannot know how we have suffered under the mad khalifas of recent years. I could tell you tales to induce nightmares. Believe me, it is in everyone's best interest that al'Mutamid is allowed to pursue his poetry in peace."

"I believe you, Farouk."

"As you are a foreigner," the physician repeated, "you cannot know that an ugly rebellion has shaken the khalifa's domain to its very foundations. Abu Ahmad and the khalifa's army are even now engaged in vicious warfare in Basrah—that is in the far south. I believe Prince Abu will eventually quench the flames of rebellion, but for now the rebel forces grow ever stronger, more brazen and brutal; their attacks are increasingly bothersome. In one incident alone more than thirty thousand died. The rebels rushed into the city at midday and slaughtered people at their prayers; the blood of the faithful flowed knee deep in the *mosqs*." Farouk paused, his head weaving back and forth sorrowfully. "A most shocking tragedy, and merely one of many. This war is a disease that must run its course; I fear it will get worse before it gets better."

"I see," I replied slowly. Indeed, I perceived full well what Farouk was telling me. The caliph was little more than an impotent idler, content to spend his time writing poems and disputing theology, leaving brother Abu to rule in his stead. The southern rebellion now occupied the caliph's army—which is why peace with the emperor of Byzantium was so important to the Sarazens just now. If these facts were known to the Byzantines, I wondered, would Basil remain content with his peace treaty?

"Perhaps," I suggested, turning to another subject on my mind, "you might offer me your thoughts on the Armenians. I know nothing of them, and my views may well be clouded by recent events."

"Ah," replied Farouk, glancing around quickly, "for that I would need to gather my thoughts. Come, I will take you back to your room." He rose and we began following another pathway. "It is no secret," he began once we were moving again, "that the Armenians came to us seeking refuge from the wicked persecutions practised upon them by unenlightened emperors in the west—refuge which the Arab lords were happy to grant as the Armenians asked nothing save to be left alone to practise their peculiar religion. In return for safety and tolerance, they vowed to regard the enemies of the khalifa as their own, and to fight shoulder-to-shoulder with their Sarazen brothers. This they have done ever since.

"But in recent years, they have grown, shall we say, discontented?" Farouk's glance searched the nearby shadows. "It has been suggested that they no longer feel the protection of the khalifa adequate reparation for their travails."

"Perhaps they believe peace between the Sarazens and the Byzantines threatens the safety they have previously enjoyed."

"Again, my friend," Farouk said, smiling and nodding, "you have captured the matter with admirable brevity and concision. Yes, they fear the peace will bring the renewal of hostilities against them."

Despite the physician's smiles, a sense of dread settled over me. I could see that anyone seeking to thwart the plans of both emperor and caliph could not have contrived a more masterful stroke: an attack on the emperor's envoy together with the rumour that the Sarazens would not abide the peace treaty effectively crushed any hope of peace between the two long-warring empires. If, however, the true source of the treachery could be revealed—and I was certain Nikos was deeply involved—the fragile peace plan might yet be salvaged.

But who held the power to accomplish this feat? The caliph, of course, and perhaps the amir—armed with the information I had provided—could effectively expose the treachery. Anyway, I thought with some small comfort, it was well out of my hands.

"I thank you," I said, "for speaking so forthrightly

about these matters. But, forgive me if I speak bluntly, why have you told me these things?"

"Men in positions of influence must often make important decisions," he observed blandly. "The best decisions are those which flow from true understanding. And, as I said before, you deserve a proper accounting."

"Once again, you have rendered your patient valuable service. Now, I think, I must concentrate whatever small abilities and resources I possess in helping free my friends and brothers who remain slaves in the mines."

"A worthy ambition, to be sure," confirmed Farouk. "I commend you to your task. Still," he stopped walking and turned to me, "I feel I must warn you, that path, should you choose it, is fraught with difficulty. Amir Sadiq has implied as much, and he is right. Nevertheless, he has given you his promise and a more valuable commodity would be difficult to imagine."

"Please, do not think me ungracious," I replied, "but my ignorance prevents me from grasping the nature of the difficulty you describe."

"The principal obstacle, I believe, lies in the manner which Faysal employed to free you."

"He killed the overseer."

"So I understand." We turned then, and I found that we were moving towards the palace once more. "Naturally, such extreme methods, however warranted, often have the effect of complicating matters far beyond our abilities to appreciate at the time."

I accepted what Farouk said, although I was beginning to grow weary of everyone telling me what difficult times we lived in and how I must be patient. I seemed always on the receiving end of such advice, but never in a position to give it. That, I thought, would have to change before I began to get my way.

My kindly physician returned me to my room then,

and I rested through the heat of the day, rising when I heard footsteps in the corridor. Kazimain came into my room expecting me to be asleep. She started when, raising her eyes from the tray in her hands, she saw me standing beside the bed. Curiously, she blushed; colour seeped into her cheeks and throat and she hastened to place the tray on the low wooden tripod. She then turned and departed abruptly, leaving me with the distinct impression that I had spoiled a surprise.

I called after her to wait, knowing she would understand nothing of what I said. As expected, she paid no heed; I listened until her footsteps could no longer be heard, and then went to the door and looked out. Though I could easily be mistaken, I believe I saw her face at the far end of the corridor—just the side of her face, peering around the corner . . . she disappeared the instant I stepped from the room.

I ate some fruit from the tray, and drank the sweet drink from the golden cup, and sat upon my bed pondering what such odd behaviour could mean. I was thus occupied when I heard footsteps in the corridor. This time, I remained seated, waiting for Kazimain to enter when she would. It was not Kazimain who came to me, however, but Faysal, and he brought with him a slender young man with short curly hair and large sad eyes. The young man was dressed in simple white trousers and a short sleeveless tunic; he was barefoot, and his right foot was tattooed with a strange blue mark.

Faysal greeted me respectfully and remarked on my recovery. He then presented the barefoot young man to me saying, "This is Mahmoud. He is to be your teacher." At my inquiring glance, he explained: "The noble Sadiq believes you to be a man of intelligence. Further, it is the amir's belief that you will accede more swiftly to your rightful rank within his household once you are master of your own words. To this end, he has determined that you are to speak like a civilized man from now on."

"The amir is too kind," I replied, my heart sinking at the prospect of having to learn yet another language.

"Be of good cheer, my friend," Faysal told me. "Mahmoud is a master of many tongues. He will soon have you speaking like a true son of the desert."

"Again," I replied, my enthusiasm flagging, "I am in the amir's debt. I will look forward to beginning tomorrow."

"The day is not so far spent that you must defer your pleasure," Faysal countered. "Now is the propitious hour for new beginnings."

"As you will," I said, yielding to Faysal's suggestion. Turning to the young man, I indicated the cushions on the floor. "Please, be seated. Let us begin."

Mahmoud bowed slightly from the waist and folded himself onto a cushion, crossing his legs and resting his hands on his knees. "It is an honour for me to instruct you, A'dan," he told me in singing Greek. "My mother was from Thessalonika, thus I have an affinity for the speech of my earliest memory. I think we shall prosper together." He waited for me to ease myself into a sitting position on a cushion, and then said, "We begin."

With this, Mahmoud began saying the letters of the Greek alphabet, interposing them with their Arabic counterparts. Faysal watched for a moment, then left the room with a smile of satisfaction on his face. Thus began a long and arduous grappling for mastery of what must be the world's most insidious speech. Wonderfully fluid and subtle, it is nonetheless fiendishly difficult to utter for one not born to it.

I might have despaired ever succeeding, but from the beginning I determined that I stood a far better chance of rescuing my friends, and taking revenge on Nikos, if I could speak Arabic. It was to Gunnar and Dugal, then, and for vengeance sake, that I dedicated my efforts. Curiously, this determination took hold in me and produced an unexpected result. For as I dwelt on it over the following days, I began to feel different within myself. This feeling festered like a boil on my soul until it suddenly burst. I remember the very moment it happened. I was standing on the roof as the sun went down on another hot, wearisome day; I was watching the dusky reds and lavenders of the sky deepen towards night, and I suddenly thought: *I will be a slave no more.*

The idea shocked me with its potency. Instantly, as if a long-sealed vessel were shattered, spilling its contents every which way over the floor, thoughts scattered everywhere. Too long had I been the unwitting victim of fate; too long had I meekly accepted as my due whatever those in authority deigned to give me. Too long had I been the dupe of circumstance, the feather blown hither and thither, the leaf tossed on eventful waves. But no more.

*I will be free,* I thought. *Men may rule me, but from now on I will be my own master. I will act, and not be acted upon. From this moment, I am a new man, and I will do what I want.*

What did I want? I wanted to see my friends free, of course, and to see Nikos dead, or in their place. But how to do it? The answer did not emerge at once. Indeed, it took me some time to work out how it might be accomplished. When I finally glimpsed the shape of my ambition, it took a form far stranger than any I could have imagined at the time.

Meanwhile, I redoubled my efforts at learning to speak, as Faysal had it, "like a civilized man." In this I did not suffer alone. Through myriad blunderings, failings, mistakes, errors, and confusion, the patient Mahmoud stood by me, commending my feeble progress and patiently correcting my lapses. It could not have been easy for him to sit with me day after day, often in bitter disappointment over his thick-headed pupil's shortcomings. Nor was it easy for me—I cannot count the times I threw myself down gasping with strangled frustration at the difficulty of making sense.

"It is for your own good, A'dan," Mahmoud would say gently, before adding: "The amir wills it." Then, once I had composed myself anew, we would begin again.

My chief and only solace through this interminable ordeal was Kazimain. She continued to bring me my meals each morning and evening—as I could not speak well enough to attend the amir's table, Sadiq had decreed that I take my meals alone in my room. This was not a punishment, I discovered; he treated his own children the same way. I found this out some time after Farouk departed, pronouncing me well enough recovered to be safely left. Employing my feeble abilities, I spoke to Kazimain one evening when she came with my food.

"The days are growing shorter now," I observed mildly.

She lowered her eyes. "Yes," she agreed. "Soon Lord Sadiq will return and you will begin taking your meals at the amir's table. Then you will see Kazimain no more."

"Truly?" I said. It was the first I had heard of anything like this.

She nodded, her head still bent to her work.

"If my speaking Arabic prevents me from seeing you, then I shall pretend not to speak at all."

She glanced up in horror. "You must not!" she warned. "Lord Sadiq would not be pleased."

"But I do not want you to go away. I like seeing you."

She did not look at me, but placed the tray of food on the tripod, turned quickly, and made to leave.

"Wait," I said. "Stay."

Kazimain hesitated. Then, unexpectedly she straightened and turned back. "I am your servant. Command me."

Her reply, if I understood it correctly, surprised me. "It is tedious eating every meal alone. Stay and talk to me. It will be good for me to speak to someone besides Mahmoud."

"Very well," she agreed. "If that is what you require."

"It is." I sat down on a cushion beside the tray, and gestured for her to join me in my meal.

"It is not allowed," she said. "But I will sit while you eat." She picked up a cushion, moved it further away and sat down. "What would you have me say to you?"

"Tell me about—a," I could not think of the word I wanted, so said, "—Kazimain. Tell me about Kazimain."

"That is a tale soon told," she said. "Your servant Kazimain is kinswoman to Lord Sadiq. My mother was the amir's sister—one of four. She died of fever eight years ago."

"I am sorry to hear it," I said. "What of your father?"

"My father was a very wealthy man; he owned many olive trees and three ships. When my mother died, he grew unhappy and lost interest in his affairs. One night when he did not come to his meal, the servants found him in his room. He was dead," she intoned without emotion. "In our city it is said he died of a wounded heart."

Though I did not understand all she said, I grasped the essence of it, and found it fascinating. I had no words to express my interest, so I merely asked, "What happened then?"

"As the amir was eldest of all his brothers, I was brought here. It is our way," she paused, then added: "Here have I been, and here will I stay—until Lord Sadiq makes a suitable marriage for me."

This last was said with the merest hint of resignation—which I understood well enough, though I did not understand the word she used to describe the marriage. "This would not please you?" I asked.

"My pleasure is to serve my lord and obey his will," she answered mildly, but I sensed a disposition in sharp conflict to her words. Then she gave me a look of such direct and open appraisal, I saw a very different young woman before me than I had known before. "You speak well," she said.

"Mahmoud is an excellent teacher," I answered. "He makes his poor pupil appear better than he is. I am only too aware of how much I do not know, and how much more I must learn. I do not think I shall join the amir's table soon."

She stood abruptly. "Then I will come again tomorrow night so that you may speak to me—if that is your command."

"It is my . . . wish," I said.

She left the room without a sound, leaving only the slight scent of jasmine lingering in the air. I finished my meal and lay on my bed looking out at the night sky, and whispering her name to the southern stars.

# 51

Through casual questioning of Mahmoud, I was able to discover that, after one delay and another, Lord Sadiq had given up waiting for Abu's oft-promised return, and had ridden to the south with a company of warriors—his *rafiq*, I was told; a word which meant companions. These particular companions however, had not been chosen for fellowship's sake, but for other qualities, such as loyalty, courage, and skill at arms.

Although my young teacher did not know why the amir had gone away, I reckoned it was all to do with the information I had given Sadiq regarding the treacherous death of the eparch and the betrayal of the peace treaty. Abu was still fighting the rebellion in the south, and it made sense that the amir would wish to hold council with his superior before attempting to repair the ruptured peace.

Meanwhile, I continued to learn all I could from Mahmoud, a remarkably intelligent fellow, whose knowledge extended far beyond language to include religion and science and music. He could play several instruments and knew many songs, and composed music which he performed and sang. He read whole portions of the Qur'an, the holy book of Islam, and we discussed what he read.

Mostly, however, we talked of ethics, a subject in which Mahmoud was particularly adept, and which the Arabs had developed into a sacred art. Simple hospitality, for example—the ordinary care of visitors observed in some fashion by most peoples—for the Arab faithful imposed enormous spiritual obligations on both host and guest which were transgressed at great peril to the soul. The list of proscriptions, prohibitions, duties, and responsibilities was endless, and the tiniest nuances parsed to the finest hair.

As my strength returned and stamina increased, my lessons were often conducted outside the walls of the amir's palace. Mahmoud took me into the city where we wandered the streets and talked about what we saw. This allowed me the opportunity to question him on the things I found puzzling about Arab ways. We always had much to discuss.

Oddly, the more I questioned, the less I understood; I came to suspect that my questions only served to expose the vast chasm of difference between the Eastern and Western mind that could not be observed from a distance. The life Mahmoud revealed to me was strange in many hundreds of ways, and I began to believe that any similarities between East and West were purely accidental, and not an affirmation of a common humanity. Certain resemblances or affinities of thought I might perceive in the Eastern races were likely to be my own invention; for upon closer scrutiny the imagined similarity was sure to alter beyond recognition, or disappear altogether.

This conclusion, however, was long in coming. I did not hold this view when wandering the streets with Mahmoud. It is always my fate to arrive at a thing too late. To think of the suffering I might have saved shames me now. Still, if I was ignorant—and, oh, I was—at least I was innocent in my ignorance. Pray, remember this.

My first impression of Ja'fariya was of immense wealth; the place was less a city than a congregation of palaces, each more ostentatious than the last. It had been built on the banks of the Tigris river by Caliph al'Mutawakkil to escape the closeness and squalor of Samarra, which itself had been built by Caliph al'Mutasim to escape the close-ness and squalor of Baghdat, a few days' journey down river. Samarra, mere shouting distance to the south of its lavish neighbour, was larger and only slightly less extrava-gant and, save for housing the caliphs and their noblemen, served in every other respect as the official centre of gov-ernment.

Clearly, no expense had been spared by the caliphs on their pleasure homes, or on those works they deemed best able to bring them credit in the eyes of men and Allah. The Great Mosq of Samarra, for example, had been conceived with an eye toward dwarfing all other rivals. From what Mahmoud told me, I reckoned that it had achieved the aim of its patron admirably well. He took me to the mosq on one of our rambles.

"Behold!" he cried, raising a hand to the edifice upon our approach. "The walls you see before you are eight hun-dred paces long and five hundred wide; they sit on founda-tions thick as ten men standing shoulder to shoulder. Forty towers crown the wall-top, and the inner yard alone can contain a hundred thousand faithful and fifty thousand can pray inside! The *minaret* is unique in all the world. Come, A'dan, I will show you."

With that, we stepped through a huge wooden door set in an even greater timber door which formed half of the pair which made an absolutely gigantic gate. There were two men in white turbans standing just inside the door; they wore long white robes with wide belts of red cloth wrapped around their waists many times. Into their belts were thrust the curious curved thin swords of the Arabs.

They regarded us impassively, and allowed us to pass without a word.

"Since the rebellion began," Mahmoud whispered as we moved away quickly, "the mosqs are guarded at all times."

He led me into the immense inner yard: a vast and virtually empty square within the many-towered walls enclosing only the hall of prayer and the minaret which, as he said, was certainly exceptional. "The khalifa was inordinately fond of Babylon's ancient artifacts," Mahmoud informed me. Indicating the steps spiralling up the outside of the prayer tower, he said, "Al'Mutasim copied his design for the prayer tower from the ruins of ziggurats which abound in the south." Mahmoud gazed in admiration at the towering minaret, then added, in a tone that left no doubt regarding the caliph's madness, "He liked to ride to the top of his tower on the back of a white donkey. He kept a herd of white donkeys solely for this purpose."

Turning away from the minaret, we moved towards a low stone basin standing in the centre of the yard; this basin, though shallow, was fully large enough to hold the entire population of Ja'fariya, and was filled with water which swirled about the stone rim where people sat washing their hands and feet before going into the prayer hall.

"The pool," explained Mahmoud, dipping his hands into the running water, "is continually replenished by fresh water from the river in such a way as to make it flow. Washing is sacred to Islam, and standing water is unclean. Therefore, the water in the pool must flow."

A large circular plinth sat near the basin, a bronze spike projecting from its surface. Though its prominence suggested some importance, I could perceive no use for the massive object. "This is the Divider of the Hours," he said when I asked what it could be. "I will show you."

Stepping to the plinth, I saw that the face of the thing

was uniformly flat, and inscribed with a bewildering array of lines both straight and curved which had been etched into the stone. "Heaven's light strikes the marker;" Mahmoud touched the bronze spike, "the shadow falls upon the line," he indicated one of the series of lines, "and as the sun moves the shadow moves, dividing out the hours of the day. By this the muezzin knows when it is time to mount the minaret and make the call to prayer."

"A sun dial," I murmured. I had heard of them, but I had never seen one—not even in Constantinople. The Christian monks in sunny climes could make good use of such a device to reckon the times of prayer, regularly spacing them throughout the day, summer or winter. But then, I reflected, I was no longer a monk and held no interest in the problems of abbey governance and the daily round.

"Come, I will take you into the prayer hall now."

"Is it permitted?" I was still finding the intricate assortment of prohibitions and allowances entirely baffling; it was impossible to guess what might be permitted or denied.

"Certainly," Mahmoud assured me. "All men are welcome in the house of prayer, Muslim and Christian alike. The same God hears our prayers, does he not?"

Mahmoud led me back to the basin where we washed our hands and feet, then proceeded to the hall where we were met by more white-turbaned guards, who regarded us closely, but made no move to hinder us in any way. We lay our sandals alongside those of many others on grass mats provided for the purpose at the doorway. The entrance to the hall was closed, not by a wooden door, but by a heavy green cloth with an Arabic word sewn in yellow.

Mahmoud took hold of the edge of the cloth and drew it back, beckoning me to enter. I stooped under the cloth and found myself in a cavernous dark space, the darkness pierced by shafts of blue light from small round windholes high in the upper reaches of the hall.

The air was still and cool, and I could hear the murmur of voices like the insect drone in an orchard. Owing to the brightness of the sun outside, it was some moments before my eyes adjusted and I could see properly, but the impression of a grove only deepened; before me marched row upon row of slender pillars, like gently tapering trees, their boles illumined by moonlight.

I took a few hesitant steps and felt as if I were walking on cushions; looking down, I saw that the great expanse of floor was spread with carpets—thousands of them—from one wall to the other, thick like moss grown deep on a forest floor.

Soon I was able to make out the forms of people kneeling or standing here and there. A low wooden beam, like a ship's rail, provided a boundary to the right and left. "Go in, go in," urged Mahmoud softly. "Only women must stay behind the rail."

Indeed, there were, I noticed, a few women kneeling in the area provided for them; they wore their shawls over their heads and knelt low so as to disappear. Mahmoud and I passed deeper into the hall, and proceeded towards the place where, in a Christian church, the altar would have been. Here there was no altar, however, nor any other sort of furniture; the only feature to distinguish the place from the rest of the hall was an empty niche, the *qiblah*, Mahmoud told me. "Kneeling thus," he indicated the niche, "we set our faces towards Makka, the holy city."

"What is the significance of this city?" I asked.

"From the beginning of time it is a holy place—the place of the Ka'aba, the House of God built by the Prophet Ibrahim," replied my teacher. "For the Faithful, Makka is the centre of the world. It is also the birthplace of the Blessed Prophet, peace be upon him, and the place where he was called and consecrated to his work. It is the destination of the *Hajj*."

I had never heard this word before, and asked what it was. Mahmoud thought for some moments before answering. "The Hajj is a journey," he said. "But unlike other journeys a man may make, it is both physical and spiritual at the same time, a journey of the body for the good of the soul."

"A pilgrimage," I suggested.

"Perhaps," he allowed ambiguously. "For the Faithful, it is this way: when a man comes to his maturity, he begins to prepare himself for the Hajj. Depending on the man, and where he lives, this preparation may take many years. But one day he orders his affairs and sets out on his way to Makka. When he arrives, he will perform the sacred rituals of our faith: he will perform the Greater Hajj and the Lesser Hajj; he will drink water from the Well of Zamzam, and make sacrifices on the plain of Min; he will make progression seven times around the Ka'aba and go inside to kiss the sacred Black Stone. These things, and others, he will do, as all the Faithful must do, if they are to stand ready before God on the Day of Judgement.

"So," concluded Mahmoud, "when we pray, we face Makka out of respect for this holy place, and to remind ourselves of the journey we must all one day make."

We talked further of such things, and then returned to the heat and sun outside, which seemed, after the cool darkness of the cave-like mosq, akin to stepping into a flaming oven. Again, it took some moments for my eyes to adjust to the light, and then I discovered that someone had taken my sandals. This struck me as most peculiar—that a thief should practise his nefarious craft at the entrance to a house of prayer—and I remarked on it as we stepped back into the street.

"Why does this surprise you?" wondered Mahmoud.

"It is, after all, the way of the world, is it not? The good man goes about his affairs with faith and good will, and the bad man looks only to satisfy his base desires, caring nothing for others, or for God."

"True," I agreed. "Yet, I did not expect to be robbed by thieves within the holy precinct."

Mahmoud laughed at my foolishness. "What better place to steal shoes?"

We walked slowly—and for me, somewhat painfully—back to the amir's palace, stopping often to rest in the shade where we found it. Once, while we sat under a tree beside the road, a man came out of a nearby house and brought us sweetened lemon water to drink. "You see?" said Mahmoud, when he had thanked the man and sent him away with a blessing. "Thieves in the temple and angels in the street. Allah is utterly mysterious, is he not?"

"Inscrutable," I agreed sourly. My feet hurt.

Later that night, when Kazimain came with my tray she brought me a bundle wrapped in blue silk. "What is this?" I asked as she placed the tray on the tripod and the bundle in my hands.

"It is a gift, Aidan," she replied, kneeling beside the tray. I do not know which surprised me more—the unexpected gift, or her use of my name.

I looked at the shimmering cloth and could think of nothing to say. Kazimain tugged at one end of the silk covering. "You must open it," she instructed, "and see what is inside."

"I do not understand," I admitted, fumbling with the smooth material. Kazimain watched me for a moment, smiling, almost glowing with delight. She was more beautiful than I had ever seen her—black hair shining, her deep brown eyes alight with joy, her smooth almond skin slightly flushed with the excitement she felt.

"It is a gift," she said, "there is nothing to understand."

With that, she pulled away the silk to reveal a new pair of sandals, good leather and finely made—far better than the ones I had lost at the mosq.

"Thank you, Kazimain," I said, mystified. "How did you know my sandals had been stolen?"

She smiled slyly, taking immense pleasure in my bewilderment.

"Did Mahmoud tell you?"

She shook her head, her mouth quivering with suppressed laughter.

"Then how did you know?"

"I was there," she said, laughing.

"There—at the mosq? I did not see you."

"Oh, but I saw you," she replied, and her smile took on a mysterious quality—as if she were keeping a secret to herself. "I was praying."

"And what were you praying for?" I asked the question glibly, without a moment's thought; I was so enjoying her laughter and was beguiled by her almost luminous presence, I merely wanted to keep her talking.

But her smile disappeared instantly. She turned her face away, and I thought I had offended her in some way. "Kazimain," I said quickly, "forgive me. I did not mean—"

"I was praying," she began, turning to face me once more; and I saw that her cheeks and throat were rosy; she was blushing. "I was praying that Allah would show me the man I am to marry." She spoke solemnly, but her eyes still held the glow of excitement.

"And did he?"

Kazimain nodded, and glanced down at her hands in her lap. "He did," she answered, her voice growing quiet.

"Who did you see?"

"I prayed that he would show me the man I am to marry," she said again, her head still bowed. "When I finished, I looked up," she raised her eyes to mine, "and I saw you, Aidan."

For the space of three heartbeats neither of us spoke. Kazimain's eyes met mine steadily and I read neither embarrassment nor uncertainty in her glance. She had confided her secret and was now measuring my response.

"Marry me, Kazimain." The words were out of my mouth before I knew what I was saying. I reached across and took her hand. "Will you be my wife?"

"I will, Aidan," she replied, softly acquiescing. Her glance did not falter. As if to emphasize her answer, she squeezed my hand.

We sat there awkwardly for a moment, looking at one another. I had asked and she answered. It was finished just like that. Very likely, she had given me her answer many times before; had I known how to listen, I might have heard.

Nevertheless, none of this surprised me; it was as if this meeting between us was foreordained by a force greater than either of us. I know I had the feeling of events wheeling swiftly over a well-travelled course to a destination long ago established. I felt as if I was merely saying the words I had been destined to say. If there was no surprise, neither was there fear or alarm. The circumstance seemed both right and natural—as if we had talked this way a thousand times, and knew well what the other would say.

"Kazimain," I said, and reached out for her. She came into my arms at once, and I felt the warmth of her embrace filling me with an unutterable certainty. *This*, I thought, holding her, *is the only truth we can know in life. Nothing else in all the world is certain—only this: that a man and woman should come together in love.*

We kissed then, and the ardour of her kiss stole my breath away. I returned her passion with all the fervour I possessed. A lifetime of vows and heart-felt disciplines had prepared me well, for in that kiss I sealed with all my soul the fate before me, embracing a mystery clothed in warm and yielding female flesh. Holding only the moment, with neither thought nor care for the future, I kissed her, and drank deep the strong wine of desire.

I knew, even as we touched, that I had never wanted anything more in all my life. All my crabbed cravings were as a cupful of pondwater beside the vast ocean of longing I felt surging through me. My head swam; my eyes blurred. I burned from inside out as if my blood and bones were consumed with liquid fire.

It was only later, after she had gone, that the awesome implications of what I had done struck me. How could this be? I could not possibly marry her. Even if I wanted to—did I?—would the amir allow it? I, a slave of undetermined rank in his house, was in no position to marry a woman of his tribe. What is more, I was a Christian and she a Muslim. The thing could not be.

I would, I decided, undo what had been done. Tomorrow, when she came with my tray, I would explain to her that it could not be, that I was wrong to suggest such a thing as marriage. It had been but the folly of the moment; I had not been thinking clearly. No doubt she felt the same; she would agree. We had both been careless, perhaps confused. It was only a tiny lapse, after all. Kazimain was intelligent; Kazimain was wise. She would not fail to see how wrong we were, how foolish we had been to imagine what could not be.

"She will understand," I told myself. "She must."

# 52

When Kazimain appeared the next morning, I was amazed and distressed to watch my late-night resolve crumble and melt away like a clump of sand overswept by a sea wave. One look at her and the desire I felt at our kiss rekindled instantly, and flared brighter and hotter than before. The glance of Kazimain's dark eyes as she came into my arms let me know she felt the same.

I clasped her to me and breathed her perfumed essence deep into my lungs, as if I would inhale her into my being. I wanted only to have her, to hold her, forever. The raw force of this feeling struck me with such intensity that it made me weak. I could only stop my limbs trembling by clutching her more tightly. I fell back on the bed and pulled her onto me. We lay there for a time, our bodies shaking with passion. She lay her head against my chest and entwined her arms around me. I felt her gentle weight upon me, and marvelled that I could have existed so long without knowing this simple pleasure and indulging it every moment of every day.

We might have remained like this all day—indeed, I would have been content to remain so for the rest of my life—but the sound of footsteps in the corridor outside roused us. Kazimain smoothed her clothes and we hastily adopted the pretence that we had simply been talking to one another as I broke my fast.

I took up a bit of bread, tore it, and began eating, swallowing my first bite as Faysal stepped into the room. His eyes flicked to Kazimain, who was pouring water from the jar into one of the cups. "Greetings," he said, "I have come to tell you that Lord Sadiq is returning. He arrives in Ja'fariya in two days' time."

"Greetings, Faysal; it is good to see you again. Please," I urged, "Sit down and eat with me. I would hear what news you bring."

He smiled to hear me speaking Arabic so well. "It would be a pleasure," he said, inclining his head. As Faysal folded himself upon a cushion beside the tray, Kazimain poured him some of the sweetened lemon water, and then, rising, made a small bow of deference and left the room, taking my heart with her.

Faysal and I ate together and he told me that the amir and Abu Ahmad had indeed spent many long hours in council, trying to decide what best to do in light of Komes Nikos's treachery. "And did they reach a decision?" I asked.

"It is not for me to say," Faysal replied. "I think, however, my Lord Sadiq will be most anxious to speak to you upon his return."

We talked of other things then—the heat and dust of desert travel, the remarkable abilities of camels in this regard, and the interminable southern rebellion. At mention of Abu's campaign, Faysal shook his head. "Word is not good, my friend," he said. "The revolt has quickly become a war and the khalifa's forces have not been able to contain it as they hoped. Many have been killed on both sides, but the rebels are growing in strength, while Abu's numbers decline."

Although Faysal did not say it, I reckoned by this that the peace with Byzantium was more important to the Arabs than ever before. The rebellion was taxing the caliphate heavily; the Arabs could not fight two different wars on two such faraway fronts and hope to survive, much less win the conflict. I understood very well the predicament the Arabs faced.

After Faysal had gone, I sat and contemplated the curious opportunity this information had created for me. As I sat thinking, it came into my mind that I was in a rare and privileged position: perhaps only one other person in all Byzantium possessed the knowledge that I possessed. And that person was the traitor Nikos, and perhaps even *he* did not guess how much the Arabs needed the peace treaty. Certainly, no one in Byzantium knew of both Nikos's treachery and the Arabs' need. This knowledge gave me power. True, I would have to return to Constantinople to realize this power—a detail which imposed its own difficulties.

But that aside, if I were to reach the emperor and inform him that an attack on the Sarazens just now would win back in one campaign all that the empire had lost to the Arab predation over the years, how long would Basil the Macedonian hesitate? To crush an enemy that has for generations bedevilled the empire would be too sweet a victory to resist. The reward would be mine to name. But could I do it? Could I betray the amir and his people— those who had saved my life—just to satisfy my bloodlust?

Oh, there was power here; I could feel it. Where power exists, danger lies close at hand. I did not cozen myself with illusions that the Sarazens would leave anyone alive who could, with a word, destroy them. I would have to act quickly to protect myself.

When Mahmoud came for me a little while later, I told him that I did not want to go into the city with him today.

"Instead," I said, "I want you to tell me about the customs of marriage observed by the Arabs."

His smile was quick, and his reply suitably oblique. Glancing at my new sandals, he said, "Would this knowledge have for you a practical application, my friend?"

"I am ever curious, Mahmoud, as you know."

"Then I will enlighten you," he said, and made to sit down.

"Not here," I told him quickly. "Come, let us go to the roof garden and enjoy the day before it grows too hot."

Once on the roof, I led the way along the more secluded pathways so that we would not be overheard. As we walked in the shade of small, fan-leafed palms and flowering creepers, Mahmoud began to instruct me in the marriage customs of his race. "It may surprise you," he said, "but there is no single practice which all Arab peoples observe. We are a nation of tribes, you see; each tribe will hold to its own particular rites in such matters."

"Then let us take the amir's tribe—for example."

"Very well," he agreed, "the people of the amir's tribe, for example, come from the southwest where more primitive customs even now prevail. The marriage rite itself is exceedingly simple: a man and woman make vows before their kindred and the woman goes to live with the man in his house. There the marriage is consummated in the usual way, a great celebration ensues, and the two families concerned are ever after united—a unity which is further enhanced by the exchange of gifts."

"What sort of gifts?" I wondered.

"Any sort at all," he answered. "The gifts can vary greatly, depending on the wealth of the respective tribes: horses and camels, for the wealthy, in addition to gold and silver; or, if the young people have no riches they may exchange tokens only." He paused, regarding me critically. "It may serve you to know that to this very day, many of the desert tribes hold to an ancient belief in the chieftain's right to grant or withhold the marriage of his kinswomen. For this reason, the prudent man always seeks to win the tribal leader's approval. Sometimes, he acquires this approval even before asking the young woman. Sometimes, this permission is granted without the bride's consent. The practice remains the same, whether a man has one wife, or many."

"I see."

"If I were to find myself in the position—for example," he mused pointedly, "of wishing to marry a woman of the amir's tribe, it would be to the amir I must address my request. Whether my appeal was granted would be entirely the amir's decision."

I had suspected that this might be the way of it. Similar customs were not unknown in the royal houses of Éire, where, it was held, certain queens in ancient times had kept more than one husband.

"You see," Mahmoud continued, "each marriage forms a bond not only between husband and wife, but between the families, and between tribes, too. The bond thus created is exceedingly strong, surviving even death, and can be broken only by the most extreme acts of violence or repudiation. The law of Islam recognizes this bond and considers it both sacred and holy."

He paused, regarding me curiously. "Touching that, I have naturally assumed both husband and wife are to share a single faith in Islam."

"Naturally," I agreed.

"Otherwise," he added delicately, "the union would not be possible. By Allah, it is strictly forbidden to marry outside the faith—and, of course, to renounce Islam is unthinkable."

"I understand," I replied, and spent the rest of the day pondering how I might gain the amir's approval. I was still deep in contemplation when Kazimain brought me my evening meal. She brought me far more than that.

"You are unhappy, beloved," she said. Putting down the tray, she knelt beside it.

"I have been thinking," I replied, leaning forward to caress her cheek with my hand. She allowed me to stroke her cheek for a moment and then kissed my palm before bending to her work.

"It is said: too much thinking," she replied, pouring my drink into a silver cup, "can bring a man to distraction, and distraction to ruin."

"I truly hope not," I said, "for I have been thinking about our marriage."

"And this has made you unhappy?" She began breaking bread.

"But I am not unhappy," I insisted. "I have been speaking to Mahmoud, who tells me that I must obtain Lord Sadiq's approval to marry you."

"This is so," she affirmed, her chin jutting in agreement. "You must go to the amir and beg on your knees if you wish to marry me."

"I will crawl over burning coals for you, Kazimain," I replied, "if it will secure the amir's approval."

"He will surely give it," she said, smiling.

"I wish I could be certain."

"Has not Lord Sadiq said that you are a guest in his house?" she said. "Hospitality decrees that the requests of a guest cannot be refused. Anything you ask will be granted."

"Anything?" I wondered. Could the claims of hospitality be made to stretch so far?

"Anyway," she continued, "it is not as if I were a woman of no account who must depend upon my kinsman for a bride gift. My father was a wealthy man—"

"So you have said."

"—a wealthy and far-thinking man who provided handsomely for his daughter. I own lands and riches in my own right, and they are mine to do with as I will." She smiled with sweet defiance. "The man who marries me will gain far more than a wife."

"Kazimain, marry me," I said, seizing her hand and kissing her palm.

"I have already said that Allah wills it." Her tone was primly impassive.

"I have nothing to give you," I warned lightly.

"Give me but yourself," she said, "and I will be satisfied." She made to rise. "And now I must go."

"So soon? But—"

"Hush," she whispered, placing her fingertips to my lips. "We must not be found out now. If anyone were to suspect, they might hinder us." She rose and hastened to the door, glanced out into the corridor, and then looked back at me. "I will come to you tonight . . ." She paused teasingly then added, "in your dreams." She kissed her fingertips and raised her hand to me, then disappeared into the corridor.

I ate my meal alone and watched the evening sky deepen to dusk, listening to the muezzin's chanting call to evening prayer. This day, I thought, had gone very well. I had risen early with the firm intention of ending our proposed union, and now I sought it more ardently than ever.

I did love Kazimain, I swear it. But it was not love for her that wakened or nurtured my desire. Christ have mercy, even as she stood offering me the gift of herself, I saw but a way to fulfill the promise I had made to my friends. Revenge was all that mattered to me. Poor Kazimain was merely a convenient means by which this vengeance might be achieved. This, and no kindly regard for that beautiful, trusting soul, is what kindled my passion. I do freely confess this so that all may know what manner of man I had become.

Of my priestly vows, I had no qualm whatsoever. God had forsaken me, and I him. That part of my life was over; insofar as I was concerned, it was God, not me, who had died in Byzantium. So be it.

The next day I prepared for the amir's return, practising what I would say to him. Kazimain and I saw each other only once, and that briefly. She said that to avoid suspicion, she had arranged for another to bring my evening meal. We parted then, and I spent a restless night turning the matter over and over in my mind.

Lord Sadiq returned as expected at midday, and his arrival threw the entire household into a flurry of excitement. I kept myself out of sight, watching the activity from the roof garden, which had become my haunt as no one else seemed ever to go there. The horses of his bodyguard clattered into the street, clearing the way. Two of the rafiq dismounted and went inside to announce their lord's arrival, while the others ranged themselves outside. Meanwhile, servants, slaves, wives, and children hastened out into the street to bid him welcome. They shouted greetings and waved squares of coloured cloth as he rode into view.

Even from my rooftop roost I could tell that the amir was in no gentle mood. Without a word he threw himself from the saddle, bowed stiffly to his wives, and then strode rapidly into the house. This, I thought, boded ill for my plans. True, I did not know what was on his mind to upset him so, but in all likelihood my request would not be greeted with delight.

Still, I did not see any other course open to me. I could wait until the amir was in a better mood, but depending on what was troubling him, I might wait in vain. In the meantime, my position as a guest in his house could change at any moment. Regardless of the outcome, my best chance was to act now.

I prepared myself for the encounter. When I heard footsteps rushing up the stairs to the roof, I knew that the moment had come.

"Lord Sadiq demands your presence," said the servant who had been sent to fetch me. "You are to come at once."

I inclined my head in submission to the request. "I am ready," I told him. "You may lead me to him."

The servant bridled at this. Was I not a slave, like him? But I had schooled my manner well. No more would I behave as a slave. Mine would be the imperious demeanour of the amir himself.

Nevertheless, as the doors were flung open to his reception room and I glimpsed the amir sitting on his great chair, his face contorted by a vicious scowl, my new-found resolve deserted me. Faysal stood behind him, arms crossed over his chest, the frown on his face matching that of his lord's. I gulped down a deep breath, gritted my teeth and forced my feet to shuffle ahead. The servant saw my dismay and smiled in derision. This angered me, and I plucked up my flagging courage and strode into the glaring amir's receiving room as if I were the Holy Roman Emperor himself.

The first words out of the amir's mouth, however, all but destroyed my fledgling determination. "You did not tell me you were a spy for the emperor," he charged. "I should have let them kill you. It would have saved me the trouble." He clapped his hands sharply, and three of his warriors rushed forth, seized me by the arms, and forced me to my knees. Another warrior approached, carrying a curved axe on a pole.

"Well?" demanded the amir. "Have you anything to say before you die?"

# 53

I will speak," I said, forcing strength to my voice. "But I will not beg for my life on my knees. You demand an explanation, Lord Sadiq, and I will give it—only, allow me to stand before you like a man."

These words both surprised and, I think, pleased the amir. Like many men of power and influence he respected courage and plain-speaking. He gave a twitch of his hand and the warriors raised me to my feet. I stood, smoothed my clothes, and stepped forward. Though trembling inside, I forced myself to appear calm and unconcerned.

"So!" snapped the amir impatiently. "You are standing like a man. Explain yourself—if you can. I am waiting."

"I will explain, lord," I said, "but as a guest in your house, I would first make one request."

His face hardened at these words and his dark eyes narrowed dangerously. Clearly, he did not like me invoking the demand of hospitality. He glowered at me murderously, his voice a coiled serpent about to strike as he inquired, "What is this request?"

"I ask your permission to marry Kazimain, your kinswoman."

Lord Sadiq stared at me as if I had lost my mind. Perhaps

I had, for until the words were out of my mouth, I had not truly intended to say them. Indeed, it had occurred to me to request my freedom instead. Had I done so, however, I would never have been able to see Kazimain again and on my own, I had no chance at all of obtaining my revenge. At the last instant, I had asked the greater boon knowing full well it would be denied. Far better, I decided, to die trying than never having tried at all. In the end, if blood were to flow, it made little difference whether I was slaughtered as a goat or a lamb.

"Marry Kazimain!" A look of amazement transformed the amir's features. He shook his head slowly as if he had been struck a blow. "Can I believe my ears?" he demanded, and stared around him as if he expected an answer. Before I could speak, he shouted. "No! It is impossible! I should kill you now and rid the world of your impudence!"

"As a guest in your house," I replied with all the composure I could muster, "I must demand that you honour the claims of hospitality."

"What do you know of such things?" he roared. "You are a slave in this house!"

"A slave I may be, lord," I conceded, "yet until such time as my position in your household has been decided, I remain a guest under your roof." He grimaced at my allusion to his own words, but said nothing. Faysal's frown, however, had altered to an expression of astonished admiration.

"The words were yours, not mine," I said. "The physician Farouk was kind enough to translate for me. If there is any doubt, I am certain he will recall the conversation."

"Yes! Yes!" Sadiq cried impatiently. He whirled away from me, stalked to his chair and flung himself down in it. He sat glaring at me for a moment. "Well? Will you yet speak?"

"I would be most happy to tell you whatever you wish

to know, lord," I replied evenly. "First, however, I require an answer to my request."

"And I have already told you!" he shouted. "It is impossible; a woman of nobility cannot marry a slave. The disgrace would be past enduring. Then there is the matter of faith: you are a Christian, she is a Muslim, and that is the end of it."

"For my part, I am willing to embrace Islam for her," I told him, squaring my shoulders. "But, if our marriage is impossible, I have nothing further to say." Strange to tell, but my pretence of defiance actually made me feel more bold. I returned Sadiq a steady gaze, courage mounting with every thumping beat of my heart.

The amir stared at me balefully. "You are a slave and a traitor," he intoned.

"A slave I may be, lord," I answered. "But I am no traitor. If someone has suggested this to you, he is either mistaken or a liar."

The amir turned his head to look at Faysal, who only gazed back in bewilderment. "Never have I encountered such audacity," declared Sadiq. "Is this the gratitude my benevolence has earned?"

"What manner of benevolence is it that seeks the death of the guest who shelters beneath the amir's protection?" I charged, and at once feared I had pressed him too far.

He growled and dismissed my question with a flick of his hand. I pressed my attack with a brazen disregard for life and limb. "Consider, O Benevolent One," I said, stepping forward a pace, "that marriage creates strong ties of blood. Naturally, a man constrained by such bonds would not betray his lord, for to do so would be to betray himself. Who but the most vile and contemptible craven would even ponder such a thing?"

Amir Sadiq cocked his head to one side and gave me a

long, grudging look, then looked away as if the sight wearied him. "No doubt it was a mistake to teach you to speak. But as you have found your tongue," he said, affecting scorn and impatience, "please continue."

"Kazimain and I wish to be married," I stated. "You say it is impossible since I am a Christian and a slave. Yet, I am willing to convert, and you hold it in your power to grant my freedom. Do it, Lord Sadiq. Perform the impossible, and men will marvel at your power—"

"Men will marvel at my foolishness!" he sneered.

"No." I shook my head slowly. "Your generosity and sagacity will become legendary. For in one bold act you will have freed a man beholden to you and secured him with ties more binding than any slave's chain could ever be—ties of loyalty and blood."

Lord Sadiq said nothing for a long moment; he simply sat staring, his gaze deep and searching. I stood assured before him, confident in my claim. Incredibly, I felt no fear. I had cast my lot and could do no more; it remained for him to decide my fate.

The amir clapped his hands and I thought he would proceed with the execution. Instead, Sadiq shouted, "Bring Kazimain!"

We waited in silence while servants went to fetch the young woman. The amir said nothing, but remained carefully watchful—as if he thought I might vanish in a wisp of smoke if he did not keep an eye on me. For myself, I bore the waiting easily, secure in my new-found confidence.

Soon, Kazimain appeared, hastened into the hall by two of the amir's bodyguard who led her to stand before the amir and then took their places with the other warriors standing behind us. Kazimain did not look at me; she kept her eyes on Lord Sadiq all the while. To her credit, she betrayed neither fear nor alarm, but maintained an impassive expression. There was, I thought, more than a hint of determination in the set of her jaw, and her glance remained keen.

"I have loved you like a daughter, Kazimain," Sadiq said quietly. "Therefore, it distresses me to hear the lies this man has been speaking about you."

"Lies, amir?" she wondered. "What lies are these?"

"He says that you two wish to be married," replied Sadiq. "He says that you have agreed to this. I suspect it is nothing more than a clumsy ruse thrown up like dust before a wind to distract me from his genuine motives. I would know the truth."

"If these are the lies that you find so distressing," she replied coolly, "then allow me to put your mind at rest." The amir's quick smirk of satisfaction faded at once as she continued, saying, "Aidan is not lying. He is telling the truth."

She said it so calmly that the amir did not seem to hear at first. He made to rise from his chair and then stopped in mid-motion and fell back again. "Kazimain," he implored, "do you know what this means?"

"I know when someone has asked me to marry," she answered smoothly. "And I know well when I have agreed."

Lord Sadiq looked from her to me and back again, tapping the arms of his chair with his fingertips. "What if I said that I thought you were saying these things merely to save his worthless life?"

"If you were to tell me such a thing, my lord," Kazimain replied without hesitation, "then I would say that it is the amir who is telling lies. The truth is that Allah has brought us together and, out of obedience, we wish to be married."

"He is a slave, Kazimain," the amir pointed out.

"Who holds the power to change that," wondered Kazimain, "if not the amir himself?"

"That is what *he* said," grumbled Sadiq. He tapped the

arms of his chair for a long moment. I could see him struggling to grasp the implications of the circumstances arrayed before him. Sure, the thing had taken a strange leap; he was no longer certain what to say or do.

Here, Faysal endeavoured to help. The amir's advisor stepped forward and bent to whisper in his ear. Sadiq listened, nodded, then said, "Before I could grant such a request as this man has made, I must be certain in my heart that he was not a spy sent here to help bring our people to destruction."

"As to that," I said, "I have offered to tell you whatever you wish to know once I have obtained my request."

"I must have more than that!" snapped the amir. "You are asking gold and rubies of me, but offering only dung and pebbles in return."

We had reached an impasse; neither of us could move without giving valuable ground to the other. Kazimain took it on herself to break the deadlock.

"My Lord Sadiq," she said, "is not a spy by nature scheming and duplicitous? What schemes has this man fomented? What duplicity have you discovered in him?"

"None," admitted the amir. "Yet, lack of discovery does not mean there has been no deception. A spy will necessarily be skilled in hiding his deceit."

"Thus," pursued Kazimain, "lack of deceit becomes proof of deception. Innocence confirms guilt. If that is what justice has become, Wise Amir, then all men stand condemned."

"You twist my words, woman!" growled the amir. Turning his face to me, he said, "The accusation has been made and is yet to be denied."

By this I knew that he was softening. I decided to risk meeting him halfway. "Were I to gain approval to marry your kinswoman, the problem would cease to be important," I pointed out.

"You are saying this to save your life," Sadiq maintained, but the fight was going out of him.

"I am saying it because it is true," I countered. "If it helps save my life, well and good. If not, you will have killed a loyal and trustworthy man, and one who has ever treated you with gratitude and honesty. I can say no more."

"If I grant you the approval you desire," said the amir, his tone that of a horse-trader seeking to make the best of a bad bargain, "will you yet treat me with honesty and loyalty?" I opened my mouth to speak my affirmation of his offer, but he stopped me with a raised finger. "And will you answer all my questions to my complete satisfaction?" He lowered his hand, inviting my reply.

"Lord Sadiq," I told him, "whether my answers will indeed satisfy you, I cannot warrant. But you have my word that I will answer your questions in all truth."

"You expect me to rely on the word of a slave?" demanded the amir.

"Even as my life depends upon yours," I said. "For my part, I have seen enough to know that you are a man of honour who makes no vow he cannot fulfil. Whatever promise you undertake, I will trust it with my life."

This response pleased him inordinately. His smile was so quick and genuine, that his anger now seemed to have been mostly bluff. I had surprised him, but his greater interest lay in learning the truth. Threats were simply the quickest and surest way to obtain it.

Turning to Kazimain, he adopted a gravid air once more, saying, "It is shameful for a woman of a noble house to marry a slave." He paused, fingering his bearded chin thoughtfully. "We cannot allow our kinswoman to bear such a disgrace. Therefore, I suppose we must do something about the rank of this man whose proposal of marriage you have accepted."

Turning to me, he proclaimed, "Aidan, you came to me a slave, but from this day you shall call no man master. With Allah, All Wise and Compassionate, as my witness, I return to you your freedom."

"Thank you, Lord Sadiq," I said, bowing with genuine gratitude.

"You are free, my friend," he said. "Go in peace."

I do not know if this last was said to trick me, or confuse me into making a blunder, but I told him, "I am content to remain at your side as long as you will have me. I would consider it both duty and joy to serve you in some small way."

Sadiq beamed with pleasure. "The choice is yours." Motioning to Faysal, who leaned near, he said, "The apartments vacated by my former advisor have been unused these past two years; see that they are prepared at once. Also, the silver formerly paid for these services will from this day be paid to Aidan."

"Lord Sadiq," I protested quickly, "I ask nothing more than I have already been given. I am a man of simple needs; it is more than enough."

"You, my friend, are a man soon to acquire a wife and, in due course, Allah willing, many children. Your days of simplicity are, I fear, quickly approaching an end. In any event, I could not possibly allow my kinswoman to marry a fellow lacking the means to support her properly."

"I am overwhelmed by your generosity, my lord, but—"

The amir raised an admonitory hand. "Try me in this," he insisted. "I know whereof I speak." He stood and spread his arms wide. "Now then, allow me to be the first of many to extol your impending marriage, and offer my felicitations."

Kazimain ran to her uncle, throwing herself into his embrace. She kissed him on both cheeks and kissed his hands also. I followed, stepping forward somewhat awk-wardly—still trying to comprehend what had just hap-pened to me—gripped his hands and embraced him. Kazimain thanked him, and I thanked him; she kissed both of us many times and, with tears gleaming in her eyes, pro-claimed it the happiest day of her life.

Then, before I could speak even a word to her, she darted away, saying that she must tell everyone what had come about. She disappeared from the hall in a rush.

"I believe you must be touched by God," the amir said, watching her go. "The man who has won Kazimain's heart has claimed a treasure worth many kingdoms. One day you must tell me how you accomplished this remarkable feat."

"That is a secret," I replied, "I shall guard with my life."

Lord Sadiq laughed at this, turned and commanded Faysal to have refreshments brought to his private rooms. Placing his hand on my shoulder, he led me from the reception hall saying, "And now, my friend, I think it time we began telling one another the truth."

# 54

The amir poured the cool sweet lemon water into golden cups, and passed one to me. He had dismissed Faysal and the other servants so that none should overhear. Leaning back on his cushions, he eyed me shrewdly and, after a sip from his cup, said, "You may speak freely. On my honour, no harm will come to you. If I placed so much as a finger to the tip of your nose, Kazimain would have me boiled in oil."

"I am your servant, Lord Sadiq. I will tell you anything you wish to know."

"Then begin by telling my why you are doing this." Before I could ask what he meant, he added, "Are your feelings for Kazimain genuine?"

"What I feel for Kazimain," I answered, "I have never felt for any other woman."

The amir smiled. "You are most adept at paring the truth to its finest point. But come, let us be done with this childish game. Since you remain reluctant to speak openly, perhaps you will allow me to begin." He sipped from his cup, watching me over the rim. When he finished, he placed the cup on the brass tray, touched the back of his hand to his mouth, and then said, "All you told me of the Armenian treachery, I repeated to Abu Ahmad. While he agreed that it explained much, he determined that it was necessary to test the validity of this information. Thus, inquiries were made through means available to the khalifa."

"Yes?"

"And it was learned that all you said was true."

"If all I said was true, then obviously, I must be a spy—is that what you thought?"

His sly smile returned. "It was determined that an additional test was required," he explained. "After all, who else could know so much? Only a spy of the emperor could possibly command such intimate knowledge."

"Would such a spy," I asked, "also arrange to have himself sold as a slave? Would this same spy arrange his own death at the hands of his torturers?"

"Misfortunes abound," answered Sadiq, "even for the emperor's spies. No doubt you were caught in Nikos's treachery along with the others and thus prevented from carrying your information back to the emperor. If I had not discovered your whereabouts, you surely would have died."

"I am truly grateful to your highness," I told him sincerely.

"Yes, and you have taken wonderful advantage of your position," he continued. "But let us make a bargain between us: I will give you a thousand denarii in silver, and I will see you safely to Trebizond where you can board a ship to take you back to Byzantium—or wherever you wish to go." He leaned forward. "All this is yours if you tell me what I wish to know."

Growing wary, I said, "Why do you suggest this bargain?"

"So that you will know that you do not have to marry Kazimain merely to obtain your freedom. Tell me the truth and I will let you walk free. Do you agree?"

"Very well," I acceded, "I agree. What do you wish to know?"

"The truth—are you a spy?"

"Yes, I am."

"I knew it!" The amir's fist struck the brass tray, upsetting the cups and spilling the drink. "I knew it!" he cried—as much in relief as vindication.

"I am a spy," I confessed again, "but perhaps not in the way you think."

"I must know the truth," Sadiq insisted. "It is of utmost importance, believe me. Who is your master? What is his purpose?"

"Everything I have told you is the truth. I was indeed a slave to Harald Bull-Roar when he came to raid Constantinople. It so happened that while we were there I was able to perform a small service for the emperor—"

"So he freed you, and took you into his service," suggested Sadiq.

"No, lord, he did not. He might have, but that is not his way. Instead, he made the Danish king part of his mercenary force and sent the Sea Wolves to guard the eparch and the merchant ships on their voyage to Trebizond. He said that if I performed a certain task for him, we would discuss my freedom when I returned."

"What was this task?"

"To watch and listen to all that was said and done in Trebizond during the peace mediations and to bring him word if I should discover anything suspicious regarding the eparch."

"The eparch!" wondered Sadiq, plainly surprised. "Did he doubt the eparch's loyalty?"

"He did not tell me why, but he seemed to me a man deeply concerned with trust and loyalty. I think he mistrusted the eparch—unnecessarily, in all events."

"He should have mistrusted this Nikos," mused the

amir. Glancing at me, he said, "So, you were to watch the eparch. That was all? Nothing else?"

"Nothing else."

"You were not to watch the Arabs, perhaps? Even a little?"

"In all truth, he said nothing to me regarding the Arabs. He had no reason to believe that I would ever be in a position to be privvy to intelligence from that quarter, amir. He did not anticipate my present situation. You must know that the emperor is as anxious for the peace as is the khalifa. Byzantium needs it as much as Samarra, if not more."

"Why is this?"

"Emperor Basil seeks the increase in trade and commerce if he is to pay for his new palaces and public buildings. The imperial city has been neglected for decades; renovation on such a massive scale requires an unending supply of wealth."

"Ya'allah!" Sadiq nodded in rueful agreement at this. "If only the rulers of this world had smaller appetites."

"Now you know the truth," I told him. "I watched and listened to what was said and done in Trebizond—for all the good that came of it. The eparch is dead, and the traitor remains free to continue his treacheries. The warring and raiding will resume, and—"

"No," said the amir earnestly, "the fighting will not resume. This is what Abu Ahmad has determined. We will abide the peace we have sought and won." He paused. "This is why I was forced to test you, my friend. I had to know what manner of man I had entrusted with the future of our people."

I did not know what he meant, but it sounded farreaching and vaguely ominous in my ears. "Your future, amir?"

Sadiq clucked his tongue over my bewilderment. "Ah,

indeed you are a sorry spy," he replied lightly. "You held the fate of the Arab people in your hands, for you knew our weakness—a thing even the notorious Nikos does not suspect."

"The rebellion?" I said. "I learned about that long ago. Had I been the sort of spy you imagined, I would have run to the emperor as soon as you left the palace."

"Obviously."

"But I stayed."

"Yes, you stayed."

"Even so, you thought me a traitor. You threatened to kill me—"

"I would certainly have killed you," Sadiq maintained firmly, "if you had lied to me." He spread his hands and placed them flat on the table as if to push the unpleasantness from him. "Please, understand; with so much at hazard, there could be no mistake."

"And Kazimain—did she know? Was she watching me?"

The amir glanced away. "Kazimain . . ." he began, and hesitated, "She knew, yes."

"I see." I nodded absently. The heatflash of anger flared quick and hot, then swiftly abated; in its place settled a sour humiliation. I had been made a fool. It came to me that I had felt exactly this same way before: upon discovering Gunnar had waited in the forest all day to see if I would run away from him; the Watching-Trial, he called it. Well, I had unwittingly undergone a second watching-trial, and found it no more to my liking than the first.

Sadiq righted the cups and poured more drink; he placed a cup before me, poured one for himself, drank, and began speaking again, his voice taking on a tone of urgency, but I was thinking: *Why must my loyalty be always put to the test? Am I so unreliable, so inconstant that those above me cannot trust me otherwise? What is it about me that fills everyone with such doubt?*

". . . Abu has agreed," the amir was saying, "it is of utmost importance. We are to leave at once, taking only—"

Hearing the last of this, I glanced up quickly.

"I am sorry, my friend," said the amir, mistaking my stricken look, "your marriage must wait a little longer, I fear. Certainly, we will return here as soon as possible, and I will gladly provide a wedding celebration to surpass all celebrations. This shall be my gift to you both, but as it is—"

"Please," I said, "where are we going?"

"To Byzantium," he answered, mildly surprised that I should ask. "Did I not just say so? The treachery of this man Nikos must not be allowed to obstruct the peace between our peoples. He must be stopped before fighting begins again."

"By all means, Lord Sadiq," I concurred, quickening to the thought. For I suddenly saw the opportunity I desired above all else: I could have my revenge, and I would not have to betray the amir to get it. "But it occurs to me that we will need help."

The amir appeared taken aback by my suggestion. "What help would you suggest?"

"I am not the only one who knows what happened in Trebizond, nor the only one who survived the ambush on the road to Sebastea. If we are to confront Komes Nikos with his crime, it seems to me that the more voices raised in condemnation, the better. You will remember that I was last seen by the emperor when I was slave to a barbarian king. If the basileus is to credit what I say, I must have help."

Sadiq regarded me with dark, unfathomable eyes. "This help, of which you speak. I suppose it has a price?" He sounded disappointed.

"Only this: obtain freedom for my friends, and we will help you stop Nikos and renew the peace."

He waited, expecting me to say more. "What else do you require?"

"That is all."

"Freedom for your friends?" wondered Sadiq, surveying me dubiously. "Nothing else? You must hate this Nikos more than I suspected."

I felt my stomach tightening into a knot of anticipation. "Can it be done?"

"Allah willing, it might be arranged," the amir replied, tapping his chin thoughtfully. "But let us understand one another: if I achieve this feat, you will go with me to Byzantium and aid me in restoring the treaty?"

"We will do whatever you ask," I vowed.

"Then we must pray the khalifa is in his right mind today," Sadiq replied, making his decision. "If you like, I will inform Kazimain that the wedding must be delayed a little."

"Thank you," I said, "but I will tell her myself."

"As you wish." Sadiq rose to his feet. "You must excuse me," he said, "there is much to be done—and quickly." He clapped his hands, and Faysal appeared as out of nowhere. "I have an urgent message for the wazir," he said. "We require an audience with the khalifa at his earliest convenience—today. Go!"

To me, he said, "Rise up, Aidan. If my new advisor is to accompany me, he must be arrayed like royalty."

The amir led me to another room where his clothes were kept in sandalwood chests. He chose a new robe and cloak for me, then summoned servants to come and prepare me for my audience. "Make him appear a nobleman," he commanded as he left the room. "For today this man must stand before the khalifa!"

When they had completed this task, Faysal came in carrying a bundle wrapped in blue silk. "For you, Aidan," he said. "The amir wishes you to have this."

I opened the bundle to reveal a knife of the kind the Irish call a *daigear*, but unlike any I had ever seen: all silver and gold of the most wonderful craftsmanship, worked into fantastic leaf-and-tendril designs and studded with rubies, emeralds, and sapphires. The blade, however, was of a metal called steel, and sharper than the cut of the keenest razor. I could hardly take my eyes from the knife long enough to thank Faysal.

"All Sarazen noblemen wear such a knife," he said. "It is called *Qadi*."

"Judgement?" I wondered. "Why that?"

"Because," said Faysal, taking the treasure and tucking it into my belt properly, "a man must sometimes rely on his own hand for justice, and when Qadi speaks, arguments cease."

Stepping away, he pronounced me an acceptable likeness of an Arab nobleman, and said, "Now you are ready to meet the khalifa. May Allah grant you favour in his sight."

# 55

The Caliph of Samarra was sitting under a fig tree in the palace *arboretum*. He had, it was explained, been sitting under the tree for five days, awaiting inspiration from the angel Gabriel for the completion of a poem recently begun.

"Perhaps," Wazir Tabataba'i suggested discreetly, "your business with the khalifa would be more auspiciously conducted another day."

"All business should be conducted in gardens under fig trees," countered the amir. "The world would be a far better place. We will be happy to greet the khalifa in his garden."

"As you will." The black-turbaned wazir bowed graciously, but I perceived a note of warning in his tone. He turned and led us through the vast, empty reception hall, his dark blue robe billowing behind him like a sail, his soft-slippered feet silent on polished green marble floors.

We walked through one enormous room after another, passing beneath blue-painted domes as big and deep as the heavenly skybowl; some were even pierced by thousands of tiny star-shaped holes to imitate the night sky. Tall pillars upheld these domes, and the grand, shapely arches. The walls of some of the rooms were covered with blue-and-green painted tiles; others were painted red or warm ochre, and decorated with gold-leaf peacock plumes. Along the walls there were chests and boxes—and in several rooms, throne-like seats—of exotic woods inlaid with gold and silver and pearl. And everywhere were rugs and carpets of the most cunningly intricate design and colour. We passed one room where the ceiling was covered with red-striped cloth that hung loosely down from a central timber pillar, so that the room entirely resembled a tent.

The wazir then led us along a wide corridor of onyx columns and out into a walled garden with a fountain in the centre, through this to an iron scroll-work gate and into the arboretum, or tree garden, where dwelt his master, awaiting divine inspiration.

I felt slightly foolish and out of place: my clothes were far more extravagant than anything I had ever worn; the turban made my head feel several times too large and dangerously unsteady; the oil on my moustache kept getting onto my lips, making them feel slippery and strange; the knife hilt dug into my hip bone, and I greatly feared wounding myself by bending over too quickly. In all it was, I suppose, a necessity, but I would have been far more at ease and confident if less had been made of me.

But the amir, having insisted on this course, had departed, leaving me to the expert ministrations of his servants. First, I had been stripped naked and washed with scented water poured from a tall, slender ewer into a huge brass bowl in which I was made to stand. My hair, long now and without a trace of tonsure anymore, was dressed with perfumed oil, and my skin as well. Then, one after another, various coloured tunics were brought and tried until they settled on one to match the red robe and cloak the amir had chosen. Next I had been given a wide black belt which wrapped my waist four times, and a pair of soft black leather boots. A long narrow strip of creamy white cloth became a turban, the end of which was secured with a ruby pin. It was as they were finishing that Faysal had entered carrying the Qadi-knife. Thrusting the blade through a fold in my belt, Faysal pronounced me ready and I was conducted to the courtyard where Sadiq was waiting.

Two milk-white horses stood in the yard and the amir was watching his grooms saddle the wonderful animals. At my approach, he turned and his handsome face brightened with genuine pleasure. "Ah! A very Prince of Persia! Please, do not let Kazimain see you, or she will never allow you out of her sight."

"Do you think me ready to stand before the khalifa?" I asked.

"My friend," intoned Sadiq seriously, "were you going to meet Allah himself, you could not look any finer. Now then, when was the last time you sat a horse?"

"I cannot remember."

Sadiq frowned. "I thought as much . . ." Turning abruptly, he called to one of the grooms. "Jalal! Take Sharwa away. Bring Yaqin instead." To me he confided, "You will find her more to your liking."

The stableman left the courtyard on the run leading one of the white horses—only to return some moments later, leading a pale grey mare with a black tail, mane, and forelegs. The sunlight on the animal's coat made it look silky. "Ah, yes," sighed the amir appreciatively. "She is a wonder, this Yaqin." He stepped to the horse and patted her smooth neck, and motioned for me to do the same. "Here, Beautiful One, is my friend Aidan," he said, speaking softly into the horse's ear. "He is a good fellow. Do not disgrace him, please."

As if in answer to the amir's request, the mare tossed her head up and down, and nuzzled Sadiq's neck. "Later," the amir said, scolding lightly, "if you behave yourself, you shall have a fig." To me, he said, "She has developed a liking for honeyed dates as well."

We watched the stablemen go about saddling the horses; they accomplished their work deftly and efficiently, handling the horses with polite firmness. "It is a sin," observed Sadiq idly, "to mistreat a horse." He clearly enjoyed his horses, and lavished great affection on them. "A very great sin. One of the worst."

"Mahmoud tells me all men shall ride such horses in paradise," I mentioned.

"That is true," Sadiq agreed. Having finished with the horses, one of the stablehands led the white horse to the amir and passed the reins to him. Lord Sadiq placed his foot in the stirrup and swung himself up into the saddle. "Let us pray, however," he said, "that we live to ride through the streets of Byzantium first."

We then made our way in slow and stately progress along the wide central street of Ja'fariya to the khalifa's palace, drawing stares and greetings from the people in the streets as we passed. Upon arriving at the palace, we were greeted by the wazir and led through one stunning room after another to our audience with the most powerful man in the whole of the Arabian empire.

Caliph al'Mutamid, by the will of Allah, Ruler of the Abbasids, Protector of the Faithful, was a round-shouldered fat man with a long, wispy grey beard and soulful dark eyes. He was arrayed like one of his fabled thousand peacocks, in lapis lazuli blue and emerald, with sparkling flashes of crimson. Each garment was interwoven with gold and silver threadwork, and a peacock plume surmounted his bulging satin turban of glistering grey. His wide belt was the same satiny stuff, and he wore a long, curved dagger with a golden, gem-studded handle protruding from the folds across his dome-shaped belly.

As the wazir had told us, the Great One sat under a large, full-leafed fig tree, propped up on *damasc* cushions, a small writing desk ready to hand should the awaited inspiration strike. Around him lay bowls of fruit and breads of various kinds—to help fortify him for his vigil, no doubt. Two braziers sent clouds of fragrant incense wafting on the soft breezes stirring beneath the leafy canopy of branches.

Had I been a poet in the khalifa's place, I believe the garden itself would have supplied inspiration enough for many great works; it appeared the very semblance of what God must have had in mind when he created Eden. Neither leaf, nor bud, nor branch, nor blade of grass was misplaced; each plant and every tree was the paragon of its kind, residing in perfect harmony with every other plant and tree. But the caliph, far from basking in the serenity of his beautiful surroundings, appeared bored and unhappy; he sat slumped in his cushions as if he had been dropped there from a great height.

At our approach, al'Mutamid roused himself from his stupor and sat up, blinking his eyes. "Tabataba'i!" he cried. "There you are! How dare you keep me waiting like this!"

"Calm yourself, excellent one," soothed the wazir with exaggerated patience. "Amir Sadiq has arrived. He wishes a word with your highness." He bowed and gestured the amir forward. "I will leave you to discuss your affairs in private."

"By all means, Tabataba'i, please stay," suggested the amir quickly. "If the khalifa has no objection, I have none."

"Let him stay," muttered the caliph irritably. His head swivelled and he passed a critical eye over me. "Who is this man? What does he want?"

"May the peace of Allah be with you, Great Khalifa. With the khalifa's kind permission, I present to your highness my advisor. His name is Aidan. He has recently joined my household."

"He is not an Arab," al'Mutamid pointed out.

"No, Majesty," replied Sadiq smoothly, "he comes from Êrlandah—a sea island far to the west."

"I have never heard of this place," grumped the khalifa, then doubt clouded his face. "Have I, Tabataba'i? Have I ever heard of this place?"

"Assuredly not, Highness," answered the wazir.

"Ah!" cried the khalifa triumphantly. "You see! You see!" He took up the corner of his robe and blew his nose. "The angels come here, you know." He gestured vaguely to the garden. The khalifa's hands were long and his fingers thin—a feature oddly out of place on a man so fat.

"Aidan has come here to help us in our relations with the emperor," the amir continued. He seemed unconcerned by his superior's shocking behaviour.

The khalifa's head swivelled towards me again. "Has he indeed?" He looked at me through narrowed eyes. "The Emperor of the West is a Christian," he informed me. "Are you a Christian also?"

I did not know what or whether to reply, but Sadiq indicated that I should answer. "Yes," I replied. "That is, I was—but no longer."

al'Mutamid nodded gravely. "They say the emperor is fond of horses."

"I believe this is true," I confirmed. "I have seen some of his horses."

"How many?"

"Your majesty?"

"How many horses did you see?"

"Six, I believe."

"Six!" roared al'Mutamid; his laughter shook the leaves

on the nearby branches. "Six! Did you hear, Tabataba'i? The emperor has but six horses! I have six *thousand*!" Abruptly, the khalifa became suspicious. "Where did you learn to speak like this?"

"I was taught in Lord Sadiq's house by an excellent teacher—a young man named Mahmoud."

"He is not an Arab, either," observed al'Mutamid wearily. He yawned, already losing interest in the proceedings.

"No, Highness," agreed Sadiq, "Mahmoud is an Egyptian."

"Ah," nodded the khalifa sagely, "that explains much." Rocking his body to one side, he delivered himself of a long, sonorous fart, and said, "What do you want, Sadiq? Why are you here?"

"We have come to beg a benevolence of you, Majesty," he answered. "Aidan has friends who, through no fault of their own, have fallen into slavery. It is my belief that they should be freed at once and allowed to return to their lands in the west."

"If we free all the slaves," al'Mutamid remarked, holding up a long finger, "there would be no one to do the work. Who would do the work, Tabataba'i?"

The wazir stepped forward quickly. "I do not believe the amir is suggesting that you free *all* the slaves. Are you, Lord Sadiq?"

"By no means, wazir," he said. "Only those known to Aidan."

"Six!" cried al'Mutamid suddenly. "Let it be the same as the emperor's horses!"

"Very well," agreed the wazir quickly, "we shall release one slave for each of the emperor's horses. I will write the decree shall I, majesty?" Without waiting for an answer, Tabataba'i stepped to the desk and knelt down. Taking up a square of parchment, he dipped the pen into a pot of ink and began to write.

But there were more than six survivors. Stepping forward, I made to object. "I beg your pardon—" I began, then halted as Sadiq warned me off with a quick motion of his hands. The khalifa's eyes rolled towards me expectantly. "Forgive me," I blustered, "I merely wished to acknowledge my gratitude for your estimable generosity. I am certain that those who are to be freed will be forever indebted to your majesty's compassion," I paused, "as for the rest—they will no doubt remain usefully, if less gratefully, employed."

Sadiq frowned. Obviously, I had pressed the matter further than was becoming a man in my precarious position. What did I care for courtesy? I just hoped above all else that Wazir Tabataba'i had caught my insinuation. If he had, however, he gave no sign.

The khalifa sniffed ostentatiously. "I am writing a poem," he informed us blithely. "It is about the duties of man before God."

"How very worshipful, Highness," said Sadiq. "No doubt, it will be most instructive. I look forward to its completion with keen anticipation."

"Prayer is a duty," the khalifa said, then paused. "I cannot think why." His face wrinkled in sudden panic. "Why is this, Tabataba'i?"

"Prayer shows the devotion of the soul to its creator," answered the wazir absently. His pen continued flowing across the parchment for a moment, then he stopped, inspected what he had written, puffed his cheeks and blew on it, then sat back. "A royal seal is required, Majesty. Would you like me to do it for you?"

The khalifa grimaced and flicked his hand impatiently in the wazir's direction. Tabataba'i rose and withdrew, saying, "I will await you in the courtyard, Amir Sadiq. You will find me there when you have concluded your business."

The wazir withdrew, leaving us to bid farewell to the khalifa. Lord Sadiq made several judicious observations of a general and pleasant nature, whereupon we prepared to make good our escape. Just as we were thanking the caliph for his charity, and bidding him farewell, the addle-pated fellow raised his hands and burst out chanting.

"Allah is the light of the heavens and earth!" cried the khalifa in a loud, cracking voice. "His light is as a pillar upon which stands a lamp in a glass, shining like starlight and glittering like a pearl, kindled from the blessed olive tree—neither of the east, nor of the west—whose fragrant oil gives light though fire touches it not. Light upon light! God guides to his light whomsoever he pleases, and sets forth parables for the instruction of the people. Allah is wise in all things; his knowledge is infinite!"

So saying, the khalifa lowered his hands; he slumped back on his cushions once again and closed his eyes. Sadiq bowed low. "Thank you for reminding me, Majesty," he said. "May God keep you well, khalifa."

"Fruit," the khalifa murmured sleepily. "We must be having some fruit. I see bowls of it here."

With a glance to me, Sadiq led the way from the garden and back through the hall to the courtyard where our horses, having been watered during our audience, were now waiting. As soon as we were beyond the hearing of the khalifa, I spoke up. "There were more than six survivors," I pointed out, and demanded: "What are we to do about the rest?"

"Be at peace," answered Sadiq placidly. "Tabataba'i will have everything in order."

"But he does not know," I objected.

"The matter was well in hand," Sadiq insisted. "You might have ruined everything with your clumsy meddling." He relented then, and said, "You worry for nothing. Have faith, Aidan."

Wazir Tabataba'i was waiting for us in the courtyard. The parchment was rolled in a bit of silk and tied with a length of the same material. He presented the roll to me, saying, "May Allah, Wise and Compassionate, speed your friends' return to freedom. It is a very great gift you have been given this day."

Not wishing to seem ungrateful, I nevertheless felt constrained to see for myself that all was in order. "Thank you, wazir," I said, and proceeded to untie the parchment. Once unrolled, I held the square between my hands and examined the graceful script closely.

"That is the royal seal of al'Mutamid," Tabataba'i said, pointing to the red embossed insignia. "Do you read Arabic?"

"Alas, no," I conceded. Handing the scroll to him, I said, "Please?"

"Of course," he smiled haughtily. "It says: 'Be it here known that the Khalifa al'Mutamid, Defender of the Faithful, has decreed that the bearer of this communication shall obtain the immediate release of certain slaves who are known to him. Anyone making bold to hinder or interfere in the execution of this decree shall be committing treason, and shall thus earn the full measure of the khalifa's wrath.'" He finished reading and looked up. "I trust this meets with your approval?"

"Indeed, it is all I could have asked. Again, I thank you, Wazir Tabataba'i."

"Do not thank *me*," the wazir said elaborately, handing me the scroll. "Thank al'Mutamid, and thank Allah the khalifa was in a reasonable mind today. It might easily have been otherwise." He bowed, touching his forehead in a sign of respect to the amir, then turned and strode away.

"Wazir Tabataba'i serves the khalifate, not the khalifa," Sadiq informed me when we were once again remounted and riding out through the palace gates. "No one knows better how to temper the royal rages." A cloud seemed to pass over the amir's face as he spoke, but I could not guess his feeling. "At all events, I knew the wazir would make the decree usefully ambiguous."

"Once more, I find myself indebted to your prudence and acumen. I will repay you if I can."

He shook his head. "There is no need. I only regret you had to see the khalifa in his infirmity, but there was no other way. Still, as the wazir has said, it was one of his better days. al'Mutamid has been known to disrobe before guests and defecate, or fly into an insatiable fury and demand all his servants be impaled on white-hot spikes." Turning in the saddle, he said, "Do not for the briefest instant believe Abu Ahmad shares any of his brother's attributes. Praise be to Allah! Abu's mind is keen as the blade at his side; he is both philosopher and prince. Eighty thousand men serve under his command, and each with but a single thought: to die for the greater glory of God and Abu."

"The people are fortunate that the khalifa has such a brother," I remarked. The amir only nodded. He said nothing more until we were dismounting in the courtyard of his palace. "Tonight," he declared, swinging down from the saddle in a single, fluid motion, "is the last night we will have in Ja'fariya. You will eat at my table. I will send Kazimain to bring you at the proper time."

"As you will, Lord Sadiq," I replied, trying to emulate his cat-like grace.

"Now, you must excuse me," he said. "I have three wives, and owe particular obligations to each. We will be gone many days, so I must do what I can to discharge my marital duties—as is proper in the sight of Allah."

"By all means," I replied, "it would be a sin to leave undone that which, for duty's sake, must be done."

"Although you are not yet a married man, I knew you

would understand." I watched him walk away, much in envy of his sense of duty.

While the amir's many servants laboured with preparations for our journey, I spent the remainder of the day thinking what I would tell Kazimain. Alas, when I heard the familiar sound of her footfall in the corridor beyond my room, I was no closer to knowing what I should say. Seeing her face—glowing with happiness as she swept into the room—only made the grim chore more difficult.

She crossed the room in two running steps and came into my arms in a rush, knocking me over onto the bed. She kissed me once, twice, three times—whereupon I lost count, drowning myself in her all-encircling embrace. When she paused to catch her breath, she held my face between her hands and looked at me, the light of her happiness a dazzling ray that lit the room even as it lit her eyes.

"I have been waiting for you all day!" she said, placing her chin against my chest and staring into my face. "The servants said you had gone to see the khalifa."

"We did that," I told her. "I went to obtain freedom for my friends." How deep were her eyes, and how dark.

"Were you successful?" she asked.

"More successful than I could have hoped," I replied, tracing the curve of her lips with a fingertip.

"Are you not pleased?"

"But I am," I said, "very well pleased."

"You do not seem pleased. You seem unhappy." She kissed me again. "The banquet tonight will cheer you," she said. "It is only the amir's family, so we can sit together."

"Kazimain . . ." I said, cupping a hand to her cheek. The words stuck in my throat.

Concern drew her brows together. "What is troubling you?"

"You will have seen the preparations—"

"Yes, the amir is going away again. They say he is going to Byzantium."

"He is," I told her, "and I am to go with him."

The light went out of her eyes as if snuffed by a cold wind. Misery enveloped her like a robe. "Why must you go?"

"I am sorry, my love," I said, reaching for her. She pulled away.

"Why?"

"It was the price for my friends' freedom," I said, adding, "and for my own."

"And you agreed to this?"

"I would have agreed to anything. Yes, I told him I would go."

"It was wrong of Lord Sadiq to treat you in such a callous manner." She leapt up. "I will go to him at once and make him see that he cannot do this."

"No, Kazimain," I stood, and held out my hand to her. "No. It must be this way. The amir needs me with him in Byzantium, and the need is such that he would have taken me with him anyway. I made the best bargain I could."

"It was wrong to make you choose!" she insisted.

"I have other reasons—" I confessed, "reasons of my own for going."

"Reasons that do not include me," she said accusingly.

"Yes," I replied. "It is difficult, I know. But I am content."

"Well, I am not!" she snapped. Her lower lip quivered, and unshed tears shimmered in her eyes.

I moved closer and put my arms around her; she nestled her head against my shoulder, and we stood for a long moment holding one another. "I am sorry, Kazimain," I whispered, stroking her long hair. "I wish it were otherwise."

"If you are going, then I will go, too." She warmed to

the idea instantly. "I will go with you. We can be together and you can show me the city, and—"

"No, my love." It hurt me to dash her quick-kindled hope. "It is too dangerous."

"For me it is too dangerous, but not for you?"

"I would not go at all if need did not compel me," I answered. "If I had my way I would stay here with you forever."

She shrugged my hands from her shoulders and stepped away, looking at me sadly. When she spoke, her voice was soft almost to breaking. "If you go, I know I will never see you again."

"I *will* come back," I insisted, but the words lacked conviction against her sorrow. "I will."

# 56

Dinner that night was meant to be a festive affair with singing, dancing, and music. Lord Sadiq reclined on cushions at the head of the long, low table with his wives, who fed him choice morsels from the various plates and platters and bowls which the kitchen servants conveyed to the banqueting room in an unfaltering stream.

I dined with Faysal and several of the amir's closest friends; across from us sat the women, who, since it was a festive meal, were invited to eat at table with the men, instead of in the women's apartments. The conversation was light and polite, with much laughter all around. Clearly, everyone was enjoying the farewell banquet. For me, however, the feast was more in the nature of an ordeal: sitting opposite Kazimain, knowing how unhappy she was, enduring her silent reproaches, and unable to cheer her or ease the burden of her sadness or even to explain myself.

The food was lavish and luxurious, and had been prepared in such a way as to delight all the senses; still, it might have been ashes in my mouth for all the joy it gave me. The music, playing soft and low through the meal, and becoming more lively once we had finished and lay back to watch the dancers, seemed interminable and grating.

Ordinarily, I would have enjoyed dinner and music, savouring the strange otherness of tastes and sounds, but in my downcast mood I merely grew fretful and uneasy. I wanted to flee the room and spend the last moments with Kazimain, alone. I wanted to hold her, to love her. I wanted to feel the softness of her skin, to feel her warm and yielding flesh in my arms. I wanted to tell her . . . Alas, there was so much I wanted to tell her, I could not think. My mind spun anxiously; my thoughts whirled like leaves in a tempest, and I could get no peace.

And then, when the meal was finished and the last of the dancers departed, the women rose from the table and disappeared through a door on the far side of the room.

I made to follow, but Faysal laid a hand on my arm. "They go to the *harim*," he informed me good-naturedly, "where no man is permitted—not even moon-eyed lovers."

"But I must speak to Kazimain," I insisted.

He shrugged. "Tomorrow you will speak to her."

*Tomorrow will be too late,* I thought, and followed the women out of the room. They crossed a torch-lit courtyard and disappeared behind a high door. The harim guard bowed his head respectfully at my approach, but made no move to step aside. "I wish to speak to Kazimain," I told him.

"You will wait here, please," he said in a soft, almost feminine voice. The guard returned a few moments later to say that Kazimain did not wish to speak to me.

"Did you tell her who asked to see her?" I challenged.

"I told her," replied the guard. "Princess Kazimain expressed her inestimable regret, and wished her future husband a good night."

"But I—" I began, and then realized I did not know what I could say to her anyway. I returned to the banquet hall and slumped heavily in my seat.

"Take my advice and eat something," urged Faysal.

"The journey will be hard and we will not find food like this on the way. Eat! Enjoy yourself."

But I could eat nothing more, and sat watching the surrounding revelry in a misery of agitation and regret. When at last the amir retired to his private quarters, and we were free to stay or go as we would, I left the continuing celebration and went to my room where I spent a restless, wakeful night.

The thin dawn light found me ill-rested and on edge. At the sound of footsteps in the corridor, I rose at once, and realized that I had been listening all night for that sound. But it was not Kazimain who entered my room—an unknown servant appeared and placed the familiar tray on the wooden stand. The servant asked if there was anything else I required, then departed. Ignoring the food, I dressed instead, and then stood staring out the windhole, watching Ja'fariya come to life beneath the sun's watery rays. I thought of going to find Kazimain, and though I would not be allowed to enter the harim, I thought I might at least send a message for her to meet me in the courtyard.

I had just decided on this plan when I once again heard footsteps in the corridor. Thinking that Kazimain had come after all, I turned expectantly. A young serving boy appeared, and my heart fell. "Please, master," said the boy, his bow quick, all but indiscernible, "I am to say the horses are ready."

I thanked the boy and, taking a last look around my little cell of a room, I picked up my parchment scroll and tucked it carefully into an inner fold of my robe. I then proceeded along the corridor, and down the stairs, through the hall, and out into the courtyard where the horses were saddled and waiting.

For the sake of speed, the amir had decided that we should travel with no more than ten of the rafiq; the amir, Faysal, and myself, brought the number to thirteen. *The same number as that of the monks who had begun the ill-fated pilgrimage*, I thought ruefully, and it seemed an unfortunate coincidence to me. I might have prayed that this pilgrimage met with better success than the last one, but God, I knew, would heed not a word anyway. So, I saved my breath for breathing.

The amir had ordered the handsome grey saddled for me, and I walked to where a groom stood holding the reins, and spoke to the horse as Sadiq had done. Yaqin tossed her head and nuzzled my neck, giving every sign that she remembered me.

"She likes you."

I turned quickly. "Kazimain! I hoped I would see you before we left. I feared—"

"What? That I would let my almost-husband go away without wishing him farewell?" She stepped nearer, and I could see that she had put off her sorrow and was now reconciled to the necessity of my leaving. Indeed, she seemed cheerful and resolute—as if she was determined to make the best of my absence.

"I would give anything to stay with you," I told her.

"I know." She smiled. "I will miss you while we are apart, but it will only make our joy the greater when we meet again."

"And I will miss you, Kazimain." I ached to take her in my arms and kiss her, but such a thing was not done; it would have brought her into disrepute among her people. I was constrained to satisfy myself with merely gazing at her, and engraving her face upon my memory.

She grew uncomfortable beneath my gaze and lowered her eyes to her hands where she held a small silk-wrapped bundle. "A gift for you," she said. I thanked her and asked what it was, preparing to open it. "No," she said, laying a warm hand upon mine. "Do not open it now. Later, when you are far from here—then open it and think of me."

"Very well." I tucked the parcel into my belt. "Kazimain, I—" Now was my chance, but I found I was no better prepared than before; words abandoned me. "I am sorry, Kazimain. I wish it could be otherwise—deeply do I wish it."

"I know," she said.

Just then Lord Sadiq emerged from the palace. Faysal signalled to the rafiq, who mounted their horses and began riding towards the gate; he then called to me: "Be mounted! We go!"

"Farewell, Kazimain," I said awkwardly. "I love you."

She raised a hand to her lips and, kissing her finger-tips, pressed them to my lips. "Go with God, my love," she whispered. "I will pray for us both every day until we are together once more."

Abruptly, she turned and hastened away. Darting between the pillars, she was gone. Faysal called again, and I climbed into the saddle and followed him out. We proceeded through the still-empty streets of Ja'fariya, the air cool where shadows yet lingered. The amir rode at the head of the column with Faysal behind, leading the three pack mules, and myself beside him.

In no time at all we passed the city gates, and proceeded along the main road which ran beside the Tigris River which, at that time of the year, was little more than a turgid stream, much withered between its rock-bound banks. The stone of the region was pale pink, and the colour had seeped into the land, making the dust and soil ruddy. The further from the city we travelled, the more desolate the surrounding hills became. We soon left the few outlying settlements—with their pink, cracked-mud hovels and tiny, scrupulously tended fields—far behind.

We rode through the morning, pausing only briefly to water the horses. I had never ridden so far all at once, and it was not long before I began to feel the ache in my legs.

Faysal observed my distress. "In a few days, you will feel like you were born to the saddle." He laughed at the face I made at this, and informed me, "Do not worry, my friend. We will rest during the heat of the day."

The sun was so hot by then that I reckoned the resting place he spoke of could not be far. But when Sadiq showed no sign of halting, I asked Faysal if he thought the amir had forgotten. "He has not forgotten, never fear," he laughed. "See the trees?" He squinted far ahead into the distance towards a dusty green clump amidst the pale pink rocks. "We can shelter there."

Indeed, we might well have sheltered there, but we did not. Upon reaching the place, we rode on. I looked back longingly, and Faysal laughed, and pointed to another clump of trees on the horizon. Alas, we passed those, too, and another as well before the amir at last turned his mount towards the welcome shade of a tamarisk grove.

The instant the mare came to a halt, I threw myself from the saddle, and only then realized how very sore I had become. It was all I could do to stand upright, and I could not take a step without wincing. "We water the horses first," Faysal said; he spoke in a kindly way, but his meaning was clear enough. I hobbled after him, leading Yaqin to the riverbank where she could drink her fill. We then unsaddled our mounts and staked them to long tethers beneath the trees so they could graze on whatever they might find.

Only then did we refresh ourselves, returning to the river a short way upstream of where the horses had drunk. There we knelt on the damp soil, splashed water over our heads, filled our mouths with water and spit it out once more. The water was too silty to drink, but it wet our mouths. We quenched our thirst from the waterskins the mules carried. And then we settled down beneath the trees to rest.

The rafiq talked in low voices among themselves, and I lay back half-asleep listening to the murmur of their speech—like the lazy drone of insects humming in the shade beneath the trees. I do not remember sleeping; indeed, I do not think I closed my eyes at all. I was simply leaning with my back against the tree, staring up through the shadowed leaves into the pale blue sky above, when all at once I saw the heavens opened up and a great golden city revealed.

I made to cry out, so the others might see this marvel, but my tongue cleaved to the roof of my mouth and I could not utter a sound, so I watched in mute amazement as the dazzling city descended slowly from the sky. The glorious place gleamed and shone with a radiance far surpassing any earthly light, and this gave me to know that I was seeing the Heavenly City itself.

As if to confirm this assumption, there came a sound like that of the ocean in full gale: a deep-booming roar of majestic and limitless power, a voice to shake the foundations of the earth. The wind-wail swelled until it filled all the world; my inward parts vibrated with the sound, and I felt as if the ground whereon I lay might crumble beneath me and flow away like water. Strangely, no one else appeared to notice either the terrible din or the sharp, bright rays of light streaming all around.

I tried to stand, to run, but had lost control of my limbs and could not move. I could but stare, transfixed as the white-clothed citizens of the Heavenly City began streaming earthward on the piercing shafts of light—angels, speeding to earth on various mercies and intercessions. The sound I heard was that of the ceaseless movement of their wings as they hurtled down.

*How,* I wondered, *was it possible that this sound was not heard among men?* For the mighty wind-roar permeated all the world, and filled the heavens. Indeed, it seemed more substantial than any mere created thing, and more enduring—a tremendous column to uphold the fabric of the world.

One of the heavenly minions flew towards me, striking down from the sky like lightning. Towering above the tree where I reclined, his face shining with all the intensity of the sun, he gazed down upon me with fearful severity. "How long?" he said, shaking the leaves on the branches with the force of his demand.

He seemed to expect an answer, but I remained mute before him, still unable to open my mouth. When I did not speak, he cried out again. "How long, O man?"

I did not understand the question. Perhaps he sensed my confusion, or heard the thought in my head, for he looked down upon me and said, "How long, Faithless One, will you offend heaven with your arrogance?"

Lifting a radiant hand, he swept his arm wide, and I saw the whole vast army of heaven encamped around us with their horses and chariots of fire. I could not endure the sight, and had to close my eyes lest they be burned to cinders in my skull.

"Remember," the angel intoned, "all flesh is grass."

Opening my eyes, I looked again; but the chariots and their shining occupants were gone, and gone, too, the heavenly messenger who had spoken to me.

I could move again and my mouth was unstopped. I looked around and was amazed to see everything precisely as it had been before. No one gave the slightest indication of having seen or heard anything. The warriors still sat talking, the horses still cropped the dry grass. Nothing had changed. I lay back against the tree and closed my eyes. Sure, the heat and sun had combined to induce a waking dream.

That is what I told myself, and I believed it, too. By the time we roused ourselves to continue on, I had persuaded myself that I had seen and heard nothing—a fleeting trick of the imagination only. If there had been anything out of the ordinary . . . sure, the others would have seen and heard it, too.

This strained certainty remained with me through the rest of the day, and I gradually put the incident from my mind. The following days bled together, each melting into the next like ice shards in the sun with nothing to distinguish one from another. We rode and rested, ate, slept, and rose to ride again. Each day's end saw the gradual advance of the ragged line of mountains to the north. After five days, we turned away from the river and proceeded northeast towards the foothills of the nearer range. "The mines are there," Sadiq told me; he pointed to a cleft low down on one of the larger crags. "We must go through that pass to reach them."

"How far is it?" I asked, anticipation quickening within me. "How many days?"

"Four, perhaps." The amir considered this for a moment. "Yes, four—if all goes well."

"And how many until we reach the mine?"

"Another day—the mountain trails are very bad."

As if to reach our destination the sooner, he pressed on with renewed vigour, driving a swifter pace. It was well after sundown when we finally stopped to make camp for the night, and I was so tired and preoccupied by the stabbing pains in my legs and thighs and back that I ate little of the stew Faysal prepared for our supper, and quickly retired in silent torment to nurse my aches.

Sleep proved elusive, however, and I lay weary and wakeful, regarding the stars in their long slow circling sweep of heaven's dome. Without the sun to inflame it, the air grew steadily cooler, and I pulled my cloak more tightly around me and listened to the soft chitter-chatter of the insects along the river course. Eventually, I grew drowsy and closed my eyes.

It seemed as if my eyelids had no more than touched one another when a voice spoke out of the darkness. "Rise, Aidan!" whispered the voice. "Follow me."

I woke and sat upright, and saw a figure dressed in white striding rapidly away. "Faysal!" I hissed aloud, not wishing to wake those sleeping around me. "Wait!"

He halted at the sound of my voice, but did not turn around. I struggled to my feet and, with limping steps, hurried after him. What was he doing, waking people in the dead of night?

I had taken no more than three or four paces when he moved on, leaving me to follow as best I could. "Faysal!" I called, trying to keep my voice down. "Wait!"

He led me a short distance along the riverbank to a place where the tamarisk grove thinned; here he stopped to wait. I hobbled as best I could over the rough rocky ground, forbearance rapidly turning to annoyance with every painful step. By the time I joined him, I was justly irritated at having been made to scramble after him in the dark.

"Well?" I demanded curtly. "What is so important you must drag me from my sleep?"

He gave no sign of having heard me, but continued gazing across the river. "Faysal," I said, more loudly, "what is wrong with you?"

At this he turned, and I found myself looking into the face of dear, dead Bishop Cadoc.

# 57

Cadoc glared at me from beneath lowered brows. "I am disappointed in you, Aidan," he said tartly. "Disappointed in the extreme—and disgusted."

His round face warped in a scowl, the good bishop clicked his tongue in sharp vexation. "Have you any notion of the trouble your disobedience is causing? The pit yawns before you, boy. Wake up!"

"Bishop Cadoc," I said, annoyance melting in the strangeness of the meeting, "how do you come to be here? I saw you killed."

"Yes, a very great gift that—and just look what you have done with it," he growled, his frown dour and disapproving. "Think you I could stand aside and watch you obliterate all that has been accomplished on your behalf from the moment you were born to now?" He glared indignantly. "Well? What have you to say for yourself?"

Unable to frame a suitable reply, I simply stared at the apparition before me. It was Bishop Cadoc, without any doubt whatever. Yet, though his features were the same, he exuded health and vitality beyond any I had known him to possess; sure, he seemed more alive than many living men, and the eyes that regarded me with such disapproval held nothing otherworldly about them, but were keen as double-edged blades. His simple monk's mantle was not white, as I supposed, but a softly glimmering material which gave a faint illumination to his face and hands—something more than moongleam, though similar—which made him appear to be standing in reflected light.

Curious, I reached out a hand to touch him—to see if his form was as solid as it appeared. "No!" He flicked up a warning hand. "Such is not permitted." Indicating a nearby rock, he said, "Now sit you down and listen to me."

Stubbornly, I stood. "I am no—"

"Sit!" he commanded, and I sat. Placing fists on his hips, the bishop of Cennanus na Ríg glowered. "Your stiff-necked pride has brought the pilgrimage dangerously close to failure."

"Me!" I cried, leaping up. "I have done nothing!"

"Sit down and listen!" the bishop commanded sternly. "Night is soon over, and I must return."

"Where?"

Ignoring the question, he said, "Lay aside your damnable pride, brother. Humble yourself before God, repent, and beg forgiveness while there is yet time." He paused and his features softened. We might have been two monks talking by moonlight, a senior churchman chastising his wayward junior.

"Look at you! Wallowing in arrogance and self-pity, drowning in doubt—and all because of a trifling disappointment and small vexations of uncertainty. What do you know of anything?"

"God abandoned *me*," I muttered, "not the other way."

"Oh, yes," he said snidely, "your precious dream. It was a great boon you were given, but you threw it away. I see now you treat *all* your gifts the same: with nothing but contempt."

"Gift!" I said. "I was meant to die in Byzantium—what manner of gift is that?"

The apparition rolled its eyes in exasperation. "You were not always so dull-witted, God save you. Many a man—a *perceptive* man, mind—would give much to know where he will die."

I could not believe what I was hearing. I stared incredulously at the bishop's softly glowing form.

"Oh, a very great boon, that," I muttered scornfully. "I went to Byzantium believing I would die, but willing to face martyrdom for Christ's sake. Indeed, I was prepared for death, but nothing happened—nothing."

"And so you were disappointed," the bishop's apparition mocked, adopting the tone of one well used to exhorting thickheaded pupils. I made no answer, but glowered sullenly back. Cadoc frowned and drew a deep breath. "Perhaps, if you had pondered the meaning of your dream more deeply—"

"What difference does it make now? It is over and done."

"I tell you the truth, Aidan mac Cainnech," he declared in solemn displeasure, "you are making me angry."

*I am mad,* I thought. Here was I, arguing with a dead man's apparition in the middle of the night. *I must be losing my mind—first angels and now the spirits of the departed. What next?*

"This is what you came to tell me?" I inquired sourly.

"No, son," he said, his voice gentling. "I came to warn you, and to encourage you." He leaned towards me earnestly. "Beware: great danger gathers about you. Forces in high places seek your destruction. Continue on the way you are going, and the abyss will claim you."

"That is encouraging," I muttered.

"That was the warning," snapped the dead bishop. "But I say to you, rejoice, brother; the race is soon run, and the prize awaits. Persevere!"

So saying, he began to move away from me—I say "move away" because while he did not so much as lift a foot, I sensed motion and he began to fade from my sight, growing rapidly smaller as if retreating across a vast distance. "Remember this: all flesh is grass!" he called, his voice dwindling away. "Keep your eyes on the prize!"

"Wait!" I cried, jumping up again.

His words drifted back to me, now very faint and far away: "All flesh is grass, Brother Aidan. The race is soon run. Farewell . . ."

Cadoc disappeared from sight, and I came to myself with a shudder and looked around. The camp was quiet and still, the men asleep. Low in the west, the moon shone brightly, but pink dawn marbled the sky in the east. I stood for a time, trying to understand what had happened to me. It had been a dream, I decided. What else could it have been? Unlike my other dreams, however, this one had caused me to get up and walk in my sleep; I had never done that before.

I felt foolish standing alone in the dark, talking to myself, so I crept back to my place beneath the tree and wrapped my robe around me and tried to go to sleep. Daylight roused the others a short time later. We broke fast on the remains of the previous night's meal, then saddled the horses and rode on.

The strange events of the previous day had cast me into a pensive humour. I rode beside Faysal, as before, but my mind was far away and preoccupied with all I had seen and heard. Time and again I kept returning to the same words: All flesh is grass. That is what the angel had told me, and Bishop Cadoc had said it, too. I found this curiously comforting: at least my spectral visitors agreed with one another.

The words themselves were from the Holy Scriptures; I had copied out enough psalms to recognize that much at least. And the prophets often likened man and his span of days to the ephemeral grass that blushed green in the dawnlight only to be blasted by the sun's all-consuming fire and blown away on the desert wind.

I thought about this as I rode along, and thought, too, how long it had been since I had contemplated anything of Holy Writ. Once it had been all my life, and now such thoughts were few and exceedingly far between. Melancholy settled over me, and I gave myself to wondering what else I could recall.

My efforts were rewarded at once: *All men are like grass, and all their glory is like the flowers of the field.* That was from one of the prophets—Isaiah, I think. And then there was one from the Psalms: *You, Lord God, sweep away men in the sleep of death; they are like the grass of the morning—though in the morning it springs up new, by evening it is dry and withered.*

Once begun, other fragments of scripture surfaced. I found the mental exercise mildly diverting—at least it relieved the monotony of the ride. *They wither more quickly than grass—such is the destiny of those who forget the Lord.* Sure, I had copied that once or twice, but though I wrung my poor brain for trying, I could in no wise remember the source. The message was clear enough, however; it made me wonder whether I had forgotten the Lord. No, I maintained, God had forgotten *me*.

Another versicle floated up from the hidden depths of memory: *Who are you that fear mortal men, who are but grass, that you forget the Lord, your Maker, who has stretched out the heavens and laid the Earth's foundations?*

The question spoke to me with such directness and force that I turned in the saddle to see if Faysal had spoken. But he rode with his head bent beneath the sun, and his eyes were closed; some of the others were dozing in the saddle, too. Clearly, no one paid any attention to me.

Again, the question resounded in my mind, and with an insistence that seemed to require an answer: *Who was I to fear mortal men and forget my Maker?* Was it fear that led to forgetting? Perhaps, but it seemed more likely that forgetting led to fear. Further, the question implied the foolishness of fearing mere mortals when the Maker of Heaven and Earth alone held power over the soul. Obviously, if fear were coinage, then God was the treasurer who demanded payment.

Oh, but it was not fear that so beset me: I was not afraid, I was angry! I had given my all to God, and he had rejected the gift. He had abandoned me, withdrawn his guiding hand and cast me adrift in a world that knew neither mercy nor justice.

As if in response to this observation, another scriptural shred floated to my attention: *Do not fret because of evil men, or be envious of those who do wrong; for like the grass they soon wither and die away.* That one I knew; it was from Psalms. Thus, I had worked myself around to the same place once more. But what did it mean, this talk of flesh and grass and fear and forgetting—what did any of it mean?

As the blistering sun reached the summit of its upward climb, we stopped to rest. I took a little water and lay down under a thornbush—the last of the trees was far behind us now, and all that gave shade or shelter in the rough, dry hills was a tough low bush with small leathery leaves and short, sharp thorns. I tried to sleep, but the ground was hard and uneven, and my mind kept returning to the questions that had occupied me during the morning.

The implication suggested by the fragments tossed up by my agitated spirit, was that I had allowed my disappointment to turn to bitterness and doubt, which had in turn corroded my faith. Perhaps that was true. But I had every right to be bitter! God had abandoned me, after all.

How long was I obliged to remain faithful to a god who no longer cared?

I did my best to put the issue behind me, but the questions gnawed at me through the day. As I could get no peace, I engaged Faysal in discussion. "Which do you think the greater boon," I asked as we rode along, climbing the ragged track up into the hills, "knowing your death, or remaining ignorant of it?"

After pondering the question for a time, he had answered, "Both positions have much to commend them."

"That is no answer—"

"Allow me to finish," he replied. "It seems to me that it is the lot of man to remain ignorant of his demise until the unhappy event overtakes him. Therefore, I am persuaded that Allah has ordained it thus for our benefit."

"Even so," I allowed, "if the choice *were* yours to make, which would you choose?"

He thought for a moment, then asked, "Is it likely that this should happen to me?"

"I suppose not, but—"

"Then an answer is not required."

"Your evasion of the question suggests you would deem such knowledge a curse, not a boon."

"I did not say that," Faysal objected. "You misconstrue my words."

"You did not say *anything*," I pointed out. "How could I misconstrue it?"

We talked in this way for a time, eventually losing interest in the pointless exchange. Later, as the men were making camp for the night, I found myself sitting next to Sadiq as he scanned the valley through which we had passed that day. The setting sun flamed the rocks and tinted the shadows violet; away to the south the sky was rose-coloured in the dusk. "There is a storm coming," Sadiq said, observing the southern sky.

"Good—a little rain will be most welcome."

"No rain this time of the year," the amir replied. "Wind."

"A sandstorm then." My heart fell at the thought.

"Yes, a sandstorm. As God wills, it may pass to the east." He turned from his inspection of the sky, and eyed me with the same severe scrutiny. "Faysal tells me you are talking about death."

"True," I conceded, and told him what we had discussed. He seemed interested in the question so I asked him whether he would consider knowledge of his death a boon?

"Of course," he replied without hesitation.

This intrigued me. "Why?" I asked, and confessed that I could see no benefit whatsoever.

"That is where you are wrong. A man armed with such knowledge would be free to accomplish mighty things."

"Free?" I wondered at the use of this word. "Why do you say free? It seems to me that such knowledge is a terrible burden."

"Terrible for some, perhaps," allowed the amir. "For others it would be liberation. If a man had foreknowledge of his death, it would follow that he would also know all the places where death could *not* claim him. Thus, he would be free from all fear, and could do whatever he pleased." A quickened intensity charged his speech. "Just think! This man would be a hero in battle, braving every danger, fighting with exquisite courage because he knew in his heart he could not be killed."

"What would happen," I pressed, "when this man came at last to the place appointed for his meeting with death?"

"Ah," replied Sadiq, turning his eyes to the valley once more, "when he came to that place he would also have no fear because he would have prepared himself properly for this meeting. Fear arises from uncertainty. Where there is perfect certainty, there is no fear."

As one who had lived with such knowledge, I found this line of reasoning unconvincing. Certainty, in my experience, only made the thing more difficult, not less.

I was still contemplating what Sadiq had said, when he rose abruptly. "Ya'Allah!" he said softly.

Glancing up, I saw that he was gazing down into the valley, his eyes fixed on the place where the trail began its long torturous climb up to the promontory on which we now sat. "What do you see?" I asked, following his gaze.

But Sadiq was already hastening away. From over his shoulder he called, "We are being followed!"

# 58

Still staring at the place Sadiq had indicated, I perceived a minute movement along the valley floor: a solitary figure, desert pale, picking its lone way slowly along the trail in the dusk. I strained my eyes to see more, and could, with difficulty, make out the form of a horse ambling behind the figure. Very soon the shadows would steal both from view.

"Get back!" Sadiq ordered, and I edged away from the overlook wondering how Sadiq could have seen the follower. Even after being shown where to look, the lone figure was all but impossible to see. The answer came to me then that the Amir had seen the figure because he knew it was there, was looking for it, and likely had been searching for some time.

Concealing ourselves among the tumbled rocks on either side of the trail, we settled down to wait—and waited long, but the follower did not appear. After a suitable period had elapsed, Sadiq left his hiding place and crept once more to the promontory where he lay on his stomach and gazed down into the valley for a moment before returning to call us from our places.

"Our friend has made camp for the night," he said. "It

is a poor thing to travel alone; I think we must persuade him to join the companionship of our fire." The amir chose four of the rafiq to accomplish this task. "Go quietly," he warned, "for we do not wish to inspire unholy fear in our guest."

The four proceeded into the valley on foot, leaving the rest to make camp. As Faysal and the others went about their chores, the blue-black twilight stain deepened in the sky and the stars began to shine. It was full dark by the time the welcome party returned with our solitary pursuer.

They came abruptly out of the night, emerging into the circle of light provided by our campfire—two warriors, leading their charge, the third coming behind, and the fourth leading a horse and donkey. We fell silent as they appeared; Sadiq stood. "I am pleased you could be persuaded to join us," he said, speaking to the figure still in darkness.

I peered into the gloom beyond the firelight and saw a slender form swathed head to foot in a pale robe.

"Come forward, friend," Sadiq invited. "Sit with us; warm yourself by our fire, and share our meat."

The figure stood silently, but made no move to accept Sadiq's invitation. Neither did the warriors move, but held themselves stiffly, as if afraid or embarrassed to stand too near the stranger.

"Please," the amir insisted, his tone growing firm. "My next appeal may be less to your liking."

Lowering the hood, the stranger stepped into the circle of light.

"Kazimain!" I cried, leaping to my feet.

"Ah, Kazimain," sighed Sadiq, shaking his head wearily.

I went to her and made to embrace her, but among the Children of Allah, it is held a sinful thing for a man and woman to be seen touching one another, so I stood uncertainly before her, aware of the eyes on us, and Lord Sadiq's inevitable displeasure. "Kazimain?" I whispered, pleading for an explanation.

She glanced at me, her dark eyes defiant; she seemed on the point of speaking, but thought better of it, stepped past me and settled herself at the fire. Sadiq stared at his kinswoman, an expression of exasperated pride and annoyance warring on his swarthy face. Annoyance won. "You should not have come," he said at last.

Kazimain, without taking the slightest regard, extended her hands towards the fire. No doubt she had foreseen this meeting and had prepared what she would do. "One would almost think you were not happy to see me, Uncle," she observed, her voice sweet and soft.

"It was a foolish thing to do." The amir frowned. He dismissed his men to their chores, and sat down, folding his legs beneath him. He placed his hands on his knees. "There are wicked men in the hills. You might have been killed," he paused, "or worse."

Kazimain raised her head and regarded him with regal disdain. "I was ever within sight of the amir," she replied coolly. "Is his arm so short that he could not protect me?"

"You have been hiding all this time?" I wondered.

"The fire is warm," she said, holding her hands before the flames. "It is a luxury I did not allow myself." She glanced at me, the merest hint of a superior smile touching her lips. "If the amir had known, he would have sent me home."

"The amir *will* send you home!" declared Sadiq firmly.

Kazimain inclined her head nicely. "If that is your decision, my kinsman, I will not disagree."

"You should not have come," Sadiq said again. "No daughter of mine would ever do such a thing."

"No doubt your unborn daughters are better behaved than I," Kazimain replied.

"Your disobedience is shameful and unbecoming." The amir's voice was growing tight with frustration.

"Forgive me, uncle," Kazimain replied, "but I do not believe you forbade me to travel. How have I disobeyed you?"

"Must I foresee every possibility?" Sadiq charged. Snatching up a small stick, he snapped it, and threw it into the fire. "This insolence is intolerable. You will return to Ja'fariya at once."

Kazimain rose. "If that is your command." She turned as if she meant to go right then.

"Ya'Allah!" muttered Sadiq. "Camels are less contentious." He looked at me, frowned, and said, "Stay, Kazimain. No one is riding anywhere tonight. Tomorrow is soon enough."

"As you will, lord." Kazimain returned to her place by the fire, the very image of meekness and compliance.

"At dawn tomorrow," Sadiq declared, "you will be escorted back to Samarra where you belong."

"I understand," she said.

We three sat together in uneasy silence for a moment. The matter was settled, and there was nothing more to say. Sadiq looked at me, and then at Kazimain, and back again; abruptly, he stood and walked away, commanding one of the men to take care of Kazimain's horse and donkey.

It was as much privacy as we were likely to get, so I wasted not a moment of it. I leaned nearer and whispered, "Kazimain, why did you come?"

"Need you ask, my love?" she stared into the fire, lest anyone see her talking to me and take offence.

"Lord Sadiq is right, it was very dangerous. You could have been hurt."

"Are you to be angry with me, too?" she asked, her brow creasing slightly.

"Not in the least, my love, I—"

"I thought you would be pleased to see me."

"I am—more than I can say—but you took a terrible risk."

Shaking her head, she said, "Perhaps, but I think it worthwhile to see you again."

She turned her face towards me at last; the firelight shimmering on her skin made my heart melt with longing. I wanted to take her in my arms and kiss her forever, but I could not so much as touch her hand. I almost squirmed with desire.

"I knew," she continued, "that if you left Samarra I would never see you again. I decided to come with you."

"And now you must go back."

"That is what Lord Sadiq has said," she agreed, but the way she said it made me wonder.

Four days later, we arrived at the enormous timber gate of the slave camp that was the caliph's silver mine. Yes, and Kazimain remained with us still, for on the morning that the amir had decreed for her return, she had respectfully pointed out that if her uncle truly cared about her safety, he would allow her to continue her journey since remaining with him and his bodyguard would undoubtedly be safer than returning alone, or with an escort of only two or three. The amir countered by saying he would send half his men, and received the reply that this proposal seemed needlessly foolhardy since it would compromise the amir's enterprise.

"On the other hand," Kazimain pointed out, "while I know little of your purposes, I am persuaded that there are times when a woman's presence may be of considerable value."

While Sadiq was none too certain about this, Faysal concurred whole-heartedly. "It is true, my lord amir," he said. "The Prophet himself, grace and peace be upon him forever, often rejoiced in the aid of his wife and kinswomen, as is well known."

In the end, Sadiq allowed himself to be persuaded—against his better judgement, it must be said—to allow his niece to continue. "But only so far and until proper arrangements can be made to send you home," he vowed. Kazimain, of course, meekly acquiesced to this, as she did to all his wishes.

Although the sun remained hot, we left the heat of the lowlands behind and entered the cooler heights of the hills, climbing steadily towards the mountains. Now and then we felt a freshening breeze on our faces, and slept more comfortably at night. Day by day, we pursued the winding trail into the hills, arriving at the mine four days after leaving the valley behind.

Sure, I was anxious to gain the freedom of my friends. From the moment when, still far off, we glimpsed the white-washed timbers of the gate—a mere glimmer in the midday sun—freeing the captives occupied my every thought. And now that we stood before the very gate—yawning open as if to mock the freedom denied to the inhabitants within—it was all I could do to keep from throwing myself from the saddle and rushing headlong to the overseer's dwelling and commanding him to unchain them and set them free.

Sadiq sagely advised against such rash behaviour. "Perhaps you would allow me the pleasure of serving you in this," he offered. "The chief overseer may balk at the request of a former slave. He will not, however, find it so easy to refuse me, I think."

As he spoke, the sick hatred welled up inside me. Again, I felt the ache of oppression in my bones and the sting of the lash; I felt the shaking frustration of enforced weakness, and the exhaustion of body and soul, the waking death of bondage. I wanted nothing more than to make those who practised this injustice suffer as I had suffered.

"I thank you, Lord Sadiq," I said, drawing myself up in the saddle, "but I will speak to him myself."

"Of course," the amir replied, "I leave the choice to you. However, I stand ready to aid you should your efforts fall short of the desired result." He regarded me, trying to read the depth of my intent. Then, with the air of a man passing on a dangerous duty, he summoned Faysal and three of his rafiq to accompany me. "Take Bara, Musa, and Nadr with you," he said, "and attend Aidan as you would attend me."

Satisfied with this preparation, Sadiq dismounted to await my return, saying, "Be wise, my friend, as Allah is wise."

I looked to Kazimain, who favoured me with an encouraging smile before replacing the veil. Then, turning in the saddle, I lifted the reins and rode through the hateful gate once more, and felt the slow heat of righteous wrath simmering in my heart. *This day,* I thought, *vengeance begins. So be it.*

We made our way along the narrow pathway through the close-huddled dwellings to the square of sun-blasted dirt outside the whitewashed house of the overseer. Keeping my saddle, I signalled Faysal to summon the man, which he did, calling out in a loud voice.

Word of our arrival, I expect, had been passed to the overseer the moment we reached the gates, for he appeared in the open doorway of the house, and stood looking out at us for a moment before emerging. I could see his white-turbaned head motionless in the dark as he gazed out at his unexpected visitors.

Faysal called again, and the overseer stepped, blinking, into the sun. "Greetings in the Holy Name," he said. "What is your business here?"

Not deigning to dismount, I addressed him from the saddle. "I have come to obtain the release of slaves."

I do not believe he recognized me at all, but I remembered him: he was the pit overseer Dugal had inadvertently struck, and who had directed our torture. He now stood in the sun, his small pig eyes all asquint, trying to work out how this unexpected demand might be turned to his advantage. The wrinkles of his sun-swarthy face arranged themselves in a shrewd expression. "Who are you to speak thus to me?"

"My name is Aidan mac Cainnech," I told him. "I am advisor to J'amal Sadiq, Amir of Samarra."

He stiffened at the name, the memory of his predecessor's treatment at the hands of the amir's men still sore to him. "The amir has no authority here," he declared. "Who makes this demand?"

"Protector of the Faithful, Khalifa al'Mutamid," I replied.

The chief overseer became sly. "You have *proof*, I presume?"

Taking the khalifa's decree, I passed it to Faysal, who leaned down from the saddle and offered it to the overseer who untied the silk band and carefully unrolled the parchment. "You *can* read, I presume?"

A frown appeared on his face as he scanned the document. After a moment, he lowered the decree and stared at me; this time he seemed to find something familiar in my face, but clearly could not think where he had seen me before.

"Come down from your lofty perch, my friend," he said, "and let us discuss this matter face to face."

Looking down on him, revulsion surged through me. God help me, I despised him. Oh, he was a vile creature.

"We have nothing to discuss," I replied. "I will tell you the names of those who are to be freed, and you will free them."

His face closed like a fist. "Names mean nothing here," he replied with an air of superiority. That was true, and I should have remembered. Thinking he had thwarted me, he allowed himself a smug sneer.

"It makes no difference," I responded coolly, "you will assemble the slaves and I will choose those I require from among them."

"*All* the slaves?" He sputtered like a pot about to boil. "But there are hundreds of slaves here—scattered everywhere in these hills. It would take the entire day to assemble them all."

"Then I suggest you begin at once."

"I would lose a day's worth of silver!" he shrieked. "Come back tomorrow," he suggested. "Come at dawn and you can see them before they begin their labour."

"Do you refuse the emissary of the khalifa?"

"You are being hasty," he said. "I must point out to you that what you ask is very difficult. There are many questions to be considered." His pained expression smoothed. "There is no need to invoke the khalifa's name; this is a matter between the two of us."

"My thoughts precisely."

"Seeing that you understand me," he said, his voice oily and insinuating, "I believe we can reach a fair *agreement*." He rubbed the fingertips of his right hand against the palm of his left.

"I understand you better than you know," I told him, my voice thick with loathing. Placing a hand to the jewelled daigear at my belt, I said, "Assemble the slaves at once, or lose your worthless tongue."

Turning to Faysal, I said, "I am going to wait in the overseer's house. See that this son of a rat does what is required of him."

"If I refuse?" the overseer said, the arrogant sneer back on his face.

"If he refuses," I said to Faysal, "kill him."

## 59

The overseer gaped, unable to decide if I was in earnest; he opened his mouth to protest, then decided to save his breath, and hastened away to begin the task of summoning and assembling the slaves. While Faysal and one of the rafiq accompanied the overseer, I dismounted, secured my horse to the whipping post and went into the overseer's house to await his return.

The interior was dim, the low wide windholes shuttered against the sun. As my eyes adjusted to the darkness, I saw a room of clutter and filth. The powder-fine red-brown dust, which was everywhere in the mines, blew in on the breeze and was never swept out again; it clung to everything, and was hard caked in the places he habitually walked.

The dwelling reeked of bitter smoke; the stink clung to the carpets and cushions on the floor. "Hashish," muttered one of the warriors scornfully, and pointed to a small iron brazier filled with ash which stood beside a large greasy leather cushion. Here then, the chief overseer spent his nights, inhaling the potent vapours of the stupefying plant. I did not like to sit down in this hovel, so I stood, and the rafiq stood with me, contemptuous of a man whose life could be read in this slovenly mess.

My thoughts turned to my friends, and I wondered what they would say when they saw that I had returned to free them. Did they think I had forgotten them? Did they imagine I had abandoned them? Or was hope yet alive in their hearts? When this day dawned and they rose to take up the tools of their torment once again, did they realize how close was their liberation? Did they sense the nearness of their freedom even now?

From somewhere high on the hill the sounding iron clanged, and after a time the first slaves began streaming down the hill paths to their accustomed places along the boundary of the sun-baked square outside the overseer's house. I watched them as they arrived, searching among the ranks for any familiar face, but saw none. The distressing thought flitted through my mind: *what if they are dead?* What if I have tarried too long and they have all succumbed to cruel labour and the lash? What if none now survived for me to set free? This was something I had never considered, but I did so now; and, had I imagined it would have done any good, I would have prayed that God had sustained them and kept them to this day.

I waited. More and more slaves were coming to the square. They saw the horses tethered to the post in the yard—where on such occasions someone among them provided an exemplary sacrifice—and wondered what new torture was at hand.

The slave throng slowly gathered. I stood in the doorway, searching the crowd, and had begun to fear I would not find anyone I knew, when I saw Jarl Harald. He stood a head or more taller than anyone around him, which should have made him easier to find. But then I realized why I had not seen him sooner: he had changed. His fine mane of flame-red hair and beard were now a matted, moth-eaten mass; his broad shoulders were bowed and he stood with a slump, his body twisted to one side, as if favouring a crippled limb. Grey-faced, the once proud lord gazed down at the ground, never raising his eyes.

With awful dread, I searched the ranks and found, to my horror, others I should have recognized before. One after another—and each more wretched than the last—I identified them. I could not bear to look at them, and turned away in a sudden panic of doubt, thinking, *It was a mistake to come. I should have left them to their fate. There can be no salvation; liberation has come too late.*

Finally, the chief overseer returned to stand uncertainly in the centre of the yard. Faysal left him in the company of the warrior named Nadr, and proceeded to the house. "The slaves are assembled," Faysal reported.

I thanked him and said, "I wish I could free them all. Would the khalifa's generosity stretch so far, do you think?"

"They are waiting," he said.

I nodded. "They will wait no longer. Captivity has ended for a fortunate few."

Stepping from the overseer's house into the full brightness of the sun, it was a moment before I could see properly. The sun scorched through the thin cloth of my robe, and my heart went out to those standing naked beneath the burning rays. At least the mines were dark and cool. Now I was making them burn in the blast furnace of the day's heat.

Faysal regarded me out of the corner of a narrowed eye, but I shook off his concern. "Let us be done with this," I murmured, striding forward once more.

Not knowing where else to begin, I went first to the place where Harald stood and pointed to him. The barbarian did not so much as glance in my direction. "Bring him here," I ordered the nearest guard, who seized Harald roughly by the arm and jerked him from his place. "Gently!" I told the guard sternly. "He is a king."

The Dane shuffled forth, his leg chains rattling on the ground; he came to stand before me, never once looking up. "I have returned," I told him. "I have come for you."

At these words, he raised his head for the first time. With pale, watery eyes he looked at me, but without recognition. My heart fell.

"Jarl Harald," I said, "it is Aidan. Do you not remember me?"

Into his dull gaze flickered a light I had never seen before—beyond mere recognition, or realization; beyond common hope, or joy. A light which was nothing less than life itself reawakening in a human soul. Awareness at its most profound and pure kindled in that spark of light and blazed in the smile that slowly spread across Harald Bull-Roar's face.

"Aidan God-speaker," he breathed. And then could say no more for the tears that choked his voice. He raised a trembling hand to me, as if he would stroke my face. I seized the hand and grasped it tight.

"Stand easy, brother," I told him. "We are soon leaving this place." Turning my eyes once more to the throng, I asked, "How many of the others still live?"

"All of them, I think," he replied nodding.

"Where are they? I do not see them."

By way of reply, the wily Dane raised his hands to his mouth, drew breath and gave out a bellowing roar. It was, I remembered, the sea marauder's war cry, now weakened and strained. He gave it again, and then cried, "Heya! Aidan has returned! Come, men, we are going home!"

The echo of Harald's shout died away to silence. I watched the gathered ranks as out from among the dead-eyed slaves came the wasted remnant of the Sea Wolf pack. My spirit writhed within me to see them shambling forth—some in pairs still, others by themselves, but all dragging their irons. Off to one side, one poor wretch hobbled towards me, his eagerness made pathetic by his lurching gait. His last steps were ill-judged and he tottered headlong to the dust. I reached down to raise him and found myself looking into Gunnar's haggard face.

"Aeddan," he said, tears streaming from his eyes. "Aeddan, thank God, you have come at last. I knew you would return. I knew you would not leave us to die in this place."

I helped him to his feet and clasped him to me. "Gunnar," I said, "forgive me, brother. I should have come sooner, forgive me."

"How should I forgive you?" Wonder made his features childlike. "You have returned. I knew you would. I never doubted."

I looked at the other slaves slowly making their way to where we stood. "Where is Dugal?" I said. "I do not see him." Once more, panic assailed me. *Have I come too late? Dugal! Where are you, brother?* "Where are the Britons?"

In the same instant, I heard a cry from across the yard. I turned and saw, stumbling forward through the press, the hulking figure of my dearest friend and brother. Vastly changed, he was—still, I knew him as I would have known my own self. "Dugal!" I cried, and hastened to meet him.

Seeing me, he half-turned and gestured to someone behind him, and then came on. We met in the centre of the yard before the whipping post where we had last seen one another, and where Bishop Cadoc had gone to death in my place. "Dugal!" I cried, my own eyes filling with tears. "Are you alive, Dugal?"

"Just so, Dána," he whispered, kneading the flesh of my shoulders with his hands. "I am."

Faysal appeared beside us just then. "We best move quickly," he reminded me. "The slaves and their masters grow restive."

To Dugal I said, "Do the Britons yet live?"

"They do," he said, and turned to the slaves looking on, their agitation increasing by the moment. No longer slack-witted, I could tell by the expressions on their faces they had begun to perceive that there would be no execution today. But the sight of strangers choosing slaves seemingly at random confused and excited them.

"Brynach! Ddewi!" At Dugal's shout two round-shouldered figures lurched from the throng. I would not have known them in a thousand years for the men they had once been. Brynach's hair was white and he walked with a stoop, and the young Ddewi had lost an eye. The hair and beards of both, like the hair and beards of all, were nasty, matted, lice-infested tangles.

I took up their hands and embraced them. "Brothers," I said, "I have come for you."

Brynach smiled; his teeth were discoloured and his gums were raw. "All praise to Christ, our Lord and Redeemer! His purposes shall not be seen to fail."

At his words my heart twisted within me. I wanted to shout at him: *Christ! How dare you thank that monster! Had it been left to God, the mines would claim your rotting bones. It is Aidan, not Christ, who frees you now!*

But I swallowed the bile and said, "We are leaving this place. Can you walk?"

"I will crawl to freedom if need be," he said, his mouth spreading in a grin. The skin of his lips split in the violence of his smile and began to bleed.

"Come, Ddewi, the day of our liberation has come. We are leaving our captivity." With the gentleness of a mother bending to an ailing child, the elder monk took hold of the younger's hand and began leading him away. It was then that I understood Ddewi had lost more than an eye only.

Some of the slaves across the yard began shouting at me. I could not make out what they wanted, nor did I want to know. My only thought now was to escape with the prize as quickly as possible. "We must go," Faysal said, his voice urgent, his eyes wary. "To wait any longer is to tempt the devil."

Pausing only long enough to make doubly certain that none of my friends was left behind, I counted eighteen Sea Wolves, and three Celts. To Faysal, I said, "Mount those who cannot walk." He hurried away, shouting orders to Bara and Nadr.

The chief overseer, who had stood aside biding his time, now pressed forward. "You take my slaves;" he protested, shaking his fist in the air, "what will you give me for them?"

Rounding on him, I said, "You have read the decree. It says nothing of payment."

"You cannot take my slaves!" he whined. "I must be paid!"

Ignoring him, I called to Faysal, "Is everyone ready?"

"Lead the way," he replied. "We will follow." He looked around at the guards, who appeared sullen and unhappy. Some shifted uneasily in their places, as if weighing the consequences of siding with the overseer.

"This way," I called, raising my hand and striding forth. I took but two steps and was stopped by Jarl Harald, who put his hand to my sleeve and said, "We cannot leave yet."

"Cannot leave?" I stared at him. "What do you mean?"

He glanced furtively towards the overseer, who still waved his arms in protest, crying his outrage at our uncaring treatment of him. Putting his mouth to my ear, Harald whispered a terse explanation.

"What?" I wondered in disbelief. "You cannot mean it."

He nodded solemnly. "We did not know you would return today," he said.

"I am sorry," I told him flatly. "There is no time."

Folding his arms across his chest, the king shook his head solemnly. "Nay."

Faysal, seeing my hesitation, hastened to my side. "We must go."

"There is a small matter yet to be resolved," I muttered, staring hard at the king, who remained adamant.

Faysal made to protest, then glanced at the Danish king, his face set in a stubborn frown. "Resolve it quickly, my friend," he relented. "I fear your decree will not detain this greedy fellow very much longer."

I looked to the slave master, who was now urgently gesturing for several of his guards to join him. There was nothing for it but to seize the lion by his beard, as it were. "Come with me," I ordered Faysal, "and bring two warriors."

Marching directly to the angry overseer, I faced him squarely. "We are leaving," I announced, "but not before the chains are removed and we have secured the bones of our brothers."

"Bones!" he brayed in disbelief. "There was nothing said about bones!"

"Listen to me well," I told him darkly as Faysal and the two rafiq came to stand behind me, "your worthless life hangs by a thread over the pit, but hear me out and you may yet save yourself."

The slave master subsided, grumbling and cursing.

"I was a slave here," I began. "On the day I left this place, two of my friends and I were to have been executed." The slow dawn of recognition broke over the man's fleshy face. "Faysal stopped the execution, but not before you killed an old man who gave himself in my place. Do you remember?"

An expression akin to fear crept into the overseer's sun-blasted features. Yes, he remembered it all now.

"Answer me!"

His eyes flicked to the two warriors whose hands moved towards the hilts of their swords. "It is possible," he allowed.

"That man was a priest of God," I said. "He was a holy man, and he was my friend. I will not allow his bones to remain in this accursed place. Therefore, we will take them with us." The overseer gaped, but did not disagree. "Now then, tell me where his body is buried."

"We do not bury slaves," the overseer informed me with smug self-assurance. "We throw their corpses to the dogs."

"If that is the way of it," I replied, my voice falling to what I hoped was a withering whisper, "you must pray to whatever god will hear you that we find his remains." I let him imagine the worst. "Show me where his body was thrown."

The overseer pointed to one of the guards. "That one knows. He will show you."

Turning to Faysal, I said, "See that the leg irons are removed, and then take the overseer into his house and wait there with him until I return."

As soon as the first slaves were freed from their leg chains, we set off: Harald, Brynach, Gunnar, Hnefi, no fewer than six other Sea Wolves, the guard and myself. Once out of sight of the yard, I took Harald by the arm, "We will take our time, but you must hurry." I told him then what I had in mind and ordered him to do the same. "Do you understand?"

Nodding, the jarl and his men hobbled off up the long slope in the direction of the mines, walking in a laborious, rolling amble; they had grown unused to moving their feet so freely. The guard watched them suspiciously. "Where are they going?" he demanded.

"Show us where you put the body of my friend," I commanded.

The guard pointed at the retreating Danes, and prepared to renew his demand.

"Now!" I told him. "I grow weary of your insolence."

The guard clamped his mouth shut, turned on his heel and led us in the opposite direction. We walked to a place behind the settlement and he showed me a small ravine, little more than a dry ditch choked with the tough little desert thorn bushes and twisted, stunted cacti. Judging from the bits of broken pottery and the stink, I guessed the refuse of the settlement was pitched down the slope. "There," the guard muttered with a downward jerk of his chin.

"We will begin searching," I told him. "Bring us a robe."

As the guard sauntered away, I told Brynach what I had in mind to do. He commended my thoughtfulness, saying, "Ah, a man after my own heart. May your compassion be rewarded forever." Then, raising his shaggy head, he said, "And Joseph made the Sons of Israel swear an oath and said, 'God will surely come to your aid, and you must carry my bones from this place.'" So Joseph's sons took up his bones and bore them out of Egypt."

"I will go down and see what I can find," I told him, and left him reciting Holy Scripture on the edge of the ravine. I picked my way carefully down the steep slope, sliding the last few steps. I found a broken stick and began poking here and there among the refuse, potsherds, and sheep dung. There were bones aplenty—mostly those of animals, but some human.

And then, half hidden under a pile of dung and shrivelled garbage, I glimpsed a wad of sun-rotted cloth and my heart missed a beat. The cloth was the coarse weave of a monk's cloak. I scraped away the refuse to reveal a tell-tale bulge. Squatting down, I lifted away the scrap of discarded clothing to reveal the discoloured skull of Bishop Cadoc.

The bone was white where the sun had scoured it, but brown where it had laid in the dirt; there were scrags of hard-baked flesh still clinging to the underside, dry and black.

Laying aside the skull, I prodded a little more and turned up a long leg bone, and a single curved rib. Here and there, I found other bones: an arm without a hand, the lumpy cradle of a pelvis, some more ribs.

"Aidan?" came a call from the edge of the ravine above. "Have you found anything?"

"Yes," I answered, and told him what I had found so far.

I do not know what I expected; Cadoc had been cut in two, the pieces carelessly heaved into the pit, and the corpse worried by dogs. No doubt, there were pieces of the good bishop scattered from one end of the ditch to the other.

"Do you want me to come down now?" Brynach called from above.

"No, brother, I think we will not find much more."

"The skull is the most needful," Brynach told me. "And the leg bones. Do you have two leg bones?"

"Just one," I replied.

"Ah, a pity," sighed Brynach. "Still, it is a handsome gesture. God is smiling even now."

I moved further down the ravine and found what appeared to be a shoulderblade. I did not take it, though, for it was gnawed rough and covered with the teeth marks—those of dogs, and smaller, sharper ones that fit a rodent's jaws. The slave guard returned while I was searching among the rocks and refuse, and I ordered him to join me, bringing the garment he had been sent to find. He came, reluctantly, dragging a long, pale yellow robe of the kind the Arabs use to repel the sun and dust when travelling.

Taking the robe, I spread it on the rocks and shifted the bones onto it. Brynach crept a little way down the slope to watch me. When I finished, he raised his hands and declaimed aloud: "When I die, bury me in the place where the man of God is buried; lay my bones beside his bones." Lowering his hands, he said, "That is from the Book of Kings. Thanks to you, Aidan, we will bear our departed brother back to his beloved soil and give him a burial proper to his station."

I made no reply, ashamed of my true purpose and wishing that I had thought of this for its own sake. I looked at the meagre offering, a pitiable reminder of a great man's existence. No doubt a more diligent search would have reclaimed more, but I was growing anxious that we had been away too long already. So, I folded the robe over the paltry assortment, gathered the ends, and carefully swung the bundle onto my back. I climbed to the top of the ravine and, with Brynach and the guard, returned to the place where I had told Harald and his men to meet us.

There was no one in sight.

# 60

should never have let them go off by themselves," I
muttered irritably. I could see the gleaming hope of
freedom, so close as to hear the whir of its golden
wings, beginning to recede. There was nothing to do but
wait; lowering the bundle of bones to the ground, we stood
in the blazing sun, shifting the powdery dust with our feet.
The slave guard, already deeply suspicious, held himself a
little to one side, watching every move.

"Those men are Danes," observed Brynach.

"That they are," I sighed.

"The same that took you away that night?"

"Near enough as makes no difference," I replied, hoping to save myself a lengthy explanation.

But Brynach only nodded thoughtfully. "The Arabs
with you," he continued, "they were here the day Cadoc
was killed. They took you away."

"True." I glanced at the British monk, hand to forehead, shielding his eyes from the sun; he seemed unconcerned that his only hope of freedom dwindled with every
drop of sweat that rolled down his neck.

"Who are they?" he asked. "And who are you, that
they should have saved you?"

I looked away, not wishing to offend, but unwilling to relate that too-lengthy tale just now. "It is not told in words of a moment," I replied. "Perhaps later, when I can properly explain."

He accepted this with good grace. "Truly, God moves in mysterious ways, and the musings of his heart are beyond discovery," he declared. "And that is a fact."

*Then God must surely be an Arab,* I thought. *Or the Emperor of Byzantium's elder brother.*

Brynach, having found his voice, was apparently keen to use it. "The Danes," he said, "where did they go?"

I was saved from having to make up an answer by a sound not unlike that of pigs being slaughtered. It seemed to come from up the hill in the direction of the mines. We all three turned as one towards the sound. "Whatever can it be?" wondered Brynach.

The sound increased, and into view came a column of Sea Wolves, marching in a ragged double rank. Between each pair was slung a weighty bundle, similar to that which contained the bishop's bones, only larger, and clearly much heavier. They were struggling down from the mines, dragging their heavy burdens, and they sang as they marched.

"Did you have to listen to that?" Brynach asked.

"Not often."

"Thank God."

"Heya!" cried Harald limping to where we stood. The column halted and the men all but collapsed upon their bundles. "We are ready to leave now," he said, gasping for breath from his exertion, "and we will not be looking back."

Brynach stared at me as I answered in Harald's tongue. "I had no idea there would be so much, or I would not have agreed," I said without enthusiasm. Any hope that we might leave unmolested had deserted me. The chief overseer would certainly not let us go when he saw how much the Sea Wolves intended to take away with them. And, as we could not avoid crossing the yard, there was nothing for it but to brazen the thing through. "If you are ready, then follow me."

Brynach and I took up our bundle and an odd procession fell in line behind us as we made our slow way back down the slope to the yard where the others stood waiting.

The overseer, who had by this time overcome his fear of the caliph's decree, came flying out of his house as we entered the yard. "What is this? What is this?" he cried, waving his arms.

"I have already told you," I replied icily. "We bear away the bones of Bishop Cadoc."

His squint-eyes narrowed to mere slits as he counted all the bundles on the ground. "So many bones?" he whined. "It is not possible."

Faysal, Nadr, Bara, and Musa took up places behind me. The gathered slaves looked on, growing excited once again. "What is he saying?" hissed Brynach anxiously.

By way of reply, I bent down and unknotted the bundle Brynach and I carried. Withdrawing the skull, I stood and thrust it before his face. "Look upon the visage of one who died by your hand," I told him. "Look long, Oppressor, and remember. His blood shall cry witness against you on Judgement Day."

The overseer blenched at this, so I continued my bluff. Putting out a hand to the Sea Wolves' bundles, I declared, "And likewise the blood of all those who suffered under the lash and died at your pleasure—all these shall rise up on the last day and condemn you before Allah, the Righteous Judge."

The slave master made bold to protest, but I stopped him before he could say a word. "Detain us now and you will surely never see Paradise."

"Be gone with you!" he shouted, angry now. Summoning a few of the guards to him, he said, "The sight of them offends me. See that they leave at once!"

I suppose he took on this guise to preserve what little dignity remained him, but he need not have worried that we would overstay our welcome. No man was more impatient to be gone than the one standing before him at that moment.

Replacing the skull, I carefully retied the bundle and gestured for Dugal to come and carry it, and instructed that Ddewi, and some of the others should be mounted on the five horses along with as many of the bundles as they could hold. Then, turning on my heel, I led my bedraggled band of Vikings and monks from the yard like the Prophet Moses escorting the Chosen out of Egypt. Realizing that we were leaving, the watching slaves began to clamour; just as we reached the street leading to the gate, they surged after us, begging—demanding—to be included in our number. All at once the overseer and his guards were fighting to keep from being trampled in the rush.

Making what haste we could, we proceeded down the single narrow street of the settlement to the gate, arriving just ahead of the oncoming mob. Behind us, I could hear the voice of the overseer crying orders for the gate to be closed at once.

"Faysal!" I yelled, shouting above the rising commotion. He raced to my side. "Run ahead and hold the gate. If they close it now we will never get free. Hurry!"

Off he ran, taking two warriors with him; the others remained behind to guard our retreat if they could. I called to Harald and Dugal. "Make for the gate, men! Hurry!"

"We are hurrying as fast as we can," Dugal answered, lumbering past; he all but dragged poor Brynach, who appeared to have scant appreciation for our predicament.

"God help us!" said Brynach, invoking divine aid and intervention on our behalf.

"Save your breath," I snarled. "God is done with us. It is we who must be saving ourselves!"

He broke off, staring at me. I pushed him on. "Go! Go! Do not stand there gawking, man. Run!"

The Danes needed no coaxing. Lugging their bundles, they slewed on through the dust, heads down, sweating and grunting with the effort. I urged them on, shouting, pointing ahead to the gate, where Faysal gestured wildly. I looked and saw the great timbers swinging slowly shut.

The opening was a hundred paces or more from where I stood. Whirling around, I looked to where the last of the Sea Wolves toiled toward freedom. We would never make it!

"Throw down your burdens," I cried. "Run! Save yourselves!"

No one paid the slightest heed. The stubborn Danes lowered their heads and laboured on. Unless the gate was held, they would be cut off; once closed, I had little hope that it would be opened again—not for me, or the amir, or anyone else.

I dashed to where Faysal was contending with the guards. "We cannot hold it any longer!" he cried.

The great timbers continued to close. Darting forward, I pushed against one of the huge cross-members with all my might, but could not so much as discourage its inevitable progress. "Help me!" I shouted. Bara and Musa leapt to my aid, and we desperately strove to slow the closure, while Faysal renewed his protestations with the gate-men. Meanwhile, the gate, groaning under its own weight, ground ahead regardless.

Dugal was first to reach the opening; bearing the bundle of bones, he hastened through pulling Brynach with him. Meanwhile, Faysal, seeing his efforts were wasted with the gatemen, ran to join us, adding his strength to ours. Even so, it was no use; our feet slid in the dust. The gate ground ahead, more slowly, but just as relentlessly as before.

We could not stop it.

A few of the first Sea Wolves hastened empty-handed through the ever-narrowing portal. They were free!

But one glance over my shoulder, and my heart fell. Harald and the remaining Danes, striving heroically with the weight of their bundles, were still too, too far away. What is more, the mad rush of slaves, despite the shackles and leg chains, was gaining on them from behind.

"Throw down the sacks!" I cried. "Save yourselves!"

The Sea Wolves responded to this, not by releasing their burdens, but by striving still harder. I saw one of them stumble and fall, pulling his partner down with him, and tripping up the two behind. Those following on were somehow able to avoid tumbling into the heap, but the accident slowed them all.

I looked to the gate and saw that the gap was now merely two men wide. And the first of the run-amok slaves had almost reached the last pair of straggling Danes.

"The gate is closing!" I called again and again. "Run for it!"

As before, my pleas met with no greater heed.

I heard a voice beside me and looked to see Dugal leaning into the gate. He had left his burden on the other side, and returned to lend his hand to halting the gate.

"Dugal!" I shouted. "Get you free, man! Go on! Go!"

He merely grimaced and bent his strength to the hopeless task.

*Will* no one *do what I tell them?* I wondered. "Go, Dugal! Save yourself!"

The gap was now but wide enough for one man to slip through. Very soon, it would close completely, and the first of the Danes was still fifty paces or more from reaching the gate.

*Kyrie eleison!* I muttered through clenched teeth. *God help us!*

More curse than prayer, I confess; it was merely the last gasp of a drowning man, as it were. But, lo and behold! the groaning timbers abruptly jolted to a halt.

I looked and saw Amir Sadiq on horseback, just beyond the opening, a rope from his saddle tied to a crosstimber of the gate. The horse was rearing, the rope taut.

Harald Bull-Roar appeared, sweat pouring down him like rain. Throwing down his bundle, he cried encouragement to his men, all but pushing them to freedom.

The gate groaned and shuddered, the top of its tall timbers quivering.

We held the great door while Harald muscled his men through the gap. The first of the fleeing slaves had reached the last of the Sea Wolves and had overtaken them. Heedless of all else, they threw themselves headlong at the door, jamming the opening and blocking the escape.

With a roar, Harald waded into them, seizing slaves and shoving them right and left. He cleared the pinched passage even as he pushed his own men through to freedom.

"Ya'Allah!" cried Faysal, the sinews in his neck and arms standing out like cords of rope. "We cannot hold it much longer!"

"Heya!" bellowed Harald. "We are free! Hurry!"

I looked and saw Harald and two other Danes, arms stretched wide holding the gate for us. The oncoming mob raced nearer.

Turning to Faysal and the others, I cried, "It is done! They are free!"

I had to repeat this in Irish for Dugal, but no one needed a second prod. In an instant, we were all of us diving for the slender opening. Faysal, Bara, and Musa squeezed past the Sea Wolves and out. But just as Dugal and I reached the opening, the gate gave out a grating sigh and juddered ahead. The Danes, unable to hold it any longer, fell back.

The timbers slammed shut with a heart-stopping crash.

Before we could even halt our steps, the enormous gate rebounded on itself and gaped open again. Shoving Dugal ahead of me, I flung myself through. I landed, sprawling on my face in the dust on the other side. Behind me, the gate banged closed once more.

Sadiq, his mount still straining at the rope, called a warning. I heard a crack like that of a whip and looked up in time to see the rope recoiling through the air. Sadiq's horse, unbalanced by the sudden snap of the rope, toppled over backwards. The amir, unable to quit the saddle, was pressed to the ground as the horse rolled over him.

My feet scarcely touched the ground as I flew to him. I snagged the reins and jerked with all my might—raising the wild-eyed, flailing animal by strength of will alone. The horse got its feet under it and, with a lurching spring, stood, shaking its head and mane.

"Amir!" I shouted, throwing aside the reins. I leaped to his side, but Sadiq did not move.

# PART FOUR

*Black in sin is yonder house,*
*Blacker still the men therein,*
*I am the white swan,*
*King over them.*
*I will go in the name of God,*
*In likeness of deer, in likeness of bear,*
*In likeness of serpent, in likeness of King,*
*In likeness of my King will I go.*
*The three shielding me and aiding me,*
*The three each step aiding me.*

# 61

The amir lay as dead, his eyes half-open. The breath had been squeezed from his lungs and he was unconscious. Two of his rafiq, who had been likewise manning ropes at the gate, rushed to help me. "Gently! Gently!" I told them, as together we rolled him onto his side; we were rewarded with a long, ragged gasp as air filled the amir's lungs. He coughed and moaned, and began breathing again.

From the far side of the towering gate came the wails of the wretches who had not been able to get out in time. The shrieks turned to screams of terror as those who stood at the gate were crushed against it by the mass of those pushing from behind.

Faysal ran to my aid. Kazimain's horse raced to where we stooped over the amir; sliding from the saddle, she rushed to her kinsman's side. She grasped his hand and began rubbing it briskly, trying to wake him. Bending to his ear, she murmured softly, her voice trembling with anxiety.

I could not make out what she said, but in a moment, the amir stirred and tried to raise his head. Kazimain bade him rest easy. "It is done," I told him. "We are free."

"Can you stand, lord?" asked Faysal.

The amir looked around, as if to ascertain who spoke. His wits returned to him then, for he nodded, and Faysal and I helped him to his feet. He swayed as if dizzy, but objected when we made to steady him. "It is nothing, it will pass," he said, shaking his head as if to clear it. "Where is my horse?"

Faysal retrieved the animal and brought it to stand before his lord. As Sadiq climbed into the saddle, the massive gate behind us began to throb and shake. My stomach squirmed as I heard the dull cracking thud of human bodies breaking against the barrier: the slaves were hurling themselves at the unyielding timber in their despair. It was a hideous sound, and one I hope never to hear again. But there was nothing to be done for them, and we were not certain of our own safety until we were far from that place.

"We must not linger here," said Faysal, glancing warily over his shoulder.

"Lead the way," Sadiq commanded. "The rafiq and I will follow." He called his warriors to him and hastily formed a phalanx to guard our escape. Faysal, meanwhile, led us swiftly away. We hastened after him, scrambling down the trail as best we could, until we came to the place just out of sight of the gate where the pack horses and supplies waited. There we paused to assemble ourselves and better order our departure.

"The chief overseer will hold you to blame for setting his slaves to riot," the amir said; he sat on his horse, watching the former captives limping towards us. "I had no idea you had so many friends."

Indeed, there were several dozen more than I had set out to free, for those who had forced their way out through the gate were now making their way to where we waited. "I am sorry, Lord Sadiq," I started, "they all—"

But the amir waved aside my explanation. "It would not have happened if the slave master had kept order. We will find a way to deal with them," he said, then cast an eye towards where the Danes stood sweating and panting around the bundles they had, risking all, borne from their captivity. "Your Sea Wolves appear to have acquired a few belongings while they toiled for the khalifa," Sadiq observed.

Jarl Harald saw the amir's appraising glance, and knew well what lay behind it. He bent to the bundle on the ground between his feet and untwisted the knots. Brynach and Dugal, their own bundle slung between them, came to stand beside me. We all watched as Harald opened the folds to reveal a mass of dull, misshapen lumps of rock, pale and watery in colour.

"Silver!" exclaimed Brynach. "Christ have mercy! They risked their lives for silver?"

"To the Danefolk, silver is worth more than life," I explained. "They risk everything for it whenever they sail beyond sight of home. Besides," I added, looking at all the sacks, "it is a fine abundance of silver."

Retrieving one of the colourless chunks, Harald marched boldly to the amir's horse and gave the lump to Sadiq, who took it in his hand, hefted it, and nodded sagely before passing it back to the Dane.

"It seems the amir approves," I observed to Harald. "The Sea Wolves will keep their treasure."

Just then, the slaves who had squeezed themselves through the gap in those confused last moments saw us and rushed forward, crying out to be allowed to journey with us. They whined most piteously: "Do not leave us! We will die in the desert! Be merciful! Take us with you!"

Sadiq and Faysal held hasty council, whereupon Faysal returned to address them. "The Lord Sadiq is moved by your pleas. In exchange for your promise to leave us in peace, we will see you safe as far as the Amida road, but no further."

Sure, they all agreed readily, and, after everyone was given water and something to eat, we started off in two long columns. Sadiq and Kazimain led the way, followed by Ddewi on my horse, with Brynach walking beside him—Ddewi was not fit enough to walk and required someone to help him keep his saddle. Dugal and I walked behind them, carrying the bishop's bones, and the Sea Wolves came next, having divided their mass of treasure into many smaller bundles and distributed the weight evenly among all eighteen. Behind came the pack animals bearing the supplies, with the other slaves after them; the amir's mounted rafiq came last.

What a long, slow line we made. And it stretched out longer and moved slower as the day wore on. We camped early; the sun was not yet down when we stopped, and we had travelled but a short distance. But the newly-freed captives could go no further. Still, we were away from the hateful mines, and the valley stretched invitingly before us.

The amir made his camp a little apart from the others, and went to sleep almost as soon as he had finished his evening meal, saying that he thought he had taken too much sun. I was eager to hear how my friends had fared, and mentioned as much to Kazimain, who said, "Go, my love. Renew your friendship. You will have much to tell one another." She turned to where, despite the still-warm dusk, Sadiq lay rolled in his robe beside the little campfire. "I would sit with the amir a little," she said.

So, I made my way to where the monks had made their camp among some great smooth, flat rocks beside the trail. Dugal and Brynach reclined, exhausted, on the rocks, and Ddewi, hunch-shouldered, sat splay-legged beneath them placidly feeding twigs and small knots of dry grass to a tiny fire.

Settling myself on a broad ledge-like stone, I said, "Well now, Dugal, here was I thinking you had given up waiting for me."

"Aidan, man," Dugal said in a lightly reproving tone, raising his head slightly, "look at you now. How were we to know it was you and not the very prince of Sarazens?"

"And who else would be coming for you?"

"Oh, it was a sweet surprise," he remarked, rolling onto his elbow, "to see you striding out so brave and bold. Where did you get that knife, Dána?"

Withdrawing the blade from my belt, I handed it to him. "It is called Qadi," I explained. "The amir gave it to me."

Dugal ran his fingers over the jewelled weapon, making appreciative noises. "Did you see this, Bryn?" he said, flourishing the gleaming blade in the air. "Had I a daigear like this, I might have rescued us myself. Ah, but you put the overseer in his place, I believe; so you did."

Ddewi laughed at this—a soft chuckle only, but it was the first indication I had that he apprehended anything of his surroundings. I looked to Brynach, who said, "Oh, he comes to himself a little sometimes. Perhaps he can recover." His gaze shifted from the younger monk to me. "I am still wondering how you came to be among these Arabs."

"That is easily told," I replied, and explained about my sojourn in Trebizond with the eparch, and the ambush on the way to Sebastea which led to my enslavement at the mine.

"It happened to us the very same way," remarked Brynach.

"Aidan believes it was no accident," Dugal informed him, and went on to describe for Brynach my assumption that the emperor's courtier had personally arranged the disasters which had overtaken us.

"But it cannot be," objected Brynach. "Nikos befriended us; he never had reason to betray us, or wish us harm." He shook his head slowly. "I am certain he was merely trying to help. The holy book was without its cover, and he—"

"The book!" What with one thing and another, I had forgotten all about Colum Cille's holy book and left it behind.

"Calm yourself, Aidan," Dugal said. "We have it still." He indicated Ddewi, idly playing with the fire.

"Ddewi," said Brynach gently, "Stand up and show us the book."

Though he gave no indication of having heard, the mute young monk rose from his place and turned towards us. Looking more closely, I saw the square shape of the cambutta beneath his ragged mantle. Taking the hem of his garment in both hands, he raised it to reveal the leather bag, its strap slung around his neck and over one shoulder; he was wearing the book on his chest.

I resisted the temptation to have him take it out of the bag, to open it and examine its pages once more; but this was neither the time nor the place. "Thank you, Ddewi," Brynach said, and he sat down again, once more as far away from us as his shattered thoughts allowed.

"Cadoc gave it to him as we stood in the yard that day," Brynach explained; I knew well which day he meant. "Poor Ddewi has not breathed a word to anyone since. I do believe that what little wit remains him he owes to the book."

"He keeps the book," Dugal observed, "and the book keeps him."

"We were to get a new cover made," Brynach lamented, "but that will not happen now."

"There are silversmiths enough in Constantinople," I remarked. "Whyever did you think to go to Trebizond in the first place?"

"Did I say we were going to Trebizond?" Brynach wondered.

"No, Dugal told me," I replied, remembering our brief conversation at the mines. "He said you wanted to go there to get a new cumtach made for the book."

"Well," Brynach allowed, "it is true we would have made harbour in Trebizond, naturally. But we were on our way to Sebastea; Cadoc wanted to see the governor."

A thin chill snaked down my ribs. "What did you say?" Although I had heard him quite plainly, I made him repeat it word for word. "You are certain—Cadoc wanted to see the governor?"

"Aye, he did," answered Brynach. "It seems the two had met once when this Honorius was a Procurator in Gaul."

"And was it before this desire was known," I asked, "or after that Nikos became interested in helping you?"

The canny Briton stared at me for a moment. "Ah, I see which way your mind is working, brother, but you are wrong," he answered with satisfaction. "I know for a fact that the voyage was Cadoc's idea entirely. He was set on going before anyone ever laid eyes on Nikos. Since we were travelling to Sebastea anyway, the bishop merely asked if anyone could be found in that place who might help us restore the book."

"Were you with them when they spoke?" I asked, my voice rising to a demand. "Did you hear Cadoc say this?"

"I was and I did," Brynach answered firmly. "And that is why I know you are wrong to think the worst of Nikos. He was trying to help us."

Despite his insistence, my suspicions remained; but nothing would be gained by hammering at Brynach, so I left the matter for the present. On the face of it, his explanation seemed logical enough: Nikos did not send the monks to Trebizond; Cadoc had it in mind to go there before Nikos became involved. Even so, the thing did not sit well with me.

Talk turned to the rigours ahead and, as night deepened around us, Gunnar appeared out of the twilight to say that Harald was asking for me. Regarding the Britons a little awkwardly, he said, "Jarl Harald would speak to you, Aeddan. If you are willing."

"Of course, Gunnar."

"I know you would rather stay with your brothers," he said doubtfully.

"Nay, nay," I answered, rising, "I should have come to you sooner. Let us go speak to him." As the monks declined to join us, I bade them good night and walked with Gunnar the short distance to the Sea Wolf camp.

There, I found men sprawled over the ground where they had fallen, exhausted by the day's exertions. I had seen Danes in similar circumstances before, of course, but this time, at least, they had not drunk so much as a single drop of öl. I looked with pity on their once-hale bodies, now wasted thin from poor food and killing labour.

Harald was leaning against a rock with his head back and his eyes closed. At my approach, however, he roused himself and made to rise. "Nay, jarl, be at ease," I said. "Please, sit and rest.

But he would not hear it. Instead, he climbed shakily onto his feet and embraced me like one of his own karlar. What is more, he called to the others and bade them to rise also, but only one or two made the attempt. "Ah, Aeddan," he breathed, and smiled, placing his arm around my shoulders. His face was sun-blasted, haggard and lined, and his eyes were dull with fatigue, but the voice he raised still held something of its former bellow when he called aloud for everyone to attend him: "See here, all you Danes!" he shouted. "This is our good friend. We are free tonight because he would not see us go down to death in the pit."

This brought not so much as a yawn from any of the Sea Wolves who might have been awake to hear it. Turning to me, King Harald said, "I would we had a sea of öl to drink your health. But, hear me, Aeddan. I, Harald Bull-Roar make this vow: half the silver we have obtained, I give to you. For without you, we would be slaves still and our wealth would avail us nothing."

"You are too generous, Jarl Harald." This pleased him and he smiled. "As it happens, I cannot accept even so much as a single lump of your silver." This pleased him still more. "What I did, I did for reasons of my own. Your freedom is all the reward I seek, and I have that."

"You speak well," Harald said, "but I would be less than a king if I did not reward you. Since you will not take silver, I charge you to name the thing you desire most, and, with all the power at my command, I will obtain it for you."

We sat down together then, and for the first time I felt an equal in his company. The feeling did not last long, however, for very soon the overtired jarl, lost in a fit of yawning, slumped onto his side and drifted off to sleep. I left the Sea Wolves to their death-like slumber, and crept away unseen to make my bed next to the amir's fire.

Although we had planned to move on the next day, we rested instead. The former slaves had spent all their strength in the escape and following march, and few were in any condition to renew their exertions. We might usefully have rested the following day as well, but Faysal, weighing our increased numbers against the rapidly dwindling provisions, suggested that if we did not make some progress, however small, we would soon be going hungry. "As it is," he suggested, "we must go to Amida and replenish our supplies."

This meant a delay, which Amir Sadiq did not like, but there was no other choice. So, setting forth at a gentle pace, we proceeded down the long, meandering trail to the valley floor, resting often. The next day, we proceeded west towards the Amida road.

Thus, upon reaching the road two days later, we turned not north to Trebizond, but south to Amida. Despite the fact that the amir no longer provided for them, many of the former captives preferred to remain close in order to travel under the protection of the rafiq. A few, however, unburdened by any such fears, left us as soon as we gained the road, eager to reach the city.

Though the former captives could not walk fast, nor for any great distance, still we journeyed at a better pace than before. Indeed, over the next days I observed a general improvement in all of the newly freed men, Britons and Danes alike: they moved more easily, and their strength increased day by day. Sure, they were strong men who had survived the mines. Even Ddewi seemed to come more to himself, as if, little by little, he remembered who he had been.

Each day I saw Kazimain, of course, but with everyone so close around us all the time, we had few opportunities to speak to one another, and these were all too brief. We contented ourselves with knowing glances, and hastily uttered words of endearment: not enough to make a man content, but it was all we had.

Then, early on the morning we were to enter Amida, she came to me. Men were breaking camp and saddling the horses, others preparing food. I turned, smiling as Kazimain hurried to where I stood talking to Dugal; one glance at the set of her jaw, and I broke off my chatter. Drawing her a little apart, I said, "You look about to burst."

"The amir says I am to stay in Amida," she told me, her voice shaking. "He intends hiring men to escort me back to Ja'fariya."

The thing had taken me unawares and before I could think what to say, she gripped my arm tightly and said, "He must not do this, Aidan."

"He fears for your safety," I muttered without conviction.

"And I fear for his!" she snapped. Taking in my bewilderment, she bent her head towards mine and confided in a low voice, not to be overheard. "He is not well."

I pulled back. "Not well?" Glancing around to where he sat breaking fast on some bread Faysal had given him, I said, "He seems in perfect health to me."

Kazimain dismissed my observation. "That is how he wants to appear," she said. "He has begun sleeping too long, and too deeply. He does not rise so quickly."

"That is no cause for worry," I suggested. "He is tired—we are all tired. Exhausted. No doubt we would all feel better for a day's rest."

Kazimain's smooth brow creased in a frown. "You are not listening!" she said. "Please, Aidan, do something. He must not leave me behind."

"I will speak to him," I promised. "If that is what you want."

This was not the right thing to say, I quickly discovered, for she stormed away and would speak to me no more.

Upon reaching Amida, late in the day, the amir ordered his tent to be erected a short distance from the settlement, and forbade the Sea Wolves to leave camp. Harald and his men were disappointed, but when Faysal explained that there was no öl of any kind, nor even wine, in all of Amida, the Danemen bore their disappointment more bravely. "Perhaps it is for the best," remarked Gunnar with stoic forbearance; "it will mean more silver to take home to Karin."

With that the Sea Wolves set about cleaning themselves; they bathed and shaved their matted beards and cut their hair, and cast off their filthy rags for simple mantles the amir provided. When they finished, much of their former swagger had returned.

The Britons, who had no silver to worry about, were also unwilling to go into the town. "I will not set foot in that accursed place," Dugal vowed.

"You have no purse," I pointed out. "Therefore, you have nothing to fear."

"Ha!" Dugal mocked. "Think you I would give the slave-traders a chance to seize me and sell me again? I never will."

Dugal was, perhaps, closer to the truth than he knew. In any event, I was prepared to stay in camp with the others and await the amir's return, but Kazimain insisted I go. "You must speak to Lord Sadiq!" she urged.

This is how I came to be standing in the slave market at Amida when I heard someone cry, "Aedan!"

# 62

The market square was awash in an uneasy flood of people, most of whom were shouting at the top of their voices, trying to make themselves heard over all the others. On this day, there were no slaves to be sold, but there were horses and donkeys, sheep and goats aplenty, and also, an animal I had seen but once or twice in Trebizond: camels; loud, shaggy, and ill-tempered creatures much favoured by those of the dry southern places. Sellers appeared to outnumber buyers, and as the sun was already stretching the shadows across the square, desperation had begun setting in. Most of the sellers were herdsmen and farmers who did not care to begin the long journey home with empty purses.

The shout came again, sharp and distinct: "Aedan!"

I stood stump-still and listened. If I was not certain I had heard it the first time, I heard it clearly now, and I began searching the busy marketplace for whoever had called me. Though the square teemed with people, no one paid the slightest attention to me. Well, the market was so noisy, I might have imagined it after all; I made to continue on my way, following the amir and Faysal about the chore of procuring supplies. Yet, even as I turned to hasten after them, out of the corner of my eye, I glimpsed the slight, wizened figure of Amet, the magus I had consulted in Trebizond.

He moved towards me, holding up his hands in a peculiar gesture of greeting—as if he feared I would flee him before he could reach me. I hastened to join him, but before I took three strides, a herd of goats moved between us and suddenly I was surrounded by the bleating animals.

Amet stopped. Gazing intently at me across a distance of fifty paces, his hands still raised, palms outward in his peculiar greeting, he called out; his mouth moved, but his words were swallowed by the din of the market and the nattering of the goats.

Cupping a hand to my ear, I shouted, "What did you say?"—whereupon he repeated his call. I heard him no better the second time, and was only able to make out a single word: Sebastea.

"I cannot hear you!" I shouted, and started towards him once again, shoving my way through the goat herd, only to have him taken from my sight by a man leading three horses. They passed before me, man and horses, and when I stepped forward again Amet was gone.

I rushed to the place where he had been standing, but the little magus was nowhere to be seen. "Amet!" I cried.

His voice came to me one last time, but further away. "Come to Sebastea, Aedan! Sebastea . . ."

Nowhere among the mass of bodies pressing all around was Amet to be found. I called his name again, but received no reply. He had vanished so completely that I quickly doubted whether I had seen him at all. Making a last inspection of the square, I turned and hurried after Faysal and the amir, who were talking to a man standing beside a wagon loaded with sacks of grain.

I quickly rejoined them, taking my place behind

Faysal just as Sadiq struck a bargain with the man for his wagonload of barley. While Faysal told the man where to deliver the grain, Sadiq turned his attention to the other matter on his mind: finding an escort to take Kazimain back to Samarra.

"The *shaykh* of this place will know men I can trust," Sadiq said.

"Lord Amir," I said, "if I may be so bold as to suggest—" I hesitated.

"Yes?" demanded the amir in a distracted way, his eyes searching the marketplace. "What? What? Speak."

"—to suggest that Kazimain should be allowed to continue the journey with us."

Amir Sadiq's eyes shifted to me; his mouth twitched into an instant frown. "Continue with us," he said, his voice leaden, "to Byzantium?"

"Yes," I replied, and could feel the resistance rise up within him.

But before he could draw breath to refuse me, Faysal spoke up, "Lord, if you please, this is the very thing I have been thinking."

Sadiq's baleful eyes swung from me to Faysal. "You are both mad." He turned abruptly. "It cannot be allowed."

"I believe she could be of great use to us," I persisted. "It may be that—"

"No," the amir said, moving away, "I have spoken and the matter is concluded."

"Lord," implored Faysal, "please reconsider. Kazimain is shrewd and resourceful, as we know. We know not what manner of reception we will face in Byzantium, and—"

"Precisely!" said the amir, rounding on us. "The very reason I cannot allow her to remain even a moment longer than necessary." Sadiq stopped abruptly. He pressed a hand to his temple and squeezed his eyes shut, as if trying very hard to think of something he had forgotten.

A strange apprehension came over Faysal's features as he stood looking on. "Amir?" he said softly.

"It is nothing—the sun," Sadiq muttered; his face had lost some of its colour and his voice its strength. "Let us finish and return to camp."

Thus was Lord Sadiq determined and there was no changing his mind. One of the merchants in the market pointed out the shaykh, and Sadiq sought his counsel in hiring trustworthy men to escort Kazimain. The two conferred, money changed hands, and that was the end of it.

Along with dry provisions of various kinds, the amir also bought a herd of sheep and some goats, three camels, and a wagon. That evening, as the supplies which had been delivered were being packed away in the wagon, I overheard Faysal and Kazimain talking in hushed, urgent voices.

I joined them and heard Faysal saying, ". . . they are to come for you in the morning. The shaykh has pledged the life of his son for your protection, and—" He broke off at my approach.

"I am sorry, Kazimain," I said. "The amir would not be persuaded. Still, perhaps it is for the best. I would feel better if I knew you were safe."

"For the best!" she snapped. The fire in her dark eyes died as quickly as it flared. "You will remember that it is not for your sake that I sought to continue this journey, but for the amir's alone. He is not well."

Her concern mystified me. Though I did not doubt its sincerity, I could not credit its cause. "So you have said," I granted. "But I see no evidence of any illness. He seems to me as much himself as ever." I shrugged, and looked to Faysal for confirmation. "Is this not so?"

"No, it is *not* so," she replied in a tone that indicated this should have been self-evident. Helpless against such overwhelming ignorance, Kazimain also appealed to Faysal. "Tell him!"

"Kazimain believes the amir was injured," Faysal explained, "at the mine—when his horse fell and rolled on him." With a light lift of his shoulders, he said, "Lord Sadiq denies anything is wrong."

There was no persuading Kazimain, and she would not be consoled. The unintentional dispute left a sour taste in my mouth, so I walked around the camp for a while to think what I might do, eventually settling with the Britons as Dugal and Brynach prepared a meal. Sadiq had determined that each of the separate parties of our company would fare better if they did their own cooking, thus relieving the Arabs of the duty. Brynach raised his eyes from the pot as I settled myself against a rock. "No doubt I have seen a more woeful countenance," he remarked, returning to his stirring, "but I do not remember when."

Ddewi, squatting nearby and tracing lines in the dust with his finger, lifted his head and laughed at Bryn's small jest. Noticing my surprise, Brynach said, "He seems to be getting better." Raising his voice, he called, "Aye, Ddewi? I say you are feeling a little better now." Ddewi had returned to his reverie and made no sign that he had heard or understood. "But you, Brother Aidan," the Briton continued, "seem a little worse. What is wrong?"

I made to dismiss his question with a shrug and a smile. "I saw a man today who was not there. A curious thing, nothing more."

"Indeed?" Brynach's eyebrows arched with interest, but he kept on stirring. "Have you ever seen him before?"

"Aidan is always seeing things," proclaimed Dugal, arriving with an armful of brushy twigs for the fire. "He has dreams and visions, and such."

I made to protest. "Dugal, no I—"

"He does!" Dugal insisted.

"The man I saw was no vision," I declared. "He was a man I met in Trebizond. I thought I saw him today in the marketplace—he called out to me. But it was crowded, and by the time I reached him, he had gone. Perhaps I did not see him at all."

Brynach frowned in disapproval of my explanation, but said no more and returned to his cooking. Dugal, breaking the twigs into smaller pieces, said, "What was it like, this Trebizond?"

At his mention of the word, something Brynach had said before squirmed uneasily in my head. Rather than answer Dugal's question, I asked one of my own. "You told me you were going to see the governor, why?"

"Cadoc desired his aid," Brynach answered.

"But not on behalf of the cumtach," I suggested. "You could have had a new cover made in Constantinople."

"That is true."

"Then why? What aid could Governor Honorius provide?"

Brynach stopped stirring. He looked from Dugal to me, and then down into the pot, as if trying to read a purpose in the bubbling liquid. "I suppose," he said, "it makes no difference now."

He gestured to Dugal to take his place at the fire, then came and settled himself on the ground facing me. "Cadoc is dead." The sadness in his voice went deeper, I thought, than grief for the beloved bishop. "He would have told you himself."

I remained silent, tingling with anticipation. Even so, his first words surprised me. "Governor Honorius was to be our advocate against Rome."

"Rome!" I wondered in amazement. "What has Rome to do with this? Why did—"

Brynach raised a hand to fend off any more questions. "It was, you might say, the true purpose for the pilgrimage." As he spoke, an image formed in my mind: men at a board—monks breaking bread and talking in quiet fellowship with one another. The image changed and I saw myself sitting with Brynach, and him beckoning me closer. *"Those I choose to be my friends call me Bryn,"* he was saying. *"May I tell you something?"*

The memory struck me with the force of a blow. Gazing at him now, I cast my mind back to that night. "That is what you were going to tell me," I said. Brynach returned my gaze with a blank expression. "The night of our first meeting—you were going to tell me, but one of the monks intruded."

He nodded slightly. "Yes, I suppose I meant to . . ."

"We should have been told," I said, my tone growing harsh. "If there was a hidden purpose to our journey—"

Dugal, silent as a stone, stared at us, trying to take in the revelation he was hearing.

"Not a *hidden* purpose—" protested Brynach quickly. "Never that."

"We should have been told," I insisted. "Tell me now."

Brynach shook his head slowly; the sadness in his eyes was raw and deep. "Do you also remember," he said softly, "that we were to go first to Ty Gwyn?"

Again, I was assailed by a sudden recollection. "Ty Gwyn," I murmured. "The storm prevented us from putting to shore."

"You do remember," Brynach confirmed.

"I also remember we were never told *why* we were to go there," I remarked tartly.

"For years, I had been travelling from abbey to abbey, hearing the complaints of abbots and bishops, detailing the grievances, so to speak, writing them down. The Book of Sins, I called it." He smiled sadly. "Rome's sins against us."

"But we sailed on without it."

"Well," Brynach shrugged, "that could not be helped.

When I finished my little red book, Bishop Cadoc had three copies made: one was kept at Ty Gwyn, one at Hy, and one at Nantes, in Gaul."

"That was where Cadoc and Honorius met," I said, recollecting our previous talk.

"Indeed," he confirmed. "Having laboured so long over our appeal, we thought to share the fruit, so to speak. The churches of Gaul are pressed as sorely as those of Britain and Éire. We hoped to enlist these brothers in our cause." He shook his head again. "We were making for Nantes when the Danes attacked us."

"But you reached Nantes," I said. "You must have retrieved your red book."

"We did, yes."

"And you brought it to Byzantium, did you not?" Brynach affirmed my question with a nod. "What happened to it?"

"We were to deliver it into the emperor's hands," Brynach replied simply, "but—" Frowning, he hesitated.

"But it was lost when your ship was attacked," I suggested, believing I had guessed the book's fate.

Brynach glanced up quickly. "By no means," he said. "The book is still in Byzantium. And that is cause for hope. Nikos, the very man you condemn out of hand—he has the book even now."

I stared in stupefaction at the senior monk, overwhelmed by the immensity of the catastrophe: the hopelessness of Bishop Cadoc's doomed trust, and Nikos's monumental treachery. I felt as if the weight of the world had shifted and rolled upon my chest.

"Nikos!" My hands balled to fists. "You gave it to Nikos! In God's name, man, why?"

Dugal, kneeling over the bubbling pot, stirdle in hand, looked from one to the other of us, a troubled expression on his face.

"Peace, brother," Brynach soothed. "We gave it to him, yes, for safe-keeping. And that is how I know he was trying to help us." Brynach's faith was as genuine as it was misplaced. "Nikos was much impressed by my thoroughness and particularity. 'Such a meticulous indictment,' he told us, 'could not fail to move the emperor.' Those were his very words."

The ache in my chest gave way to a hollow feeling. I felt as if I were a gourd, ripe to bursting, split down the middle and scooped out in a single, devastating swipe. Nevertheless, like murky sediment settling in a pool, the thing was gradually coming clear. I pressed on. "What of the governor? What was his place in this?"

"Cadoc knew him well; the two had been friends in Gaul. Cadoc, then a priest, baptized Honorius into the faith. In respect of this singular blessing, Honorius always held that if Cadoc ever required his aid, he would give it. So it was that the bishop hoped to claim that promise. Over the years, Honorius had risen to a position of considerable influence; he was to guide us to the prize we sought."

Almost fearfully, I said, "This prize—what was it?"

"A dispensation from the emperor," Brynach replied, his voice taking on strength once more, "for the free practice of our faith."

I could make no sense of this. "Have you lost your mind, brother? Whatever can you mean? We *are* free," I asserted, forgetting for the moment that I was done with such things and no longer cared one way or the other. "We owe allegiance to no earthly king."

"Not if Rome has its way," countered Brynach blackly. "Even now the Pope is raising the cry of heresy against us."

"Heresy!" I could not imagine what Brynach was talking about. "It is absurd."

"But true just the same," replied the monk. "The Pope

would bring *all* who call themselves Christian beneath his sway. We have always vexed Rome, I think, with our different ways. The Pope would have us bow the knee to his authority."

"So you hoped to appeal to a higher authority," I mused, hopelessness settling over me once more.

"There is no higher authority on earth than the emperor himself," Brynach declared, growing earnest. "He can grant us the peace we seek. Once we reach Sebastea," he said quickly, "we can—"

His words, combined with his rekindled intensity, filled me with alarm. "The pilgrimage is ended," I said ruthlessly, my tone growing harsh. "We are returning to Trebizond, and then travelling on to Constantinople. It is finished," I stated flatly. "The pilgrimage ended in disaster long ago."

Brynach opened his mouth, and then closed it again without speaking. He rose and went back to his place at the cooking pot. I thought the matter ended there; however, I was gravely mistaken.

# 63

**M**y mind squirmed like an eel caught in the eagle's grasp. Upset by Brynach's talk, disturbed, angry, I walked a long time, watching night descend through a ruddy desert sky, trying to regain my peace and composure. The more I walked however, the more agitated I became—but obscurely so: I did not know what I was anxious about, nor could I discern the source of my aggravation. All the while, my thoughts spun and shifted, flitting first one way and then another, but never finding rest.

Once, I felt as if I were about to burst with a sudden blazing insight. I waited, almost panting with anticipation. But nothing came, so I made my way back to camp and found a place to be alone with my troubled thoughts. Was it, I wondered, something Brynach had said that now sat so ill with me?

Tossed by the turmoil of my unsatisfactory meditations, I heard, but did not attend, a soft, strangled sound. It came again, and I turned to see Dugal, his head bent, shuffling towards me, hands covering his face. Even in the darkness, I could see his broad shoulders curved down as under an unseen burden. He came to where I sat on my solitary rock a short distance from camp.

"Dugal?"

In a moment, he raised his face. I expected tears, but his eyes were dry. The torment he felt was etched in every line of his face, however, and his voice was raw when he spoke. "Christ have mercy!" he said. "It is all because of me."

"Sit you down," I told him sternly. Still preoccupied by my own concerns I had no inclination towards gentleness and understanding. "Tell me now, what ails you?"

"All the evil that has befallen us—" he said, his voice cracking with regret, "it is all because of me. God have mercy on my soul, I am the cause of our afflictions."

"Tch!" I clicked my tongue at him. "Listen to you, now. Even if you were the Devil incarnate, you could not have wrought such havoc."

In his shame, he bent his head to his hands, and covered his face, murmuring, "Jonah . . . I am Jonah."

Rising to my knees, I leaned towards him, placing a hand on his shoulder. "Hear me, Dugal," I said firmly. "The fault is not yours. The misfortunes which have befallen us are the work of a zealot who shrinks not from murder, or any other crime, to further his wicked purpose."

"The man you describe is me," came the muffled reply. "I am that Jonah."

"Do not be a fool," I told him bluntly. "The man I describe is Komes Nikos. The iniquity is his alone."

Dugal, however, would not be comforted. "You do not understand," he said, his cry a very wound. "From the beginning—before ever we left Éire . . ." He shook his head, overwhelmed by misery.

"Stop that, Dugal. Look at me." I spoke severely, trying to brace him with sharp speech and firm purpose. "Look me in the eye, man, and tell me what you did."

Slowly, a man crushed by his burden of guilt, Dugal

raised his head. There were tears in his eyes now. He pushed them away with the heels of his hands.

"Well? I am waiting."

"I cheated my way onto the ship," he said at last.

"What ship?" I could not imagine what he was talking about.

"*Our* ship—*Bán Gwydd*," he said; once loosed, the words came tumbling out. "I knew I would never be chosen like you, Aidan. But I knew also I could not let you go on pilgrimage without me. So, with God as my witness, I schemed and plotted night and day for a way to get aboard that ship. I steeled myself to do whatever vile thing came to hand so that I might be included with you. The Devil placed the chance in my hand and I seized it." Dugal gazed forlornly at me with damp eyes. "God save me, I did the deed without thinking twice."

"You pushed Libir on the path," I said, remembering our leave-taking, and the slippery rocks leading down to the little ship.

The change in Dugal's demeanor was wonderful to behold. The pain in his eyes passed through bewilderment and arrived at amazement. "You knew?"

"Dugal! I have always known!"

"You knew," he said again. "Yet, you never breathed a word."

"Of course, I knew. Listen to me now: Libir was old; he could not have endured the journey—he would have died in the shipwreck, and if not then, he certainly would have been killed any number of times after. Most likely, you saved his life."

Dugal stared, not willing to believe what I was saying.

"Did you really think God would curse us to ruin because you took an old man's place in a boat?" I demanded.

"But I hurt him," he replied dully. "I hurt him, Aidan. Our misfortunes came upon us through my prideful sin."

"Put that out of your mind," I told him. "Whatever happens in this world happens. That is all. The only misfortune is thinking God cares. Hear me, Dugal: He does not care. Still less does He intervene in our affairs one way or another."

My words stung him; I could see it in his eyes. He did not expect such venom from me, and was shocked by what I said. After a moment, he said, "I would feel better if I confessed."

"You have already confessed," I pointed out, my anger subsiding.

"Would you hear my confession, Aidan?"

"No," I told him. "But confess by all means, if it will make you feel better; get Brynach to shrive you. I want no part of it."

Dugal nodded glumly and climbed to his feet. I watched as he approached Brynach; the two talked, whereupon the elder monk led Dugal a little apart, and the two knelt together to pray. God help me, I could not bear to see them, so turned my back, pulled my robe around my shoulders, lay down and tried to sleep. The cool desert air was still and soft, the sky bright, and my mind kept circling, circling endlessly, unable to alight and unwilling to rest.

In the end, I gave up and simply stared at the stars. Even that was no good. For, though I watched the glowing opalescent sky, I saw only the black chain of deceit stretching back and back—to Byzantium. I thought of Nikos and his treachery, but instead of allowing myself to renew my rage and hatred—which is what I always did whenever his memory crossed my mind—this time I considered him dispassionately: a riddle to be solved, rather than a serpent to be killed.

Strangely, my mind ceased flitting restlessly from thought to thought, and a profound calm eased into my spirit. I began to see the difficulty in a cool, clear light. It came to me that both Eparch Nicephorus and Bishop Cadoc had been betrayed by Nikos. Why? Neither man, so far as I knew, had ever so much as heard of the other, and yet Nikos went out of his way to destroy them. What was it that united the two men as objects of Nikos's treachery?

Well, there was only one answer: both men knew Governor Honorius. Indeed, both had been going to see him, and both had been attacked. Honorius, then, lay at the centre of this mystery.

So then, what was it about the governor that Nikos feared? Whatever the answer, I reasoned, it must be terrible in its import: hundreds of people had died to keep it hidden—and those were just the ones I knew. How many more had been sacrificed, and why?

Try as I might, I could not get beyond the *why*?

Gazing up at the glowing sky-vault above me, my mind turned again to my vision of the afternoon: Amet standing in the centre of the marketplace, hailing me, calling me. *Come to Sebastea,* he had said. *Sebastea . . .*

I was on my feet before I knew it, and stumbling through the sleeping camp. Kneeling over the sleeping Brynach, I took him by the shoulder. He came awake at my touch.

"How did you know the governor was in Sebastea?" I said, my voice shaking with excitement.

"Peace, brother," he said, and made to rise.

"Answer me! How did you know?" I demanded, already guessing what he would say.

"Nikos told us," Brynach replied. "He said the governor always spent the summer there."

A thin, icy chill trickled along my ribs. Oh, Nikos was cunning as a viper and just as poisonous. He knew, even before setting foot in Trebizond that the governor would not be joining us there. He had sent the monks, not to Honorius's home in Trebizond, but to Sebastea where he knew the governor could be found; and, when the eparch had concluded the treaty, then Nikos diverted us to Sebastea, too.

Nikos was, it seemed, always sending people to Sebastea, but none of them ever arrived. Why?

My quick-kindled excitement died. I had thought myself close to solving the riddle. But the more I probed, the more the mystery deepened, and now I was no nearer a solution than before. I returned to my sleeping place, dispirited and disgusted, to wrestle with thoughts that would not yield.

A pale white dawn found me awake still, unrested and aching in head and heart. Slowly, the camp began to stir; I lay listening to the idle talk of the amir's warriors as they built up the fires once more. Thus, I was already alert when I heard Kazimain approach, her footfall soft in the dust.

"Aidan," she said tentatively. Her voice quivered.

"My love," I replied, rolling over to look at her. She appeared to have slept no better than I; her hair was unbound, and the corners of her eyes were red. "Kazimain?"

"It is Lord Sadiq." Her hand was shaking, so I grasped it; her fingers were cold. "I cannot wake him."

I was beside the amir in an instant. In swift steps I entered the tent, knelt over him and pressed my hand to the side of his neck, much as Farouk had done to me countless times. The amir's skin was warm to the touch, and I could feel the rapid flutter of a strong pulse beneath my fingertips; his breath was quick and shallow. He seemed to sleep, but it was a false repose. There was a faint mist of sweat on his brow.

Touching his shoulder, I jostled him gently, but firmly. "Lord Sadiq," I said, "wake you now." I repeated this three times, but the amir made no sound, neither did he move.

"You see how he is," Kazimain said, peering over my shoulder.

"Where is Faysal?"

"He did not eat anything last night," she replied. "He said he was not hungry . . . It is not like the amir to sleep so long . . ."

"Kazimain," I said sharply, drawing her back. "Where is Faysal?"

"Out there—" She gestured vaguely behind her. "I did not—" She looked at me, frightened now. "I woke you instead."

"Wake him now and tell him to bring some water."

She nodded and backed from the tent. Straightening the amir's head, I began to gently remove his turban. So far as I knew, he had not changed it since the incident at the gate. As the long strip of cloth unwound, I held my breath, fearing what I would find.

As the last length came away, I put the cloth aside and examined the amir's head. To my relief there was no injury that I could see; so I began to search, lightly lifting his matted dark hair to see the scalp beneath. By the time Kazimain returned, I had completed my examination, finding nothing unusual.

Kazimain knelt beside me, worried still, but better composed. Faysal appeared a moment later, with a jar of water. He poured from the jar into a small bowl, and brought it to the amir's lips. I placed my hand behind the amir's head and raised it to receive the water. As I lifted, the amir moaned, as if in pain, but he did not wake.

"Wait," I told Faysal. "There is something here." To Kazimain I said, "Let us turn him over."

Half-lifting, half-rolling, we placed the amir on his side, and I quickly found the place my fingers had touched.

The wound was little more than a deep-coloured

bruise at the base of his skull. But when I probed with my fingers, rather than solid bone beneath the skin, I felt pulpy flesh. "Here," I said, guiding Kazimain's fingers to the place. "But gently, gently."

The amir moaned again as Kazimain touched the wound; she pulled back her hand as if she had burned her fingers. "The bone is crushed," she gasped, her voice dwindling to a whisper.

"Faysal," I commanded, "ride to Amida. Bring a physician at once."

He stared at me. "I do not think there is a physician in Amida."

"Go, man," I snapped. "Hurry!"

Faysal inclined his head in acknowledgement of the command—a gesture I had seen him make a thousand times, but always to Lord Sadiq, never to anyone else. He left the tent, and Kazimain and I attempted to get the amir to drink some water, but succeeded only in wetting his chin and the side of his face.

"Stay with him," I told Kazimain, "I will fetch Brynach. He is learned in many things; he may know what to do."

Upon emerging from the tent, one of the rafiq met me and announced that Kazimain's escort had arrived and was ready to take her away. I looked to where the warrior pointed and saw six men on horseback. "Tell them they must wait," I said, and hurried on.

Brynach, Dugal, and Ddewi had risen and lit a fire to take the chill from the morning air. Upon hearing of the amir's distress, Brynach nodded and said, "Have no fear for Lord Sadiq. We have among us one who is many-gifted in the healing arts." He put out his hand to Ddewi, who sat with hand extended before the crackling fire, his features placid.

"You cannot mean—" I protested.

Brynach nodded.

"But he is not himself. His mind—he does not even know where he is. Sure, he cannot do anything."

"Are you God now that you know what a man is capable of doing?" There was no rancour in Brynach's tone. He turned to regard Ddewi with satisfaction. "He is hiding within himself. We have but to coax him into the daylight once more."

"Your faith is laudable," I said, struggling to keep the contempt out of my voice. "But it is the amir—I fear for his life. And if any ill should befall him at Ddewi's hands . . ."

Brynach blithely waved aside my objection. "It is right to bear concern for one another, but your fears betray a lack of faith."

"It is not a matter of faith," I declared harshly, "but one of expedience. Ddewi does not even remember his own name. What if I were to entrust to him the care of the amir, and Lord Sadiq died?"

Brynach placed a hand on my shoulder in a fatherly way. "O, man of little faith, trust God, and see what he will do."

In my experience, all that came of trusting God was that matters went from bad to worse—and usually so rapidly as to steal the very breath away.

Despite Brynach's faith-blinded confidence, I would not have allowed Ddewi to so much as sit quietly in the amir's tent, if Faysal had not returned to camp with the unhappy word that there was no physician in Amida.

"No one?" I growled.

He shrugged. "A few old women sit with those who are ill."

Dugal, having seen Faysal's lathered horse, joined us, and as Bryn explained what was happening, I asked, "What happens when someone falls seriously ill?"

"They die."

"No doubt," put in Brynach, "this has come about that God's glory may be increased."

"No doubt," I muttered sourly.

"Be of good cheer, brother," Dugal exhorted. "It may be that this will be the saving of them both."

With that, everyone turned to me expectantly, awaiting my decision. "Where else," I asked Faysal, "can we find a physician?"

"Samarra or Baghdat," he answered.

But, strange to say, it was not Faysal's voice I heard; it was Amet's, calling me across the marketplace. *Come to Sebastea . . .*

Oh, Brynach was right, it was a matter of faith—not as he imagined it, however. It was not God, or even Ddewi, who vied for my faith. The question was this: could I trust my vision? I had trusted once, and it had proven false. If it proved so again, the amir would pay with his life.

Samarra was a long way behind us now, and Baghdat further still. Even if we rode night and day, we could not reach either place before many days had passed and, looking at him now, I doubted whether the amir could endure the journey. Well, the choice was clear at least, if not easily made.

I felt a touch at my arm. "Aidan?" Faysal asked. "What are you thinking?"

"Faysal, listen. There may be another choice. What about Sebastea?"

He considered this for a moment. "It may be closer," he allowed. "It is a sizeable city."

"I think we should go there."

Faysal hesitated; I was on the point of urging again when Kazimain spoke up. "We must do what is most expedient," she said. "We do not know how long he can endure."

"Very well," replied Faysal. "I yield to your judgement."

Turning to Brynach, who was bending over Ddewi, whispering in his ear, I said: "Bring Ddewi to the tent. I will allow him to tend Lord Sadiq until we get to Sebastea. However, Kazimain will remain with him to see that he does no harm."

Dugal and Brynach, each taking an arm, raised the unwitting monk between them, and led him towards the tent, Brynach speaking low to his young charge the while. It was not a sight to inspire the highest confidence. I watched them walk away, misgiving deep and dire rising within me. *May God help us all,* I thought, but it was a cold-hearted wish with neither hope nor faith in it at all.

After escorting Ddewi to the amir's side, Dugal returned to where I stood talking to Faysal about how best to proceed. "Never fear, Aidan," Dugal told me, "all things work together for the good of those who love God."

Faysal, regarding the big monk curiously, asked, "Please, what is he saying?"

"He said not to worry, that God ever toils for good," I translated roughly, if enthusiastically.

"We have a similar saying," Faysal replied. "The Faithful say, 'All is as Allah wills.' It is the same thing, I think."

Faysal began to organize the arrangements which would enable Sadiq to travel, doing for the amir what he once did for me. "We may leave for Sebastea shortly; I will let you know when we are ready, he told me."

While Faysal undertook the required preparations, I went to Jarl Harald and explained to the Danes why we yet lingered in camp. Gunnar, Hnefi, and some of the others crowded around to hear the news. I told them Lord Sadiq had fallen ill in the night, and that we were going to Sebastea to find a physician. Harald accepted this with good grace, saying that he would personally carry the Arab jarl on his back if it meant he could recover the sooner.

"We owe him a great debt of honour," he said, and meant just that.

Then, having set the Sea Wolves the chore of breaking camp, I returned to Sadiq's tent. Brynach and Ddewi knelt beside the amir; Kazimain, who stood over them, turned to meet me as I entered. "It is remarkable," she said. "Already Lord Sadiq rests more easily."

"What did he do?"

"He merely touched the amir with his hands while he prayed."

I did not doubt her, but attributed the observation more to her own desire to see her kinsman healed than anything Ddewi might have done.

"God willing, he will sleep now," Brynach informed us.

"He was sleeping before," I retorted. I cannot say why I took offence at the monk; I know he meant only good. But his assurance rankled me, and I bristled at his unquestioning confidence: it made of the amir's injury a trivial thing. And, of course, nothing is simple.

Brynach gazed at me curiously. Forcing a more reasonable tone, I said, "Make him ready. I have already given orders to break camp."

Leaving the tent, I hastened to where Kazimain's escort was waiting. "Our plans have changed," I told the head man. "You are no longer needed. Thank the shaykh and tell him that the amir wishes you to keep the money you have been paid. Lord Sadiq may have need of your services another day."

For good or ill, the decision was made. I turned my face towards Sebastea.

# 64

Owing to the heat, we took to travelling at night, setting out at dusk and continuing until mid-morning when the sun's blistering rays became too hot. Fortunately, the moon was in a quarter to aid us, so we did not lack for light; the well-worn trail shone with a pale phantom glow allowing us to push a relentless pace towards Sebastea. It was here that the camels—truly disagreeable beasts in every way—displayed their chief, perhaps only, virtue: they could move quickly and with little need for rest or water, and this while carrying loads that would crush a horse.

Thus, we journeyed swiftly, pressing ever northward through the cramped and crooked valleys, more often than not in sight of the Tigris's murky waters. One night we passed a tiny, fly-blown holding on the riverbank and Faysal, after conversing with a few of the holding's inhabitants, returned to inform us that it was the last Arab settlement we would see. Sebastea, he was told, lay three days' journey to the north and a little east, and Trebizond a further seven days north and west. Beyond Sebastea, however, there was a good road, and Faysal assured me the journey would be less arduous. Sometime during the night we crossed the much-disputed border into imperial lands.

We did what little we could to make the amir comfortable. Ddewi remained steadfastly at Lord Sadiq's side, eating and sleeping nearby, and walking with the horses and sling. Kazimain always rode with them, and assured me that the young monk, though quiet and withdrawn, was constantly alert to his duty, performing many small tasks which, taken together, seemed to produce a beneficial effect.

For his part, the amir was not often conscious, and even when he woke seemed unable to rouse himself so much as to lift his head from his bed. I feared the worst, and we pushed as swift and relentless a pace as could be achieved without further endangering him.

Thus it was with a feeling of great relief that after three nights I glimpsed the white walls of Sebastea shimmering in the dawnlight of a day already hazy with heat. We proceeded to the city and adopted the amir's practice of establishing camp a short distance outside the city walls. While the rafiq and Danes prepared the tents, Faysal and I hastened to procure the services of a physician.

Arabs were a common sight in the busy streets of Sebastea so no one made bold to hinder us as we made our way to the marketplace. There, I selected the most prosperous-looking money-changer—a gold and silver merchant with a red-and-blue striped canopy over his stall—and asked him who was the most skilled physician in the city.

"Theodore of Sykeon is the man you seek," replied the merchant without hesitation. Regarding Faysal and myself shrewdly, he added, "I must caution you however, his services will not be bought cheaply. This, I find, is the rule with all men who ply their arts at the pinnacle of perfection, and the excellent Theodore is no exception."

I thanked the merchant, and inquired where Theodore

could be found, that we might secure his services without delay. But the merchant would not send us away like errand boys. "Only tell me where you are staying and I will have one of my servants bring him to you."

I thanked him for his thoughtfulness, but declined. "The need is urgent, and we are anxious that there should be no delay. I think it best to arrange matters ourselves."

"Make no mistake," the gold merchant replied graciously, "it is not compassion, but self-interest that prompts me. For if you are men who do not shrink from engaging the very best for your ailing friend, then I think such men may require other services while sojourning in Sebastea," he allowed himself an appreciative glance at the Qadi's jewelled handle protruding from my belt, "perhaps the services of a money-changer. Should this need arise, I hope you will deem it necessary to look no further than your humble servant, Hadjidakis."

With that, he took up and rang a small brass bell, and a slender and barefoot youth appeared. "Now then," Hadjidakis said, "where are you staying?" I told him, and he relayed the information to the young man, speaking in a language I did not understand. The youth nodded once and darted away into the thronging marketplace. "You may return to your friend in confidence: Theodore of Sykeon will be with you shortly. Unless," he said hopefully, "there is anything else I can do for you?"

"A small matter comes to mind," I said. "We have business with the governor. I am told he resides in the city. Is this so?"

"Indeed so," he answered. "Even now Exarch Honorius occupies a palace in the street next to the forum. It is not difficult to find. Ask anyone, they will tell you the way."

I thanked Hadjidakis again, and we made our way back to camp, returning only a few moments before the physician himself appeared. A man of mature years, small-boned and neat-featured, he was dressed simply and impeccably in a white linen cloak and mantle. A gold chain hung heavily around his neck and a blue hat of soft cloth sat far back on his head. He arrived in a covered chair borne by four Ethiope slaves led by the youth in Hadjidakis' employ. Upon ascertaining that he had not been led astray, the physician paid the youth with a bronze coin, then ordered his slaves to lower the chair.

"I am Theodore," he said simply, making a small bow. "If you would kindly take me to the sufferer, I will make my examination now."

I conducted the physician to the amir's tent and entered to find Kazimain and Ddewi, as always, by his side. "Here is the physician," I told them, "he has come to tend Amir Sadiq. We will leave him to make his examination."

"There is no need," Theodore replied affably. "Please, stay, my friends, if you will. I may have cause to question you about his care."

This impressed Kazimain, who, when I had translated the physician's words, replied that Theodore put her in mind of Farouk, which she considered a very auspicious sign. Ddewi favoured the newcomer with a sharply appraising glance of his solitary eye, but said nothing.

As the tent was somewhat crowded, I elected to wait outside and instructed Theodore to come to me when he finished. Upon emerging from the tent, I met Faysal lingering by the entrance. "I believe we have done the best for Lord Sadiq," I told him.

"Pray Allah it is enough."

Leading him a few paces from the tent, I said, "Faysal, I would like your opinion of a thing I have been considering." So saying, I began to relate my suspicions regarding the governor's place in Nikos's treachery.

He listened, nodding now and again to himself. "You

have learned something of subtlety, my friend," he said appreciatively. "If the governor stands at the heart of the mystery, then we must go to him and see what we can learn."

Theodore emerged from the amir's tent just then. Stepping quickly to where we stood, he said, "I have concluded my examination." He spoke with clipped efficiency. "The amir is in distress by reason of a head wound—as you know. The bone at the base of his skull has been crushed. It is my belief that bleeding inside the skull has brought about his unfortunate condition."

"Will he live?" I asked.

"The injury is severe," he said with smooth evasion. "That he remains alive even now is a credit to the young man who attends him." He looked from me to Faysal and back again. "Yet, I am puzzled."

"Yes?"

"The wound is in no way recent;" he said, "and I see by your camp that you have been travelling. Is this so?"

"We have come from Amida," I told him. "There was no help for him there, so we came north to obtain the best care for the amir."

Theodore shook his head in amazement. "Then the young man's skill is more extraordinary than I imagined. Together we will undertake the healing of Lord Sadiq." Placing his palms together neatly, he said, "I trust this meets with your approval?"

"As you will," Faysal replied. "We defer to your learning and judgement."

"Then, if you will excuse me, I must send for certain of my tools. This evening we must perform a most delicate operation. I need time to prepare." With that he hastened to speak to his slaves, two of whom departed on the run. Returning to the tent, Theodore bowed once in our direction and then entered.

"Come, Faysal," I said, "I think we must pay a visit to the governor."

We found our way to the forum quickly and easily; the many-pillared colonnade in the heart of the city could be seen from any of several approaches. Once there, locating the street Hadjidakis had mentioned posed no greater difficulty. The governor's house was large, with a single door opening almost directly onto the street, save for two steps rising between two ornate columns. A guardsman stood outside in the street, spear in hand, a shield slung over his shoulder. People passed him without a glance, however, and from this I deduced that he was a familiar feature of the place. Leaving Faysal to watch the house from across the street, I strode to the house.

"I was told the governor is in residence," I said upon greeting the guard, who regarded me with bored suspicion.

"He is receiving no one," the guard replied in a tone that suggested he had said this too many times for his own liking.

"That is truly unfortunate," I sighed. "I have travelled a very great distance to see him. Perhaps you might allow my name to be put forward."

Without bothering to reply, the guard motioned me on with his spear. Clearly, his was not the final authority. Once inside however, I was met by another, more formidable obstacle in the person of an official in a robe and mantle of faded green; he wore a braided thong around his neck on which was affixed a large metal box, and sat at a table in the centre of a spacious vestibule, writing on a vellum roll. He deigned not to notice me as I came to stand before him. Two more equally bored-looking guards stood either side of a door directly behind him.

"If you please," I said, "I was told the governor is in residence."

The official raised his eyes from the document before him and all but yawned in my face. "He is seeing no one. Leave your name and come back tomorrow."

"I have travelled a very great distance." Leaning close, I confided, "It is a matter of some delicacy involving a very great deal of money." Reaching into my sleeve, I pulled out one of the silver coins Faysal had given me and placed it on the table. "I would be most grateful if the governor could be notified."

Obtaining no response, I placed another coin beside the first. The official finally lay aside his pen. His lips curled in a smile, but his eyes remained cold. "Perhaps I may be of service. My name is Casius; I am Proconsul of Sebastea. What is the nature of your business with Exarch Honorius?"

Thinking quickly, I said, "It concerns property belonging to my betrothed wife."

"Property, you say?"

"Yes, it is a delicate matter, and I should not like to say too much about it to anyone except the governor. When do you think he might see me?"

"This is not a matter for the exarch's arbitration," Casius informed me flatly. "I suggest you place your matter before the magister or, better still, your local apographeus."

"Ah, yes, well, it was, in fact, the magister who suggested I come here." Once given to the lie, I became brazen. "He said that inasmuch as Honorius was a friend of my father's, the governor would want to advise me personally."

The proconsul—if indeed he *was* the proconsul—hesitated; I could see him calculating his next response. "Why did you not tell me the governor was a friend of yours in the first place?"

"A friend, as I say, of my father's," I corrected. "Would that have made a difference?"

"I will put your name forward," he said, taking up his long reed pen once more; he dipped it in the ink pot and scratched something on the vellum. "Perhaps the exarch will see you."

"All the better if that could be arranged," I said, laying a third coin on the table. "There have been rumours that the governor is ill, you know. I am certain Honorius's friends in Trebizond will welcome reassurances of his health."

He stopped writing and tapped his teeth with the pen. "These rumours—what are they saying?"

"Oh, one thing and another," I replied casually. "They think it strange that he should remain so long in Sebastea when he has such a splendid residence in Trebizond."

Casius made up his mind at once. Pushing back his chair, he rose. "Wait here." With that, he stepped to the guarded door, opened it, and disappeared into the room beyond—returning a few moments later. "This business," he said, "I believe you told me it concerns your betrothed also?"

"Yes," I lied, "so it does."

"Fetch her," the proconsul said. "Return with the woman, and the governor will see you."

I knew I had gained a prize. "Very well," I said, "I will do as you suggest." Thanking the man, I told him to expect us shortly, then departed before he could change his mind.

In the street once more, I hurried from the house, motioning Faysal to follow. "The governor is there," I told him as he fell into step beside me. I explained how I had convinced them to let me see him, and said, "I thought Kazimain might assist us."

"Undoubtedly," he agreed, "but will they allow you to speak to him alone?"

"That remains to be seen," I said, "but I have a plan."

We made quick work of returning to camp, apprising Kazimain of the difficulties, and proceeding once more to the city. We approached to within a hundred paces of the palace, where I paused and turned to Kazimain. "Are you ready?" I asked. "Once we have entered, we are committed. If you have any doubts, speak now. It is not too late to abandon the scheme."

"You need have no fear for me," she said. "I am well able to do my part."

"Good," I said, drawing a deep breath. "We begin."

Raising the hood of her mantle, Kazimain covered her head in the manner of Christian women, and offered me her arm; taking it, I pulled her close, and together we walked to the governor's house.

As before, I was met by a man at a table—a different man, this time, but as listless and bored as the first. I told him that Proconsul Casius had arranged for me to speak with the governor. The man looked at me, and then at Kazimain, and said, interest quickening his heavy features, "Yes, I believe he mentioned it. But he failed to tell me precisely why you wanted to see the exarch."

"It is a matter of some delicacy, as I have already explained," I replied. The fellow stared at me with insolent indifference, so I added, "But I suppose it would do no harm to tell you that it involves the property of my betrothed." I indicated Kazimain beside me. "Her brother refuses to relinquish her share."

"Why," asked the man, apathy seeping back into his face, "should this concern the exarch?"

"In light of my family's long friendship, and the particular injustice involved, it has been suggested that Honorius might be persuaded to at least give us the benefit of his counsel."

"You know Exarch Honorius?"

"Oh, yes," I replied, with conviction, "very well. He is an old friend of my father's. I have been many times in his house in Trebizond." That last was true at least.

Again, this produced the desired result. The fellow pushed himself up from his chair and said, "I will see what can be done."

As Casius before him, he stepped to the door and disappeared into the room beyond. The guards, after eyeing Kazimain from head to heel, turned their flagging attention once more to the study of the painted wall opposite, and we to a lengthy wait.

After a while, the inner door opened and I stood, thinking that we would be summoned. But a short, plump old woman emerged, carrying a bundle of clothing. The bundle was unwieldy and, as she reached the door to the street, she lost her grip and the load slipped from her hands. "My laundry!" she cried, scrabbling after it.

"Allow me, mother," I said, stooping quickly to gather it for her. Taking the clothes, the washerwoman sniffed at me, and proceeded on her way.

I sat down to wait once more, and had begun thinking that the man was not coming back, when the door opened and the proconsul addressed us. "The exarch will see you now."

We stepped to the door, and the man put his hand to my arm, stopping me. Fearing I had somehow been discovered, my heart lurched inside my chest. But the man merely said, "Exarch Honorius has not been feeling well of late. He requires rest. You must be brief and to the point."

"I understand."

"Also," the man tightened his grip on my arm, "I would say nothing regarding the rumours in Trebizond if I were you. It is a highly sensitive issue just now and I feel it would complicate your position unnecessarily."

"Very well," I allowed reluctantly, "if that is what you advise."

"It is."

"Then I will say nothing," I agreed, and the official opened the door and allowed us into the room.

Governor Honorius was a big man with a full head of white hair. His shoulders and hands were broad, and his features generous. But he sat slumped in his chair as if he lacked the will ever to rise again, and his eyes were dark-circled and sunken; his flesh had the unhealthy pallor I had learned to associate with captivity. He was sitting in a large chair, behind which stood two more guards with spears and short swords. Casius was present, standing at his right hand; the other official stepped behind us to close the door and remained there.

"Thank you for seeing us, governor," I said quickly, anxious to speak first. "I bring greetings from my father, Nicephorus."

At this name Honorius's eyes quickened with interest, much as I had hoped. He searched my face, but without recognition. "I fear you have the better of me."

"Forgive me, governor," I said. "I was but a small boy when last we met. It has been many years. I should not have presumed upon your memory."

He looked at me hopefully. "Of course, I do remember you now."

Before I could reply, the first official, Casius, spoke up. "I believe that you said it was a matter involving property," he announced. "I have already explained that it is not a matter for the exarch's involvement. Is that not so?"

"That is so," replied Honorius, his voice going strangely dead.

"So you see—" offered the second official hurriedly, "I fear you have—"

"A moment more, please," I said firmly. "The property in question is the inheritance rightfully due my bride, to be passed to her upon her betrothal and to be used as her dowry."

"Yes, yes," said the governor in a distracted way. "These matters can be very—"

"Her brother," I said—turning to Kazimain, I put my hand on her shoulder and gave it a firm squeeze—"refuses to relinquish her share, and our wedding is needlessly—"

All at once Kazimain began to weep. She buried her face in her hands and wailed. The official closest to the door advanced threateningly. "Why is she crying?" he demanded.

"She is very distraught," I explained, "as anyone might imagine. Our wedding has been—"

"Tell her to be quiet," he growled, "or she will have to leave."

"Please, my love," I said, squeezing her shoulder again, "you must try to control yourself."

Kazimain responded with a wail, and sobbed more loudly. "Take her out of here," ordered Casius.

The second man stepped closer and made to lay hold of her. Kazimain stepped aside, ran to the governor's chair, and threw herself before him. She wrapped her arms around his legs and wailed, tears streaming down her cheeks. The governor peered down in startled amazement. The two officials leapt forward and tried to pry her loose, shouting, "Stop that! Get up!"

I rushed to help them. "Here now," I said. "Here now. You must desist at once, my darling." I pawed ineffectually at Kazimain, stepping first this way and then that, entangling myself in their efforts.

"Get out of the way!" shouted the second official. Shoving me roughly aside, the two raised Kazimain to her feet and began dragging her away. "Guards! The door!" The two guards hastened to open the door.

Stepping quickly to the governor's side, I whispered, "We are here to help you, Honorius."

"Help me?" He seemed bewildered by the suggestion. "I am a prisoner here."

"We can free you. We will come for you tonight."

The old man clutched at my sleeve. "It is too late for me," he said. "No one can help me. The emperor—" His fingers raked at my arm. "Listen to me! You must warn him—"

"I have men with me," I told him. "We will come for you tonight. Be ready."

Proconsul Casius and one of the guards' returned before either of us could say more. I stepped back abruptly, and said aloud, "Pray accept my apology, governor. My bride is overwrought. If the dowry is not forthcoming—"

"Enough!" the official said, almost stumbling in his haste to pry me from Honorius's side. "Get out! Had I known what a disturbance you would create, I never would have allowed you to waste the exarch's time in such a disgraceful way."

"I beg your pardon," I said, stepping smoothly away. At the door, I paused and turned once more to the governor. "I will deliver your greetings to my father. He will be greatly cheered to know that you are feeling better now."

Honorius gaped at me, his mouth working to speak words I could not catch. I was pushed through the vestibule and out the door so fast that I collided with Kazimain who was already in the street, a frowning guard at her side. "You need trouble yourselves no further," Casius called angrily from the door. "Should you return, the exarch has given orders not to admit you. There is nothing further he can do."

The guard watched us until we were out of sight. But once we had turned the corner, I grabbed Kazimain and hugged her tightly. "Excellent!" I cried.

She put her arms around my neck, smiling, and then

remembered herself and abruptly pulled away. "Was it what you wanted?"

"You were magnificent!"

"Do you think they believed us?"

"It does not matter," I replied. "We have seen Honorius, and he is alive—that is all we need to know."

Kazimain gazed at me, her eyes shining. "Was I magnificent? Truly?"

"That you were, my love." Turning away, my mind was already leaping to the task before us. "Hurry," I called over my shoulder, "we have much to do before nightfall."

# 65

t would be best," Theodore was saying, "if no one remained inside the tent while the *cheirourgia* is performed."

Glancing at Kazimain, pale and drawn but determined, I said, "We will stay."

"Then you must remain silent," Theodore replied. "I warn you now, there will be an issue of blood. Do not be frightened at this; it is a feature of the procedure."

I relayed the physician's words to Kazimain and she nodded, never taking her eyes from the amir's prostrate form. Sadiq's hair was clipped short and the back of his head shaved smooth; he had been given a strong, soporific drug called *opium* made from the juice of certain flowers common in the east. Turned face down on a bed of cushions, Sadiq now slept soundly, with Ddewi at his head on one side and Theodore on the other. The amir's arms were bound to his body with cords, and his legs were also tied together.

Selecting a small, razor-like knife from among the various tools spread upon a cloth-covered brass platter beside him, Theodore nodded to Ddewi, who took the amir's head between his hands. "We begin," he said.

With deft, unhesitating strokes Theodore pierced the skin at the base of the amir's skull and opened a circular flap of skin, which he lifted and pinned up out of the way with a needle, much as a tailor might do with a scrap of cloth. Kazimain folded her hands and pressed them to her lips.

Blood ran freely from the wound as Theodore replaced the knife and regarded his handiwork for a moment. Apparently satisfied, he then took up a small powdery stone and applied it to several places along the edge of the cut he had made, and the bleeding diminished considerably. A look of wonder appeared on Ddewi's face.

Selecting another, longer-bladed knife, Theodore leaned forward and began gently scraping at the wound, and I soon saw the glimmer of white bone. "Since you are here," the physician said, speaking with slow concentration, "you might as well be of use to me. Come and hold the lamp a little higher."

With a look and a nod, Theodore positioned me and directed the light where he wanted it to fall. I held the brass lamp as he bent to the study of his work, probing now and then with the tip of the long blade held lightly in his fingers.

After a few moments, he breathed a whispered, "Ah, yes!" To Ddewi, he said, "You were right, my friend. It is a small fragment of bone which has become dislodged and has caused the bleeding inside the skull."

Replacing the knife upon the tray, Theodore took up a strange tool; shaped like a pair of miniature tongs, but with elongated pincers at the end, it had loops for his thumb and finger with which he operated it. Using this, he bent to his work and in a moment I heard a wet, sucking sound and he raised the instrument into the light. A nasty, jagged piece of pink-white bone the size of a man's thumbnail glistened between the pincers' jaws.

"Here," he announced, "is the source of the amir's infirmity." Dropping the bit of bone onto the brass tray with a pattering chink, he said, "Now his healing can begin."

Replacing the tongs, he took up another cloth, doubled it and spread it carefully over the cushion beside the amir's head. "We will turn him now," said Theodore, and together Ddewi and the physician rolled the amir onto his side. Black blood oozed from the wound onto the cloth. The healer watched the flow with satisfaction, remarking to Ddewi on its colour and turgid consistency.

"You may replace the lamp," Theodore told me. "There is nothing more to be done until the wound has drained. That will take some time, I think. Refresh yourselves, my friends. I will summon you when the procedure commences anew."

"Very well," I said, and moved to where Kazimain was standing, her hands still clenched to her chin. "Come, we will walk a little before I go."

"I am staying," she said, shaking her head.

Leaving her to her vigil, I stepped through the tent flap to find Faysal hovering just outside. "All is well," I told him. "They are nearly finished."

"Praise be to Allah," he sighed with audible relief.

Glancing at the dusky sky, I said, "We must leave or the gates will be closed. Is everything ready?"

"Seven have been sent into the city already," he replied. "The rest ride with us. I have saddled one of the pack horses for Exarch Honorius. We await your command."

The setting sun shone red as it disappeared below the horizon; away to the east, a new-risen slice of moon gleamed dully and two stars had begun to glow. It would be a warm, clear night, with enough light to make our way without torches.

"It is a good night for an escape," I said, touching the handle of the knife tucked into my belt. "Come, the governor is waiting."

A few moments later, Faysal and I and the three remaining rafiq were riding towards Sebastea, leaving the Sea Wolves behind to guard the camp. Jarl Harald had all but begged to be allowed to undertake the raid, but I considered the Danes were not yet fit enough to fight. Also, their appearance would have roused undue suspicion in the city. "It is but a small errand," I told him, "and we need someone to guard the camp, after all. Nurse your strength for the battle to come."

Thus, we proceeded to the city gates, leading a pack horse burdened with bundles of straw wrapped in sacking. Appearing as merchants arriving late to the city, we passed easily through the gate without so much as a glance from the guards squatting around their little cooking fire in the shadow of the gateman's hut.

"Getting into the city is easy," I had told Faysal on my return from the city. "But getting out again—that will be difficult."

"Leave it to me," he replied. Faysal had made most of the preparations for our night raid—and with such efficiency, I wondered at his skill. And then I remembered how he had rescued me, and reflected that where such furtive activities were concerned, Faysal did not lack practice.

Once past the gates, we made our way quickly to an inn near the marketplace that Kazimain and I had identified on our visit that morning. There we joined the warriors who had entered Sebastea earlier; four of them were sitting outside the inn, and the other three were standing in the street a little distance away. At our approach one of the rafiq raised his eyes and gave an imperceptible nod. Faysal dismounted and summoned the man, and the two spoke together quietly for a moment.

"Sayid has found a small gate on the northern wall," Faysal said when he returned. "He believes it will serve our purpose."

"Good," I said, looking towards the inn. "We might as well have something to eat—it will help the time go more quickly."

We lingered over our meal, sitting unobtrusively in a corner of the main room, until the innkeeper closed his shutters for the night. Then, leaving a silver coin on the table, Faysal and I quit the inn and proceeded quickly and quietly to the forum. Several prostitutes hailed us as we passed, offering their services from the shadows of the pillars. I had not anticipated this, and worried that their loud solicitations brought attention to us. Even so, Sebastea's citizens were used to the noise they made, for the few people still about in the streets paid us no heed.

Creeping along the dark and narrow streets, we came to the governor's house. I did not see the warriors, but Faysal assured me they were hidden nearby, watching for the signal. "We can stand over there," I said, pointing to a niche in the wall formed by a disused doorway. We had planned merely to watch the house for a while, to make certain everyone was asleep inside. The house, as I have said, fronted directly onto the street and, as we passed by, I saw that the door was open.

"This is better than I could have hoped," I told Faysal, already revising the plan in my head. "I will go alone."

"Wait!" he warned. "This is not right." He turned around and made a gesture with his arms. In a moment, we were joined by three warriors, blades in hand. "Now we will go in," Faysal said. "The others will keep watch outside."

We slipped silently into the shadowed doorway. I put my hand to the door and pushed—it swung open easily and I stepped into the vestibule. Someone had thoughtfully left a lamp burning on a stand beside the door, but there was no one in the room. We stood for a moment, listening, but heard not a sound. I glanced at Faysal, who shrugged, unable to think why the door should be unsecured.

Taking up the lamp, I led the search of the house, which, in the Byzantine manner, comprised two floors, one atop the other joined by stairs. I did not know which of the many rooms might be the governor's, but decided to look for Honorius on the upper floor first, reasoning that if I were holding a man a captive in his own residence, I would keep him as far away from the front door as possible.

From my previous visit, I knew the stairs were not to be found beyond the large door that opened onto the vestibule, so I turned and went through a smaller archway which led onto a short corridor. Once in the corridor, I saw two more arches: the left opened onto a small court-yard, and the right gave onto stairs.

Motioning to Faysal, I indicated that I would go up first. Keeping my lamp low, I climbed the steps quickly, and paused at the top to listen. The house was silent; it might have been a tomb. Satisfied that we had not yet alerted the guards to our presence, I gestured to the rest to follow.

The room at the top of the steps was a smaller copy of the vestibule below, but with a door leading to interior rooms. As below, so above: the door was open. I stepped to the door, put my hand to the polished wood, and was about to push it when Faysal put his hand to my arm. "Allow me," he breathed, drawing his long knife from his belt.

Without the slightest sound, he slipped into the room. I heard a muffled grunt of surprise, and then the door swung wide. Faysal motioned me inside. "Now we know why there are no guards," he said, taking the lamp from my hands.

In the fitful light I saw Honorius lying on a bed soaked in blood. Eyes wide and bulging, his mouth open in a final, silent scream, his throat had been sliced open from ear to ear. The room stank of urine and faeces, and the sickly-sweet odour of blood. Everything was deathly silent, save for the droning buzz of flies gathering in the darkness.

Sitting next to the body was an old woman. She looked impassively at Faysal and me, then turned her eyes once more to the governor.

"He is dead," she said softly, and I recognized her then as the washerwoman I had met earlier in the day. "I brought his clothes."

"Woman, how long have you been here?" I asked, squatting down beside her.

"They killed him," she said, and put a plump red hand to her face. I heard an odd, strangled sound; she was sobbing.

Leaving her for the moment, I put a hand to the corpse's cheek; the skin was cold to the touch. Even in the dim and flickering lamplight, I could tell the blood had begun to congeal. His murderers had left nothing to chance: hands bound behind him, his throat had been cut to keep his screams from being heard, and he had been stabbed several times in the chest for good measure.

"He has been dead some time," Faysal observed.

"I told him we would come for him," I said, remembering our brief meeting. "He said no one could save him—that it was too late."

Faysal touched my arm and indicated the old woman. I looked and saw that she was clutching a small white packet to her bosom with her free hand. Bending to her once more, I said, "Mother, what have you there?"

Reaching out, I put my hand to the packet. The old woman raised her face, fearful now. "I am an honest woman!" she cried, growing suddenly agitated. "Three years I have worked in this house! Three years! I have never stolen so much as a thread!"

"I believe you," I said. "What do you hold there?"

"I am no thief," she insisted, clutching the packet more tightly. "Ask anyone—ask the governor! He will tell you I am an honest woman."

"Please?" I asked, tugging the packet gently from her.

"I found it," she told me. "It was there," she said, pointing at a pile of clothing folded neatly on the floor. "He left it there for me to find. I swear it! I took nothing! I am no thief."

"Peace, old woman," I said, trying to soothe her. "We make no accusations."

"They try to trick you sometimes," she told me breathlessly. "They leave things for you to find, and then they say you steal them. I am no thief." She shook a finger at the packet in my hand. "I found it. I did not steal it."

Faysal brought the lamp near, and I bent to my examination. "It is parchment," I said, turning it over in the light, "bound with a strip of cloth . . . and, here—here is the governor's seal." Above the seal, written in a thin, spidery hand were two words: the first was *basileus,* I could not make out the second. "It may be for the emperor."

Slipping the cloth band from the packet, I made to break the seal. Faysal counselled against it, saying, "I think we should leave before someone finds us."

The old laundress had begun sobbing again. "Three years I have worked for this house!" she moaned. "I am an honest woman. Where will I find another house?"

"Come," Faysal urged, "we can do nothing here."

Stuffing the packet into my belt, I turned to the old woman. "You do not have to stay here. You can come with us if you wish."

She looked at me with her damp eyes, then glanced at

the governor's body. "I wash his clothes," she said. "I am an old woman. I will stay with him."

Stepping quickly to the door, Faysal motioned me to follow. I rose slowly. "The danger is past," I said. "I do not think the killers will return. You can get help in the morning." The old woman made no reply, but turned her gaze once more upon the bloodied body lying beside her.

Back down the stairs, through the corridor and into the vestibule, we fled. With trembling hand, I returned the lamp to its stand, and crept to the door. I put my hand to the handle, pulled open the door slightly, and slipped out.

Sayid appeared at once, stepping from the shadows to motion me forward. "Swiftly!" he hissed. "Someone comes."

Glancing to where he pointed, I saw a man ambling towards us; he was, perhaps, thirty paces away. Even as I looked, the man halted. "He has seen us," Faysal said. "Hurry! This way!"

Faysal turned and fled down the street. In the same instant, the man began shouting. "Thieves! Robbers!" he cried, his voice echoing down the empty street. "Help! Thieves! Robbers!"

We ran to the inn where we had left the horses under Nadr's vigilant eye; he passed me the reins to my mount and I swung up into the saddle. "Lead the way," I called. "We are behind you."

At a sign from Faysal, Sayid rode out; I could still hear the fellow crying for help as we clattered back along the deserted street—passing the startled man once more. Despite his cries of robber and thief, the streets remained empty and quiet; save for a skulking dog or two that barked as we passed, Sebastea slept undisturbed.

Upon reaching the north wall, we turned off the main street and continued along a narrow passageway until we came to an unused guard tower, beneath which a small, lean-to hut had been erected beside the low wooden gate.

Sayid dismounted before the hut, and slapped the crude door with his hand. A thin weasel of a fellow poked out his head, squinted at the mounted warriors and complained, "I never agreed to so many!"

"Be quiet!" warned Sayid. "Open the gate."

"But you never said there would be so many," the gateman protested, stepping cautiously out of his hut.

"You are well paid for the work of a moment," Sayid said. "Now open the gate."

The gateman withdrew his keys reluctantly. "Opening the gate is, as you say, the work of a moment," he allowed. "Forgetting what I have seen this night . . . whether such a thing is possible, I am far from certain."

"Perhaps," said Faysal, jingling coins in his hand, "these will help you to perform the impossible." Leaning from the saddle, he extended his hand.

The gateman reached expectantly towards the offered coins. Faysal raised his hand. "When the others are through the gate," he said. "Not before."

"The others?" wondered the gateman, his eyes growing wide. "I see no one here. Oh, already I am becoming so forgetful."

The oily fellow turned to his task and, in a few moments, the gate creaked open. A steep road led away from the wall, blue-white in the moonlight against the black of high-mounded banks. The gateway was narrow and low, forcing us to bend double in the saddle. Once beyond the wall and its banked-earth ramparts, the road swung towards the east. We rode west, however, and made our way more slowly across fields and grazing land, arriving back at camp as the last light of a setting moon traced the domes and spires of the city in lingering silver.

When daylight transmuted night's silver to morning's red gold, I would, I believed, at last hold the answer to the mystery of Nikos's betrayal.

# 66

Your business in Trebizond can wait," Theodore said bluntly. "The amir must not be moved."

"You said he would be able to travel."

"In a few days, perhaps," the physician allowed, "and even that is too soon. The amir has survived a most delicate procedure. Now he must rest if his wound is to heal properly. Given time, I have no doubt he will regain his former strength and well-being."

"Unfortunately, there is no time," I insisted. "Need is upon us; as you see, we must leave at once."

We spoke outside the tent as men broke camp and prepared to depart. Faysal stood nearby, a frown deepening on his brown face.

"Then I suggest you leave the amir with me. My house is large; I will care for him there. Never fear, I am well acquainted with the requirements of noblemen. When Lord Sadiq has recovered sufficiently, he can follow."

"Your offer is tempting as it is gracious," I replied. "However, we are hard pressed to continue our journey as best we may. The amir himself would agree—indeed, he would demand it if I did not."

"Then, it is my duty to tell you that the amir will not survive such a journey. If you persist, you will kill him."

Shouldering this grim responsibility, I replied, "We are grateful for your service." Motioning Faysal to join us, I said, "Faysal will reward you now. Go in peace."

The physician accepted his payment and said no more. He collected his tools, woke his slaves, and departed, his dire pronouncement hanging over me like a curse. Once he had gone, I commanded the rafiq to make ready the amir's riding sling, and by the time the rose-pink sun cleared the eastern ridge, we were well along the Trebizond road. Speed was our most reliable ally, I reckoned, for if we maintained the pace I had begun, we would reach Trebizond before news of the governor's death. Any messengers would be forced to go by the same road on which we journeyed; to do otherwise would take too long, and should anyone try to overtake us, we would certainly apprehend them long before they could come near. Not forgetting the last time I had travelled this same road, I kept scouts ranging far ahead to prevent us rushing into another ambush.

Though I bitterly regretted the urgency, I pressed ahead relentlessly, my cold heart fixed on Byzantium and the confrontation to come. Time and again, my hand strayed to the folded document beneath my robe. That square scrap of parchment, hastily scrawled in Honorius's hand, exposed the wicked heart of Nikos's treachery.

Upon our return to camp, I had immediately opened the packet and read out the letter contained within. That Honorius had written it, I had no doubt; I recognized both the hand and signature from the letter the eparch had received. Faysal, holding a torch near, watched the expression on my face as the dire truth came clear.

Lowering the document, I glanced at Faysal, eager in the torchlight. Even as I spoke the words, my mind was leaping ahead to what must be done to prevent the terrible act they described. "Nikos plans to murder the emperor," I said.

"For this they killed the governor?" he observed.

"And everyone else who came too near," I told him, and explained: "Honorius was taken prisoner because he found out about the plot and tried to warn the emperor. They kept him alive because they found his office useful to further their aims."

"It says this?" wondered Faysal, tapping the parchment with a finger.

"Oh, yes," I replied, "and much else besides." I passed the document to Faysal and held the torch while he read.

The letter, signed and sealed by the governor, provided damning evidence of Nikos's treachery—though even Honorius did not perceive the full extent of the plot. But I knew.

What is more, I was confident that I now possessed all the scattered fragments of the mosaic and that I had assembled them aright. The resulting picture may not have been pleasant; but it was true.

It seems that while making one of his periodic visits to the southern region, word had reached Exarch Honorius of a rumour that the emperor was to be killed by someone close to the throne. Upon further investigation, he had learned that the conspiracy originated in a city called Tephrike, and was thought to be the work of an Armenian named Chrysocheirus. Though I knew neither the city nor the man, I knew the word the governor used to describe them: Paulician.

Upon reading this, I recalled Bishop Arius telling me that after their expulsion from Constantinople, the Paulicians had fled east where their continual raiding, as much as their alliance with the Arabs, had eventually roused the anger of the emperor, who had ordered reprisals against the cult. The emperor was Basil, of course, and from Honorius's description, I gathered that Tephrike was the central stronghold of the Paulicians, and Chrysocheirus had been their leader; he was, like many of the sect's members, of Armenian descent. He was also kinsman to a courtier well placed in the imperial palace—an ambitious young man named Nikos.

Thus, the mystery had at last come clear. In order to maintain hostilities between the Sarazens and the empire, from which the cult benefited, the peace initiative had to be stopped; and for his part in the persecution, the emperor had been marked for death.

My brother monks simply had the great misfortune of wandering into Nikos's elaborate snare. Their unwitting desire to see Honorius had brought them to Nikos' attention, and they had been eliminated. In much the same way, the eparch had been dealt with as well. When Honorius discovered the plot, he was taken prisoner; and, when his usefulness came to an end, he was killed. So far as Nikos knew, no one remained alive to confront him with his crimes.

Oh, but he had not reckoned on the resilience of the Irish spirit, the determined strength of barbarians, nor the tenacity and resourcefulness of Arab resolve.

True, I had no special concern for the emperor; I confess it freely. My sympathies were entirely otherwise. The poor and powerless—like the blessed Bishop Cadoc, and all those women and children killed in the ambush—claimed my small store of compassion. The emperor had his bodyguard of Farghanese mercenaries; he had his ships and his soldiers and his fortresses. But it was the weak and innocent who always suffered in the clash, and who protected them?

God alone, it seemed; and time and again, he proved himself a highly unreliable defender. If anything were to be done to help those in harm's way this time, it would be myself, not God, who shouldered the burden.

Still, all my efforts would be worth less than nothing if Nikos's plot succeeded. I had long ago vowed that if I ever got free, I would see Nikos's head nailed to the Magnaura Gate and his corpse trampled in the Hippodrome. Driven by my singular desire for revenge—rekindled to a fine and handsome blaze by Honorius's letter—my thoughts flew towards Trebizond and Harald's waiting ships. How I ached to be in Byzantium with my hands around Nikos's throat.

Faysal finished reading and lowered the parchment, his face grim in the flickering torchlight. "The conspiracy against the emperor must not be allowed to succeed," he intoned softly. "For the sake of the peace treaty, we must expose it. The amir would not be pleased if we allowed anything to stand in our way."

"My thoughts exactly," I replied. "Then we agree—it is on to Byzantium as quickly as possible."

Alas, so many of our number were afoot we could not move with anything near the speed I desired. Indeed, I seriously considered going on ahead myself, perhaps taking a few men for protection, but we would need every available man to help crew the ships and I would gain nothing if, arriving in Trebizond, we were unable to sail at once.

Thus, I had no better alternative than to proceed as best and as fast as circumstances allowed—ever mindful of the amir's infirmity. Sebastea lay some small distance behind us when we stopped to rest that first day, taking shelter from the hammering sun in an olive grove beside the road. While the rafiq and Danes drew water from the well that supplied the grove, Kazimain and Ddewi tended Lord Sadiq, and Brynach, Dugal, and myself sat down to talk.

"It appears," Brynach began as soon as we were settled, "that we have embarked on a mission of some urgency." His gaze was direct and his manner straightforward, as if addressing an equal. "Are we to know its aim?"

"Indeed, and I would value your counsel, brother," I replied, and began to detail the convoluted path by which we had arrived at the place we now occupied. The elder monk listened, nodding thoughtfully from time to time—as if what I said supplied the answers to questions of long-standing concern. I finished by explaining my speculations on what had happened to the governor. "Regretfully, Honorius was killed before we could rescue him. I have no doubt the deed was carried out by the same faction of which Nikos is a member."

"This faction," Brynach asked, "have you discovered its identity?"

"They are Armenians, for the most part," I told him, "and adherents to a heretical sect known as Paulicians."

"I have never heard of them," said Dugal, struggling to imagine why these people should wish him ill.

"Nor I," replied Brynach. "But then, there are many sects. Not all of them are heretical."

"Perhaps not," I conceded. "As it happens, they were cast out of the Holy Church and driven from Constantinople several years ago. Their faith has been anathematized, and their leaders declared enemies of the emperor. Persecution has forced them to become secretive."

"Granting what you say is true," Brynach said somewhat doubtfully, "why would these Paulicians concern themselves with us? We have done nothing to rouse either their wrath or interest."

"So far as I can see," I answered, "their aim is twofold: they hope to thwart the peace between Byzantium and the Sarazens, and they are also intent on murdering the emperor. Governor Honorius learned of their plans and was preparing to warn the emperor when he was made prisoner."

"What has that to do with us?" wondered Dugal, still struggling to imagine why people he had never heard of, much less seen, should wish harm on a handful of Irish monks.

"The eparch and his skilful negotiation of the peace was a threat to the Paulicians because the treaty abolished their safety in Arab lands from which they are allowed to raid with impunity," I explained. "The monks of Kells were merely unlucky—Cadoc wanted to see the governor, and Nikos could not risk allowing you to meet with Honorius and then returning to warn the emperor of the plot against him."

"We wandered into a hornets' nest unaware," mused Dugal, shaking his head at the wild caprices of fortune.

"That you did, brother."

Brynach, frowning under the oppressive weight this distressing knowledge produced in him, lifted woeful eyes to me. "So we are hastening to Byzantium to warn the emperor," he concluded.

"To warn the emperor, yes," I agreed, and added, "but also to bring Nikos to justice. I mean to confront him with his crimes and see him die the death he so richly deserves."

"What if you cannot reach the emperor?" Dugal wondered. "We were many days waiting to see him, and sure, we never did."

"We have the amir with us," I reminded him. "The emperor will be more than eager to meet with the man who can deliver peace with the Arabs. If we can but keep Lord Sadiq alive, the basileus will see us, never fear; and what is more, once he sees the governor's letter he will believe us." I saw no reason to mention my own pledge to bring word to the basileus, who would be more than eager to hear what I had to tell him.

Later, we left the shaded grove and moved out once more, some riding, most walking, silent as the shadows stretching along the road: a curious *karwán*, made up of horses and camels, lithe Sarazens and lumbering Sea Wolves, Christians and Muhammedans, veiled Kazimain and bearded Irish monks, the stricken amir in his swaying sling, and Faysal and myself walking side by side, leading the ungainly company. We had not been joined together by choice: our unlikely allegiance had been formed by circumstance and fate—*kismet*, the Arabs called it—but was no less strong for that.

Though the sun was still hot, the air was beginning to lose its heat. By the time the far hills turned purple in the dusky light, night's chill had begun seeping into the land. We journeyed through starlit night, silently, wrapped in our cloaks for warmth—only to cast them off again when the sun spread the eastern sky with its blood-red glow. When the heat-blast became unbearable, we sheltered in whatever shade we could find, thus completing the circle.

Each day was a duplicate of the one before—save that the land began to change as the hills became rough and craggy, the valleys deeper and more narrow. Though I saw Kazimain daily, we spoke infrequently, and then only about the amir's precarious condition; it occupied her every thought. She wore her worry well, bearing up with admirable fortitude; even so, the journey exacted its price. With each passing day, the distance between us grew the more. Concerns of my own prevented me from crossing the divide; I confess I did but stand aside and watch that gap increase.

Then we reached the place I dreaded most—where the road passed beneath high cliffs and the emperor's envoy had been ambushed.

Little remained of that iniquitous outrage and the bloody butchery that followed; I suppose anything of value had long since been scavenged by other travellers on this road. Even so, a few signs persisted: the ragged heaps of rock along the cliffside where scores lay buried, killed in their unsuspecting sleep; haphazard scatterings of sun-bleached bones picked clean by bird and beast; a few broken spears, and a battered shield or two. That was all. Little enough, as I say, to mark the magnitude of the tragedy.

Though the days remained bright, a thick soul-hugging gloom settled over me. While all around me moved in sun-dazzling brilliance, I walked in winter bleak and grey. Over the next days, I thought about the ambush, all that had gone before, and all that had come after. I dreamed of reprisal and justice; more, I dreamed of satisfaction: eye for eye, flesh for flesh, life for life.

Into this desert melancholy, the dead bishop's words came back to me: *All flesh is grass, Brother Aidan*. But so immersed was I in my dreams of vengeance, that I could discern no meaning to the riddle. Eating little, sleeping less, I thought of nothing and no one save myself and the fearful retribution I held within my grasp.

All else dwindled to insignificance against the all-consuming hunger for revenge. When at last the walls of Trebizond appeared on the plain below us—and beyond the city the clean blue sweep of the sea, glittering in the early-morning light—that craving was honed keen and sharp as a blade in the gut.

What is more, I felt well-armed and ready to strike. True, returning to Constantinople might mean my own death—it was a possibility I had not forgotten—but I no longer cared. Despite my vision and previous apprehension, I wanted nothing more than to see Nikos on his knees begging for his worthless life before the disembowelling spear. Beside that, my own demise was of no account. If I perished, so be it. I meant to collect the blood debt for those who had been so brutally slaughtered.

# 67

Since our presence in Trebizond was impossible to hide, I attempted to make our appearance both brief and unassuming. We would linger in the city only so long as it took to provision the ships. Once aboard, we would sail immediately—thereby thwarting any interference from the duplicitous magister and his unseen minions. Accordingly, I held counsel with Jarl Harald to discuss how this might be accomplished.

"Before anyone knows to stop us, we will be gone," Harald said confidently; he had regained his former bluff manner, if not his entire strength. The Danes are a sturdy race; hardship seems only to make them stronger. Harald and his men had recovered from the privations of slavery wonderfully well; they were almost completely restored and eager as I was to return to Constantinople. "I will go to the harbour and make the necessary preparations. When I send word, you come and we will sail at once."

"What if the ships are not there anymore?" I asked. Never once did Harald display the slightest doubt, but insisted his ships would still be waiting for his return and that the crews would be ready. While I wondered at his simple faith, he laughed at my unbelief.

"You will see," Harald said, and chose men to go with him. They were soon lost in the early-morning bustle and crush of people making their way into the city. Meanwhile, I explained our plans to Faysal. "What if his ships are not there any longer?" Faysal wondered, scanning the crowded road uneasily.

"Harald says his men would starve to death before they would abandon their king."

"They are so loyal, these Wolves of the Sea?"

We settled ourselves outside the city gates to wait, hoping Harald's trust in his men was not woefully misplaced. The king had been absent a long time, after all. But before the sun had passed midday, one of the Danes returned. "The ships are soon sea-ready. Jarl Harald says come to the harbour now."

Trebizond appeared exactly as we had left it; nothing had changed—which surprised me somewhat, for I felt a lifetime had passed since I had last threaded my way through the narrow streets to the harbour. This time, however, I was painfully aware of the attention we were attracting, and feared that the city's soldiers would appear at any moment to challenge us; but we passed unhindered, and proceeded directly to the wharf where the four longships lay at anchor.

Once there, we were greeted warmly by the Danes, forty-four in all, who had stayed behind. Gunnar stood on the quayside with happy tears streaming down his face, while his friends pounded him joyfully on the back. Sure, I too was overcome by the sight of Tolar and Thorkel and the rest, looking much the same as the day we had left them on the wharf. While the world had turned through its three seasons they had stood at their duty and guarded the dragon-headed ships against the expectation of their king's imminent return: an exemplary feat of pure childlike faith.

The Sea Wolves' jubilation at the appearance of their king and comrades was nothing beside their amazement at the wealth the Jarl brought with him. Their rejoicing, however, was soon swallowed in the feverish rush to board everyone and set off. We were, of course, forced to abandon the horses and camels; Faysal chose three men to stay behind and look after the animals, charging them to establish camp outside the walls and await the amir's return.

"They are so loyal, these rafiq?" I asked, turning his question back on him.

"Allah willing, they will wait until their beards grow to touch the ground," he replied.

"And then?"

"They will shave, and wait some more."

What with his crew so brutally decimated, Harald no longer commanded enough Sea Wolves to man four ships, and had been forced to the onerous expediency of hiring seamen to help man the ships—Greek fishermen, mostly, who agreed to go to Constantinople where they could find work on other ships. He hired fifty-three, and would have taken more, but there were no more to be had at any price.

As soon as the last water cask was lashed to its companions, and the last of the rafiq scrambled aboard, the Sea Wolves took up their long oars and pushed away from the wharf. As the wind was favourable, Harald ordered the handsome red-and-white banded sails to be raised while the ships were still in harbour. Although such practice was certain to draw the harbour master's condemnation, the jarl cared nothing for that, thinking only to get away as swiftly as possible. Thus, in less time than it takes to tell it, the four longships sped from Trebizond like wild geese loosed after lengthy captivity.

Harald, glad to be his own master once more, took his place at the sternpost and commanded Thorkel, the pilot, to steer a course that kept us far from sight of land. I asked him if this unaccustomed caution arose from fear of Sarazen pirates, but he spat and said, "The emperor owes me much silver for my pains, and the sooner we reach Miklagård, the sooner I will be paid."

I could but marvel at the audacity of the man. Even after all that had happened, he still considered himself in the emperor's employ, and meant to collect his wages. Nor had he forgotten the debt Nikos owed him—an account he meant to collect in blood.

The tented platform behind the mast, where Harald was wont to keep his treasure, became the amir's sickbed. As soon as we departed the harbour, I went to see how he fared. Faysal and Ddewi had hung the amir's sling between the mast and one of the supports of the platform; Sadiq lay covered only by a cloth of the lightest material. He seemed peacefully asleep, and if not for the white band swathing his head instead of his customary turban, he might merely have been a man taking a well-deserved rest.

"There is little change," Kazimain informed me when I asked. She appeared haggard, her eyes dull and her skin pallid; her lips were dry and cracked. The journey and its consequent demands of caring for her stricken kinsman had used her cruelly.

"Has he woken?"

Not trusting her voice, she merely shook her head.

"The worst is behind us," I said, trying to comfort her. "He can rest for a time now—at least until we reach Constantinople."

At this, Ddewi raised his head and regarded me with interest. "How long?" he asked. The question, though simple, surprised me; it was the first time I had heard him speak since escaping the mines.

"No fewer than twelve days," I answered. "Thorkel says if the wind stays fair, we shall make good time."

"Twelve days," he mused, returning his gaze to the amir's unmoving form. "That is good."

Kazimain noticed my look of mild surprise, and smiled. "Yes," she said, "he speaks now. No doubt, you have been too busy to notice."

"I am sorry, Kazimain. If I have seemed preoccupied, it is not—"

"Shhh," she soothed. "I did not speak so to rebuke you, my love. I know your thoughts are elsewhere."

She returned to her duty, and I curled myself into the curve of the bow to take a nap. No sooner had I closed my eyes, however, than Harald's bellow roused me. "That one may be trouble," he said, pointing to a square red sail visible against the buff-coloured hills. Another ship with a blue-and-white striped sail could be seen moving eastward along the coast, following the established sea path.

"Perhaps he will turn aside when he reaches deeper water," I suggested.

"Perhaps," agreed Harald doubtfully. "We must keep our eyes on him, I think. He is very fast, that one."

The red ship did not turn into the sea lane when he reached deep water; he proceeded on steadily, following our wake, seemingly content to hold back as the distant hills dwindled behind us. Harald read this as a bad omen. "He is waiting until we are out of sight of land," Harald said. "Then he will make his move. We have a little time yet to prepare."

Signalling to the other three ships, Harald brought them nearer so that we sailed more closely together. He ordered all the provisions to be lashed down and secured, and for weapons to be placed at the ready. The Sea Wolves placed their shields along the rails, which served to raise the sides of the ships and so better protect those inside. Spears were set upright in the leather oar holders between the shields, ready at hand.

My brother monks saw the activity and asked what it meant. I told them about the red ship, saying, "Harald thinks they may be pirates."

"I think he is right," Dugal agreed. "The ship that attacked us on the way to Trebizond had red sails, too."

"We will pray to God for deliverance," Bryn said staunchly. Dugal regarded the spears thoughtfully.

"You would be better employed," I advised, "praying to the wind that it does not fail."

The red ship drew ever nearer—until we could see the narrow prow plainly above the sea swell. Then she slackened her pace to match our own, hanging back what seemed a respectful distance, her master exercising obvious caution. "What does he want, this one?" mused Harald aloud, cupping his hands to his eyes to shield them from the sun-glare. "Why does he wait?"

"Perhaps," I suggested, "he is simply a merchant who wishes to travel in our company."

"And perhaps he is waiting for his friends," the jarl replied contemptuously. "We are four against one, after all."

By day's end the red ship had come no closer, neither had she altered her course by so much as a hair. She kept her distance through the night, and when morning came the red sail was still in place. With the dawn came a more forceful breeze, blowing out of the southwest. Thinking to increase the distance between ourselves and the red ship, Harald altered the course slightly to take advantage of the fresh wind.

The longships leapt forward at once, and very soon the red ship was seen to be growing smaller. "We are leaving them behind!" shouted Dugal. "Praise God!"

Faysal was of the same opinion and looked upon the dwindling red sail as an auspicious sign. I could not help noticing, however, that none of the Sea Wolves shared this optimistic view. Not even when the strange ship disappeared from view completely, did they relax their vigilance. Since they were masters of seacraft and warfare, I allowed my mood to be guided by their example, and remained wary.

Harald's manoeuvre gained us a space of peace—at least, once the sail disappeared we did not see the red ship again the rest of that day, nor the following night. All day long, we anxiously scanned the horizon for any sign of the red ship, but saw nothing. It seemed that the monk's prayers had done their work.

Night was far gone when the moon finally rose, and Harald sent a man up the mast to watch the horizon. I dozed at the prow, half-awake, listening for the warning cry from the mast-top. It came at dawn, when the Sea Wolf called down from his perch that he saw the red once more. We gathered at the rail and gazed into the dawn-misted distance, waiting to sight the tell-tale spot on the horizon.

Alas, when it came into view, it was not one ship only this time; it was two. The call came down from the mast lookout: "Two ships! I see two!"

We leaned over the rail, each holding his breath, straining for a glimpse. In a little while, we were able to confirm the lookout's observation: two sails—one ahead, and one slightly behind and to the right of the first—emerged from the sea haze. As midday approached, it became clear that they pursued a course directly towards us. By evening, despite Harald Bull-Roar's best efforts, they had gained on us.

"They are done with waiting," Gunnar mused, his face glowing in the last of a golden dusk. He and Tolar, inseparable now that they were reunited, had come to stand beside me as I looked out at the relentlessly approaching vessels. "Now they will catch us if they can."

"Can we outrun them?" I asked.

"Nay," Gunnar said, shaking his head slowly. "That is what we have been trying to do all day. They are very fast, these small ships." He looked at the pirate vessels, now running a short way to the west of our close-clustered fleet. "But never fear, Aeddan," he added reassuringly, "we still outnumber them. If they try to attack, we can easily divide them. It is a difficult thing to board four longships at once, I think—even for Arab pirates."

Forced to bow to the Sea Wolves' superior wisdom, I thought to inform Kazimain of our position, and was surprised when Ddewi emerged to summon me. "The amir has awakened," he said, smiling with quiet excitement. "He is asking for you."

"Indeed?" Following Ddewi into the tented enclosure, I found the amir talking quietly to Kazimain. The days aboard ship had been good for him, it seemed. He had been able to sleep in peace without being continually jostled by horses and awakened at every turn.

"Greetings, Lord Sadiq!" I exclaimed upon entering, "I am glad to see you awake. Ddewi tells me you are feeling better."

"Truly," he replied. "Allah willing, I shall soon feel strong enough to take up my sword and do battle with the sea raiders."

"Ah, that is why I came," I said, settling myself just inside the entrance; Kazimain and Ddewi shifted aside to allow me room to sit, "but I see you have heard already."

"The walls of my palace are cloth," he said, raising a hand limply to the tented enclosure; "it would have been more surprising if I had not heard." He paused, and licked his lips. Ddewi, alert to his needs, instantly produced a cup of water; the amir waved it aside. When he spoke again, his voice was soft, but his gaze direct. "The attack—when will it come?"

"The Danes do not think the raiders will try to take us

at night," I replied. "It is likely they will wait until tomorrow."

"That, I fear, is too soon for me," the amir said with a slight, dry smile. The skin stretched across his cheekbones was pale as parchment and very thin. "Tell these pirates they must wait a little longer if they wish to fight the Lion of Samarra."

"Of course, Lord Sadiq, I shall tell them at first opportunity. In any case, Harald thinks it will be a disappointing battle. He is confident that two ships of raiders cannot defeat four longships of Sea Wolves."

"Tell your King Harald that overconfidence is a pernicious enemy," the amir advised. "The raiders know themselves outnumbered, and still they come. Does this not speak a word of caution to you?"

Kazimain leaned forward, placing her hand on Sadiq's shoulder. "Uncle, speak no more. Rest now."

"Well," I said lightly, "if the wind holds good we may outrun them after all." Rising to leave, I promised to come and see him again soon.

"Tell King Harald what I said," the amir urged as I withdrew.

"I will tell him."

Kazimain followed me out, and we made our way to the prow where we could speak more easily without being overheard. "He is getting better," she said, quiet insistence giving her a determined air. "Ddewi hopes he will be ready to walk again soon." She paused, looking out at the flat milk-blue horizon. Her brow furrowed, but whether in thought or worry, I could not tell, so waited for her to speak again. In a moment, she turned to me and said, "What will happen when we reach Byzantium?"

"I fear we will have more than enough trouble just getting there," I indicated the double set of red sails, still coursing off to the west, closer now, "without worrying what comes after."

"What do you want to happen?" she persisted.

"I want everything to be like it was," I began. "I want—"

I was cut off by Harald's sudden cry. "Down sail!" he bellowed. "To oars!"

Sure, his roar shook the very mast to its quivering top. Suddenly, everyone was scrambling to the rowing benches. Glancing seaward, I saw what had alarmed Harald: the red ships had abruptly changed course and were now charging straight at us.

I ran to Harald's side where he stood gripping the rail as if it was a spear. "The waiting is over," he said. "Now the fighting begins."

# 68

Slamming the oaken oar into the slot, I leapt onto the bench, recalling the last time I had tried my hand at rowing. It was in *Bán Gwydd*; we were fleeing the Sea Wolves, and I had never held an oar before. It was with a peculiar regret that I perceived I was no better oarsman now. The long timber was unwieldy in my hands, and cursedly awkward. I found myself alternately plunging the blade too deep, or merely swiping up a spray.

Gunnar, seeing my difficulty, took his place on the bench before me. "See here, Aeddan, man!" he called over his shoulder. "Just you do what I do, and all will be well."

I ceased my frenzied thrashing and watched him perform a few strokes: he pushed the oar forward and dipped it slightly before dragging it back, taking the strain in his shoulders and letting the blade glide through the water. Imitating his example, the oar became slightly less cumbersome, and the rowing easier.

Dugal and Brynach also settled nearby, and I told them to follow Gunnar's lead, which they did, very quickly acquiring the skill—especially Dugal, who with his strength could easily match the best of the Danes.

"We must be calling him Dugal Bull-Rower from now on," called Hnefi from his bench opposite Dugal's.

Those nearby laughed at his small jest, and I translated the joke for Dugal, saying, "This is praise indeed, coming from Hnefi."

"Tell him I will match him stroke for stroke and we will see who tires first," replied Dugal.

Soon every available hand on every ship was wielding an oar. Alas, now was the extent of the Sea King's losses cruelly apparent: of those who had sailed from Bjorvika with Harald, barely one in four survived; more than one hundred and seventy had begun the journey, and only forty-four remained alive. Thus, despite the aid of the Greek fishermen, the rowing benches were not crowded, and even with the help of the Arab rafiq—who were no seamen—the ships fared but little faster.

I soon realized, however, that Harald's aim was not to outrun the raiders, but simply to turn the longships into the wind and hope the raiders could not close on us. If we succeeded in holding them off long enough, there was always a chance we might achieve enough distance to allow us to catch a favourable wind and sail out of danger.

At first, the strategy appeared to work—and wonderfully well. As the longships swung onto their new course, the red ships turned to follow and we saw the sails fall slack. Moments later, the red ships slowed; having no oars, the raiders foundered in the water.

The Sea Wolves saw it and cheered. But then the raiders hauled the sails tight, and began pegging back and forth at long angles to the wind—a tactic which brought groans from the Danes.

"They know something of sailing, these raiders," Gunnar said. "They cannot catch us, but neither will we lose them. We must keep rowing and hope the wind falls."

Row we did, watching the red ships coursing relentlessly

back and forth over our wake as the sun slowly arced across the empty blue vault of heaven. As the day grew long and muscles tired, dark oaths took the place of the easy laughter. The Greeks complained that they had been hired on as seamen, not slaves; and upon learning their complaint, Harald told them they could either row or swim, the choice was theirs—although rowers could hope for additional reward upon reaching our destination.

Others may have grumbled, but I relished my long toil on the hard bench, considering that each stroke of the oars drove us closer to Byzantium and Nikos's day of reckoning.

Sitting on my rough bench, I imagined how it would be:

We would sail into Theodosius Harbour, swarm through the gate, and make our way to the imperial palace, where, in a blaze of righteous fury, we would confront the astonished Nikos with his treasons and treacheries. Upon hearing the confession from the wretch's lips, the grateful emperor would deliver him into our hands for execution— which would be duly effected, but only after a particularly excruciating period of torture specially prepared by the Sea Wolves. The emperor, whose life we had so narrowly saved, would reward us fabulously, of course, and we would leave that accursed place forever.

The dream, pleasant as it was, came to an end when, early the next morning, the wind changed quarter, gusting smartly from the southeast. The red ships were keen to the change. Even as the Danes raced to raise sails, the raiders were swinging effortlessly back onto course.

"Up sail!" cried Harald, as Thorkel hauled at the steering oar, sending the ships onto a new course. Sea Wolves shipped oars and scrambled to the ropes to raise the sail. There came a groan and a crack as the mast took the weight and the great square sail snapped full. I felt the ship hesitate as the prow bit into the waves, only to spring ahead as the dragonhead came bounding up once more. In the space of three heartbeats the longships were flying before the wind like low-swooping gulls.

Oh, but the red ships were faster still. With each swell and surge of the waves, they came the closer, ever narrowing the distance between us. Soon we could see the hulls above the water, and only a little while later, we could make out figures aboard the raiding vessels. The Sea Wolves fell to counting them in an effort to reckon the number of the enemy, arguing over the estimates, and counting again.

It seemed there were at least thirty raiders aboard each of the red ships, while we had only a hundred and twenty-four men in all—Greeks, Irish, Danes, and Sarazens together. Also, we were four ships to their two, and even if we were outmanoeuvred, each raider ship would, as Gunnar had pointed out, find boarding two longships at once a most difficult chore.

But the raiders had something very different in mind, as we quickly learned to our deep and utter dismay.

The first attack came as, standing at the rails, we saw a white puff of smoke sweep up from the side of the nearest red ship. We heard a whirring whoosh like an entire flock of swans whistling through the air overhead. There sounded a sharp report from across the water. Crack! In the self-same instant, the mast was struck as by an unseen hand, shaking the tall timber to the keel beam, whereupon the topmost tip sprouted bright red-blue flames. The Sea Wolves gaped in disbelief at this dire wonder, and asked one another what it could mean. The Greeks, however, knew all too well, and threw up their hands in horror.

I became aware of someone shouting in Arabic. "Get down!" he called, and I turned to see Faysal clambering over the empty rowing benches in an effort to reach me. "Aidan!" he cried. "Tell them—tell everyone to get down!"

As he was speaking, a cry went up from those at the

rail: another white cloud of smoke puffed out, followed by the strange whirring noise, and suddenly the sea gushed up over the hull to rain over everyone. I dashed seawater from my eyes and when I looked again, behold! the sea was burning with bright red-blue flames.

"It is Greek fire," Faysal told me. "The Byzantines use it against our ships in war. It is a liquid fire that burns everything it touches, and can only be extinguished with sand."

The sea hissed and sizzled where the strange flames danced, before sinking abruptly and throwing up a thick white cloud of steam. "We have no sand—what can we do?" I wondered, seeing no way to prevent the raiders from throwing the stuff. They seemed able to hurl it from a distance with startling ease and impunity.

"Let godly men pray to God," Faysal declared. "There is no deliverance apart from Allah!"

Harald Bull-Roar was once more master of his own ships and soul, however, and threw himself into their defence with breathtaking zeal. His stentorian call rising above the cries of the men, he commanded our small fleet to split, each ship to go its separate way; this strategy forced the raiders to confine their attack to individual vessels and choose their marks more carefully.

Thus, we were driven back to the rowing benches, in an effort to move the ships. In less time than it takes to tell, the Sea Wolf pack was scattering in four different directions, and the red raiders were struggling to turn around without losing their wind advantage.

Two Viking ships succeeded in crossing safely behind the raiders, leaving only Harald's dragonship and the remaining longship in harm's way. Thorkel skillfully guided us onto a glancing course, turning the unprotected hull away from the attacker, thereby reducing our presentation many times over—the efficacy of which was amply demonstrated with the next attack. For, as we swung onto our new heading, the nearest red ship spewed forth another flaming missile.

This time, upon seeing the tell-tale puff of smoke, I was able to follow the progress of the hissing object as it hurtled through the sky to strike the water a scant few paces from the rail. The next attempt cast up spray the same distance from the opposite rail, which brought a taunting clamour from the Danes as they mocked their attacker's lack of skill. They did not, I noticed, slacken the pace of their rowing, however, but continued with renewed dedication.

Seeing the dragonship had slipped their grasp, the red ship turned its attention to the longship nearest us, and with devastating result.

White smoke belched out from the hull near the prow and I heard a whir in the air, and then a splintering crash. Flames appeared on the hull of our sister vessel, leaping and licking in long reddish-blue tongues, running wildly along the rail, spilling into the ship and into the water.

Sea Wolves stripped off their siarcs and commenced beating at the flames with their clothes, which only served to spread the fire the more. The ship itself began to burn, throwing up an oily black smoke.

Harald, standing at the sternpost, called for his pilot to turn our ship, and, heedless of our own safety, we rowed to the aid of our companions.

Two more fiery missiles sank harmlessly into the sea before a fourth struck the sail of the burning longship, spilling a brilliant torrent over the surface of the sail and raining down fiery droplets onto those below.

We lowered our heads and hunched our backs, driving the dragonship forward. Out of the corner of my eye, I glimpsed a figure leaping to the rail; in the same motion a line snaked out across the distance between the two ships.

I looked and saw Jarl Harald tugging mightily on the hook-ended rope, which was now firmly attached to the burning longship. He roared for his men, and three Sea Wolves ran to help him drag the two ships together.

Within moments, the rowers on the near side of the ship were pulling in their oars and standing to help our comrades into our boat. One after another they fled the fire; several sailors were singed, but none were badly burned. And no sooner had all been taken aboard, than it was up oars and shove the burning vessel away before the flames could spread.

Harald commanded everyone to return to their rowing, calling a cadence for speed. I thought we would try to escape now, keeping the flaming longship between us and our attackers. But the Sea King was dauntless and bold, choosing to counter the raiders' attack and gain, if possible, victory. In this, he showed his true mettle.

Instead of turning tail and fleeing, Harald ordered Thorkel to bring the dragonprow sharply around behind the burning craft—a perilous scheme since the vessel was now almost completely engulfed in flames: the square sail was a vast, shimmering curtain of fire; smoke rolled thick and black from the blazing hull.

Slowly the dragonship turned, passing alongside the doomed vessel prow to stern—so close that the flame-roar drowned out all other sound, so close I could feel the heat-blast on my face.

One gust of the fitful wind and our own ship would be caught up in the blaze. Crouching low, I rowed as best I could, keeping one eye on the sail overhead and hoping against hope the wind did not shift. Not so Harald Bull-Roar; he lashed the grapple rope to the sternpost and called Thorkel to make for the red ships.

Cursing his sorry fate, Thorkel laboured over the steering oar, working it this way and that, fighting to keep the line smooth and clean so as not to waste a single stroke of the rowers' blades—a chore made much the more difficult since we were now towing a burning wreck.

"Faster!" roared Harald, his voice booming out in exhortation to his oarsmen. "Huh! Huh! Huh! Huh!" he grunted his encouragement.

Aided by the rescued seamen, we plied the oars and the doughty pilot brought the dragonprow around sharply, driving straight for the nearest red raider. As the further red ship swung away, the raider in our path prepared to loose his fiery projectiles.

Twice I heard the whirring whistle of the missiles as they passed—so near that I smelled the acrid oily pitch scent as they sped by. The third time we were not so lucky.

Closing on the red ship—we could see the enemy now, and see also the bronze tube at the prow by which, through unknown means, the Greek fire vomited forth— the distance decreasing with every juddering thump of my heart, I saw the white smoke belch from the brazen tube, heard the whiz of the weapon and saw it soar straight towards the open hull.

Brave Dugal saw it, too, and up he jumped, holding out his hands as if to catch the thing.

"Dugal!" I shouted with all my might. "No!"

Down and down it came, plummeting from heaven with the speed of a falling rock. Up Dugal reached, straining for his catch. The projectile sailed over his head. Dugal leaped, hands high. He must have got a hand to the missile, for it appeared to bounce from his fingertips and up into the lower part of the sail, which arrested its flight. The thing slid from the sail and fell into the bottom of the ship.

I saw then that the missile was nothing more than a rounded earthen jar, made to shatter and spill out its vile liquid. But this particular jar did not burst. Perhaps in diverting the jar into the sail, Dugal kept it from breaking.

Certainly, he saved us, for even as it landed with a hollow thump on the hull timbers, Dugal scooped it up and dived for the prow.

As Dugal ran, a portion of the Greek fire spilled down the side of the pot and splattered onto the handle of an oar. Blue-red flames instantly started up where the stuff touched, setting the wood alight. The startled Sea Wolf stood up and flung the oar into the sea before it could do any damage.

Meanwhile, Dugal scrambled with the terrible jar to the dragonhead prow, took aim, and hurled it back at the red ship.

It was an act of valour worthy of a hero, and had we been but a few hundred paces closer, it would have been magnificent. As it was, the jar simply plunged into the water and sank with a bubbling hiss.

Still, the Sea Wolves, greatly inspired by this display of courage, cheered him as heartily as if he had driven the enemy ship under the waves with a mighty clout.

Closer now, Harald called for us to row faster, and faster still. Already, my heart was pounding with the exertion; my breath came in raking gasps and I could feel the burning deep in my lungs. My hands were raw, and there was blood on the oar grip. The muscles of my back and shoulders were a knotted mass. Heedless of the pain, I plied my oar with grim determination, sweat pouring from me.

The dragonship, streaming rapidly through the waves, bore straightaway towards the raiders. I could hear the enemy yelling, and when I hazarded a look, I saw them scurrying around the bronze throwing tube, desperate to ready the foul instrument to spew again.

The dragonship was closing swiftly now; the pirates, believing themselves about to be rammed, braced for the impact, while their helmsman headed the enemy vessel directly onto us to force a glancing blow.

Now did Harald's daring show its genius, for at the last possible moment, he ordered Thorkel to turn hard aside. Then, lofting a war axe, he leapt to the sternpost and with two quick chops, severed the rope which bound us to the burning ship.

Suddenly loosed, and with no one to steer her, the flaming longship slewed sideways in the water. The enemy pilot tried to turn aside, but it was already too late: the raiders struck the burning vessel amidships and the mast gave out a deep sighing groan, teetered, and then plunged like an axe-felled tree to strike the red ship's cross-member where it hung, catching the sail alight and showering flames into the hull below.

The sight brought the Sea Wolves to their feet; they leapt onto the benches and onto the rail where they cried their joyful acclamation at the enemy's demise. I cheered, too. Before I knew it, my feet were on the rail and my voice was loud in jubilation as I shook my fists in the air.

I felt hands on me and looked down into Dugal's face; he was grinning with relief, but holding tight to me lest I should tumble overboard. He said something, but his voice was overwhelmed in the glad commotion, and I could not hear a word he said. "Yes!" I shouted in reply. "It is a splendid sight!"

Harald allowed the Sea Wolves only a moment's celebration, and then ordered everyone back to the oars. We rowed clear of the burning wrecks, which were now inextricably entangled and drifting dangerously in the waves. Casting a last look over my shoulder as the dragonship swung away, I saw the red ship's sail fully ablaze and falling in great fiery patches onto the heads of the Arab pirates as they screamed in terror, their pitiable cries swallowed in the smoke billowing from the flaming hull to flatten on the breeze and spread over the water.

Leaving the wailing enemy to the doom he had

prepared for us, Harald turned his attention to the second red ship.

Standing at the sternpost, his bull voice belling, the Sea King called cadence as we rowed to engage the raiders in combat. "Huh! Huh! Huh! Huh!" he bellowed. It soon became apparent that the two remaining longships had not only been able to stay clear of the raiders' fire-throwing prow, but had somehow navigated themselves into position behind the red ship and beyond reach of hand-thrown missiles. They were now angling for the attack, one on either side of the enemy vessel, keeping the raider ship between them.

The red vessel appeared to be trying to swing about in order to confront her attackers, but to no avail. The oar-driven longships could easily remain out of reach. Preoccupied with this difficulty, the red ship did not immediately see the dragonship ploughing a wave-furrow straight towards her.

Thorkel steered a course that would bring us up from the rear to come alongside the red ship—a much-loved Sea Wolf tactic, allowing them to grapple onto the other boat and, once the defenders were subdued, to board and loot the vessel. I knew the strategy well: it had been used to ruinous effect on little *Bán Gwydd*.

Whether it would have been successful against the red ship is a matter for eternal speculation. Before we could close on them, the raiders discovered our swift-charging onslaught. The Arab enemy took one look at the dragon-ship leaping through the waves in its eagerness to devour them, changed course and fled before the wind.

We might have made good the chase, and caught them, but Harald knew better than to exhaust his men with hard rowing and then expect them to win a battle. Instead, he broke off pursuit, and signalled the two remaining longships to follow him.

Thus, we turned aside, leaving the burning ships behind. There were men in the water by now; forced to choose between a fiery death or a watery grave, many had chosen the latter. Three half-drowned pirates bobbed into view just a spear's throw from the rail on my side of the ship. They hailed us in the name of Jesu as we drew near, but the rest of their speech was incomprehensible to me.

The Danes were for killing them—indeed, several Sea Wolves already had their spears out of the holders and were taking aim, when Faysal put a stop to it. Seizing the nearest spearman by the arm, he prevented the warrior from throwing while shouting to me to tell them not to kill the pirates.

"Save them!" Faysal urged. "They are not Arabs, they are Armenians. Such captives may prove useful to us in Byzantium."

I relayed his words to Harald, who grudgingly agreed and ordered the men to rescue the survivors instead.

The captives were in all respects similar to the raiders who had attacked us on the road to Sebastea, and like those others their appearance was such that, until they spoke, I could not tell them from Arabs. "How did you know they were Armenians?" I asked Faysal. "Was it from their speech?"

"As Allah lives I knew even before they spoke," he replied with a shrewd smile. "The Sarazens do not yet possess the secret of the Greek fire. The method of its making is a carefully guarded secret which we have yet to penetrate. That these men use it can only mean that someone from within the imperial service has given the secret to them."

So it was that three soggy Armenians joined our company, snatched from the sea, to be bound hand and foot and carried to Constantinople as further proof of Nikos's treachery.

Standing at the sternpost, Harald Bull-Roar called, "Up sail!" and commanded Thorkel to resume our previous course. Then, as the proud dragonprow swung around, Jarl Harald lofted the war axe and bellowed his victory call.

"To Miklagård!" he bawled. "Death to our enemies!"

# PART FIVE

Thou shalt not be left in the land of
   the wicked,
Thou shalt not be bent in the courts
   of the false;
Thou shalt rise victorious above them
As rise the waves above the shore.
Christ himself is shepherd over thee,
Enfolding thee on every side;
He will not forsake thee head nor heel,
Nor let evil come anigh.

# 69

T en days after the sea battle, one of the Danes scrambled up the mast and hailed us to the sight of Miklagård, the Great Golden City. The call brought Lord Sadiq from his bed and, with Kazimain and Ddewi in attendance, he came to see the gleaming domes and towers of Constantinople.

Since the battle he had appeared often, if briefly, to walk the length of the ship a few times and take the air. On these occasions, he spoke to me—and through me to Harald—giving every indication of making a fair recovery. Though he still slept much of the time, striving to recapture his strength through rest, I formed the impression that he was indeed returning to health.

Standing at the rail, we watched the city emerge from the heat haze, shimmering atop its high-humped hills—like a dazzling white pearl couched on a bed of dusty green and grey.

"This is the much-vaunted City of Gold?" asked Kazimain. Owing to the presence of so many foreigners, she was forced to wear the veil continually, and though I could see her eyes, I could not discern the thought behind her words.

"That it is," I replied, and reflected how different this arrival seemed from the first. Then I had approached the city in fear and trembling, with dread in my bones, convinced that death awaited me the moment I set foot on the quay. Oh, but that was a different man from the one that looked out over the rail. The eyes that now beheld Byzantium belonged to a harder Aidan, stronger and more wise.

"I thought," Kazimain said, "it would be a bigger place."

Glancing to where the amir stood talking quietly to Faysal, I said, "Lord Sadiq seems very well. It is good to see him hale once more." Turning back to the glistering white of the city, we watched in silence for a time, my thoughts drifting inevitably towards events to come. After awhile, I said, "We are close now, Kazimain. Truly, I can feel it— justice lies within my grasp."

"You are so confident, my love."

"We have but to present ourselves to the emperor and reveal the plot against him, and our enemies will be destroyed."

"Allah alone shapes the future," Kazimain chided gently, moving away. "Only Allah may say what will be."

*How wrong you are, my love*, I thought, *the future belongs to those who dare seize it for themselves.*

I did not know whether Nikos employed spies, and if so whether they worked the harbours of Byzantium, but I considered it likely. In any event, the sudden appearance of three Viking longships would no doubt arouse some small interest, even among the jaded denizens of Constantinople. And while I did not care to warn our enemies unnecessarily, I could think of no way to avoid it; ships must come to port, and men must disembark.

Once again, I deemed speed our surest hope. If we could reach the emperor shortly after making port, we might strike before the foe knew we had landed; failing that, we could at least forestall any but the most hastily mounted opposition.

Still, it was a risk. After all we had endured, I reckoned it a poor exchange that we must trust fate and fortune to such uncertainty. As we drew nearer and the city loomed ever larger, its crowded harbours lining the stout walls, its famed seven hills rising above all, the thought occurred to me to change our approach.

"Jarl Harald!" I cried from the rail. "Make for Hormisdas Harbour!"

He regarded me with surprise but gave the command. As the ship swung around unexpectedly, the amir demanded to know why we had suddenly altered course.

I explained that since, so far as I knew, Harald's were the only longships in the emperor's employ, our arrival in the imperial harbour could but warn Nikos that we had returned. "We will attract the least notice passing among the foreign vessels of Hormisdas Harbour, and our arrival will not be marked if we use the Barbarians' Gate."

The amir grimaced at the term, but accepted my suggestion with good grace. "No doubt it is but a gate like any other," he remarked. "Humility also has its benefits."

We proceeded slowly into the crowded port, steeling ourselves for the impending confrontation. Alas, deeds taking place in Byzantium's black and twisted heart had long since rendered our small subterfuge a meaningless gesture.

Closer, we saw that the bay was heavily crowded—ships from every part of the world rode at anchor before us, thick on the water.

"I think something is wrong here." Harald scanned the clutter of masts cramming the quayside ahead—a veritable forest. "It is not as it was before."

At first I did not comprehend his meaning. The quayside appeared exactly as I remembered it. However, Dugal, standing beside me at the rail, confirmed Harald's observation when he said, "I did not think this place ever knew a moment's peace."

"Jarl Harald was just saying he thinks something is wrong, but I cannot—"

And then I saw it: the harbour was strangely becalmed. None of the sea-going vessels were moving. The lack of activity on the part of the larger craft had escaped my notice because the usual number of small boats still plied the clogged waters, busily ferrying passengers to and fro. These, however, accounted for the only movement in the harbour. All the big ships—and there were hundreds— remained motionless. I saw ships sitting low in the water, fully laden, but none were making for the docks to unload their goods.

What is more, the wharf appeared more than usually crowded; all along its length, people were thronged in dense knots, and swarmed around the gates, but the crowds, like the ships, were motionless, and I saw no one carrying cargo.

Turning back to the rail, I hailed the nearest boatman and, as soon as he had drawn near, inquired why none of the ships were docking or unloading. "The harbour is closed," the boatman answered. "And the gates."

Harald joined me and demanded to know what I had learned. Upon receiving my reply, the king said, "Ask him why this has happened."

Turning once again to the boatman, I asked, and was appalled at the answer I received. The sun in the sky seemed to dim, and I felt the same awful impotent frustration I had felt the day Bishop Cadoc was murdered.

"What does he say?" asked Harald impatiently. Brynach and Faysal needed no translation, and both at once besieged the boatman with questions. Faysal then hastened to rouse the amir with the tidings.

Gripping the rail between my hands, I turned to King Harald who was awaiting my reply. "He says—" I replied, my voice hollow in my ears, "—the emperor is dead."

Unable to credit the words, I said them again, "The emperor is dead. They have closed the harbours and gates to all foreigners." Looking past Harald along the line of those crowding the rail, I said, "I must tell the amir."

"The amir has heard," said a tired voice behind me. "We have come too late."

Sadiq stepped to the rail, Faysal beside him; the amir nodded to Faysal, who called down to the boatman. The two talked for a moment, whereupon Faysal turned and said, "He says the Golden Gate remains open."

Upon further questioning, and payment of a silver coin, the boatman went on to explain that in times of great import—such as an imperial birth, wedding, or death—the various entrances to the city were closed to allow the soldiery to assume other duties. The Golden Gate, however, was never shut, save in time of war; but owing to the crush of people, gaining entry into the city would be very difficult.

This I relayed to Harald, whereupon the jarl called the men to oars, and soon we were sliding slowly along the city's great southern wall towards the district known as Psamathia. Although we found no proper harbour there, the water proved deep enough for secure anchorage—indeed many ships were already berthed there, prow to shore, while waiting to take on goods or provisions, or to make repairs before undertaking voyages.

Thorkel quickly found a place to drop anchor, and commanded the ships to be lashed together. We then formed a landing party.

Harald reckoned he should be the first to go ashore; he had it in mind to proceed directly to the palace and settle accounts with whoever the new emperor might be.

"You are a striking figure, Jarl Harald. What if someone were to recognize you?" I argued. "We cannot risk warning Nikos unnecessarily. If he escapes us now, all we have endured will be for nothing. We cannot allow that to happen."

Jarl Harald did not like it, but in the end was persuaded to wait, at least until we could see how matters stood at court. It was agreed that Brynach and myself should go, along with Dugal to act as bodyguard. We hailed a small boat and Harald gave us each a handful of silver coins; he also gave Dugal a sword. The incident put me in mind of the day the monks of Kells first set off, when Lord Aengus offered him a blade, which Bishop Cadoc refused. This time, however, Dugal took it.

As Faysal arranged with the boatman to take us to shore, the amir called me to him. "You must be very careful, Aidan," he advised, stroking his beard thoughtfully. "Our enemies are men without souls." Then, raising his dark eyes to mine, he warned: "Do not become one of them." He stood for a time gazing at me, then left, saying, "Bring me word when you return."

"Of course, Lord Sadiq," I replied, and watched him stoop like an old man as he entered his tented chamber.

A moment later, Faysal called that the boat was waiting. Brynach and Dugal were already boarded. Before sliding over the rail to join them, I glanced at the tented platform and saw Kazimain watching, her veil to one side. She was frowning because of the sun in her eyes, but it seemed in that moment an expression of utter disapproval and sorrow. Then she saw me, and the glower vanished in her smile. Still, I wondered whether her true feelings were not more truly declared in the frown.

The Greek sailors began clamouring for their pay and release. Leaving Faysal and Harald to deal with them, I lowered myself into the waiting boat. As the boatman worked the oar, I instructed Brynach and Dugal, speaking in our common tongue so as not to be overheard, "I think it best if we pretend to be traders. Should anyone ask, we will tell them we have come to buy spices and oil."

"To look at us," put in Dugal, fanning his billowy mantle, "you would not think us monks."

"A small deception," Brynach observed. "But if you think it necessary, I have no objection."

"I would feel better for it," I told him. "Since we are traders, and have been travelling for many days, our ignorance of affairs in Constantinople will not appear suspicious."

Brynach eyed me dubiously. "Do you believe him so powerful, this Nikos, that we must practise such deceits?"

"Ships sail at his command, and high officials die in their beds," I spat, anger flaring instantly. "You yourself have suffered at his hands, and watched your brothers succumb to his intrigues one after another. How is it you have seen all this and still do not believe?"

"Oh, I believe," replied Brynach slowly, "make no mistake. I believe him to be no more than a man—a wicked, hateful man, perhaps, but human nonetheless. But you, Aidan—you make him out a demon with powers over the very air and light."

"Until I see him dead and in his grave," I replied coldly, "I will believe him the Devil incarnate, and treat with him accordingly."

"It is our Lord Christ who upholds and protects us," Brynach said firmly. "We have nothing to fear."

"Sure, he has shown himself a sorry protector," I snapped. "Look around you, Brother Brynach, we have been beset with death and disaster at every turn, and our great good God has done nothing!"

"We are still alive," Dugal pointed out. His mild, unwitting faith irritated me.

"Yes, and how many others are *not* alive!" My anger drew the boatman's attention; he raised his eyebrows. Lowering my voice, I forced myself to remain calm. "I wonder whether our dead brothers, or the two hundred and more who fell in the ambush, would share your smug appraisal."

"I had no idea you felt so ill-used," Brynach replied, adopting a calm, unperturbed tone.

"Say nothing of my feelings," I said coldly. "But tell me, if you can, how many more people must die before you understand how little God cares?"

Dugal, taken aback by the force of my outburst, stared at me as if at a stranger.

Unable to make them see the stark futility of their faith, I shut my mouth and turned my face away until the boat bumped against the low stone quay, and we disembarked. I paid the boatman, and started at once for the gate, which we could see rising above the squatting hovels that spread like an unwholesome crust over the muck and mire of the marshlands along the wide stinking ditch beneath Constantinople's western wall. These were the homes, so to speak, of the day-labourers who unloaded the ships and carried the goods to and from the markets. This day the harbours were closed, and the workers idle; they watched us as we passed.

Picking our way through refuse heaps and reeking mud, we came to the Egnatian Way, the road which passed through the Golden Gate, eventually becoming The Mese and leading directly to the forum and the palace. Upon reaching the road, we saw that the wide, stone-paved expanse had become a river of humanity—and a turgid river at that, moving with almost imperceptible slowness, albeit with ear-numbing clamour towards the pale yellow gate far, far ahead.

There seemed no other choice but to join the throng jostling its slow way towards the city. This we did, pushing our way in behind a group of men carrying large stuffed bags made of heavy sackcloth. We shuffled slowly along together for a time, the five throwing off their weighty burdens every now and then to give themselves a rest before moving on again. It was during one such lull in the march that I spoke to them, offering to help shoulder the weight of their sacks.

"Your offer is generous, my friend," the leader of the group told me, "but we have no money with which to repay your kindness."

"We have come to the city to make our fortune," another said—a young man with a dark feather-wisp smudge of moustache. The head man gave him a disapproving look which he blithely ignored, and announced: "We are the best potters in all Nicea."

"Have you travelled far?" I asked.

"Not as far as you, by the look of it," answered the leader dourly.

"We have been some time in the east," I volunteered. "Is this road always so crowded?"

"You must be the only men in all Byzantium who do not know what has happened," the chief potter said, regarding us dubiously.

"The basileus is dead!" the young man informed me with undisguised pleasure.

"Truly?" I asked, trying to sound suitably amazed.

Dugal joined in, saying, "When did this happen?" His Greek was not good, and the men stared at him before answering.

"Six days ago," said another potter, unable to resist any longer. Indicating the sack on the ground between his feet, he said, "We have made funeral bowls which we will sell in the markets here." So saying, the man untied the mouth of the bag, reached in and grabbed what appeared to be a handful of straw. From the straw, he withdrew a pale blue and white bowl, finely made, if somewhat small and shallow. He offered me the bowl to examine, and I saw the inside had been decorated with an image of a man wearing a crown and holding a spear in one hand and a cross in the other. Below the man, who appeared to be standing atop one of the city's domes, was the word *Basil*.

"It is very handsome," I said, passing it to Brynach for his appreciative appraisal.

"City people will pay very much for this fine work," he said proudly. "And we have made three hundred of these bowls to sell."

"The emperor's funeral," I mused, steering the conversation back onto course, "is it to be soon?"

"Why, it is tomorrow," replied the leader. Then leaning close, he confided the secret of their hoped-for success: "We are going to sell our bowls outside the Hagia Sophia." Taking the bowl from Dugal, he put his finger on the image of the dome and gave me a conspiratorial wink. "We know where the funeral procession will pass."

"I wish you well," I said. "It seems we have chosen a poor time to come to the city."

"A poor time," agreed one of the potters, "if you hoped to sup with the emperor!" Everyone laughed at this outrageous suggestion. "But maybe not so bad if you have something to sell."

"Especially," continued the second potter, "if you stay long enough to welcome the new emperor." So saying, he withdrew another bowl, the same as the first in every detail—the same man with spear and cross standing atop the same dome—save for the inscription which read, *Leo*. "We have made three hundred of these also."

"You have sown your seed with admirable forethought," Brynach said. "I wish you a bountiful harvest." He paused and asked, "Is it known how the emperor died?"

"They are saying it was a hunting accident," the chief potter confided with a gossip's enthusiasm. "It happened at the summer palace at Apamea."

"A stag pulled him from his horse and gored him," added

the youth helpfully. "They say the emperor was dragged twenty miles before they could get him free of the beast."

"That is not certain, Issacius," cautioned his elder. "It is a sin to repeat rumours."

"The emperor's guards were with him and they saw everything that happened," continued the youth, his zeal unabated.

"No one saw what happened," asserted one of the other potters. "I heard the basileus had ridden ahead, and no one knew anything was wrong until they saw his horse running away. That is why the Farghanese were too far away to help."

"They gave chase and cornered the stag," continued the second potter with a dark look at the youth. "One of the bodyguard had to cut the emperor's belt to free him from the stag's antlers."

"Yes, but the beast escaped into the forest." The youth paused to enjoy the effect of his next announcement. "It took the emperor *nine days* to die."

"Nothing good comes of repeating rumours," the chief potter scolded. To us he said, "The truth is that we have heard many things. Some say one thing, and some say another, and they cannot all be right. I think no one really knows what happened. Therefore, it is perhaps best to say as little as possible."

"A wise course," I agreed. We talked about the possible funeral preparations and the various imperial ceremonies, and when I judged we had learned what we could from the potters, I bade them farewell.

Leaving the enforced procession, we made our way back to the ships. Dugal led the way, and I followed, heedless of the muck and stink, mindful only of the scheme taking shape in my mind.

## 70

Your plan possesses the elegance of simplicity," observed Lord Sadiq approvingly when I told him. "A proper splendour will make it irresistible."

Accordingly, the amir chose a villa on the Golden Horn, a magnificent house—even larger than that of Governor Honorius' in Trebizond—with dozens of rooms on two floors, and a central courtyard which boasted a fountain. Even by Constantinopolitan standards it was an opulent, if not ostentatious, abode. The amir explained, "Only the most alluring bait silences the shriek of the trap."

"Lord Sadiq, *you* are the bait in this trap," I reminded him.

We took residence and, under cover of darkness, spirited thirty Sea Wolves and three Armenian pirates into the house. The next morning we sent Faysal and all eight of the rafiq, arrayed in fine new clothes, to the imperial palace to place Lord Sadiq's petition before the Imperial Prefect, requesting an audience with the new emperor.

"There was no mistake," Faysal said upon his return. "The fellow knew the house well. He told me many foreign emissaries make use of it while staying in the city."

"And he said he would send someone to interview the amir?" I asked. Faysal nodded. "When?"

"Tomorrow, or the next day," Faysal replied. "The prefect was quite upset that we have arrived unannounced. But I explained that, owing to the emperor's untimely death, we were unable to make our presence known until now."

"And he believed you?"

Faysal smiled. "I gave him no reason to believe otherwise."

"What of the soldier?" wondered Sadiq. "Did you have any difficulty locating him?"

"None whatever, lord," Faysal answered. "All was as Aidan said it would be. I spoke with the man—"

"Did anyone see you?" I interrupted.

"It is difficult to say," Faysal said. "But I took pains to be as discreet as possible."

"Will he help us?"

"He said we could trust him to take whatever actions necessary to see justice accomplished."

"Then it is in Allah's hands," Sadiq observed.

The trap was set. That Nikos, now bearing dead Nicephorus' title must come to pay a visit to the amir, I doubted not at all. Visiting foreign dignitaries had long been part of his court function, after all, allowing him to remain close to the throne. Also, no one knew better than Nikos himself what had been done to destroy the peace treaty between Byzantium and the Sarazens. He could not risk having that treaty come to life again at such an inappropriate moment.

Thus, when Nikos learned that Amir Sadiq had arrived and requested audience with the new emperor, he would certainly make it his concern to deal with the matter personally. We had but to wait for Eparch Nikos to come to us, and when he did, I would be ready. I steeled myself for that meeting, and I told myself that soon, soon it would be over.

I ate little and slept ill, my mind whirling with thoughts of what I would do when I finally saw him. Time and again, my hand strayed to the Qadi knife for reassurance. I am no warrior, and considered that I might be killed, but I no longer feared death. Nikos, I vowed, would never leave the house alive. If I could not accomplish his death, Harald and the Sea Wolves would.

Every possibility had been anticipated, save one: the speed with which Nikos sprung the trap. His arrival was so quick on the heels of Faysal's petition that I feared he had penetrated our deception.

Two mounted komes, dressed in their distinctive yellow and blue, arrived mid-morning, rapped respectfully at the door, and informed Faysal of the eparch's imminent arrival.

I had barely enough time to alert Lord Sadiq, hasten the Danes into position, and take up my own hiding place before the eparch himself appeared. He came with ten of the imperial bodyguard, the Farghanese—five of which took up position outside the house; the remaining five entered with him, watchful, bristling.

My heart, already pounding with an excitement of anticipation, beat even faster at my first glimpse of Eparch Nikos. His dark hair was longer, more closely observant of the moment's affectations at court, I suppose, and he was more richly clothed than when last I had seen him: wearing flowing black trousers, a long black tunic with voluminous white sleeves, held at his slim waist with a wide black belt which boasted a huge silver buckle in the shape of a spearblade. His manner was smoothly superior as always, his quick eyes just as keen, his smile tight and cold.

Faysal, ever the perfect servant, conducted the three officials to the courtyard which, in the eastern manner, had been furnished with a wide low table and cushions under a striped canopy. He brought them to the table and bade them to sit, then departed, saying, "I beg your pardon to inform the amir of your arrival."

After a suitably decorous interval, Lord Sadiq appeared, regal in his flowing robes of creamy white and turquoise. The three courtiers rose in a show of respect, receiving a slight bow from Sadiq, who then invited his guests to sit with him at table, and offered them refreshment of fruit, cake, and sweet drinks. This they did, under the vigilant eyes of the imperial bodyguard who had ranged themselves at the courtyard portals.

"How enjoyable to see you again, Amir Sadiq," Nikos said, beginning the proceedings. "Your journey was pleasant, I trust." Without waiting for a response, he added, "I must say, your arrival, agreeable though it is, has taken us somewhat by surprise."

"Truly?" The amir inquired, mild concern crossing his brow. "Eparch Nicephorus and I agreed that I should come to arrange suitable lodging for the Arab delegation prior to the arrival of the khalifa. Indeed, Khalifa al'Mutamid is eagerly anticipating his meeting with the emperor in the spring."

"As it happens, recent events have rather overshadowed affairs at court just now. The palace has been in turmoil, as you might imagine," he suggested delicately.

"The imperial funeral, of course," Sadiq responded with equal tact. "Appropriate gifts of condolence will be despatched to Emperor Leo at once, of course. And if our inauspicious arrival has disturbed the emperor, I will make official apologies."

"Please accept my assurance that apologies will not be necessary," replied Nikos with a thin, dismissive smile. Upon hearing this, it occurred to me why he had responded to our petition so promptly: the emperor did not yet know of the amir's arrival. If Nikos had his way, the emperor never would.

"Indeed," Nikos continued, "it is I who must beg your pardon, for I see now where the problem has arisen." He placed the palms of his hands together. "It is with the greatest regret that I must inform you that Eparch Nicephorus is, I fear, no longer living."

Sadiq stared for a moment. "I am sorry to hear it," he said at last, and with genuine feeling. "He was a good man. I was proud to call him my friend."

"Naturally, as happens in these situations," Nikos resumed placidly, "his unfortunate death has left various matters unattended. I myself have been struggling to shoulder many of the burdens he bore so effortlessly."

"Was it a long illness?"

"He passed quickly," Nikos replied. "But then, his age was against him, I suppose." Consummate liar that he was, I almost believed him when he paused sorrowfully, and added, "Poor Nicephorus, I truly miss him. It happened shortly after our return from Trebizond. In many ways, I am still trying to come to terms with his death. It has left something of a void in imperial affairs—and now that his emperor has followed him, so to speak . . ." He paused, as if reflecting on the impossible hardships of his position. Then, appearing to brush all the unpleasantness aside, and taking up his staff of office once more, he said, "Well, the affairs of the empire go on. That is why I have come, Amir Sadiq. How may I help you?"

"Before we begin, I feel I must seek your indulgence," Sadiq said, "but it seems I have exhausted my meagre store of Greek. With your permission, I will ask Faysal to translate for me."

Nikos nodded his consent, whereupon Faysal, who had been standing apart, took his place at the amir's left hand. This artifice served a useful tool for Sadiq, permitting him time to frame his replies, and the leisure to study his guest's responses.

"As you know, the treaty is very important to the khalifa, and to the Arab people," Sadiq said through Faysal, which was entirely true. "I would not like to think the Eparch Nicephorus's untimely demise had diminished our hopes for peace in any way."

"Then allow me to reassure the amir," replied Nikos when Faysal had finished translating. "The prospect for peace is as bright as it has ever been."

"That is good," agreed Sadiq sagely. "Those who have been influential in this matter will be remembered. I am certain the khalifa would desire me to dispense such rewards as I deem fitting. Rest assured I will do so with liberality."

All this I saw and heard from my hiding place, and marvelled at the amir's skill in guiding the conversation to its desired end.

"As always, your thoughtfulness is commendable, Lord Sadiq. Nothing would please me more than to serve you in this. If you will allow me, I will personally take your gift to the emperor. This would allow me the opportunity of presenting these sentiments on your behalf. The basileus will, I believe, appreciate your gesture."

"Very well," acceded the amir, when Faysal had translated for him. "Would you like to see what I have prepared for the emperor?"

"By all means," answered Nikos agreeably.

"It is in the next room," he said, rising. "Come, I will show you."

At this, I felt my heart seize in my chest. Flattening my back against the column, I touched the jewelled daigear at my belt and then the governor's letter beneath my siarc, closed my eyes, and drew a deep breath. *Courage*, I told myself. *It is soon over.*

The amir led his guests to a room opening onto the corridor surrounding the courtyard. The room was bare, save for a coil of braided leather rope on the floor. Nikos entered the room behind Sadiq, glanced quickly around, and said, "Where is the gift?"

"It is here," Sadiq assured him.

"Where?" Nikos, suspicion well roused, stepped away from the amir.

"But *you* are to be the gift, Eparch Nikos," Lord Sadiq said. He raised his hands and clapped them twice very loud. There came a clatter from the courtyard as the unsuspecting Farghanese were swiftly overpowered and disarmed by a swarm of vengeful Danes.

Nikos and the two komes turned as one towards the sound just as I stepped into the doorway. His eyes met mine, and suspicion turned instantly to hot rage. For my own part, however, I felt my heart grow very cold. This was proceeding far, far easier than I could have imagined.

"You!" Nikos snarled. "How dare you!" His eyes darted from me to the amir, and back. "Do you know who I am?"

"Oh, I think we all know you very well," I replied, stepping into the room. "You are a liar and a murderer, a very serpent in the guise of a man. Today, however, the doom which you so richly deserve and have so long evaded has ensnared you, *Eparch* Nikos."

Harald and six Sea Wolves appeared behind me at that moment, just as we had planned. "The guards are resting peacefully," he told me, and I passed this information along to the others as the Danes took hold of Nikos and his aides.

The komes, frightened by the disaster overtaking them, began shouting and clamouring to be released at once.

I directed Hnefi and Gunnar to remove the two quaking komes, and they were hauled, white-faced and shaking, from the room.

Nikos, livid with rage, glowered hatefully at me. "I thought you dead."

"Then consider this revenge from beyond the grave," I told him.

"Revenge—for Nicephorus, that wizened little turd of a man? That is absurd."

"For Nicephorus, yes," I told him. "But no less for the Danes in the eparch's bodyguard, and all the merchants, and their women and children."

"You are insane," Nikos retorted indignantly. "Merchants and children? I have no idea what you are talking about."

"I am talking about the ambush on the road to Sebastea which you arranged," I said.

"Which I myself narrowly escaped," Nikos corrected smoothly.

"Is that what you told the emperor?"

"This is what the emperor believes, and you cannot prove otherwise," he said, and the sneer was back in his voice. It was all I could do to keep from seizing him by the throat then and there.

"Perhaps not," I conceded, trying to keep my voice level. "But there are other crimes to answer." Turning my head, I called over my shoulder: "Brynach! Dugal! Ddewi! Come here."

A moment later, the three monks stepped into the room. Nikos stared; clearly, he had not expected to meet them again, much less in my company. I stared, too, for they had devised for themselves monkish robes similar to those they had worn at the abbey; moreover, they had shaved their beards, cut their hair, and renewed their tonsures so that they now looked much the way they would have when Nikos had last seen them.

I suppose I had grown used to their shaggy appearance, but seeing them in their priestly garb brought me up short; it reminded me that I had once been of the Célé Dé.

792 ⊠ STEPHEN R. LAWHEAD

Nikos recovered his composure instantly. Oh, he was subtle and he was sure. "Who are these men?" he demanded.

"Like the others in this house," I replied, "they are men who would make accusation against you. Indeed, we have all been eagerly awaiting this moment for a very long time."

"I have done nothing," he insisted. "I will not listen to your *accusations*."

"The emperor will listen," Brynach said stoutly. "And may God have mercy on your soul."

"Of what do you accuse me? Poor weather and pirates?" Nikos said, spitting the words maliciously. "The emperor will laugh at you and your ridiculous complaints."

"I doubt the emperor will laugh," I told him. "Indeed, when news of your death reaches him, I expect he will shed a fleeting tear before appointing another to your place."

"Spare me your tiresome threats," Nikos scoffed. "If you can make good your accusations, then take me to the emperor and we will see who laughs—and who dies."

Brynach, alarmed by my intention to kill Nikos, interceded, "Brother, you cannot kill him like this. We must take him before the emperor, and let God's Vice-Regent on Earth be his judge."

Lord Sadiq also interposed. "Do not stain yourself with his killing, my friend. It is better that the basileus should learn what manner of man has been serving him." He gazed at me earnestly. "If not for your own sake, then for the sake of the peace, and all those who will suffer if it is not achieved."

I hesitated, and Nikos thought he saw his chance. "Come then," he demanded, snapping his fingers imperiously. "Take me to the emperor at once!"

Nikos's easy mastery of the situation should have sent a warning tingling through me. Oh, but I had waited long and endured much in pursuit of my vengeance; I was so anxious that it might slip away, I rushed headlong towards the confrontation, blindly heedless of the end.

## 71

H old out your hands," I commanded. Nikos, hatred burning from every pore, slowly extended his hands. Indicating the coil of rope, I called to the Danes, "Tie him."

Harald himself took part in trussing Nikos securely. Nor was he gentle with the windings and knots. When he was finished, he drew Nikos's gold-handled sword and put the blade to his ribs. "He will not be escaping this time, I think."

Thus we departed for the Great Palace, eighteen barbarians, ten Sarazens, and a handful of monks, leading one baleful eparch and three Armenian pirates through the streets of Constantinople: a strange procession, perhaps. But no more strange than that which had brought the thieving quaestor to justice.

The imperial guards and the two komes remained at the villa, bound hand to foot, where they were watched over by a dozen disgruntled Sea Wolves, who would rather have been among their comrades going to the palace.

Nikos walked along, head down, eyes on the ground, neither speaking, nor struggling. He knew well enough when to keep his mouth shut; I reckon he was biding his time and saving his breath for when it would serve him best. Once he stumbled and would have fallen, but Harald reached out a hand and steadied him. Had Nikos's look been a blade, Jarl Harald would have lost his hand. As it was, Nikos turned his eyes once more to the ground without a word.

The only time he spoke was to confirm his name to the scholarae at the gate, who was understandably reluctant to allow our party into the palace precinct without better authority than he possessed. This difficulty had been anticipated, of course. "We are an official delegation," I declared. "Please summon the Chief of the Palace Guard."

The soldier stared, uncertainly. "But I—"

"All is well," I assured him. "We will wait here until he can attend us."

With a last backward glance, the soldier departed, leaving us in the company of his fellow guards. He was gone longer than I imagined it would take—enough time for me to begin thinking our ruse had been discovered. *Patience,* I thought, smiling at the staring, suspicious scholarii; *brazen it out and we are soon finished.*

My resolve was soon rewarded when, a few moments later, I stood looking into the face of my friend, Justin.

"So," he said, his aspect solemn as his voice, "you have returned at last." His eyes flicked from me to those with me, taking in the Arabs and barbarians at a glance. "What do you want?"

I felt a sudden queasiness ripple through my inward parts. Had I misjudged my old friend?

"It is good to see you, Justin," I said. "You helped me once—"

"And now you expect me to help you again," he observed, his voice hard.

Nikos, seeing his chance, announced, "They have taken me against my will. I demand you seize them at once."

Justin turned his face slowly towards the disturbance. "Who are you to make demands of the emperor's men?"

"I am Nikos, Eparch of Constantinople," he snapped in exasperation. "Make them release me at once and I will see you rewarded."

"Will you now?" Turning to me, he said, "What do you intend with him?"

"We intend bringing him to justice," I replied.

"Then I fear you will be disappointed, friend," he said. "There is no justice in this world—here least of all."

"You helped me once," I reminded him quickly. "Please, for the sake of the righteousness you once cared about, help me again."

Justin regarded me dully, his expression unfathomable. Then, shaking his head slowly, I saw a smile begin spreading across his face. "There are other gates, you know. Why must you always come to mine?" Then he seized me by the arms and embraced me like a brother. Turning to the worried scholarii, he said, "These men here have important business with the emperor. We will provide an escort. Follow me."

With that, we were ushered through the gates and into the palace precinct beyond. At each impediment, Justin called upon his personal authority to remove the obstacle and allow us to proceed. So it was that we eventually came to be standing in a large hall called the Onopodion, which formed the entrance to the Daphne Palace, where the new basileus was staying until his preferred residence, the Octagon, could be refurbished for his use. We were admitted into the marbled hall with its blue-painted ceiling, and had come under the severe scrutiny of the magister officiorum—not the same who had served Basil, but another—who was distressed to see the eparch in the rough company of so many strange people, most of them barbarians.

He was on the point of calling out the emperor's Farghanese bodyguard, but Justin presented himself and patiently allayed his fears, assuming full responsibility for the attending company. Nikos—the hidden swordpoint jabbing painfully in his side—remained belligerently silent. "Explain to the basileus that the eparch seeks immediate audience," Justin commanded, "and I will alert the bodyguard."

The magister, perhaps relieved to have the matter taken from his shoulders, scuttled through a smaller door which opened within a massive great door the size of a city gate. Now, like everyone who came into the palace precinct for any reason, we waited.

Having come this far, Nikos recovered some of his swagger. "What do you expect will happen in there?" he inquired shrewdly. I glanced around to see him regarding me with undiluted loathing.

Harald drew back a hand to quiet him, but I intervened with a word and shake of my head. "I expect you to be condemned for your crimes," I replied. "And then I expect you will die."

Nikos shook his head with slow superiority. "Then friend Justin is right: you *will* be disappointed."

"We shall see."

"Let me tell you what is going to happen."

Annoyed by his insolence, I turned my face away and made no reply.

"You will go before the emperor with your trifling complaints, all of which I will deny," said Nikos, smug in his certainty. "Lacking any form of convincing proof, the emperor will have your tongues cut out for lying; you will be scourged and condemned to death in the emperor's mines."

His use of the word brought me sharply around once more. "You know so much about mines, do you, Nikos?" I spat, stepping closer. "Do you also know about death?"

"I know the punishment the emperor reserves for his dearest enemies."

"Was Bishop Cadoc an enemy?" I demanded. "And the monks of Éire—were they the emperor's enemies?" Stepping closer, I felt the anger leaping up within me. "Was Eparch Nicephorus an enemy? What of the children on the road to Sebastea? Were they enemies, too?" I stepped closer, my anger rising. "Was Exarch Honorius an enemy, Nikos? And what of the emperor's own mercenaries, King Harald and his Danes, who were in the employ of Basil himself. Are they also enemies?"

He gazed back at me mildly unconcerned, betraying neither fear, nor remorse. Why? Did he require more strenuous convincing?

Putting my hand into my siarc, I brought out the parchment square. "Do you recognize the seal?" I asked. "It is Honorius's seal. He wrote this before your conspirators murdered him."

Nikos looked blandly at the letter, offering an indifferent shrug.

"I saw Honorius before he was killed. I tried to free him. He left this for me." I held the letter before his face. "If you think I lack convincing proof," I said, my voice thick with hatred, "you are wrong. Honorius knew about your plot to kill Emperor Basil. He knew, and he wrote what he knew in this letter."

A strange expression of glee appeared on Nikos's face. "My plot?" he asked with a laugh. "Is that what you believe? Is that why I am made to stand here, bound like a slave for the galley?"

Nikos's laugh roused the interest of the others. Faysal and Brynach translated for their companions, but Harald moved to my side and demanded, "What is he telling you?"

"He shows no concern that the emperor should learn of his crimes."

The jarl's eyes narrowed. Seizing Nikos by the hair, he pressed the swordpoint harder. "By Odin, I will show him cause for concern."

To Nikos, I said, "Do you deny plotting to kill Emperor Basil?"

"How ignorant you are," Nikos replied, his voice tight against the pain in his side. "So righteous, so quick to judge. You know less than nothing, and presume to sit in judgement over me! Let me go, and get out while you can."

"Say what you like, I know you conspired with others to take the emperor's life," I told him, anger turning to rage. "Honorius discovered your treachery, so you took him captive and murdered him. You had Bishop Cadoc and my brother monks killed, too, for no other reason than that they wanted to see the governor. You could not risk having them return to tell the emperor what they saw."

Harald released his grip on the captive's head, but the sword remained firmly in place. "To tell the *basileus* what they saw?" wondered Nikos; he could not resist displaying his supremacy. "Your Greek is appalling as ever!" His mocking laugh sounded hollow in the voluminous hall. "I think *usurper* was the word you meant."

I stared at him, trying to make sense of what he was telling me. Harald demanded to know what Nikos said. "He is saying Basil was not the rightful emperor," I replied.

"Do not listen to him," Harald advised. "He is a liar practising his craft."

Ignoring Harald, I glared at Nikos. "What do you mean?"

"Still fumbling in the dark?" Nikos wondered. "Well, I am certain Leo can explain it so that even you and your trained barbarians can understand."

"Usurper—you called Basil a usurper—what did you mean?"

Nikos only laughed at me.

Rage burning within me, I forced myself to turn and walk a few paces away. Harald called after me, "What is he saying?"

Faysal and Brynach hastened to where I stood. "What does he mean?" they asked, confused as I was by what they had heard.

"Quiet!" I shouted. "Let me think!"

Out of the turmoil of my thoughts emerged a memory, clear as a vision: I saw Justin and myself sitting together over a meal. Justin, leaning over the table, was speaking low, and with what at the time I considered malicious delight: *"Even the emperor's friends say Basil the Macedonian's ascension owes less to divine appointment, than to the skillful application of the blade."* Once again I saw him draw his forefinger knife-like across his throat.

*"Any sorrow at Michael's passing was buried along with his blood-sodden corpse . . . It was well known he seduced and bedded Basil's wife—and not once only, but many times, and that Basil knew. Indeed, some claim that one of our emperor's sons is not his own."*

At the time I had rebuked Justin for repeating wicked and slanderous rumours. Instead, I should have been praising him for telling the truth!

Raising my eyes, I saw Justin watching me solemnly. Oh, yes, he knew.

"Aidan," called the amir, standing with Kazimain a few paces away. "Do not heed him. Wait for the emperor."

I made no reply, but addressed Nikos instead. "You were acting for Leo."

Nikos said nothing, but words were no longer necessary—his sly, superior sneer confirmed everything. I saw his lips curve so smoothly and with such easy indifference, I knew we had risked all and lost.

Fool! I shrieked inwardly, shaken by my own stupidity and ignorance.

Sick dread stole over me, swallowing the rage in gloom. There could be no justice: The King of Kings, Elect of Christ, God's Vice-Regent on Earth was bloody with the self-same crime for which I sought Nikos's condemnation.

In that moment of revelation, I saw the last light of hope snuffed out. Evil reigned. All was futility and bleak, bleak despair. I stood impotent before powers too great for me to know, and too mighty for me to resist.

There was a movement beside me. I felt a hand on my shoulder. "Do not listen to him," Dugal said.

Harald called to me again, but I could hear nothing for the pounding howl of the void screaming in my ears.

Stepping to where Nikos stood, the sneer ripe on his smirking face, I drew the daigear from my belt.

"Cut me loose," commanded the eparch arrogantly. He extended his hands so that I could sever his bonds, and I began sawing at the leather cords.

Harald reached out to stay my hand, and some of the others cried out for me to stop. But I continued slicing at the cords.

"Perhaps you are more intelligent than I thought, priest." Nikos pulled his hands free as the loosened cords fell away. "Or, should I say fallen priest? Look at them," he sneered, indicating the clean-shaven monks. "God's servants, spreading the gospel, imparting doctrine—Ha! Dogs returning to their own vomit. Look at them! A bag of shit knows more of faith."

I said nothing, but stared impassively at him.

"I used to be like you," Nikos said, rubbing his wrists. "I used to be a true believer. And then, like you, I learned the truth." He smiled, triumphant in his victory. "We are the same, you and I."

"Indeed," I agreed, "we are more alike than you know."

Raising the jewelled knife, I plunged it deep into his wicked heart.

# 72

Nikos looked down at the knife protruding from his chest, then raised his eyes once more. "Barbarian!" he spat, trembling with rage.

Reaching for the bejewelled handle, he made to pluck the daigear from his body. But I took hold of it first, shoving the blade to the hilt and then twisting it. I felt the sharp metal scrape hard against bone.

Nikos's hands gripped mine in a grotesque mockery of friendship. He tried again to pull the blade from his chest, but I held fast.

I heard the others shouting, their voices a meaningless confusion behind me. I heard my name, but the sound held no meaning. Icy serenity pervaded my soul; I felt tranquil, empty—as if all the anger and hatred I had carried for so long had been extinguished in this single act, leaving nothing behind.

"What have you done?" whispered Nikos, rage melting into bewilderment. He looked at me with a profoundly puzzled expression, his eyes glittering strangely.

"All they that take the sword, shall also perish with the sword," I replied. The words came to my tongue of themselves.

"Fool!" he shouted, tearing my hands away at last. He lurched backwards, clutching at the daigear as if it were a serpent that had sunk its fangs into him.

Perhaps his strength was already failing, or perhaps the wide metal blade had wedged somehow against bone, for he grasped the knife and tried to pluck it out but the daigear did not move. Raising his head, he shrieked aloud and with shaking hands, pulled again. Blood trickled gently from the wound, seeping from around the blade, but the daigear remained stuck fast.

Frantic now, Nikos grasped the weapon with both hands and, with a tremendous, sobbing cry, dragged the daigear from his chest. A swift-spreading dark stain appeared against the black of his siarc. "You will die for this," he said, his voice hoarse in the strained silence of the hall. "You will all die."

A snaking tendril of blood appeared at the side of his mouth as he spoke. Nikos lifted a hand to his lips, touched his fingertips to the blood and then held them before his eyes as the colour drained from his face.

Nikos coughed, spewing blood, raised the daigear and took a step towards me. I stood before him unresisting, willing to receive the blade into my own breast. To die in Byzantium was my fated end, and if this was how death found me, so be it.

The wounded eparch took another step, holding the knife so as to strike. But the step became a lurch as his legs abruptly lost their strength. Nikos crashed to his knees, the blade spinning from his grasp and clattering onto the stone floor.

Clutching at my legs, he hauled himself up, his mouth working to frame a word. His eyes beseeched, but the word was never spoken, for even as he gave it utterance, a great gush of blood surged up from his gullet and out of his mouth.

"An eye for an eye," I muttered. "A life for a life."

With a groan, he made to rise, clutching at me and trying to gather his legs under him, to stand one last time. He gained one leg and, shaking violently, somehow pulled himself into an unsteady crouch.

Nikos, bent nearly double, raised his head and gazed furiously around, his eyes glassy and unseeing. Beads of sweat glistened on his pale flesh. Pressing both hands to his chest, he lurched and fell heavily onto his back. With a deep, rattling groan, he rolled onto his side and was seized with a spasm of coughing. Blood issued forth in a brilliant crimson cascade, and he lay his head down on the floorstones.

I did not realize he was dead until Harald, bending over him, pushed him onto his back once more. There came a slow, gurgling hiss as the air fled his lungs.

Someone spoke, and I looked up to see Dugal standing beside me. I stepped towards him, and my legs turned to water. Dugal grabbed my arm and bore me up in his strong grasp. I saw his mouth move, but could make no sense of his words.

A rushing sound filled my ears, and I felt a heavy pressure inside my head. Squeezing my eyes shut, I gasped for air, fighting for my breath. The sound and pressure dissipated, and my breath returned.

"Aidan . . . Aidan?"

Opening my eyes, I found myself looking into Dugal's face. Brynach had joined him, and they were both staring at me with troubled expressions. Dugal held me by the arms, shaking me lightly; they were both talking to me, but I made no response.

I looked away from them to Nikos lying on his back on the floor, gazing up at the blue sky-painted ceiling. Still, I felt nothing: neither hatred, nor remorse, nor elation, nor any other emotion, save only the familiar dull emptiness. I knew what I had done, and I was fully aware of everyone's shock and dismay. The scholarii, amazed at what had happened, lowered their spears and made as if to guard the body, but their reaction had come too late. Frightened now, and finding themselves outnumbered by barbarians, one of them began shouting and beating on the door, calling for help. Justin merely stood aside looking on.

In a moment, the smaller door opened within the larger and the magister appeared once more. He took one swift glance at the corpse on the floor, and retreated, his hands fluttering in agitation. We heard him go crying into the room beyond and, as the great door swung slowly open, two imperial guards appeared. Taking positions beside the entrance, they crouched there, spears at the ready. More guards hastened towards us, weapons drawn, their leather shoes slapping the polished stone floor. The magister officiorum stood in the doorway, wringing his hands, and behind him Basileus Leo advanced with swift and terrible dignity.

I faced him calmly; indeed, I was astonished at my own clarity and presence of mind. It seemed as if, having crossed some unknown divide, I now stood on the other side, myself once more.

Regarding the new emperor, I observed a tall, narrow-faced man—the length of his features was emphasized by his long dark beard—wearing a simple white robe of common cloth, and a cloak of the same stuff. The only evidence of his imperial rank was a crown made of flat plaques of gold joined to form a narrow band; the centre of each plaque held a different gem, and two beaded strands joined the band to hang down either side of his head. His high and noble brow creased in a frown as he halted in the doorway to take in the tableau before him, his large dark eyes searching out each and all.

No one moved. No one spoke.

Lowering his gaze to the body on the floor, he paused as if contemplating an obscure text, the meaning of which eluded him. Finally, raising his eyes to the living once more, he said, "So!"

"Blessed basileus," began the magister, stepping to the emperor's side. "Eparch Nikos has been killed. He—"

Basileus Leo silenced the courtier with a practised flick of his hand.

Ignoring the magister, Leo said, "Will someone tell me what has taken place?" Though low, his voice echoed loud in the thick hush of the domed Onopodion.

I found the question extraordinary. Clearly, he could see what had happened, and in any case the magister had just told him. Yet, he made no judgement, nor did he rush to a conclusion, but waited for an explanation.

Unexpectedly, Faysal was first to reply. He stepped forward several paces, pressed his hands to his chest and bowed low. He then rose, declaring: "Wise basileus, allow me to present to your majesty, Lord J'Amal Sadiq, Amir of the Abbasid Sarazens, Servant of Allah, and Emissary of Khalifa al'Mutamid, Defender of the Faithful."

At this Lord Sadiq stepped forward. "May the peace of Allah be with you and with your people, Wise basileus." He made a slight bow of respect, touching his fingertips to his forehead. "Perhaps, with your majesty's indulgence, I may be permitted to offer an interpretation of events which I have myself witnessed," the amir said, his much-deprecated Greek not only flawless, but eloquent.

"Greetings, Amir Sadiq, in the name of the Lord Christ," said Leo, inclining his head stiffly. Extending his hand towards the eparch's body, he said, "Your arrival has taken us somewhat unawares, as have events." He glanced to where Nikos lay. "Nevertheless, it is our distinct pleasure to welcome you, Lord Sadiq, and we are most eager to hear your explanation. Speak, we beg you, and shed some light on this dark adventure."

"Basileus, to my considerable distress, I have this day discovered an evil treachery practised against my people—and yours," Sadiq replied. "A deed of devastating wickedness contrived to impede the treaty of peace which was negotiated by myself and Eparch Nicephorus in Trebizond, on behalf of Emperor Basil of Constantinople and the Khalifa al'Mutamid of Samarra."

I watched Leo closely for any sign of knowledge or complicity, but saw not the slightest twinge or flutter of recognition. Indeed, the astonishment which appeared on his elongated countenance was, I believe, wholly genuine. "Tell us more, we pray you, Lord Sadiq," said Leo, and with a gesture ordered his guards to stand at their ease; the spears were raised and swords sheathed.

"Only recently have I learned that the treaty of which I speak never reached Constantinople," the amir resumed, speaking with kingly poise, "by reason of Eparch Nicephorus' murder. Indeed, I myself was attacked aboard ship to prevent this unhappy news reaching your ears." Here, Sadiq turned and indicated the three Armenians. "I have no doubt you will obtain sufficient confirmation of my tale from these captives we have brought with us and now deliver to your care."

Leo's slow gaze took in the pirates, and then the host of barbarians, Sarazens, and monks. "These are most distressing tidings, Lord Sadiq," he remarked at last, his voice appropriately subdued.

"No less distressing, I believe, is the fact that the man responsible for these and other crimes was a courtier very close to the imperial throne."

It was all true, of course, but I marvelled at Sadiq's ability to colour the harsh facts with coolly disinterested oratory. Leo, too, appeared impressed by the manner in which the amir elucidated his revelations. The basileus professed himself ignorant of the events, and beseeched the amir to continue.

"It is my special pleasure to offer your majesty the agreeable report that the criminal responsible for these and other iniquitous transgressions was apprehended and did condemn himself out of his own mouth." He gazed impassively at the body on the floor. "Judgement is now in the hands of Almighty God, before whom all men must one day stand."

Nodding slowly, Leo looked once more upon the bloody corpse before him. "It may have been better," he observed dryly, "if the criminal could have answered a more mundane tribunal first."

"A thousand pardons, basileus," replied Lord Sadiq, "I can but express my deepest regret. Human frailty is the burden we all must bear as best we can, majesty, and events raced beyond our feeble ability to order them to a more acceptable conclusion. Nevertheless, I have the utmost confidence that the matter has been satisfactorily resolved, and that justice, ever the prerogative of the One True God, has been served."

Extending his hand towards the body, Sadiq concluded, "Allah's judgement is ever swift. Let us say that it was perhaps somewhat more swift in this instance than is commonly anticipated."

Emperor Leo turned and called an order to his guards, two of whom departed on the run. Turning back to us, he said, "The body of the offender will be dealt with in a manner consonant with his crimes." He moved to the doorway. "Yet, if we may prevail upon you to attend us further, we would hear more of the means and methods of the subjects introduced to us just now."

"Indeed, basileus," remarked the amir boldly, "I also believe there remains a claim to answer and debts to be settled."

With that, Leo turned and led the way into the throne-room. Amir Sadiq followed, attended by Kazimain; Jarl Harald came next, surrounded by the Danes; Justin and the gate guards followed. Brynach, Ddewi and Dugal, looking lost and confused, approached me, dazed expressions on their faces. "Aidan, why?" was all they could say.

How could I tell them what I did not know myself? I turned and followed the retinue, passing the body lying with its face in a thickening pool of blood. Out of the corner of my eye, I saw Faysal stoop and retrieve something from the floor; he brought it to me.

"The Qadi has spoken," he said, and I saw that he had wiped the blade clean. Faysal tucked the weapon into my belt once more, saying, "All is as Allah wills. May Allah be praised."

# 73

ay the peace of Allah attend you all your days, Wise Basileus," said Amir Sadiq. "Truth is more often bitter than sweet, yet it strengthens all who partake. Taste then, if you will, that your judgement may be seasoned with discernment."

Thus spoke the amir, relating all that had happened: the embassy to Trebizond and the long season of negotiation leading to the initial peace agreement; the hateful tribulations that followed—including the brutal massacre on the Sebastea road, the murder of the governor, and the enslavement of the survivors in the mines.

Leo listened, sitting not on his golden throne, but on a simple camp chair of the kind military commanders often employed. The image of a general ordering battle was furthered by the double rank of Farghanese bodyguards ranged behind him. The imperial frown had returned as Leo contemplated the story Sadiq unfolded before him.

When at last the amir finished, he said, "The accord which we offer has been secured at a fearful price. Few were brave, fewer still knew the reason for their torment, but such sacrifice as theirs should not be dishonoured by those who wield power and authority. The Sarazens stand ready to renew the treaty that has been so dearly purchased."

Leo, a thoughtful expression on his long face, nodded. "Peace between our peoples is a noble—and it must be said, costly—ambition, Lord Sadiq. With your approval, we will cause the treaty to be rewritten. Naturally, this will require your close participation."

"The successful completion of the peace treaty is of foremost importance," Sadiq said. "To this end, I have come to Constantinople, and to this end, I place myself at your service."

Basileus Leo next turned his attention to the Danes. Accordingly, Jarl Harald was summoned, and took his place before the emperor. He motioned for me to join him, which I did.

"Sovereign Lord," I said, "with permission, I will translate the king's words for your majesty's benefit."

Inclining his head in assent, the emperor said, "We give you leave to speak."

I gave a slight nod to Harald, who immediately proceeded to lay his claims before the emperor. "Most Noble Emperor," he said, his voice a low thunder in the great room, "I am Harald Bull-Roar, Jarl of the Danes of Skania, and servant of the Emperor Basil, who took me into his service to provide for the protection of his ships. This I have done with unrivalled skill and courage, to the cost of one ship and all save sixty brave men."

"You will forgive us, Lord Harald," replied Leo when I had relayed the king's words, "if we profess no knowledge of this agreement. Be that as it may, I am aware that my predecessor often pursued such arrangements. What were you to be paid for these services?"

"Great Leader," answered Harald, speaking through me, "the agreed recompense was one thousand nomismi for the king and his ships and eight denarii for each man, each month, to be paid upon completion of duties in Trebizond and safe return to Constantinople."

Harald, having thought of something to add, nudged me and spoke again. "Basileus, Jarl Harald respectfully requests the cost of one fine ship and the lives of one hundred and twelve loyal men to be taken into account." Harald thought of yet one more circumstance to add: "Not forgetting the hardships of slavery endured by the king and his men during the time of their service to the emperor."

The emperor's frown had deepened on his narrow face. He considered his answer before making his reply, chin on fist, regarding the hulking Danes all the while. This gave me good opportunity to observe the emperor; I was still undecided how much of Nikos's schemes he was party to. I think that some small part of me yet wanted to believe the best, so I watched him for any hopeful sign.

"Lord Harald," began Leo in his deep voice, "we are mindful of the enormous sacrifices you and your men have made on behalf of the empire. We are aware that provision is often allowed for the widows of soldiers killed in imperial service. Therefore, we propose to extend this compensation to you, in addition to a remittance for your ship. The logothete will call upon you tomorrow to agree on the amounts and arrange payment. We trust you will find this acceptable?"

"Great Sovereign," replied Harald, when I had translated the emperor's offer, "insofar as mere treasure can ever replace men of courage in the service of their lord and the hearts of their kinfolk, I deem your majesty's offer acceptable, and will receive your servant with all courtesy."

The magister officiorum, standing at the emperor's right hand, duly recorded the agreement on his wax tablet. When he finished, Emperor Leo stood and declared the proceedings concluded. I could not help but notice that nothing further had been mentioned of Nikos. While Amir Sadiq and Harald may have been content to allow the matter to end, I was not; I reckoned the monks of Kells and Hy still had a claim to be settled.

Even as the emperor rose to dismiss the assembly, I made bold to speak. "Lord and emperor," I said, stepping before him, "there is yet a debt to be reconciled."

He paused, glancing back over his shoulder to see who had called him. "Yes? And what is that?"

Indicating Brynach, Dugal, and Ddewi, standing a little apart from the Danes, I said, "My brother monks have also suffered much at the hands of those to whom authority had been given. They came on pilgrimage to make entreaty before the emperor. Thirteen left Éire, and only those survive who stand before you now."

The emperor appeared distracted. He glanced at the monks, and seemed inclined to sit down again, but thought better of it and remained standing. "We are sympathetic to your plight," he intoned, "and we are not unmoved by it. Be that as it may, we are persuaded that pilgrimage is wont to be a perilous undertaking, and any that would be a pilgrim must count the cost.

"Therefore, we can but share your sorrow at the loss of your brothers, and offer our heartfelt condolences."

With that, Leo turned away again. Brynach and the others looked on in startled confusion at the emperor's abrupt rejection. Seeing that the emperor meant to terminate the audience anyway, I determined there was nothing to be lost by pushing the matter further.

"With all respect, lord and basileus," I remarked, speaking up once more, "it was not the natural predation of seawaves or the dangers of the trail that led these holy men to their deaths, but the wanton actions of a depraved and ambitious man who traded on the authority granted him by the throne you now possess."

"That man," replied Leo quickly, "as we have been so pithily reminded, has been summoned to the Eternal

Judgement Seat to answer for his crimes, which, we have no doubt, were deserving of the punishment exacted. We are persuaded that the manner of his death, while unlawful, has secured a rough equity. Therefore, we are content to leave affairs as they stand." He regarded me sternly. "If you are wise, you will follow our example."

Returning his stern gaze, I replied, "Wise Lord, I pray you do not mistake me. These men ask no compensation for their loss, but will bear it for the sake of the petition that compelled them to seek audience with the Lord and Emperor, Elect of Christ, God's Vice-Regent on Earth. That petition remains to be heard."

"If that is so," replied Leo curtly, "it must be placed before us through the organs of state which exist for such purposes. We will, of course, consider it in due course."

The emperor's manner baffled and provoked me; it seemed extraordinary, especially in light of his willingness to dispose of the other claims so efficiently. Harald's settlement would cost the imperial treasury dearly, but the monks were not asking for so much as a single denarius. Why, then did he resist so?

It occurred to me then that of the three debts presented to him, this was the one for which he could make no restitution. The Arabs would be happy to see the treaty restored, and the Danes could be bought off with silver—but the monks would only be satisfied with justice, and Leo knew he could not offer that.

Sure, I had my answer. Even so, I resolved to hear the truth from his own mouth.

"Sovereign Lord," I said, fearless now, having neither self-respect nor honour to lose, "before leaving for Trebizond, the basileus took me into his employ also—to be, he said, his eyes and ears in that foreign place, and to bring him word of all that happened there. In short, I was to be his spy."

Leo, wanting to leave, regarded me distractedly. "As the basileus is dead, and the peace treaty is to be rewritten, we can see no value in resuming an occupation whose purpose has ceased."

"With all respect," I replied quickly, "I have information regarding certain matters which would reward careful consideration."

This intrigued Leo, I could see; he was curious to learn what I knew, but could not allow anyone else to hear. He made up his mind at once; declaring the audience ended, he ordered his visitors to wait in the outer hall, and his bodyguard to remove themselves a discreet distance so that we might talk together without being overheard.

"We find you an obdurate emissary," he said, resuming his seat. "What is your purpose in pursuing these matters?"

"Lord and emperor," I answered, "in light of the recent tragedy which has overtaken the empire, I could in no wise remain easy in my mind if I did not tell you that Basil's suspicions regarding betrayal were not unfounded."

"The former emperor was a very suspicious and fearful man," Leo allowed, and I noted that he never referred to Basil as his father. "Which of his many fears did he confide to you?"

"That men were plotting to kill him," I answered. It was not true, of course; but in light of Basil's murder, he might have been.

"And were they?" inquired Leo. The question was asked casually, but the keenness with which he regarded me gave me to know that I had pricked his interest.

"Yes, lord," I answered bluntly. "The conspiracy was discovered by Exarch Honorius, for which knowledge the governor was also murdered. I carry his sealed letter," I touched the parchment beneath my siarc, "which testifies to this fact, and was meant to serve as a warning to the emperor. Unfortunately, we arrived in Constantinople too late to prevent the consummation of the hateful act."

"The emperor died in an accident," Leo replied coolly. "I am told he rode too far ahead of the hunt—always an ill-advised thing to do in any circumstance—and it ended in the disaster for which the empire is still in mourning."

I had hoped he would be curious to know what the letter contained, but Emperor Leo was too canny to be caught like that. Still, I had but one more chance and nothing to lose, so I took it: "Eparch Nikos left no doubt about the veracity of these reports involving wild stags and runaway horses."

Leo folded one hand into the other and looked at me over the fist. "The eparch," he said slowly, "may have wished to create suspicions of his own, for purposes of his own. While his crimes, as you suggest, may once have demanded answers, he is now beyond questioning. We must be satisfied with the end which Heaven, in its infinite wisdom, has ordained."

That was all he said, and I understood that it was over at last. Not only had I failed to gain even so much as a hint of wrongdoing, much less a confession, Leo would simply lay all blame for every wrong on Nikos' head. I had provided him with the perfect scapegoat; dead, Nikos provided exoneration and absolution. Sick at heart, I stood looking on in despair.

Leo shifted, as if he would leave, but something held him. Regarding me with a sour expression, he said, "As you have not answered, we will ask you once again: what is it that you want?"

"Sovereign lord," I replied, almost desperately, "I came to Byzantium a monk with nothing save the faith that sustained me. Now even that poor possession has been taken from me. I have seen the innocent slaughtered in their hundreds—men, women, and children whose only wrongdoing was to cross Nikos's path. I saw the blessed Bishop Cadoc torn apart by horses and his body hacked to pieces.

I myself have endured slavery and torture, but that was nothing beside the dissolution of my faith."

I paused, swallowing hard, knowing that the next words I spoke might well bring about the fulfillment of my darkling dream, my death in Byzantium. I stumbled on, heedless of consequences. "I came here today seeking justice for those who died; yes, and revenge for myself, I will not deny it. When I learned there could be no justice, I undertook revenge lest that, too, escape me."

Leo accepted this without remark, and without the slightest indication of concern or anger or even surprise. So, I pushed ahead.

"Before he died, Nikos gave me to know that he killed Basil, and that the one who now wears the crown endorsed his crimes and conspired with him. You have asked what I want, and it is this: was he speaking the truth?"

Leo sat for a long moment, gazing at me with his dark, deep-set eyes as if at a problem that resisted every solution. Drawing himself up, he spoke at last. "We see that you have endeavoured good on behalf of the imperial throne," he told me, "and this at fearful expense to yourself. Would that you had asked us to restore your silver; we would have given it you a thousand times over. But you desire a thing even the basileus cannot bestow: the renewing of your faith." An expression of regret softened his features. "I am sorry," he said, one man speaking to another.

He rose from his chair, slowly unfolding his long form to stand tall and slender before me—so unlike Basil in every way. "Truly, I am sorry," he said again.

I made no move, nor spoke any word. There was nothing more to say. Shorn of my last hope, bereft of all belief, I simply gazed back at him, a numb, hollow creature of wood and bone.

Tall and regal, Leo moved away, but then turned after only a few paces. "If Eparch Nikos overreached himself in pursuit of his ambitions," he said, voicing what had already become the official explanation for all wrongdoing, "we see that his sins have borne their bitter fruit. It may not be to your liking, but we hold that justice is satisfied."

He hesitated, his lips pressed into a hard line as he regarded me almost angrily. I have seen such expressions before, usually when a person is warring within himself. With Leo, the battle was swiftly over.

"You ask for the truth," he said, his voice low to a whisper, "perhaps you will recognize it when we tell you this: Nikos did not kill my father."

Basileus Leo motioned one of the guards to come forward. The soldier took my arm and, under the gaze of the emperor, I was led from the room. But upon reaching the huge door, I glanced back and he was gone.

*Yes,* I thought bitterly, *I could yet recognize the truth when I heard it.*

Brynach was waiting for me as I stepped from the room. The Danes, I could see, were huddled together across the hall, deep in discussion—about what they would do with their increased wealth, I suppose. Sadiq and Faysal were head-to-head, speaking together in low tones; Kazimain stood near, looking lost and forlorn.

"The emperor wished to speak to you," Brynach suggested hopefully.

"He did," I allowed, glancing to the place where Nikos had fallen. The body was gone and three young servants were scattering wood dust over the floor to draw up the blood; soon that would be gone, too, leaving, perhaps, only a slight ruddy tint to the smooth stone to mark what had happened in this room. Dugal and Ddewi stood nearby watching the cleaners, and I motioned them to join us.

"Tell us, brother, what did he say to you?" Brynach asked, eager for a word that would redeem the pilgrimage.

"He said justice was served," I told him scornfully.

"But there is no justice in this place; there is only debt and the collection of debts."

"Did you tell him about the book?" wondered Ddewi. "Did you tell him we brought a gift for the imperial library?" He put his hand on the leather bag he carried beneath his siarc. The simple action cut me to the bone. He had borne this burden of love without complaint, and would go on bearing it.

"Ddewi," I said, "the emperor is not worthy of our gift. Men of faith gave their lives for its safe-keeping, and I would not demean their sacrifice."

Ddewi appeared disappointed. "Then what are we to do with it?"

"Carry it back with you," I told him. "Take it home, Ddewi, where it will be a treasure of inspiration to all who see it."

"What of our petition?" Brynach, ever hopeful, could not help himself. "Did you tell him why we came?"

"No, Bryn, I did not," I replied bluntly.

The Briton's face fell. "Why?" he asked, his eyes searching me for an answer. "It was our last chance."

"It was no chance at all," I said. "Shake the dust of this place from your feet, leave and never look back. I tell you the truth: make your peace with Rome, there is no protection here."

We left the palace then, crossing the reception hall to the outer doors. Dugal, who had remained silent before, fell into step behind me. "Did Leo own the deed?" he asked.

"He told me that Nikos did not kill his father."

"Sure, that was a lie, Aidan."

"No, Dugal," I replied from my wooden heart, "that, at least, was the truth."

The doors opened and we stepped out into the light of a day grown unimaginably bright.

# 74

Harald Bull-Roar, in a mood of jubilant anticipation, declared a feast to celebrate his great good fortune. Dauntless battlechief that he was, he arrayed himself for war and led his brave Sea Wolves into the fearsome markets to face the cunning tradesmen of Constantinople and secure the necessary provisions. They returned some while later, much wounded in pride and pocket, but victorious, bringing with them six casks of Cypriot wine, a dozen bags of bread, bundles of charcoal, and the carcasses of several pigs and three bullocks, ready-spitted and dressed for the roasting pit.

Wasting not a moment, they set the charcoal to life and put the meat to the flame. Then they opened the first of the casks and slaked their thirst with dark red wine, easing their hunger with loaves of good flatbread while waiting for the pigs to roast. It was not in Harald to forget his bread allowance, and he had collected it, still warm from the oven, despite the fact that not a man among them spoke Greek. I could only imagine how they had made their wishes known to the unfortunate baker.

The Arabs, beguiled by the Danes' irresistible good will, joined easily into the festivities. Some of the rafiq helped prepare the food and showed their hosts how to mix wine with water for best flavour and less devastating effect. Although Sadiq did not drink wine, he allowed the others to do as they would, and by way of blessing the occasion, sent Faysal to procure additional delicacies of a variety and array to make the long tables groan: dates, sweetmeats, olives both black and green, cakes in honey syrup, pots of thickened milk sweetened and flavoured with almonds, and several kinds of fruit unknown to me.

As eventide shadows stole across the courtyard and the heat of the day dissipated into the brilliant pinks and purples of a warm Mediterranean night, the merrymaking burst into song and dance to the delight of all—save myself and my brother monks. They were lamenting the failure of the pilgrimage, but I was grieving for a greater loss.

Owing to the sound of raucous singing and the rhythmic thump of improvised drumming emanating from the banqueting rooms, I did not hear the others as they approached. "Brother Aidan," announced Brynach firmly, "we would speak with you."

I turned to see the three of them standing uncertainly nearby. "Come then, and sit down," I said. "My solitude is large enough to share."

They stepped closer, but stood over me and would not sit—as if what they had to say should not be compromised by informality. Brynach gave out their concern at once. "We have been thinking and praying about the events of the day," he said, "and we believe you have acted rashly. We think we should go to the emperor and present our petition. If we tell him why we have come and what it means, he will take pity on us and give us the aid we so desperately need."

I raised my eyes to look at his face, earnest and determined in the twilight. Stars were beginning to shine in the sky, and the delicious scent of roasting meat curled along the gently wafting breeze of the courtyard. I drew the aroma deep into my lungs as I took a breath to answer. "You have seen, yet you still do not understand," I told him. "What more do you require to convince you? Would you have me explain it again?"

The three looked at each other. Dugal replied, "Yes, brother. Unless you tell us we cannot understand."

"Then hear me," I said, standing to address them. "This is the way of it: when greed and power conspire together, let all men beware. You have heard this said, and now, through bitter experience, you know it to be true. Moreover, when those who uphold justice are far more guilty than those whom they must judge, there is neither hope nor redemption. Why believe the unrighteous judge will honour the truth, or look beyond his own interests to protect yours?"

"If that were so," Brynach observed, "nothing in this world would be safe, or certain."

"Nothing *is* safe," I said flatly. "But one thing, and one thing only is certain: the innocent will suffer."

"I do wonder at your words," Brynach confessed, not without compassion. "It is unlike you—unlike the man I once knew."

"I am *not* the man I was! That man is long since dead. But what of that? He deserved no better fate than all the rest who died along the way."

"How can you speak so, brother?" the elder monk chided gently. "God has guided and protected you through all things to now. He has showered his favour upon you. Even now he holds you in the palm of his loving hand."

I turned my face away. "Speak to Cadoc and the others of God's protection," I muttered. "Do not speak to me. Sure, I know full well how God cares for those who trust him."

My bitterness stung them, and they stared at one

another in dismay. After a moment, Ddewi plucked up his courage. "Are you saying these things because you killed Nikos and now you fear to stand before the emperor once more?"

So, that was on their minds. Why not? They did not know what I knew. "Listen to me," I said sharply, "and heed me well. Put away any notion that you will receive favour from the emperor's hand. Do not be deceived: he is no God-fearing man. Nikos was acting on behalf of Leo from the beginning. What Nikos did, he did for Leo, as much as for his own insatiable ambition."

"But, Aidan," objected Dugal, "you said Leo told the truth when he said Nikos did not kill the emperor."

A great weariness drew over me. They still did not comprehend the enormity of the evil allowed to flourish in Byzantium's holy palaces. I shook my head in despair. "Think, Dugal. All of you, think! Think what it means. Leo said that Nikos did not kill his *father*—and that was the truth." Dugal and the others gaped at me, baffled and hurt.

"Do you still not see it?" I said, my voice lashing at their ignorance. "Emperor Basil was *not* Leo's father." I let this sink in for a moment, before proceeding, "This is the way of it: Michael seduced and bedded many noblewomen of his court; one of them was Basil's wife. Basil knew this; indeed, he even encouraged it because it gave him a hold over the emperor. When a son was born of the adulterous union, he used the occasion to advance himself."

"Leo is *Michael's* son?" wondered Brynach in amazement.

"Yes, and in exchange for keeping the boy as his own, Basil was raised to the purple and made co-sovereign. When Michael's profligacy no longer served him, Basil arranged the old emperor's murder—some say he even did the deed himself—and then claimed the throne outright. Years pass, and the unloved boy grows up determined to avenge his true father's death. To this end, Nikos was employed by Leo; to this end the wicked scheme was laid—long before we ever thought to come to Byzantium."

I could see them struggling against this hard truth.

"We should tell someone," suggested Dugal weakly. "The emperor should be made to answer for his crimes."

I did not allow them the luxury of false hope. "The emperor is sovereign of the church, and judge over all, answerable only to God himself. Who do you propose to tell? God? I tell you He already knows, and does nothing."

"We could tell the Patriarch of Constantinople," suggested Brynach, more out of desperation than hope.

"The patriarch," I said savagely, "the same who owes his appointment and continued survival to the emperor— do you think he would listen? Even if he did, the only one who could prove the truth of our accusations was Nikos, and I silenced him forever." My voice became mocking. "I killed Nikos, yet his master and protector—the very same whose commands Nikos obeyed and for whom he died— shed not a tear. It seems our Holy Emperor was only too happy to heap all the blame for the hardship and havoc his schemes have wreaked onto Nikos's bloodied head. The deaths of monks and Danes and Arabs, the murder of the eparch and the governor, and who knows how many of his own subjects—all this will now be buried with Nikos and his name.

"Oh, it was a very great service I performed for the emperor. And out of his considerable gratitude, the Wise Basileus has allowed me to keep my life."

The others stared at me, stunned.

"There can be no justice here," I concluded, grim with the hopelessness of it. "Basil was never the rightful emperor; Leo, as Michael's bastard, has a valid claim to the throne, but he, like the man who raised him, is a schemer and murderer."

The water trickling in the fountain grew loud in the silence that followed. I saw that the moon had risen and poured soft light into the many-shadowed courtyard.

"I know now what Nikos meant," Brynach said, "when he called Basil usurper." Looking at me, he asked, "What did he mean when he called you a fallen priest?"

I made no reply.

"Aidan," he said gently, "are you still one of us?"

I could not bear the hurt and sadness in their eyes any more, so I looked away when I answered. "No," I said softly. "I ceased being a priest long ago."

After a moment, Brynach said, "No one is ever far from the reach of God's swift sure hand. I will pray for you, brother."

"If you like," I replied. Brynach accepted this and did not press me further. A wave of laughter from the banqueting room washed across the courtyard just then. "You should go and enjoy the feast," I told them. "Rejoice with those who rejoice."

"Will you be joining us, Dána?" asked Dugal.

"Perhaps," I allowed. "In a little while."

They departed, leaving me to myself once more. It was only after they had gone, that I became aware of Kazimain, standing across the courtyard in the shadow of a column. She was watching me, waiting. I rose at once, but before I could go to her, she strode towards me purposefully, her jaw set, her lips firm. I had seen the look before.

"You were speaking to your kinsmen," she said, lifting her veil. "I did not wish to intrude." Glancing down, she folded her hands before her as she ordered the words she had prepared.

"You are never an intrusion, my love," I said lightly.

"Aidan, please, it is hard for me to say this." She paused, and when she spoke again, her voice had taken on a determined tone. "I shall not marry you," she said simply.

"What?"

"We will not be married, Aidan."

"Why?" I said, astonished by the abruptness of her announcement. She lowered her eyes to her folded hands. "Why are you saying this, Kazimain? Nothing has changed between us."

She shook her head slowly. "No, my love, *you* have changed."

Unable to answer, I merely stared at her, a cold familiar numbness spreading outward from my heart.

She raised her head and looked at me, her dark eyes grave and serious. "I am sorry, Aidan."

"Kazimain, tell me, how have I changed?"

"Need you ask?"

"I *do* ask," I insisted, though in my heart I knew she was right. Without knowing precisely why, I felt like a thief caught in the act of robbery, or a liar discovered in his falsehood.

"I have observed you these last many days. It is clear to me that you are no longer a man of faith."

"I am no longer a Christian, it is true," I told her, "so the difference in our beliefs need not pose any difficulty to our marriage. I love you, Kazimain."

"But it is not love we are talking about," she said gently, "it is belief. I see that you are no longer a Christian, *not* because you renounced your faith in the Christ, but because you have abandoned God. Having forsaken God, you no longer believe in anything. Aidan, it is forbidden for a woman of Islam to marry an infidel. To do so is death."

There was nothing but pity in her eyes as she said this; nevertheless, I felt the last small square of solid ground crumbling away beneath my feet. "But in Samarra—"

"In Samarra it was different," she said sharply; "*you* were different. I knew you were disappointed, but when I saw you in the mosq I thought you were a man who yet put his trust in God. I know now that you believe in nothing higher than yourself." Lowering her head, she added, half to herself, "I hoped for what cannot be."

"Kazimain, please," I said, clinging desperately to the last remaining certainty I possessed. Though it cut me deep, there was no disputing what she said. I had enough honesty left in my heart to recognize the truth when I heard it.

"We are betrothed no more."

I cannot say the strength of her resolve surprised me. She was, after all, the same Sarazen princess who had defied her uncle and risked all to follow us into the desert alone. She had shown herself steadfast in every way, and she demanded no less from the man who would share her life. Sure, a blind man could have seen I was not her equal. Once, perhaps, but no longer.

"If only we could have stayed in Samarra," I said, accepting the finality of her declaration at last. "I would have married you, Kazimain. We would have been happy there."

This touched her, I think, for her manner softened towards me, and she stretched a hand to my face. "I would have followed you to the end of the earth," she whispered. Then, as if this admission would recoil upon her, she pulled away, straightened, and added, "Even so, it is finished between us."

Gathering her robes about her, she lowered the veil once more. "I will pray God grants you peace, Aidan."

I watched her move away, slender and regal, her head high. She turned as she reached the colonnade and, looking back, called, "Farewell, my love." Stepping into the shadows, she disappeared, leaving only the faint, lingering scent of oranges and sandalwood in the air.

*Farewell, Kazimain. I have loved you, and love you still. No other woman will ever own my heart; it is forever yours.*

I stayed alone in the courtyard for a long time, listening to the sounds of the celebration, and marking the slow progression of the stars overhead. In the end, I did not join the revelry, but remained in the courtyard all night, wretched and alone.

Never had I felt so rejected and forsaken. I wept that night for the loss of my faith, no less than for the loss of my love. The last frail cord that bound me to the world and to myself had been severed, and I was now a soul wholly adrift.

# 75

When the Logothete of the Treasury arrived at midday the next day, he found a somewhat groggy King Harald surrounded by a ragged band of bleary barbarians, the splintered remains of six wine casks, and an assortment of scattered bones and broken dishes. Upon presentation of the imperial official, the jarl revived wonderfully well and, after graciously offering the logothete a haunch of congealed pork—which the courtier declined with equal grace—the two sat down to reckon accounts.

Naturally, I was required to sit with them so as to translate for Harald. As on similar occasions, I was very soon moved to a kind of awe at the wily Dane's ability to exploit the latent opportunities of any situation. Armed with a modest array of weapons, he nevertheless used them with impressive skill: now wheedling, now cajoling, then pouting, coaxing, or demanding; he could shout, shaking the rooftrees with anger, yet never lose his temper; he could cozen with a convincing display of good-natured ignorance one moment, and the next perform the most intricate calculations with bewildering speed and accuracy.

By the time the logothete departed, he seemed a dazed

and broken man. And why not? Harald had triumphed utterly, conceding a few minor battles along the way, while sweeping the field and winning the war. The imperial coffers were lightened by more than sixty thousand silver denarii, making Harald and the few surviving Sea Wolves wealthy men one and all.

When, later in the day, the payment arrived—half in silver denarii, and the other half in gold solidi, contained in five stout iron-bound sea boxes, as agreed—I helped Jarl Harald make his mark on the vellum scroll the courtier produced to record the Danes' receipt of the payment.

When the official and his men had gone, Harald offered me a share of the wealth. "Take it, Aeddan," he urged. "If not for you, none of us would be alive to enjoy our good fortune. Yours is a debt of gratitude we cannot easily repay, but it would cheer me greatly to see you accept it."

"Nay, Jarl Harald," I told him. "The losses represented by that treasure were yours alone. Give it to the widows and orphans of the men who will not be coming home."

"I will provide for them, never fear," the king said. "But there is more than enough. Please, take something."

Again, I declined, but Harald prevailed on me to take a generous measure of gold solidi to assist myself and the other monks on our return journey. The suggestion made sense, and I accepted the coins, whereupon the Sea King departed saying he would find another way to repay me. He then declared another feast—this one to celebrate their new wealth. The festivities occupied them the rest of the day and far into the night. When the revelry reached a fine, expansive mood, the Danes fell to boasting recklessly of all they would do with the riches they carried home with them. Gunnar and Hnefi took it upon themselves to surpass one another.

"When I get home," declared Hnefi loudly, "I will have a ship trimmed in gold!"

"One ship only?" wondered Gunnar. "I myself will have a whole fleet of ships, each larger than the last, with mast and oars of gold."

"Well and good," continued Hnefi grandly, "but I will also have a drinking hall larger than Odin's—with a hundred vats of öl to slake the thirst of all my karlar, of which I shall have a thousand."

"Well, that may do for you," conceded Gunnar loftily, "but such a mean hut would never do for me, for I will have ten-thousand karlar, each with his own öl vat."

Hnefi laughed scornfully. "You would need a hall far larger than Valhalla to hold them all!"

"Well then," Gunnar smiled at the ease with which he had trapped Hnefi, "I shall have such a hall—larger than Valhalla, so that each of my noblemen will have a place at table to feast with me. And a hundred skalds to sing my praise by day and night."

And so it went, each striving to better the other in outrageous displays of greed made glorious by dint of ever-more-extravagant boasts. Those looking on called encouragement to the two contenders, laughing loudly, and praising each new height of imagined excess.

I sat listening, bone-aching exhaustion stealing over me as I looked from one beaming Sea Wolf face to the next. They were so like children, so simple and uncomplicated in their pleasures and desires, unaware of anything save the present moment, to which they gave their unstinting attention. I gazed at them and wished I could return to that quality of innocence. Then, weary with the weight of all that had happened in the last two days, I crept away to my bed.

Despite their late-night revelry, the Danes rose early the next morning and hastened to the wharf at Psamathia where the ships were moored. As Constantinople resumed its normal busy pace, the other gates were opened once more and Harald brought the three longships around to the small harbour which served the great houses along the Golden Horn—the better, he said, to keep an eye on the provisioning for the voyage home.

"When will you leave?" I asked him. We were standing on the quay at the place called the Venetian Quarter, watching some of the Danes load sacks of grain into the longships.

He squinted at the sky and looked out at the sea, then called something to Thorkel, who was ordering the storage of the supplies as they arrived. Receiving a grunted reply, Harald turned back to me, and answered, "Tomorrow. It is a long time we have been away from Skania—a very long time, and the men are eager to return to their wives and kinfolk. The weather is good. We will leave tomorrow."

"I understand," I said, unsettled by the suddenness of the departure. "Sure, I will come down and see you away."

"Yes," Harald said, clapping a big hand to my shoulder, "you do that, Aeddan."

He moved off then, but I watched him as he walked along the wharf, looking at the ships; occasionally he hailed someone on board, or paused to put his hands on the keel, or thump the side with his fist. I left the wharf after a while, as Harald and Thorkel were waving their arms at a small man aboard a sleek little merchant vessel with yellow sails.

Later, when some of the Sea Wolves returned from their various errands in the city, Gunnar and Tolar came to me, bearing a large bag between them. "Jarl Harald says we must be leaving tomorrow," Gunnar said simply. "We will miss you, Aeddan."

"I will miss you, too," I replied. "But you have Karin and Ulf to think about. And Tolar has his kinfolk. They will all be glad to see the both of you again."

"Heya," Gunnar allowed, "and I will be glad to see

them. I tell you the truth, Aeddan, when I get home I will never go a-viking again. Tolar and I have discussed this, and we both agree we are getting too old for these adventures." Tolar nodded emphatically.

"A wise decision," I told them.

"We brought you a gift to remember our friendship," Gunnar said. Reaching into the bag, he brought out a small pottery bowl, and placed it in my hands. The bowl was shallow, but finely made; the inside had been decorated in blue and white with the image of a man wearing a crown and holding a spear in one hand and a cross in the other. Below the man, who seemed to be standing atop Saint Sophia's dome, was the word *Leo*.

"It is a splendid bowl, Gunnar. But I cannot take it. Karin would be delighted with a bowl like this. You must give it to her instead."

"Nay, nay," he said. "That one is for you, Aeddan. We have six more just like it."

We parted then, and I promised to come down to the ship to see them away. "Sit at table with us tonight," Gunnar invited. "We will drink together one last time."

"Tonight then," I agreed.

But I did not sit with them that night. Everywhere around me, the life I had known was ending; all were going their own way now, and I could not prevent that, nor would I have wished to—far from it! I was relieved that the tribulation was over. Still, I could not find it in me to sit with them and raise cups in honour of a friendship that was, like everything else around me, dying.

The next morning, Jarl Harald bade Lord Sadiq and Faysal farewell. "If you should come north to Skania," Harald said, speaking through me, "you will be welcome in my hall. We will sit together and feast like kings."

"And should you ever venture south again," the amir replied, "you have but to speak my name to anyone, and you will be brought at once to my palace where you will be welcomed as a noble friend."

They embraced one another then, and Harald took his leave. I walked with the Danes down the steep narrow streets to the wharf; Dugal came as well, but kept to himself and said nothing along the way. Since our talk in the courtyard, he and the others had not had much to say to me. I did not know if they were shunning me, or if they were merely uncertain about how things stood and did not wish to make matters worse between us.

In their eagerness to go home, the Danes made for the ships and scrambled aboard the moment we reached the harbour. Some paused long enough to call a parting word—even Hnefi bade me a breezy farewell.

A fair few, toiling under the weight of newly-acquired treasures, required the aid of their comrades to get aboard, but all three ships were ready to up sails in a surprisingly short time.

Thorkel was first to take his leave. He called from his place at the tiller, saying, "Perhaps we meet again one day, Aeddan, heya?"

"Farewell, Thorkel! See that you keep a steady course now."

"Never fear! I have my map!" he replied with a wave, then turned his attention to the sail.

Gunnar and Tolar came to where Dugal and I stood watching. "You are a good fellow," Gunnar told me. Tolar echoed the sentiment: "Heya," he said.

"I owe you a great debt, Aeddan," Gunnar continued, regarding me with sad eyes. "I shall be very sorry if I do not find a way to make good my reckoning." To which Tolar added, "Indeed."

"You owe me nothing," I replied lightly. "Go home to your wife and son. And if you think of me at all, remember also your promise not to go a-viking anymore. It would please me to think of you enjoying your wealth—instead of skinning poor pilgrims for plunder."

Gunnar became contrite. "We are done with that, by Odin." Tolar nodded and spat.

"Then I am glad."

Gunnar gathered me in an enormous, bone-cracking embrace. "Farewell, Aeddan . . ." he whispered, and then turned away quickly.

Tolar, against all nature, also embraced me, then stepped away with a smile. "You are not so bad, I think," he said meaningfully.

"You are not so bad, either," I told him, and watched him redden with embarrassment. "Go in peace, Tolar—and see you keep an eye on Gunnar."

"That will not be hard, for I am buying a holding next to his that we might be wealthy farmers together," he said, speaking more words than I had ever heard him utter in a single breath.

King Harald was the last to take his leave. He came to where I stood, and presented the small man I had seen him speaking with the previous day. "This man is master of the Venetian ship," he told me, pointing to the yellow-sailed vessel. "He has agreed to take you and your brother priests home to Irlandia. I have paid him to do this, and he has promised to make an easy sailing for you, and to feed you well."

Harald indicated the man, and made a presenting motion with his hands. The fellow glanced at the big Dane uncertainly, and then turned to me and said, "I give you good greeting, my friends. I am Pietro. You are, I believe, to accompany me on my return voyage. That, at least, is my understanding." He spoke fine Latin with a refined, yet easy intonation.

"So it would appear," I confirmed. "Forgive me if I seem doubtful, but I knew nothing about this until now."

"Worry for nothing," Pietro said. "My ship I place at your service." Glancing once more at Harald, who stood beaming at the both of us, he said, "I leave you to your farewells, but come to me when you are finished and we will make our plans."

So saying, the elegant little fellow bowed himself away. Harald smiled with satisfaction. "I brought you here, so it is only right that I should see you home again," he explained. "I searched for the best ship, and his is almost as good as my own. He has sailed from here many times, and I think he is a good pilot. But I told him that if ever word should come to me that you were ill treated, I shall come and slit him throat to belly like a fish."

"Do you suppose he understood you?" I wondered.

Harald's smile broadened. "Who can say?" He clapped me on the back then, and said, "I leave you now, Aeddan Truth-Sayer. You were a good slave, I shall be sorry to see you no more."

"You were a splendid master, Jarl Harald," I told him. We embraced like brothers, and he turned and hurried to the ship.

Within moments of Harald's climbing aboard, the Sea Wolves took up the oars and pushed away from the wharf. As the ship glided out into the channel, I saw Gunnar standing at the dragonhead prow, waving to me. I waved back, and then came the command in Harald's loud voice to man the oars, and Gunnar disappeared.

I felt a presence, and noticed that Dugal, who had kept himself apart, had rejoined me. "That is that," he said, and I sensed some relief in his tone.

"Yes," I said. "That is that."

I watched until the longships had passed from sight down the Golden Horn, then led Dugal to where the Venetian ship lay at anchor, explaining how Harald had arranged for our journey home.

"The Sea Wolf did that for us?" wondered Dugal, much impressed.

The ship's master met us as we approached. He bade us board and satisfy ourselves that his was, indeed, in every way, a splendid vessel. "We have been many days awaiting the last of our trade goods—silk cloth and pepper, and bowls of glass and silver," he said. "We should have left six days ago, but the emperor's funeral caused a small delay. God willing, the ship will be loaded by this evening and we shall be ready to sail this time tomorrow."

"So soon?" I said, and then thought, *Why not? There is nothing to hold us here any longer.*

Pietro hesitated. "The season grows late, and we should not look upon the good weather as a gift that will last forever. However, we could wait a day or two longer, if you prefer."

I thanked him for the offer. "That will not be necessary," I replied, and wondered just how much Harald had paid him. "We will be ready tomorrow."

"Very well," Pietro said, inclining his head as if acquiescing to my wishes. "I will send a man to collect your things in the morning."

Returning to the villa, I informed Brynach and Ddewi of the arrangements Harald had made for us, and our imminent departure. "So soon?" Bryn wondered aloud.

"Pietro said he would wait until we were ready," I explained. "But I could see nothing to hold us here. I know it is not much time," I allowed; "if I had thought you wanted to stay on—"

"No," Brynach said quickly, "no—you are right. There is nothing more for us here." He paused, looking thoughtful. "And is it still your plan to return with us? I thought—"

"Where else would I go?" I said, then added quickly,

"So, then, you have one last day in Byzantium. There must be something you wish to do in the city before we leave."

"I was always hoping to pray in the Church of the Holy Wisdom," Brynach replied; Ddewi and Dugal nodded their agreement. "I would like that. The brothers at Christ Pantocrator were going to take us, but then . . . well, it makes no matter."

"Go," I urged. "All three of you—go now. There are guides aplenty eager to show you the wonders of Constantinople for the price of a loaf." I gave him one of Harald's gold solidii. They protested such extravagance, but I had nothing smaller to give them and suggested it was little enough payment for their pains and bade them to enjoy the day.

They held quick council between them and decided to do it without delay. "Will you not come with us, Aidan?" inquired Dugal, regarding me with concern.

"There is nothing more I care to see or do in this city," I answered. "Besides, I would only steal your joy. Go and say your prayers, Dugal, and never fear—I will be here when you return."

No sooner had they left, than Faysal appeared to say that Lord Sadiq desired to speak with me. I had been expecting a summons of some kind, and now that it had come, I found I was unready to face him. Guilt about how Kazimain and I had parted was, I suppose, making me dread a confrontation.

As I expected, he was not happy. After a simple, if somewhat austere greeting, he bade me sit down, and said, "Kazimain has told me that you two are not to be married. While I doubt neither her word nor her honour, I would hear it from your lips also."

"It is true," I replied. "I have broken my vow, and we have parted."

Sharp disapproval pursed the amir's lips into a frown.

"That is not how Kazimain put it," he informed me, "but as this is a matter between a man and a woman, I will not interfere if your mind is made up. As to that, I offered to persuade you to change your mind, but Kazimain does not wish it." He paused, trying to read my thought from the expression on my face.

When he spoke again, he said, "There is a place for you in my court. I have need of a man of your considerable abilities. Stay with me, Aidan, and I will see that you rise to your rightful estate." He paused. "You need not marry my kinswoman to gain my favour, you have earned my highest esteem many times over with your exemplary deeds and character."

"I fear you flatter me too highly, Lord Sadiq," I said. "And your offer is tempting, but I cannot accept it."

The amir nodded silently, accepting my decision gracefully. "What will you do?"

"Return to Éire," I answered. I would complete the pilgrimage, see it through. That, at least, I could do.

"Forgive me for saying so, but though you return to your home a thousand times, you will not be happy there anymore," the amir warned. "You have seen too much of the world and its ways to hide away in your monastery."

"You may be right," I conceded. "Still, it is my home."

Sadiq gazed at me, and seemed to soften. "I wish you well, my friend." He rose, signalling an end to our talk. "Still, if you should ever come again to Samarra, you will find me ready to receive you and resume our friendship."

"I am grateful, Lord Sadiq. But my heart is hungry, and will not be satisfied until I have seen Éire again."

"Go in peace, Aidan," said the amir, raising his hands in blessing. "May Allah, Wise and Merciful, make straight your path and protect you from Satan's wiles, and may the Lord of Hosts grant you peace in his celestial palaces forever."

Placing his fingertips to his forehead, he then touched his heart, saying, "Sala'am, Aidan, and farewell."

We ate together for the last time that night; the amir insisted on providing a feast to send us on our way. The rafiq and the monks attended and the talk was light and pleasant—Faysal and I were kept busy translating for everyone. All through the meal, I looked for Kazimain to join us, but the evening ended and she did not appear.

Nor did I see her the next morning when Pietro's man collected our few bundled belongings and we left the villa for the waiting ship. Though we had made our farewells the night before, Faysal insisted on accompanying us to the wharf. He said it was to make certain that we did not get lost and fall into misfortune. Just before I climbed aboard, I offered Faysal the Qadi as a parting gift, but he refused, saying that if I ever returned to Byzantium again, I would certainly need a good knife. Crossing his hands over his chest, he bowed, and bespoke the peace of Allah for our voyage. He then stood on the quayside watching us until we passed from sight.

That was the last I saw of any of them.

# 76

I will say nothing of our homeward voyage—save that it was at every point the opposite of our outgoing journey. The ship was both stout and swift, the weather warm and mild, the company of Pietro and his crew, cordial—even the food, which the Venetians prepared with skill and exuberance, was more than agreeable. Thus, we enjoyed comforts I had not imagined to exist among seafaring folk.

Though we urged the sturdy little ship's master to put first into their home port for the sake of his cargo, he would not have it any other way but that he delivered us safely to our destination as agreed. The more we tried to persuade him, the more adamant he grew. "You," he declared, "are my foremost concern. I will not rest until you are once again among your brother priests."

Again, I wondered how much Harald had paid to secure this kind of treatment—and what accompanying threats he might have added as further inducement—but, as there was nothing to be done, we simply sat back and allowed the days to drift pleasantly by . . . until one morning, Pietro came to us and said, "If you would like to see your homeland once again, follow me."

We made our way to the prow where he pointed to a low-rising blue eminence floating on the horizon. "There is Ierne," he said. "You must tell me now where you wish to make landfall."

We held council, and decided that Brynach had the best reckoning of the Irish coast, so he should guide the ship to our destination. This he did, and by nightfall we had reached the bay at the mouth of the Boann River.

Rather than tempt the rocky shoreline at dusk, Pietro dropped anchor in the bay and waited until morning. We passed an excruciating night—within shouting distance of our cherished homeland, but unable to cross over until morning.

When dawnlight finally came, we proceeded slowly upriver to Inbhir Pátraic and made landfall at the wooden wharf. "See now!" cried Dugal as his feet touched the planking. "We have crossed three seas without so much as getting our feet wet!"

Indeed, in light of our previous voyage, it was a remarkable achievement. We all agreed that our Venetian shipmates were fine sailors, and praised them extravagantly, much to their delight. Pietro liked the look of the settlement, and decided to stay a day or two to trade. He asked if we would translate for him; "I will pay you handsomely," he said. "You have been good company aboard my ship. I would like to do this for you."

Bryn thanked him and said that, tempting though his offer might be, we had been away a long time and were anxious to return to the abbey which still lay two days' walk inland. "Yet, where trade is the subject," he added, "I think you will find that, with the people hereabouts, silver speaks for itself."

We bade farewell to Pietro and all his men in turn, and then climbed up the twisting, narrow path to the clifftop where we were greeted by a small crowd of folk who had seen the ship and gathered in anticipation of news and trade.

The head man pushed his way forward to welcome us. An expression of honest astonishment appeared on his face when he realized who it was that stood before him. "Hoo!" he cried. "Look at you now! Look at you! Returned from foreign lands as hale as the day you left!" Glancing around quickly, he searched among us and then scanned the cliff trail and wharf below. "Michael bless me, where are the others? Where are all the rest? Are they coming after?"

"Greetings, Ladra," Brynach answered. "Yes, we have returned—we four alone. Alas, no more will be coming after."

This caused a ripple of comment through the crowd. Ladra looked from one to the other of us, and said, "Well, well, however it may be, welcome home. You have much to tell, and we would hear it gladly."

"That, I fear, must wait a little," Brynach replied. "Our first duty is to make our return known to our brothers at the abbey. The day is good and we are well rested; I think we must make for Kells straightaway."

Ladra's face fell, and the people groaned. Pointing to the wharf below, I said, "There stands a man with ready silver. Would you keep him standing on the wharf until he grows weary and sails away to find more willing traders elsewhere?"

This caused a mild tumult as the people hastened down to meet Pietro and make him properly welcome. The resulting commotion allowed us to slip through the crowd and proceed on our way unhindered by hospitality, however well-meaning. Shouldering our various bundles, we started off.

Oh, it was fine to feel the soft turf beneath my feet and smell the cool, damp mistful air. Blissful green of every shade met the gaze at every turn, a soothing balm for eyes grown accustomed to the dry, colourless rock-bound wastes of the east. All that day I walked in a wonder of recollection: each hill and every tree seemed a miracle created anew to refresh the soul and delight the senses.

To be in Éire again, and know the place as for the first time—there is no finer thing.

We walked until midday and rested by the river, then walked again until nightfall took the path from us. Though we had no food with us, we did not count it a hardship, for to sleep once more under the summer stars and breath the still, soft fragrant air of that peaceful land was sustenance enough.

Rising before dawn, we proceeded on our way eagerly, and with such vigour and pace that by eventide we came in sight of Cenannus na Ríg. We paused at the last hillside to look across the valley at the stone-encircled settlement, too overcome with the upsurge of mingled feelings to speak: the happiness of safe return entwining sorrow for our dear brothers who did not now stand beside us.

Then, even as we stood looking on, there came the clear, clean sound of the abbey bell tolling vespers. At the third stroke, Dugal was striding down the hill, and by the fifth he was running. Down we flew, racing as fast as we could go; I ran behind Dugal, and Brynach and Ddewi followed hard behind. We reached the abbey gate out of breath and weary, but thankful to be so.

"Home!" Dugal cried, his face glowing with the exertion and jubilation. "Aidan, man, we are home!"

His cry brought the porter from his hut. He took one look at us and dashed for his bell and began ringing it to announce our arrival. "God bless you, brothers! Welcome!" he shouted, trying to make himself heard above the bell.

"Paulinus!" hollered Dugal jovially. "Leave off your bell ringing, we cannot hear a thing!"

Brother Paulinus came and stood before us, eager in the twilight, bursting with questions and welcome. From the chapel monks were already streaming towards us, and in less than the space of three heartbeats we were surrounded on all sides by our good brothers, all shouting glad welcome and slapping our backs and praising God and all the company of heaven for our safe return.

Then, even then—in the midst of all the merriment—I felt once more the vile serpent rear its head in my soul. Alas, it had not died with Nikos, it had only slept. To see all those dear brothers, their faces so joyful, and to hear them praise for our keeping the same God who had given so many others over to death made my spirit writhe within me. Even as I stood with the cries of happiness resounding in my ears, I could feel the poison seeping from my wounded soul.

The pain was almost past enduring. It was all I could do to remain among them, smiling, laughing, accepting their good wishes—when all I wanted was escape. I saw Dugal go down on his knees to beg forgiveness of Libir for pushing him down on the rocks—I turned away as the bitter bile rose in my throat.

Then Abbot Fraoch was standing before us, his arms outspread in welcome, acclaiming our arrival. Behind him, grinning with pleasure at the sight of us, stood Ruadh, the abbey secnab and my own dear confessor. "Behold!" Fraoch said, his broken voice raised in a happy rasp of salutation. "The wayfarers have returned! The pilgrimage is completed. Let the Lord Christ be praised for his faithful and steadfast protection!"

There followed a burst of renewed acclaim, which the good abbot allowed to continue a while, before raising his hands for silence. "Brothers, it is right to welcome our kinsmen with praise and thanksgiving," he said. "However, I see that only four have returned where thirteen set out, and it would be a shameful thing not to ask after those whose absence demands explanation."

Brynach stepped forward and related the unhappy tidings that we were indeed the only survivors of the pilgrimage and that all the rest were dead, having exchanged the white martyrdom for that of the red. This brought murmurs of sorrow and lament from the throng—especially for the deceased monks who had set out from our own community.

Bryn then motioned for Dugal to come forward. The big monk shouldered his way to the fore and took the carefully wrapped bundle from off his back and placed it on the ground at Abbot Fraoch's feet.

"Aidan here," Dugal said with a nod in my direction, "was not content to allow our blessed Bishop Cadoc's mortal bones to remain among the godless in pagan lands. We have brought the bishop's relics home to be buried with all honour and respect."

The abbot regarded the bundled bones sorrowfully. "Ah, well," he said. "Ah, mo croi, it is a grief to me, and to us all. Christ have mercy." Raising his eyes once more, he said, "Thank you, Brother Dugal. Thank you, Brother Aidan. It was good of you to be so mindful of the sympathies of others. We are, all of us, beholden to your tender thoughtfulness."

Ha! I thought, anger flaring up within me. Shall I tell you how he died? Shall I tell you how this godly man's life was cruelly torn from him and his body thrown into the refuse pit with no more tender thought than yesterday's joint of mutton? Shall I tell you that the only reason his bones were retrieved at all was so that a band of godless barbarians could salvage their pilfered treasure? Shall I tell you the truth of God's steadfast protection?

I said none of these things, of course, but merely acknowledged the abbot's sentiments with a reverent nod.

Abbot Fraoch then said, "Vespers have been rung, and the prayers begun. Let us go to the chapel and give thanks to God for the pilgrims' safe return."

Everyone began talking at once, pelting us with questions and clamouring to be heard; we were swept up by the well-wishing throng and carried to the doors of the chapel. There I was to endure a time of prayer more onerous to me than a hundred days of slavery in the caliph's mines. At least when it was finally over the abbot allowed us to retreat to the cells which had been prepared for us.

He forbade anyone to ask any more questions of us that night, and dismissed us to our sleep. "I can see you are tired from your long journey," he said. "Go now to your rest, and we will await your tales in the morning."

Thus, I was spared having to talk any more about the tribulations we had survived. I left the church in despair, and made my way to the cells; Dugal walked beside me, pleased to be back among his friends and familiar surroundings once more. "Ah, mo croi," he sighed with contentment. "It is good. Do you not think so, Dána?"

"Yes," I replied.

"I tell you the truth," he declared, "there were times I did not think we would ever see this place again."

"Nor did I," I said, and thought: And now that we are here once more, I wonder what was so important. What were we trying to do? What did it mean?

"Are you sad, Aidan?" Dugal asked.

"No, just a little tired," I said, to avoid further conversation on the subject. "I did not foresee having to answer so many questions."

"You have been to Byzantium," Dugal observed simply, "and they have not. Sure, they are curious. You cannot blame them for that."

There was food in the cell—a loaf of brown bread and a little honey mead for our homecoming. I ate alone by the

light of a single beeswax candle and went to sleep thinking
how quiet it was . . . only to be awakened at dawn by the
tolling of the matin bell signalling the beginning of the
daily round.

I had not heard that sound for a very long time, but
the moment I heard it my heart sank—to think that all the
time I had been away, the same bell had rung the call to
maiden prayers day after day after day, and nothing, absolutely nothing had changed. The monastery was still the
same as the day I left; its work went on in the same,
unchanging way, as it had before my birth and would after
I was dust in an unknown grave.

Despair, renewed with the morning, washed over me
in black waves. I had been to Byzantium, and beyond. I
had beheld wonders of unrivalled wealth and power. I had
served Arab potentates, and endured the life of a slave. I
had loved a Sarazen princess—Christ have mercy, had I
been a better man, I would be married now! Oh, Kazimain,
forgive this wretch of a fool.

Truly, I had partaken of life unimaginable to the simple brotherhood of the abbey. And now, here I was, once
more among the monks of Kells, and nothing had
changed—save myself, and that not for the better.

I lay on my straw pallet in the pearl-grey light of
dawn, staring up at the bleak stone ceiling of my cell,
drowning in the futility that whelmed me over and pulled
me down and down into the depths of hopelessness. I
pressed my eyes shut to stay the tears, but they leaked
from beneath my eyelids anyway and rolled down my
cheeks.

How could I brave the day? How could I brave the
innocent interest my every word held for those who had
remained behind? How could I brave the endless, ignorant
questions and satisfy the credulous, ignorant curiosity?
What was I to do?

I remained in my cell until after the bell for prime, and then went to Ruadh's hut. He was not there, but I went in anyway and sat down on the floor to wait until he came. As I waited, I looked around at the bare stone room with its narrow windhole in the wall and the thin straw sleeping pallet on the floor, the leather bulga hanging by its strap from the wooden peg above the pallet, the shallow basin of water at the foot of the bed, the iron candletree, the stone shelf with its small wooden cross—everything exactly as I remembered it, exactly as it had been the day I had gone away.

The room spoke a lonely psalm to me, a hymn of desolation and barren futility. I felt like running out again, but presently heard footsteps approaching. A moment later, Ruadh entered the room.

"There you are, Aidan," he said, crossing to his chair—as if resuming a discussion that had been diverted by a temporary interruption. "When I did not see you in the hall, nor at prayers, I thought I might find you here."

"You always know me better than I know myself," I told him.

"I always did," he said, and smiled. He folded his hands in his lap and gazed at me for a time, smiling to himself. "Welcome home, Aidan," he breathed at last. "It is good to see you again."

"And good to see you, secnab," I said.

"Is it?" He lifted an eyebrow inquiringly. "The expression on your face tells a different tale." He paused, but when I did not deny it, he continued, "I have been talking to Brynach. He says it was your decision to bring the book home with you."

"Did he say what led me to that decision?"

"Yes," Ruadh answered, "but I would hear it from you."

"The pilgrimage failed," I told him, and all the bitterness

I felt came surging up once more. "There was nothing to be done."

"He said you spoke to the emperor alone."

"I did, yes. What else did Brynach tell you?"

"He said you saved their lives."

That day, once so full in my memory, now seemed remote. I shook my head slowly. Here, in the unvaried simplicity of the abbey, my former life was already dwindling away to nothing.

I looked at Ruadh—my anamcara, my soul's good friend—for many years he had patiently listened to my dreams and confessions, guiding me, prodding me, helping me in any of a thousand ways with his wise counsel. He knew me better than any other, but even Ruadh would never understand more than the tiniest fragment of all that had happened. How could I tell him—where could I begin?

"It was nothing," I said. "Anyone else would have done the same."

We talked a little more—mostly about the abbey and resuming my duties in the scriptorium—and when I rose to leave, Ruadh walked with me outside. "It will take time to return, Aidan. You must not expect to come back as if nothing happened."

Over the next days, I avoided talking about the pilgrimage. When anyone asked a question, I replied with vague, dismissive answers, and eventually the brothers stopped asking. Life in the monastery went on, after all, and what was done was done. I resumed my work, and the daily round. The work I had once viewed with such pride and delight was dry tedium to me now, the very scratch of the pen set my teeth on edge and the words I wrote held no meaning. Prayer became merely a way to escape the scriptorium; and though I knelt in the chapel with all the rest, I never opened my heart to God.

How could I pray? I knew God for what he was: a

monstrous betrayer of souls—demanding honour and worship and obedience, demanding life and love, promising protection and healing and sanctuary. And then, when need was greatest and the longed-for sanctuary required . . . nothing. In return for years of slavish devotion, he gave nothing, less than nothing, in return.

Each day as I knelt in the chapel, listening to the simple brothers speak their prayers, I thought, *Lies! All lies! How can anyone believe a single word?*

Thus, the wounded animal that was my heart sickened and began devouring itself in its misery. I sank further and further beneath the weight of malignant grief. When Brynach and Ddewi departed to return to their abbey in Britain, I did not see them away or say farewell. Dugal chastised me about it later, but I did not care. I was a world of woe unto myself, and the days passed unnoticed and unheeded.

One day I rose to see that winter had come again to Kells, and realized I had not been aware of the season's change. The greyness of the land and sky was the greyness of my own benighted soul. Standing before my cell, I looked out across the muddy yard to our little church and recoiled in disgust. After the glittering splendour of Hagia Sophia and the towers of the Great Mosq, our rude stone structure appeared a mean, ill-made thing. I looked around at all the places I had once thought sublime in their humble simplicity, and found them coarse, ugly, vulgar, and repugnant against the glowing reality of all I had seen and done in Byzantium.

I realized then, to my horror, that the shining verity of my memory was swiftly receding, replaced by emptiness, by a gathering gloom of shadows moving in an ever-increasing void. Soon there would be nothing left—soon not even the shadows would remain, and the darkness would be complete.

Oh, but once my memories had pulsed with the blood-heat of life. In desperation, I forced myself to recall that once I had walked with kings and conversed in languages never heard in this land. Once I had stood at the prow of a Sea Wolf ship and sailed oceans unknown to seamen here. I had ridden horses through desert lands, and dined on exotic foods in Arab tents. I had roamed Constantinople's fabled streets, and bowed before the Holy Roman Emperor's throne. I had been a slave, a spy, a sailor. Advisor and confidant of lords, I had served Arabs, Byzantines, and barbarians. I had worn a captive's rags, and the silken robes of a Sarazen prince. Once I had held a jewelled knife and taken a life with my own hand. Yes, and once I had held a loving woman in my arms and kissed her warm and willing lips.

Would that I had died in Byzantium!

Death would have been far, far better than the gnawing, aching emptiness that was now my life. I bent my head and moaned for the hopelessness of it. That night, I went for the last time to my confessor's hut.

# 77

I can stay here no longer," I told him, hopelessness making me blunt.

"Sure, you surprise me, Aidan. I thought you had left us long ago," Ruadh replied, then motioned me into his cell and bade me sit. Lowering himself into his chair, he pressed his hands together and asked, "What did you expect to find?"

His question, like his placid demeanour, took me unawares; I had to ask him to repeat himself, for I was not certain I had heard properly.

"Your pilgrimage, Aidan—what did you expect to find in Byzantium?"

"Truly?" I asked, provoked by his subtle insinuation that I was somehow to blame for my misery. "I expected to meet my death," I answered, and told him of the vision I had dreamed the night before I left.

"A curious dream, certainly," Ruadh conceded mildly. He thought for a moment, gazing at the wooden cross on its stone shelf. "Pilgrimage is called the White Martyrdom," he mused. "Yet, we say the pilgrim seeks not the place of his death, but the place of his resurrection. A curious thing to say," he observed, "unless the pilgrim was in some way already dead."

He let the words do their work. Then, directing his gaze to me, he said, "I have heard from Bryn and Dugal most of what happened. Naturally, they know very little about your sojourn with the Sea Wolves and Sarazens, but I think I understand enough from what they have told me to know how it was with you." He smiled unexpectedly. "Aidan, you have experienced a life which your brothers can scarce begin to imagine. You have seen more than most men could see in ten lifetimes. You have been richly blessed."

"Blessed!" I choked on the word. "Cursed, you mean."

Disregarding my outburst, he continued, "So I ask you again, what did you expect?"

"I expected God to honour his word," I replied. "That, at least, if nothing else. I thought I could depend on the truth. But I have learned there is no truth. The innocent are everywhere slaughtered—they die pleading for God to save them, and death takes them anyway. Faith's own guardians are inconstant liars, and Christ's holy church is a nest of vipers; the emperor, God's Co-ruler on Earth, is a vile, unholy murderer."

"Life is a school of the spirit, Aidan," Ruadh intoned with gentle insistence. "Learning is our soul's requirement, and suffering our most persuasive teacher."

"Oh, aye, it is a school," I agreed, feeling the throbbing ache of futility. "It is a terrible school wherein we learn harsh and bitter lessons. We begin by trusting, and learn there is no one worthy of our trust. We learn that we are all alone in this world, and our cries go unheeded. We learn that death is the only certainty. Yes, we all die: most in agony and torment, some in misery, and the fortunate few in peace, but we all die. Death is God's one answer to all our prayers."

"Do not blaspheme, Aidan," cautioned the secnab sternly.

"Blaspheme!" I challenged angrily. "Why, I speak the very heart of God's own truth, brother. How is that blasphemy? We put our trust in the Lord God, and were proved fools for believing. We endured slavery and torture and death, and God lifted not a finger to save us. I saw our own blessed Bishop Cadoc hacked to pieces before my eyes and God—the God he loved and served all his days—did not so much as lift a finger to ease his suffering."

Ruadh regarded me severely, his brow creased in disapproval. "As he did nothing when His beloved son died on the cross," my anamcara pointed out. "We are closest to Christ when sharing the world's misery. Think you Jesu came to remove our pains? Wherever did you get that notion? The Lord came, not to remove our suffering, but to show us the way through it to the glory beyond. We can overcome our travails. That is the promise of the cross."

"A promise worth as much as the empty air," I said. "Thirteen monks left this abbey, and only four returned. We paid a fearful price—and all for nothing! All our torment accounted for nothing, and accomplished no purpose. No good came of it. The only fortunate ones, that I can see, are the barbarians: they went out for plunder and came back wealthier than they could have imagined. At least they got what they wanted."

Ruadh was silent for a time. "Aidan, have you lost your faith?" he asked at last.

"I did not lose my faith—it was stolen from me," I growled. "God abandoned *me*!"

"So this is why you wish to leave," the secnab observed. He did not try to dissuade me, and for that I was grateful. "Do you have any idea where you might go?"

"No," I said. "I only know that there is no place for me here any more."

"I think you are right," agreed my wise anamcara gently. "I think you should leave."

Again, his attitude surprised me. "Truly?"

"Oh, yes—truly. Anyone who has suffered as you have, and who feels the way you feel, should not remain here." He regarded me with fatherly compassion. "Winter is a hard time, however. Stay at least until the spring— until Eastertide, say."

"And what shall I do until then?" I wondered.

"Until then," he replied, "you can use the time to think about what you might like to do when you leave."

"Very well," I agreed. It seemed a sensible plan, and I had no other. "I will stay until the Eastertide."

Having made the decision, life became easier for me in some ways. Sure, I did not feel such a Judas. I began looking to the coming spring and thinking where I should go and what I should do. In the end, I decided to return to my own people. Even if I did not stay with them, I could at least remain there until I found a better place. I was still a nobleman of my clan, after all; though it had been many years since I had visited the settlement, they would not turn me away.

Slowly, the days dwindled down, and like a slow, white tide the long winter receded. Spring came and, with the approach of Eastertide, I began to think what I would tell Dugal; he knew nothing of my decision to leave the abbey. Yet, as often as I prepared myself to raise the subject with him, when the moment came I found better reason to refrain.

Nevertheless, as the land warmed to a mild and pleasant spring I determined that come what may, I would tell him at the first opportunity. Three days before Easter, I went looking for him, but I could not find him anywhere. One of the brothers told me he thought Dugal was following his seasonal custom, helping the shepherds with the lambing in the next valley.

I found my friend there, sitting on the hillside, watching

the flock. He greeted me warmly, and I sat down beside him. "Brother," I said, "I have a burden on my heart."

"Speak then," he said, "if it would lighten the load for sharing." I noticed he did not look at me, but kept his eyes on the sheep as they grazed. Perhaps he already sensed my leaving in the way I had behaved towards him all winter.

"Dugal, I—" the words stuck in my throat. I swallowed hard and pushed ahead. "Dugal, I am leaving. I cannot—"

I broke off just then, for Dugal leapt to his feet. "Listen!" he cried, pointing across the valley.

Looking where he pointed, I saw the figure of a man— a monk, one of the shepherds—flying down the hill as fast as he could run. He was shouting as he ran, but I could not make out the words. "What is he saying?"

"Shh!" Dugal hissed urgently, cupping a hand to his ear. "Listen!"

The shout came again and I heard it this time. "Wolves!" I said. "He has seen a wolf."

"Not a wolf," Dugal replied, already turning away. "*Sea Wolves!*"

Together we raced back to the abbey, stumbling over the winter stubble in the unploughed fields. We arrived breathless to raise the alarm; within three heartbeats the entire monastery was in well-ordered upheaval as monks scurried everywhere in a grimly determined effort to hide the abbey's treasures: the cups and plate used for the Holy Sacraments; candleholders, the altar cloth; the manuscripts and those books precious to us whether or not their covers had any value.

Fortunately, the warning was timely so that when the dread raiders came in sight, we were ready. Abbot Fraoch would meet them at the gate, and offer the cattle and grain, if they would but leave the buildings unmolested.

Accordingly, he summoned me to him. "You can speak to them in their own tongue, I believe," he said.

"Aye, he speaks like a very Sea Wolf himself," replied Dugal helpfully.

"Good," said the abbot, and related the message I should convey.

"I will try," I replied, "though it may not be of any help. They are difficult to persuade at best, and will not listen to anyone when the silverlust is on them."

"Do what you can," the abbot said. "We will uphold you in prayer."

Ruadh, taking his place beside the abbot, said, "We will all be praying for you, Aidan."

I thought how best to meet the raiders, and decided that if I went out a little way from the gate alone, I might stand the best chance of blunting the attack. Once they reached the abbey, they would not likely hear a word anyone said. So, as the rest of the monks gathered at the gate to watch, I walked out along the trail to meet the marauders face to face.

I could see them now. Having crossed the stream, they were already striding up the long sloping hill: a raiding party of at least thirty Vikings, the leaf-shaped blades of their long spears glinting in the sunlight as they came.

I heard a softly rumbling noise behind me. Glancing back over my shoulder, I saw the brothers of the abbey kneeling, hands clasped, their voices raised in fervent prayer, beseeching God on my behalf.

When I turned back, the Sea Wolves were closer. I could make out individuals in the foreranks, and tried to establish which one might be their war leader. The huge, hulking Dane towering over his swordbrothers seemed a likely choice, and then I noticed that beside this giant strode a figure whose gait, whether in daylight or darkness, I would always recognize.

An instant later, my feet were flying to meet them, shouting, "Harald! Gunnar! It is me, Aidan!"

The next thing I knew, Harald Bull-Roar's voice was bellowing in reply, and I was swept into the familiar bone-crushing ritual that passed for welcome among the sea-braving Danes. "I knew we would find you if we kept looking," Gunnar said proudly. "I told them, and here you are."

"Indeed, he told us so often that we could not rest a day until we found you," Jarl Harald explained. "We have been looking for you since the ice began to melt."

The monks, having seen me beswarmed by Vikings, now came running to my defence—though what they thought to do, I cannot guess. Dugal was among the first, and I called to him, "All is well! Tell the others, there is nothing to fear. It is Jarl Harald come to visit!"

Dugal succeeded in slowing the onrushing monks, who approached uncertainly, gawking at the strange-looking barbarians, and murmuring in low, astonished voices. Taking Harald and Gunnar each by the arm, I led them to where Abbot Fraoch and Ruadh were standing, and said, "I present Jarl Harald Bull-Roar, King of the Danes of Skania, and his karl, Gunnar Warhammer."

"Give the king our best greeting, and welcome him in the name of our Lord Christ," the abbot said. "Tell him he and his men are to be our honoured guests."

This I told Harald, resplendent in a blue cloak and handsome trousers of deepest red. He stepped before the assembled monks gleaming with gold and silver at throat and wrist; his long red beard was brushed and its ends braided. He wore seven silver bands on each arm, and seven silver brooches secured his cloak.

Upon receiving our good abb's greeting, he inclined his head regally, and motioned to one of his karlar to come near. The man handed him a bulky leather bundle, which Harald took and commenced unwrapping. A moment later, the white blaze of silver dazzled our eyes.

The monks gasped and murmured in amazement at the sight, and it took me a moment to understand the significance of what I was seeing. "A cumtach?" Yes, but what a book cover! It was solid silver embossed with the image of a cross; a square-cut ruby adorned each of the arms and a cluster of emeralds decorated the centre. "Jarl Harald, truly! I have never seen its equal."

"It is for your holy book," the king declared, placing the treasure in Abbot Fraoch's hands. He made a bow and explained, "The first cover was lost to the Jarl of Miklagård, a fact which vexes me sorely. This one will serve to replace it, I think. It is made from some of the silver we got in the Sarazen mines. If not for Aeddan, none of us would be alive now to enjoy our treasure."

The abbot could hardly believe his ears when I translated the jarl's words. "It is a rare and magnificent gift, Lord Harald," replied Fraoch, impressed almost beyond reason. "And completely unexpected. We are at a loss to thank you properly."

To this, the Danish king replied, "Do not thank me," he said. "The treasure is not a gift; we have come to trade and bring that in payment."

"Trade?" wondered the abbot when I told him what Harald had said. I looked to Gunnar, who stood at the king's shoulder fairly trembling with suppressed excitement.

Turning to me, Harald Bull-Roar declared, "Ever since Aeddan returned to fetch us from the slave pit, Gunnar has not ceased telling us of this God of yours. It is all he talks about. He will have it no other way but that we must build a church for the Christ, and begin worshipping him in Skania.

"I have vowed to build the church, but we have no one to teach us what to do. Therefore, if we are to get any peace, you must come with us, I think."

Before I could think what to say, Gunnar seized me, "Come, brother. I want Ulf to be a priest, and there is no better man to teach him."

I looked at Gunnar, the bright happiness of our reunion fading at his words. "Would you had said anything but that," I told him. "I cannot go with you. I am no priest anymore."

"Not a priest?" wondered Gunnar, still smiling. "How can this be?"

Before I could explain further, Abbot Fraoch spoke up and asked me to entreat the Danemen to stay with us and observe the Easter celebration. Harald, always ready for a feast, readily agreed, and we proceeded into the hall where they were offered cups of mead in welcome.

The abbot determined to show the Danes around the abbey and explain each and every detail of monastic life, including the Holy Mass which would mark the beginning of our Eastertide feastday observance. Thus, it fell to me to interpret the abb's instructions. Harald proclaimed himself interested in everything, and it fair exhausted me translating between the two of them. We examined the chapel and oratory, the tower and its bell, the monks' cells, the guest lodge, and even the interiors of the storehouses. Of all the places they saw, the Danes liked the scriptorium best.

"Look here!" cried Harald, seizing a new-copied vellum leaf. "It is like the book Aeddan had."

The Sea Wolves proceeded to examine the work of all the monks, making much over the cunning designs and beautiful colours of the leaves upon which the scribes toiled. Fraoch insisted on showing them how the pigments were ground and made into ink, how the gold was painstakingly applied, and how the various skins were assembled to make a book. The Danes exclaimed like children, gaining their first glimmering of understanding.

Owing to this lengthy distraction, it was not until after

our evening meal that I found another chance to speak to Gunnar alone. "This is a very good place," he said approvingly. "We shall build such a place in Skania, I think."

"By all means," I agreed. "But I—"

"Karin would have liked this," he said. "Helmuth, too."

"It is too bad they could not come with you," I replied. "But, Gunnar, I cannot—" The look of sadness on Gunnar's broad face halted me.

"They died while I was a-viking," he sighed. "Ylva said it was a bad winter, and the fever got them and they died. First Helmuth and then Karin. Many others died as well— it was very bad, I think."

"Gunnar, I am sorry to hear it," I told him.

"Heya," he sighed, shaking his head sadly. We sat together in silence for a moment—but only for a moment, for he suddenly smiled, and said, "But I have a daughter now—born in the spring after I left. She is just like her mother, and I have named her Karin."

His smile grew wistful. "Ylva is my wife now, so it is not so bad. Ah, but I miss Karin, Aeddan. She was good to me, and I miss her." He paused, remembering his good wife, then added, "But everyone dies, and I will see her again in heaven, heya?"

Despair cast its dark cloak over me, and I said, "You see how unreliable this God is, and yet you still want to build a church? Truly, Gunnar, you are better off without it."

Gunnar regarded me in disbelief. "How can you speak so, Aeddan—especially after all we have seen?"

"It is *because* of all we have seen that I speak as I do," I retorted. "God cares nothing for us. Pray if it makes you feel better; do good if it pleases you, but God remains unmoved and unconcerned either way."

Gunnar was quiet for a moment, gazing at the little stone chapel. "The people of Skania pray to many gods who neither hear nor care," Gunnar said. "But I remember the day you told me about Jesu who came to live among the fisherfolk, and was nailed to a tree by the skalds and Romans and hung up to die. And I remember thinking, this Hanging God is unlike any of the others; this god suffers, too, just like his people.

"I remember also that you told me he was a god of love and not revenge, so that anyone who calls on his name can join him in his great feasting hall. I ask you now, does Odin do this for those who worship him? Does Thor suffer with us?"

"This is the great glory of our faith," I murmured, thinking of Ruadh's words to me—but changing them to reflect Gunnar's sentiment, "that Christ suffers with us and, through his suffering, draws us near to himself."

"Just so!" agreed Gunnar eagerly. "You are a wise man, Aeddan. I knew you would understand. This is most important, I think."

"You find this comforting?"

"Heya," he said. "Do you remember when the mine overseer was going to kill us? There we were, our bodies were broken, our skin blackened by the sun—how hot it was! Remember?"

"Sure, it is not a thing a man easily forgets."

"Well, I was thinking this very thing. I was thinking: I am going to die today, but Jesu also died, so he knows how it is with me. And I was thinking, would he know me when I came to him? Yes! Sitting in his hall, he will see me sail into the bay, and he will run down to meet me on the shore; he will wade into the sea and pull my boat onto the sand and welcome me as his wayfaring brother. Why will he do this? Because he too has suffered, and he knows, Aeddan, he *knows*." Beaming, Gunnar concluded, "Is that not good news?"

I agreed that it was, and Gunnar was so full of joy at this thought that I did not have the heart to tell him I could not come and be his priest. Later that night, after our guests had been made as comfortable as possible in the guest lodge, I lay down to sleep and instead found myself thinking how strange it was that Gunnar should come to faith this way.

Sure, I myself had told him most of what he knew. But he had endured the same hardships, and suffered all that I had suffered, and more—at least, I had not lost wife and friends to fever while a slave in foreign lands—yet Gunnar's travails created in him a kinship with Christ, while mine produced only separation. This seemed very strange to me. Stranger still, I fell asleep wondering not what was wrong with Gunnar, but what was wrong with me?

The thought dogged me into the next day. It was Passion Day, the commemoration of Christ's death, and the beginning of the Eastertide celebrations. The monks do no work on this day, and so we had leisure to entertain our guests. Abbot Fraoch, never one to miss an opportunity of spreading the faith, called me to him and asked me to assemble the Danes so that he could address them. This I did, and he extended to them the invitation to be baptized.

"Do you think this wise?" I asked, while Harald and the others considered the offer. "They know nothing of Christianity. They have had no instruction."

"I merely open the door," the abb told me. "Let the Good Lord bring in whoever he will." Lifting a hand to where the Danes conferred, he said, "Look at them, Aidan. They have come here to get a priest and build a church. This is the favourable Day of the Lord! Let them seal their faith—now while the spirit is moving. There will be plenty of time for instruction later."

Harald spoke up then, saying, "We have held council over this matter, and it is decided that Gunnar is willing. Therefore, he should be baptized now."

I relayed the answer to the abbot, who professed himself

well pleased, and at once led the whole body of monks and
Danes out from the monastery and down the path to the
stream where we often bathed. There, Fraoch put off his
robe and strode into the water in his mantle; in order to act
as translator for the proceedings, I was required to join him.
He called Gunnar into the water, saying, "Let him who
would rise with Christ also die with him."

Putting off his clothes, Gunnar stepped into the stream
and waded to where we stood. The abbot asked him the
three needful questions: Do you renounce evil? Do you
embrace Christ? Will you remain his faithful servant until
the end of your life?

To each of these Gunnar answered a resounding
HEYA! Whereupon we took him by the arms and laid
him down in the water and raised him up again into the
new life of faith. The abbot took his vial of holy oil and
made the sign of the cross on Gunnar's forehead, saying,
"I sign you with the cross of Christ, now and henceforth
your lord, redeemer and friend. Go forth, Gunnar
Warhammer, and live to God's glory by the light that is in
you."

Gunnar embraced me and the abbot both, thanked us,
and went up out of the stream rejoicing. He was then given
a new white mantle to wear and welcomed by the monks
of the abbey as a brother in Christ; then, taken with the
wonder of the moment, the brothers began singing to him
the baptism blessing:

> *Pour down upon him thy grace, Everliving;*
> *Give to him virtue and growth,*
> *Give to him strength and guidance,*
> *Give to him faith and loving kindness,*
> *That he may stand in thy presence happy*
> *for ever and ever and three times for ever.*
> *Amen!*

The entire ritual so impressed the watching Sea Wolves that they all threw off their clothes and clambered into the water to be baptized, too. Harald demanded to be next, and was accorded this honour by the abbot, who summoned Ruadh and Cellach, and some of the others to help. The ceremony occupied us well into the day, and when we gathered at twilight for the Passion Day vespers, it was with the addition of thirty new converts. I translated the words of the prayers and the psalms for them, and they professed to find it all very pleasant, even enjoyable.

Throughout the evening meal, and the whole of the next day I was made to explain what it all meant as the neophyte Christians wanted to know if they would be invincible in battle now, and forever lucky in all their dealings.

"No," I told them. "Indeed, it is the other way entirely. If my life is any example, then you will be supremely unlucky and forever vulnerable to every harm under heaven."

The thought sat ill with me, I believe, for I found it hard to sleep and could get no rest for thrashing about on my bed. Some little while before dawn I woke, rose, and left my cell to find that the abbey had vanished in the night. All around me I could see a featureless expanse stretching in every direction flat to the horizon, without feature, without colour, with neither hill, nor rock, nor tree—a desert place of howling wind and bone-aching emptiness.

*What has happened to the abbey?* I wondered. *Where has everyone gone?*

Even as I struggled to comprehend the enormity of this disaster, I heard high above me the sound of an eagle crying as it flew. I raised my eyes and saw, soaring alone in the empty sky, the great bird, wings outstretched, keen eyes searching for a place to rest.

Suddenly, I was with that eagle, looking, longing for a place to rest. On and on, searching and searching, but never finding; over wilderness and wasteland the bird soared with only the sound of the wind's dull whine through wide-spread feathertips for company. I felt the bone-aching weariness dragging on those broad wings as they swept the empty sky, but still that wonderful bird flew on, vistas of emptiness on every side, and never a resting place to be found.

Then, even as those great, good wings faltered, I glimpsed, far away to the east, the faint ruddy glow of the sun rising above the world-cloaking mist. Higher and higher rose the sun, growing gradually brighter, shining like red-gold in the fireglow of heaven's forge.

My eyes were dazzled by the radiance of the sun; I could not bear the sight and had to look away. When I looked back, however, wonder of wonders! It was no longer the sun rising up, but an enormous, gleaming city, arrayed on seven hills: Constantinople—but as I had never seen it, alive with a brilliance of wonders: towers, domes, basilicas, bridges, triumphal arches, churches, and palaces—all of them glittering and gleaming. Each hilltop glowed with perfect splendour, radiant with the light of its own beauty, illumined by the twin fires of faith and holiness: Byzantium, the City of Gold, sparkling like a treasure of unsurpassed magnificence.

The weary eagle saw the New Rome rising before it, and took heart, lifting its wings with strength renewed. At last, I thought, the worthy bird is saved, for somewhere in such a city the eagle will certainly find a place of rest.

Closer and closer, the eagle flew, each wingbeat bearing it swiftly nearer to the haven of the golden city. The proud bird, its heart quickening at the sight of such an extravagant reward for its long perseverance, descended, spreading wide its wings as it prepared to land upon the highest tower. But as the eagle swooped lower, the city suddenly changed. Oh, it was not a city at all, but a giant, ravening beast with the hindquarters of a lion, and the foreparts of a dragon, its skin of scaly gold and claws of glass, and an enormous gaping maw of a mouth lined with swords for teeth.

The eagle twisted in the air and cried in alarm, beating its wings in retreat. But the golden beast stretched out its long, snake-like neck and plucked the weary bird from the sky as it fled. The jaws shut and the eagle vanished.

The sharp clash of the great golden beast's jaws brought me from the dream. I awoke at once, and could still hear the echo receding through the empty air. I looked around at the familiar surroundings of the abbey, my limbs shaking from the swiftly-fading sound. But it was not the snap of monstrous jaws that made me quake within myself; I heard instead the echo of Bishop Cadoc's dread admonition: All flesh is grass.

*Everyone dies*, Gunnar had said. *All flesh is grass,* said Cadoc. *What did you expect, Aidan?*

Did you really think that Christ would blunt the spear-points, deflect the lash, cause the chains to melt away when they touched your skin? Did you expect to walk in sunlight and not feel the heat, or to go without water and not grow thirsty? Did you think that all the hatred would turn to brotherly love the moment you strode into view? Did you think both storms and tempers would calm because of the tonsure on your head?

Did you believe that God would shield you forever from the hurt and pain of this sin-riven world? That you would be spared the injustice and strife others were forced to endure? That disease would no longer afflict you, that you would live forever untouched by the tribulations of common humanity?

Fool! All these things Christ suffered, and more.

Aidan, you have been blind. You have beheld the truth, stared long upon it, yet failed to perceive so much as the smallest glimpse of all that was shown you. Sure, this is the heart of the great mystery: that God became man, shouldering the weight of suffering so that on the final day none could say, "Who are you to judge the world? What do you know of injustice? What do you know of torture, sickness, poverty? How dare you call yourself a righteous God! What do you know of death?"

*He knows, Aidan, he knows!*

Gunnar, untutored barbarian that he was, had discerned this central truth, while I, for all my monkish learning, had forever failed to grasp it. In Gunnar, this understanding had kindled hope and faith, even as my lack of understanding had brought me to hopelessness.

Oh, but with the coming of the dawn on Resurrection Day, Holy Easter, my vision had been revived. And in the restoring of the dream, I was myself restored. I saw Byzantium once more, and knew that I would die there. This time, however, there was no fear. I believed—for now I knew what Lord Sadiq had said was true—that perfect certainty cast out fear, and that a man forearmed with such faith was truly free.

As the sun rose on our Resurrection Day celebrations, I knew the liberation of a soul set free. During the Service of the Sacraments, I translated Abbot Fraoch's words for the Danemen, and as they spoke the prayer of repentance for the first time, I also repented of my blindness, doubt, and fear. God had not forsaken me, but had upheld me even in my despair. This thought humbled me, and as the abbot raised the chalice from the altar I stood with contrite heart, thinking, *Kyrie eleison! Lord have mercy . . . Christ have mercy!*

Then, as our good abb offered the chalice for the renewal of God's eternal blessing, I renewed my priestly vows.

# Epilogue

Aidan mac Cainnech returned to Skania, the land of his former captivity, and adopted it as his home. For nearly fifty years, he preached the Good News to the Danish tribes, establishing four churches during an active and eventful ministry. Of these, his favourite remained the church Jarl Harald and Gunnar built for him at Bjorvika, within sight of the sea.

In the third year of his sojourn among the Danes, Aidan was joined by his great friend and brother, Dugal, who served faithfully by his side for twenty-three years. The two monks spent many long northern nights together remembering their adventures as young men, and it was Dugal who persuaded Aidan to record his experiences for the amusement and edification of their kinsmen and friends in Éire and Britain.

Gunnar Silverbags and Ylva produced many fine children, contributing liberally to both the treasury and enrolment of Aidan's school at Bjorvika. Harald Bull-Roar, having returned from Byzantium with more wealth than he ever managed to spend, died at a theng from injuries sustained during a particularly exciting wrestling match.

In the year of Our Lord, 943, Bishop Aidan mac

Cainnech made his third and final pilgrimage to Byzantium, accompanied by Abbot Ulf and his three sons, together with Harald Bull-Roar's grandson, Olaf Open-Hand, who had assumed command of his grandfather's sturdy fleet. Upon their arrival, all were warmly received by the Holy Roman Emperor Constantine Porphyrogenitus, a pious and godly man, who, in recognition of the venerable priest's long obedience, accorded him many honours.

Though far advanced in years, Bishop Aidan established the *Caithair Culdich*—Chair of the Culdees, or Célé Dé—at the Patriarchal School of Constantinople. There he spent his last days as teacher and advisor to the emperor's court, and there the esteemed monk died in the winter of 949, full of grace and wisdom.

Saint Aidan's tomb can be found in the Chapel of the Holy Fathers, in the shadow of the Hagia Sophia. Additional grave markers have been erected in the grounds of each of the four churches begun by him in what is now Sweden, Denmark, and Norway. A small memorial stone can also be found at Kells, and another on the island of Iona, ancient Hy, where some of his bones were taken for burial so that the Celtic Church might ever rejoice in the memory of Aidan mac Cainnech.